EVERYMAN,
I WILL GO WITH THEE,
AND BE THY GUIDE,
IN THY MOST NEED
TO GO BY THY SIDE

GEORGE ELIOT

Daniel Deronda

with an Introduction by A. S. Byatt

EVERYMAN'S LIBRARY

163

First included in Everyman's Library, 1964
Introduction © A. S. Byatt, 1999
Bibliography and Chronology © Everyman Publishers plc, 2000
Typography by Peter B. Willberg

ISBN 1-85715-163-1

A CIP catalogue record for this book is available from the
British Library

Published by Everyman Publishers plc,
Gloucester Mansions, 140A Shaftesbury Avenue,
London WC2H 8HD

Distributed by Random House (UK) Ltd.,
20 Vauxhall Bridge Road, London SW1V 2SA

DANIEL DERONDA

CONTENTS

———

INTRODUCTION

Daniel Deronda is a startling and unexpected novel. When first met, it appears to be the culmination of the ample Victorian novel, long, intensely moral, full of details of social and cultural life. But in fact it resembles no other English fiction very much, and its ambitions are not simply English. There are ways in which it harks back to Sir Walter Scott, Eliot's early hero, and founder of the European novel, and there are ways in which it resembles the sweeping melodrama, and the spiritual materialism, of Balzac, dead in 1850. George Eliot is Britain's great European novelist. She read German, French, Spanish, Italian, Greek, and Latin. She was at home in the literatures of those languages. The author of *Daniel Deronda* has learned from Jane Austen and Shakespeare, is in competition with Bulwer Lytton and the new sensation novels of Wilkie Collins – but she is also profoundly influenced by Goethe and German religious thought, by Renan, Michelet and Balzac. She has also learned from the most recent science of her time – the ideas of Darwin, and the sociological beliefs about the development of societies. *Daniel Deronda* sets out to describe Jewish mysticism, and the Jewish search for a national identity and home. Yet its success depends on the extraordinary depiction of a spoiled, unkind, beautiful girl of limited intelligence, who becomes one of the unforgettable characters in the history of the novel.

F. R. Leavis included Eliot in his Great Tradition, remarking that she was the 'English Tolstoy'. He felt that *Daniel Deronda* fell into two parts – a successful novel about the English aristocracy, and an unsuccessful Jewish novel. He pointed out also that Henry James's *Portrait of a Lady*, with its ambitious heroine trapped by a cold sadist, was a reworking of the English half, and that Isabel Archer and Osmond were less powerful and original characters than Gwendolen and Grandcourt. He made the suggestion that the 'English' part could be published perhaps without the Jewish part, and no truthful critic could fail to understand the responses behind those desires. The Jewish part is heavily written, shot through with a kind of Victorian sentiment and earnestness that has not worn well. It is easy, quoting Eliot's defensive remarks about this innovatory material, which her readers might find difficult, and also her remarks about her design of the novel, which she felt to be an indissoluble whole, to argue that it must be read complete or not at all. It is possible indeed to describe its coherence, its interweaving of themes and repetitions of scenes, as though it was a complete, intelligently articulated work of art. The fact of the readerly discomfort with many of the sentimental scenes in Mordecai's family remains.

A look at the opening of the book gives some idea both of the intricacy and of the dramatic intensity of this novel. The epigraph to the whole work reads like a moralizing speech from a seventeenth-century Revenge drama by Webster or Ford, or possibly like a Romantic imitation of that form by Shelley or Coleridge. It begins 'Let thy chief terror be of thine own soul...' This is immediately followed by a chapter-epigraph in the voice of George Eliot's comfortable, speculative, prose-narrative persona, about beginnings, scientific and poetic, world history and epic, with a glancing reference to Goethe's Faust, and a context that includes the history of the stars. Which is followed in turn by a simple question, 'Was she beautiful or not beautiful?', followed by more –

and what was the secret of form or expression which gave the dynamic quality to her glance? Was the good or the evil genius dominant in those beams? Probably the evil; else why was the effect that of unrest rather than of undisturbed charm? Why was the wish to look again felt as coercion and not as a longing in which the whole being consents?

She who raised these questions in Daniel Deronda's mind was occupied in gambling...

This is Gwendolen seen through the eye of Deronda. She is playing games of chance in a European 'scene of dull, gas-poisoned absorption' amongst a cosmopolitan crowd of ghoulish and vulture-like creatures. Their whole relationship is contained in it – the suggestion of uneasy sexual chemistry, the moral judgement and concern of the man, the woman's losing game with hazard. Eliot had seen Byron's grand-niece,

INTRODUCTION

Miss Leigh, feverishly losing money in Homburg in 1872, and had remarked that there was 'very little dramatic "Stoff" to be picked up by watching'. But the image had persisted. Gillian Beer has brilliantly described the connection of Deronda's first question with Darwin's new theories of sexual selection and the descent of man. It is also connected, I think, to Goethe's novella, *Die Wahlverwandtschaften* (*Elective Affinities*), which turns on an image of chemical attraction for the involuntary movements of affections between human beings. Goethe's image of good and evil stands next to his scientific idea of chance conjunctions, with its overtones of unwilled determinism. *Daniel Deronda* could be said to be a novel in which the melodramatic plot is controlled by chance and the random (under which, as so often, appears to exist a more rigid form of ineluctable fate). When Eliot wrote *Middlemarch* she was interested in the probable, the typical human and natural event – her intention was, she said, echoing a phrase Lyell used in his description of long geological processes, 'to show the gradual action of ordinary causes rather than exceptional'. *Daniel Deronda* is about matters neither ordinary nor gradual. It is not held together, as *Middlemarch* is, by a web of metaphors about interconnection of people, things and ideas. It is constructed around flashing brief images of sudden light and dark, demons, snakes and cold-blooded nixies. It is a cosmic myth, a world history, and a morality play.

*

To understand the ambitions of the Jewish plot of the novel completely, the reader would need to retrace Eliot's historical reading – Milman's *History of the Jews*, Ewald's *History of the Jews* and the illuminating writings on the Talmud of Eliot's friend, Emanuel Deutsch. Much the best introduction to all this that I have read is Elinor Shaffer's chapter on *Daniel Deronda* in '*Kubla Khan' and the Fall of Jerusalem*, where Shaffer uses her own learning about biblical criticism to illuminate the moment-to-moment drama of Eliot's novel. She argues persuasively that Deronda corresponds to Ernest Renan's secular portrait of Jesus in his *Vie de Jésus*, which she describes as 'something like a case history in the pathology of messianic claims'. Deronda, like Renan's Christ, is beautiful, attractive to women and accepting their devotion, capable of unconscious cruelty and self-deception. Deronda, she says, 'is not "like-able"; no more than Will Ladislaw in *Middlemarch* is he meant to be "satisfactory" or (as Raymond Williams has put it) "one of us" '. Despite his upbringing by the English squirearchy he has an 'Oriental' sensibility, and softness – the Meyricks refer to him as Cameralzaman, the beautiful prince from *The Arabian Nights*. Shaffer identifies a 'streak of ardent hypocrisy and tender cruelty' in his treatment of his Magdalen, Gwen-dolen – this is perhaps going a little too far, but is more to the point, and makes him much more interesting, than treating him as a virtuous and stick-like hero. Shaffer also discusses the novel's relations with Matthew Arnold's distinction between Hebraism and Hellenism in the British character. She points out that Arnold discusses the Celtic character – imaginative, superstitious, aware of the marvellous – as contributing what the rigid Jewish monotheism did not give to the Christian religion. Arnold quotes Renan's essay 'On the Study of Celtic Literature': the supremely Celtic quality 'is to react against the despotism of fact'. Shaffer does not quote, though she well might, Eliot's notebook entries on Gwendolen the Celtic goddess: 'Gwen is considered as the British Venus ... Gwen-dolen or the Lady of the bow, or perhaps from Gwendal, white browed, was, it seems, an ancient British Goddess, probably the moon.'

Eliot is working out both a cosmic myth, an ironic realist narrative of conversion and charisma, and an international, inter-racial epic. Feuerbach's *Essence of Christianity*, which she translated wonderfully, rigorously rejects superhuman divin-ities, and sets up the good of the species as the goal of moral growth and attention. *Homo homini deus est* – man is man's true god, both in fact and as an ideal purpose. All Eliot's novels are about increasing human understanding, and imagination of other humans. In *Daniel Deronda* the hero discovers his mission as the leader of his people in search of a national home – much as the gypsy heroine of Eliot's poem *The Spanish Gypsy* had already discovered hers. Beyond those biologically ingrained sympathies are wider ones still. Shaffer points out that Eliot has been criticized for comparing the disappointed suitor Rex to medieval Florence: 'Now, however, it seemed that his inward peace was hardly more stable than that of republican Florence, and his heart no better than the alarm-bell that made work slack and tumult busy.' This is, she says, part of a constant reference to Dante in the novel. Gwendolen is early presented as incurious about religion 'in the same way that some people dislike arithmetic and accounts . . . it had not occurred to her, any more than it had occurred to her to enquire into the conditions of colonial property and banking, on which, as she had had many opportunities of knowing, the family fortune was dependent.' Eliot asks a rhetorical question about her small preoccupations in the context of the American Civil War – showing both Gwendolen's blindness to large issues, and the inextricable entanglement of her womanhood and her fate with the wider human movements.

Could there be a slenderer, more insignificant thread in human history than this consciousness of a girl, busy with her small inferences of the way in which she could make her life pleasant? – in a time, too, when ideas were with fresh vigour making armies of themselves, and the universal kinship was declaring itself fiercely: when women on the other side of the world would not mourn for the husbands and sons who died bravely in a common cause, and men stinted of bread on our side of the world heard of that willing loss and were patient: a time when the soul of man was waking to pulses which had for centuries been beating in him unfelt, until their full sum made a new life of terror or of joy.

What in the midst of that mighty drama are girls and their blind visions? They are the Yea or Nay of that good for which men are enduring and fighting. In these delicate vessels is borne onward through the ages the treasure of human affections.

Nation and race and species are the human immortality – and girls and women are the vessels in which it is passed onwards. The novel – including the interesting epigraphs – is full of references to women in general, as objects for sale and barter, as persecutors and victims, as mothers, wives, widows and daughters. In both the Jewish and the English plots there are women who struggle to find a use for their energies, a place to put down roots, a modicum of freedom. Mirah is an

object of barter to her father; Gwendolen sells her freedom
to Grandcourt in exchange for her mother's comfort. Miss
Arrowpoint sees truly, and chooses the restless and homeless
European Jewish musician – the 'Wandering Jew' – over a
rich match in the English upper classes. The movement of
women and their feelings are bound up both in images of
space and confinement, and in their relations to art and the
making of art. I find it poignant that it was to the dying
Jew, Emanuel Deutsch, that Eliot wrote words of attempted
comfort about the feminist Mary Wollstonecraft, which contain a narrative germ she later used for the Jewish heroine,
the singer, Mirah: 'Dear Rabbi,' she wrote, 'Remember, it has
happened to many to be glad they did not commit suicide,
though they once ran for the final leap, or as Mary Wollstonecraft did, wetted their garments well in the rain, hoping
to sink the better when they plunged.'

Gwendolen is a wonderful study in rootlessness and insecur-
ity. Her agoraphobia, her fears, her small cruelties to sisters
and lovers are all traced swiftly and with a few sharp touches
back to her disturbed childhood, the death of her father, her
mother's remarriage, the death of her stepfather. 'Pity that
Offendene was not the home of Miss Harleth's childhood, or
endeared to her by family memories! A human life, I think,
should be well rooted in some spot of a native land, where it
may get the love of tender kinship for the face of earth, for
the labours men go forth to ...' The whole of this paragraph
is one of George Eliot's great and subtle tributes to the sense
of belonging in the English countryside she grew up with, and
describes with unsentimental love. Daniel has had a secure
and loving upbringing, but is also rootless, an orphan, with
unknown parents. All Eliot's novels are critical of the staid
stabilities and ignorant complacencies of English society, but
Daniel Deronda treats this ignorance as a form of cruelty
and even wickedness. Grandcourt triumphs over Gwendolen
because of his inertia, his lethargy, his refusal to imagine. He
treats her as he treats his dogs, with a careless sadism.
Gwendolen accepts him because he 'is not ridiculous', but his
well-bred façade covers a malignant nullity. Eliot points out
that he does not even try to understand why, or how, his wife

does not love him, because he doesn't care whether she does or not, and cannot conceive of anyone being actually repelled by him.

All George Eliot's powerful heroines – Maggie Tulliver, Dorothea Brooke, Gwendolen – are attractive because they have an excess of energy, and all are destroyed or damaged by dullness and inertia, by the conventions of their society and the expectations of conventional men. Marriage, the happy ending of the fairy-tale, is a trap and a tragedy for Dorothea and Gwendolen. Dorothea sees her marriage to Casaubon as 'a perpetual struggle of energy with fear', and Gwendolen, who has been a spirited virgin huntress, riding, excelling at archery, brandishing her little whip as an instrument of control, finds herself trapped inside a yacht, floating aimlessly, with a husband compared to 'a dangerous serpent ornamentally coiled in her cabin without invitation'.

Women's energies, in nineteenth-century women's novels generally, in George Eliot's particularly, and in Eliot's own life, are interwoven with women's relations to good and bad art. Dorothea is overcome by the great alien art of Rome on her honeymoon – her previous experience had been with 'art chiefly of the hand-screen sort'. The good and the powerful women of *Daniel Deronda* are artists. Miss Arrowpoint chooses European art over English good breeding, as I said. Mirah is a true singer, who knows the pure smallness of her talent and resists her father's attempts to exploit and corrupt it. Daniel's mother, the Alcharisi, is part of a line of powerful singers in fiction, in the novels of Mme de Staël and George Sand, as well as in George Eliot's own interesting poem, 'Armgart'. She has renounced marriage, motherhood, and her Jewish roots for art, and makes an impassioned speech about her own energies which is dreadfully moving, despite the fact that the reader is hearing it, as the reader first saw Gwendolen, through Daniel. Daniel, ever-quick in sympathy, tries to tell her he ' "can imagine the hardship of an enforced renunciation" '.

'No,' said the Princess, shaking her head, and folding her arms with an air of decision. 'You are not a woman. You may try – but you can never imagine what it is to have a man's force of genius in you, and yet to suffer the slavery of being a girl. To have a pattern cut out –

"this is the Jewish woman; this is what you must be; this is what you are wanted for; a woman's heart must be of such a size and no larger, else it must be pressed small, like Chinese feet; her happiness is to be made as cakes are, by a fixed receipt." '

Daniel, as Jenny Uglow points out, sees both his mother and Gwendolen as serpent-women: 'Her worn beauty had a strangeness in it as if she were not quite a human mother, but a Melusina, who had ties with some world which is independent of ours.'

   Gwendolen's own attempts at art are very interesting. It is suggestive that as a child she killed her sister's canary for interrupting her singing with its own shrill notes. The charades, in which she poses as Hermione from *The Winter's Tale*, are related to Emma Hamilton's famous 'Attitudes', to the theatricals in *Mansfield Park*, and most importantly to the tableaux in Goethe's *Elective Affinities*, another tale about bored and limited provincial upper classes making pointless imitation art. Indeed the vivacious and thoughtlessly cruel Luciane in that clever, cold tale, who instigates the dressing-up, has many things in common with Eliot's more profound and terrible study of triviality. In *Daniel Deronda* Gwendolen is posing as Hermione, the woman-statue in a state of suspended animation, who is able to return to life and movement. She is frozen with terror and fear when the panel flies open revealing a fleeing figure, and a dead face – a premonition, or, as Ignês Sodré has suggested, an image of Gwendolen's desire to kill her stepfather, and unconscious fear of having succeeded? One of the most terrible scenes in the novel is the one in which Gwendolen asks Klesmer, the true artist, for advice about how to earn her living by art. It is significant, ironically and sadly, that at that moment she sees art as a way out of marriage: 'The inmost fold of her questioning now, was whether she need take a husband at all – whether she could not achieve substantiality for herself and know gratified ambition without bondage.' She cannot – and Klesmer's definition of genius as ' "a great capacity for receiving discipline" ' reminds us that *Daniel Deronda* is the final novel of a provincial English-woman who, against all the odds, and with ferocious application of intelligence and imagination, had become generally recognized as one of Europe's great writers. Like Deronda she was bothered by 'spiritual daughters' and disciples, like Klesmer she was aware of the gap between complacent artiness and the true, powerful thing itself. But unlike the cautious social sketcher of her earlier fictions, she knew that she could do it, and do it supremely well. The brilliant, rapid confidence of her intricate portrait of Gwendolen shows that.

The Italian critic, Franco Moretti, in *The Way of the World*, his interesting book on the European *Bildungsroman*, argues that George Eliot is almost alone amongst English novelists in writing about adult human beings whose fates are settled by their own inner psychological structures, strengths and weaknesses, and not by a desire to return to the innocence of childhood, which is threatened by fairy-tale villains and witches (David Copperfield, Jane Eyre). For him *Middlemarch* is the great novel, and *Daniel Deronda* and *Felix Holt* fail because their heroes are not primarily interesting as individuals, but as representative figures, who '*sacrifice* their individuality' in a way typical of the coming age of the masses; they are 'the first *functionaries* of abstract beliefs'. Moretti suggests, but does not explore the idea, that the use of the ancient forms of fairy-tale and romantic fable, in which, as Todorov says, everything is connected by a fatal necessity, is part of the representation of this new world, in which the connection between the individual and the society he meets and measures himself against is uncertain. What he is not quite arguing is that the 'sensation novel' with its melodrama, and the novel of abstract beliefs, are somehow linked. What he does say as a specific criticism of *Daniel Deronda* is that Eliot has chosen an old form to represent what she feels to be a new historical movement, and has failed more or less honourably. I think that this can be accepted, to an extent, as a critical understanding. But I would add that Eliot's repeated insistence on the importance of the insignificant consciousness of her silly girl in the large and incomprehensible world she fails to master is part of the final flowering of the *Bildungsroman*, and a triumphant part.

A. S. Byatt

SELECT BIBLIOGRAPHY

BIOGRAPHIES
ASHTON, ROSEMARY, *George Eliot: A Life*, Hamish Hamilton, 1996.
HAIGHT, GORDON S., *George Eliot: A Biography*, Oxford University Press, 1968. Standard scholarly life.

OTHER WRITINGS BY GEORGE ELIOT RELEVANT TO *DANIEL DERONDA*
George Eliot's Daniel Deronda Notebooks, ed. Jane Irwin, Cambridge University Press, 1996.
The George Eliot Letters, ed. Gordon S. Haight, 9 vols, Yale University Press, 1945–6, 1978.
George Eliot: Selected Essays, Poems and Other Writings, ed. A. S. Byatt and Nicholas Warren, Penguin, 1990. A wide selection of George Eliot's non-fiction writings, including extracts from her translations of Feuerbach and Strauss.
The Journals of George Eliot, ed. Margaret Harris, Cambridge University Press, 1999.
Selected Critical Writings of George Eliot, ed. Rosemary Ashton, Oxford University Press (World's Classics), 1992.
Selections from George Eliot's Letters, ed. Gordon S. Haight, Yale University Press, 1985. A very well-chosen one-volume selection of the letters.
The Essence of Christianity, Ludwig Feuerbach, translated by George Eliot, Prometheus Books, 1989.

BIBLIOGRAPHIES
HANDLEY, GRAHAM, *State of the Art: George Eliot, A Guide through the Critical Maze*, Bristol Press, 1990.
LEVINE, GEORGE, *An Annotated Bibliography of George Eliot*, Harvester, 1988.

CRITICAL LITERATURE
BEER, GILLIAN, *Darwin's Plots*, Routledge & Kegan Paul, 1983. A broad study of Darwinian metaphor, and Darwinian themes in Victorian fiction. Has an excellent chapter on *Daniel Deronda* and Darwin's theories of sexual selection.
BYATT, A. S. & SODRÉ, IGNÊS, *Imagining Characters*, Chatto & Windus, Vintage, 1995. Dialogues between a novelist and a psychoanalyst on six novels by women, with a discussion of *Daniel Deronda*.

CARROLL, DAVID, ed., *George Eliot: The Critical Heritage*, Routledge, 1971. A selection of reviews of George Eliot's novels, from contemporary critics to the twentieth century. Excellent introduction.

HAIGHT, GORDON S., ed., *A Century of George Eliot Criticism*, Methuen, 1966. A good selection of articles on George Eliot's novels from 1858 to 1962.

MORETTI, FRANCO, *The Way of the World*, Verso, 1987. A study of the European *Bildungsroman*, with a provocative discussion of *Daniel Deronda*.

SHAFFER, ELINOR, *'Kubla Khan' and the Fall of Jerusalem*, Cambridge University Press, 1975. A study of the Higher Criticism of the Bible, and its presence in European literature. A brilliant chapter on *Daniel Deronda*.

UGLOW, JENNY, *George Eliot*, Virago, 1987. Much the best introductory study of Eliot's life and work, full of surprising observations.

About the Introducer:

A. S. BYATT was Senior Lecturer in English and American Literature at University College, London, before becoming a full-time writer. Her fiction includes *The Virgin in the Garden*, *Possession* (for which she won the Booker Prize in 1990), *Angels and Insects* and *Elementals*. Her critical work includes studies of Wordsworth and Coleridge and of Iris Murdoch. She is also the author of *Imagining Characters: Six Conversations about Women Writers* (with Ignês Sodré). She was appointed a CBE in 1990 and a OBE in 1999.

CHRONOLOGY

DATE	AUTHOR'S LIFE	LITERARY CONTEXT
1819	Born Mary Ann Evans at Arbury Farm, Warwickshire, 22 November.	Scott: *Ivanhoe*; *The Bride of Lammermoor*.
1820		
1824		Goethe: *Wilhelm Meisters Lehrjahre* (1795) trans. Carlyle as *Wilhelm Meister's Apprenticeship*.
1829		Balzac: *La Comédie humaine* (17 vols, to 1848).
1830		Stendhal: *Le Rouge et le Noir*. Charles Lyell: *Principles of Geology* (to 1833).
1831		Hugo: *Notre-Dame de Paris*.
1832		George Sand: *Indiana*. Death of Goethe and Sir Walter Scott.
1833		George Sand: *Lélia*.
1837		Dickens: *Pickwick Papers*.
1838		Charles Hennell: *An Inquiry into the Origins of Christianity*.
1840		
1841	Meets freethinking Coventry group, the Brays and Hennells.	Dickens: *The Old Curiosity Shop*.
1842	Stops attending church.	
1844–6	Translates David Friedrich Strauss, *Das Leben Jesu* (1835), as *The Life of Jesus*.	
1845		Disraeli: *Sybil, or The Two Nations*.
1846		
1847		C. Brontë: *Jane Eyre*. E. Brontë: *Wuthering Heights*. Thackeray: *Vanity Fair* (to 1848).
1848		Dickens: *Dombey and Son*. Marx and Engels: *The Communist Manifesto*. Elizabeth Gaskell: *Mary Barton: A Tale of Manchester Life*.

HISTORICAL EVENTS

Birth of Victoria.

Death of George III; accession of George IV.
Repeal of Combination Acts. *Westminster Review* founded.

Catholic Emancipation.

Death of George IV; accession of William IV. The 'Bourgeois Revolution'
in France: flight of Charles X and accession of Louis-Philippe.
The first great railway, between Liverpool and Manchester, opened.

First Parliamentary Reform Act.

Factory Act, regulating child labour. Start of Oxford Movement; Newman
launches 'Tracts for the Times'. Abolition of slavery in the British Empire.
Queen Victoria comes to the throne.
Chartists demand reform, including universal suffrage.

Marriage of the Queen to Prince Albert.
Newman's Tract XC.
Income tax introduced. 'Young England' Movement.

Irish potato famine.

Repeal of the Corn Laws under Sir Robert Peel. Railway expansion.

Revolutions in Europe; Chartist unrest in England. Pre-Raphaelite
Brotherhood founded.

DATE	AUTHOR'S LIFE	LITERARY CONTEXT
1849	Death of her father. She travels abroad with her friends Charles and Cara Bray, and remains for eight months in Geneva.	
1850		First publication of Wordsworth's *Prelude*. Death of Wordsworth and Balzac. Herbert Spencer: *Social Statics*. Dickens: *David Copperfield*.
1851	Lodges with John Chapman in London from January. Chapman introduces her to George Henry Lewes in October.	
1852–4	Assistant Editor of the *Westminster Review* (London). John Chapman was Editor.	
1852		Thackeray: *Henry Esmond*.
1853		Comte: *Cours de philosophie positive* (1830–42) trans. Harriet Martineau as *Positive Philosophy*. Dickens: *Bleak House*.
1854	Translates Ludwig Feuerbach, *Das Wesen des Christenthums* (1841), as *The Essence of Christianity*. Published by Chapman under the name Marian Evans. Travels to Germany as the wife of Lewes, with whom she lived until his death.	Dickens: *Hard Times*. Coventry Patmore: *The Angel in the House* (to 1863).
1854–6		
1855		Lewes: *Life of Goethe*. Elizabeth Gaskell: *North and South*. Turgenev: *Russian Life in the Interior or the Experiences of a Sportsman*, trans. J. D. Meiklejohn.
1855–6	Translates Spinoza, *Ethics*: published by Chapman.	
1857	First published fiction, three stories in *Blackwood's Magazine*, which appeared in the following year under the title *Scenes of Clerical Life*. John Blackwood was to remain her publisher and trusted friend.	Flaubert: *Madame Bovary*. Elizabeth Gaskell: *The Life of Charlotte Brontë*. Dickens: *Little Dorrit*. Trollope: *Barchester Towers*. Lewes: *Sea-side Studies*.
1858		

CHRONOLOGY

Mazzini's short-lived Roman republic falls to French army. Other European revolutions suppressed and period of reaction follows.

Don Pacifico incident. Public Libraries Act.

Great Exhibition at the Crystal Palace. Second census records a population of 17,927,609 in England and Wales as compared with 8,872,980 in 1801. Foundation of Royal School of Mines – first state institution for scientific research and teaching.

Louis Napoleon proclaimed Emperor of France.

British Medical Association founded. Dissenters allowed to matriculate at Oxford.

Crimean War.
Palmerston becomes Prime Minister (to 1858).

Dissenters allowed to matriculate at Cambridge.

Indian Mutiny. Matrimonial Causes Act.

Jews admitted to Parliament.

DATE	AUTHOR'S LIFE	LITERARY CONTEXT
1859	First published novel: *Adam Bede*.	Darwin: *The Origin of Species*. J. S. Mill: *On Liberty*.
1860	*The Mill on the Floss*.	Collins: *The Woman in White*.
1861	*Silas Marner*.	Dickens: *Great Expectations*.
1862		Tolstoy: *Childhood, Boyhood and Youth*, trans. Malwida von Meysenbug.
1862–3	*Romola* published in parts in the *Cornhill Magazine*.	Hugo: *Les Misérables* (1862). Death of Thackeray (1863).
1864–5		Trollope: *Can You Forgive Her?* Dickens: *Our Mutual Friend*.
1866	*Felix Holt, the Radical*.	Elizabeth Gaskell: *Wives and Daughters*.
1867		Turgenev: *Fathers and Sons* (1862), trans. Eugene Schuyler.
1868	*The Spanish Gypsy, a dramatic poem*.	Collins: *The Moonstone*.
1869		Turgenev: *Liza* (English version of *A Nest of Gentlefolk*), trans. W. R. S. Ralston. Trollope: *Phineas Finn*. J. S. Mill: *The Subjection of Women*. Arnold: *Culture and Anarchy*.
1869–71	A number of poems published including *The Legend of Jubal*. Writing *Middlemarch*.	
1870		Death of Dickens.
1870–71		
1871–2	*Middlemarch* published, first in eight parts, then in 1873 in four volumes, and in one volume in 1874.	
1873		Trollope: *The Eustace Diamonds*.
1874		Hardy: *Far from the Madding Crowd*.
1876	*Daniel Deronda*.	James: *Roderick Hudson*.
1877–8		
1878	Lewes dies. George Eliot finishes his work *Problems of Life and Mind*.	Hardy: *The Return of the Native*. James: *Daisy Miller*.
1879	*Impressions of Theophrastus Such* (essays).	Meredith: *The Egoist*.
1880	Marries John Walter Cross, 6 May. Dies in London, 22 December.	
1881		James: *The Portrait of a Lady*.

CHRONOLOGY

DANIEL DERONDA

Let thy chief terror be of thine own soul:
There, 'mid the throng of hurrying desires
That trample o'er the dead to seize their spoil,
Lurks vengeance, footless, irresistible
As exhalations laden with slow death,
And o'er the fairest troop of captured joys
Breathes pallid pestilence.

BOOK I
The Spoiled Child

I

Men can do nothing without the make-believe of a beginning. Even Science, the strict measurer, is obliged to start with a make-believe unit, and must fix on a point in the stars' unceasing journey when his sidereal clock shall pretend that time is at Nought. His less accurate grandmother Poetry has always been understood to start in the middle; but on reflection it appears that her proceeding is not very different from his; since Science, too, reckons backwards as well as forwards, divides his unit into billions, and with his clock-finger at Nought really sets off *in medias res*. No retrospect will take us to the true beginning; and whether our prologue be in heaven or on earth, it is but a fraction of that all-presupposing fact with which our story sets out.

WAS she beautiful or not beautiful? and what was the secret of form or expression which gave the dynamic quality to her glance? Was the good or the evil genius dominant in those beams? Probably the evil; else why was the effect that of unrest rather than of undisturbed charm? Why was the wish to look again felt as coercion and not as a longing in which the whole being consents?

She who raised these questions in Daniel Deronda's mind was occupied in gambling: not in the open air under a southern sky, tossing coppers on a ruined wall, with rags about her limbs; but in one of those splendid resorts which the enlightenment of ages has prepared for the same species of pleasure at a heavy cost of gilt mouldings, dark-toned colour and chubby nudities, all correspondingly heavy – forming a suitable condenser for human breath belonging, in great part, to the highest fashion, and not easily procurable to be breathed in elsewhere in the like proportion, at least by persons of little fashion.

It was near four o'clock on a September day, so that the atmosphere was well-brewed to a visible haze. There was deep stillness, broken only by a light rattle, a light chink, a

3

small sweeping sound, and an occasional monotone in French, such as might be expected to issue from an ingeniously constructed automaton. Round two long tables were gathered two serried crowds of human beings, all save one having their faces and attention bent on the tables. The one exception was a melancholy little boy, with his knees and calves simply in their natural clothing of epidermis, but for the rest of his person in a fancy dress. He alone had his face turned towards the doorway, and fixing on it the blank gaze of a bedizened child stationed as a masquerading advertisement on the platform of an itinerant show, stood close behind a lady deeply engaged at the roulette-table.

About this table fifty or sixty persons were assembled, many in the outer rows, where there was occasionally a deposit of new comers, being mere spectators, only that one of them, usually a woman, might now and then be observed putting down a five-franc piece with a simpering air, just to see what the passion of gambling really was. Those who were taking their pleasure at a higher strength, and were absorbed in play, showed very distant varieties of European type: Livonian and Spanish, Græco-Italian and miscellaneous German, English aristocratic and English plebeian. Here certainly was a striking admission of human equality. The white bejewelled fingers of an English countess were very near touching a bony, yellow, crab-like hand stretching a bared wrist to clutch a heap of coin – a hand easy to sort with the square, gaunt face, deep-set eyes, grizzled eye-brows, and ill-combed scanty hair which seemed a slight metamorphosis of the vulture. And where else would her ladyship have graciously consented to sit by that dry-lipped feminine figure prematurely old, withered after short bloom like her artificial flowers, holding a shabby velvet reticule before her, and occasionally putting in her mouth the point with which she pricked her card? There too, very near the fair countess, was a respectable London tradesman, blond and soft-handed, his sleek hair scrupulously parted behind and before, conscious of circulars addressed to the nobility and gentry, whose distinguished patronage enabled him to take his holidays fashionably, and to a certain extent in their distinguished company. Not his the gambler's passion that nullifies appetite, but a well-fed leisure, which in the intervals of winning money in business and spending it showily, sees no better resource than winning money in play and spending it yet more showily – reflecting always that Providence had never manifested any disapprobation of his amusement, and dispassionate enough to leave off if the sweetness of winning much and seeing others lose had turned to the sourness of losing much and seeing others win. For the vice of gambling lay in losing money at it. In his bearing there might be something of the tradesman, but in his pleasures he was fit to rank with the owners of the oldest titles. Standing close to his chair was a handsome Italian, calm, statuesque, reaching across him to place the first pile of napoleons from a new bagful just brought him by an envoy with a scrolled moustache. The pile was in half a minute pushed over to an old bewigged woman with eyeglasses pinching her nose. There was a slight gleam, a faint mumbling smile about the lips of the old woman; but the statuesque Italian remained impassive, and – probably secure in an infallible system which placed his foot on the neck of chance – immediately prepared a new pile. So did a man with the air of an emaciated beau or worn-out libertine, who looked at life through one eyeglass, and held out his hand tremulously when he asked for change. It could surely be no severity of system, but rather some dream of white crows, or the induction that the eighth of the month was lucky, which inspired the fierce yet tottering impulsiveness of his play.

But while every single player differed markedly from every other, there was a certain uniform negativeness of expression which had the effect of a mask – as if they had all eaten of some root that for the time compelled the brains of each to the same narrow monotony of action.

Deronda's first thought when his eyes fell on this scene of dull, gas-poisoned absorption was that the gambling of Spanish shepherd-boys had seemed to him more enviable: – so far Rousseau might be justified in maintaining that art and science had done a poor service to mankind. But suddenly he felt the moment become dramatic. His attention was arrested by a young lady who, standing at an angle not far from him, was the last to whom his eyes travelled. She was bending and speaking English to a middle-aged lady seated at play beside her; but the next instant she returned to her play, and showed the full height of a graceful figure, with a face which might possibly be looked at without admiration, but could hardly be passed with indifference.

The inward debate which she raised in Deronda gave to his eyes a growing expression of scrutiny, tending farther and farther away from the glow of mingled undefined sensibilities forming admiration. At one moment they followed the movements of the figure, of the arms and hands, as this problematic sylph bent forward to deposit her stake with an air of firm choice; and the next they returned to the face which, at present unaffected by beholders, was directed steadily towards the game. The sylph was a winner; and as her taper fingers, delicately gloved in pale-grey, were adjusting the coins which had been pushed towards her in order to pass them back again to the winning point, she looked round her with a survey too markedly cold and neutral not to have in it a little of that nature which we call art concealing an inward exultation.

But in the course of that survey her eyes met Deronda's, and instead of averting them as she would have desired to do, she was unpleasantly conscious that they were arrested – how long? The darting sense that he was measuring her and looking down on her as an inferior, that he was of different quality from the human dross around her, that he felt himself in a region outside and above her, and was examining her as a specimen of a lower order, roused a tingling resentment which stretched the moment with conflict. It did not bring the blood to her cheeks, but sent it away from her lips. She controlled herself by the help of an inward defiance, and without other sign of emotion than this lip-paleness turned to her play. But Deronda's gaze seemed to have acted as an evil eye. Her stake was gone. No matter; she had been winning ever since she took to roulette with a few napoleons at command, and had a considerable reserve. She had begun to believe in her luck, others had begun to believe in it: she had visions of being followed by a *cortège* who would worship her as a goddess of luck and watch her play as a directing augury. Such things had been known of male gamblers; why should not a woman have a like supremacy? Her friend and chaperon who had not wished her to play at first was beginning to approve, only administering the prudent advice to stop at the right moment and carry money back to England – advice to which Gwendolen had replied that she cared for the excitement of play, not the winnings. On that supposition the present moment ought to have made the flood-tide in her eager experience of gambling. Yet when her next stake was swept away, she felt the orbits of her eyes getting hot, and the certainty she had (without looking) of that man still watching her was something like a pressure which begins to be torturing. The more reason to her why she should not flinch, but go on playing as if she were indifferent to loss or gain. Her friend touched her elbow and proposed that they should quit the table. For reply Gwendolen put ten louis on the same spot: she was in that mood of defiance in which the mind loses sight of any end beyond the satisfaction of enraged resistance; and with the puerile stupidity of a dominant impulse includes luck among its objects of defiance. Since she was not winning strikingly, the next best thing was to lose strikingly. She controlled her muscles, and showed no tremor of mouth or hands. Each time her stake was swept off she doubled it. Many were now watching her, but the sole observation she was conscious of was Deronda's, who, though she never looked towards him, she was sure had not moved away.

Such a drama takes no long while to play out: development and catastrophe can often be measured by nothing clumsier than the moment-hand. 'Faites votre jeu, mesdames et messieurs,' said the automatic voice of destiny from between the moustache and imperial of the croupier; and Gwendolen's arm was stretched to deposit her last poor heap of napoleons. 'Le jeu ne va plus,' said destiny. And in five seconds Gwendolen turned from the table, but turned resolutely with her face towards Deronda and looked at him. There was a smile of irony in his eyes as their glances met; but it was at least better that he should have kept his attention fixed on her than that he should have disregarded her as one of an insect swarm who had no individual physiognomy. Besides, in spite of his superciliousness and irony, it was difficult to believe that he did not admire her spirit as well as her person: he was young, handsome, distinguished in appearance – not one of those ridiculous and dowdy Philistines who thought it incumbent on them to blight the gaming-table with a sour look of protest as they passed by it. The general conviction that we are admirable does not easily give way before a single negative; rather when any of Vanity's large family, male or female, find their performance received coldly, they are apt to believe that a little more of it will win over the unaccountable dissident. In Gwendolen's habits of mind it had been taken for granted that she knew what was admirable and that she herself was admired. This basis of her thinking had received a disagreeable concussion, and reeled a little, but was not easily to be overthrown.

In the evening the same room was more stiflingly heated, was brilliant with gas and with the costumes of many ladies who floated their trains along it or were seated on the ottomans.

The Nereid in sea-green robes and silver ornaments, with a pale sea-green feather fastened in silver falling backward over her green hat and light-brown hair, was Gwendolen Harleth. She was under the wing or rather soared by the shoulder of the lady who had sat by her at the roulette-table; and with them was a gentleman with a white moustache and clipped hair: solid-browed, stiff, and German. They were walking about or standing to chat with acquaintances; and Gwendolen was much observed by the seated groups.

'A striking girl – that Miss Harleth – unlike others.'

'Yes; she has got herself up as a sort of serpent now, all green and silver, and winds her neck about a little more than usual.'

'Oh, she must always be doing something extraordinary. She is that kind of girl, I fancy. Do you think her pretty, Mr. Vandernoodt?'

'Very. A man might risk hanging for her – I mean, a fool might.'

'You like a *nez retroussé* then, and long narrow eyes?'

'When they go with such an *ensemble*.'

'The *ensemble du serpent*?'

'If you will. Woman was tempted by a serpent: why not man?'

'She is certainly very graceful. But she wants a tinge of colour in her cheeks: it is a sort of Lamia beauty she has.'

'On the contrary, I think her complexion one of her chief charms. It is a warm paleness: it looks thoroughly healthy. And that delicate nose with its gradual little upward curve is distracting. And then her mouth – there never was a prettier mouth, the lips curl backwards so finely, eh, Mackworth?'

'Think so? I cannot endure that sort of mouth. It looks so self-complacent, as if it knew its own beauty – the curves are too immovable. I like a mouth that trembles more.'

'For my part I think her odious,' said a dowager. 'It is wonderful what unpleasant girls get into vogue. Who are these Langens? Does anybody know them?'

'They are quite *comme il faut*. I have dined with them several times at the *Russie*. The baroness is English. Miss Harleth calls her cousin. The girl herself is thoroughly well-bred, and as clever as possible.'

'Dear me! And the baron?'

'A very good furniture picture.'

'Your baroness is always at the roulette-table,' said Mackworth. 'I fancy she has taught the girl to gamble.'

'Oh, the old woman plays a very sober game; drops a ten-franc piece here and there. The girl is more headlong. But it is only a freak.'

'I hear she has lost all her winnings to-day. Are they rich? Who knows?'

'Ah, who knows? Who knows that about anybody?' said Mr. Vandernoodt, moving off to join the Langens.

The remark that Gwendolen wound her neck about more than usual this evening was true. But it was not that she might carry out the serpent idea more completely: it was that she watched for any chance of seeing Deronda, so that she might inquire about this stranger, under whose measuring gaze she was still wincing. At last her opportunity came.

'Mr. Vandernoodt, you know everybody,' said Gwendolen, not too eagerly, rather with a certain languor of utterance which she sometimes gave to her clear soprano. 'Who is that near the door?'

'There are half a dozen near the door. Do you mean that old Adonis in the George the Fourth wig?'

'No, no; the dark-haired young man on the right with the dreadful expression.'

'Dreadful, do you call it? I think he is an uncommonly fine fellow.'

'But who is he?'

'He is lately come to our hotel with Sir Hugo Mallinger.'

'Sir Hugo Mallinger?'

'Yes. Do you know him?'

'No.' (Gwendolen coloured slightly.) 'He has a place near us, but he never comes to it. What did you say was the name of that gentleman near the door?'

'Deronda – Mr. Deronda.'

'What a delightful name! Is he an Englishman?'

'Yes. He is reported to be rather closely related to the Baronet. You are interested in him?'

'Yes. I think he is not like young men in general.'

'And you don't admire young men in general?'

'Not in the least. I always know what they will say. I can't at all guess what this Mr. Deronda would say. What *does* he say?'

'Nothing, chiefly. I sat with his party for a good hour last night on the terrace, and he never spoke – and was not smoking either. He looked bored.'

'Another reason why I should like to know him. I am always bored.'

'I should think he would be charmed to have an introduction. Shall I bring it about? Will you allow it, Baroness?'

'Why not? – since he is related to Sir Hugo Mallinger. It is a new *rôle* of yours, Gwendolen, to be always bored,' continued Madame von Langen, when Mr. Vandernoodt had moved away. 'Until now you have always seemed eager about something from morning till night.'

'That is just because I am bored to death. If I am to leave off play I must break my arm or my collar-bone. I must make something happen; unless you will go into Switzerland and take me up the Matterhorn.'

'Perhaps this Mr. Deronda's acquaintance will do instead of the Matterhorn.'

'Perhaps.'

But Gwendolen did not make Deronda's acquaintance on this occasion. Mr. Vandernoodt did not succeed in bringing him up to her that evening, and when she re-entered her own room she found a letter recalling her home.

11

II

This man contrives a secret 'twixt us two,
That he may quell me with his meeting eyes
Like one who quells a lioness at bay.

THIS was the letter Gwendolen found on her table: –

DEAREST CHILD, – I have been expecting to hear
from you for a week. In your last you said the Langens
thought of going to Baden. How could you be so thought-
less as to leave me in uncertainty about your address? I am
in the greatest anxiety lest this should not reach you. In any
case you were to come home at the end of September, and I
must now entreat you to return as quickly as possible, for if
you spent all your money it would be out of my power to
send you any more, and you must not borrow of the
Langens, for I could not repay them. This is the sad
truth, my child – I wish I could prepare you for it better –
but a dreadful calamity has befallen us all. You know
nothing about business and will not understand it; but
Grapnell and Co. have failed for a million and we are
totally ruined – your aunt Gascoigne as well as I, only
that your uncle has his benefice, so that by putting down
their carriage and getting interest for the boys, the family
can go on. All the property our poor father saved for us goes
to pay the liabilities. There is nothing I can call my own. It
is better you should know this at once, though it rends my
heart to have to tell it you. Of course we cannot help
thinking what a pity it was that you went away just when
you did. But I shall never reproach you, my dear child; I
would save you from all trouble if I could. On your way
home you will have time to prepare yourself for the change
you will find. We shall perhaps leave Offendene at once,
for we hope that Mr. Haynes, who wanted it before, may be
ready to take it off my hands. Of course we cannot go to the
Rectory – there is not a corner there to spare. We must get
some hut or other to shelter us, and we must live on your
uncle Gascoigne's charity, until I see what else can be

done. I shall not be able to pay the debts to the tradesmen besides the servants' wages. Summon up your fortitude, my dear child, we must resign ourselves to God's will. But it is hard to resign one's self to Mr. Lassman's wicked recklessness, which they say was the cause of the failure. Your poor sisters can only cry with me and give me no help. If you were once here, there might be a break in the cloud. I always feel it impossible that you can have been meant for poverty. If the Langens wish to remain abroad perhaps you can put yourself under some one else's care for the journey. But come as soon as you can to your afflicted and loving mamma,

FANNY DAVILOW.

The first effect of this letter on Gwendolen was half-stupefying. The implicit confidence that her destiny must be one of luxurious ease, where any trouble that occurred would be well clad and provided for, had been stronger in her own mind than in her mamma's, being fed there by her youthful blood and that sense of superior claims which made a large part of her consciousness. It was almost as difficult for her to believe suddenly that her position had become one of poverty and humiliating dependence, as it would have been to get into the strong current of her blooming life the chill sense that her death would really come. She stood motionless for a few minutes, then tossed off her hat and automatically looked in the glass. The coils of her smooth light-brown hair were still in order perfect enough for a ball-room; and as on other nights, Gwendolen might have looked lingeringly at herself for pleasure (surely an allowable indulgence); but now she took no conscious note of her reflected beauty, and simply stared right before her as if she had been jarred by a hateful sound and was waiting for any sign of its cause. By-and-by she threw herself in the corner of the red velvet sofa, took up the letter again and read it twice deliberately, letting it at last fall on the ground, while she rested her clasped hands on her lap and sat perfectly still, shedding no tears. Her impulse was to survey and resist the situation rather than to wail over it. There was no inward exclamation of 'Poor mamma!' Her mamma had never seemed to get much enjoyment out of life, and if Gwendolen had been at this moment disposed to feel pity she would have bestowed it on herself – for was she not naturally and rightfully the chief object of her mamma's anxiety too? But it was anger, it was resistance that possessed her; it was bitter vexation that she had lost her gains at roulette, whereas if her luck had continued through this one day she would have had a handsome sum to carry home, or she might have gone on playing and won enough to support them all. Even now was it not possible? She had only four napoleons left in her purse, but she possessed some ornaments which she could pawn: a practice so common in stylish society at German baths that there was no need to be ashamed of it; and even if she had not received her mamma's letter, she would probably have decided to raise money on an Etruscan necklace which she happened not to have been wearing since her arrival; nay, she might have done so with an agreeable sense that she was living with some intensity and escaping humdrum. With ten louis at her disposal and a return of her former luck, which seemed probable, what could she do better than go on playing for a few days? If her friends at home disapproved of the way in which she got the money, as they certainly would, still the money would be there. Gwendolen's imagination dwelt on this course and created agreeable consequences, but not with un-broken confidence and rising certainty as it would have done if she had been touched with the gambler's mania. She had gone to the roulette-table not because of passion, but in search of it: her mind was still sanely capable of picturing balanced probabilities, and while the chance of winning allured her, the chance of losing thrust itself on her with alternate strength and made a vision from which her pride shrank sensitively. For she was resolved not to tell the Langens that any misfortune had befallen her family, or to make herself in any way indebted to their compassion; and if she were to pawn her jewellery to any observable extent, they would interfere by inquiries and remonstrances. The course that held the least risk of intolerable annoyance was to raise money on her necklace early in the morning, tell the Langens that her mamma desired her immediate return without giving a reason, and take the train for Brussels that evening. She had no maid with her, and the Langens might make difficulties about her returning alone, but her will was peremptory.

Instead of going to bed she made as brilliant a light as she could and began to pack, working diligently, though all the while visited by the scenes that might take place on the coming day – now by the tiresome explanations and farewells, and the whirling journey towards a changed home, now by the alternative of staying just another day and standing again at the roulette-table. But always in this latter scene there was the presence of that Deronda, watching her with exasperating irony, and – the two keen experiences were inevitably revived together – beholding her again forsaken by luck. This importunate image certainly helped to sway her resolve on the side of immediate departure, and to urge her packing to the point which would make a change of mind inconvenient. It had struck twelve when she came into her room, and by the time she was assuring herself that she had left out only what was necessary, the faint dawn was stealing through the white blinds and dulling her candles. What was the use of going to bed? Her cold bath was refreshment enough, and she saw that a slight trace of fatigue about the eyes only made her look the more interesting. Before six o'clock she was completely equipped in her grey travelling dress even to her felt hat, for she meant to walk out as soon as she could count on seeing other ladies on their way to the springs. And happening to be seated sideways before the long strip of mirror between her two windows she turned to look at herself, leaning her elbow on the back of the chair in an attitude that might have been chosen for her portrait. It is possible to have a strong self-love without any

15

self-satisfaction, rather with a self-discontent which is the more intense because one's own little core of egoistic sensibility is a supreme care; but Gwendolen knew nothing of such inward strife. She had a *naïve* delight in her fortunate self, which any but the harshest saintliness will have some indulgence for in a girl who had every day seen a pleasant reflection of that self in her friends' flattery as well as in the looking-glass. And even in this beginning of troubles, while for lack of anything else to do she sat gazing at her image in the growing light, her face gathered a complacency gradual as the cheerfulness of the morning. Her beautiful lips curled into a more and more decided smile, till at last she took off her hat, leaned forward and kissed the cold glass which had looked so warm. How could she believe in sorrow? If it attacked her, she felt the force to crush it, to defy it, or run away from it, as she had done already. Anything seemed more possible than that she could go on bearing miseries, great or small.

Madame von Langen never went out before breakfast, so that Gwendolen could safely end her early walk by taking her way homeward through the Obere Strasse in which was the needed shop, sure to be open after seven. At that hour any observers whom she minded would be either on their walks in the region of the springs, or would be still in their bedrooms; but certainly there was one grand hotel, the *Czarina*, from which eyes might follow her up to Mr. Wiener's door. This was a chance to be risked: might she not be going in to buy something which had struck her fancy? This implicit falsehood passed through her mind as she remembered that the *Czarina* was Deronda's hotel; but she was then already far up the Obere Strasse, and she walked on with her usual floating movement, every line in her figure and drapery falling in gentle curves attractive to all eyes except those which discerned in them too close a resemblance to the serpent, and objected to the revival of serpent-worship. She looked neither to the right hand nor to the left, and transacted her business in the shop with a coolness which gave little Mr. Wiener nothing to remark

except her proud grace of manner, and the superior size
and quality of the three central turquoises in the necklace
she offered him. They had belonged to a chain once her
father's; but she had never known her father; and the
necklace was in all respects the ornament she could most
conveniently part with. Who supposes that it is an impossible contradiction to be superstitious and rationalizing at
the same time? Roulette encourages a romantic superstition as to the chances of the game, and the most prosaic
rationalism as to human sentiments which stand in the way
of raising needful money. Gwendolen's dominant regret
was that after all she had only nine louis to add to the four
in her purse: these Jew pawnbrokers were so unscrupulous
in taking advantage of Christians unfortunate at play! But
she was the Langens' guest in their hired apartment, and
had nothing to pay there: thirteen louis would do more
than take her home; even if she determined on risking
three, the remaining ten would more than suffice, since
she meant to travel right on, day and night. As she turned
homewards, nay entered and seated herself in the *salon* to
await her friends and breakfast, she still wavered as to her
immediate departure, or rather she had concluded to tell
the Langens simply that she had had a letter from her
mamma desiring her return, and to leave it still undecided
when she should start. It was already the usual breakfast
time, and hearing some one enter as she was leaning back
rather tired and hungry with her eyes shut, she rose expecting to see one or other of the Langens – the words which
might determine her lingering at least another day, ready-
formed to pass her lips. But it was the servant bringing in a
small packet for Miss Harleth, which had that moment
been left at the door. Gwendolen took it in her hand and
immediately hurried into her own room. She looked paler
and more agitated than when she had first read her
mamma's letter. Something – she never quite knew what –
revealed to her before she opened the packet that it contained the necklace she had just parted with. Underneath
the paper it was wrapt in a cambric handkerchief and

17

within this was a scrap of torn-off note-paper, on which was written with a pencil in clear but rapid handwriting – '*A stranger who has found Miss Harleth's necklace returns it to her with the hope that she will not again risk the loss of it.*'

Gwendolen reddened with the vexation of wounded pride. A large corner of the handkerchief seemed to have been recklessly torn off to get rid of a mark; but she at once believed in the first image of 'the stranger' that presented itself to her mind. It was Deronda; he must have seen her go into the shop; he must have gone in immediately after, and redeemed the necklace. He had taken an unpardonable liberty, and had dared to place her in a thoroughly hateful position. What could she do? – Not, assuredly, act on her conviction that it was he who had sent her the necklace, and straightway send it back to him: that would be to face the possibility that she had been mistaken; nay, even if the 'stranger' were he and no other, it would be something too gross for her to let him know that she had divined this, and to meet him again with that recognition in their minds. He knew very well that he was entangling her in helpless humiliation: it was another way of smiling at her ironically, and taking the air of a supercilious mentor. Gwendolen felt the bitter tears of mortification rising and rolling down her cheeks. No one had ever before dared to treat her with irony and contempt. One thing was clear: she must carry out her resolution to quit this place at once; it was impossible for her to reappear in the public *salon*, still less stand at the gaming-table with the risk of seeing Deronda. Now came an importunate knock at the door: breakfast was ready. Gwendolen with a passionate movement thrust necklace, cambric, scrap of paper and all into her *nécessaire*, pressed her handkerchief against her face, and after pausing a minute or two to summon back her proud self-control, went to join her friends. Such signs of tears and fatigue as were left seemed accordant enough with the account she at once gave of her having been called home, for some reason which she feared might be a trouble of her mamma's; and of her having sat up to do her packing, instead of waiting for help from her friend's maid. There was much protestation, as she had expected, against her travelling alone, but she persisted in refusing any arrangements for companionship. She would be put into the ladies' compartment and go right on. She could rest exceedingly well in the train, and was afraid of nothing.

In this way it happened that Gwendolen never reappeared at the roulette-table, but set off that Thursday evening for Brussels, and on Saturday morning arrived at Offendene, the home to which she and her family were soon to say a last goodbye.

III

'Let no flower of the spring pass by us: let us crown ourselves with rose-buds before they be withered.'

– BOOK OF WISDOM.

PITY that Offendene was not the home of Miss Harleth's childhood, or endeared to her by family memories! A human life, I think, should be well rooted in some spot of a native land, where it may get the love of tender kinship for the face of earth, for the labours men go forth to, for the sounds and accents that haunt it, for whatever will give that early home a familiar unmistakable difference amidst the future widening of knowledge: a spot where the definiteness of early memories may be inwrought with affection, and kindly acquaintance with all neighbours, even to the dogs and donkeys, may spread not by sentimental effort and reflection, but as a sweet habit of the blood. At five years old, mortals are not prepared to be citizens of the world, to be stimulated by abstract nouns, to soar above preference into impartiality; and that prejudice in favour of milk with which we blindly begin, is a type of the way body and soul must get nourished at least for a time. The best introduction to astronomy is to think of the nightly heavens as a little lot of stars belonging to one's own homestead.

But this blessed persistence in which affection can take root had been wanting in Gwendolen's life. Offendene had been chosen as her mamma's home simply for its nearness to Pennicote Rectory, and it was only the year before that Mrs. Davilow, Gwendolen, and her four half-sisters (the governess and the maid following in another vehicle) had been driven along the avenue for the first time on a late October afternoon when the rooks were cawing loudly above them, and the yellow elm leaves were whirling.

The season suited the aspect of the old oblong red-brick house, rather too anxiously ornamented with stone at every line, not excepting the double row of narrow windows and the large square portico. The stone encouraged a greenish lichen, the brick a powdery grey, so that though the building was rigidly rectangular there was no harshness in the physiognomy which it turned to the three avenues cut east, west, and south in the hundred yards' breadth of old plantation encircling the immediate grounds. One would have liked the house to have been lifted on a knoll, so as to look beyond its own little domain to the long thatched roofs of the distant villages, the church towers, the scattered homesteads, the gradual rise of surging woods, and the green breadths of undulating park which made the beautiful face of the earth in that part of Wessex. But though standing thus behind a screen amid flat pastures, it had on one side a glimpse of the wider world in the lofty curves of the chalk downs, grand steadfast forms played over by the changing days.

The house was but just large enough to be called a mansion, and was moderately rented, having no manor attached to it, and being rather difficult to let with its sombre furniture and faded upholstery. But inside and outside it was what no beholder could suppose to be inhabited by retired tradespeople: a certainty which was worth many conveniences to tenants who not only had the taste that shrinks from new finery, but also were in that border-territory of rank where annexation is a burning topic; and to take up her abode in a house which had once sufficed for dowager countesses gave a perceptible tinge to Mrs. Davilow's satisfaction in having an establishment of her own. This, rather mysteriously to Gwendolen, appeared suddenly possible on the death of her step-father Captain Davilow, who had for the last nine years joined his family only in a brief and fitful manner, enough to reconcile them to his long absences; but she cared much more for the fact than for the explanation. All her prospects had become more agreeable in consequence. She had disliked their former way of life, roving from one foreign watering-place or Parisian apartment to another, always feeling new antipathies to new suites of hired furniture, and meeting new people under conditions which made her appear of little importance; and the variation of having passed two years at a showy school, where on all occasions of display she had been put foremost, had only deepened her sense that so exceptional a person as herself could hardly remain in ordinary circumstances or in a social position less than advantageous. Any fear of this latter evil was banished now that her mamma was to have an establishment; for on the point of birth Gwendolen was quite easy. She had no notion how her maternal grandfather got the fortune inherited by his two daughters; but he had been a West Indian – which seemed to exclude further question; and she knew that her father's family was so high as to take no notice of her mamma, who nevertheless preserved with much pride the miniature of a Lady Molly in that connection. She would probably have known much more about her father but for a little incident which happened when she was twelve years old. Mrs. Davilow had brought out, as she did only at wide intervals, various memorials of her first husband, and while showing his miniature to Gwendolen recalled with a fervour which seemed to count on a peculiar filial sympathy, the fact that dear papa had died when his little daughter was in long clothes. Gwendolen, immediately thinking of the unlovable step-father whom she had been acquainted with the greater part of her life while her frocks were short, said –

'Why did you marry again, mamma? It would have been nicer if you had not.'

Mrs. Davilow coloured deeply, a slight convulsive movement passed over her face, and straightway shutting up the memorials she said, with a violence quite unusual in her –

'You have no feeling, child!'

Gwendolen, who was fond of her mamma, felt hurt and ashamed, and had never since dared to ask a question about her father.

This was not the only instance in which she had brought on herself the pain of some filial compunction. It was always arranged, when possible, that she should have a small bed in her mamma's room; for Mrs. Davilow's motherly tenderness clung chiefly to her eldest girl, who had been born in her happier time. One night under an attack of pain she found that the specific regularly placed by her bedside had been forgotten, and begged Gwendolen to get out of bed and reach it for her. That healthy young lady, snug and warm as a rosy infant in her little couch, objected to step out into the cold, and lying perfectly still, grumbled a refusal. Mrs. Davilow went without the medicine and never reproached her daughter; but the next day Gwendolen was keenly conscious of what must be in her mamma's mind, and tried to make amends by caresses which cost her no effort. Having always been the pet and pride of the household, waited on by mother, sisters, governess, and maids, as if she had been a princess in exile, she naturally found it difficult to think her own pleasure less important than others made it, and when it was positively thwarted felt an astonished resentment apt, in her cruder days, to vent itself in one of those passionate acts which look like a contradiction of habitual tendencies. Though never even as a child thoughtlessly cruel, nay, delighting to rescue drowning insects and watch their recovery, there was a disagreeable silent remembrance of her having strangled her sister's canary-bird in a final fit of exasperation at its shrill singing which had again and again jarringly interrupted her own. She had taken pains to buy a white mouse for her sister in retribution, and though inwardly excusing herself on the ground of a peculiar sensitiveness which was a mark of her general superiority, the thought of that infelonious murder had always made her wince. Gwendolen's nature was not remorseless, but she liked to make her penances easy, and now that she was twenty and more, some of her native force had turned into a self-control by which she guarded herself from penitential humiliation. There was more show of fire and will in her than ever, but there was more calculation underneath it.

On this day of arrival at Offendene, which not even Mrs. Davilow had seen before – the place having been taken for her by her brother-in-law Mr. Gascoigne – when all had got down from the carriage, and were standing under the porch in front of the open door, so that they could have both a general view of the place and a glimpse of the stone hall and staircase hung with sombre pictures, but enlivened by a bright wood fire, no one spoke: mamma, the four sisters, and the governess all looked at Gwendolen, as if their feelings depended entirely on her decision. Of the girls, from Alice in her sixteenth year to Isabel in her tenth, hardly anything could be said on a first view, but that they were girlish, and that their black dresses were getting shabby. Miss Merry was elderly and altogether neutral in expression. Mrs. Davilow's worn beauty seemed the more pathetic for the look of entire appeal which she cast at Gwendolen, who was glancing round at the house, the landscape, and the entrance hall with an air of rapid judgment. Imagine a young race-horse in the paddock among untrimmed ponies and patient hacks.

'Well, dear, what do you think of the place?' said Mrs. Davilow at last, in a gentle deprecatory tone.

'I think it is charming,' said Gwendolen, quickly. 'A romantic place; anything delightful may happen in it; it would be a good background for anything. No one need be ashamed of living here.'

'There is certainly nothing common about it.'

'Oh it would do for fallen royalty or any sort of grand poverty. We ought properly to have been living in splendour, and have come down to this. It would have been as romantic as could be. But I thought my uncle and aunt Gascoigne would be here to meet us, and my cousin Anna,' added Gwendolen, her tone changed to sharp surprise.

'We are early,' said Mrs. Davilow; and entering the hall, she said to the housekeeper who came forward, 'You expect Mr. and Mrs. Gascoigne?'

'Yes, madam: they were here yesterday to give particular orders about the fires and the dinner. But as to fires, I've had 'em in all the rooms for the last week, and everything is well aired. I could wish some of the furniture paid better for all the cleaning it's had, but I *think* you'll see the brasses have been done justice to. I *think* when Mr. and Mrs. Gascoigne come, they'll tell you nothing's been neglected. They'll be here at five, for certain.'

This satisfied Gwendolen, who was not prepared to have their arrival treated with indifference; and after tripping a little way up the matted stone staircase to take a survey there, she tripped down again, and followed by all the girls looked into each of the rooms opening from the hall – the dining-room all dark oak and worn red satin damask, with a copy of snarling, worrying dogs from Snyders over the sideboard, and a Christ breaking bread over the mantelpiece; the library with a general aspect and smell of old brown leather; and lastly, the drawing-room, which was entered through a small antechamber crowded with venerable knick-knacks.

'Mamma, mamma, pray come here!' said Gwendolen, Mrs. Davilow having followed slowly in talk with the housekeeper. 'Here is an organ. I will be Saint Cecilia; some one shall paint me as Saint Cecilia. Jocosa (this was her name for Miss Merry), let down my hair. See, mamma!'

She had thrown off her hat and gloves, and seated herself before the organ in an admirable pose, looking upward; while the submissive and sad Jocosa took out the one comb which fastened the coil of hair, and then shook out the mass till it fell in a smooth light-brown stream far below its owner's slim waist.

Mrs. Davilow smiled and said, 'A charming picture, my dear!' not indifferent to the display of her pet, even in the presence of a housekeeper. Gwendolen rose and laughed with delight. All this seemed quite to the purpose on entering a new house which was so excellent a background.

'What a queer, quaint, picturesque room!' she went on, looking about her. 'I like these old embroidered chairs, and the garlands on the wainscot, and the pictures that may be anything. That one with the ribs – nothing but ribs and darkness – I should think that is Spanish, mamma.'

'Oh *Gwendolen*!' said the small Isabel, in a tone of astonishment, while she held open a hinged panel of the wainscot at the other end of the room.

Every one, Gwendolen first, went to look. The opened panel had disclosed the picture of an upturned dead face, from which an obscure figure seemed to be fleeing with outstretched arms. 'How horrible!' said Mrs. Davilow, with a look of mere disgust; but Gwendolen shuddered silently, and Isabel, a plain and altogether inconvenient child with an alarming memory, said –

'You will never stay in this room by yourself, Gwendolen.'

'How dare you open things which were meant to be shut up, you perverse little creature?' said Gwendolen, in her angriest tone. Then snatching the panel out of the hand of the culprit, she closed it hastily, saying, 'There is a lock – where is the key? Let the key be found, or else let one be made, and let nobody open it again; or rather, let the key be brought to me.'

At this command to everybody in general Gwendolen turned with a face which was flushed in reaction from her chill shudder, and said, 'Let us go up to our own room, mamma.'

The housekeeper on searching found the key in the drawer of a cabinet close by the panel, and presently handed it to Bugle, the lady's maid, telling her significantly to give it to her Royal Highness.

'I don't know who you mean, Mrs. Startin,' said Bugle, who had been busy upstairs during the scene in the drawing-room, and was rather offended at this irony in a new servant.

'I mean the young lady that's to command us all – and well worthy for looks and figure,' replied Mrs. Startin in propitiation. 'She'll know what key it is.'

'If you have laid out what we want, go and see to the others, Bugle,' Gwendolen had said, when she and Mrs. Davilow entered their black and yellow bedroom, where a pretty little white couch was prepared by the side of the black and yellow catafalque known as 'the best bed.' 'I will help mamma.'

But her first movement was to go to the tall mirror between the windows, which reflected herself and the room completely, while her mamma sat down and also looked at the reflection.

'That is a becoming glass, Gwendolen; or is it the black and gold colour that sets you off?' said Mrs. Davilow, as Gwendolen stood obliquely with her three-quarter face turned towards the mirror, and her left hand brushing back the stream of hair.

'I should make a tolerable Saint Cecilia with some white roses on my head,' said Gwendolen, – 'only, how about my nose, mamma? I think saints' noses never in the least turn up. I wish you had given me your perfectly straight nose; it would have done for any sort of character – a nose of all work. Mine is only a happy nose; it would not do so well for tragedy.'

'Oh, my dear, any nose will do to be miserable with in this world,' said Mrs. Davilow, with a deep, weary sigh, throwing her black bonnet on the table, and resting her elbow near it.

'Now, mamma!' said Gwendolen in a strongly remonstrant tone, turning away from the glass with an air of vexation, 'don't begin to be dull here. It spoils all my pleasure, and everything may be so happy now. What have you to be gloomy about *now*?'

'Nothing, dear,' said Mrs. Davilow, seeming to rouse herself, and beginning to take off her dress. 'It is always enough for me to see you happy.'

'But you should be happy yourself,' said Gwendolen, still discontentedly, though going to help her mamma with caressing touches. 'Can nobody be happy after they are quite young? You have made me feel sometimes as if nothing were of any use. With the girls so troublesome, and Jocosa so dreadfully wooden and ugly, and everything make-shift about us, and you looking so dull – what was the use of my being anything? But now you *might* be happy.'

'So I shall, dear,' said Mrs. Davilow, patting the cheek that was bending near her.

'Yes, but really. Not with a sort of make-believe,' said Gwendolen with resolute perseverance. 'See what a hand and arm! – much more beautiful than mine. Any one can see you were altogether more beautiful.'

'No, no, dear. I was always heavier. Never half so charming as you are.'

'Well, but what is the use of my being charming, if it is to end in my being dull and not minding anything? Is that what marriage always comes to?'

'No, child, certainly not. Marriage is the only happy state for a woman, as I trust you will prove.'

'I will not put up with it if it is not a happy state. I am determined to be happy – at least not to go on muddling away my life as other people do, being and doing nothing remarkable. I have made up my mind not to let other people interfere with me as they have done. Here is some warm water ready for you, mamma,' Gwendolen ended, proceeding to take off her own dress and then waiting to have her hair wound up by her mamma.

There was silence for a minute or two, till Mrs. Davilow said, while coiling the daughter's hair, 'I am sure I have never crossed you, Gwendolen.'

'You often want me to do what I don't like.'

'You mean, to give Alice lessons?'

'Yes. And I have done it because you asked me. But I don't see why I should, else. It bores me to death, she is so slow. She has no ear for music, or language, or anything else. It would be much better for her to be ignorant, mamma: it is her *rôle*, she would do it well.'

'That is a hard thing to say of your poor sister, Gwendolen, who is so good to you, and waits on you hand and foot.'

'I don't see why it is hard to call things by their right names and put them in their proper places. The hardship is for me to have to waste my time on her. Now let me fasten up your hair, mamma.'

'We must make haste. Your uncle and aunt will be here soon. For heaven's sake, don't be scornful to *them*, my dear child, or to your cousin Anna, whom you will always be going out with. Do promise me, Gwendolen. You know, you can't expect Anna to be equal to you.'

'I don't want her to be equal,' said Gwendolen, with a toss of her head and a smile, and the discussion ended there.

When Mr. and Mrs. Gascoigne and their daughter came, Gwendolen, far from being scornful, behaved as prettily as possible to them. She was introducing herself anew to relatives who had not seen her since the comparatively unfinished age of sixteen, and she was anxious – no, not anxious, but resolved that they should admire her.

Mrs. Gascoigne bore a family likeness to her sister. But she was darker and slighter, her face was unworn by grief, her movements were less languid, her expression more alert and critical as that of a rector's wife bound to exert a beneficent authority. Their closest resemblance lay in a non-resistant disposition, inclined to imitation and obedience; but this, owing to the difference in their circumstances, had led them to very different issues. The younger sister had been indiscreet, or at least unfortunate in her marriages; the elder believed herself the most enviable of wives, and her pliancy had ended in her sometimes taking shapes of surprising definiteness. Many of her opinions, such as those on church government and the character of Archbishop Laud, seemed too decided under every alteration to have been arrived at otherwise than by a wifely receptiveness. And there was much to encourage trust in her husband's authority. He had some agreeable virtues, some striking advantages, and the failings that were imputed to him all leaned toward the side of success.

One of his advantages was a fine person, which perhaps was even more impressive at fifty-seven than it had been earlier in life. There were no distinctively clerical lines in the face, no official reserve or ostentatious benignity of expression, no tricks of starchiness or of affected ease: in his Inverness cape he could not have been identified except as a gentleman with handsome dark features, a nose which began with an intention to be aquiline but suddenly became straight, and iron-grey hair. Perhaps he owed this freedom from the sort of professional make-up which penetrates skin tones and gestures and defies all drapery, to the fact that he had once been Captain Gaskin, having taken orders and a diphthong but shortly before his engagement to Miss Armyn. If any one had objected that his preparation for the clerical function was inadequate, his friends might have asked who made a better figure in it, who preached better or had more authority in his parish? He had a native gift for administration, being tolerant both of opinions and conduct, because he felt himself able to overrule them, and was free from the irritations of conscious feebleness. He smiled pleasantly at the foible of a taste which he did not share – at floriculture or antiquarianism for example, which were much in vogue among his fellow-clergymen in the diocese: for himself, he preferred following the history of a campaign, or divining from his knowledge of Nesselrode's motives what would have been his conduct if our cabinet had taken a different course. Mr. Gascoigne's tone of thinking after some long-quieted fluctuations had become ecclesiastical rather than theological; not the modern Anglican, but what he would have called sound English, free from nonsense: such as became a man who looked at a national religion by daylight, and saw it in its relations to other things. No clerical magistrate had greater weight at sessions, or less of mischievous impracticableness in relation to worldly affairs. Indeed, the worst imputation thrown out against him was worldliness: it could not be proved that he forsook the less fortunate, but it was not to be denied that the friendships he cultivated were of a kind likely to be useful to the father of six sons and two daughters; and bitter observers – for in Wessex, say ten years ago, there were persons whose bitterness may now seem incredible – remarked that the colour of his opinions had changed in consistency with this principle of action. But cheerful, successful worldliness has a false air of being more selfish than the acrid, unsuccessful kind, whose secret history is summed up in the terrible words, 'Sold, but not paid for.'

Gwendolen wondered that she had not better remembered how very fine a man her uncle was; but at the age of sixteen she was a less capable and more indifferent judge. At present it was a matter of extreme interest to her that she was to have the near countenance of a dignified male relative, and that the family life would cease to be entirely, insipidly feminine. She did not intend that her uncle should control her, but she saw at once that it would be altogether agreeable to her that he should be proud of introducing her as his niece. And there was every sign of his being likely to feel that pride. He certainly looked at her with admiration as he said –

'You have outgrown Anna, my dear,' putting his arm tenderly round his daughter, whose shy face was a tiny copy of his own, and drawing her forward. 'She is not so old as you by a year, but her growing days are certainly over. I hope you will be excellent companions.'

He did give a comparing glance at his daughter, but if he saw her inferiority he might also see that Anna's timid appearance and miniature figure must appeal to a different taste from that which was attracted by Gwendolen, and that the girls could hardly be rivals. Gwendolen, at least, was aware of this, and kissed her cousin with real cordiality as well as grace, saying, 'A companion is just what I want. I am so glad we are come to live here. And mamma will be much happier now she is near you, aunt.'

The aunt trusted indeed that it would be so, and felt it a blessing that a suitable home had been vacant in their uncle's parish. Then, of course, notice had to be taken of the four other girls whom Gwendolen had always felt to be superfluous: all of a girlish average that made four units utterly unimportant, and yet from her earliest days an obtrusive influential fact in her life. She was conscious of having been much kinder to them than could have been expected. And it was evident to her that her uncle and aunt also felt it a pity there were so many girls: – what rational person could feel otherwise, except poor mamma, who never would see how Alice set up her shoulders and lifted her eyebrows till she had no forehead left, how Bertha and Fanny whispered and tittered together about everything, or how Isabel was always listening and staring and forgetting where she was, and treading on the toes of her suffering elders.

'You have brothers, Anna,' said Gwendolen, while the sisters were being noticed. 'I think you are enviable there.'

'Yes,' said Anna, simply, 'I am very fond of them. But of course their education is a great anxiety to papa. He used to say they made me a tomboy. I really was a great romp with Rex. I think you will like Rex. He will come home before Christmas.'

'I remember I used to think you rather wild and shy. But it is difficult now to imagine you a romp,' said Gwendolen, smiling.

'Of course I am altered now; I am come out, and all that. But in reality I like to go blackberrying with Edwy and Lotta as well as ever. I am not very fond of going out; but I dare say I shall like it better now you will be often with me. I am not at all clever, and I never know what to say. It seems so useless to say what everybody knows, and I can think of nothing else, except what papa says.'

'I shall like going out with you very much,' said Gwendolen, well disposed towards this *naïve* cousin. 'Are you fond of riding?'

'Yes, but we have only one Shetland pony amongst us. Papa says he can't afford more, besides the carriage-horses and his own nag. He has so many expenses.'

'I intend to have a horse and ride a great deal now,' said Gwendolen, in a tone of decision. 'Is the society pleasant in this neighbourhood?'

'Papa says it is, very. There are the clergymen all about, you know; and the Quallons and the Arrowpoints, and

Lord Brackenshaw, and Sir Hugo Mallinger's place where there is nobody – that's very nice, because we make picnics there – and two or three families at Wancester; oh, and old Mrs. Vulcany at Nuttingwood, and –'

But Anna was relieved of this tax on her descriptive powers by the announcement of dinner, and Gwendolen's question was soon indirectly answered by her uncle, who dwelt much on the advantages he had secured for them in getting a place like Offendene. Except the rent, it involved no more expense than an ordinary house at Wancester would have done.

'And it is always worth while to make a little sacrifice for a good style of house,' said Mr. Gascoigne, in his easy, pleasantly confident tone, which made the world in general seem a very manageable place of residence. 'Especially where there is only a lady at the head. All the best people will call upon you; and you need give no expensive dinners. Of course I have to spend a good deal in that way; it is a large item. But then I get my house for nothing. If I had to pay three hundred a-year for my house I could not keep a table. My boys are too great a drain on me. You are better off than we are, in proportion; there is no great drain on you now, after your house and carriage.'

'I assure you, Fanny, now the children are growing up, I am obliged to cut and contrive,' said Mrs. Gascoigne. 'I am not a good manager by nature, but Henry has taught me. He is wonderful for making the best of everything; he allows himself no extras, and gets his curates for nothing. It is rather hard that he has not been made a prebendary or something, as others have been, considering the friends he has made, and the need there is for men of moderate opinions in all respects. If the Church is to keep its position, ability and character ought to tell.'

'Oh, my dear Nancy, you forget the old story – thank Heaven, there are three hundred as good as I. And ultimately we shall have no reason to complain, I am pretty sure. There could hardly be a more thorough friend than Lord Brackenshaw, your landlord, you know, Fanny. Lady

Brackenshaw will call upon you. And I have spoken for Gwendolen to be a member of our Archery Club – the Brackenshaw Archery Club – the most select thing anywhere. That is, if she has no objection,' added Mr. Gascoigne, looking at Gwendolen with pleasant irony.

'I should like it of all things,' said Gwendolen. 'There is nothing I enjoy more than taking aim – and hitting,' she ended, with a pretty nod and smile.

'Our Anna, poor child, is too short-sighted for archery. But I consider myself a first-rate shot, and you shall practise with me. I must make you an accomplished archer before our great meeting in July. In fact, as to neighbourhood, you could hardly be better placed. There are the Arrowpoints – they are some of our best people. Miss Arrowpoint is a delightful girl: – she has been presented at court. They have a magnificent place – Quetcham Hall – worth seeing in point of art; and their parties, to which you are sure to be invited, are the best things of the sort we have. The archdeacon is intimate there, and they have always a good kind of people staying in the house. Mrs. Arrowpoint is peculiar, certainly; something of a caricature, in fact; but well-meaning. And Miss Arrowpoint is as nice as possible. It is not all young ladies who have mothers as handsome and graceful as yours and Anna's.'

Mrs. Davilow smiled faintly at this little compliment, but the husband and wife looked affectionately at each other, and Gwendolen thought, 'My uncle and aunt, at least, are happy; they are not dull and dismal.' Altogether, she felt satisfied with her prospects at Offendene, as a great improvement on anything she had known. Even the cheap curates, she incidentally learned, were almost always young men of family, and Mr. Middleton, the actual curate, was said to be quite an acquisition: it was only a pity he was so soon to leave.

But there was one point which she was so anxious to gain that she could not allow the evening to pass without taking her measures towards securing it. Her mamma, she knew, intended to submit entirely to her uncle's judgment with regard to expenditure; and the submission was not merely prudential, for Mrs. Davilow, conscious that she had always been seen under a cloud as poor dear Fanny, who had made a sad blunder with her second marriage, felt a hearty satisfaction in being frankly and cordially identified with her sister's family, and in having her affairs canvassed and managed with an authority which presupposed a genuine interest. Thus the question of a suitable saddle-horse, which had been sufficiently discussed with mamma, had to be referred to Mr. Gascoigne; and after Gwendolen had played on the piano, which had been provided from Wancester, had sung to her hearers' admiration, and had induced her uncle to join her in a duet – what more softening influence than this on any uncle who would have sung finely if his time had not been too much taken up by graver matters? – she seized the opportune moment for saying, 'Mamma, you have not spoken to my uncle about my riding.'

'Gwendolen desires above all things to have a horse to ride – a pretty, light, lady's horse,' said Mrs. Davilow, looking at Mr. Gascoigne. 'Do you think we can manage it?'

Mr. Gascoigne projected his lower lip and lifted his handsome eyebrows sarcastically at Gwendolen, who had seated herself with much grace on the elbow of her mamma's chair.

'We could lend her the pony sometimes,' said Mrs. Gascoigne, watching her husband's face, and feeling quite ready to disapprove if he did.

'That might be inconveniencing others, aunt, and would be no pleasure to me. I cannot endure ponies,' said Gwendolen. 'I would rather give up some other indulgence and have a horse.' (Was there ever a young lady or gentleman not ready to give up an unspecified indulgence for the sake of the favourite one specified?)

'She rides so well. She has had lessons and the riding-master said she had so good a seat and hand she might be trusted with any mount,' said Mrs. Davilow, who, even if she had not wished her darling to have the horse, would not have dared to be lukewarm in trying to get it for her.

'There is the price of the horse – a good sixty with the best chance, and then his keep,' said Mr. Gascoigne, in a tone which, though demurring, betrayed the inward presence of something that favoured the demand. 'There are the carriage-horses – already a heavy item. And remember what you ladies cost in toilet now.'

'I really wear nothing but two black dresses,' said Mrs. Davilow, hastily. 'And the younger girls, of course, require no toilet at present. Besides, Gwendolen will save me so much by giving her sisters lessons.' Here Mrs. Davilow's delicate cheek showed a rapid blush. 'If it were not for that, I must really have a more expensive governess, and masters besides.'

Gwendolen felt some anger with her mamma, but carefully concealed it.

'That is good – that is decidedly good,' said Mr. Gascoigne, heartily, looking at his wife. And Gwendolen, who, it must be owned, was a deep young lady, suddenly moved away to the other end of the long drawing-room, and busied herself with arranging pieces of music.

'The dear child has had no indulgences, no pleasures,' said Mrs. Davilow, in a pleading undertone. 'I feel the expense is rather imprudent in this first year of our settling. But she really needs the exercise – she needs cheering. And if you were to see her on horseback, it *is* something splendid.'

'It is what we could not afford for Anna,' said Mrs. Gascoigne. 'But she, dear child, would ride Lotta's donkey, and think it good enough.' (Anna was absorbed in a game with Isabel, who had hunted out an old backgammon-board, and had begged to sit up an extra hour.)

'Certainly, a fine woman never looks better than on horseback,' said Mr. Gascoigne. 'And Gwendolen has the figure for it. I don't say the thing should not be considered.'

'We might try it for a time, at all events. It can be given up, if necessary,' said Mrs. Davilow.

'Well, I will consult Lord Brackenshaw's head groom. He is my *fidus Achates* in the horsey way.'

'Thanks,' said Mrs. Davilow, much relieved. 'You are very kind.'

'That he always is,' said Mrs. Gascoigne. And later that night, when she and her husband were in private, she said –

'I thought you were almost too indulgent about the horse for Gwendolen. She ought not to claim so much more than your own daughter would think of. Especially before we see how Fanny manages on her income. And you really have enough to do without taking all this trouble on yourself.'

'My dear Nancy, one must look at things from every point of view. This girl is really worth some expense: you don't often see her equal. She ought to make a first-rate marriage, and I should not be doing my duty if I spared my trouble in helping her forward. You know yourself she has been under a disadvantage with such a father-in-law, and a second family, keeping her always in the shade. I feel for the girl. And I should like your sister and her family now to have the benefit of your having married rather a better specimen of our kind than she did.'

'Rather better! I should think so. However, it is for me to be grateful that you will take so much on your shoulders for the sake of my sister and her children. I am sure I would not grudge anything to poor Fanny. But there is one thing I have been thinking of, though you have never mentioned it.'

'What is that?'

'The boys. I hope they will not be falling in love with Gwendolen.'

'Don't presuppose anything of the kind, my dear, and there will be no danger. Rex will never be at home for long together, and Warham is going to India. It is the wiser plan to take it for granted that cousins will not fall in love. If you begin with precautions, the affair will come in spite of them. One must not undertake to act for Providence in these matters, which can no more be held under the hand than a brood of chickens. The boys will have nothing, and Gwendolen will have nothing. They can't marry. At the worst there would only be a little crying, and you can't save boys and girls from that.'

Mrs. Gascoigne's mind was satisfied: if anything did happen, there was the comfort of feeling that her husband would know what was to be done, and would have the energy to do it.

IV

'*Gorgibus.* – ...Je te dis que le mariage est une chose sainte et sacrée, et que c'est faire en honnêtes gens, que de débuter par là.
'*Madelon.* – Mon Dieu! que si tout le monde vous ressemblait, un roman serait bientôt fini! La belle chose que ce serait, si d'abord Cyrus épousait Mandane, et qu'Aronce de plain-pied fût marié à Clélie! ...Laissez-nous faire à loisir le tissu de notre roman, et n'en pressez pas tant la conclusion.'

– MOLIÈRE: *Les Précieuses Ridicules.*

IT would be a little hard to blame the Rector of Pennicote that in the course of looking at things from every point of view, he looked at Gwendolen as a girl likely to make a brilliant marriage. Why should he be expected to differ from his contemporaries in this matter, and wish his niece a worse end of her charming maidenhood than they would approve as the best possible? It is rather to be set down to his credit that his feelings on the subject were entirely good-natured. And in considering the relation of means to ends, it would have been mere folly to have been guided by the exceptional and idyllic – to have recommended that Gwendolen should wear a gown as shabby as Griselda's in order that a marquis might fall in love with her, or to have insisted that since a fair maiden was to be sought, she should keep herself out of the way. Mr. Gascoigne's calculations were of the kind called rational, and he did not even think of getting a too frisky horse in order that Gwendolen might be threatened with an accident and be rescued by a man of property. He wished his niece well, and he meant her to be seen to advantage in the best society of the neighbourhood.

Her uncle's intention fell in perfectly with Gwendolen's own wishes. But let no one suppose that she also contemplated a brilliant marriage as the direct end of her witching the world with her grace on horseback, or with any other accomplishment. That she was to be married some time or other she would have felt obliged to admit; and that her marriage would not be of a middling kind, such as most

girls were contented with, she felt quietly, unargumenta-
tively sure. But her thoughts never dwelt on marriage as
the fulfilment of her ambition; the dramas in which she
imagined herself a heroine were not wrought up to that
close. To be very much sued or hopelessly sighed for as a
bride was indeed an indispensable and agreeable guarantee of womanly power; but to become a wife and wear all
the domestic fetters of that condition, was on the whole a
vexatious necessity. Her observation of matrimony had
inclined her to think it rather a dreary state, in which a
woman could not do what she liked, had more children
than were desirable, was consequently dull, and became
irrevocably immersed in humdrum. Of course marriage
was social promotion; she could not look forward to a single
life; but promotions have sometimes to be taken with
bitter herbs – a peerage will not quite do instead of leader-
ship to the man who meant to lead; and this delicate-
limbed sylph of twenty meant to lead. For such passions
dwell in feminine breasts also. In Gwendolen's, however,
they dwelt among strictly feminine furniture, and had no
disturbing reference to the advancement of learning or the
balance of the constitution; her knowledge being such as
with no sort of standing-room or length of lever could have
been expected to move the world. She meant to do what
was pleasant to herself in a striking manner; or rather,
whatever she could do so as to strike others with admiration and get in that reflected way a more ardent sense of
living, seemed pleasant to her fancy.

'Gwendolen will not rest without having the world at
her feet,' said Miss Merry, the meek governess: – hyperbolical words which have long come to carry the most
moderate meanings; for who has not heard of private persons having the world at their feet in the shape of some
half-dozen items of flattering regard generally known in a
genteel suburb? And words could hardly be too wide or
vague to indicate the prospect that made a hazy largeness
about poor Gwendolen on the heights of her young self-
exultation. Other people allowed themselves to be made

slaves of, and to have their lives blown hither and thither like empty ships in which no will was present: it was not to be so with her, she would no longer be sacrificed to creatures worth less than herself, but would make the very best of the chances that life offered her, and conquer circumstance by her exceptional cleverness. Certainly, to be settled at Offendene, with the notice of Lady Brackenshaw, the archery club, and invitations to dine with the Arrowpoints, as the highest lights in her scenery, was not a position that seemed to offer remarkable chances; but Gwendolen's confidence lay chiefly in herself. She felt well equipped for the mastery of life. With regard to much in her lot hitherto, she held herself rather hardly dealt with, but as to her 'education' she would have admitted that it had left her under no disadvantages. In the schoolroom her quick mind had taken readily that strong starch of unexplained rules and disconnected facts which saves ignorance from any painful sense of limpness; and what remained of all things knowable, she was conscious of being sufficiently acquainted with through novels, plays, and poems. About her French and music, the two justifying accomplishments of a young lady, she felt no ground for uneasiness; and when to all these qualifications, negative and positive, we add the spontaneous sense of capability some happy persons are born with, so that any subject they turn attention to impresses them with their own power of forming a correct judgment on it, who can wonder if Gwendolen felt ready to manage her own destiny?

There were many subjects in the world – perhaps the majority – in which she felt no interest, because they were stupid; for subjects are apt to appear stupid to the young as light seems dim to the old; but she would not have felt at all helpless in relation to them if they had turned up in conversation. It must be remembered that no one had disputed her power or her general superiority. As on the arrival at Offendene, so always, the first thought of those about her had been, what will Gwendolen think? – if the footman trod heavily in creaking boots or if the laundress's work was

41

unsatisfactory, the maid said 'This will never do for Miss Harleth;' if the wood smoked in the bedroom fireplace, Mrs. Davilow, whose own weak eyes suffered much from this inconvenience, spoke apologetically of it to Gwendolen. If, when they were under the stress of travelling, she did not appear at the breakfast-table till every one else had finished, the only question was, how Gwendolen's coffee and toast should still be of the hottest and crispest; and when she appeared with her freshly-brushed light-brown hair streaming backward and awaiting her mamma's hand to coil it up, her long brown eyes glancing bright as a wave-washed onyx from under their long lashes, it was always she herself who had to be tolerant – to beg that Alice who sat waiting on her would not stick up her shoulders in that frightful manner, and that Isabel instead of pushing up to her and asking questions would go away to Miss Merry.

Always she was the princess in exile, who in time of famine was to have her breakfast-roll made of the finest-bolted flour from the seven thin ears of wheat, and in a general decampment was to have her silver fork kept out of the baggage. How was this to be accounted for? The answer may seem to lie quite on the surface: – in her beauty, a certain unusualness about her, a decision of will which made itself felt in her graceful movements and clear unhesitating tones, so that if she came into the room on a rainy day when everybody else was flaccid and the use of things in general was not apparent to them, there seemed to be a sudden, sufficient reason for keeping up the forms of life; and even the waiters at hotels showed the more alacrity in doing away with crumbs and creases and dregs with struggling flies in them. This potent charm, added to the fact that she was the eldest daughter, towards whom her mamma had always been in an apologetic state of mind for the evils brought on her by a step-father, may seem so full a reason for Gwendolen's domestic empire, that to look for any other would be to ask the reason of daylight when the sun is shining. But beware of arriving at conclusions without comparison. I remember having seen the same assiduous, apologetic attention awarded to persons who were not at all beautiful or unusual, whose firmness showed itself in no very graceful or euphonious way, and who were not eldest daughters with a tender, timid mother, compunctious at having subjected them to inconveniences. Some of them were a very common sort of men. And the only point of resemblance among them all was a strong determination to have what was pleasant, with a total fearlessness in making themselves disagreeable or dangerous when they did not get it. Who is so much cajoled and served with trembling by the weak females of a household as the unscrupulous male – capable, if he has not free way at home, of going and doing worse elsewhere? Hence I am forced to doubt whether even without her potent charm and peculiar filial position Gwendolen might not still have played the queen in exile, if only she had kept her inborn energy of egoistic desire, and her power of inspiring fear as to what she might say or do. However, she had the charm, and those who feared her were also fond of her; the fear and the fondness being perhaps both heightened by what may be called the iridescence of her character – the play of various, nay, contrary tendencies. For Macbeth's rhetoric about the impossibility of being many opposite things in the same moment, referred to the clumsy necessities of action and not to the subtler possibilities of feeling. We cannot speak a loyal word and be meanly silent, we cannot kill and not kill in the same moment; but a moment is room wide enough for the loyal and mean desire, for the outlash of a murderous thought and the sharp backward stroke of repentance.

V

'Her wit
Values itself so highly, that to her
All matter else seems weak.'
– *Much Ado about Nothing*.

GWENDOLEN'S reception in the neighbourhood fulfilled her uncle's expectations. From Brackenshaw Castle to the Firs at Wancester, where Mr. Quallon the banker kept a generous house, she was welcomed with manifest admiration, and even those ladies who did not quite like her, felt a comfort in having a new, striking girl to invite; for hostesses who entertain much must make up their parties as ministers make up their cabinets, on grounds other than personal liking. Then, in order to have Gwendolen as a guest, it was not necessary to ask any one who was disagreeable, for Mrs. Davilow always made a quiet, picturesque figure as a chaperon, and Mr. Gascoigne was everywhere in request for his own sake.

Among the houses where Gwendolen was not quite liked, and yet invited, was Quetcham Hall. One of her first invitations was to a large dinner party there, which made a sort of general introduction for her to the society of the neighbourhood; for in a select party of thirty and of well-composed proportions as to age, few visitable families could be entirely left out. No youthful figure there was comparable to Gwendolen's as she passed through the long suite of rooms adorned with light and flowers, and, visible at first as a slim figure floating along in white drapery, approached through one wide doorway after another into fuller illumination and definiteness. She had never had that sort of promenade before, and she felt exultingly that it befitted her: any one looking at her for the first time might have supposed that long galleries and lackeys had always been a matter of course in her life; while her cousin Anna, who was really more familiar with these things, felt almost as much embarrassed as a rabbit suddenly deposited in that well-lit space.

'Who is that with Gascoigne?' said the archdeacon, neglecting a discussion of military manœuvres on which, as a clergyman, he was naturally appealed to. And his son, on the other side of the room – a hopeful young scholar, who had already suggested some 'not less elegant than ingenious' emendations of Greek texts – said nearly at the same time, 'By George, who is that girl with the awfully well-set head and jolly figure?'

But to a mind of general benevolence, wishing everybody to look well, it was rather exasperating to see how Gwendolen eclipsed others: how even the handsome Miss Lawe, explained to be the daughter of Lady Lawe, looked suddenly broad, heavy, and inanimate; and how Miss Arrowpoint, unfortunately also dressed in white, immediately resembled a *carte-de-visite* in which one would fancy the skirt alone to have been charged for. Since Miss Arrowpoint was generally liked for the amiable unpretending way in which she wore her fortunes, and made a softening screen for the oddities of her mother, there seemed to be some unfitness in Gwendolen's looking so much more like a person of social importance.

'She is not really so handsome, if you come to examine her features,' said Mrs. Arrowpoint, later in the evening, confidentially to Mrs. Vulcany. 'It is a certain style she has, which produces a great effect at first, but afterwards she is less agreeable.'

In fact, Gwendolen, not intending it, but intending the contrary, had offended her hostess, who, though not a splenetic or vindictive woman, had her susceptibilities. Several conditions had met in the Lady of Quetcham which to the reasoners in that neighbourhood seemed to have an essential connection with each other. It was occasionally recalled that she had been the heiress of a fortune gained by some moist or dry business in the city, in order fully to account for her having a squat figure, a harsh parrot-like voice, and a systematically high head-dress; and since

45

these points made her externally rather ridiculous, it appeared to many only natural that she should have what are called literary tendencies. A little comparison would have shown that all these points are to be found apart; daughters of aldermen being often well-grown and well-featured, pretty women having sometimes harsh or husky voices, and the production of feeble literature being found compatible with the most diverse forms of physique, masculine as well as feminine.

Gwendolen, who had a keen sense of absurdity in others, but was kindly disposed towards any one who could make life agreeable to her, meant to win Mrs. Arrowpoint by giving her an interest and attention beyond what others were probably inclined to show. But self-confidence is apt to address itself to an imaginary dullness in others; as people who are well-off speak in a cajoling tone to the poor, and those who are in the prime of life raise their voice and talk artificially to seniors, hastily conceiving them to be deaf and rather imbecile. Gwendolen, with all her cleverness and purpose to be agreeable, could not escape that form of stupidity: it followed in her mind, unreflectingly, that because Mrs. Arrowpoint was ridiculous she was also likely to be wanting in penetration, and she went through her little scenes without suspicion that the various shades of her behaviour were all noted.

'You are fond of books as well as of music, riding, and archery, I hear,' Mrs. Arrowpoint said, going to her for a *tête-à-tête* in the drawing-room after dinner: 'Catherine will be very glad to have so sympathetic a neighbour.' This little speech might have seemed the most graceful politeness, spoken in a low melodious tone; but with a twang fatally loud, it gave Gwendolen a sense of exercising patronage when she answered gracefully –

'It is I who am fortunate. Miss Arrowpoint will teach me what good music is: I shall be entirely a learner. I hear that she is a thorough musician.'

'Catherine has certainly had every advantage. We have a first-rate musician in the house now – Herr Klesmer;

perhaps you know all his compositions. You must allow me to introduce him to you. You sing, I believe. Catherine plays three instruments, but she does not sing. I hope you will let us hear you. I understand you are an accomplished singer.'

'Oh no! – "die Kraft ist schwach, allein die Lust ist gross," as Mephistopheles says.'

'Ah, you are a student of Goethe. Young ladies are so advanced now. I suppose you have read everything.'

'No, really. I shall be so glad if you will tell me what to read. I have been looking into all the books in the library at Offendene, but there is nothing readable. The leaves all stick together and smell musty. I wish I could write books to amuse myself, as you can! How delightful it must be to write books after one's own taste instead of reading other people's! Home-made books must be so nice.'

For an instant Mrs. Arrowpoint's glance was a little sharper, but the perilous resemblance to satire in the last sentence took the hue of girlish simplicity when Gwendolen added –

'I would give anything to write a book!'

'And why should you not?' said Mrs. Arrowpoint, encouragingly. 'You have but to begin as I did. Pen, ink, and paper are at everybody's command. But I will send you all I have written with pleasure.'

'Thanks. I shall be so glad to read your writings. Being acquainted with authors must give a peculiar understanding of their books: one would be able to tell then which parts were funny and which serious. I am sure I often laugh in the wrong place.' Here Gwendolen herself became aware of danger, and added quickly, 'In Shakespeare, you know, and other great writers that we can never see. But I always want to know more than there is in the books.'

'If you are interested in any of my subjects I can lend you many extra sheets in manuscript,' said Mrs. Arrowpoint – while Gwendolen felt herself painfully in the position of the young lady who professed to like potted sprats. 'These are things I dare say I shall publish eventually: several friends have urged me to do so, and one doesn't like to be obstinate. My Tasso, for example – I could have made it twice the size.'

'I dote on Tasso,' said Gwendolen.

'Well, you shall have all my papers, if you like. So many, you know, have written about Tasso; but they are all wrong. As to the particular nature of his madness, and his feelings for Leonora, and the real cause of his imprisonment, and the character of Leonora, who, in my opinion, was a cold-hearted woman, else she would have married him in spite of her brother – they are all wrong. I differ from everybody.'

'How very interesting!' said Gwendolen. 'I like to differ from everybody. I think it is so stupid to agree. That is the worst of writing your opinions: you make people agree with you.'

This speech renewed a slight suspicion in Mrs. Arrowpoint, and again her glance became for a moment examining. But Gwendolen looked very innocent, and continued with a docile air.

'I know nothing of Tasso except the *Gerusalemme Liberata*, which we read and learned by heart at school.'

'Ah, his life is more interesting than his poetry. I have constructed the early part of his life as a sort of romance. When one thinks of his father Bernardo, and so on, there is so much that must be true.'

'Imagination is often truer than fact,' said Gwendolen, decisively, though she could no more have explained these glib words than if they had been Coptic or Etruscan. 'I shall be so glad to learn all about Tasso – and his madness especially. I suppose poets are always a little mad.'

'To be sure – "the poet's eye in a fine frenzy rolling;" and somebody says of Marlowe –

> "For that fine madness still he did maintain,
>   Which always should possess the poet's brain."'

'But it was not always found out, was it?' said Gwendolen, innocently. 'I suppose some of them rolled their eyes in private. Mad people are often very cunning.'

Again a shade flitted over Mrs. Arrowpoint's face; but the entrance of the gentlemen prevented any immediate mischief between her and this too quick young lady, who had over-acted her *naïveté*.

'Ah, here comes Herr Klesmer,' said Mrs. Arrowpoint, rising; and presently bringing him to Gwendolen she left them to a dialogue which was agreeable on both sides, Herr Klesmer being a felicitous combination of the German, the Sclave, and the Semite, with grand features, brown hair floating in artistic fashion, and brown eyes in spectacles. His English had little foreignness except its fluency; and his alarming cleverness was made less formidable just then by a certain softening air of silliness which will sometimes befall even Genius in the desire of being agreeable to Beauty.

Music was soon begun. Miss Arrowpoint and Herr Klesmer played a four-handed piece on two pianos which convinced the company in general that it was long, and Gwendolen in particular that the neutral, placid-faced Miss Arrowpoint had a mastery of the instrument which put her own execution out of the question – though she was not discouraged as to her often-praised touch and style. After this every one became anxious to hear Gwendolen sing; especially Mr. Arrowpoint; as was natural in a host and a perfect gentleman, of whom no one had anything to say but that he had married Miss Cuttler, and imported the best cigars; and he led her to the piano with easy politeness. Herr Klesmer closed the instrument in readiness for her, and smiled with pleasure at her approach; then placed himself at the distance of a few feet so that he could see her as she sang.

Gwendolen was not nervous: what she undertook to do she did without trembling, and singing was an enjoyment to her. Her voice was a moderately powerful soprano (some one had told her it was like Jenny Lind's), her ear good, and she was able to keep in tune, so that her singing gave pleasure to ordinary hearers, and she had been used to unmingled applause. She had the rare advantage of look- ing almost prettier when she was singing than at other times, and that Herr Klesmer was in front of her seemed not disagreeable. Her song, determined on beforehand, was a favourite aria of Bellini's, in which she felt quite sure of herself.

'Charming!' said Mr. Arrowpoint, who had remained near, and the word was echoed around without more insincerity than we recognize in a brotherly way as human. But Herr Klesmer stood like a statue – if a statue can be imagined in spectacles; at least, he was as mute as a statue. Gwendolen was pressed to keep her seat and double the general pleasure, and she did not wish to refuse; but before resolving to do so, she moved a little towards Herr Klesmer, saying with a look of smiling appeal, 'It would be too cruel to a great musician. You cannot like to hear poor amateur singing.'

'No, truly; but that makes nothing,' Herr Klesmer, suddenly speaking in an odious German fashion with staccato endings, quite unobservable in him before, and apparently depending on a change of mood, as Irishmen resume their strongest brogue when they are fervid or quarrelsome. 'That makes nothing. It is always acceptable to see you sing.'

Was there ever so unexpected an assertion of superiority? at least before the late Teutonic conquests? Gwendolen coloured deeply, but, with her usual presence of mind, did not show an ungraceful resentment by moving away immediately; and Miss Arrowpoint, who had been near enough to overhear (and also to observe that Herr Klesmer's mode of looking at Gwendolen was more conspicuously admiring than was quite consistent with good taste), now with the utmost tact and kindness came close to her and said –

'Imagine what I have to go through with this professor! He can hardly tolerate anything we English do in music. We can only put up with his severity, and make use of it to find out the worst that can be said of us. It is a little comfort to know that; and one can bear it when every one else is admiring.'

'I should be very much obliged to him for telling me the worst,' said Gwendolen, recovering herself. 'I dare say I have been extremely ill taught, in addition to having no talent – only liking for music.' This was very well expressed considering that it had never entered her mind before.

'Yes, it is true; you have not been well taught,' said Herr Klesmer, quietly. Woman was dear to him, but music was dearer. 'Still, you are not quite without gifts. You sing in tune, and you have a pretty fair organ. But you produce your notes badly; and that music which you sing is beneath you. It is a form of melody which expresses a puerile state of culture – a dandling, canting, see-saw kind of stuff – the passion and thought of people without any breadth of horizon. There is a sort of self-satisfied folly about every phrase of such melody: no cries of deep, mysterious passion – no conflict – no sense of the universal. It makes men small as they listen to it. Sing now something larger. And I shall see.'

'Oh, not now. By-and-by,' said Gwendolen, with a sinking of heart at the sudden width of horizon opened round her small musical performance. For a young lady desiring to lead, this first encounter in her campaign was startling. But she was bent on not behaving foolishly, and Miss Arrowpoint helped her by saying –

'Yes, by-and-by. I always require half an hour to get up my courage after being criticized by Herr Klesmer. We will ask him to play to us now: he is bound to show us what is good music.'

To be quite safe on this point Herr Klesmer played a composition of his own, a fantasia called *Freudvoll, Leidvoll, Gedankenvoll* – an extensive commentary on some melodic ideas not too grossly evident; and he certainly fetched as much variety and depth of passion out of the piano as that moderately responsive instrument lends itself to, having an imperious magic in his fingers that seemed to send a nerve-thrill through ivory key and wooden hammer, and compel the strings to make a quivering lingering speech for him.

Gwendolen, in spite of her wounded egoism, had fullness of nature enough to feel the power of this playing, and it gradually turned her inward sob of mortification into an excitement which lifted her for the moment into a desperate indifference about her own doings, or at least a determination to get a superiority over them by laughing at them as if they belonged to somebody else. Her eyes had become brighter, her cheeks slightly flushed, and her tongue ready for any mischievous remarks.

'I wish you would sing to us again, Miss Harleth,' said young Clintock, the archdeacon's classical son, who had been so fortunate as to take her to dinner, and came up to renew conversation as soon as Herr Klesmer's performance was ended. 'That is the style of music for me. I never can make anything of this tip-top playing. It is like a jar of leeches, where you can never tell either beginnings or endings. I could listen to your singing all day.'

'Yes, we should be glad of something popular now – another song from you would be a relaxation,' said Mrs. Arrowpoint, who had also come near with polite intentions.

'That must be because you are in a puerile state of culture, and have no breadth of horizon. I have just learned that. I have been taught how bad my taste is, and am feeling growing pains. They are never pleasant,' said Gwendolen, not taking any notice of Mrs. Arrowpoint, and looking up with a bright smile at young Clintock.

Mrs. Arrowpoint was not insensible to this rudeness, but merely said, 'Well, we will not press anything disagreeably:' and as there was a perceptible outrush of imprisoned conversation just then, and a movement of guests seeking each other, she remained seated where she was, and looked round her with the relief of the hostess at finding she is not needed.

'I am glad you like this neighbourhood,' said young Clintock, well pleased with his station in front of Gwendolen.

'Exceedingly. There seems to be a little of everything and not much of anything.'

'That is rather equivocal praise.'

'Not with me. I like a little of everything; a little absurd-ity, for example, is very amusing. I am thankful for a few queer people; but much of them is a bore.'

(Mrs. Arrowpoint, who was hearing this dialogue, per-ceived quite a new tone in Gwendolen's speech, and felt a revival of doubt as to her interest in Tasso's madness.)

'I think there should be more croquet, for one thing,' said young Clintock; 'I am usually away, but if I were more here I should go in for a croquet club. You are one of the archers, I think. But depend upon it croquet is the game of the future. It wants writing up, though. One of our best men has written a poem on it, in four cantos; – as good as Pope. I want him to publish it. You never read anything better.'

'I shall study croquet to-morrow. I shall take to it instead of singing.'

'No, no, not that; but do take to croquet. I will send you Jenning's poem, if you like. I have a manuscript copy.'

'Is he a great friend of yours?'

'Well, rather.'

'Oh, if he is only rather, I think I will decline. Or, if you send it me, will you promise not to catechize me upon it and ask me which part I like best? Because it is not so easy to know a poem without reading it as to know a sermon without listening.'

'Decidedly,' Mrs. Arrowpoint thought, 'this girl is double and satirical. I shall be on my guard against her.'

But Gwendolen, nevertheless, continued to receive polite attentions from the family at Quetcham, not merely because invitations have larger grounds than those of per-sonal liking, but because the trying little scene at the piano had awakened a kindly solicitude towards her in the gentle mind of Miss Arrowpoint, who managed all the invitations and visits, her mother being otherwise occupied.

VI

'Croyez vous m'avoir humiliée pour m'avoir appris que la terre
tourne autour du soleil? Je vous jure que je ne m'en estime pas
moins.'

              −FONTENELLE: *Pluralité des Mondes*.

THAT lofty criticism had caused Gwendolen a new sort of
pain. She would not have chosen to confess how unfortunate she thought herself in not having had Miss
Arrowpoint's musical advantages, so as to be able to question Herr Klesmer's taste with the confidence of thorough
knowledge; still less, to admit even to herself that Miss
Arrowpoint each time they met raised an unwonted feeling
of jealousy in her: not in the least because she was an
heiress, but because it was really provoking that a girl
whose appearance you could not characterize except by
saying that her figure was slight and of middle stature, her
features small, her eyes tolerable and her complexion sallow, had nevertheless a certain mental superiority which
could not be explained away – an exasperating thoroughness in her musical accomplishment, a fastidious discrimination in her general tastes, which made it
impossible to force her admiration and kept you in awe of
her standard. This insignificant-looking young lady of
four-and-twenty, whom any one's eyes would have passed
over negligently if she had not been Miss Arrowpoint,
might be suspected of a secret opinion that Miss
Harleth's acquirements were rather of a common order;
and such an opinion was not made agreeable to think of by
being always veiled under a perfect kindness of manner.

But Gwendolen did not like to dwell on facts which
threw an unfavourable light on herself. The musical magus
who had so suddenly widened her horizon was not always
on the scene; and his being constantly backwards and
forwards between London and Quetcham soon began to
be thought of as offering opportunities for converting
him to a more admiring state of mind. Meanwhile, in the

manifest pleasure her singing gave at Brackenshaw Castle, the Firs, and elsewhere, she recovered her equanimity, being disposed to think approval more trustworthy than objection, and not being one of the exceptional persons who have a parching thirst for a perfection undemanded by their neighbours. Perhaps it would have been rash to say then that she was at all exceptional inwardly, or that the unusual in her was more than her rare grace of movement and bearing, and a certain daring which gave piquancy to a very common egoistic ambition, such as exists under many clumsy exteriors and is taken no notice of. For I suppose that the set of the head does not really determine the hunger of the inner self for supremacy: it only makes a difference sometimes as to the way in which the supremacy is held attainable, and a little also to the degree in which it can be attained; especially when the hungry one is a girl, whose passion for doing what is remarkable has an ideal limit in consistency with the highest breeding and perfect freedom from the sordid need of income. Gwendolen was as inwardly rebellious against the restraints of family conditions, and as ready to look through obligations into her own fundamental want of feeling for them, as if she had been sustained by the boldest specula- tions; but she really had no such speculations, and would at once have marked herself off from any sort of theoretical or practically reforming women by satirizing them. She rejoiced to feel herself exceptional; but her horizon was that of the genteel romance where the heroine's soul poured out in her journal is full of vague power, originality, and general rebellion, while her life moves strictly in the sphere of fashion; and if she wanders into a swamp, the pathos lies partly, so to speak, in her having on her satin shoes. Here is a restraint which nature and society have provided on the pursuit of striking adventure; so that a soul burning with a sense of what the universe is not, and ready to take all existence as fuel, is nevertheless held captive by the ordinary wirework of social forms and does nothing particular.

This commonplace result was what Gwendolen found herself threatened with even in the novelty of the first winter at Offendene. What she was clear upon was, that she did not wish to lead the same sort of life as ordinary young ladies did; but what she was not clear upon was, how she should set about leading any other, and what were the particular acts which she would assert her freedom by doing. Offendene remained a good background, if anything would happen there; but on the whole the neighbourhood was in fault.

Beyond the effect of her beauty on a first presentation, there was not much excitement to be got out of her earliest invitations, and she came home after little sallies of satire and knowingness, such as had offended Mrs. Arrowpoint, to fill the intervening days with the most girlish devices. The strongest assertion she was able to make of her individual claims was to leave out Alice's lessons (on the principle that Alice was more likely to excel in ignorance), and to employ her with Miss Merry, and the maid who was understood to wait on all the ladies, in helping to arrange various dramatic costumes which Gwendolen pleased herself with having in readiness for some future occasions of acting in charades or theatrical pieces, occasions which she meant to bring about by force of will or contrivance. She had never acted – only made a figure in *tableaux vivants* at school; but she felt assured that she could act well, and having been once or twice to the Théâtre Français, and also heard her mamma speak of Rachel, her waking dreams and cogitations as to how she would manage her destiny sometimes turned on the question whether she should become an actress like Rachel, since she was more beautiful than that thin Jewess. Meanwhile the wet days before Christmas were passed pleasantly in the preparation of costumes, Greek, Oriental, and Composite, in which Gwendolen attitudinized and speechified before a domestic audience, including even the housekeeper, who was once pressed into it that she might swell the notes of applause; but having shown herself unworthy by observing that Miss Harleth looked far more like a queen in her own dress than in that baggy thing with her arms all bare, she was not invited a second time.

'Do I look as well as Rachel, mamma?' said Gwendolen one day when she had been showing herself in her Greek dress to Anna, and going through scraps of scenes with much tragic intention.

'You have better arms than Rachel,' said Mrs. Davilow; 'your arms would do for anything, Gwen. But your voice is not so tragic as hers: it is not so deep.'

'I can make it deeper if I like,' said Gwendolen, provisionally; then she added, with decision, 'I think a higher voice is more tragic: it is more feminine; and the more feminine a woman is, the more tragic it seems when she does desperate actions.'

'There may be something in that,' said Mrs. Davilow, languidly. 'But I don't know what good there is in making one's blood creep. And if there is anything horrible to be done, I should like it to be left to the men.'

'Oh mamma, you are so dreadfully prosaic! As if all the great poetic criminals were not women! I think the men are poor cautious creatures.'

'Well, dear, and you – who are afraid to be alone in the night – I don't think you would be very bold in crime, thank God.'

'I am not talking about reality, mamma,' said Gwendolen, impatiently. Then, her mamma being called out of the room, she turned quickly to her cousin, as if taking an opportunity, and said, 'Anna, do ask my uncle to let us get up some charades at the Rectory. Mr. Middleton and Warham could act with us – just for practice. Mamma says it will not do to have Mr. Middleton consulting and rehearsing here. He is a stick, but we could give him suitable parts. Do ask; or else I will.'

'Oh, not till Rex comes. He is so clever, and such a dear old thing, and he will act Napoleon looking over the sea. He looks just like Napoleon. Rex can do anything.'

'I don't in the least believe in your Rex, Anna,' said Gwendolen, laughing at her. 'He will turn out to be like those wretched blue and yellow water-colours of his which you hang up in your bedroom and worship.'

'Very well, you will see,' said Anna. 'It is not that I know what is clever, but he has got a scholarship already, and papa says he will get a fellowship, and nobody is better at games. He is cleverer than Mr. Middleton and everybody but you calls Mr. Middleton clever.'

'So he may be in a dark-lantern sort of way. But he *is* a stick. If he had to say "Perdition catch my soul, but I do love her," he would say it in just the same tone as, "Here endeth the second lesson."'

'Oh Gwendolen!' said Anna, shocked at these promiscuous allusions. 'And it is very unkind of you to speak so of him, for he admires you very much. I heard Warham say one day to mamma, "Middleton is regularly spoony upon Gwendolen." She was very angry with him; but I know what it means. It is what they say at college for being in love.'

'How can I help it?' said Gwendolen, rather contemptuously. 'Perdition catch my soul if I love *him*.'

'No, of course; papa, I think, would not wish it. And he is to go away soon. But it makes me sorry when you ridicule him.'

'What shall you do to me when I ridicule Rex?' said Gwendolen, wickedly.

'Now, Gwendolen, dear, you *will not*?' said Anna, her eyes filling with tears. 'I could not bear it. But there really is nothing in him to ridicule. Only you may find out things. For no one ever thought of laughing at Mr. Middleton before you. Every one said he was nice-looking, and his manners perfect. I am sure I have always been frightened at him because of his learning and his square-cut coat, and his being a nephew of the bishop's and all that. But you will not ridicule Rex – promise me.' Anna ended with a beseeching look which touched Gwendolen.

'You are a dear little coz,' she said, just touching the tip of Anna's chin with her thumb and fore-finger. 'I don't ever want to do anything that will vex you. Especially if Rex is to make everything come off – charades and everything.'

And when at last Rex was there, the animation he brought into the life at Offendene and the Rectory, and his ready partnership in Gwendolen's plans, left her no inclination for any ridicule that was not of an open and flattering kind, such as he himself enjoyed. He was a fine open-hearted youth, with a handsome face strongly resembling his father's and Anna's, but softer in expression than the one, and larger in scale than the other: a bright, healthy, loving nature, enjoying ordinary innocent things so much that vice had no temptation for him, and what he knew of it lay too entirely in the outer courts and little-visited chambers of his mind for him to think of it with great repulsion. Vicious habits were with him 'what some fellows did' – 'stupid stuff' which he liked to keep aloof from. He returned Anna's affection as fully as could be expected of a brother whose pleasures apart from her were more than the sum total of hers; and he had never known a stronger love.

The cousins were continually together at the one house or the other – chiefly at Offendene, where there was more freedom, or rather where there was a more complete sway for Gwendolen; and whatever she wished became a ruling purpose for Rex. The charades came off according to her plans; and also some other little scenes not contemplated by her in which her acting was more impromptu. It was at Offendene that the charades and tableaux were rehearsed and presented, Mrs. Davilow seeing no objection even to Mr. Middleton's being invited to share in them, now that Rex too was there – especially as his services were indispensable; Warham, who was studying for India with a Wancester 'coach,' having no time to spare, and being generally dismal under a cram of everything except the answers needed at the forthcoming examination, which might disclose the welfare of our Indian Empire to be

DANIEL DERONDA

somehow connected with a quotable knowledge of Browne's Pastorals.

Mr. Middleton was persuaded to play various grave parts, Gwendolen having flattered him on his enviable immobility of countenance; and, at first a little pained and jealous at her comradeship with Rex, he presently drew encouragement from the thought that this sort of cousinly familiarity excluded any serious passion. Indeed, he occasionally felt that her more formal treatment of himself was such a sign of favour as to warrant his making advances before he left Pennicote, though he had intended to keep his feelings in reserve until his position should be more assured. Miss Gwendolen, quite aware that she was adored by this unexceptionable young clergyman with pale whiskers and square-cut collar, felt nothing more on the subject than that she had no objection to be adored: she turned her eyes on him with calm mercilessness and caused him many mildly agitating hopes by seeming always to avoid dramatic contact with him – for all meanings, we know, depend on the key of interpretation.

Some persons might have thought beforehand that a young man of Anglican leanings, having a sense of sacredness much exercised on small things as well as great, rarely laughing save from politeness, and in general regarding the mention of spades by their naked names as rather coarse, would not have seen a fitting bride for himself in a girl who was daring in ridicule, and showed none of the special grace required in the clergyman's wife; or, that a young man informed by theological reading would have reflected that he was not likely to meet the taste of a lively, restless young lady like Miss Harleth. But are we always obliged to explain why the facts are not what some persons thought beforehand? The apology lies on their side, who had that erroneous way of thinking.

As for Rex, who would possibly have been sorry for poor Middleton if he had been aware of the excellent curate's inward conflict, he was too completely absorbed in a first passion to have observation for any person or thing. He did not observe Gwendolen; he only felt what she said or did, and the back of his head seemed to be a good organ of information as to whether she was in the room or out. Before the end of the first fortnight he was so deeply in love that it was impossible for him to think of his life except as bound up with Gwendolen's. He could see no obstacles, poor boy; his own love seemed a guarantee of hers, since it was one with the unperturbed delight in her image, so that he could no more dream of her giving him pain than an Egyptian could dream of snow. She sang and played to him whenever he liked, was always glad of his companionship in riding, though his borrowed steeds were often comic, was ready to join in any fun of his, and showed a right appreciation of Anna. No mark of sympathy seemed absent. That because Gwendolen was the most perfect creature in the world she was to make a grand match, had not occurred to him. He had no conceit – at least, not more than goes to make up the necessary gum and consistence of a substantial personality: it was only that in the young bliss of loving he took Gwendolen's perfection as part of that good which had seemed one with life to him, being the outcome of a happy, well-embodied nature.

One incident which happened in the course of their dramatic attempts impressed Rex as a sign of her unusual sensibility. It showed an aspect of her nature which could not have been preconceived by any one who, like him, had only seen her habitual fearlessness in active exercises and her high spirits in society.

After a good deal of rehearsing it was resolved that a select party should be invited to Offendene to witness the performances which went with so much satisfaction to the actors. Anna had caused a pleasant surprise; nothing could be neater than the way in which she played her little parts; one would even have suspected her of hiding much sly observation under her simplicity. And Mr. Middleton answered very well by not trying to be comic. The main source of doubt and retardation had been Gwendolen's desire to appear in her Greek dress. No word for a charade would occur to her either waking or dreaming that suited her purpose of getting a statuesque pose in this favourite costume. To choose a motive from Racine was of no use, since Rex and the others could not declaim French verse, and improvised speeches would turn the scene into burlesque. Besides, Mr. Gascoigne prohibited the acting of scenes from plays: he usually protested against the notion that an amusement which was fitting for every one else was unfitting for a clergyman; but he would not in this matter overstep the line of decorum as drawn in that part of Wessex, which did not exclude his sanction of the young people's acting charades in his sister-in-law's house – a very different affair from private theatricals in the full sense of the word.

Everybody of course was concerned to satisfy this wish of Gwendolen's, and Rex proposed that they should wind up with a tableau in which the effect of her majesty would not be marred by any one's speech. This pleased her thoroughly, and the only question was the choice of the tableau.

'Something pleasant, children, I beseech you,' said Mrs. Davilow; 'I can't have any Greek wickedness.'

'It is no worse than Christian wickedness, mamma,' said Gwendolen, whose mention of Rachelesque heroines had called forth that remark.

'And less scandalous,' said Rex. 'Besides, one thinks of it as all gone by and done with. What do you say to Briseis being led away? I would be Achilles, and you would be looking round at me – after the print we have at the Rectory.'

'That would be a good attitude for me,' said Gwendolen, in a tone of acceptance. But afterwards she said with decision, 'No. It will not do. There must be three men in proper costume, else it will be ridiculous.'

'I have it!' said Rex, after a little reflection. 'Hermione as the statue in the Winter's Tale! I will be Leontes and Miss Merry Paulina, one on each side. Our dress won't signify,' he went on laughingly; 'it will be more

Shakespearian and romantic if Leontes looks like Napoleon, and Paulina like a modern spinster.'

And Hermione was chosen; all agreeing that age was of no consequence; but Gwendolen urged that instead of the mere tableau there should be just enough acting of the scene to introduce the striking up of the music as a signal for her to step down and advance; when Leontes, instead of embracing her, was to kneel and kiss the hem of her garment, and so the curtain was to fall. The antechamber with folding-doors lent itself admirably to the purposes of a stage, and the whole of the establishment, with the addition of Jarrett the village carpenter, was absorbed in the preparations for an entertainment which, considering that it was an imitation of acting, was likely to be successful, since we know from ancient fable that an imitation may have more chance of success than the original.

Gwendolen was not without a special exultation in the prospect of this occasion, for she knew that Herr Klesmer was again at Quetcham, and she had taken care to include him among the invited.

Klesmer came. He was in one of his placid silent moods, and sat in serene contemplation, replying to all appeals in benignant-sounding syllables more or less articulate – as taking up his cross meekly in a world overgrown with amateurs, or as careful how he moved his lion paws lest he should crush a rampant and vociferous mouse.

Everything indeed went off smoothly and according to expectation – all that was improvised and accidental being of a probable sort – until the incident occurred which showed Gwendolen in an unforeseen phase of emotion. How it came about was at first a mystery.

The tableau of Hermione was doubly striking from its dissimilarity with what had gone before: it was answering perfectly, and a murmur of applause had been gradually suppressed while Leontes gave his permission that Paulina should exercise her utmost art and make the statue move.

Hermione, her arm resting on a pillar, was elevated by about six inches, which she counted on as a means of

DANIEL DERONDA

showing her pretty foot and instep, when at the given signal she should advance and descend.

'Music, awake her, strike!' said Paulina (Mrs. Davilow, who by special entreaty had consented to take the part in a white burnous and hood).

Herr Klesmer, who had been good-natured enough to seat himself at the piano, struck a thunderous chord – but in the same instant, and before Hermione had put forth her foot, the movable panel, which was on a line with the piano, flew open on the right opposite the stage and disclosed the picture of the dead face and the fleeing figure brought out in pale definiteness by the position of the wax-lights. Every one was startled, but all eyes in the act of turning towards the opened panel were recalled by a piercing cry from Gwendolen, who stood without change of attitude, but with a change of expression that was terrifying in its terror. She looked like a statue into which a soul of Fear had entered: her pallid lips were parted; her eyes, usually narrowed under their long lashes, were dilated and fixed. Her mother, less surprised than alarmed, rushed towards her, and Rex too could not help going to her side. But the touch of her mother's arm had the effect of an electric charge; Gwendolen fell on her knees and put her hands before her face. She was still trembling, but mute, and it seemed that she had self-consciousness enough to aim at controlling her signs of terror, for she presently allowed herself to be raised from her kneeling posture and led away, while the company were relieving their minds by explanation.

'A magnificent bit of *plastik* that!' said Klesmer to Miss Arrowpoint. And a quick fire of undertoned question and answer went round.

'Was it part of the play?'

'Oh no, surely not. Miss Harleth was too much affected. A sensitive creature!'

'Dear me! I was not aware that there was a painting behind that panel; were you?'

'No; how should I? Some eccentricity in one of the Earl's family long ago, I suppose.'

'How very painful! Pray shut it up.'

'Was the door locked? It is very mysterious. It must be the spirits.'

'But there is no medium present.'

'How do you know that? We must conclude that there is, when such things happen.'

'Oh, the door was not locked; it was probably the sudden vibration from the piano that sent it open.'

This conclusion came from Mr. Gascoigne, who begged Miss Merry if possible to get the key. But this readiness to explain the mystery was thought by Mrs. Vulcany unbecoming in a clergyman, and she observed in an undertone that Mr. Gascoigne was always a little too worldly for her taste. However, the key was produced, and the rector turned it in the lock with an emphasis rather offensively rationalizing – as who should say, 'It will not start open again' – putting the key in his pocket as a security.

However, Gwendolen soon reappeared, showing her usual spirits, and evidently determined to ignore as far as she could the striking change she had made in the part of Hermione.

But when Klesmer said to her, 'We have to thank you for devising a perfect climax: you could not have chosen a finer bit of *plastik*,' there was a flush of pleasure in her face. She liked to accept as a belief what was really no more than delicate feigning. He divined that the betrayal into a passion of fear had been mortifying to her, and wished her to understand that he took it for good acting. Gwendolen cherished the idea that now he was struck with her talent as well as her beauty, and her uneasiness about his opinion was half turned to complacency.

But too many were in the secret of what had been included in the rehearsals, and what had not, and no one besides Klesmer took the trouble to soothe Gwendolen's imagined mortification. The general sentiment was that the incident should be let drop.

There had really been a medium concerned in the starting open of the panel: one who had quitted the room in haste and crept to bed in much alarm of conscience. It was the small Isabel, whose intense curiosity, unsatisfied by the brief glimpse she had had of the strange picture on the day of arrival at Offendene, had kept her on the watch for an opportunity of finding out where Gwendolen had put the key, of stealing it from the discovered drawer when the rest of the family were out, and getting on a stool to unlock the panel. While she was indulging her thirst for knowledge in this way, a noise which she feared was an approaching footstep alarmed her; she closed the door and attempted hurriedly to lock it, but failing and not daring to linger, she withdrew the key and trusted that the panel would stick, as it seemed well inclined to do. In this confidence she had returned the key to its former place, stilling any anxiety by the thought that if the door were discovered to be unlocked nobody could know how the unlocking came about. The inconvenient Isabel, like other offenders, did not foresee her own impulse to confession, a fatality which came upon her the morning after the party, when Gwendolen said at the breakfast-table, 'I know the door was locked before the housekeeper gave me the key, for I tried it myself afterwards. Some one must have been to my drawer and taken the key.'

It seemed to Isabel that Gwendolen's awful eyes had rested on her more than on the other sisters, and without any time for resolve she said with a trembling lip, 'Please forgive me, Gwendolen.'

The forgiveness was sooner bestowed than it would have been if Gwendolen had not desired to dismiss from her own and every one else's memory any case in which she had shown her susceptibility to terror. She wondered at herself in these occasional experiences, which seemed like a brief remembered madness, an unexplained exception from her normal life; and in this instance she felt a peculiar vexation that her helpless fear had shown itself, not, as usual, in solitude, but in well-lit company. Her ideal was to be daring in speech and reckless in braving dangers, both moral and physical; and though her practice fell far behind her ideal, this shortcoming seemed to be due to the pettiness of circumstances, the narrow theatre which life offers to a girl of twenty, who cannot conceive herself as anything else than a lady, or as in any position which would lack the tribute of respect. She had no permanent consciousness of other fetters, or of more spiritual restraints, having always disliked whatever was presented to her under the name of religion, in the same way that some people dislike arithmetic and accounts: it had raised no other emotion in her, no alarm, no longing; so that the question whether she believed it had not occurred to her, any more than it had occurred to her to inquire into the conditions of colonial property and banking, on which, as she had had many opportunities of knowing, the family fortune was dependent. All these facts about herself she would have been ready to admit, and even, more or less indirectly, to state. What she unwillingly recognized and would have been glad for others to be unaware of, was that liability of hers to fits of spiritual dread, though this fountain of awe within her had not found its way into connection with the religion taught her or with any human relations. She was ashamed and frightened, as at what might happen again, in remembering her tremor on suddenly feeling herself alone, when, for example, she was walking without companionship and there came some rapid change in the light. Solitude in any wide scene impressed her with an undefined feeling of immeasurable existence aloof from her, in the midst of which she was helplessly incapable of asserting herself. The little astronomy taught her at school used sometimes to set her imagination at work in a way that made her tremble; but always when some one joined her she recovered her indifference to the vastness in which she seemed an exile; she found again her usual world in which her will was of some avail, and the religious nomenclature belonging to this world was no more identified for her with those uneasy impressions of awe than her uncle's surplices seen out of use at the rectory. With human ears and eyes about her, she had always hitherto recovered her confidence, and felt the possibility of winning empire. To her mamma and others her fits of timidity or terror were sufficiently accounted for by her 'sensitiveness' or the 'excitability of her nature;' but these explanatory phrases required conciliation with much that seemed to be blank indifference or rare self-mastery. Heat is a great agent and a useful word, but considered as a means of explaining the universe it requires an extensive knowledge of differences; and as a means of explaining character 'sensitiveness' is in much the same predicament. But who, loving a creature like Gwendolen, would not be inclined to regard every peculiarity in her as a mark of pre-eminence? That was what Rex did. After the Hermione scene he was more persuaded than ever that she must be instinct with all feeling, and not only readier to respond to a worshipful love, but able to love better than other girls. Rex felt the summer on his young wings and soared happily.

VII

THE first sign of the unimagined snowstorm was like the transparent white cloud that seems to set off the blue. Anna was in the secret of Rex's feeling; though for the first time in their lives he had said nothing to her about what he most thought of, and he only took it for granted that she knew it. For the first time, too, Anna could not say to Rex what was continually in her mind. Perhaps it might have been a pain which she would have had to conceal, that he should so soon care for some one else more than for herself, if such a feeling had not been thoroughly neutralized by doubt and anxiety on his behalf. Anna admired her cousin – would have said with simple sincerity, 'Gwendolen is always very good to me,' and held it in the order of things for herself to be entirely subject to this cousin; but she looked at her with mingled fear and distrust, with a puzzled contemplation as of some wondrous and beautiful animal whose nature was a mystery, and who, for anything Anna knew, might have an appetite for devouring all the small creatures that were her own particular pets. And now Anna's heart was sinking under the heavy conviction which she dared not utter, that Gwendolen would never care for Rex. What she herself held in tenderness and reverence had constantly seemed indifferent to Gwendolen, and it was easier to imagine her scorning Rex than returning any tenderness of his. Besides, she was always thinking of being something extraordinary. And poor Rex! Papa would be angry with him, if he knew. And of course he was too young to be in love in that way; and she, Anna, had thought that it would be years and years before anything of that sort came, and that she would be Rex's housekeeper ever so long. But what a heart must that be which did not return his love! Anna, in the prospect of his suffering, was beginning to dislike her too fascinating cousin.

It seemed to her, as it did to Rex, that the weeks had been filled with a tumultuous life evident to all observers: if he had been questioned on the subject he would have said that he had no wish to conceal what he hoped would be an engagement which he should immediately tell his father of; and yet for the first time in his life he was reserved not only about his feelings but – which was more remarkable to Anna – about certain actions. She, on her side, was nervous each time her father or mother began to speak to her in private lest they should say anything about Rex and Gwendolen. But the elders were not in the least alive to this agitating drama, which went forward chiefly in a sort of pantomime extremely lucid in the minds thus expressing themselves, but easily missed by spectators who were running their eyes over the Guardian or the Clerical Gazette, and regarded the trivialities of the young ones with scarcely more interpretation than they gave to the actions of lively ants.

'Where are you going, Rex?' said Anna one grey morning when her father had set off in the carriage to the sessions, Mrs. Gascoigne with him, and she had observed that her brother had on his antigropelos, the utmost approach he possessed to a hunting equipment.

'Going to see the hounds throw off at the Three Barns.'

'Are you going to take Gwendolen?' said Anna, timidly.

'She told you, did she?'

'No, but I thought— Does papa know you are going?'

'Not that I am aware of. I don't suppose he would trouble himself about the matter.'

'You are going to use his horse?'

'He knows I do that whenever I can.'

'Don't let Gwendolen ride after the hounds, Rex,' said Anna, whose fears gifted her with second-sight.

'Why not?' said Rex, smiling rather provokingly.

'Papa and mamma and aunt Davilow all wish her not to. They think it is not right for her.'

'Why should you suppose she is going to do what is not right?'

'Gwendolen minds nobody sometimes,' said Anna, getting bolder by dint of a little anger.

'Then she would not mind me,' said Rex, perversely making a joke of poor Anna's anxiety.

'Oh Rex, I cannot bear it. You will make yourself very unhappy.' Here Anna burst into tears.

'Nannie, Nannie, what on earth is the matter with you?' said Rex, a little impatient at being kept in this way, hat on and whip in hand.

'She will not care for you one bit – I know she never will!' said the poor child in a sobbing whisper. She had lost all control of herself.

Rex reddened and hurried away from her out of the hall door, leaving her to the miserable consciousness of having made herself disagreeable in vain.

He did think of her words as he rode along: they had the unwelcomeness which all unfavourable fortune-telling has, even when laughed at; but he quickly explained them as springing from little Anna's tenderness, and began to be sorry that he was obliged to come away without soothing her. Every other feeling on the subject, however, was quickly merged in a resistant belief to the contrary of hers, accompanied with a new determination to prove that he was right. This sort of certainty had just enough kinship to doubt and uneasiness to hurry on a confession which an untouched security might have delayed.

Gwendolen was already mounted and riding up and down the avenue when Rex appeared at the gate. She had provided herself against disappointment in case he did not appear in time by having the groom ready behind her, for she would not have waited beyond a reasonable time. But now the groom was dismissed, and the two rode away in delightful freedom. Gwendolen was in her highest spirits, and Rex thought that she had never looked so lovely before: her figure, her long white throat, and the curves of her cheek and chin were always set off to perfection by the compact simplicity of her riding dress. He could not conceive a more perfect girl; and to a youthful lover like Rex it seems that the fundamental identity of the good, the true, and the beautiful, is already extant and manifest in the object of his love. Most observers would have held it more than equally accountable that a girl should have like impressions about Rex, for in his handsome face there was nothing corresponding to the undefinable stinging quality – as it were a trace of demon ancestry – which made some beholders hesitate in their admiration of Gwendolen.

It was an exquisite January morning in which there was no threat of rain, but a grey sky making the calmest background for the charms of a mild winter scene: – the grassy borders of the lanes, the hedgerows sprinkled with red berries and haunted with low twitterings, the purple bareness of the elms, the rich brown of the furrows. The horses' hoofs made a musical chime, accompanying their young voices. She was laughing at his equipment, for he was the reverse of a dandy, and he was enjoying her laughter: the freshness of the morning mingled with the freshness of their youth; and every sound that came from their clear throats, every glance they gave each other, was the bubbling outflow from a spring of joy. It was all morning to them, within and without. And thinking of them in these moments one is tempted to that futile sort of wishing – if only things could have been a little otherwise then, so as to have been greatly otherwise after! – if only these two

beautiful young creatures could have pledged themselves
to each other then and there, and never through life have
swerved from that pledge! For some of the goodness
which Rex believed in was there. Goodness is a large,
often a prospective word; like harvest, which at one
stage when we talk of it lies all underground, with an
indeterminate future: is the germ prospering in the
darkness? at another, it has put forth delicate green blades,
and by-and-by the trembling blossoms are ready to be
dashed off by an hour of rough wind or rain. Each stage
has its peculiar blight, and may have the healthy life
choked out of it by a particular action of the foul land
which rears or neighbours it, or by damage brought from
foulness afar.

'Anna had got it into her head that you would want to
ride after the hounds this morning,' said Rex, whose secret
associations with Anna's words made this speech seem
quite perilously near the most momentous of subjects.

'Did she?' said Gwendolen, laughingly. 'What a little
clairvoyante she is!'

'Shall you?' said Rex, who had not believed in her
intending to do it if the elders objected, but confided in
her having good reasons.

'I don't know. I can't tell what I shall do till I get there.
Clairvoyantes are often wrong: they foresee what is likely. I
am not fond of what is likely; it is always dull. I do what is
unlikely.'

'Ah, there you tell me a secret. When once I knew what
people in general would be likely to do, I should know you
would do the opposite. So you would have come round to a
likelihood of your own sort. I shall be able to calculate on
you. You couldn't surprise me.'

'Yes, I could. I should turn round and do what was likely
for people in general,' said Gwendolen, with a musical
laugh.

'You see you can't escape some sort of likelihood. And
contradictoriness makes the strongest likelihood of all. You
must give up a plan.'

'No, I shall not. My plan is to do what pleases me.' (Here should any young lady incline to imitate Gwendolen, let her consider the set of her head and neck: if the angle there had been different, the chin protrusive and the cervical vertebræ a trifle more curved in their position, ten to one Gwendolen's words would have had a jar in them for the sweet-natured Rex. But everything odd in her speech was humour and pretty banter, which he was only anxious to turn towards one point.)

'Can you manage to feel only what pleases you?' said he.

'Of course not; that comes from what other people do. But if the world were pleasanter, one would only feel what was pleasant. Girls' lives are so stupid: they never do what they like.'

'I thought that was more the case of the men. They are forced to do hard things, and are often dreadfully bored, and knocked to pieces too. And then, if we love a girl very dearly we want to do as she likes, so after all you have your own way.'

'I don't believe it. I never saw a married woman who had her own way.'

'What should you like to do?' said Rex, quite guilelessly, and in real anxiety.

'Oh, I don't know! – go to the North Pole, or ride steeplechases, or go to be a queen in the East like Lady Hester Stanhope,' said Gwendolen flightily. Her words were born on her lips, but she would have been at a loss to give an answer of deeper origin.

'You don't mean you would never be married?'

'No; I didn't say that. Only when I married, I should not do as other women do.'

'You might do just as you liked if you married a man who loved you more dearly than anything else in the world,' said Rex, who, poor youth, was moving in themes outside the curriculum in which he had promised to win distinction. 'I know one who does.'

'Don't talk of Mr. Middleton, for heaven's sake,' said Gwendolen, hastily, a quick blush spreading over her face and neck; 'that is Anna's chant. I hear the hounds. Let us go on.'

She put her chestnut to a canter, and Rex had no choice but to follow her. Still he felt encouraged. Gwendolen was perfectly aware that her cousin was in love with her; but she had no idea that the matter was of any consequence, having never had the slightest visitation of painful love herself. She wished the small romance of Rex's devotion to fill up the time of his stay at Pennicote, and to avoid explanations which would bring it to an untimely end. Besides, she objected, with a sort of physical repulsion, to being directly made love to. With all her imaginative delight in being adored, there was a certain fierceness of maidenhood in her.

But all other thoughts were soon lost for her in the excitement of the scene at the Three Barns. Several gentlemen of the hunt knew her, and she exchanged pleasant greetings. Rex could not get another word with her. The colour, the stir of the field had taken possession of Gwendolen with a strength which was not due to habitual association, for she had never yet ridden after the hounds – only said she should like to do it, and so drawn forth a prohibition; her mamma dreading the danger, and her uncle declaring that for his part he held that kind of violent exercise unseemly in a woman, and that whatever might be done in other parts of the country, no lady of good position followed the Wessex hunt: no one but Mrs. Gadsby, the yeomanry captain's wife, who had been a kitchen-maid and still spoke like one. This last argument had some effect on Gwendolen, and had kept her halting between her desire to assert her freedom and her horror of being classed with Mrs. Gadsby.

Some of the most unexceptionable women in the neighbourhood occasionally went to see the hounds throw off; but it happened that none of them were present this morning to abstain from following, while Mrs. Gadsby, with her doubtful antecedents grammatical and otherwise, was not visible to make following seem unbecoming. Thus

Gwendolen felt no check on the animal stimulus that came from the stir and tongue of the hounds, the pawing of the horses, the varying voices of men, the movement hither and thither of vivid colour on the background of green and grey stillness: – that utmost excitement of the coming chase which consists in feeling something like a combination of dog and horse, with the superadded thrill of social vanities and consciousness of centaur-power which belong to human kind.

Rex would have felt more of the same enjoyment if he could have kept nearer to Gwendolen, and not seen her constantly occupied with acquaintances, or looked at by would-be acquaintances, all on lively horses which veered about and swept the surrounding space as effectually as a revolving lever.

'Glad to see you here this fine morning, Miss Harleth,' said Lord Brackenshaw, a middle-aged peer of aristocratic seediness in stained pink, with easy-going manners which would have made the threatened Deluge seem of no consequence. 'We shall have a first-rate run. A pity you don't go with us. Have you ever tried your little chestnut at a ditch? you wouldn't be afraid, eh?'

'Not the least in the world,' said Gwendolen. And this was true; she was never fearful in action and companionship. 'I have often taken him at some rails and a ditch too, near—'

'Ah, by Jove!' said his lordship, quietly, in notation that something was happening which must break off the dialogue; and as he reined off his horse, Rex was bringing his sober hackney up to Gwendolen's side when — the hounds gave tongue, and the whole field was in motion as if the whirl of the earth were carrying it; Gwendolen along with everything else; no word of notice to Rex, who without a second thought followed too. Could he let Gwendolen go alone? under other circumstances he would have enjoyed the run, but he was just now perturbed by the check which had been put on the impetus to utter his love, and get utterance in return, an impetus which could not at once resolve itself into a totally different sort of chase, at least with the consciousness of being on his father's grey nag, a good horse enough in his way, but of sober years and ecclesiastical habits. Gwendolen on her spirited little chestnut was up with the best, and felt as secure as an immortal goddess, having, if she had thought of risk, a core of confidence that no ill luck would happen to her. But she thought of no such thing, and certainly not of any risk there might be for her cousin. If she had thought of him, it would have struck her as a droll picture that he should be gradually falling behind, and looking round in search of gates: a fine lithe youth, whose heart must be panting with all the spirit of a beagle, stuck as if under a wizard's spell on a stiff clerical hackney, would have made her laugh with a sense of fun much too strong for her to reflect on his mortification. But Gwendolen was apt to think rather of those who saw her than of those whom she could not see; and Rex was soon so far behind that if she had looked she would not have seen him. For I grieve to say that in the search for a gate, along a lane lately mended, Primrose fell, broke his knees, and undesignedly threw Rex over his head.

Fortunately a blacksmith's son who also followed the hounds under disadvantages, namely, on foot (a loose way of hunting which had struck some even frivolous minds as immoral), was naturally also in the rear, and happened to be within sight of Rex's misfortune. He ran to give help which was greatly needed, for Rex was a good deal stunned, and the complete recovery of sensation came in the form of pain. Joel Dagge on this occasion showed himself that most useful of personages, whose knowledge is of a kind suited to the immediate occasion: he not only knew perfectly well what was the matter with the horse, how far they were both from the nearest public-house and from Pennicote Rectory, and could certify to Rex that his shoulder was only a bit out of joint, but also offered experienced surgical aid.

'Lord, sir, let me shove it in again for you! I's see Nash the bone-setter do it, and done it myself for our little Sally twice over. It's all one and the same, shoulders is. If you'll trusten to me and tighten your mind up a bit, I'll do it for you in no time.'

'Come then, old fellow,' said Rex, who could tighten his mind better than his seat in the saddle. And Joel managed the operation, though not without considerable expense of pain to his patient, who turned so pitiably pale while tightening his mind, that Joel remarked, 'Ah, sir, you aren't used to it, that's how it is. I's see lots and lots o' joints out. I see a man with his eye pushed out once – that was a rum go as ever I see. You can't have a bit o' fun wi'out such a sort o' things. But it went in again. I's swallowed three teeth mysen, as sure as I'm alive. Now, sirrey' (this was addressed to Primrose), 'come alonk – you mustn't make believe as you can't.'

Joel being clearly a low character, it is happily not necessary to say more of him to the refined reader, than that he helped Rex to get home with as little delay as possible. There was no alternative but to get home, though all the while he was in anxiety about Gwendolen, and more miserable in the thought that she too might have had an accident, than in the pain of his own bruises and the annoyance he was about to cause his father. He comforted himself about her by reflecting that every one would be anxious to take care of her, and that some acquaintance would be sure to conduct her home.

Mr. Gascoigne was already at home, and was writing letters in his study, when he was interrupted by seeing poor Rex come in with a face which was not the less handsome and ingratiating for being pale and a little distressed. He was secretly the favourite son, and a young portrait of the father; who, however, never treated him with any partiality – rather, with an extra rigour. Mr. Gascoigne having inquired of Anna, knew that Rex had gone with Gwendolen to the meet at the Three Barns.

'What's the matter?' he said, hastily, not laying down his pen.

'I'm very sorry, sir; Primrose has fallen down and broken his knees.'

'Where have you been with him?' said Mr. Gascoigne, with a touch of severity. He rarely gave way to temper.

'To the Three Barns to see the hounds throw off.'

'And you were fool enough to follow?'

'Yes, sir. I didn't go at any fences, but the horse got his leg into a hole.'

'And you got hurt yourself, I hope, eh?'

'I got my shoulder put out, but a young blacksmith put it in again for me. I'm just a little battered, that's all.'

'Well, sit down.'

'I'm very sorry about the horse, sir. I knew it would be a vexation to you.'

'And what has become of Gwendolen?' said Mr. Gascoigne, abruptly. Rex, who did not imagine that his father had made any inquiries about him, answered at first with a blush which was the more remarkable for his previous paleness. Then he said, nervously –

'I am anxious to know – I should like to go or send at once to Offendene – but she rides so well, and I think she would keep up – there would most likely be many round her.'

'I suppose it was she who led you on, eh?' said Mr. Gascoigne, laying down his pen, leaning back in his chair, and looking at Rex with more marked examination.

'It was natural for her to want to go; she didn't intend it beforehand – she was led away by the spirit of the thing. And of course I went when she went.'

Mr. Gascoigne left a brief interval of silence, and then said with quiet irony, 'But now you observe, young gentleman, that you are not furnished with a horse which will enable you to play the squire to your cousin. You must give up that amusement. You have spoiled my nag for me, and that is enough mischief for one vacation. I shall beg you to get ready to start for Southampton tomorrow and join Stillfox, till you go up to Oxford with him. That will be good for your bruises as well as your studies.'

Poor Rex felt his heart swelling and comporting itself as if it had been no better than a girl's.

'I hope you will not insist on my going immediately, sir.'

'Do you feel too ill?'

'No, not that – but—' here Rex bit his lips and felt the tears starting, to his great vexation; then he rallied and tried to say more firmly, 'I want to go to Offendene – but I can go this evening.'

'I am going there myself. I can bring word about Gwendolen, if that is what you want.'

Rex broke down. He thought he discerned an intention fatal to his happiness, nay, his life. He was accustomed to believe in his father's penetration, and to expect firmness. 'Father, I can't go away without telling her that I love her, and knowing that she loves me.'

Mr. Gascoigne was inwardly going through some self-rebuke for not being more wary, and was now really sorry for the lad; but every consideration was subordinate to that of using the wisest tactics in the case. He had quickly made up his mind, and could answer the more quietly –

'My dear boy, you are too young to be taking moment-ous, decisive steps of that sort. This is a fancy which you have got into your head during an idle week or two: you must set to work at something and dismiss it. There is every reason against it. An engagement at your age would be totally rash and unjustifiable; and moreover, alliances between first cousins are undesirable. Make up your mind to a brief disappointment. Life is full of them. We have all got to be broken in; and this is a mild beginning for you.'

'No, not mild. I can't bear it. I shall be good for nothing. I shouldn't mind anything, if it were settled between us. I could do anything then,' said Rex, impetuously. 'But it's of no use to pretend that I will obey you. I can't do it. If I said I would, I should be sure to break my word. I should see Gwendolen again.'

'Well, wait till to-morrow morning that we may talk of the matter again – you will promise me that,' said Mr. Gascoigne, quietly; and Rex did not, could not refuse.

The Rector did not even tell his wife that he had any other reason for going to Offendene that evening than his desire to ascertain that Gwendolen had got home safely. He found her more than safe – elated. Mr. Quallon, who had won the brush, had delivered the trophy to her, and she had brought it before her, fastened on the saddle; more than that, Lord Brackenshaw had conducted her home, and had shown himself delighted with her spirited riding. All this was told at once to her uncle, that he might see how well justified she had been in acting against his advice; and the prudential Rector did feel himself in a slight difficulty, for at that moment he was particularly sensible that it was his niece's serious interest to be well regarded by the Brackenshaws, and their opinion as to her following the hounds really touched the essence of his objection. However, he was not obliged to say anything immediately, for Mrs. Davilow followed up Gwendolen's brief triumphant phrases with –

'Still, I do hope you will not do it again, Gwendolen. I should never have a moment's quiet. Her father died by an accident, you know.'

Here Mrs. Davilow had turned away from Gwendolen, and looked at Mr. Gascoigne.

'Mamma, dear,' said Gwendolen, kissing her merrily, and passing over the question of the fears which Mrs. Davilow had meant to account for, 'children don't take after their parents in broken legs.'

Not one word had yet been said about Rex. In fact there had been no anxiety about him at Offendene. Gwendolen had observed to her mamma, 'Oh, he must have been left far behind, and gone home in despair,' and it could not be denied that this was fortunate so far as it made way for Lord Brackenshaw's bringing her home. But now Mr. Gascoigne said, with some emphasis, looking at Gwendolen –

'Well, the exploit has ended better for you than for Rex.'

'Yes, I dare say he had to make a terrible round. You have not taught Primrose to take the fences, uncle,' said

Gwendolen, without the faintest shade of alarm in her looks and tone.

'Rex has had a fall,' said Mr. Gascoigne, curtly, throwing himself into an arm-chair, resting his elbows and fitting his palms and fingers together, while he closed his lips and looked at Gwendolen, who said –

'Oh, poor fellow! he is not hurt, I hope?' with a correct look of anxiety, such as elated mortals try to superinduce when their pulses are all the while quick with triumph; and Mrs. Davilow, in the same moment, uttered a low 'Good heavens! There!'

Mr. Gascoigne went on: 'He put his shoulder out, and got some bruises, I believe.' Here he made another little pause of observation; but Gwendolen, instead of any such symptoms as pallor and silence, had only deepened the compassionateness of her brow and eyes, and said again, 'Oh, poor fellow! it is nothing serious, then?' and Mr. Gascoigne held his diagnosis complete. But he wished to make assurance doubly sure, and went on still with a purpose.

'He got his arm set again rather oddly. Some blacksmith – not a parishioner of mine – was on the field – a loose fish, I suppose, but handy, and set the arm for him immediately. So after all, I believe, I and Primrose come off worst. The horse's knees are cut to pieces. He came down in a hole, it seems, and pitched Rex over his head.'

Gwendolen's face had allowably become contented again, since Rex's arm had been reset; and now, at the descriptive suggestions in the latter part of her uncle's speech, her elated spirits made her features less manageable than usual; the smiles broke forth, and finally a descending scale of laughter.

'You are a pretty young lady – to laugh at other people's calamities,' said Mr. Gascoigne, with a milder sense of disapprobation than if he had not had counteracting reasons to be glad that Gwendolen showed no deep feeling on the occasion.

'Pray forgive me, uncle. Now Rex is safe, it is so droll to fancy the figure he and Primrose would cut – in a lane all by themselves – only a blacksmith running up. It would make a capital caricature of "Following the hounds."'

Gwendolen rather valued herself on her superior freedom in laughing where others might only see matter for seriousness. Indeed, the laughter became her person so well that her opinion of its gracefulness was often shared by others; and it even entered into her uncle's course of thought at this moment, that it was no wonder a boy should be fascinated by this young witch – who, however, was more mischievous than could be desired.

'How can you laugh at broken bones, child?' said Mrs. Davilow, still under her dominant anxiety. 'I wish we had never allowed you to have the horse. You will see that we were wrong,' she added, looking with a grave nod at Mr. Gascoigne – 'at least I was, to encourage her in asking for it.'

'Yes, seriously, Gwendolen,' said Mr. Gascoigne, in a judicious tone of rational advice to a person understood to be altogether rational, 'I strongly recommend you – I shall ask you to oblige me so far – not to repeat your adventure to-day. Lord Brackenshaw is very kind, but I feel sure that he would concur with me in what I say. To be spoken of as the young lady who hunts by way of exception, would give a tone to the language about you which I am sure you would not like. Depend upon it, his lordship would not choose that Lady Beatrice or Lady Maria should hunt in this part of the country, if they were old enough to do so. When you are married, it will be different: you may do whatever your husband sanctions. But if you intend to hunt, you must marry a man who can keep horses.'

'I don't know why I should do anything so horrible as to marry without *that* prospect, at least,' said Gwendolen, pettishly. Her uncle's speech had given her annoyance, which she could not show more directly; but she felt that she was committing herself, and after moving carelessly to another part of the room, went out.

'She always speaks in that way about marriage,' said Mrs. Davilow; 'but it will be different when she has seen the right person.'

'Her heart has never been in the least touched, that you know of?' said Mr. Gascoigne.

Mrs. Davilow shook her head silently. 'It was only last night she said to me, "Mamma, I wonder how girls manage to fall in love. It is easy to make them do it in books. But men are too ridiculous."'

Mr. Gascoigne laughed a little, and made no further remark on the subject. The next morning at breakfast he said –

'How are your bruises, Rex?'

'Oh, not very mellow yet, sir; only beginning to turn a little.'

'You don't feel quite ready for a journey to Southampton?'

'Not quite,' answered Rex, with his heart metaphorically in his mouth.

'Well, you can wait till to-morrow, and go to say goodbye to them at Offendene.'

Mrs. Gascoigne, who now knew the whole affair, looked steadily at her coffee lest she also should begin to cry, as Anna was doing already.

Mr. Gascoigne felt that he was applying a sharp remedy to poor Rex's acute attack, but he believed it to be in the end the kindest. To let him know the hopelessness of his love from Gwendolen's own lips might be curative in more ways than one.

'I can only be thankful that she doesn't care about him,' said Mrs. Gascoigne, when she joined her husband in his study. 'There are things in Gwendolen I cannot reconcile myself to. My Anna is worth two of her, with all her beauty and talent. It looks so very ill in her that she will not help in the schools with Anna – not even in the Sunday-school. What you or I advise is of no consequence to her; and poor Fanny is completely under her thumb. But I know you think better of her,' Mrs. Gascoigne ended with a deferential hesitation.

'Oh, my dear, there is no harm in the girl. It is only that she has a high spirit, and it will not do to hold the reins too tight. The point is, to get her well married. She has a little too much fire in her for her present life with her mother and sisters. It is natural and right that she should be married soon – not to a poor man, but one who can give her a fitting position.'

Presently Rex, with his arm in a sling, was on his two miles' walk to Offendene. He was rather puzzled by the unconditional permission to see Gwendolen, but his father's real ground of action could not enter into his conjectures. If it had, he would first have thought it horribly cold-blooded, and then have disbelieved in his father's conclusions.

When he got to the house, everybody was there but Gwendolen. The four girls, hearing him speak in the hall, rushed out of the library, which was their schoolroom, and hung round him with compassionate inquiries about his arm. Mrs. Davilow wanted to know exactly what had happened, and where the blacksmith lived, that she might make him a present; while Miss Merry, who took a subdued and melancholy part in all family affairs, doubted whether it would not be giving too much encouragement to that kind of character. Rex had never found the family troublesome before, but just now he wished them all away and Gwendolen there, and he was too uneasy for good-natured feigning. When at last he had said, 'Where is Gwendolen?' and Mrs. Davilow had told Alice to go and see if her sister were come down, adding, 'I sent up her breakfast this morning. She needed a long rest,' – Rex took the shortest way out of his endurance by saying almost impatiently, 'Aunt, I want to speak to Gwendolen – I want to see her alone.'

'Very well, dear; go into the drawing-room. I will send her there,' said Mrs. Davilow, who had observed that he was fond of being with Gwendolen, as was natural, but had not thought of this as having any bearing on the realities of life: it seemed merely part of the Christmas holidays which were spinning themselves out.

Rex for his part felt that the realities of life were all hanging on this interview. He had to walk up and down the drawing-room in expectation for nearly ten minutes – ample space for all imaginative fluctuations; yet, strange to say, he was unvaryingly occupied in thinking what and how much he could do, when Gwendolen had accepted him, to satisfy his father that the engagement was the most prudent thing in the world, since it inspired him with double energy for work. He was to be a lawyer, and what reason was there why he should not rise as high as Eldon did? He was forced to look at life in the light of his father's mind.

But when the door opened and she whose presence he was longing for entered, there came over him suddenly and mysteriously a state of tremor and distrust which he had never felt before. Miss Gwendolen, simple as she stood there, in her black silk, cut square about the round white pillar of her throat, a black band fastening her hair which streamed backwards in smooth silky abundance, seemed more queenly than usual. Perhaps it was that there was none of the latent fun and tricksiness which had always pierced in her greeting of Rex. How much of this was due to her presentiment from what he had said yesterday that he was going to talk of love? How much from her desire to show regret about his accident? Something of both. But the wisdom of ages has hinted that there is a side of the bed which has a malign influence if you happen to get out on it; and this accident befalls some charming persons rather frequently. Perhaps it had befallen Gwendolen this morning. The hastening of her toilet, the way in which Bugle used the brush, the quality of the shilling serial mistakenly written for her amusement, the probabilities of the coming day, and, in short, social institutions generally, were all objectionable to her. It was not that she was out of temper, but that the world was not equal to the demands of her fine organism.

However it might be, Rex saw an awful majesty about her as she entered and put out her hand to him without the least approach to a smile in eyes or mouth. The fun which had moved her in the evening had quite evaporated from the image of his accident, and the whole affair seemed stupid to her. But she said with perfect propriety, 'I hope you are not much hurt, Rex; I deserve that you should reproach me for your accident.'

'Not at all,' said Rex, feeling the soul within him spreading itself like an attack of illness. 'There is hardly anything the matter with me. I am so glad you had the pleasure: I would willingly pay for it by a tumble, only I was sorry to break the horse's knees.'

Gwendolen walked to the hearth and stood looking at the fire in the most inconvenient way for conversation, so that he could only get a side view of her face.

'My father wants me to go to Southampton for the rest of the vacation,' said Rex, his baritone trembling a little.

'Southampton! That's a stupid place to go to, isn't it?' said Gwendolen, chilly.

'It would be to me, because you would not be there.'

Silence.

'Should you mind about my going away, Gwendolen?'

'Of course. Every one is of consequence in this dreary country,' said Gwendolen, curtly. The perception that poor Rex wanted to be tender made her curl up and harden like a sea-anemone at the touch of a finger.

'Are you angry with me, Gwendolen? Why do you treat me in this way all at once?' said Rex, flushing, and with more spirit in his voice, as if he too were capable of being angry.

Gwendolen looked round at him and smiled. 'Treat you? Nonsense! I am only rather cross. Why did you come so very early? You must expect to find tempers in dishabille.'

'Be as cross with me as you like – only don't treat me with indifference,' said Rex, imploringly. 'All the happiness of my life depends on your loving me – if only a little – better than any one else.'

He tried to take her hand, but she hastily eluded his grasp and moved to the other end of the hearth, facing him.

'Pray don't make love to me! I hate it.' She looked at him fiercely.

Rex turned pale and was silent, but could not take his eyes off her, and the impetus was not yet exhausted that made hers dart death at him. Gwendolen herself could not have foreseen that she should feel in this way. It was all a sudden, new experience to her. The day before she had been quite aware that her cousin was in love with her – she did not mind how much, so that he said nothing about it; and if any one had asked her why she objected to love-making speeches, she would have said laughingly, 'Oh, I am tired of them all in the books.' But now the life of passion had begun negatively in her. She felt passionately averse to this volunteered love.

To Rex at twenty the joy of life seemed at an end more absolutely than it can do to a man at forty. But before they had ceased to look at each other, he did speak again.

'Is that the last word you have to say to me, Gwendolen? Will it always be so?'

She could not help seeing his wretchedness and feeling a little regret for the old Rex who had not offended her. Decisively, but yet with some return of kindliness, she said –

'About making love? Yes. But I don't dislike you for anything else.'

There was just a perceptible pause before he said a low 'good-bye,' and passed out of the room. Almost immediately after, she heard the heavy hall-door bang behind him.

Mrs. Davilow too had heard Rex's hasty departure, and presently came into the drawing-room, where she found Gwendolen seated on the low couch, her face buried, and her hair falling over her figure like a garment. She was sobbing bitterly. 'My child, my child, what is it?' cried the mother, who had never before seen her darling struck down in this way, and felt something of the alarmed anguish that women feel at the sight of overpowering sorrow in a strong man; for this child had been her ruler. Sitting down by her with circling arms, she pressed her cheek against Gwendolen's head, and then tried to draw it upward. Gwendolen gave way, and letting her head rest against her mother, cried out sobbingly, 'Oh mamma, what can become of my life? there is nothing worth living for!'

'Why, dear?' said Mrs. Davilow. Usually she herself had been rebuked by her daughter for involuntary signs of despair.

'I shall never love anybody. I can't love people. I hate them.'

'The time will come, dear, the time will come.'

Gwendolen was more and more convulsed with sobbing; but putting her arms round her mother's neck with an almost painful clinging, she said brokenly, 'I can't bear any one to be very near me but you.'

Then the mother began to sob, for this spoiled child had never shown such dependence on her before: and so they clung to each other.

VIII

What name doth Joy most borrow
When life is fair?
     'To-morrow.'
What name doth best fit Sorrow
In young despair?
     'To-morrow.'

THERE was a much more lasting trouble at the Rectory. Rex arrived there only to throw himself on his bed in a state of apparent apathy, unbroken till the next day, when it began to be interrupted by more positive signs of illness. Nothing could be said about his going to Southampton: instead of that, the chief thought of his mother and Anna was how to tend this patient who did not want to be well, and from being the brightest, most grateful spirit in the household, was metamorphosed into an irresponsive dull-eyed creature who met all affectionate attempts with a murmur of 'Let me alone.' His father looked beyond the crisis, and believed it to be the shortest way out of an unlucky affair; but he was sorry for the inevitable suffering, and went now and then to sit by him in silence for a few minutes, parting with a gentle pressure of his hand on Rex's blank brow, and a 'God bless you, my boy.' Warham and the younger children used to peep round the edge of the door to see this incredible thing of their lively brother being laid low; but fingers were immediately shaken at them to drive them back. The guardian who was always there was Anna, and her little hand was allowed to rest within her brother's, though he never gave it a welcoming pressure. Her soul was divided between anguish for Rex and reproach of Gwendolen.

'Perhaps it is wicked of me, but I think I never *can* love her again,' came as the recurrent burthen of poor little Anna's inward monody. And even Mrs. Gascoigne had an angry feeling towards her niece which she could not refrain from expressing (apologetically) to her husband.

'I know of course it is better, and we ought to be thankful that she is not in love with the poor boy; but really, Henry, I think she is hard: she has the heart of a coquette. I cannot help thinking that she must have made him believe something, or the disappointment would not have taken hold of him in that way. And some blame attaches to poor Fanny; she is quite blind about that girl.'

Mr. Gascoigne answered imperatively. 'The less said on that point the better, Nancy. I ought to have been more awake myself. As to the boy, be thankful if nothing worse ever happens to him. Let the thing die out as quickly as possible; and especially with regard to Gwendolen – let it be as if it had never been.'

The Rector's dominant feeling was that there had been a great escape. Gwendolen in love with Rex in return would have made a much harder problem, the solution of which might have been taken out of his hands. But he had to go through some further difficulty.

One fine morning Rex asked for his bath, and made his toilet as usual. Anna, full of excitement at this change, could do nothing but listen for his coming down, and at last hearing his step, ran to the foot of the stairs to meet him. For the first time he gave her a faint smile, but it looked so melancholy on his pale face that she could hardly help crying.

'Nannie!' he said, gently, taking her hand and leading her slowly along with him to the drawing-room. His mother was there, and when she came to kiss him, he said, 'What a plague I am!'

Then he sat still and looked out of the bow-window on the lawn and shrubs covered with hoar-frost, across which the sun was sending faint occasional gleams – something like that sad smile on Rex's face, Anna thought. He felt as if he had had a resurrection into a new world, and did not know what to do with himself there, the old interests being left behind. Anna sat near him, pretending to work, but really watching him with yearning looks. Beyond the garden hedge there was a road where waggons and carts sometimes went on field-work: a railed opening was made in the hedge, because the upland with its bordering wood and clump of ash-trees against the sky was a pretty sight. Presently there came along a waggon laden with timber; the horses were straining their grand muscles, and the driver having cracked his whip, ran along anxiously to guide the leader's head, fearing a swerve. Rex seemed to be shaken into attention, rose and looked till the last quivering trunk of the timber had disappeared, and then walked once or twice along the room. Mrs. Gascoigne was no longer there, and when he came to sit down again, Anna, seeing a return of speech in her brother's eyes, could not resist the impulse to bring a little stool and seat herself against his knee, looking up at him with an expression which seemed to say, 'Do speak to me.' And he spoke.

'I'll tell you what I am thinking of, Nannie. I will go to Canada, or somewhere of that sort.' (Rex had not studied the character of our colonial possessions.)

'Oh Rex, not for always!'

'Yes; to get my bread there. I should like to build a hut, and work hard at clearing, and have everything wild about me, and a great wide quiet.'

'And not take me with you?' said Anna, the big tears coming fast.

'How could I?'

'I should like it better than anything; and settlers go with their families. I would sooner go there than stay here in England. I could make the fires, and mend the clothes, and cook the food; and I could learn how to make the bread before we went. It would be nicer than anything – like playing at life over again, as we used to do when we made our tent with the drugget, and had our little plates and dishes.'

'Father and mother would not let you go.'

'Yes, I think they would when I explained everything. It would save money; and papa would have more to bring up the boys with.'

There was further talk of the same practical kind at intervals, and it ended in Rex's being obliged to consent that Anna should go with him when he spoke to his father on the subject.

Of course it was when the Rector was alone in his study. Their mother would become reconciled to whatever he decided on; but mentioned to her first, the question would have distressed her.

'Well, my children!' said Mr. Gascoigne, cheerfully, as they entered. It was a comfort to see Rex about again.

'May we sit down with you a little, papa?' said Anna. 'Rex has something to say.'

'With all my heart.'

It was a noticeable group that these three creatures made, each of them with a face of the same structural type – the straight brow, the nose suddenly straightened from an intention of being aquiline, the short upper lip, the short but strong and well-hung chin: there was even the same tone of complexion and set of the eye. The grey-haired father was at once massive and keen-looking; there was a perpendicular line in his brow which when he spoke with any force of interest deepened; and the habit of ruling gave him an air of reserved authoritativeness. Rex would have seemed a vision of the father's youth, if it had been possible to imagine Mr. Gascoigne without distinct plans and without command, smitten with a heart sorrow, and having no more notion of concealment than a sick animal; and Anna was a tiny copy of Rex, with hair drawn back and knotted, her face following his in its changes of expression, as if they had one soul between them.

'You know all about what has upset me, father,' Rex began, and Mr. Gascoigne nodded.

'I am quite done up for life in this part of the world. I am sure it will be no use my going back to Oxford. I couldn't do any reading. I should fail, and cause you expense for nothing. I want to have your consent to take another course, sir.'

Mr. Gascoigne nodded more slowly, the perpendicular line on his brow deepened, and Anna's trembling increased.

'If you would allow me a small outfit, I should like to go to the colonies and work on the land there.' Rex thought the vagueness of the phrase prudential; 'the colonies' necessarily embracing more advantages, and being less capable of being rebutted on a single ground than any particular settlement.

'Oh, and with me, papa,' said Anna, not bearing to be left out from the proposal even temporarily. 'Rex would want some one to take care of him, you know – some one to keep house. And we shall never, either of us, be married. And I should cost nothing, and I should be so happy. I know it would be hard to leave you and mamma; but there are all the others to bring up, and we two should be no trouble to you any more.'

Anna had risen from her seat, and used the feminine argument of going closer to her papa as she spoke. He did not smile, but he drew her on his knee and held her there, as if to put her gently out of the question while he spoke to Rex.

'You will admit that my experience gives me some power of judging for you, and that I can probably guide you in practical matters better than you can guide your-self.'

Rex was obliged to say, 'Yes, sir.'

'And perhaps you will admit – though I don't wish to press that point – that you are bound in duty to consider my judgment and wishes?'

'I have never yet placed myself in opposition to you, sir.' Rex in his secret soul could not feel that he was bound not to go to the colonies, but to go to Oxford again – which was the point in question.

'But you will do so if you persist in setting your mind towards a rash and foolish procedure, and deafening your-self to considerations which my experience of life assures me of. You think, I suppose, that you have had a shock which has changed all your inclinations, stupefied your brains, unfitted you for anything but manual labour, and given you a dislike to society? Is that what you believe?'

'Something like that. I shall never be up to the sort of work I must do to live in this part of the world. I have not the spirit for it. I shall never be the same again. And without any disrespect to you, father, I think a young fellow should be allowed to choose his way of life, if he does nobody any harm. There are plenty to stay at home, and those who like might be allowed to go where there are empty places.'

'But suppose I am convinced on good evidence – as I am – that this state of mind of yours is transient, and that if you went off as you propose, you would by-and-by repent, and feel that you had let yourself slip back from the point you have been gaining by your education till now? Have you not strength of mind enough to see that you had better act on my assurance for a time, and test it? In my opinion, so far from agreeing with you that you should be free to turn yourself into a colonist and work in your shirt-sleeves with spade and hatchet – in my opinion you have no right whatever to expatriate yourself until you have honestly endeavoured to turn to account the education you have received here. I say nothing of the grief to your mother and me.'

'I'm very sorry; but what can I do? I can't study – that's certain,' said Rex.

'Not just now, perhaps. You will have to miss a term. I have made arrangements for you – how you are to spend the next two months. But I confess I am disappointed in you, Rex. I thought you had more sense than to take up such ideas – to suppose that because you have fallen into a very common trouble, such as most men have to go through, you are loosened from all bonds of duty – just as if your brain had softened and you were no longer a responsible being.'

What could Rex say? Inwardly he was in a state of rebellion, but he had no arguments to meet his father's;

and while he was feeling, in spite of anything that might be said, that he should like to go off to 'the colonies' tomorrow, it lay in a deep fold of his consciousness that he ought to feel – if he had been a better fellow he would have felt – more about his old ties. This is the sort of faith we live by in our soul-sicknesses.

Rex got up from his seat, as if he held the conference to be at an end. 'You assent to my arrangement then?' said Mr. Gascoigne, with that distinct resolution of tone which seems to hold one in a vice.

There was a little pause before Rex answered, 'I'll try what I can do, sir. I can't promise.' His thought was, that trying would be of no use.

Her father kept Anna, holding her fast, though she wanted to follow Rex. 'Oh papa,' she said, the tears coming with her words when the door had closed; 'it is very hard for him. Doesn't he look ill?'

'Yes, but he will soon be better; it will all blow over. And now, Anna, be as quiet as a mouse about it all. Never let it be mentioned when he is gone.'

'No, papa. But I would not be like Gwendolen for anything – to have people fall in love with me so. It is very dreadful.'

Anna dared not say that she was disappointed at not being allowed to go to the colonies with Rex; but that was her secret feeling, and she often afterwards went inwardly over the whole affair, saying to herself, 'I should have done with going out, and gloves, and crinoline, and having to talk when I am taken to dinner – and all that!'

I like to mark the time, and connect the course of individual lives with the historic stream, for all classes of thinkers. This was the period when the broadening of gauge in crinolines seemed to demand an agitation for the general enlargement of churches, ball-rooms, and vehicles. But Anna Gascoigne's figure would only allow the size of skirt manufactured for young ladies of fourteen.

IX

I'll tell thee, Berthold, what men's hopes are like:
A silly child that, quivering with joy,
Would cast its little mimic fishing-line
Baited with loadstone for a bowl of toys
In the salt ocean.

EIGHT months after the arrival of the family at
Offendene, that is to say in the end of the following June,
a rumour was spread in the neighbourhood which to many
persons was matter of exciting interest. It had no reference
to the results of the American war, but it was one which
touched all classes within a certain circuit round Wancester:
the corn-factors, the brewers, the horse-dealers, and
saddlers, all held it a laudable thing, and one which was to
be rejoiced in on abstract grounds, as showing the value of
an aristocracy in a free country like England; the blacksmith in the hamlet of Diplow felt that a good time had
come round; the wives of labouring men hoped their nim-
ble boys of ten or twelve would be taken into employ by the
gentlemen in livery; and the farmers about Diplow
admitted, with a tincture of bitterness and reserve, that a
man might now again perhaps have an easier market or
exchange for a rick of old hay or a waggon-load of straw. If
such were the hopes of low persons not in society, it may be
easily inferred that their betters had better reasons for
satisfaction, probably connected with the pleasures of life
rather than its business. Marriage, however, must be considered as coming under both heads; and just as when a visit
of Majesty is announced, the dream of knighthood or a
baronetcy is to be found under various municipal night-
caps, so the news in question raised a floating indeterminate vision of marriage in several well-bred imaginations.

The news was that Diplow Hall, Sir Hugo Mallinger's
place, which had for a couple of years turned its white
window-shutters in a painfully wall-eyed manner on its
fine elms and beeches, its lilied pool and grassy acres

specked with deer, was being prepared for a tenant, and was for the rest of the summer and through the hunting season to be inhabited in a fitting style both as to house and stable. But not by Sir Hugo himself: by his nephew Mr. Mallinger Grandcourt, who was presumptive heir to the baronetcy, his uncle's marriage having produced nothing but girls. Nor was this the only contingency with which fortune flattered young Grandcourt, as he was pleasantly called; for while the chance of the baronetcy came through his father, his mother had given a baronial streak to his blood, so that if certain intervening persons slightly painted in the middle distance died, he would become a baron and peer of this realm.

It is the uneven allotment of nature that the male bird alone has the tuft, but we have not yet followed the advice of hasty philosophers who would have us copy nature entirely in these matters; and if Mr. Mallinger Grandcourt became a baronet or a peer, his wife would share the title – which in addition to his actual fortune was certainly a reason why that wife, being at present unchosen, should be thought of by more than one person with sympathetic interest as a woman sure to be well provided for.

Some readers of this history will doubtless regard it as incredible that people should construct matrimonial prospects on the mere report that a bachelor of good fortune and possibilities was coming within reach, and will reject the statement as a mere outflow of gall: they will aver that neither they nor their first cousins have minds so unbridled; and that in fact this is not human nature, which would know that such speculations might turn out to be fallacious, and would therefore not entertain them. But, let it be observed, nothing is here narrated of human nature generally: the history in its present stage concerns only a few people in a corner of Wessex – whose reputation, however, was unimpeached, and who, I am in the proud position of being able to state, were all on visiting terms with persons of rank.

There were the Arrowpoints, for example, in their beautiful place at Quetcham: no one could attribute sordid views in relation to their daughter's marriage to parents who could leave her at least half a million; but having affectionate anxieties about their Catherine's position (she having resolutely refused Lord Slogan, an unexceptionable Irish peer, whose estate wanted nothing but drainage and population), they wondered, perhaps from something more than a charitable impulse, whether Mr. Grandcourt was good-looking, of sound constitution, virtuous or at least reformed, and if liberal-conservative, not too liberal-conservative; and without wishing anybody to die, thought his succession to the title an event to be desired.

If the Arrowpoints had such ruminations, it is the less surprising that they were stimulated in Mr. Gascoigne, who for being a clergyman was not the less subject to the anxieties of a parent and guardian; and we have seen how both he and Mrs. Gascoigne might by this time have come to feel that he was overcharged with the management of young creatures who were hardly to be held in with bit or bridle, or any sort of metaphor that would stand for judicious advice.

Naturally, people did not tell each other all they felt and thought about young Grandcourt's advent: on no subject is this openness found prudentially practicable – not even on the generation of acids, or the destination of the fixed stars; for either your contemporary with a mind turned towards the same subjects may find your ideas ingenious and forestall you in applying them, or he may have other views on acids and fixed stars, and think ill of you in consequence. Mr. Gascoigne did not ask Mr. Arrowpoint if he had any trustworthy source of information about Grandcourt considered as a husband for a charming girl; nor did Mrs. Arrowpoint observe to Mrs. Davilow that if the possible peer sought a wife in the neighbourhood of Diplow, the only reasonable expectation was that he would offer his hand to Catherine, who, however, would not accept him unless he were in all respects fitted to secure her happiness. Indeed, even to his wife the Rector was silent as to the contemplation of any matrimonial result, from the probability that Mr. Grandcourt would see Gwendolen at the next Archery Meeting; though Mrs. Gascoigne's mind was very likely still more active in the same direction. She had said interjectionally to her sister, 'It would be a mercy, Fanny, if that girl were well married!' to which Mrs. Davilow, discerning some criticism of her darling in the fervour of that wish, had not chosen to make any audible reply, though she had said inwardly, 'You will not get her to marry for your pleasure;' the mild mother becoming rather saucy when she identified herself with her daughter.

To her husband Mrs. Gascoigne said, 'I hear Mr. Grandcourt has two places of his own, but he comes to Diplow for the hunting. It is to be hoped he will set a good example in the neighbourhood. Have you heard what sort of young man he is, Henry?'

Mr. Gascoigne had not heard; at least, if his male acquaintances had gossiped in his hearing, he was not disposed to repeat their gossip, or give it any emphasis in his own mind. He held it futile, even if it had been becoming, to show any curiosity as to the past of a young man whose birth, wealth, and consequent leisure made many habits venial which under other circumstances would have been inexcusable. Whatever Grandcourt had done, he had not ruined himself; and it is well known that in gambling, for example, whether of the business or holiday sort, a man who has the strength of mind to leave off when he has only ruined others, is a reformed character. This is an illustration merely: Mr. Gascoigne had not heard that Grandcourt had been a gambler; and we can hardly pronounce him singular in feeling that a landed proprietor with a mixture of noble blood in his veins was not to be an object of suspicious inquiry like a reformed character who offers himself as your butler or footman. Reformation, where a man can afford to do without it, can hardly be other than genuine. Moreover, it was not certain on any showing hitherto that Mr. Grandcourt had needed reformation more than other young men in the ripe youth of five-and-thirty; and, at any rate, the significance of what he had been must be determined by what he actually was.

Mrs. Davilow, too, although she would not respond to her sister's pregnant remark, could not be inwardly indifferent to an event that might promise a brilliant lot for Gwendolen. A little speculation on 'what may be' comes naturally, without encouragement – comes inevitably in the form of images, when unknown persons are mentioned; and Mr. Grandcourt's name raised in Mrs. Davilow's mind first of all the picture of a handsome, accomplished, excellent young man whom she would be satisfied with as a husband for her daughter; but then came the further speculation – would Gwendolen be satisfied with him? There was no knowing what would meet that girl's taste or touch her affections – it might be something else than excellence; and thus the image of the perfect suitor gave way before a fluctuating combination of qualities that might be imagined to win Gwendolen's heart. In the difficulty of arriving at the particular combination which would ensure that result, the mother even said to herself, 'It would not signify about her being in love, if she would only accept the right person.' For whatever marriage had been for herself, how could she the less desire it for her daughter? The difference her own misfortunes made was, that she never dared to dwell much to Gwendolen on the desirableness of marriage, dreading an answer something like that of the future Madame Roland, when her gentle mother urging the acceptance of a suitor, said, 'Tu seras heureuse, ma chère.' 'Oui, maman, comme toi.'

In relation to the problematic Mr. Grandcourt least of all would Mrs. Davilow have willingly let fall a hint of the aerial castle-building which she had the good taste to be ashamed of; for such a hint was likely enough to give an adverse poise to Gwendolen's own thought, and make her detest the desirable husband beforehand. Since that scene after poor Rex's farewell visit, the mother had felt a new sense of peril in touching the mystery of her child's feeling, and in rashly determining what was her welfare: only she could think of welfare in no other shape than marriage.

The discussion of the dress that Gwendolen was to wear at the Archery Meeting was a relevant topic, however; and when it had been decided that as a touch of colour on her white cashmere, nothing, for her complexion, was comparable to pale green – a feather which she was trying in her hat before the looking-glass having settled the question – Mrs. Davilow felt her ears tingle when Gwendolen, suddenly throwing herself into the attitude of drawing her bow, said with a look of comic enjoyment –

'How I pity all the other girls at the Archery Meeting – all thinking of Mr. Grandcourt! And they have not a shadow of a chance.'

Mrs. Davilow had not presence of mind to answer immediately, and Gwendolen turned quickly round towards her saying, wickedly –

'Now you know they have not, mamma. You and my uncle and aunt – you all intend him to fall in love with me.'

Mrs. Davilow, piqued into a little stratagem, said, 'Oh, my dear, that is not so certain. Miss Arrowpoint has charms which you have not.'

'I know. But they demand thought. My arrow will pierce him before he has time for thought. He will declare himself my slave – I shall send him round the world to bring me back the wedding-ring of a happy woman – in the mean time all the men who are between him and the title will die of different diseases – he will come back Lord Grandcourt – but without the ring – and fall at my feet. I shall laugh at him – he will rise in resentment – I shall laugh more – he will call for his steed and ride to Quetcham, where he will find Miss Arrowpoint just married to a needy musician, Mrs. Arrowpoint tearing her cap off, and Mr. Arrowpoint standing by. Exit Lord Grandcourt, who returns to Diplow, and like M. Jabot, *change de linge*.'

Was ever any young witch like this? You thought of hiding things from her – sat upon your secret and looked innocent, and all the while she knew by the corner of your eye that it was exactly five pounds ten you were sitting on! As well turn the key to keep out the damp! It was probable that by dint of divination she already knew more than any one else did of Mr. Grandcourt. That idea in Mrs. Davilow's mind prompted the sort of question which often comes without any other apparent reason than the faculty of speech and the not knowing what to do with it.

'Why, what kind of man do you imagine him to be, Gwendolen?'

'Let me see!' said the witch, putting her fore-finger to her lips with a little frown, and then stretching out the finger with decision. 'Short – just above my shoulder – trying to make himself tall by turning up his moustache and keeping his beard long – a glass in his right eye to give him an air of distinction – a strong opinion about his waist-coat, but uncertain and trimming about the weather, on which he will try to draw me out. He will stare at me all the while, and the glass in his eye will cause him to make horrible faces, especially when he smiles in a flattering way. I shall cast down my eyes in consequence, and he will perceive that I am not indifferent to his attentions. I shall dream that night that I am looking at the extraordinary face of a magnified insect – and the next morning he will make me an offer of his hand; the sequel as before.'

'That is a portrait of some one you have seen already, Gwen. Mr. Grandcourt may be a delightful young man for what you know.'

'Oh yes,' said Gwendolen, with a high note of careless admission, taking off her best hat and turning it round on her hand contemplatively. 'I wonder what sort of behaviour a delightful young man would have!' Then, with a merry change of face, 'I know he would have hunters and racers, and a London house and two country houses, – one with battlements and another with a veranda. And I feel sure that with a little murdering he might get a title.'

The irony of this speech was of the doubtful sort that has some genuine belief mixed up with it. Poor Mrs. Davilow felt uncomfortable under it, her own meanings being usually literal and in intention innocent; and she said, with a distressed brow –

'Don't talk in that way, child, for heaven's sake! You do read such books – they give you such ideas of everything. I declare when your aunt and I were your age we knew nothing about wickedness. I think it was better so.'

'Why did you not bring me up in that way, mamma?' said Gwendolen. But immediately perceiving in the crushed look and rising sob that she had given a deep wound, she tossed down her hat and knelt at her mother's feet, crying –

'Mamma, mamma! I was only speaking in fun. I meant nothing.'

'How could I, Gwendolen?' said poor Mrs. Davilow, unable to hear the retractation, and sobbing violently while she made the effort to speak. 'Your will was always too strong for me – if everything else had been different.'

This disjointed logic was intelligible enough to the daughter. 'Dear mamma, I don't find fault with you – I love you,' said Gwendolen, really compunctious. 'How can you help what I am? Besides, I am very charming. Come, now.' Here Gwendolen with her handkerchief gently rubbed away her mother's tears. 'Really – I am contented with myself. I like myself better than I should have liked my aunt and you. How dreadfully dull you must have been!'

Such tender cajolery served to quiet the mother, as it had often done before after like collisions. Not that the collisions had often been repeated at the same point; for in the memory of both they left an association of dread with the particular topics which had occasioned them: Gwendolen dreaded the unpleasant sense of compunction towards her mother, which was the nearest approach to self-condemnation and self-distrust that she had known; and Mrs. Davilow's timid maternal conscience dreaded whatever had brought on the slightest hint of reproach.

Hence, after this little scene, the two concurred in excluding Mr. Grandcourt from their conversation.

When Mr. Gascoigne once or twice referred to him, Mrs. Davilow feared lest Gwendolen should betray some of her alarming keen-sightedness about what was probably in her uncle's mind; but the fear was not justified. Gwendolen knew certain differences in the characters with which she was concerned as birds know climate and weather; and, for the very reason that she was determined to evade her uncle's control, she was determined not to clash with him. The good understanding between them was much fostered by their enjoyment of archery together: Mr. Gascoigne, as one of the best bowmen in Wessex, was gratified to find the elements of like skill in his niece; and Gwendolen was the more careful not to lose the shelter of his fatherly indulgence, because since the trouble with Rex both Mrs. Gascoigne and Anna had been unable to hide what she felt to be a very unreasonable alienation from her. Towards Anna she took some pains to behave with a regretful affectionateness; but neither of them dared to mention Rex's name, and Anna, to whom the thought of him was part of the air she breathed, was ill at ease with the lively cousin who had ruined his happiness. She tried dutifully to repress any sign of her changed feeling; but who in pain can imitate the glance and hand-touch of pleasure?

This unfair resentment had rather a hardening effect on Gwendolen, and threw her into a more defiant temper. Her uncle too might be offended if she refused the next person who fell in love with her; and one day when that idea was in her mind she said –

'Mamma, I see now why girls are glad to be married – to escape being expected to please everybody but themselves.'

Happily, Mr. Middleton was gone without having made any avowal; and notwithstanding the admiration for the handsome Miss Harleth, extending perhaps over thirty square miles in a part of Wessex well studded with families whose members included several disengaged young men, each glad to seat himself by the lively girl with whom it was so easy to get on in conversation, – notwithstanding these grounds for arguing that Gwendolen was likely to have other suitors more explicit than the cautious curate, the fact was not so.

Care has been taken not only that the trees should not sweep the stars down, but also that every man who admires a fair girl should not be enamoured of her, and even that every man who is enamoured should not necessarily declare himself. There are various refined shapes in which the price of corn, known to be a potent cause in this relation, might, if inquired into, show why a young lady, perfect in person, accomplishments, and costume, has not the trouble of rejecting many offers; and Nature's order is certainly benignant in not obliging us one and all to be desperately in love with the most admirable mortal we have ever seen. Gwendolen, we know, was far from holding that supremacy in the minds of all observers. Besides, it was but a poor eight months since she had come to Offendene, and some inclinations become manifest slowly, like the sunward creeping of plants.

In face of this fact that not one of the eligible young men already in the neighbourhood had made Gwendolen an offer, why should Mr. Grandcourt be thought of as likely to do what they had left undone?

Perhaps because he was thought of as still more eligible; since a great deal of what passes for likelihood in the world is simply the reflex of a wish. Mr. and Mrs. Arrowpoint, for example, having no anxiety that Miss Harleth should make a brilliant marriage, had quite a different likelihood in their minds.

X

1st Gent. What woman should be? Sir, consult the taste
Of marriageable men. This planet's store
In iron, cotton, wool, or chemicals –
All matter rendered to our plastic skill,
Is wrought in shapes responsive to demand:
The market's pulse makes index high or low,
By rule sublime. Our daughters must be wives,
And to be wives must be what men will choose:
Men's taste is woman's test. You mark the phrase?
'Tis good, I think? – the sense well winged and poised
With t's and s's.

2d Gent.   Nay, but turn it round:
Give us the test of taste. A fine *menu* –
Is it to-day what Roman epicures
Insisted that a gentleman must eat
To earn the dignity of dining well?

BRACKENSHAW PARK, where the Archery Meeting was held, looked out from its gentle heights far over the neighbouring valley to the outlying eastern downs and the broad slow rise of cultivated country hanging like a vast curtain towards the west. The castle, which stood on the highest platform of the clustered hills, was built of rough-hewn limestone, full of lights and shadows made by the dark dust of lichens and the washings of the rain. Masses of beech and fir sheltered it on the north, and spread down here and there along the green slopes like flocks seeking the water which gleamed below. The archery-ground was a carefully-kept enclosure on a bit of table-land at the farthest end of the park, protected towards the south-west by tall elms and a thick screen of hollies, which kept the gravel walk and the bit of newly-mown turf where the targets were placed in agreeable afternoon shade. The Archery Hall with an arcade in front showed like a white temple against the greenery on the northern side.

What could make a better background for the flower-groups of ladies, moving and bowing and turning their necks as it would become the leisurely lilies to do if they took to locomotion? The sounds too were very pleasant to hear, even when the military band from Wancester ceased to play: musical laughs in all the registers and a harmony of happy friendly speeches, now rising towards mild excitement, now sinking to an agreeable murmur.

No open-air amusement could be much freer from those noisy, crowding conditions which spoil most modern pleasures; no Archery Meeting could be more select, the number of friends accompanying the members being restricted by an award of tickets, so as to keep the maximum within the limits of convenience for the dinner and ball to be held in the castle. Within the enclosure no plebeian spectators were admitted except Lord Brackenshaw's tenants and their families, and of these it was chiefly the feminine members who used the privilege, bringing their little boys and girls or younger brothers and sisters. The males among them relieved the insipidity of the entertainment by imaginative betting, in which the stake was 'anything you like,' on their favourite archers; but the young maidens, having a different principle of discrimination, were considering which of those sweetly-dressed ladies they would choose to be, if the choice were allowed them. Probably the form these rural souls would most have striven for as a tabernacle was some other than Gwendolen's – one with more pink in her cheeks and hair of the most fashionable yellow; but among the male judges in the ranks immediately surrounding her there was unusual unanimity in pronouncing her the finest girl present.

No wonder she enjoyed her existence on that July day. Pre-eminence is sweet to those who love it, even under mediocre circumstances: perhaps it is not quite mythical that a slave has been proud to be bought first; and probably a barn-door fowl on sale, though he may not have understood himself to be called the best of a bad lot, may have a self-informed consciousness of his relative importance, and strut consoled. But for complete enjoyment the outward and the inward must concur. And that concurrence was happening to Gwendolen.

Who can deny that bows and arrows are among the prettiest weapons in the world for feminine forms to play with? They prompt attitudes full of grace and power, where that fine concentration of energy seen in all marksmanship, is freed from associations of bloodshed. The time-honoured British resource of 'killing something' is no longer carried on with bow and quiver; bands defending their passes against an invading nation fight under another sort of shade than a cloud of arrows; and poisoned darts are harmless survivals either in rhetoric or in regions comfortably remote. Archery has no ugly smell of brimstone; breaks nobody's shins, breeds no athletic monsters; its only danger is that of failing, which for generous blood is enough to mould skilful action. And among the Brackenshaw archers the prizes were all of the nobler symbolic kind: not property to be carried off in a parcel, degrading honour into gain; but the gold arrow and the silver, the gold star and the silver, to be worn for a time in sign of achievement and then transferred to the next who did excellently. These signs of pre-eminence had the virtue of wreaths without their inconveniences, which might have produced a melancholy effect in the heat of the ball-room. Altogether the Brackenshaw Archery Club was an institution framed with good taste, so as not to have by necessity any ridiculous incidents.

And to-day all incalculable elements were in its favour. There was mild warmth, and no wind to disturb either hair or drapery or the course of the arrow; all skilful preparation had fair play, and when there was a general march to extract the arrows, the promenade of joyous young creatures in light speech and laughter, the graceful movement in common towards a common object, was a show worth looking at. Here Gwendolen seemed a Calypso among her nymphs. It was in her attitudes and movements that every one was obliged to admit her surpassing charm.

'That girl is like a high-mettled racer,' said Lord Brackenshaw to young Clintock, one of the invited spectators.

'First chop! tremendously pretty too,' said the elegant Grecian, who had been paying her assiduous attention; 'I never saw her look better.'

Perhaps she had never looked so well. Her face was beaming with young pleasure in which there were no malign rays of discontent; for being satisfied with her own chances, she felt kindly towards everybody and was satisfied with the universe. Not to have the highest distinction in rank, not to be marked out as an heiress, like Miss Arrowpoint, gave an added triumph in eclipsing those advantages. For personal recommendation she would not have cared to change the family group accompanying her for any other: her mamma's appearance would have suited an amiable duchess; her uncle and aunt Gascoigne with Anna made equally gratifying figures in their way; and Gwendolen was too full of joyous belief in herself to feel in the least jealous though Miss Arrowpoint was one of the best archeresses.

Even the reappearance of the formidable Herr Klesmer, which caused some surprise in the rest of the company, seemed only to fall in with Gwendolen's inclination to be amused. Short of Apollo himself, what great musical *maestro* could make a good figure at an archery meeting? There was a very satirical light in Gwendolen's eyes as she looked towards the Arrowpoint party on their first entrance, when the contrast between Klesmer and the average group of English county people seemed at its utmost intensity in the close neighbourhood of his hosts – or patrons, as Mrs. Arrowpoint would have liked to hear them called, that she might deny the possibility of any longer patronizing genius, its royalty being universally acknowledged. The contrast might have amused a graver personage than Gwendolen. We English are a miscellaneous people, and any chance fifty of us will present many varieties of animal architecture or facial ornament; but it must be admitted that our prevailing expression is not that of a lively, impassioned race, preoccupied with the ideal and carrying the real as a mere make-weight. The strong point of the English gentleman pure is the easy style of his figure and clothing; he objects to marked ins and outs in his costume, and he also objects to looking inspired.

Fancy an assemblage where the men had all that ordinary stamp of the well-bred Englishman, watching the entrance of Herr Klesmer – his mane of hair floating backward in massive inconsistency with the chimney-pot hat, which had the look of having been put on for a joke above his pronounced but well-modelled features and powerful clear-shaven mouth and chin; his tall thin figure clad in a way which, not being strictly English, was all the worse for its apparent emphasis of intention. Draped in a loose garment with a Florentine berretta on his head, he would have been fit to stand by the side of Leonardo da Vinci; but how when he presented himself in trousers which were not what English feeling demanded about the knees? – and when the fire that showed itself in his glances and the movements of his head, as he looked round him with curiosity, was turned into comedy by a hat which ruled that mankind should have well-cropped hair and a staid demeanour, such, for example, as Mr. Arrowpoint's, whose nullity of face and perfect tailoring might pass everywhere without ridicule? One sees why it is often better for greatness to be dead, and to have got rid of the outward man.

Many present knew Klesmer, or knew of him; but they had only seen him on candle-light occasions when he appeared simply as a musician, and he had not yet that supreme, world-wide celebrity which makes an artist great to the most ordinary people by their knowledge of his great expensiveness. It was literally a new light for them to see him in – presented unexpectedly on this July afternoon in an exclusive society: some were inclined to laugh, others felt a little disgust at the want of judgment shown by the Arrowpoints in this use of an introductory card.

'What extreme guys those artistic fellows usually are!' said young Clintock to Gwendolen. 'Do look at the figure he cuts, bowing with his hand on his heart to Lady

Brackenshaw – and Mrs. Arrowpoint's feather just reaching his shoulder.'

'You are one of the profane,' said Gwendolen. 'You are blind to the majesty of genius. Herr Klesmer smites me with awe; I feel crushed in his presence; my courage all oozes from me.'

'Ah, you understand all about his music.'

'No, indeed,' said Gwendolen, with a light laugh; 'it is he who understands all about mine and thinks it pitiable.' Klesmer's verdict on her singing had been an easier joke to her since he had been struck by her *plastik*.

'It is not addressed to the ears of the future, I suppose. I'm glad of that: it suits mine.'

'Oh, you are very kind. But how remarkably well Miss Arrowpoint looks to-day! She would make quite a fine picture in that gold-coloured dress.'

'Too splendid, don't you think?'

'Well, perhaps a little too symbolical – too much like the figure of Wealth in an allegory.'

This speech of Gwendolen's had rather a malicious sound, but it was not really more than a bubble of fun. She did not wish Miss Arrowpoint or any one else to be out of the way, believing in her own good fortune even more than in her skill. The belief in both naturally grew stronger as the shooting went on, for she promised to achieve one of the best scores – a success which astonished every one in a new member; and to Gwendolen's temperament one success determined another. She trod on air, and all things pleasant seemed possible. The hour was enough for her, and she was not obliged to think of what she should do next to keep her life at the due pitch.

'How does the scoring stand, I wonder?' said Lady Brackenshaw, a gracious personage who, adorned with two fair little girls and a boy of stout make, sat as lady paramount. Her lord had come up to her in one of the intervals of shooting. 'It seems to me that Miss Harleth is likely to win the gold arrow.'

'Gad, I think she will, if she carries it on! she is running Juliet Fenn hard. It is wonderful for one in her first year. Catherine is not up to her usual mark,' continued his lordship, turning to the heiress's mother who sat near. 'But she got the gold arrow last time. And there's a luck even in these games of skill. That's better. It gives the hinder ones a chance.'

'Catherine will be very glad for others to win,' said Mrs. Arrowpoint, 'she is so magnanimous. It was entirely her considerateness that made us bring Herr Klesmer instead of Canon Stopley, who had expressed a wish to come. For her own pleasure, I am sure she would rather have brought the Canon; but she is always thinking of others. I told her it was not quite *en règle* to bring one so far out of our own set; but she said, "Genius itself is not *en règle*; it comes into the world to make new rules." And one must admit that.'

'Ay, to be sure,' said Lord Brackenshaw, in a tone of careless dismissal, adding quickly, 'For my part, I am not magnanimous; I should like to win. But, confound it! I never have the chance now. I'm getting old and idle. The young ones beat me. As old Nestor says – the gods don't give us everything at one time: I was a young fellow once, and now I am getting an old and wise one. Old, at any rate; which is a gift that comes to everybody if they live long enough, so it raises no jealousy.' The Earl smiled comfortably at his wife.

'Oh my lord, people who have been neighbours twenty years must not talk to each other about age,' said Mrs. Arrowpoint. 'Years, as the Tuscans say, are made for the letting of houses. But where is our new neighbour? I thought Mr. Grandcourt was to be here to-day.'

'Ah, by the way, so he was. The time's getting on too,' said his lordship, looking at his watch. 'But he only got to Diplow the other day. He came to us on Tuesday and said he had been a little bothered. He may have been pulled in another direction. Why, Gascoigne!' – the Rector was just then crossing at a little distance with Gwendolen on his arm, and turned in compliance with the call – 'this is a little

113

DANIEL DERONDA

too bad; you not only beat us yourself, but you bring up your niece to beat all the archeresses.'

'It *is* rather scandalous in her to get the better of elder members,' said Mr. Gascoigne, with much inward satisfaction curling his short upper lip. 'But it is not my doing, my lord. I only meant her to make a tolerable figure, without surpassing any one.'

'It is not my fault either,' said Gwendolen, with pretty archness. 'If I am to aim, I can't help hitting.'

'Ay, ay, that may be a fatal business for some people,' said Lord Brackenshaw, good-humouredly; then taking out his watch and looking at Mrs. Arrowpoint again – 'The time's getting on, as you say. But Grandcourt is always late. I notice in town he's always late, and he's no bowman – understands nothing about it. But I told him he must come; he would see the flower of the neighbourhood here. He asked about you – had seen Arrowpoint's card. I think you had not made his acquaintance in town. He has been a good deal abroad. People don't know him much.'

'No; we are strangers,' said Mrs. Arrowpoint. 'But that is not what might have been expected. For his uncle Sir Hugo Mallinger and I are great friends when we meet.'

'I don't know; uncles and nephews are not so likely to be seen together as uncles and nieces,' said his lordship, smiling towards the Rector. 'But just come with me one instant, Gascoigne, will you? I want to speak a word about the clout-shooting.'

Gwendolen chose to go too and be deposited in the same group with her mamma and aunt until she had to shoot again. That Mr. Grandcourt might after all not appear on the archery-ground, had begun to enter into Gwendolen's thought as a possible deduction from the completeness of her pleasure. Under all her saucy satire, provoked chiefly by her divination that her friends thought of him as a desirable match for her, she felt something very far from indifference as to the impression she would make on him. True, he was not to have the slightest power over her (for Gwendolen had not considered that the desire to

114

conquer is itself a sort of subjection); she had made up her mind that he was to be one of those complimentary and assiduously admiring men of whom even her narrow experience had shown her several with various-coloured beards and various styles of bearing; and the sense that her friends would want her to think him delightful, gave her a resistant inclination to presuppose him ridiculous. But that was no reason why she could spare his presence: and even a passing prevision of trouble in case she despised and refused him, raised not the shadow of a wish that he should save her that trouble by showing no disposition to make her an offer. Mr. Grandcourt taking hardly any notice of her, and becoming shortly engaged to Miss Arrowpoint, was not a picture which flattered her imagination.

Hence Gwendolen had been all ear to Lord Bracken-shaw's mode of accounting for Grandcourt's non-appearance; and when he did arrive, no consciousness – not even Mrs. Arrowpoint's or Mr. Gascoigne's – was more awake to the fact than hers, although she steadily avoided looking towards any point where he was likely to be. There should be no slightest shifting of angles to betray that it was of any consequence to her whether the much-talked-of Mr. Mallinger Grandcourt presented himself or not. She became again absorbed in the shooting, and so resolutely abstained from looking round observantly that, even supposing him to have taken a conspicuous place among the spectators, it might be clear she was not aware of him. And all the while the certainty that he was there made a distinct thread in her consciousness. Perhaps her shooting was the better for it: at any rate, it gained in precision, and she at last raised a delightful storm of clapping and applause by three hits running in the gold – a feat which among the Brackenshaw archers had not the vulgar reward of a shilling poll-tax, but that of a special gold star to be worn on the breast. That moment was not only a happy one to herself – it was just what her mamma and her uncle would have chosen for her. There was a general falling into ranks to give her space that she might advance conspicuously to receive the gold star from the hands of Lady Brackenshaw; and the perfect movement of her fine form was certainly a pleasant thing to behold in the clear afternoon light when the shadows were long and still. She was the central object of that pretty picture, and every one present must gaze at her. That was enough: she herself was determined to see nobody in particular, or to turn her eyes any way except towards Lady Brackenshaw, but her thoughts undeniably turned in other ways. It entered a little into her pleasure that Herr Klesmer must be observing her at a moment when music was out of the question, and his superiority very far in the background; for vanity is as ill at ease under indifference as tenderness is under a love which it cannot return; and the unconquered Klesmer threw a trace of his malign power even across her pleasant consciousness that Mr. Grandcourt was seeing her to the utmost advantage, and was probably giving her an admiration unmixed with criticism. She did not expect to admire *him*, but that was not necessary to her peace of mind.

Gwendolen met Lady Brackenshaw's gracious smile without blushing (which only came to her when she was taken by surprise), but with a charming gladness of expression, and then bent with easy grace to have the star fixed near her shoulder. That little ceremony had been over long enough for her to have exchanged playful speeches and received congratulations as she moved among the groups who were now interesting themselves in the results of the scoring; but it happened that she stood outside examining the point of an arrow with rather an absent air when Lord Brackenshaw came up to her and said –

'Miss Harleth, here is a gentleman who is not willing to wait any longer for an introduction. He has been getting Mrs. Davilow to send me with him. Will you allow me to introduce Mr. Mallinger Grandcourt?'

BOOK II
Meeting Streams

XI

The beginning of an acquaintance whether with persons or things
is to get a definite outline for our ignorance.

MR. GRANDCOURT'S wish to be introduced had no
suddenness for Gwendolen; but when Lord Brackenshaw
moved aside a little for the prefigured stranger to come
forward and she felt herself face to face with the real man,
there was a little shock which flushed her cheeks and
vexatiously deepened with her consciousness of it. The
shock came from the reversal of her expectations:
Grandcourt could hardly have been more unlike all her
imaginary portraits of him. He was slightly taller than
herself, and their eyes seemed to be on a level; there was
not the faintest smile on his face as he looked at her, not a
trace of self-consciousness or anxiety in his bearing; when
he raised his hat he showed an extensive baldness surrounded with a mere fringe of reddish blond hair, but he
also showed a perfect hand; the line of feature from brow to
chin undisguised by beard was decidedly handsome, with
only moderate departures from the perpendicular, and the
slight whisker too was perpendicular. It was not possible
for a human aspect to be freer from grimace or solicitous
wrigglings; also it was perhaps not possible for a breathing
man wide awake to look less animated. The correct
Englishman, drawing himself up from his bow into rigidity,
assenting severely, and seeming to be in a state of internal
drill, suggests a suppressed vivacity, and may be suspected
of letting go with some violence when he is released from
parade; but Grandcourt's bearing had no rigidity, it
inclined rather to the flaccid. His complexion had a faded
fairness resembling that of an actress when bare of the
artificial white and red; his long narrow grey eyes

117

expressed nothing but indifference. Attempts at description are stupid: who can all at once describe a human being? even when he is presented to us we only begin that knowledge of his appearance which must be completed by innumerable impressions under differing circumstances. We recognize the alphabet; we are not sure of the language. I am only mentioning the points that Gwendolen saw by the light of a prepared contrast in the first minutes of her meeting with Grandcourt: they were summed up in the words, 'He is not ridiculous.' But forthwith Lord Brackenshaw was gone, and what is called conversation had begun, the first and constant element in it being that Grandcourt looked at Gwendolen persistently with a slightly exploring gaze, but without change of expression, while she only occasionally looked at him with a flash of observation a little softened by coquetry. Also, after her answers there was a longer or shorter pause before he spoke again.

'I used to think archery was a great bore,' Grandcourt began. He spoke with a fine accent, but with a certain broken drawl, as of a distinguished personage with a distinguished cold on his chest.

'Are you converted to-day?' said Gwendolen.

(Pause, during which she imagined various degrees and modes of opinion about herself that might be entertained by Grandcourt.)

'Yes, since I saw you shooting. In things of this sort one generally sees people missing and simpering.'

'I suppose you are a first-rate shot with a rifle.'

(Pause, during which Gwendolen, having taken a rapid observation of Grandcourt, made a brief graphic description of him to an indefinite hearer.)

'I have left off shooting.'

'Oh, then, you are a formidable person. People who have done things once and left them off make one feel very contemptible, as if one were using cast-off fashions. I hope you have not left off all follies, because I practise a great many.'

(Pause, during which Gwendolen made several interpretations of her own speech.)

'What do you call follies?'

'Well, in general, I think whatever is agreeable is called a folly. But you have not left off hunting, I hear.'

(Pause, wherein Gwendolen recalled what she had heard about Grandcourt's position, and decided that he was the most aristocratic-looking man she had ever seen.)

'One must do something.'

'And do you care about the turf? – or is that among the things you have left off?'

(Pause, during which Gwendolen thought that a man of extremely calm, cold manners might be less disagreeable as a husband than other men, and not likely to interfere with his wife's preferences.)

'I run a horse now and then; but I don't go in for the thing as some men do. Are you fond of horses?'

'Yes, indeed: I never like my life so well as when I am on horseback, having a great gallop. I think of nothing. I only feel myself strong and happy.'

(Pause, wherein Gwendolen wondered whether Grandcourt would like what she said, but assured herself that she was not going to disguise her tastes.)

'Do you like danger?'

'I don't know. When I am on horseback I never think of danger. It seems to me that if I broke my bones I should not feel it. I should go at anything that came in my way.'

(Pause, during which Gwendolen had run through a whole hunting season with two chosen hunters to ride at will.)

'You would perhaps like tiger-hunting or pig-sticking. I saw some of that for a season or two in the East. Everything here is poor stuff after that.'

'*You* are fond of danger, then?'

(Pause, wherein Gwendolen speculated on the probability that the men of coldest manners were the most adventurous, and felt the strength of her own insight, supposing the question had to be decided.)

'One must have something or other. But one gets used to it.'

'I begin to think I am very fortunate, because everything is new to me: it is only that I can't get enough of it. I am not used to anything except being dull, which I should like to leave off as you have left off shooting.'

(Pause, during which it occurred to Gwendolen that a man of cold and distinguished manners might possibly be a dull companion; but on the other hand she thought that most persons were dull, that she had not observed husbands to be companions – and that after all she was not going to accept Grandcourt.)

'Why are you dull?'

'This is a dreadful neighbourhood. There is nothing to be done in it. That is why I practised my archery.'

(Pause, during which Gwendolen reflected that the life of an unmarried woman who could not go about and had no command of anything must necessarily be dull through all the degrees of comparison as time went on.)

'You have made yourself queen of it. I imagine you will carry the first prize.'

'I don't know that. I have great rivals. Did you not observe how well Miss Arrowpoint shot?'

(Pause, wherein Gwendolen was thinking that men had been known to choose some one else than the woman they most admired, and recalled several experiences of that kind in novels.)

'Miss Arrowpoint? No – that is, yes.'

'Shall we go now and hear what the scoring says? Every one is going to the other end now – shall we join them? I think my uncle is looking towards me. He perhaps wants me.'

Gwendolen found a relief for herself by thus changing the situation: not that the *tête-à-tête* was quite disagreeable to her; but while it lasted she apparently could not get rid of the unwonted flush in her cheeks and the sense of surprise which made her feel less mistress of herself than usual. And this Mr. Grandcourt, who seemed to feel

his own importance more than he did hers – a sort of
unreasonableness few of us can tolerate – must not take
for granted that he was of great moment to her, or that
because others speculated on him as a desirable match she
held herself altogether at his beck. How Grandcourt had
filled up the pauses will be more evident hereafter.

'You have just missed the gold arrow, Gwendolen,' said
Mr. Gascoigne. 'Miss Juliet Fenn scores eight above you.'

'I am very glad to hear it. I should have felt that I was
making myself too disagreeable – taking the best of everything,' said Gwendolen, quite easily.

It was impossible to be jealous of Juliet Fenn, a girl as
middling as mid-day market in everything but her archery
and her plainness, in which last she was noticeably like her
father: underhung and with receding brow resembling that
of the more intelligent fishes. (Surely, considering the
importance which is given to such an accident in female
offspring, marriageable men, or what the new English calls
'intending bridegrooms,' should look at themselves dis-
passionately in the glass, since their natural selection of a
mate prettier than themselves is not certain to bar the
effect of their own ugliness.)

There was now a lively movement in the mingling
groups, which carried the talk along with it. Every one
spoke to every one else by turns, and Gwendolen, who
chose to see what was going on around her now, observed
that Grandcourt was having Klesmer presented to him by
some one unknown to her – a middle-aged man with dark
full face and fat hands, who seemed to be on the easiest
terms with both, and presently led the way in joining the
Arrowpoints, whose acquaintance had already been made
by both him and Grandcourt. Who this stranger was she did
not care much to know; but she wished to observe what
was Grandcourt's manner towards others than herself.
Precisely the same; except that he did not look much at
Miss Arrowpoint, but rather at Klesmer, who was speaking
with animation – now stretching out his long fingers
horizontally, now pointing downwards with his fore-finger,

now folding his arms and tossing his mane, while he addressed himself first to one and then the other, including Grandcourt, who listened with an impassive face and narrow eyes, his left fore-finger in his waistcoat-pocket, and his right slightly touching his thin whisker.

'I wonder which style Miss Arrowpoint admires most,' was a thought that glanced through Gwendolen's mind while her eyes and lips gathered rather a mocking expression. But she would not indulge her sense of amusement by watching as if she were curious, and she gave all her animation to those immediately around her, determined not to care whether Mr. Grandcourt came near her again or not.

He did come, however, and at a moment when he could propose to conduct Mrs. Davilow to her carriage. 'Shall we meet again in the ball-room?' she said, as he raised his hat at parting. The 'yes' in reply had the usual slight drawl and perfect gravity.

'You were wrong for once, Gwendolen,' said Mrs. Davilow during their few minutes' drive to the castle.

'In what, mamma?'

'About Mr. Grandcourt's appearance and manners. You can't find anything ridiculous in him.'

'I suppose I could if I tried, but I don't want to do it,' said Gwendolen, rather pettishly; and her mamma was afraid to say more.

It was the rule on these occasions for the ladies and gentlemen to dine apart, so that the dinner might make a time of comparative ease and rest for both. Indeed the gentlemen had a set of archery stories about the epicurism of the ladies, who had somehow been reported to show a revoltingly masculine judgment in venison, even asking for the fat – a proof of the frightful rate at which corruption might go on in women, but for severe social restraint. And every year the amiable Lord Brackenshaw, who was something of a *gourmet*, mentioned Byron's opinion that a woman should never be seen eating, – introducing it with a confidential – 'The fact is' – as if he were for the first time admitting his concurrence in that sentiment of the refined poet.

In the ladies' dining-room it was evident that Gwendolen was not a general favourite with her own sex; there were no beginnings of intimacy between her and other girls, and in conversation they rather noticed what she said than spoke to her in free exchange. Perhaps it was that she was not much interested in them, and when left alone in their company had a sense of empty benches. Mrs. Vulcany once remarked that Miss Harleth was too fond of the gentlemen; but we know that she was not in the least fond of them – she was only fond of their homage – and women did not give her homage. The exception to this willing aloofness from her was Miss Arrowpoint, who often managed unostentatiously to be by her side, and talked to her with quiet friendliness.

'She knows, as I do, that our friends are ready to quarrel over a husband for us,' thought Gwendolen, 'and she is determined not to enter into the quarrel.'

'I think Miss Arrowpoint has the best manners I ever saw,' said Mrs. Davilow, when she and Gwendolen were in a dressing-room with Mrs. Gascoigne and Anna, but at a distance where they could have their talk apart.

'I wish I were like her,' said Gwendolen.

'Why? Are you getting discontented with yourself, Gwen?'

'No; but I am discontented with things. She seems contented.'

'I am sure you ought to be satisfied to-day. You must have enjoyed the shooting. I saw you did.'

'Oh, that is over now, and I don't know what will come next,' said Gwendolen, stretching herself with a sort of moan and throwing up her arms. They were bare now: it was the fashion to dance in the archery dress, throwing off the jacket; and the simplicity of her white cashmere with its border of pale green set off her form to the utmost. A thin line of gold round her neck, and the gold star on her breast, were her only ornaments. Her smooth soft hair piled up into a grand crown made a clear line about her brow. Sir Joshua would have been glad to take her portrait; and he would have had an easier task than the historian at least in this, that he would not have had to represent the truth of change – only to give stability to one beautiful moment.

'The dancing will come next,' said Mrs. Davilow. 'You are sure to enjoy that.'

'I shall only dance in the quadrille. I told Mr. Clintock so. I shall not waltz or polk with any one.'

'Why in the world do you say that all on a sudden?'

'I can't bear having ugly people so near me.'

'Whom do you mean by ugly people?'

'Oh, plenty.'

'Mr. Clintock, for example, is not ugly.' Mrs. Davilow dared not mention Grandcourt.

'Well, I hate woollen cloth touching me.'

'Fancy!' said Mrs. Davilow to her sister who now came up from the other end of the room. 'Gwendolen says she will not waltz or polk.'

'She is rather given to whims, I think,' said Mrs. Gascoigne, gravely. 'It would be more becoming in her to behave as other young ladies do on such an occasion as this; especially when she has had the advantage of first-rate dancing lessons.'

'Why should I waltz if I don't like it, aunt? It is not in the Catechism.'

'My *dear*!' said Mrs. Gascoigne, in a tone of severe check, and Anna looked frightened at Gwendolen's daring. But they all passed on without saying more.

Apparently something had changed Gwendolen's mood since the hour of exulting enjoyment in the archery-ground. But she did not look the worse under the chandeliers in the ball-room, where the soft splendour of the scene and the pleasant odours from the conservatory could not but be soothing to the temper, when accompanied with the consciousness of being pre-eminently sought for. Hardly a dancing man but was anxious to have her for a partner, and each whom she accepted was in a state of melancholy remonstrance that she would not waltz or polk.

'Are you under a vow, Miss Harleth?' – 'Why are you so cruel to us all?' – 'You waltzed with me in February.' – 'And you who waltz so perfectly!' – were exclamations not without piquancy for her. The ladies who waltzed, naturally thought that Miss Harleth only wanted to make herself particular; but her uncle when he overheard her refusal supported her by saying –

'Gwendolen has usually good reasons.' He thought she was certainly more distinguished in not waltzing, and he wished her to be distinguished. The archery ball was intended to be kept at the subdued pitch that suited all dignities clerical and secular: it was not an escapement for youthful high spirits, and he himself was of opinion that the fashionable dances were too much of a romp.

Among the remonstrant dancing men, however, Mr. Grandcourt was not numbered. After standing up for a quadrille with Miss Arrowpoint, it seemed that he meant to ask for no other partner. Gwendolen observed him frequently with the Arrowpoints, but he never took an opportunity of approaching her. Mr. Gascoigne was sometimes speaking to him; but Mr. Gascoigne was everywhere. It was in her mind now that she would probably after all not have the least trouble about him: perhaps he had looked at her without any particular admiration, and was too much used to everything in the world to think of her as more than one of the girls who were invited in that part of the country. Of course! It was ridiculous of elders to entertain notions about what a man would do, without having seen him even through a telescope. Probably he meant to marry Miss Arrowpoint. Whatever might come, she, Gwendolen, was not going to be disappointed: the affair was a joke whichever way it turned, for she had never committed herself even by a silent confidence in anything Mr. Grandcourt would do. Still, she noticed that he did sometimes quietly and gradually change his position according to hers, so that he could see her whenever she was dancing, and if he did not admire her – so much the worse for him.

This movement for the sake of being in sight of her was more direct than usual rather late in the evening, when Gwendolen had accepted Klesmer as a partner; and that wide-glancing personage, who saw everything and nothing by turns, said to her when they were walking, 'Mr. Grandcourt is a man of taste. He likes to see you dancing.'

'Perhaps he likes to look at what is against his taste,' said Gwendolen, with a light laugh: she was quite courageous with Klesmer now. 'He may be so tired of admiring that he likes disgust for a variety.'

'Those words are not suitable to your lips,' said Klesmer, quickly, with one of his grand frowns, while he shook his hand as if to banish the discordant sounds.

'Are you as critical of words as of music?'

'Certainly I am. I should require your words to be what your face and form are – always among the meanings of a noble music.'

'That is a compliment as well as a correction. I am obliged for both. But do you know I am bold enough to wish to correct *you*, and require you to understand a joke?'

'One may understand jokes without liking them,' said the terrible Klesmer. 'I have had opera books sent me full of jokes; it was just because I understood them that I did not like them. The comic people are ready to challenge a man because he looks grave. "You don't see the witticism, sir?" "No, sir, but I see what you meant." Then I am what we call ticketed as a fellow without *esprit*. But in fact,' said Klesmer, suddenly dropping from his quick narrative to a reflective tone, with an impressive frown, 'I am very sensible to wit and humour.'

'I am glad you tell me that,' said Gwendolen, not without some wickedness of intention. But Klesmer's thoughts had flown off on the wings of his own statement, as their habit was, and she had the wickedness all to herself. 'Pray, who is that standing near the card-room door?' she went on, seeing there the same stranger with whom Klesmer had been in animated talk on the archery-ground. 'He is a friend of yours, I think.'

'No, no; an amateur I have seen in town: Lush, a Mr. Lush – too fond of Meyerbeer and Scribe – too fond of the mechanical-dramatic.'

'Thanks. I wanted to know whether you thought his face and form required that his words should be among the meanings of noble music?' Klesmer was conquered, and flashed at her a delightful smile which made them quite friendly until she begged to be deposited by the side of her mamma.

Three minutes afterwards her preparations for Grandcourt's indifference were all cancelled. Turning her head after some remark to her mother, she found that he had made his way up to her.

'May I ask if you are tired of dancing, Miss Harleth?' he began, looking down with his former unperturbed expression.

'Not in the least.'

'Will you do me the honour – the next – or another quadrille?'

'I should have been very happy,' said Gwendolen, looking at her card, 'but I am engaged for the next to Mr. Clintock – and indeed I perceive that I am doomed for every quadrille: I have not one to dispose of.' She was not sorry to punish Mr. Grandcourt's tardiness, yet at the same time she would have liked to dance with him. She gave him a charming smile as she looked up to deliver her answer, and he stood still looking down at her with no smile at all.

'I am unfortunate in being too late,' he said, after a moment's pause.

'It seemed to me that you did not care for dancing,' said Gwendolen. 'I thought it might be one of the things you had left off.'

'Yes, but I have not begun to dance with you,' said Grandcourt. Always there was the same pause before he took up his cue. 'You make dancing a new thing – as you make archery.'

'Is novelty always agreeable?'

'No, no – not always.'

'Then I don't know whether to feel flattered or not. When you had once danced with me there would be no more novelty in it.'

'On the contrary; there would probably be much more.'

'That is deep. I don't understand.'

'Is it difficult to make Miss Harleth understand her power?' Here Grandcourt had turned to Mrs. Davilow, who, smiling gently at her daughter, said –

'I think she does not generally strike people as slow to understand.'

'Mamma,' said Gwendolen, in a deprecating tone, 'I am adorably stupid, and want everything explained to me – when the meaning is pleasant.'

'If you are stupid, I admit that stupidity is adorable,' returned Grandcourt, after the usual pause, and without change of tone. But clearly he knew what to say.

'I begin to think that my cavalier has forgotten me,' Gwendolen observed after a little while. 'I see the quadrille is being formed.'

'He deserves to be renounced,' said Grandcourt.

'I think he is very pardonable,' said Gwendolen.

'There must have been some misunderstanding,' said Mrs. Davilow. 'Mr. Clintock was too anxious about the engagement to have forgotten it.'

But now Lady Brackenshaw came up and said, 'Miss Harleth, Mr. Clintock has charged me to express to you his deep regret that he was obliged to leave without having the pleasure of dancing with you again. An express came from his father the archdeacon: something important: he was obliged to go. He was *au désespoir*.'

'Oh, he was very good to remember the engagement under the circumstances,' said Gwendolen. 'I am sorry he was called away.' It was easy to be politely sorrowful on so felicitous an occasion.

'Then I can profit by Mr. Clintock's misfortune?' said Grandcourt. 'May I hope that you will let me take his place?'

'I shall be very happy to dance the next quadrille with you.'

The appropriateness of the event seemed an augury, and as Gwendolen stood up for the quadrille with Grandcourt, there was a revival in her of the exultation – the sense of carrying everything before her, which she had felt earlier in the day. No man could have walked through the quadrille with more irreproachable ease than Grandcourt; and the absence of all eagerness in his attention to her suited his partner's taste. She was now convinced that he meant to distinguish her, to mark his admiration of her in a noticeable way; and it began to appear probable that she would have it in her power to reject him, whence there was a pleasure in reckoning up the advantages which would make her rejection splendid, and in giving Mr. Grandcourt his utmost value. It was also agreeable to divine that his exclusive selection of her to dance with, from among all the unmarried ladies present, would attract observation; though she studiously avoided seeing this, and at the end of the quadrille walked away on Grandcourt's arm as if she had been one of the shortest sighted instead of the longest and widest sighted of mortals. They encountered Miss Arrowpoint, who was standing with Lady Brackenshaw and a group of gentlemen. The heiress looked at Gwendolen invitingly and said, 'I hope you will vote with us, Miss Harleth, and Mr. Grandcourt too, though he is not an archer.' Gwendolen and Grandcourt paused to join the group, and found that the voting turned on the project of a picnic archery meeting to be held in Cardell Chase, where the evening entertainment would be more poetic than a ball under chandeliers – a feast of sunset lights along the glades and through the branches and over the solemn tree-tops.

Gwendolen thought the scheme delightful – equal to playing Robin Hood and Maid Marian; and Mr. Grandcourt, when appealed to a second time, said it was a thing to be done; whereupon Mr. Lush, who stood behind Lady Brackenshaw's elbow, drew Gwendolen's notice by saying, with a familiar look and tone, to Grandcourt, 'Diplow would be a good place for the meeting, and more convenient: there's a fine bit between the oaks towards the north gate.'

Impossible to look more unconscious of being addressed than Grandcourt; but Gwendolen took a new survey of the speaker, deciding, first, that he must be on terms of intimacy with the tenant of Diplow, and, secondly, that she would never, if she could help it, let him come within a yard of her. She was subject to physical antipathies, and Mr. Lush's prominent eyes, fat though not clumsy figure, and strong black grey-besprinkled hair of frizzy thickness, which, with the rest of his prosperous person, was enviable to many, created one of the strongest of her antipathies. To be safe from his looking at her, she murmured to Grandcourt, 'I should like to continue walking.'

He obeyed immediately; but when they were thus away from any audience, he spoke no word for several minutes, and she, out of a half-amused, half-serious inclination for experiment, would not speak first. They turned into the large conservatory, beautifully lit up with Chinese lamps. The other couples there were at a distance which would not have interfered with any dialogue, but still they walked in silence until they had reached the farther end where there was a flush of pink light, and the second wide opening into the ball-room. Grandcourt, when they had half turned round, paused and said languidly –

'Do you like this kind of thing?'

If the situation had been described to Gwendolen half an hour before, she would have laughed heartily at it, and could only have imagined herself returning a playful, satirical answer. But for some mysterious reason – it was a mystery of which she had a faint wondering consciousness – she dared not be satirical: she had begun to feel a wand over her that made her afraid of offending Grandcourt.

'Yes,' she said, quietly, without considering what 'kind of thing' was meant – whether the flowers, the scents, the ball in general, or this episode of walking with Mr. Grandcourt in particular. And they returned along the conservatory without farther interpretation. She then proposed to go and sit down in her old place, and they walked among scattered couples preparing for the waltz to the spot where Mrs. Davilow had been seated all the evening. As they approached it her seat was vacant, but she was coming towards it again, and, to Gwendolen's shuddering annoyance, with Mr. Lush at her elbow. There was no avoiding the confrontation: her mamma came close to her before they had reached the seats, and, after a quiet greeting smile, said innocently, 'Gwendolen, dear, let me present Mr. Lush to you.' Having just made the acquaintance of this personage, as an intimate and constant companion of Mr. Grandcourt's, Mrs. Davilow imagined it altogether desirable that her daughter also should make the acquaintance.

It was hardly a bow that Gwendolen gave – rather, it was the slightest forward sweep of the head away from the physiognomy that inclined itself towards her, and she immediately moved towards her seat, saying, 'I want to put on my burnous.' No sooner had she reached it, than Mr. Lush was there, and had the burnous in his hand: to annoy this supercilious young lady, he would incur the offence of forestalling Grandcourt; and, holding up the garment close to Gwendolen, he said, 'Pray, permit me?' But she, wheeling away from him as if he had been a muddy hound, glided on to the ottoman, saying, 'No, thank you.'

A man who forgave this would have much Christian feeling, supposing he had intended to be agreeable to the young lady; but before he seized the burnous Mr. Lush had ceased to have that intention. Grandcourt quietly took the drapery from him, and Mr. Lush, with a slight bow, moved away.

'You had perhaps better put it on,' said Mr. Grandcourt, looking down on her without change of expression.

'Thanks; perhaps it would be wise,' said Gwendolen, rising, and submitting very gracefully to take the burnous on her shoulders.

After that, Mr. Grandcourt exchanged a few polite speeches with Mrs. Davilow, and, in taking leave, asked permission to call at Offendene the next day. He was evidently not offended by the insult directed towards his friend. Certainly, Gwendolen's refusal of the burnous from Mr. Lush was open to the interpretation that she wished to receive it from Mr. Grandcourt. But she, poor child, had had no design in this action, and was simply following her antipathy and inclination, confiding in them as she did in the more reflective judgments into which they entered as sap into leafage. Gwendolen had no sense that these men were dark enigmas to her, or that she needed any help in drawing conclusions about them – Mr. Grandcourt at least. The chief question was, how far his character and ways might answer her wishes; and unless she were satisfied about that, she had said to herself that she would not accept his offer.

Could there be a slenderer, more insignificant thread in human history than this consciousness of a girl, busy with her small inferences of the way in which she could make her life pleasant? – in a time, too, when ideas were with fresh vigour making armies of themselves, and the universal kinship was declaring itself fiercely: when women on the other side of the world would not mourn for the husbands and sons who died bravely in a common cause, and men stinted of bread on our side of the world heard of that willing loss and were patient: a time when the soul of man was waking to pulses which had for centuries been beating in him unheard, until their full sum made a new life of terror or of joy.

What in the midst of that mighty drama are girls and their blind visions? They are the Yea or Nay of that good for which men are enduring and fighting. In these delicate vessels is borne onward through the ages the treasure of human affections.

XII

'O gentlemen, the time of life is short;
To spend that shortness basely were too long,
If life did ride upon a dial's point,
Still ending at the arrival of an hour.'
– SHAKESPEARE: *Henry IV.*

ON the second day after the Archery Meeting, Mr.
Henleigh Mallinger Grandcourt was at his breakfast-table
with Mr. Lush. Everything around them was agreeable:
the summer air through the open windows, at which the
dogs could walk in from the old green turf on the lawn; the
soft, purplish colouring of the park beyond, stretching
towards a mass of bordering wood; the still life in the
room, which seemed the stiller for its sober antiquated
elegance, as if it kept a conscious, well-bred silence, unlike
the restlessness of vulgar furniture.

Whether the gentlemen were agreeable to each other
was less evident. Mr. Grandcourt had drawn his chair aside
so as to face the lawn, and, with his left leg over another
chair, and his right elbow on the table, was smoking a large
cigar, while his companion was still eating. The dogs –
half-a-dozen of various kinds were moving lazily in and
out, or taking attitudes of brief attention – gave a vacillating preference first to one gentleman, then to the other;
being dogs in such good circumstances that they could play
at hunger, and liked to be served with delicacies which
they declined to put into their mouths; all except Fetch,
the beautiful liver-coloured water-spaniel, which sat with
its fore-paws firmly planted and its expressive brown face
turned upward, watching Grandcourt with unshaken constancy. He held in his lap a tiny Maltese dog with a tiny
silver collar and bell, and when he had a hand unused by
cigar or coffee-cup, it rested on this small parcel of animal
warmth. I fear that Fetch was jealous, and wounded that her
master gave her no word or look; at last it seemed that she
could bear this neglect no longer, and she gently put

her large silky paw on her master's leg. Grandcourt looked at her with unchanged face for half a minute, and then took the trouble to lay down his cigar while he lifted the unimpassioned Fluff close to his chin and gave it caressing pats, all the while gravely watching Fetch, who, poor thing, whimpered interruptedly, as if trying to repress that sign of discontent, and at last rested her head beside the appealing paw, looking up with piteous beseeching. So, at least, a lover of dogs must have interpreted Fetch, and Grandcourt kept so many dogs that he was reputed to love them; at any rate, his impulse to act just in this way started from such an interpretation. But when the amusing anguish burst forth in a howling bark, Grandcourt pushed Fetch down without speaking, and, depositing Fluff carelessly on the table (where his black nose predominated over a salt-cellar), began to look to his cigar, and found, with some annoyance against Fetch as the cause, that the brute of a cigar required relighting. Fetch, having begun to wail, found, like others of her sex, that it was not easy to leave off; indeed, the second howl was a louder one, and the third was like unto it.

'Turn out that brute, will you?' said Grandcourt to Lush, without raising his voice or looking at him – as if he counted on attention to the smallest sign.

And Lush immediately rose, lifted Fetch, though she was rather heavy and he was not fond of stooping, and carried her out, disposing of her in some way that took him a couple of minutes before he returned. He then lit a cigar, placed himself at an angle where he could see Grandcourt's face without turning, and presently said –

'Shall you ride or drive to Quetcham to-day?'

'I am not going to Quetcham.'

'You did not go yesterday.'

Grandcourt smoked in silence for half a minute and then said –

'I suppose you sent my card and inquiries.'

'I went myself at four, and said you were sure to be there shortly. They would suppose some accident prevented you from fulfilling the intention. Especially if you go to-day.'

Silence for a couple of minutes. Then Grandcourt said, 'What men are invited here with their wives?'

Lush drew out a note-book. 'The Captain and Mrs. Torrington come next week. Then there are Mr. Hollis, and Lady Flora, and the Cushats, and the Gogoffs.'

'Rather a ragged lot,' remarked Grandcourt after a while. 'Why did you ask the Gogoffs? When you write invitations in my name, be good enough to give me a list, instead of bringing down a giantess on me without my knowledge. She spoils the look of the room.'

'You invited the Gogoffs yourself, when you met them in Paris.'

'What has my meeting them in Paris to do with it? I told you to give me a list.'

Grandcourt, like many others, had two remarkably different voices. Hitherto we have heard him speaking in a superficial interrupted drawl suggestive chiefly of languor and *ennui*. But this last brief speech was uttered in subdued, inward, yet distinct tones, which Lush had long been used to recognize as the expression of a peremptory will.

'Are there any other couples you would like to invite?'

'Yes; think of some decent people, with a daughter or two. And one of your damned musicians. But not a comic fellow.'

'I wonder if Klesmer would consent to come to us when he leaves Quetcham. Nothing but first-rate music will go down with Miss Arrowpoint.'

Lush spoke carelessly, but he was really seizing an opportunity and fixing an observant look on Grandcourt, who now for the first time turned his eyes towards his companion, but slowly, and without speaking until he had given two long luxurious puffs, when he said, perhaps in a lower tone than ever, but with a perceptible edge of contempt –

'What in the name of nonsense have I to do with Miss Arrowpoint and her music?'

'Well, something,' said Lush, jocosely. 'You need not give yourself much trouble, perhaps. But some forms must be gone through before a man can marry a million.'

'Very likely. But I am not going to marry a million.'

'That's a pity – to fling away an opportunity of this sort, and knock down your own plans.'

'*Your* plans, I suppose you mean.'

'You have some debts, you know, and things may turn out inconveniently after all. The heirship is not *absolutely* certain.'

Grandcourt did not answer and Lush went on.

'It really is a fine opportunity. The father and mother ask for nothing better, I can see, and the daughter's looks and manners require no allowances, any more than if she hadn't a sixpence. She is not beautiful; but equal to carrying any rank. And she is not likely to refuse such prospects as you can offer her.'

'Perhaps not.'

'The father and mother would let you do anything you liked with them.'

'But I should not like to do anything with them.'

Here it was Lush who made a little pause before speaking again, and then he said in a deep voice of remonstrance, 'Good God, Grandcourt! after your experience, will you let a whim interfere with your comfortable settlement in life?'

'Spare your oratory. I know what I am going to do.'

'What?' Lush put down his cigar and thrust his hands into his side pockets, as if he had to face something exasperating, but meant to keep his temper.

'I am going to marry the other girl.'

'Have you fallen in love?' This question carried a strong sneer.

'I am going to marry her.'

'You have made her an offer already, then?'

'No.'

'She is a young lady with a will of her own, I fancy. Extremely well fitted to make a rumpus. She would know what she liked.'

'She doesn't like you,' said Grandcourt, with the ghost of a smile.

'Perfectly true,' said Lush, adding again in a markedly sneering tone, 'However, if you and she are devoted to each other, that will be enough.'

Grandcourt took no notice of this speech, but sipped his coffee, rose, and strolled out on the lawn, all the dogs following him.

Lush glanced after him a moment, then resumed his cigar and lit it, but smoked slowly, consulting his beard with inspecting eyes and fingers, till he finally stroked it with an air of having arrived at some conclusion, and said, in a subdued voice –

'Check, old boy!'

Lush, being a man of some ability, had not known Grandcourt for fifteen years without learning what sort of measures were useless with him, though what sort might be useful remained often dubious. In the beginning of his career he held a fellowship, and was near taking orders for the sake of a college living, but not being fond of that prospect accepted instead the office of travelling companion to a marquis, and afterwards to young Grandcourt, who had lost his father early, and who found Lush so convenient that he had allowed him to become prime minister in all his more personal affairs. The habit of fifteen years had made Grandcourt more and more in need of Lush's handiness, and Lush more and more in need of the lazy luxury to which his transactions on behalf of Grandcourt made no interruption worth reckoning. I cannot say that the same lengthened habit had intensified Grandcourt's want of respect for his companion since that want had been absolute from the beginning, but it had confirmed his sense that he might kick Lush if he chose – only he never did choose to kick any animal, because the act of kicking is a compromising attitude, and a gentleman's dogs should be kicked for him. He only said things which might have exposed himself to be kicked if his confidant had been a man of independent spirit. But what son of a vicar who has stinted his wife and daughters of calico in order to send his male offspring to Oxford, can keep an independent spirit when he is bent on dining with high discrimination, riding good horses, living generally in the most luxuriant honey-blossomed clover – and all without working? Mr. Lush had passed for a scholar once, and had still a sense of scholarship when he was not trying to remember much of it; but the bachelors' and other arts which soften manners are a time-honoured preparation for sinecures; and Lush's present comfortable provision was as good as a sinecure in not requiring more than the odour of departed learning. He was not unconscious of being held kickable, but he preferred counting that estimate among the peculiarities of Grandcourt's character, which made one of his incalculable moods or judgments as good as another. Since in his own opinion he had never done a bad action, it did not seem necessary to consider whether he should be likely to commit one if his love of ease required it. Lush's love of ease was well satisfied at present, and if his puddings were rolled towards him in the dust, he took the inside bits and found them relishing.

This morning, for example, though he had encountered more annoyance than usual, he went to his private sitting-room and played a good hour on the violoncello.

XIII

'Philistia, be thou glad of me!'

GRANDCOURT having made up his mind to marry Miss Harleth showed a power of adapting means to ends. During the next fortnight there was hardly a day on which by some arrangement or other he did not see her, or prove by emphatic attentions that she occupied his thoughts. His cousin Mrs. Torrington was now doing the honours of his house, so that Mrs. Davilow and Gwendolen could be invited to a large party at Diplow in which there were many witnesses how the host distinguished the dowerless beauty, and showed no solicitude about the heiress. The world – I mean Mr. Gascoigne and all the families worth speaking of within visiting distance of Pennicote – felt an assurance on the subject which in the Rector's mind converted itself into a resolution to do his duty by his niece and see that the settlements were adequate. Indeed, the wonder to him and Mrs. Davilow was that the offer for which so many suitable occasions presented themselves had not been already made; and in this wonder Grandcourt himself was not without a share. When he had told his resolution to Lush he had thought that the affair would be concluded more quickly, and to his own surprise he had repeatedly promised himself in a morning that he would to-day give Gwendolen the opportunity of accepting him, and had found in the evening that the necessary formality was still unaccomplished. This remarkable fact served to heighten his determination on another day. He had never admitted to himself that Gwendolen might refuse him, but – heaven help us all! – we are often unable to act on our certainties; our objection to a contrary issue (were it possible) is so strong that it rises like a spectral illusion between us and our certainty: we are rationally sure that the blind-worm cannot bite us mortally, but it would be so intolerable to be bitten, and the creature has a biting look – we decline to handle it.

139

He had asked leave to have a beautiful horse of his brought for Gwendolen to ride. Mrs. Davilow was to accompany her in the carriage, and they were to go to Diplow to lunch, Grandcourt conducting them. It was a fine mid-harvest time, not too warm for a noon-day ride of five miles to be delightful: the poppies glowed on the borders of the fields, there was enough breeze to move gently like a social spirit among the ears of uncut corn, and to wing the shadow of a cloud across the soft grey downs; here the sheaves were standing, there the horses were straining their muscles under the last load from a wide space of stubble, but everywhere the green pastures made a broader setting for the corn-fields, and the cattle took their rest under wide branches. The road lay through a bit of country where the dairy-farms looked much as they did in the days of our forefathers – where peace and permanence seemed to find a home away from the busy change that sent the railway train flying in the distance.

But the spirit of peace and permanence did not penetrate poor Mrs. Davilow's mind so as to overcome her habit of uneasy foreboding. Gwendolen and Grandcourt cantering in front of her, and then slackening their pace to a conversational walk till the carriage came up with them again, made a gratifying sight; but it served chiefly to keep up the conflict of hopes and fears about her daughter's lot. Here was an irresistible opportunity for a lover to speak and put an end to all uncertainties, and Mrs. Davilow could only hope with trembling that Gwendolen's decision would be favourable. Certainly if Rex's love had been repugnant to her, Mr. Grandcourt had the advantage of being in complete contrast with Rex; and that he had produced some quite novel impression on her seemed evident in her marked abstinence from satirical observations, nay, her total silence about his characteristics, a silence which Mrs. Davilow did not dare to break. 'Is he a man she would be happy with?' – was a question that inevitably arose in the mother's mind. 'Well, perhaps as happy as she would be with any one else – or as most other women are' – was the answer with which she tried to quiet herself; for she could not imagine Gwendolen under the influence of any feeling which would make her satisfied in what we traditionally call 'mean circumstances.'

Grandcourt's own thought was looking in the same direction: he wanted to have done with the uncertainty that belonged to his not having spoken. As to any further uncertainty – well, it was something without any reasonable basis, some quality in the air which acted as an irritant to his wishes.

Gwendolen enjoyed the riding, but her pleasure did not break forth in girlish unpremeditated chat and laughter as it did on that morning with Rex. She spoke a little, and even laughed, but with a lightness as of a far-off echo: for her too there was some peculiar quality in the air – not, she was sure, any subjugation of her will by Mr. Grandcourt, and the splendid prospects he meant to offer her; for Gwendolen desired every one, that dignified gentleman himself included, to understand that she was going to do just as she liked, and that they had better not calculate on her pleasing them. If she chose to take this husband she would have him know that she was not going to renounce her freedom, or according to her favourite formula, 'not going to do as other women did.'

Grandcourt's speeches this morning were, as usual, all of that brief sort which never fails to make a conversational figure when the speaker is held important in his circle. Stopping so soon, they give signs of a suppressed and formidable ability to say more, and have also the meritorious quality of allowing lengthiness to others.

'How do you like Criterion's paces?' he said, after they had entered the park and were slackening from a canter to a walk.

'He is delightful to ride. I should like to have a leap with him if it would not frighten mamma. There was a good wide channel we passed five minutes ago. I should like to have a gallop back and take it.'

'Pray do. We can take it together.'

'No, thanks. Mamma is so timid – if she saw me it might make her ill.'

'Let me go and explain. Criterion would take it without fail.'

'No – indeed – you are very kind – but it would alarm her too much. I dare take any leap when she is not by; but I do it, and don't tell her about it.'

'We can let the carriage pass, and then set off.'

'No, no, pray don't think of it any more; I spoke quite randomly,' said Gwendolen; she began to feel a new objection to carrying out her own proposition.

'But Mrs. Davilow knows I shall take care of you.'

'Yes, but she would think of you as having to take care of my broken neck.'

There was a considerable pause before Grandcourt said, looking towards her, 'I should like to have the right always to take care of you.'

Gwendolen did not turn her eyes on him: it seemed to her a long while that she was first blushing, and then turning pale, but to Grandcourt's rate of judgment she answered soon enough, with the lightest flute-tone and a careless movement of the head, 'Oh, I am not sure that I want to be taken care of: if I chose to risk breaking my neck, I should like to be at liberty to do it.'

She checked her horse as she spoke, and turned in her saddle, looking towards the advancing carriage. Her eyes swept across Grandcourt as she made this movement, but there was no language in them to correct the carelessness of her reply. At that very moment she was aware that she was risking something – not her neck, but the possibility of finally checking Grandcourt's advances, and she did not feel contented with the possibility.

'Damn her!' thought Grandcourt, as he too checked his horse. He was not a wordy thinker, and this explosive phrase stood for mixed impressions which eloquent interpreters might have expanded into some sentences full of an irritated sense that he was being mystified, and a determination that this girl should not make a fool of him. Did she want him to throw himself at her feet and declare that he was dying for her? It was not by that gate that she would enter on the privileges he could give her. Or did she expect him to write his proposals? Equally a delusion. He would not make his offer in any way that could place him definitely in the position of being rejected. But as to her accepting him, she had done it already in accepting his marked attentions; and anything which happened to break them off would be understood to her disadvantage. She was merely coquetting, then?

However, the carriage came up, and no further *tête-à-tête* could well occur before their arrival at the house, where there was abundant company, to whom Gwendolen, clad in riding-dress, with her hat laid aside, clad also in the repute of being chosen by Mr. Grandcourt, was naturally a centre of observation; and since the objectionable Mr. Lush was not there to look at her, this stimulus of admiring attention heightened her spirits, and dispersed, for the time, the uneasy consciousness of divided impulses which threatened her with repentance of her own acts. Whether Grandcourt had been offended or not there was no judging: his manners were unchanged, but Gwendolen's acuteness had not gone deeper than to discern that his manners were no clue for her and because these were unchanged she was not the less afraid of him.

She had not been at Diplow before except to dine; and since certain points of view from the windows and the garden were worth showing, Lady Flora Hollis proposed after luncheon, when some of the guests had dispersed, and the sun was sloping towards four o'clock, that the remaining party should make a little exploration. Here came frequent opportunities when Grandcourt might have retained Gwendolen apart and have spoken to her unheard. But no! He indeed spoke to no one else, but what he said was nothing more eager or intimate than it had been in their first interview. He looked at her not less than usual; and some of her defiant spirit having come

143

back, she looked full at him in return, not caring – rather preferring – that his eyes had no expression in them.

But at last it seemed as if he entertained some contrivance. After they had nearly made the tour of the grounds, the whole party paused by the pool to be amused with Fetch's accomplishment of bringing a water-lily to the bank like Cowper's spaniel Beau, and having been disappointed in his first attempt insisted on his trying again.

Here Grandcourt, who stood with Gwendolen outside the group, turned deliberately, and fixing his eyes on a knoll planted with American shrubs, and having a winding path up it, said languidly –

'This is a bore. Shall we go up there?'

'Oh, certainly – since we are exploring,' said Gwendolen. She was rather pleased, and yet afraid.

The path was too narrow for him to offer his arm, and they walked up in silence. When they were on the bit of platform at the summit Grandcourt said –

'There is nothing to be seen here: the thing was not worth climbing.'

How was it that Gwendolen did not laugh? She was perfectly silent, holding up the folds of her robe like a statue, and giving a harder grasp to the handle of her whip, which she had snatched up automatically with her hat when they had first set off.

'What sort of place do you like?' said Grandcourt.

'Different places are agreeable in their way. On the whole, I think, I prefer places that are open and cheerful. I am not fond of anything sombre.'

'Your place at Offendene is too sombre.'

'It is, rather.'

'You will not remain there long, I hope.'

'Oh yes, I think so. Mamma likes to be near her sister.'

Silence for a short space.

'It is not to be supposed that *you* will always live there, though Mrs. Davilow may.'

'I don't know. We women can't go in search of adventures – to find out the North-West Passage or the source of

the Nile, or to hunt tigers in the East. We must stay where
we grow, or where the gardeners like to transplant us. We
are brought up like the flowers, to look as pretty as we can,
and be dull without complaining. That is my notion about
the plants: they are often bored, and that is the reason why
some of them have got poisonous. What do you think?'
Gwendolen had run on rather nervously, lightly whipping
the rhododendron bush in front of her.

'I quite agree. Most things are bores,' said Grandcourt,
his mind having been pushed into an easy current, away
from its intended track. But after a moment's pause he
continued in his broken, refined drawl –

'But a woman can be married.'

'Some women can.'

'You certainly, unless you are obstinately cruel.'

'I am not sure that I am not both cruel and obstinate.'
Here Gwendolen suddenly turned her head and looked
full at Grandcourt, whose eyes she had felt to be upon her
throughout their conversation. She was wondering what
the effect of looking at him would be on herself rather than
on him.

He stood perfectly still, half a yard or more away from
her; and it flashed through her thought that a sort of lotos-
eater's stupor had begun in him and was taking possession
of her. Then he said –

'Are you as uncertain about yourself as you make others
about you?'

'I am quite uncertain about myself; I don't know how
uncertain others may be.'

'And you wish them to understand that you don't care?'
said Grandcourt, with a touch of new hardness in his tone.

'I did not say that,' Gwendolen replied, hesitatingly,
and turning her eyes away whipped the rhododendron
bush again. She wished she were on horseback that she
might set off on a canter. It was impossible to set off
running down the knoll.

'You do care, then,' said Grandcourt, not more quickly,
but with a softened drawl.

'Ha! my whip!' said Gwendolen, in a little scream of distress. She had let it go – what could be more natural in a slight agitation? – and – but this seemed less natural in a gold-handled whip which had been left altogether to itself – it had gone with some force over the immediate shrubs, and had lodged itself in the branches of an azalea half-way down the knoll. She could run down now, laughing prettily, and Grandcourt was obliged to follow; but she was beforehand with him in rescuing the whip, and continued on her way to the level ground, when she paused and looked at Grandcourt with an exasperating brightness in her glance and a heightened colour, as if she had carried a triumph, and these indications were still noticeable to Mrs. Davilow when Gwendolen and Grandcourt joined the rest of the party.

'It is all conquetting,' thought Grandcourt; 'the next time I beckon she will come down.'

It seemed to him likely that this final beckoning might happen the very next day, when there was to be a picnic archery meeting in Cardell Chase, according to the plan projected on the evening of the ball.

Even in Gwendolen's mind that result was one of two likelihoods that presented themselves alternately, one of two decisions towards which she was being precipitated, as if they were two sides of a boundary-line, and she did not know on which she should fall. This subjection to a possible self, a self not to be absolutely predicted about, caused her some astonishment and terror: her favourite key of life – doing as she liked – seemed to fail her, and she could not foresee what at a given moment she might like to do. The prospect of marrying Grandcourt really seemed more attractive to her than she had believed beforehand that any marriage could be: the dignities, the luxuries, the power of doing a great deal of what she liked to do, which had now come close to her, and within her choice to secure or to lose, took hold of her nature as if it had been the strong odour of what she had only imagined and longed for before. And Grandcourt himself? He seemed as little of a flaw in his fortunes as a lover and husband could possibly be. Gwendolen wished to mount the chariot and drive the plunging horses herself, with a spouse by her side who would fold his arms and give her his countenance without looking ridiculous. Certainly with all her perspicacity, and all the reading which seemed to her mamma dangerously instructive, her judgment was consciously a little at fault before Grandcourt. He was adorably quiet and free from absurdities – he would be a husband *en suite* with the best appearance a woman could make. But what else was he? He had been everywhere, and seen everything. *That* was desirable, and especially gratifying as a preamble to his supreme preference for Gwendolen Harleth. He did not appear to enjoy anything much. That was not necessary: and the less he had of particular tastes or desires, the more freedom his wife was likely to have in following hers. Gwendolen conceived that after marriage she would most probably be able to manage him thoroughly.

How was it that he caused her unusual constraint now? – that she was less daring and playful in her talk with him than with any other admirer she had known? That absence of demonstrativeness which she was glad of, acted as a charm in more senses than one, and was slightly benumbing. Grandcourt after all was formidable – a handsome lizard of a hitherto unknown species, not of the lively, darting kind. But Gwendolen knew hardly anything about lizards, and ignorance gives one a large range of probabilities. This splendid specimen was probably gentle, suitable as a boudoir pet: what may not a lizard be, if you know nothing to the contrary? Her acquaintance with Grandcourt was such that no accomplishment suddenly revealed in him would have surprised her. And he was so little suggestive of drama, that it hardly occurred to her to think with any detail how his life of thirty-six years had been passed: in general, she imagined him always cold and dignified, not likely ever to have committed himself. He had hunted the tiger – had he ever been in love, or made love? The one experience and the other seemed alike remote in Gwendolen's fancy from the Mr. Grandcourt who had come to Diplow in order apparently to make a chief epoch in her destiny – perhaps by introducing her to that state of marriage which she had resolved to make a state of greater freedom than her girlhood. And on the whole she wished to marry him; he suited her purpose; her prevailing, deliberate intention was, to accept him.

But was she going to fulfil her deliberate intention? She began to be afraid of herself, and to find out a certain difficulty in doing as she liked. Already her assertion of independence in evading his advances had been carried farther than was necessary, and she was thinking with some anxiety what she might do on the next occasion.

Seated according to her habit with her back to the horses on their drive homewards, she was completely under the observation of her mamma, who took the excitement and changefulness in the expression of her eyes, her unwonted absence of mind and total silence, as unmistakable signs that something unprecedented had occurred between her and Grandcourt. Mrs. Davilow's uneasiness determined her to risk some speech on the subject: the Gascoignes were to dine at Offendene, and in what had occurred this morning there might be some reason for consulting the Rector; not that she expected him any more than herself to influence Gwendolen, but that her anxious mind wanted to be disburthened.

'Something has happened, dear?' she began, in a tender tone of question.

Gwendolen looked round, and seeming to be roused to the consciousness of her physical self, took off her gloves and then her hat, that the soft breeze might blow on her head. They were in a retired bit of the road, where the long afternoon shadows from the bordering trees fell across it, and no observers were within sight. Her eyes continued to meet her mother's, but she did not speak.

'Mr. Grandcourt has been saying something? – Tell me, dear.' The last words were uttered beseechingly.

'What am I to tell you, mamma?' was the perverse answer.

'I am sure something has agitated you. You ought to confide in me, Gwen. You ought not to leave me in doubt and anxiety.' Mrs. Davilow's eyes filled with tears.

'Mamma, dear, please don't be miserable,' said Gwendolen, with pettish remonstrance. 'It only makes me more so. I am in doubt myself.'

'About Mr. Grandcourt's intentions?' said Mrs. Davilow, gathering determination from her alarms.

'No; not at all,' said Gwendolen, with some curtness, and a pretty little toss of the head as she put on her hat again.

'About whether you will accept him, then?'

'Precisely.'

'Have you given him a doubtful answer?'

'I have given him no answer at all.'

'He *has* spoken so that you could not misunderstand him?'

'As far as I would let him speak.'

'You expect him to persevere?' Mrs. Davilow put this question rather anxiously, and receiving no answer, asked another. 'You don't consider that you have discouraged him?'

'I dare say not.'

'I thought you liked him, dear,' said Mrs. Davilow, timidly.

'So I do, mamma, as liking goes. There is less to dislike about him than about most men. He is quiet and *distingué*.' Gwendolen so far spoke with a pouting sort of gravity; but suddenly she recovered some of her mischievousness, and her face broke into a smile as she added – 'Indeed he has all the qualities that would make a husband tolerable – battlement, veranda, stables, &c., no grins and no glass in his eye.'

'Do be serious with me for a moment, dear. Am I to understand that you mean to accept him?'

'Oh pray, mamma, leave me to myself,' said Gwendolen, with a pettish distress in her voice.

And Mrs. Davilow said no more.

When they got home Gwendolen declared that she would not dine. She was tired, and would come down in the evening after she had taken some rest. The probability that her uncle would hear what had passed did not trouble her. She was convinced that whatever he might say would be on the side of her accepting Grandcourt, and she wished to accept him if she could. At this moment she would willingly have had weights hung on her own caprice.

Mr. Gascoigne did hear – not Gwendolen's answers repeated verbatim, but a softened generalized account of them. The mother conveyed as vaguely as the keen Rector's questions would let her the impression that Gwendolen was in some uncertainty about her own mind, but inclined on the whole to acceptance. The result was that the uncle felt himself called on to interfere: he did not conceive that he should do his duty in withholding direction from his niece in a momentous crisis of this kind. Mrs. Davilow ventured a hesitating opinion that perhaps it would be safer to say nothing – Gwendolen was so sensitive (she did not like to say wilful). But the Rector's was a firm mind, grasping its first judgments tenaciously and acting on them promptly, whence counterjudgments were no more for him than shadows fleeting across the solid ground to which he adjusted himself.

This match with Grandcourt presented itself to him as a sort of public affair; perhaps there were ways in which it might even strengthen the Establishment. To the Rector, whose father (nobody would have suspected it, and nobody was told) had risen to be a provincial corn-dealer, aristocratic heirship resembled regal heirship in excepting its possessor from the ordinary standard of moral judgments. Grandcourt, the almost certain baronet, the probable peer, was to be ranged with public personages, and was a match to be accepted on broad general grounds national and ecclesiastical. Such public personages, it is true, are often in the nature of giants which an ancient community may have felt pride and safety in possessing, though, regarded privately, these born eminences must often have been inconvenient and even noisome. But of the future husband personally Mr. Gascoigne was disposed to think the best. Gossip is a sort of smoke that comes from the dirty tobacco-pipes of those who diffuse it: it proves nothing but the bad taste of the smoker. But if Grandcourt had really made any deeper or more unfortunate experiments in folly than were common in young men of high prospects, he was of an age to have finished them. All accounts can be suitably wound up when a man has not ruined himself, and the expense may be taken as an insurance against future error. This was the view of practical wisdom; with reference to higher views, repentance had a supreme moral and religious value. There was every reason to believe that a woman of well-regulated mind would be happy with Grandcourt.

It was no surprise to Gwendolen on coming down to tea to be told that her uncle wished to see her in the dining-room. He threw aside the paper as she entered and greeted her with his usual kindness. As his wife had remarked, he always 'made much' of Gwendolen, and her importance had risen of late. 'My dear,' he said, in a fatherly way, moving a chair for her as he held her hand, 'I want to speak to you on a subject which is more momentous than any other with regard to your welfare. You will guess what I mean. But I shall speak to you with perfect directness: in such matters I consider myself bound to act as your father. You have no objection, I hope?'

'Oh dear no, uncle. You have always been very kind to me,' said Gwendolen, frankly. This evening she was willing, if it were possible, to be a little fortified against her troublesome self, and her resistant temper was in abeyance. The Rector's mode of speech always conveyed a thrill of authority, as of a word of command: it seemed to take for granted that there could be no wavering in the audience, and that every one was going to be rationally obedient.

'It is naturally a satisfaction to me that the prospect of a marriage for you – advantageous in the highest degree – has

DANIEL DERONDA

presented itself so early. I do not know exactly what has passed between you and Mr. Grandcourt, but I presume there can be little doubt, from the way in which he has distinguished you, that he desires to make you his wife.'

Gwendolen did not speak immediately, and her uncle said with more emphasis –

'Have you any doubt of that yourself, my dear?'

'I suppose that is what he has been thinking of. But he may have changed his mind to-morrow,' said Gwendolen.

'Why to-morrow? Has he made advances which you have discouraged?'

'I think he meant – he began to make advances – but I did not encourage them. I turned the conversation.'

'Will you confide in me so far as to tell me your reasons?'

'I am not sure that I had any reasons, uncle.' Gwendolen laughed rather artificially.

'You are quite capable of reflecting, Gwendolen. You are aware that this is not a trivial occasion, and that it concerns your establishment for life under circumstances which may not occur again. You have a duty here both to yourself and your family. I wish to understand whether you have any ground for hesitating as to your acceptance of Mr. Grandcourt.'

'I suppose I hesitate without grounds.' Gwendolen spoke rather poutingly, and her uncle grew suspicious.

'Is he disagreeable to you personally?'

'No.'

'Have you heard anything of him which has affected you disagreeably?' The Rector thought it impossible that Gwendolen could have heard the gossip he had heard, but in any case he must endeavour to put all things in the right light for her.

'I have heard nothing about him except that he is a great match,' said Gwendolen, with some sauciness; 'and that affects me very agreeably.'

'Then, my dear Gwendolen, I have nothing further to say than this: you hold your fortune in your own hands – a fortune such as rarely happens to a girl in your circumstances – a fortune in fact which almost takes the question out of the range of mere personal feeling, and makes your acceptance of it a duty. If Providence offers you power and position – especially when unclogged by any conditions that are repugnant to you – your course is one of responsibility, into which caprice must not enter. A man does not like to have his attachment trifled with: he may not be at once repelled – these things are matters of individual disposition. But the trifling may be carried too far. And I must point out to you that in case Mr. Grandcourt were repelled without your having refused him – without your having intended ultimately to refuse him, your situation would be a humiliating and painful one. I, for my part, should regard you with severe disapprobation, as the victim of nothing else than your own coquetry and folly.'

Gwendolen became pallid as she listened to this admonitory speech. The ideas it raised had the force of sensations. Her resistant courage would not help her here, because her uncle was not urging her against her own resolve; he was pressing upon her the motives of dread which she already felt; he was making her more conscious of the risks that lay within herself. She was silent, and the Rector observed that he had produced some strong effect.

'I mean this in kindness, my dear.' His tone had softened.

'I am aware of that, uncle,' said Gwendolen, rising and shaking her head back, as if to rouse herself out of painful passivity. 'I am not foolish. I know that I must be married some time – before it is too late. And I don't see how I could do better than marry Mr. Grandcourt. I mean to accept him, if possible.' She felt as if she were reinforcing herself by speaking with this decisiveness to her uncle.

But the Rector was a little startled by so bare a version of his own meaning from those young lips. He wished that in her mind his advice should be taken in an infusion of sentiments proper to a girl, and such as are presupposed in the advice of a clergyman, although he may not consider them always appropriate to be put forward. He wished his niece parks, carriages, a title – everything that would make this world a pleasant abode; but he wished her not to be cynical – to be, on the contrary, religiously dutiful, and have warm domestic affections.

'My dear Gwendolen,' he said, rising also, and speaking with benignant gravity, 'I trust that you will find in marriage a new fountain of duty and affection. Marriage is the only true and satisfactory sphere of a woman, and if your marriage with Mr. Grandcourt should be happily decided upon, you will have probably an increasing power, both of rank and wealth, which may be used for the benefit of others. These considerations are something higher than romance. You are fitted by natural gifts for a position which, considering your birth and early prospects, could hardly be looked forward to as in the ordinary course of things; and I trust that you will grace it not only by those personal gifts, but by a good and consistent life.'

'I hope mamma will be the happier,' said Gwendolen, in a more cheerful way, lifting her hands backward to her neck and moving towards the door. She wanted to waive those higher considerations.

Mr. Gascoigne felt that he had come to a satisfactory understanding with his niece, and had furthered her happy settlement in life by furthering her engagement to Grandcourt. Meanwhile there was another person to whom the contemplation of that issue had been a motive for some activity, and who believed that he too on this particular day had done something towards bringing about a favourable decision in *his* sense – which happened to be the reverse of the Rector's.

Mr. Lush's absence from Diplow during Gwendolen's visit had been due not to any fear on his part of meeting that supercilious young lady, or of being abashed by her frank dislike, but to an engagement from which he expected important consequences. He was gone in fact to the Wancester Station to meet a lady accompanied by a maid and two children, whom he put into a fly, and afterwards followed to the hotel of the Golden Keys in that town. An impressive woman, whom many would turn to look at again in passing; her figure was slim and sufficiently tall, her face rather emaciated, so that its sculpturesque beauty was the more pronounced, her crisp hair perfectly black, and her large anxious eyes also what we call black. Her dress was soberly correct, her age perhaps physically more advanced than the number of years would imply, but hardly less than seven-and-thirty. An uneasy-looking woman: her glance seemed to presuppose that people and things were going to be unfavourable to her, while she was nevertheless ready to meet them with resolution. The children were lovely – a dark-haired girl of six or more, a fairer boy of five. When Lush incautiously expressed some surprise at her having brought the children, she said with a sharp-edged intonation –

'Did you suppose I should come wandering about here by myself? Why should I not bring all four if I liked?'

'Oh certainly,' said Lush, with his usual fluent *non-chalance*.

He stayed an hour or so in conference with her, and rode back to Diplow in a state of mind that was at once hopeful and busily anxious as to the execution of the little plan on which his hopefulness was based. Grandcourt's marriage to Gwendolen Harleth would not, he believed, be much of a good to either of them, and it would plainly be fraught with disagreeables to himself. But now he felt confident enough to say inwardly, 'I will take odds that the marriage will never happen.'

XIV

I will not clothe myself in wreck – wear gems
Sawed from cramped finger-bones of women drowned;
Feel chilly vaporous hands of ireful ghosts
Clutching my necklace; trick my maiden breast
With orphans' heritage. Let your dead love
Marry its dead.

GWENDOLEN looked lovely and vigorous as a tall, newly-opened lily the next morning: there was a reaction of young energy in her, and yesterday's self-distrust seemed no more than the transient shiver on the surface of a full stream. The roving archery match in Cardell Chase was a delightful prospect for the sport's sake: she felt herself beforehand moving about like a wood-nymph under the beeches (in appreciative company), and the imagined scene lent a charm to further advances on the part of Grandcourt – not an impassioned lyrical Daphnis for the wood-nymph, certainly: but so much the better. Today Gwendolen foresaw him making slow conversational approaches to a declaration, and foresaw herself awaiting and encouraging it according to the rational conclusion which she had expressed to her uncle.

When she came down to breakfast (after every one had left the table except Mrs. Davilow) there were letters on her plate. One of them she read with a gathering smile, and then handed it to her mamma, who, on returning it, smiled also, finding new cheerfulness in the good spirits her daughter had shown ever since waking, and said –

'You don't feel inclined to go a thousand miles away?'

'Not exactly so far.'

'It was a sad omission not to have written again before this. Can't you write now – before we set out this morning?'

'It is not so pressing. To-morrow will do. You see they leave town to-day. I must write to Dover. They will be there till Monday.'

'Shall I write for you, dear – if it teases you?'

Gwendolen did not speak immediately, but after sipping her coffee answered brusquely, 'Oh no, let it be; I will write to-morrow.' Then feeling a touch of compunction, she looked up and said with playful tenderness, 'Dear, old, beautiful mamma!'

'Old, child, truly.'

'Please don't, mamma! I meant old for darling. You are hardly twenty-five years older than I am. When you talk in that way my life shrivels up before me.'

'One can have a great deal of happiness in twenty-five years, my dear.'

'I must lose no time in beginning,' said Gwendolen, merrily. 'The sooner I get my palaces and coaches, the better.'

'And a good husband who adores you, Gwen,' said Mrs. Davilow, encouragingly.

Gwendolen put out her lips saucily and said nothing.

It was a slight drawback on her pleasure in starting that the Rector was detained by magistrate's business and would probably not be able to get to Cardell Chase at all that day. She cared little that Mrs. Gascoigne and Anna chose not to go without him, but her uncle's presence would have seemed to make it a matter of course that the decision taken would be acted on. For decision in itself began to be formidable. Having come close to accepting Grandcourt, Gwendolen felt this lot of unhoped-for fullness rounding itself too definitely: when we take to wishing a great deal for ourselves, whatever we get soon turns into mere limitation and exclusion. Still there was the reassuring thought that marriage would be the gate into a larger freedom.

The place of meeting was a grassy spot called Green Arbour, where a bit of hanging wood made a sheltering amphitheatre. It was here that the coachful of servants with provisions had to prepare the picnic meal; and a warden of the Chase was to guide the roving archers so as to keep them within the due distance from this centre, and hinder them from wandering beyond the limit which had been fixed on – a curve that might be drawn through certain well-known points, such as the Double Oak, the Whispering Stones, and the High Cross. The plan was, to take only a preliminary stroll before luncheon, keeping the main roving expedition for the more exquisite lights of the afternoon. The muster was rapid enough to save every one from dull moments of waiting, and when the groups began to scatter themselves through the light and shadow made here by closely neighbouring beeches and there by rarer oaks, one may suppose that a painter would have been glad to look on. This roving archery was far prettier than the stationary game, but success in shooting at variable marks was less favoured by practice, and the hits were distributed among the volunteer archers otherwise than they would have been in target-shooting. From this cause, perhaps, as well as from the twofold distraction of being preoccupied and wishing not to betray her preoccupation, Gwendolen did not greatly distinguish herself in these first experiments, unless it were by the lively grace with which she took her comparative failure. She was in her white and green as on the day of the former archery meeting, when it made an epoch for her that she was introduced to Grandcourt; he was continually by her side now, yet it would have been hard to tell from mere looks and manner that their relation to each other had at all changed since their first conversation. Still there were other grounds that made most persons conclude them to be, if not engaged already, on the eve of being so. And she believed this herself. As they were all returning towards Green Arbour in divergent groups, not thinking at all of taking aim but merely chatting, words passed which seemed really the beginning of that end – the beginning of her acceptance. Grandcourt said, 'Do you know how long it is since I first saw you in this dress?'

'The archery meeting was on the 25th, and this is the 13th,' said Gwendolen, laughingly. 'I am not good at calculating, but I will venture to say that it must be nearly three weeks.'

A little pause, and then he said, 'That is a great loss of time.'

'That your knowing me has caused you? Pray don't be uncomplimentary: I don't like it.'

Pause again. 'It is because of the gain, that I feel the loss.'

Here Gwendolen herself left a pause. She was thinking, 'He is really very ingenious. He never speaks stupidly.' Her silence was so unusual, that it seemed the strongest of favourable answers, and he continued –

'The gain of knowing you makes me feel the time I lose in uncertainty. Do *you* like uncertainty?'

'I think I do, rather,' said Gwendolen, suddenly beaming on him with a playful smile. 'There is more in it.'

Grandcourt met her laughing eyes with a slow, steady look right into them, which seemed like vision in the abstract, and said, 'Do you mean more torment for me?'

There was something so strange to Gwendolen in this moment that she was quite shaken out of her usual self-consciousness. Blushing and turning away her eyes, she said, 'No, that would make me sorry.'

Grandcourt would have followed up this answer, which the change in her manner made apparently decisive of her favourable intention; but he was not in any way overcome so as to be unaware that they were now, within sight of everybody, descending the slope into Green Arbour, and descending it at an ill-chosen point where it began to be inconveniently steep. This was a reason for offering his hand in the literal sense to help her; she took it, and they came down in silence, much observed by those already on the level – among others by Mrs. Arrowpoint, who happened to be standing with Mrs. Davilow. That lady had now made up her mind that Grandcourt's merits were not such as would have induced Catherine to accept him, Catherine having so high a standard as to have refused Lord Slogan. Hence she looked at the tenant of Diplow with dispassionate eyes.

'Mr. Grandcourt is not equal as a man to his uncle, Sir Hugo Mallinger – too languid. To be sure, Mr. Grandcourt is a much younger man, but I shouldn't wonder if Sir Hugo were to outlive him, notwithstanding the difference of years. It is ill calculating on successions,' concluded Mrs. Arrowpoint, rather too loudly.

'It is indeed,' said Mrs. Davilow, able to assent with quiet cheerfulness, for she was so well satisfied with the actual situation of affairs that her habitual melancholy in their general unsatisfactoriness was altogether in abeyance.

I am not concerned to tell of the food that was eaten in that green refectory, or even to dwell on the glories of the forest scenery that spread themselves out beyond the level front of the hollow; being just now bound to tell a story of life at a stage when the blissful beauty of earth and sky entered only by narrow and oblique inlets into the consciousness, which was busy with a small social drama almost as little penetrated by a feeling of wider relations as if it had been a puppet-show. It will be understood that the food and champagne were of the best – the talk and laughter too, in the sense of belonging to the best society, where no one makes an invidious display of anything in particular, and the advantages of the world are taken with that high-bred depreciation which follows from being accustomed to them. Some of the gentlemen strolled a little and indulged in a cigar, there being a sufficient interval before four o'clock – the time for beginning to rove again. Among these, strange to say, was Grandcourt; but not Mr. Lush, who seemed to be taking his pleasure quite generously to-day by making himself particularly serviceable, ordering everything for everybody, and by this activity becoming more than ever a blot on the scene to Gwendolen, though he kept himself amiably aloof from her, and never even looked at her obviously. When there was a general move to prepare for starting, it appeared that the bows had all been put under the charge of Lord Brackenshaw's valet, and Mr. Lush was concerned to save ladies the trouble of fetching theirs from the carriage where they were propped. He did not intend to bring Gwendolen's, but she, fearful lest he should do so, hurried to fetch it herself. The valet seeing her approach met her with it, and giving it into her hand gave also a letter addressed to her. She asked no question about it, perceived at a glance that the address was in a lady's handwriting (of the delicate kind which used to be esteemed feminine before the present uncial period), and moving away with her bow in her hand, saw Mr. Lush coming to fetch other bows. To avoid meeting him she turned aside and walked with her back towards the stand of carriages, opening the letter. It contained these words –

'*If Miss Harleth is in doubt whether she should accept Mr. Grandcourt, let her break from her party after they have passed the Whispering Stones and return to the spot. She will then hear something to decide her, but she can only hear it by keeping this letter a strict secret from every one. If she does not act according to this letter, she will repent, as the woman who writes it has repented. The secrecy Miss Harleth will feel herself bound in honour to guard.*'

Gwendolen felt an inward shock, but her immediate thought was, 'It is come in time.' It lay in her youthfulness that she was absorbed by the idea of the revelation to be made, and had not even a momentary suspicion of contrivance that could justify her in showing the letter. Her mind gathered itself up at once into the resolution that she would manage to go unobserved to the Whispering Stones; and thrusting the letter into her pocket she turned back to rejoin the company, with that sense of having something to conceal which to her nature had a bracing quality and helped her to be mistress of herself.

It was a surprise to every one that Grandcourt was not, like the other smokers, on the spot in time to set out roving with the rest. 'We shall alight on him by-and-by,' said Lord Brackenshaw; 'he can't be gone far.' At any rate, no man could be waited for. This apparent forgetfulness might be taken for the distraction of a lover so absorbed in thinking of the beloved object as to forget an appointment which would bring him into her actual presence. And the good-natured Earl gave Gwendolen a distant jocose hint to that effect, which she took with suitable quietude. But the thought in her own mind was, 'Can he too be starting away from a decision?' It was not exactly a pleasant thought to her; but it was near the truth. 'Starting away,' however, was not the right expression for the languor of intention that came over Grandcourt, like a fit of diseased numbness, when an end seemed within easy reach: to desist then, when all expectation was to the contrary, became another gratification of mere will, sublimely independent of definite motive. At that moment he had begun a second large cigar in a vague, hazy obstinacy which, if Lush or any other mortal who might be insulted with impunity had interrupted by overtaking him with a request for his return, would have expressed itself by a slow removal of his cigar to say, in an under-tone, 'You'll be kind enough to go to the devil, will you?'

But he was not interrupted, and the rovers set off without any visible depression of spirits, leaving behind only a few of the less vigorous ladies, including Mrs. Davilow, who preferred a quiet stroll free from obligation to keep up with others. The enjoyment of the day was soon at its highest pitch, the archery getting more spirited and the changing scenes of the forest from roofed grove to open glade growing lovelier with the lengthening shadows, and the deeply felt but undefinable gradations of the mellowing afternoon. It was agreed that they were playing an extemporized 'As you like it;' and when a pretty compliment had been turned to Gwendolen about her having the part of Rosalind, she felt the more compelled to be surpassing in liveliness. This was not very difficult to her, for the effect of what had happened to-day was an excitement which needed a vent, a sense of adventure rather than alarm, and a straining towards the management of her retreat so as not to be impeded.

The roving had been lasting nearly an hour before the arrival at the Whispering Stones, two tall conical blocks that learned towards each other like gigantic grey-mantled figures. They were soon surveyed and passed by with the remark that they would be good ghosts on a starlit night. But a soft sunlight was on them now, and Gwendolen felt daring. The stones were near a fine grove of beeches where the archers found plenty of marks.

'How far are we from Green Arbour now?' said Gwendolen, having got in front by the side of the warden.

'Oh, not more than half a mile, taking along the avenue we're going to cross up there: but I shall take round a couple of miles, by the High Cross.'

She was falling back among the rest, when suddenly they seemed all to be hurrying obliquely forward under the guidance of Mr. Lush, and lingering a little where she was, she perceived her opportunity of slipping away. Soon she was out of sight, and without running she seemed to herself to fly along the ground and count the moments nothing till she found herself back again at the Whispering Stones. They turned their blank grey sides to her: what was there on the other side? If there were nothing after all? That was her only dread now – to have to turn back again in mystification; and walking round the right-hand stone without pause, she found herself in front of some one whose large dark eyes met hers at a foot's distance. In spite of expectation she was startled and shrank back, but in doing so she could take in the whole figure of this stranger and perceive that she was unmistakably a lady, and one who must once have been exceedingly handsome. She perceived, also, that a few yards from her were two children seated on the grass.

'Miss Harleth?' said the lady.

'Yes.' All Gwendolen's consciousness was wonder.

'Have you accepted Mr. Grandcourt?'

'No.'

'I have promised to tell you something. And you will promise to keep my secret. However you may decide, you will not tell Mr. Grandcourt, or any one else, that you have seen me?'

'I promise.'

'My name is Lydia Glasher. Mr. Grandcourt ought not to marry any one but me. I left my husband and child for him nine years ago. Those two children are his, and we have two others – girls – who are older. My husband is dead now, and Mr. Grandcourt ought to marry me. He ought to make that boy his heir.'

She looked towards the boy as she spoke, and Gwendolen's eyes followed hers. The handsome little fellow was puffing out his cheeks in trying to blow a tiny trumpet which remained dumb. His hat hung backward by a string, and his brown curls caught the sun-rays. He was a cherub.

The two women's eyes met again, and Gwendolen said proudly, 'I will not interfere with your wishes.' She looked as if she were shivering, and her lips were pale.

'You are very attractive, Miss Harleth. But when he first knew me, I too was young. Since then my life has been broken up and embittered. It is not fair that he should be happy and I miserable, and my boy thrust out of sight for another.'

These words were uttered with a biting accent, but with a determined abstinence from anything violent in tone or manner. Gwendolen, watching Mrs. Glasher's face while she spoke, felt a sort of terror: it was as if some ghastly vision had come to her in a dream and said, 'I am a woman's life.'

'Have you anything more to say to me?' she asked in a low tone, but still proudly and coldly. The revulsion within her was not tending to soften her. Every one seemed hateful.

'Nothing. You know what I wished you to know. You can inquire about me if you like. My husband was Colonel Glasher.'

'Then I will go,' said Gwendolen, moving away with a ceremonious inclination, which was returned with equal grace.

In a few minutes Gwendolen was in the beech grove again, but her party had gone out of sight and apparently had not sent in search of her, for all was solitude till she had reached the avenue pointed out by the warden. She determined to take this way back to Green Arbour, which she reached quickly; rapid movement seeming to her just now a means of suspending the thoughts which might prevent her from behaving with due calm. She had already made up her mind what step she would take.

Mrs. Davilow was of course astonished to see Gwendolen returning alone, and was not without some uneasiness which the presence of other ladies hindered her from showing. In answer to her words of surprise Gwendolen said –

'Oh, I have been rather silly. I lingered behind to look at the Whispering Stones, and the rest hurried on after something, so I lost sight of them. I thought it best to come home by the short way – the avenue that the warden had told me of. I'm not sorry after all. I had had enough walking.'

'Your party did not meet Mr. Grandcourt, I presume,' said Mrs. Arrowpoint, not without intention.

'No,' said Gwendolen, with a little flash of defiance and a light laugh. 'And we didn't see any carvings on the trees either. Where can he be? I should think he has fallen into the pool or had an apoplectic fit.'

With all Gwendolen's resolve not to betray any agitation, she could not help it that her tone was unusually high and hard, and her mother felt sure that something unpropitious had happened.

Mrs. Arrowpoint thought that the self-confident young lady was much piqued, and that Mr. Grandcourt was probably seeing reason to change his mind.

'If you have no objection, mamma, I will order the carriage,' said Gwendolen. 'I am tired. And every one will be going soon.'

Mrs. Davilow assented; but by the time the carriage was announced as ready – the horses having to be fetched from the stables on the warden's premises – the roving party reappeared, and with them Mr. Grandcourt.

'Ah, there you are!' said Lord Brackenshaw, going up to Gwendolen, who was arranging her mamma's shawl for the drive. 'We thought at first you had alighted on Grandcourt and he had taken you home. Lush said so. But after that we met Grandcourt. However, we didn't suppose you could be in any danger. The warden said he had told you a near way back.'

'You are going?' said Grandcourt, coming up with his usual air, as if he did not conceive that there had been any omission on his part. Lord Brackenshaw gave place to him and moved away.

'Yes, we are going,' said Gwendolen, looking busily at her scarf which she was arranging across her shoulders Scotch fashion.

'May I call at Offendene to-morrow?'

'Oh yes, if you like,' said Gwendolen, sweeping him from a distance with her eyelashes. Her voice was light and sharp as the first touch of frost.

Mrs. Davilow accepted his arm to lead her to the carriage; but while that was happening, Gwendolen with incredible swiftness had got in advance of them and had sprung into the carriage.

'I got in, mamma, because I wished to be on this side,' she said, apologetically. But she had avoided Grandcourt's touch: he only lifted his hat and walked away – with the not unsatisfactory impression that she meant to show herself offended by his neglect.

The mother and daughter drove for five minutes in silence. Then Gwendolen said, 'I intend to join the Langens at Dover, mamma. I shall pack up immediately on getting home, and set off by the early train. I shall be at Dover almost as soon as they are; we can let them know by telegraph.'

'Good heavens, child! what can be your reason for saying so?'

'My reason for saying it, mamma, is that I mean to do it.'

'But why do you mean to do it?'

'I wish to go away.'

'Is it because you are offended with Mr. Grandcourt's odd behaviour in walking off to-day?'

'It is useless to enter into such questions. I am not going in any case to marry Mr. Grandcourt. Don't interest yourself further about him.'

'What can I say to your uncle, Gwendolen? Consider the position you place me in. You led him to believe only last night that you had made up your mind in favour of Mr. Grandcourt.'

'I am very sorry to cause you annoyance, mamma dear, but I can't help it,' said Gwendolen, with still harder resistance in her tone. 'Whatever you or my uncle may think or do, I shall not alter my resolve, and I shall not tell my reason. I don't care what comes of it. I don't care if I never marry any one. There is nothing worth caring for. I believe all men are bad, and I hate them.'

'But need you set off in this way, Gwendolen?' said Mrs. Davilow, miserable and helpless.

'Now, mamma, don't interfere with me. If you have ever had any trouble in your own life, remember it, and don't interfere with me. If I am to be miserable, let it be by my own choice.'

The mother was reduced to trembling silence. She began to see that the difficulty would be lessened if Gwendolen went away.

And she did go. The packing was all carefully done that evening, and not long after dawn the next day Mrs. Davilow accompanied her daughter to the railway station. The sweet dews of morning, the cows and horses looking over the hedges without any particular reason, the early travellers on foot with their bundles, seemed all very melancholy and purposeless to them both. The dingy torpor of the railway station, before the ticket could be taken, was still worse. Gwendolen had certainly hardened in the last twenty-four hours: her mother's trouble evidently counted for little in her present state of mind, which did not

167

essentially differ from the mood that makes men take to worse conduct when their belief in persons or things is upset. Gwendolen's uncontrolled reading, though consisting chiefly in what are called pictures of life, had somehow not prepared her for this encounter with reality. Is that surprising? It is to be believed that attendance at the *opéra bouffe* in the present day would not leave men's minds entirely without shock, if the manners observed there with some applause were suddenly to start up in their own families. Perspective, as its inventor remarked, is a beautiful thing. What horrors of damp huts, where human beings languish, may not become picturesque through aerial distance! What hymning of cancerous vices may we not languish over as sublimest art in the safe remoteness of a strange language and artificial phrase! Yet we keep a repugnance to rheumatism and other painful effects when presented in our personal experience.

Mrs. Davilow felt Gwendolen's new phase of indifference keenly, and as she drove back alone, the brightening morning was sadder to her than before.

Mr. Grandcourt called that day at Offendene, but nobody was at home.

XV

'*Festina lente* – celerity should be contempered with cunctation.'
SIR THOMAS BROWNE.

GWENDOLEN, we have seen, passed her time abroad in the new excitement of gambling, and in imagining herself an empress of luck, having brought from her late experience a vague impression that in this confused world it signified nothing what any one did, so that they amused themselves. We have seen, too, that certain persons, mysteriously symbolized as Grapnell and Co., having also thought of reigning in the realm of luck, and being also bent on amusing themselves, no matter how, had brought about a painful change in her family circumstances; whence she had returned home – carrying with her, against her inclination, a necklace which she had pawned and some one else had redeemed.

While she was going back to England, Grandcourt was coming to find her; coming, that is, after his own manner – not in haste by express straight from Diplow to Leubronn, where she was understood to be; but so entirely without hurry that he was induced by the presence of some Russian acquaintances to linger at Baden-Baden and make various appointments with them, which, however, his desire to be at Leubronn ultimately caused him to break. Grandcourt's passions were of the intermittent, flickering kind: never flaming out strongly. But a great deal of life goes on without strong passion: myriads of cravats are carefully tied, dinners attended, even speeches made proposing the health of august personages, without the zest arising from a strong desire. And a man may make a good appearance in high social positions – may be supposed to know the classics, to have his reserves on science, a strong though repressed opinion on politics, and all the sentiments of the English gentleman, at a small expense of vital energy. Also, he may be obstinate or persistent at the same low rate, and may even show sudden impulses which have a false air of dæmonic strength because they seem inexplicable, though perhaps their secret lies merely in the want of regulated channels for the soul to move in – good and sufficient ducts of habit, without which our nature easily turns to mere ooze and mud, and at any pressure yields nothing but a spurt or a puddle.

Grandcourt had not been altogether displeased by Gwendolen's running away from the splendid chance he was holding out to her. The act had some piquancy for him. He liked to think that it was due to resentment of his careless behaviour in Cardell Chase, which, when he came to consider it, did appear rather cool. To have brought her so near a tender admission, and then to have walked headlong away from further opportunities of winning the consent which he had made her understand him to be asking for, was enough to provoke a girl of spirit; and to be worth his mastering it was proper that she should have some spirit. Doubtless she meant him to follow her, and it was what he meant too. But for a whole week he took no measures towards starting, and did not even inquire where Miss Harleth was gone. Mr. Lush felt a triumph that was mingled with much distrust; for Grandcourt had said no word to him about her, and looked as neutral as an alligator: there was no telling what might turn up in the slowly-churning chances of his mind. Still, to have put off a decision was to have made room for the waste of Grandcourt's energy.

The guests at Diplow felt more curiosity than their host. How was it that nothing more was heard of Miss Harleth? Was it credible that she had refused Mr. Grandcourt? Lady Flora Hollis, a lively middle-aged woman, well endowed with curiosity, felt a sudden interest in making a round of calls with Mrs. Torrington, including the Rectory, Offendene, and Quetcham, and thus not only got twice over, but also discussed with the Arrowpoints, the information that Miss Harleth was gone to Leubronn with some old friends, the Baron and Baroness von Langen; for the immediate agitation and disappointment of Mrs. Davilow and the Gascoignes had resolved itself into a wish that Gwendolen's disappearance should not be interpreted as anything eccentric or needful to be kept secret. The Rector's mind, indeed, entertained the possibility that the marriage was only a little deferred, for Mrs. Davilow had not dared to tell him of the bitter determination with which Gwendolen had spoken. And in spite of his practical ability, some of his experience had petrified into maxims and quotations. Amaryllis fleeing desired that her hiding-place should be known; and that love will find out the way 'over the mountain and over the wave' may be said without hyperbole in this age of steam. Gwendolen, he conceived, was an Amaryllis of excellent sense but coquettish daring; the question was, whether she had dared too much.

Lady Flora, coming back charged with news about Miss Harleth, saw no good reason why she should not try whether she could electrify Mr. Grandcourt by mentioning it to him at table; and in doing so shot a few hints of a notion having got abroad that he was a disappointed adorer. Grandcourt heard with quietude, but with attention; and the next day he ordered Lush to bring about a decent reason for breaking up the party at Diplow by the end of another week, as he meant to go yachting to the Baltic or somewhere – it being impossible to stay at Diplow as if he were a prisoner on parole, with a set of people whom he had never wanted. Lush needed no clearer announcement that Grandcourt was going to Leubronn; but he might go after the manner of a creeping billiard-ball and stick on the way. What Mr. Lush intended was to make himself indispensable so that he might go too, and he succeeded; Gwendolen's repulsion for him being a fact that only amused his patron, and made him none the less willing to have Lush always at hand.

This was how it happened that Grandcourt arrived at the *Czarina* on the fifth day after Gwendolen had left Leubronn, and found there his uncle, Sir Hugo Mallinger, with his family, including Deronda. It is not necessarily a pleasure either to the reigning power or the heir presumptive when their separate affairs – a touch of gout, say, in the one, and a touch of wilfulness in the other – happen to bring them to the same spot. Sir Hugo was an easy-tempered man, tolerant both of differences and defects; but a point of view different from his own concerning the settlement of the family estates fretted him rather more than if it had concerned Church discipline or the ballot, and faults were the less venial for belonging to a person whose existence was inconvenient to him. In no case could Grandcourt have been a nephew after his own heart; but as the presumptive heir to the Mallinger estates he was the sign and embodiment of a chief grievance in the baronet's life – the want of a son to inherit the lands, in no portion of which had he himself more than a life-interest. For in the ill-advised settlement which his father, Sir Francis, had chosen to make by will, even Diplow with its modicum of land had been left under the same conditions as the ancient and wide inheritance of the two Toppings – Diplow, where Sir Hugo had lived and hunted through many a season in his younger years, and where his wife and daughters ought to have been able to retire after his death.

This grievance had naturally gathered emphasis as the years advanced, and Lady Mallinger, after having had three daughters in quick succession, had remained for eight years till now that she was over forty without producing so much as another girl; while Sir Hugo, almost twenty years older, was at a time of life when, notwithstanding the fashionable retardation of most things from dinners to marriages, a man's hopefulness is apt to show signs of wear, until restored by second childhood.

In fact, he had begun to despair of a son, and this confirmation of Grandcourt's interest in the estates certainly tended to make his image and presence the more unwelcome; but, on the other hand, it carried circumstances which disposed Sir Hugo to take care that the relation between them should be kept as friendly as possible. It led him to dwell on a plan which had grown up side by side with his disappointment of an heir; namely, to try and secure Diplow as a future residence for Lady Mallinger and her daughters, and keep this pretty bit of the family inheritance for his own offspring in spite of that disappointment. Such knowledge as he had of his nephew's disposition and affairs encouraged the belief that Grandcourt might consent to a transaction by which he would get a good sum of ready money, as an equivalent for his prospective interest in the domain of Diplow and the moderate amount of land attached to it. If, after all, the unhoped-for son should be born, the money would have been thrown away, and Grandcourt would have been paid for giving up interests that had turned out good for nothing; but Sir Hugo set down this risk as *nil*, and of late years he had husbanded his fortune so well by the working of mines and the sale of leases that he was prepared for an outlay.

Here was an object that made him careful to avoid any quarrel with Grandcourt. Some years before, when he was making improvements at the Abbey, and needed Grandcourt's concurrence in his felling an obstructive mass of timber on the demesne, he had congratulated himself on finding that there was no active spite against him in his nephew's peculiar mind; and nothing had since occurred to make them hate each other more than was compatible with perfect politeness, or with any accommodation that could be strictly mutual.

Grandcourt, on his side, thought his uncle a superfluity and a bore, and felt that the list of things in general would be improved whenever Sir Hugo came to be expunged. But he had been made aware through Lush, always a useful medium, of the baronet's inclinations concerning Diplow, and he was gratified to have the alternative of the money in his mind: even if he had not thought it in the least likely that he would choose to accept it, his sense of power would have been flattered by his being able to refuse what Sir Hugo desired. The hinted transaction had told for something among the motives which had made him ask for a year's tenancy of Diplow, which it had rather annoyed Sir Hugo to grant, because the excellent hunting in the neighbourhood might decide Grandcourt not to part with his chance of future possession; – a man who has two places, in one of which the hunting is less good, naturally desiring a third where it is better. Also, Lush had thrown out to Sir Hugo the probability that Grandcourt would woo and win Miss Arrowpoint, and in that case ready money might be less of a temptation to him. Hence, on this unexpected meeting at Leubronn, the baronet felt much curiosity to know how things had been going on at Diplow, was bent on being as civil as possible to his nephew, and looked forward to some private chat with Lush.

Between Deronda and Grandcourt there was a more faintly marked but peculiar relation, depending on circumstances which have yet to be made known. But on no side was there any sign of suppressed chagrin on the first meeting at the *table d'hôte*, an hour after Grandcourt's arrival; and when the quartette of gentlemen afterwards met on the terrace, without Lady Mallinger, they moved off together to saunter through the rooms, Sir Hugo saying as they entered the large *saal* –

'Did you play much at Baden, Grandcourt?'

'No; I looked on and betted a little with some Russians there.'

'Had you luck?'

'What did I win, Lush?'

'You brought away about two hundred,' said Lush.

'You are not here for the sake of the play, then?' said Sir Hugo.

'No; I don't care about play now. It's a confounded strain,' said Grandcourt, whose diamond ring and demeanour, as he moved along playing slightly with his whisker, were being a good deal stared at by rouged foreigners interested in a new milord.

'The fact is somebody should invent a mill to do amusements for you, my dear fellow,' said Sir Hugo, 'as the Tartars get their praying done. But I agree with you;

I never cared for play. It's monotonous – knits the brain up into meshes. And it knocks me up to watch it now. I suppose one gets poisoned with the bad air. I never stay here more than ten minutes. But where's your gambling beauty, Deronda? Have you seen her lately?'

'She's gone,' said Deronda, curtly.

'An uncommonly fine girl, a perfect Diana,' said Sir Hugo, turning to Grandcourt again. 'Really worth a little straining to look at her. I saw her winning, and she took it as coolly as if she had known it all beforehand. The same day Deronda happened to see her losing like wildfire, and she bore it with immense pluck. I suppose she was cleaned out, or was wise enough to stop in time. How do you know she's gone?'

'Oh, by the Visitor-list,' said Deronda, with a scarcely perceptible shrug. 'Vandernoodt told me her name was Harleth, and she was with the Baron and Baroness von Langen. I saw by the list that Miss Harleth was no longer there.'

This held no further information for Lush than that Gwendolen had been gambling. He had already looked at the list, and ascertained that Gwendolen had gone, but he had no intention of thrusting this knowledge on Grandcourt before he asked for it; and he had not asked, finding it enough to believe that the object of search would turn up somewhere or other.

But now Grandcourt had heard what was rather piquant, and not a word about Miss Harleth had been missed by him. After a moment's pause he said to Deronda –

'Do you know those people – the Langens?'

'I have talked with them a little since Miss Harleth went away. I knew nothing of them before.'

'Where is she gone – do you know?'

'She is gone home,' said Deronda, coldly, as if he wished to say no more. But then, from a fresh impulse, he turned to look markedly at Grandcourt, and added, 'But it is possible you know her. Her home is not far from Diplow: Offendene, near Wancester.'

Deronda, turning to look straight at Grandcourt who was on his left hand, might have been a subject for those old painters who liked contrasts of temperament. There was a calm intensity of life and richness of tint in his face that on a sudden gaze from him was rather startling, and often made him seem to have spoken, so that servants and officials asked him automatically, 'What did you say, sir?' when he had been quite silent. Grandcourt himself felt an irritation, which he did not show except by a slight movement of the eyelids, at Deronda's turning round on him when he was not asked to do more than speak. But he answered, with his usual drawl, 'Yes, I know her,' and paused with his shoulder towards Deronda, to look at the gambling.

'What of her, eh?' asked Sir Hugo of Lush, as the three moved on a little way. 'She must be a new-comer at Offendene. Old Blenny lived there after the dowager died.'

'A little too much of her,' said Lush, in a low, significant tone; not sorry to let Sir Hugo know the state of affairs.

'Why? how?' said the baronet. They all moved out of the *salon* into a more airy promenade.

'He has been on the brink of marrying her,' Lush went on. 'But I hope it's off now. She's a niece of the clergyman – Gascoigne – at Pennicote. Her mother is a widow with a brood of daughters. This girl will have nothing, and is as dangerous as gunpowder. It would be a foolish marriage. But she has taken a freak against him, for she ran off here without notice, when he had agreed to call the next day. The fact is, he's here after her; but he was in no great hurry, and between his caprice and hers they are likely enough not to get together again. But of course he has lost his chance with the heiress.'

Grandcourt joining them said, 'What a beastly den this is! – a worse hole than Baden. I shall go back to the hotel.'

When Sir Hugo and Deronda were alone, the baronet began –

'Rather a pretty story. That girl has some drama in her. She must be worth running after – has *de l'imprévu*. I think her appearance on the scene has bettered my chance of getting Diplow, whether the marriage comes off or not.'

'I should hope a marriage like that would not come off,' said Deronda, in a tone of disgust.

'What! are you a little touched with the sublime lash?' said Sir Hugo, putting up his glasses to help his short sight in looking at his companion. 'Are you inclined to run after her?'

'On the contrary,' said Deronda, 'I should rather be inclined to run away from her.'

'Why, you would easily cut out Grandcourt. A girl with her spirit would think you the finer match of the two,' said Sir Hugo, who often tried Deronda's patience by finding a joke in impossible advice. (A difference of taste in jokes is a great strain on the affections.)

'I suppose pedigree and land belong to a fine match,' said Deronda, coldly.

'The best horse will win in spite of pedigree, my boy. You remember Napoleon's *mot* – *Je suis ancêtre*,' said Sir Hugo, who habitually undervalued birth, as men after dining well often agree that the good of life is distributed with wonderful equality.

'I am not sure that I want to be an ancestor,' said Deronda. 'It doesn't seem to me the rarest sort of origination.'

'You won't run after the pretty gambler, then?' said Sir Hugo, putting down his glasses.

'Decidedly not.'

This answer was perfectly truthful; nevertheless it had passed through Deronda's mind that under other circumstances he should have given way to the interest this girl had raised in him, and tried to know more of her. But his history had given him a stronger bias in another direction. He felt himself in no sense free.

XVI

Men, like planets, have both a visible and an invisible history. The astronomer threads the darkness with strict deduction, accounting so for every visible arc in the wanderer's orbit; and the narrator of human actions, if he did his work with the same completeness, would have to thread the hidden pathways of feeling and thought which lead up to every moment of action, and to those moments of intense suffering which take the quality of action – like the cry of Prometheus, whose chained anguish seems a greater energy than the sea and sky he invokes and the deity he defies.

DERONDA'S circumstances, indeed, had been exceptional. One moment had been burnt into his life as its chief epoch – a moment full of July sunshine and large pink roses shedding their last petals on a grassy court enclosed on three sides by a Gothic cloister. Imagine him in such a scene: a boy of thirteen, stretched prone on the grass where it was in shadow, his curly head propped on his arms over a book, while his tutor, also reading, sat on a camp-stool under shelter. Deronda's book was Sismondi's History of the Italian Republics: – the lad had a passion for history, eager to know how time had been filled up since the Flood, and how things were carried on in the dull periods. Suddenly he let down his left arm and looked at his tutor, saying in purest boyish tones –

'Mr. Fraser, how was it that the popes and cardinals always had so many nephews?'

The tutor, an able young Scotchman who acted as Sir Hugo Mallinger's secretary, roused rather unwillingly from his political economy, answered with the clear-cut, emphatic chant which makes a truth doubly telling in Scotch utterance –

'Their own children were called nephews.'

'Why?' said Deronda.

'It was just for the propriety of the thing; because, as you know very well, priests don't marry, and the children were illegitimate.'

Mr. Fraser, thrusting out his lower lip and making his chant of the last word the more emphatic for a little impatience at being interrupted, had already turned his eyes on his book again, while Deronda, as if something had stung him, started up in a sitting attitude with his back to the tutor.

He had always called Sir Hugo Mallinger his uncle, and when it once occurred to him to ask about his father and mother, the baronet had answered, 'You lost your father and mother when you were quite a little one; that is why I take care of you.' Daniel then straining to discern something in that early twilight, had a dim sense of having been kissed very much, and surrounded by thin, cloudy, scented drapery, till his fingers caught in something hard, which hurt him, and he began to cry. Every other memory he had was of the little world in which he still lived. And at that time he did not mind about learning more, for he was too fond of Sir Hugo to be sorry for the loss of unknown parents. Life was very delightful to the lad, with an uncle who was always indulgent and cheerful – a fine man in the bright noon of life, whom Daniel thought absolutely perfect, and whose place was one of the finest in England, at once historical, romantic, and home-like: a picturesque architectural outgrowth from an abbey, which had still remnants of the old monastic trunk. Diplow lay in another county, and was a comparatively landless place which had come into the family from a rich lawyer on the female side, who wore the perruque of the Restoration; whereas the Mallingers had the grant of Monk's Topping under Henry the Eighth, and ages before had held the neighbouring lands of King's Topping, tracing indeed their origin to a certain Hugues le Malingre, who came in with the Conqueror, – and also apparently with a sickly complexion, which had been happily corrected in his descendants. Two rows of these descendants, direct and collateral, females of the male line, and males of the female, looked down in the gallery over the cloisters on the nephew Daniel as he walked there: men in armour with pointed beards and arched eyebrows, pinched ladies in hoops and ruffs with no face to speak of; grave-looking men in black velvet and stuffed hips, and fair, frightened women holding little boys by the hand; smiling politicians in magnificent perruques, and ladies of the prize-animal kind, with rosebud mouths and full eyelids, according to Lely; then a generation whose faces were revised and embellished in the taste of Kneller, and so on through refined editions of the family types in the time of Reynolds and Romney, till the line ended with Sir Hugo and his younger brother Henleigh. This last had married Miss Grandcourt, and taken her name along with her estates, thus making a junction between two equally old families, impaling the three Saracens' heads proper and three bezants of the one with the tower and falcons *argent* of the other, and, as it happened, uniting their highest advantages in the prospects of that Henleigh Mallinger Grandcourt who is at present more of an acquaintance to us than either Sir Hugo or his nephew Daniel Deronda.

In Sir Hugo's youthful portrait with rolled collar and high cravat, Sir Thomas Lawrence had done justice to the agreeable alacrity of expression and sanguine temperament still to be seen in the original, but had done something more than justice in slightly lengthening the nose, which was in reality shorter than might have been expected in a Mallinger. Happily the appropriate nose of the family reappeared in his younger brother, and was to be seen in all its refined regularity in his nephew Mallinger Grandcourt. But in the nephew Daniel Deronda the family faces of various types, seen on the walls of the gallery, found no reflex. Still he was handsomer than any of them, and when he was thirteen might have served as model for any painter who wanted to image the most memorable of boys: you could hardly have seen his face thoroughly meeting yours without believing that human creatures had done nobly in times past, and might do more nobly in time to come. The finest childlike faces have this consecrating power, and make us shudder anew at all the grossness and basely-wrought griefs of the world, lest they should enter here and defile.

But at this moment on the grass among the rose-petals, Daniel Deronda was making a first acquaintance with those griefs. A new idea had entered his mind, and was beginning to change the aspect of his habitual feelings as happy careless voyagers are changed when the sky suddenly threatens and the thought of danger arises. He sat perfectly still with his back to the tutor, while his face expressed rapid inward transition. The deep blush, which had come when he first started up, gradually subsided; but his features kept that indescribable look of subdued activity which often accompanies a new mental survey of familiar facts. He had not lived with other boys, and his mind showed the same blending of child's ignorance with surprising knowledge which is oftener seen in bright girls. Having read Shakespeare as well as a great deal of history, he could have talked with the wisdom of a bookish child about men who were born out of wedlock and were held unfortunate in consequence, being under disadvantages which required them to be a sort of heroes if they were to work themselves up to an equal standing with their legally born brothers. But he had never brought such knowledge into any association with his own lot, which had been too easy for him ever to think about it – until this moment when there had darted into his mind with the magic of quick comparison, the possibility that here was the secret of his own birth, and that the man whom he called uncle was really his father. Some children, even younger than Daniel, have known the first arrival of care, like an ominous irremovable guest in their tender lives, on the discovery that their parents, whom they had imagined able to buy everything, were poor and in hard money troubles. Daniel felt the presence of a new guest who seemed to come with an enigmatic veiled face, and to carry dimly-conjectured, dreaded revelations. The ardour which he had given to the imaginary world in his books suddenly rushed towards his own history and spent its pictorial

DANIEL DERONDA

energy there, explaining what he knew, representing the
unknown. The uncle whom he loved very dearly took the
aspect of a father who held secrets about him – who had
done him a wrong – yes, a wrong: and what had become of
his mother, from whom he must have been taken away? –
Secrets about which he, Daniel, could never inquire; for to
speak or be spoken to about these new thoughts seemed
like falling flakes of fire to his imagination. Those who
have known an impassioned childhood will understand
this dread of utterance about any shame connected with
their parents. The impetuous advent of new images took
possession of him with the force of fact for the first time
told, and left him no immediate power for the reflection
that he might be trembling at a fiction of his own. The
terrible sense of collision between a strong rush of feeling
and the dread of its betrayal, found relief at length in big
slow tears, which fell without restraint until the voice of
Mr. Fraser was heard saying –

'Daniel, do you see that you are sitting on the bent
pages of your book?'

Daniel immediately moved the book without turning
round, and after holding it before him for an instant, rose
with it and walked away into the open grounds, where he
could dry his tears unobserved. The first shock of suggestion past, he could remember that he had no certainty how
things really had been, and that he had been making conjectures about his own history, as he had often made stories
about Pericles or Columbus, just to fill up the blanks
before they became famous. Only there came back certain
facts which had an obstinate reality, – almost like the
fragments of a bridge, telling you unmistakably how the
arches lay. And again there came a mood in which his
conjectures seemed like a doubt of religion, to be banished
as an offence, and a mean prying after what he was not
meant to know; for there was hardly a delicacy of feeling
this lad was not capable of. But the summing up of all
his fluctuating experience at this epoch was, that a
secret impression had come to him which had given him

182

something like a new sense in relation to all the elements of his life. And the idea that others probably knew things concerning him which they did not choose to mention, and which he would not have had them mention, set up in him a premature reserve which helped to intensify his inward experience. His ears were open now to words which before that July day would have passed by him unnoted; and round every trivial incident which imagination could connect with his suspicions, a newly-roused set of feelings were ready to cluster themselves.

One such incident a month later wrought itself deeply into his life. Daniel had not only one of those thrilling boy voices which seem to bring an idyllic heaven and earth before our eyes, but a fine musical instinct, and had early made out accompaniments for himself on the piano, while he sang from memory. Since then he had had some teaching, and Sir Hugo, who delighted in the boy, used to ask for his music in the presence of guests. One morning after he had been singing 'Sweet Echo' before a small party of gentlemen whom the rain had kept in the house, the baronet, passing from a smiling remark to his next neighbour, said –

'Come here, Dan!'

The boy came forward with unusual reluctance. He wore an embroidered holland blouse which set off the rich colouring of his head and throat, and the resistant gravity about his mouth and eyes as he was being smiled upon, made their beauty the more impressive. Every one was admiring him.

'What do you say to being a great singer? Should you like to be adored by the world and take the house by storm, like Mario and Tamberlik?'

Daniel reddened instantaneously, but there was a just perceptible interval before he answered with angry decision –

'No; I should hate it.'

'Well, well, well!' said Sir Hugo, with surprised kindliness intended to be soothing. But Daniel turned away quickly, left the room, and going to his own chamber threw himself on the broad window-sill, which was a favourite retreat of his when he had nothing particular to do. Here he could see the rain gradually subsiding with gleams through the parting clouds which lit up a great reach of the park, where the old oaks stood apart from each other, and the bordering wood was pierced with a green glade which met the eastern sky. This was a scene which had always been part of his home – part of the dignified ease which had been a matter of course in his life. And his ardent clinging nature had appropriated it all with affection. He knew a great deal of what it was to be a gentleman by inheritance, and without thinking much about himself – for he was a boy of active perceptions and easily forgot his own exist-ence in that of Robert Bruce – he had never supposed that he could be shut out from such a lot, or have a very different part in the world from that of the uncle who petted him. It is possible (though not greatly believed in at present) to be fond of poverty and take it for a bride, to prefer scoured deal, red quarries, and whitewash for one's private surroundings, to delight in no splendour but what has open doors for the whole nation, and to glory in having no privilege except such as nature insists on; and noble-men have been known to run away from elaborate ease and the option of idleness, that they might bind themselves for small pay to hard-handed labour. But Daniel's tastes were altogether in keeping with his nurture: his disposition was one in which everyday scenes and habits beget not *ennui* or rebellion, but delight, affection, aptitudes; and now the lad had been stung to the quick by the idea that his uncle – perhaps his father – thought of a career for him which was totally unlike his own, and which he knew very well was not thought of among possible destinations for the sons of English gentlemen. He had often stayed in London with Sir Hugo, who to indulge the boy's ear had carried him to the opera to hear the great tenors, so that the image of a singer taking the house by storm was very vivid to him; but now, spite of his musical gift, he set himself bitterly against the notion of being dressed up to sing before all those fine people who would not care about him except as a wonderful toy. That Sir Hugo should have thought of him in that position for a moment, seemed to Daniel an unmistakable proof that there was something about his birth which threw him out from the class of gentlemen to which the baronet belonged. Would it ever be mentioned to him? Would the time come when his uncle would tell him everything? He shrank from the prospect: in his imagination he preferred ignorance. If his father had been wicked – Daniel inwardly used strong words, for he was feeling the injury done him as a maimed boy feels the crushed limb which for others is merely reckoned in an average of accidents – if his father had done any wrong, he wished it might never be spoken of to him: it was already a cutting thought that such knowledge might be in other minds. Was it in Mr. Fraser's? Probably not, else he would not have spoken in that way about the pope's nephews: Daniel fancied, as older people do, that every one else's consciousness was as active as his own on a matter which was vital to him. Did Turvey the valet know? – and old Mrs. French the housekeeper? – and Banks the bailiff, with whom he had ridden about the farms on his pony? – And now there came back the recollection of a day some years before when he was drinking Mrs. Banks's whey, and Banks said to his wife with a wink and a cunning laugh, 'He features the mother, eh?' At that time little Daniel had merely thought that Banks made a silly face, as the common farming men often did – laughing at what was not laughable; and he rather resented being winked at and talked of as if he did not understand everything. But now that small incident became information: it was to be reasoned on. How could he be like his mother and not like his father? His mother must have been a Mallinger, if Sir Hugo were his uncle. But no! His father might have been Sir Hugo's brother and have changed his name, as Mr. Henleigh Mallinger did when he married Miss Grandcourt. But then, why had he never heard Sir Hugo speak of his brother Deronda, as he spoke of his brother Grandcourt? Daniel had never before cared about the family tree – only about that ancestor who had killed three Saracens in one encounter. But now his mind turned to a cabinet of estate-maps in the library, where he had once seen an illuminated parchment hanging out, that Sir Hugo said was the family tree. The phrase was new and odd to him – he was a little fellow then, hardly more than half his present age – and he gave it no precise meaning. He knew more now and wished that he could examine that parchment. He imagined that the cabinet was always locked, and longed to try it. But here he checked himself. He might be seen; and he would never bring himself near even a silent admission of the sore that had opened in him.

It is in such experiences of boy or girlhood, while elders are debating whether most education lies in science or literature, that the main lines of character are often laid down. If Daniel had been of a less ardently affectionate nature, the reserve about himself and the supposition that others had something to his disadvantage in their minds, might have turned into a hard, proud antagonism. But inborn lovingness was strong enough to keep itself level with resentment. There was hardly any creature in his habitual world that he was not fond of; teasing them occasionally, of course – all except his uncle, or 'Nunc,' as Sir Hugo had taught him to say; for the baronet was the reverse of a strait-laced man, and left his dignity to take care of itself. Him Daniel loved in that deep-rooted filial way which makes children always the happier for being in the same room with father or mother, though their occupations may be quite apart. Sir Hugo's watch-chain and seals, his handwriting, his mode of smoking and of talking to his dogs and horses, had all a rightness and charm about them to the boy which went along with the happiness of morning and breakfast-time. That Sir Hugo had always been a Whig, made Tories and Radicals equally opponents of the truest and best; and the books he had written were all seen under the same consecration of loving belief which differenced what was his from what was not his, in spite of general resemblance. Those writings were various, from volumes of travel in the brilliant style, to articles on things in general, and pamphlets on political crises; but to Daniel they were alike in having an unquestionable rightness by which other people's information could be tested.

Who cannot imagine the bitterness of a first suspicion that something in this object of complete love was *not* quite right? Children demand that their heroes should be fleckless, and easily believe them so: perhaps a first discovery to the contrary is hardly a less revolutionary shock to a passionate child than the threatened downfall of habitual beliefs which makes the world seem to totter for us in maturer life.

But some time after this renewal of Daniel's agitation it appeared that Sir Hugo must have been making a merely playful experiment in his question about the singing. He sent for Daniel into the library, and looking up from his writing as the boy entered threw himself sideways in his arm-chair. 'Ah, Dan!' he said kindly, drawing one of the old embroidered stools close to him. 'Come and sit down here.'

Daniel obeyed, and Sir Hugo put a gentle hand on his shoulder, looking at him affectionately.

'What is it, my boy? Have you heard anything that has put you out of spirits lately?'

Daniel was determined not to let the tears come, but he could not speak.

'All changes are painful when people have been happy, you know,' said Sir Hugo, lifting his hand from the boy's shoulder to his dark curls and rubbing them gently. 'You can't be educated exactly as I wish you to be without our parting. And I think you will find a great deal to like at school.'

This was not what Daniel expected, and was so far a relief, which gave him spirit to answer –

'Am I to go to school?'

'Yes, I mean you to go to Eton. I wish you to have the education of an English gentleman; and for that it is necessary that you should go to a public school in

187

preparation for the university: Cambridge I mean you to go to; it was my own university.'

Daniel's colour came and went.

'What do you say, sirrah?' said Sir Hugo, smiling.

'I should like to be a gentleman,' said Daniel, with firm distinctness, 'and go to school, if that is what a gentleman's son must do.'

Sir Hugo watched him silently for a few moments, thinking he understood now why the lad had seemed angry at the notion of becoming a singer. Then he said tenderly –

'And so you won't mind about leaving your old Nunc?'

'Yes, I shall,' said Daniel, clasping Sir Hugo's caressing arm with both his hands. 'But shan't I come home and be with you in the holidays?'

'Oh yes, generally,' said Sir Hugo. 'But now I mean you to go at once to a new tutor, to break the change for you before you go to Eton.'

After this interview Daniel's spirit rose again. He was meant to be a gentleman, and in some unaccountable way it might be that his conjectures were all wrong. The very keenness of the lad taught him to find comfort in his ignorance. While he was busying his mind in the construction of possibilities, it became plain to him that there must be possibilities of which he knew nothing. He left off brooding, young joy and the spirit of adventure not being easily quenched within him, and in the interval before his going away he sang about the house, danced among the old servants, making them parting gifts, and insisted many times to the groom on the care that was to be taken of the black pony.

'Do you think I shall know much less than the other boys, Mr. Fraser?' said Daniel. It was his bent to think that every stranger would be surprised at his ignorance.

'There are dunces to be found everywhere,' said the judicious Fraser. 'You'll not be the biggest; but you've not the makings of a Porson in you, or a Leibniz either.'

'I don't want to be a Porson or a Leibniz,' said Daniel. 'I would rather be a greater leader, like Pericles or Washington.'

'Ay, ay; you've a notion they did with little parsing, and less algebra,' said Fraser. But in reality he thought his pupil a remarkable lad, to whom one thing was as easy as another if he had only a mind to it.

Things went very well with Daniel in his new world, except that a boy with whom he was at once inclined to strike up a close friendship talked to him a great deal about his home and parents, and seemed to expect a like expansiveness in return. Daniel immediately shrank into reserve, and this experience remained a check on his naturally strong bent towards the formation of intimate friendships. Every one, his tutor included, set him down as a reserved boy, though he was so good-humoured and unassuming, as well as quick both at study and sport, that nobody called his reserve disagreeable. Certainly his face had a great deal to do with that favourable interpretation; but in this instance the beauty of the closed lips told no falsehood.

A surprise that came to him before his first vacation, strengthened the silent consciousness of a grief within, which might be compared in some ways with Byron's susceptibility about his deformed foot. Sir Hugo wrote word that he was married to Miss Raymond, a sweet lady whom Daniel must remember having seen. The event would make no difference about his spending the vacation at the Abbey; he would find Lady Mallinger a new friend whom he would be sure to love, – and much more to the usual effect when a man, having done something agreeable to himself, is disposed to congratulate others on his own good fortune, and the deducible satisfactoriness of events in general.

Let Sir Hugo be partly excused until the grounds of his action can be more fully known. The mistakes in his behaviour to Deronda were due to that dullness towards what may be going on in other minds, especially the minds of children, which is among the commonest deficiencies even in good-natured men like him, when life has been generally easy to themselves, and their energies have been quietly spent in feeling gratified. No one was better aware than he that Daniel was generally suspected to be his own son. But he was pleased with that suspicion; and his imagination had never once been troubled with the way in which the boy himself might be affected, either then or in the future, by the enigmatic aspect of his circumstances. He was as fond of him as could be and meant the best by him. And considering the lightness with which the preparation of young lives seems to lie on respectable consciences, Sir Hugo Mallinger can hardly be held open to exceptional reproach. He had been a bachelor till he was five-and-forty, had always been regarded as a fascinating man of elegant tastes; what could be more natural, even according to the index of language, than that he should have a beautiful boy like the little Deronda to take care of? The mother might even perhaps be in the great world – met with in Sir Hugo's residences abroad. The only person to feel any objection was the boy himself, who could not have been consulted. And the boy's objections had never been dreamed of by anybody but himself.

By the time Deronda was ready to go to Cambridge, Lady Mallinger had already three daughters – charming babies, all three, but whose sex was announced as a melancholy alternative, the offspring desired being a son: if Sir Hugo had no son the succession must go to his nephew Mallinger Grandcourt. Daniel no longer held a wavering opinion about his own birth. His fuller knowledge had tended to convince him that Sir Hugo was his father, and he conceived that the baronet, since he never approached a communication on the subject, wished him to have a tacit understanding of the fact, and to accept in silence what would be generally considered more than the due love and nurture. Sir Hugo's marriage might certainly have been felt as a new ground of resentment by some youths in Deronda's position, and the timid Lady Mallinger with her fast-coming little ones might have been images to scowl at, as likely to divert much that was disposable in the feelings and possessions of the baronet from one who felt his own claim to be prior. But hatred of innocent human obstacles was a form of moral stupidity not in Deronda's grain; even the indignation which had long mingled itself with his affection for Sir Hugo took the quality of pain rather than of temper; and as his mind ripened to the idea of tolerance towards error, he habitually linked the idea with his own silent grievances.

The sense of an entailed disadvantage – the deformed foot doubtfully hidden by the shoe, makes a restlessly active spiritual yeast, and easily turns a self-centred, unloving nature into an Ishmaelite. But in the rarer sort, who presently see their own frustrated claim as one among a myriad, the inexorable sorrow takes the form of fellowship and makes the imagination tender. Deronda's early-wakened susceptibility, charged at first with ready indignation and resistant pride, had raised in him a premature reflection on certain questions of life; it had given a bias to his conscience, a sympathy with certain ills, and a tension of resolve in certain directions, which marked him off from other youths much more than any talents he possessed.

One day near the end of the Long Vacation, when he had been making a tour in the Rhineland with his Eton tutor, and was come for a farewell stay at the Abbey before going to Cambridge, he said to Sir Hugo –

'What do you intend me to be, sir?' They were in the library, and it was the fresh morning. Sir Hugo had called him in to read a letter from a Cambridge Don who was to be interested in him; and since the baronet wore an air at once business-like and leisurely, the moment seemed propitious for entering on a grave subject which had never yet been thoroughly discussed.

'Whatever your inclination leads you to, my boy. I thought it right to give you the option of the army, but you shut the door on that, and I was glad. I don't expect you to choose just yet – by-and-by, when you have looked about you a little more and tried your mettle among older men. The university has a good wide opening into the forum. There are prizes to be won, and a bit of good fortune often gives the turn to a man's taste. From what I see and hear, I should think you can take up anything you like. You are in deeper water with your classics than I ever got into, and if you are rather sick of that swimming, Cambridge is the place where you can go into mathematics with a will, and disport yourself on the dry sand as much as you like. I floundered along like a carp.'

'I suppose money will make some difference, sir,' said Daniel, blushing. 'I shall have to keep myself by-and-by.'

'Not exactly. I recommend you not to be extravagant – yes, yes, I know – you are not inclined to that; – but you need not take up anything against the grain. You will have a bachelor's income – enough for you to look about with. Perhaps I had better tell you that you may consider yourself secure of seven hundred a-year. You might make yourself a barrister – be a writer – take up politics. I confess that is what would please me best. I should like to have you at my elbow and pulling with me.'

Deronda looked embarrassed. He felt that he ought to make some sign of gratitude, but other feelings clogged his tongue. A moment was passing by in which a question about his birth was throbbing within him, and yet it seemed more impossible than ever that the question should find vent – more impossible than ever that he could hear certain things from Sir Hugo's lips. The liberal way in which he was dealt with was the more striking because the baronet had of late cared particularly for money, and for making the utmost of his life-interest in the estate by way of providing for his daughters; and as all this flashed through Daniel's mind it was momentarily within his imagination that the provision for him might come in some way from his mother. But such vaporous conjecture passed away as quickly as it came.

Sir Hugo appeared not to notice anything peculiar in Daniel's manner, and presently went on with his usual chatty liveliness.

'I'm glad you have done some good reading outside your classics, and have got a grip of French and German. The truth is, unless a man can get the prestige and income of a Don and write donnish books, it's hardly worth while for him to make a Greek and Latin machine of himself and be able to spin you out pages of the Greek dramatists at any verse you'll give him as a cue. That's all very fine, but in practical life nobody does give you the cue for pages of Greek. In fact it's a nicety of conversation which I would have you attend to – much quotation of any sort, even in English, is bad. It tends to choke ordinary remark. One couldn't carry on life comfortably without a little blindness to the fact that everything has been said better than we can put it ourselves. But talking of Dons, I have seen a Don make a capital figure in society; and occasionally he can shoot you down a cartload of learning in the right place, which will tell in politics. Such men are wanted; and if you have any turn for being a Don, I say nothing against it.'

'I think there's not much chance of that. Quicksett and Puller are both stronger than I am. I hope you will not be much disappointed if I don't come out with high honours.'

'No, no. I should like you to do yourself credit, but for God's sake don't come out as a superior expensive kind of idiot, like young Brecon, who got a Double First, and has been learning to knit braces ever since. What I wish you to get is a passport in life. I don't go against our university system: we want a little disinterested culture to make head against cotton and capital, especially in the House. My Greek has all evaporated: if I had to construe a verse on a sudden, I should get an apoplectic fit. But it formed my taste. I dare say my English is the better for it.'

On this point Daniel kept a respectful silence. The enthusiastic belief in Sir Hugo's writings as a standard, and in the Whigs as the chosen race among politicians, had gradually vanished along with the seraphic boy's face.

He had not been the hardest of workers at Eton. Though some kinds of study and reading came as easily as boating to him, he was not of the material that usually makes the first-rate Eton scholar. There had sprung up in him a meditative yearning after wide knowledge which is likely always to abate ardour in the fight for prize acquirement in narrow tracks. Happily he was modest, and took any second-rateness in himself simply as a fact, not as a marvel necessarily to be accounted for by a superiority. Still Mr. Fraser's high opinion of the lad had not been altogether belied by the youth: Daniel had the stamp of rarity in a subdued fervour of sympathy, an activity of imagination on behalf of others, which did not show itself effusively, but was continually seen in acts of considerateness that struck his companions as moral eccentricity. 'Deronda would have been first-rate if he had more ambition' – was a frequent remark about him. But how could a fellow push his way properly when he objected to swop for his own advantage, knocked under by choice when he was within an inch of victory, and, unlike the great Clive, would rather be the calf than the butcher? It was a mistake, however, to suppose that Deronda had not his share of ambition: we know he had suffered keenly from the belief that there was a tinge of dishonour in his lot; but there are some cases, and his was one of them, in which the sense of injury breeds – not the will to inflict injuries and climb over them as a ladder, but – a hatred of all injury. He had his flashes of fierceness, and could hit out upon occasion, but the occasions were not always what might have been expected. For in what related to himself his resentful impulses had been early checked by a mastering affectionateness. Love has a habit of saying 'Never mind' to angry self, who, sitting down for the nonce in the lower place, by-and-by gets used to it. So it was that as Deronda approached manhood his feeling for Sir Hugo, while it was getting more and more mixed with criticism, was gaining in that sort of allowance which reconciles criticism with tenderness. The dear old beautiful home and everything within it,

Lady Mallinger and her little ones included, were consecrated for the youth as they had been for the boy – only with a certain difference of light on the objects. The altarpiece was no longer miraculously perfect, painted under infallible guidance, but the human hand discerned in the work was appealing to a reverent tenderness safer from the gusts of discovery. Certainly Deronda's ambition, even in his spring-time, lay exceptionally aloof from conspicuous, vulgar triumph, and from other ugly forms of boyish energy; perhaps because he was early impassioned by ideas, and burned his fire on those heights. One may spend a good deal of energy in disliking and resisting what others pursue, and a boy who is fond of somebody else's pencil-case may not be more energetic than another who is fond of giving his own pencil-case away. Still, it was not Deronda's disposition to escape from ugly scenes: he was more inclined to sit through them and take care of the fellow least able to take care of himself. It had helped to make him popular that he was sometimes a little compromised by this apparent comradeship. For a meditative interest in learning how human miseries are wrought – as precocious in him as another sort of genius in the poet who writes a Queen Mab at nineteen – was so infused with kindliness that it easily passed for comradeship. Enough. In many of our neighbours' lives, there is much not only of error and lapse, but of a certain exquisite goodness which can never be written or even spoken – only divined by each of us, according to the inward instruction of our own privacy.

The impression he made at Cambridge corresponded to his position at Eton. Every one interested in him agreed that he might have taken a high place if his motives had been of a more pushing sort, and if he had not, instead of regarding studies as instruments of success, hampered himself with the notion that they were to feed motive and opinion – a notion which set him criticizing methods and arguing against his freight and harness when he should have been using all his might to pull. In the beginning his work at the university had a new zest for him: indifferent to the continuation of the Eton classical drill, he applied himself vigorously to mathematics, for which he had shown an early aptitude under Mr. Fraser, and he had the delight of feeling his strength in a comparatively fresh exercise of thought. That delight, and the favourable opinion of his tutor, determined him to try for a mathematical scholarship in the Easter of his second year: he wished to gratify Sir Hugo by some achievement, and the study of the higher mathematics, having the growing fascination inherent in all thinking which demands intensity, was making him a more exclusive worker than he had been before.

But here came the old check which had been growing with his growth. He found the inward bent towards comprehension and thoroughness diverging more and more from the track marked out by the standards of examination: he felt a heightening discontent with the wearing futility and enfeebling strain of a demand for excessive retention and dexterity without any insight into the principles which form the vital connections of knowledge. (Deronda's undergraduateship occurred fifteen years ago, when the perfection of our university methods was not yet indisputable.) In hours when his dissatisfaction was strong upon him he reproached himself for having been attracted by the conventional advantage of belonging to an English university, and was tempted towards the project of asking Sir Hugo to let him quit Cambridge and pursue a more independent line of study abroad. The germs of this inclination had been already stirring in his boyish love of universal history, which made him want to be at home in foreign countries, and follow in imagination the travelling students of the middle ages. He longed now to have the sort of apprenticeship to life which would not shape him too definitely, and rob him of the choice that might come from a free growth. One sees that Deronda's demerits were likely to be on the side of reflective hesitation, and this tendency was encouraged by his position: there was no need for him to get an immediate income, or to fit himself in haste for a profession; and his sensibility to the half-known facts of his parentage made him an excuse for lingering longer than others in a state of social neutrality. Other men, he inwardly said, had a more definite place and duties. But the project which flattered his inclination might not have gone beyond the stage of ineffective brooding, if certain circumstances had not quickened it into action.

The circumstances arose out of an enthusiastic friendship which extended into his after-life. Of the same year with himself, and occupying small rooms close to his, was a youth who had come as an exhibitioner from Christ's Hospital, and had eccentricities enough for a Charles Lamb. Only to look at his pinched features and blond hair hanging over his collar reminded one of pale quaint heads by early German painters; and when this faint colouring was lit up by a joke, there came sudden creases about the mouth and eyes which might have been moulded by the soul of an aged humorist. His father, an engraver of some distinction, had been dead eleven years, and his mother had three girls to educate and maintain on a meagre annuity. Hans Meyrick – he had been daringly christened after Holbein – felt himself the pillar, or rather the knotted and twisted trunk, round which these feeble climbing plants must cling. There was no want of ability or of honest well-meaning affection to make the prop trustworthy: the ease and quickness with which he studied might serve him to win prizes at Cambridge, as he had done among the Blue Coats, in spite of irregularities. The only danger was, that the incalculable tendencies in him might be fatally timed, and that his good intentions might be frustrated by some act which was not due to habit but to capricious, scattered impulses. He could not be said to have any one bad habit; yet at longer or shorter intervals he had fits of impish recklessness, and did things that would have made the worst habits.

197

Hans in his right mind, however, was a lovable creature, and in Deronda he had happened to find a friend who was likely to stand by him with the more constancy, from compassion for these brief aberrations that might bring a long repentance. Hans, indeed, shared Deronda's rooms nearly as much as he used his own: to Deronda he poured himself out on his studies, his affairs, his hopes; the poverty of his home, and his love for the creatures there; the itching of his fingers to draw, and his determination to fight it away for the sake of getting some sort of plum that he might divide with his mother and the girls. He wanted no confidence in return, but seemed to take Deronda as an Olympian who needed nothing – an egotism in friendship which is common enough with mercurial, expansive natures. Deronda was content, and gave Meyrick all the interest he claimed, getting at last a brotherly anxiety about him, looking after him in his erratic moments, and contriving by adroitly delicate devices not only to make up for his friend's lack of pence, but to save him from threatening chances. Such friendship easily becomes tender: the one spreads strong sheltering wings that delight in spreading, the other gets the warm protection which is also a delight. Meyrick was going in for a classical scholarship, and his success, in various ways momentous, was the more probable from the steadying influence of Deronda's friendship.

But an imprudence of Meyrick's, committed at the beginning of the autumn term, threatened to disappoint his hopes. With his usual alternation between unnecessary expense and self-privation, he had given too much money for an old engraving which fascinated him, and to make up for it, had come from London in a third-class carriage with his eyes exposed to a bitter wind and any irritating particles the wind might drive before it. The consequence was a severe inflammation of the eyes, which for some time hung over him the threat of a lasting injury. This crushing trouble called out all Deronda's readiness to devote himself, and he made every other occupation secondary to that of being companion and eyes to Hans, working with him and for him at his classics, that if possible his chance of the classical scholarship might be saved. Hans, to keep the knowledge of his suffering from his mother and sisters, alleged his work as a reason for passing the Christmas at Cambridge, and his friend stayed up with him.

Meanwhile Deronda relaxed his hold on his mathematics, and Hans, reflecting on this, at length said, 'Old fellow, while you are hoisting me you are risking yourself. With your mathematical cram one may be like Moses or Mahomet or somebody of that sort who had to cram, and forgot in one day what it had taken him forty to learn.'

Deronda would not admit that he cared about the risk, and he had really been beguiled into a little indifference by double sympathy: he was very anxious that Hans should not miss the much-needed scholarship, and he felt a revival of interest in the old studies. Still, when Hans, rather late in the day, got able to use his own eyes, Deronda had tenacity enough to try hard and recover his lost ground. He failed, however; but he had the satisfaction of seeing Meyrick win.

Success, as a sort of beginning that urged completion, might have reconciled Deronda to his university course; but the emptiness of all things, from politics to pastimes, is never so striking to us as when we fail in them. The loss of the personal triumph had no severity for him, but the sense of having spent his time ineffectively in a mode of working which had been against the grain, gave him a distaste for any renewal of the process, which turned his imagined project of quitting Cambridge into a serious intention. In speaking of his intention to Meyrick he made it appear that he was glad of the turn events had taken – glad to have the balance dip decidedly, and feel freed from his hesitations; but he observed that he must of course submit to any strong objection on the part of Sir Hugo.

Meyrick's joy and gratitude were disturbed by much uneasiness. He believed in Deronda's alleged preference, but he felt keenly that in serving him Daniel had placed himself at a disadvantage in Sir Hugo's opinion, and he said mournfully, 'If you had got the scholarship, Sir Hugo would have thought that you asked to leave us with a better grace. You have spoilt your luck for my sake, and I can do nothing to mend it.'

'Yes, you can; you are to be a first-rate fellow. I call that a first-rate investment of my luck.'

'Oh, confound it! You save an ugly mongrel from drowning, and expect him to cut a fine figure. The poets have made tragedies enough about signing oneself over to wickedness for the sake of getting something plummy; I shall write a tragedy of a fellow who signed himself over to be good, and was uncomfortable ever after.'

But Hans lost no time in secretly writing the history of the affair to Sir Hugo, making it plain that but for Deronda's generous devotion he could hardly have failed to win the prize he had been working for.

The two friends went up to town together: Meyrick to rejoice with his mother and the girls in their little home at Chelsea; Deronda to carry out the less easy task of opening his mind to Sir Hugo. He relied a little on the baronet's general tolerance of eccentricities, but he expected more opposition than he met with. He was received with even warmer kindness than usual, the failure was passed over lightly, and when he detailed his reasons for wishing to quit the university and go to study abroad, Sir Hugo sat for some time in a silence which was rather meditative than surprised. At last he said, looking at Daniel with examination, 'So you don't want to be an Englishman to the backbone after all?'

'I want to be an Englishman, but I want to understand other points of view. And I want to get rid of a merely English attitude in studies.'

'I see; you don't want to be turned out in the same mould as every other youngster. And I have nothing to say against your doffing some of our national prejudices. I feel the better myself for having spent a good deal of my time abroad. But, for God's sake, keep an English cut, and don't become indifferent to bad tobacco! And – my dear boy – it is good to be unselfish and generous; but don't carry that too far. It will not do to give yourself to be melted down for the benefit of the tallow-trade; you must know where to find yourself. However, I shall put no veto on your going. Wait until I can get off Committee, and I'll run over with you.'

So Deronda went according to his will. But not before he had spent some hours with Hans Meyrick, and been introduced to the mother and sisters in the Chelsea home. The shy girls watched and registered every look of their brother's friend, declared by Hans to have been the salvation of him, a fellow like nobody else, and, in fine, a brick. They so thoroughly accepted Deronda as an ideal, that when he was gone the youngest set to work, under the criticism of the two elder girls, to paint him as Prince Camaralzaman.

XVII

'this is truth the poet sings,
That a sorrow's crown of sorrow is remembering happier things.'
– TENNYSON: *Locksley Hall*.

ON a fine evening near the end of July, Deronda was rowing himself on the Thames. It was already a year or more since he had come back to England, with the understanding that his education was finished, and that he was somehow to take his place in English society; but though, in deference to Sir Hugo's wish, and to fence off idleness, he had begun to read law, this apparent decision had been without other result than to deepen the roots of indecision. His old love of boating had revived with the more force now that he was in town with the Mallingers, because he could nowhere else get the same still seclusion which the river gave him. He had a boat of his own at Putney, and whenever Sir Hugo did not want him, it was his chief holiday to row till past sunset and come in again with the stars. Not that he was in a sentimental stage; but he was in another sort of contemplative mood perhaps more common in the young men of our day – that of questioning whether it were worth while to take part in the battle of the world: I mean, of course, the young men in whom the unproductive labour of questioning is sustained by three or five per cent on capital which somebody else has battled for. It puzzled Sir Hugo that one who made a splendid contrast with all that was sickly and puling should be hampered with ideas which, since they left an accomplished Whig like himself unobstructed, could be no better than spectral illusions; especially as Deronda set himself against authorship – a vocation which is understood to turn foolish thinking into funds.

Rowing in his dark-blue shirt and skull-cap, his curls closely clipped, his mouth beset with abundant soft waves of beard, he bore only disguised traces of the seraphic boy 'trailing clouds of glory.' Still, even one who had never seen him since his boyhood might have looked at him with slow recognition, due perhaps to the peculiarity of the gaze which Gwendolen chose to call 'dreadful,' though it had really a very mild sort of scrutiny. The voice, sometimes audible in subdued snatches of song, had turned out merely a high baritone; indeed, only to look at his lithe powerful frame and the firm gravity of his face would have been enough for an experienced guess that he had no rare and ravishing tenor such as nature reluctantly makes at some sacrifice. Look at his hands: they are not small and dimpled, with tapering fingers that seem to have only a deprecating touch: they are long, flexible, firmly-grasping hands, such as Titian has painted in a picture where he wanted to show the combination of refinement with force. And there is something of a likeness, too, between the faces belonging to the hands – in both the uniform pale-brown skin, the perpendicular brow, the calmly penetrating eyes. Not seraphic any longer: thoroughly terrestrial and manly; but still of a kind to raise belief in a human dignity which can afford to acknowledge poor relations.

Such types meet us here and there among average conditions; in a workman, for example, whistling over a bit of measurement and lifting his eyes to answer our question about the road. And often the grand meanings of faces as well as of written words may lie chiefly in the impressions of those who look on them. But it is precisely such impressions that happen just now to be of importance in relation to Deronda, rowing on the Thames in a very ordinary equipment for a young Englishman at leisure, and passing under Kew Bridge with no thought of an adventure in which his appearance was likely to play any part. In fact, he objected very strongly to the notion, which others had not allowed him to escape, that his appearance was of a kind to draw attention; and hints of this, intended to be complimentary, found an angry resonance in him, coming from mingled experiences, to which a clue has already been given. His own face in the glass had during many years been associated for him with thoughts of some one whom he must be like – one about whose character and lot he continually wondered, and never dared to ask.

In the neighbourhood of Kew Bridge, between six and seven o'clock, the river was no solitude. Several persons were sauntering on the towing-path, and here and there a boat was plying. Deronda had been rowing fast to get over this spot, when becoming aware of a great barge advancing towards him, he guided his boat aside, and rested on his oar within a couple of yards of the river-bank. He was all the while unconsciously continuing the low-toned chant which had haunted his throat all the way up the river – the gondolier's song in the 'Otello,' where Rossini has worthily set to music the immortal words of Dante –

> 'Nessun maggior dolore
> Che ricordarsi del tempo felice
> Nella miseria:'

and, as he rested on his oar, the pianissimo fall of the melodic wail 'nella miseria' was distinctly audible on the brink of the water. Three or four persons had paused at various spots to watch the barge passing the bridge, and doubtless included in their notice the young gentleman in the boat; but probably it was only to one ear that the low vocal sounds came with more significance than if they had been an insect murmur amidst the sum of current noises. Deronda, awaiting the barge, now turned his head to the river-side, and saw at a few yards' distance from him a figure which might have been an impersonation of the misery he was unconsciously giving voice to: a girl hardly more than eighteen, of low slim figure, with most delicate little face, her dark curls pushed behind her ears under a large black hat, a long woollen cloak over her shoulders. Her hands were hanging down clasped before her, and her eyes were fixed on the river with a look of immovable, statue-like despair. This strong arrest of his attention made him cease singing: apparently his voice had entered her inner world without her having taken any note of whence it came, for when it suddenly ceased she changed her attitude slightly, and, looking round with a frightened glance, met Deronda's face. It was but a couple of moments, but that seems a long while for two people to look straight at each other. Her look was something like that of a fawn or other gentle animal before it turns to run away: no blush, no special alarm, but only some timidity which yet could not hinder her from a long look before she turned. In fact, it seemed to Deronda that she was only half-conscious of her surroundings: was she hungry, or was there some other cause of bewilderment? He felt an outleap of interest and compassion towards her; but the next instant she had turned and walked away to a neighbouring bench under a tree. He had no right to linger and watch her: poorly-dressed, melancholy women are common sights; it was only the delicate beauty, the picturesque lines and colour of the image that were exceptional, and these conditions made it the more markedly impossible that he should obtrude his interest upon her. He began to row away, and was soon far up the river; but no other thoughts were busy enough quite to expel that pale image of unhappy girlhood. He fell again and again to speculating on the probable romance that lay behind that loneliness and look of desolation; then to smile at his own share in the prejudice that interesting faces must have interesting adventures; then to justify himself for feeling that sorrow was the more tragic when it befell delicate, childlike beauty.

'I should not have forgotten the look of misery if she had been ugly and vulgar,' he said to himself. But there was no denying that the attractiveness of the image made it like-lier to last. It was clear to him as an onyx cameo: the brown-black drapery, the white face with small, small features and dark, long-lashed eyes. His mind glanced over the girl-tragedies that are going on in the world, hidden, unheeded, as if they were but tragedies of the copse or hedgerow, where the helpless drag wounded wings forsakenly, and streak the shadowed moss with the red moment-hand of their own death. Deronda of late, in his solitary excursions, had been occupied chiefly with uncertainties about his own course; but those uncertainties, being much at their leisure, were wont to have such wide-sweeping connections with all life and history that the new image of helpless sorrow easily blent itself with what seemed to him the strong array of reasons why he should shrink from getting into that routine of the world which makes men apologize for all its wrong-doing, and take opinions as mere professional equipment – why he should not draw strongly at any thread in the hopelessly-entangled scheme of things.

He used his oars little, satisfied to go with the tide and be taken back by it. It was his habit to indulge himself in that solemn passivity which easily comes with the lengthening shadows and mellowing light, when thinking and desiring melt together imperceptibly, and what in other hours may have seemed argument takes the quality of passionate vision. By the time he had come back again with the tide past Richmond Bridge the sun was near setting; and the approach of his favourite hour – with its deepening stillness, and darkening masses of tree and building between the double glow of the sky and the river – disposed him to linger as if they had been an unfinished strain of music. He looked out for a perfectly solitary spot where he could lodge his boat against the bank, and throwing himself on his back with his head propped on the cushions, could watch out the light of sunset and the opening of that bead-roll which some oriental poet describes as God's call to the little stars, who each answer, 'Here am I.' He chose a spot in the bend of the river just opposite Kew Gardens, where he had a great breadth of water before him reflecting the glory of the sky, while he himself was in shadow. He lay with his hands behind his head propped on a level with the boat's edge, so that he could see all around him, but could not be seen by any one at a few yards' distance; and for a long while he never turned his eyes from the view right in front of him. He was forgetting everything else in a half-speculative, half-involuntary identification of himself with the objects he was looking at, thinking how far it might be possible habitually to shift his centre till his own personality would be no less outside him than the land-scape, – when the sense of something moving on the bank opposite him where it was bordered by a line of willow-bushes, made him turn his glance thitherward. In the first moment he had a darting presentiment about the moving figure; and now he could see the small face with the strange dying sunlight upon it. He feared to frighten her by a sudden movement, and watched her with motionless attention. She looked round, but seemed only to gather security from the apparent solitude, hid her hat among the willows, and immediately took off her woollen cloak. Presently she seated herself and deliberately dipped the cloak in the water, holding it there a little while, then taking it out with effort, rising from her seat as she did so. By this time Deronda felt sure that she meant to wrap the wet cloak round her as a drowning-shroud; there was no longer time to hesitate about frightening her. He rose and seized his oar to ply across; happily her position lay a little below him. The poor thing, overcome with terror at this sign of discovery from the opposite bank, sank down on the brink again, holding her cloak but half out of the water. She crouched and covered her face as if she kept a faint hope that she had not been seen, and that the boatman was accidentally coming towards her. But soon he was within brief space of her, steadying his boat against the bank, and speaking, but very gently –

'Don't be afraid. ... You are unhappy. ... Pray, trust me. ... Tell me what I can do to help you.'

She raised her head and looked up at him. His face now was towards the light, and she knew it again. But she did not speak for a few moments which were a renewal of their former gaze at each other. At last she said in a low sweet voice, with an accent so distinct that it suggested foreign-ness and yet was not foreign, 'I saw you before;' ... and then added, dreamily, after a like pause, 'nella miseria.'

Deronda, not understanding the connection of her thought, supposed that her mind was weakened by distress and hunger.

'It was you, singing?' she went on, hesitatingly – 'Nessun maggior dolore.' ... The mere words themselves uttered in her sweet undertones seemed to give the melody to Deronda's ear.

'Ah, yes,' he said, understanding now, 'I am often singing them. But I fear you will injure yourself staying here. Pray let me carry you in my boat to some place of safety. And that wet cloak – let me take it.'

He would not attempt to take it without her leave, dreading lest he should scare her. Even at his words, he fancied that she shrank and clutched the cloak more tenaciously. But her eyes were fixed on him with a question in them as she said, 'You look good. Perhaps it is God's command.'

'Do trust me. Let me help you. I will die before I will let any harm come to you.'

She rose from her sitting posture, first dragging the saturated cloak and then letting it fall on the ground – it was too heavy for her tired arms. Her little woman's figure as she laid her delicate chilled hands together one over the other against her waist, and went a step backward while she leaned her head forward as if not to lose her sight of his face, was unspeakably touching.

'Great God!' the words escaped Deronda in a tone so low and solemn that they seemed like a prayer become unconsciously vocal. The agitating impression this forsaken girl was making on him stirred a fibre that lay close to his deepest interest in the fates of women – 'perhaps my mother was like this one.' The old thought had come now with a new impetus of mingled feeling, and urged that exclamation in which both East and West have for ages concentrated their awe in the presence of inexorable calamity.

The low-toned words seemed to have some reassurance in them for the hearer: she stepped forward close to the boat's side, and Deronda put out his hand, hoping now that she would let him help her in. She had already put her tiny hand into his which closed round it, when some new thought struck her, and drawing back she said –

'I have nowhere to go – nobody belonging to me in all this land.'

'I will take you to a lady who has daughters,' said Deronda, immediately. He felt a sort of relief in gathering that the wretched home and cruel friends he imagined her to be fleeing from were not in the near background. Still she hesitated, and said more timidly than ever –

'Do you belong to the theatre?'

'No; I have nothing to do with the theatre,' said Deronda, in a decided tone. Then beseechingly, 'I will put you in perfect safety at once; with a lady, a good woman; I am sure she will be kind. Let us lose no time: you will make yourself ill. Life may still become sweet to you. There are good people – there are good women who will take care of you.'

She drew backward no more, but stepped in easily, as if she were used to such action, and sat down on the cushions.

'You had a covering for your head,' said Deronda.

'My hat?' (she lifted up her hands to her head). 'It is quite hidden in the bush.'

'I will find it,' said Deronda, putting out his hand deprecatingly as she attempted to rise. 'The boat is fixed.'

He jumped out, found the hat, and lifted up the saturated cloak, wringing it and throwing it into the bottom of the boat.

'We must carry the cloak away, to prevent any one who may have noticed you from thinking you have been drowned,' he said cheerfully, as he got in again and presented the old hat to her. 'I wish I had any other garment than my coat to offer you. But shall you mind throwing it over your shoulders while we are on the water? It is quite an ordinary thing to do, when people return late and are not enough provided with wraps.' He held out the coat towards her with a smile, and there came a faint melancholy smile in answer, as she took it and put it on very cleverly.

'I have some biscuits – should you like them?' said Deronda.

'No; I cannot eat. I had still some money left to buy bread.'

He began to ply his oar without further remark, and they went along swiftly for many minutes without speaking. She did not look at him, but was watching the oar, leaning forward in an attitude of repose, as if she were beginning to feel the comfort of returning warmth and the prospect of life instead of death. The twilight was deepening; the red flush was all gone and the little stars were giving their answer one after another. The moon was rising, but was still entangled among trees and buildings. The light was not such that he could distinctly discern the expression of her features or her glance, but they were distinctly before him nevertheless – features and a glance which seemed to have given a fuller meaning for him to the human face. Among his anxieties one was dominant: his first impression about her, that her mind might be disordered, had not been quite dissipated: the project of suicide was unmistakable, and gave a deeper colour to every other suspicious sign. He longed to begin a conversation, but abstained, wishing to encourage the confidence that might induce her to speak first. At last she did speak.

'I like to listen to the oar.'

'So do I.'

'If you had not come, I should have been dead now.'

'I cannot bear you to speak of that. I hope you will never be sorry that I came.'

'I cannot see how I shall be glad to live. The *maggior dolore* and the *miseria* have lasted longer than the *tempo felice*.' She paused and then went on dreamily, – '*Dolore – miseria* – I think those words are alive.'

Deronda was mute: to question her seemed an unwarrantable freedom; he shrank from appearing to claim the authority of a benefactor, or to treat her with the less reverence because she was in distress. She went on, musingly –

'I thought it was not wicked. Death and life are one before the Eternal. I know our fathers slew their children and then slew themselves, to keep their souls pure. I meant it so. But now I am commanded to live. I cannot see how I shall live.'

'You will find friends. I will find them for you.'

She shook her head and said mournfully, 'Not my mother and brother. I cannot find them.'

'You are English? You must be – speaking English so perfectly.'

She did not answer immediately, but looked at Deronda again, straining to see him in the doubtful light. Until now she had been watching the oar. It seemed as if she were half roused, and wondered which part of her impressions was dreaming and which waking. Sorrowful isolation had benumbed her sense of reality, and the power of distinguishing outward and inward was continually slipping away from her. Her look was full of wondering timidity, such as the forsaken one in the desert might have lifted to the angelic vision before she knew whether his message were in anger or in pity.

'You want to know if I am English?' she said at last, while Deronda was reddening nervously under a gaze which he felt more fully than he saw.

'I want to know nothing except what you like to tell me,' he said, still uneasy in the fear that her mind was wandering. 'Perhaps it is not good for you to talk.'

'Yes, I will tell you. I am English-born. But I am a Jewess.'

Deronda was silent, inwardly wondering that he had not said this to himself before, though any one who had seen delicate-faced Spanish girls might simply have guessed her to be Spanish.

'Do you despise me for it?' she said presently in low tones, which had a sadness that pierced like a cry from a small dumb creature in fear.

'Why should I?' said Deronda. 'I am not so foolish.'

'I know many Jews are bad.'

'So are many Christians. But I should not think it fair for you to despise me because of that.'

211

'My mother and brother were good. But I shall never find them. I am come a long way – from abroad. I ran away: but I cannot tell you – I cannot speak of it. I thought I might find my mother again – God would guide me. But then I despaired. This morning when the light came, I felt as if one word kept sounding within me – Never! never! But now – I begin – to think—' her words were broken by rising sobs – 'I am commanded to live – perhaps we are going to her.'

With an outburst of weeping she buried her head on her knees. He hoped that this passionate weeping might relieve her excitement. Meanwhile he was inwardly picturing in much embarrassment how he should present himself with her in Park Lane – the course which he had at first unreflectingly determined on. No one kinder and more gentle than Lady Mallinger; but it was hardly probable that she would be at home; and he had a shuddering sense of a lackey staring at this delicate, sorrowful image of womanhood – of glaring lights and fine staircases, and perhaps chilling suspicious manners from lady's-maid and housekeeper that might scare the mind already in a state of dangerous susceptibility. But to take her to any other shelter than a home already known to him was not to be contemplated: he was full of fears about the issue of the adventure which had brought on him a responsibility all the heavier for the strong and agitating impression this childlike creature had made on him. But another resource came to mind: he could venture to take her to Mrs. Meyrick's – to the small home at Chelsea, where he had been often enough since his return from abroad to feel sure that he could appeal there to generous hearts, which had a romantic readiness to believe in innocent need and to help it. Hans Meyrick was safe away in Italy, and Deronda felt the comfort of presenting himself with his charge at a house where he would be met by a motherly figure of quakerish neatness, and three girls who hardly knew of any evil closer to them than what lay in history books and dramas, and would at once associate a lovely Jewess with

Rebecca in 'Ivanhoe,' besides thinking that everything they did at Deronda's request would be done for their idol, Hans. The vision of the Chelsea home once raised, Deronda no longer hesitated.

The rumbling thither in the cab after the stillness of the water seemed long. Happily his charge had been quiet since her fit of weeping, and submitted like a tired child. When they were in the cab, she laid down her hat and tried to rest her head, but the jolting movement would not let it rest: still she dozed, and her sweet head hung helpless first on one side, then on the other.

'They are too good to have any fear about taking her in,' thought Deronda. Her person, her voice, her exquisite utterance, were one strong appeal to belief and tenderness. Yet what had been the history which had brought her to this desolation? He was going on a strange errand – to ask shelter for this waif. Then there occurred to him the beautiful story Plutarch somewhere tells of the Delphic women: how when the Mænads, outworn with their torch-lit wanderings, lay down to sleep in the market-place, the matrons came and stood silently round them to keep guard over their slumbers; then, when they waked, ministered to them tenderly and saw them safely to their own borders. He could trust the women he was going to for having hearts as good.

Deronda felt himself growing older this evening and entering on a new phase in finding a life to which his own had come – perhaps as a rescue; but how to make sure that snatching from death was rescue? The moment of finding a fellow-creature is often as full of mingled doubt and exultation as the moment of finding an idea.

XVIII

Life is a various mother: now she dons
Her plumes and brilliants, climbs the marble stairs
With head aloft, nor ever turns her eyes
On lackeys who attend her; now she dwells
Grim-clad up darksome alleys, breathes hot gin,
And screams in pauper riot.
                                    But to these
She came a frugal matron, neat and deft,
With cheerful morning thoughts and quick device
To find the much in little.

MRS. MEYRICK'S house was not noisy: the front parlour
looked on the river, and the back on gardens, so that
though she was reading aloud to her daughters, the window
could be left open to freshen the air of the small double
room where a lamp and two candles were burning. The
candles were on a table apart for Kate, who was drawing
illustrations for a publisher; the lamp was not only for the
reader but for Amy and Mab, who were embroidering satin
cushions for 'the great world.'

Outside, the house looked very narrow and shabby, the
bright light through the holland blind showing the heavy
old-fashioned window-frame; but it is pleasant to know
that many such grim-walled slices of space in our foggy
London have been, and still are the homes of a culture the
more spotlessly free from vulgarity, because poverty has
rendered everything like display an impersonal question,
and all the grand shows of the world simply a spectacle
which rouses no petty rivalry or vain effort after possession.

The Meyricks' was a home of that kind; and they all
clung to this particular house in a row because its interior
was filled with objects always in the same places, which for
the mother held memories of her marriage time, and for
the young ones seemed as necessary and uncriticized a part
of their world as the stars of the Great Bear seen from the
back windows. Mrs. Meyrick had borne much stint of other
matters that she might be able to keep some engravings
specially cherished by her husband; and the narrow spaces

of wall held a world-history in scenes and heads which the children had early learned by heart. The chairs and tables were also old friends preferred to new. But in these two little parlours with no furniture that a broker would have cared to cheapen except the prints and piano, there was space and apparatus for a wide-glancing, nicely-select life, open to the highest things in music, painting, and poetry. I am not sure that in the times of greatest scarcity, before Kate could get paid work, these ladies had always had a servant to light their fires and sweep their rooms; yet they were fastidious in some points, and could not believe that the manners of ladies in the fashionable world were so full of coarse selfishness, petty quarrelling, and slang as they are represented to be in what are called literary photographs. The Meyricks had their little oddities, streaks of eccentricity from the mother's blood as well as the father's, their minds being like mediæval houses with unexpected recesses and openings from this into that, flights of steps and sudden outlooks.

But mother and daughters were all united by a triple bond – family love; admiration for the finest work, the best action; and habitual industry. Hans's desire to spend some of his money in making their lives more luxurious had been resisted by all of them, and both they and he had been thus saved from regrets at the threatened triumph of his yearning for art over the attractions of secured income – a triumph that would by-and-by oblige him to give up his fellowship. They could all afford to laugh at his Gavarnicaricatures and to hold him blameless in following a natural bent which their unselfishness and independence had left without obstacle. It was enough for them to go on in their old way, only having a grand treat of opera-going (to the gallery) when Hans came home on a visit.

Seeing the group they made this evening, one could hardly wish them to change their way of life. They were all alike small, and so in due proportion with their miniature rooms. Mrs. Meyrick was reading aloud from a French book: she was a lively little woman, half French, half

Scotch, with a pretty articulateness of speech that seemed to make daylight in her hearer's understanding. Though she was not yet fifty, her rippling hair, covered by a quakerish net cap, was chiefly grey, but her eyebrows were brown as the bright eyes below them; her black dress, almost like a priest's cassock with its row of buttons, suited a neat figure hardly five feet high. The daughters were to match the mother, except that Mab had Hans's light hair and complexion, with a bossy irregular brow and other quaintnesses that reminded one of him. Everything about them was compact, from the firm coils of their hair, fastened back *à la Chinoise*, to their grey skirts in puritan nonconformity with the fashion, which at that time would have demanded that four feminine circumferences should fill all the free space in the front parlour. All four, if they had been wax-work, might have been packed easily in a fashionable lady's travelling trunk. Their faces seemed full of speech, as if their minds had been shelled, after the manner of horse-chestnuts, and become brightly visible. The only large thing of its kind in the room was Hafiz, the Persian cat, comfortably poised on the brown leather back of a chair, and opening his large eyes now and then to see that the lower animals were not in any mischief.

The book Mrs. Meyrick had before her was Erckmann-Chatrian's *Histoire d'un Conscrit*. She had just finished reading it aloud, and Mab, who had let her work fall on the ground while she stretched her head forward and fixed her eyes on the reader, exclaimed –

'I think that is the finest story in the world.'

'Of course, Mab!' said Amy, 'it is the last you have heard. Everything that pleases you is the best in its turn.'

'It is hardly to be called a story,' said Kate. 'It is a bit of history brought near us with a strong telescope. We can see the soldiers' faces: no, it is more than that – we can hear everything – we can almost hear their hearts beat.'

'I don't care what you call it,' said Mab, flirting away her thimble. 'Call it a chapter in Revelations. It makes me want to do something good, something grand. It makes me so sorry for everybody. It makes me like Schiller – I want to take the world in my arms and kiss it. I must kiss you instead little mother!' She threw her arms round her mother's neck.

'Whenever you are in that mood, Mab, down goes your work,' said Amy. 'It would be doing something good to finish your cushion without soiling it.'

'Oh – oh – oh!' groaned Mab, as she stooped to pick up her work and thimble. 'I wish I had three wounded conscripts to take care of.'

'You would spill their beef-tea while you were talking,' said Amy.

'Poor Mab! don't be hard on her,' said the mother. 'Give me the embroidery now, child. You go on with your enthusiasm, and I will go on with the pink and white poppy.'

'Well, ma, I think you are more caustic than Amy,' said Kate, while she drew her head back to look at her drawing.

'Oh – oh – oh!' cried Mab again, rising and stretching her arms. 'I wish something wonderful would happen. I feel like the deluge. The waters of the great deep are broken up, and the windows of heaven are opened. I must sit down and play the scales.'

Mab was opening the piano while the others were laughing at this climax, when a cab stopped before the house, and there forthwith came a quick rap of the knocker.

'Dear me!' said Mrs. Meyrick, starting up, 'it is after ten, and Phœbe is gone to bed.' She hastened out, leaving the parlour door open.

'Mr. Deronda!' The girls could hear this exclamation from their mamma. Mab clasped her hands, saying in a loud whisper, 'There now! Something *is* going to happen;' Kate and Amy gave up their work in amazement. But Deronda's tone in reply was so low that they could not hear his words, and Mrs. Meyrick immediately closed the parlour door.

'I know I am trusting to your goodness in a most extraordinary way,' Deronda went on, after giving his brief narrative, 'but you can imagine how helpless I feel with a young creature like this on my hands. I could not go with her among strangers, and in her nervous state I should dread taking her into a house full of servants. I have trusted to your mercy. I hope you will not think my act unwarrantable.'

'On the contrary. You have honoured me by trusting me. I see your difficulty. Pray bring her in. I will go and prepare the girls.'

While Deronda went back to the cab, Mrs. Meyrick turned into the parlour again and said, 'Here is somebody to take care of instead of your wounded conscripts, Mab: a poor girl who was going to drown herself in despair. Mr. Deronda found her only just in time to save her. He brought her along in his boat, and did not know what else it would be safe to do with her, so he has trusted us and brought her here. It seems she is a Jewess, but quite refined, he says – knowing Italian and music.'

The three girls, wondering and expectant, came forward and stood near each other in mute confidence that they were all feeling alike under this appeal to their compassion. Mab looked rather awe-stricken, as if this answer to her wish were something preternatural.

Meanwhile Deronda going to the door of the cab where the pale face was now gazing out with roused observation, said, 'I have brought you to some of the kindest people in the world: there are daughters like you. It is a happy home. Will you let me take you to them?'

She stepped out obediently, putting her hand in his and forgetting her hat; and when Deronda led her into the full light of the parlour where the four little women stood awaiting her, she made a picture that would have stirred much duller sensibilities than theirs. At first she was a little dazed by the sudden light, and before she had concentrated her glance he had put her hand into the mother's. He was inwardly rejoicing that the Meyricks were so small: the dark-curled head was the highest among them. The poor wanderer could not be afraid of these gentle faces so near hers; and now she was looking at each of them in turn while the mother said, 'You must be weary, poor child.'

'We will take care of you – we will comfort you – we will love you,' cried Mab, no longer able to restrain herself, and taking the small right hand caressingly between both her own. This gentle welcoming warmth was penetrating the bewildered one: she hung back just enough to see better the four faces in front of her, whose goodwill was being reflected in hers, not in any smile, but in that undefinable change which tells us that anxiety is passing into contentment. For an instant she looked up at Deronda, as if she were referring all this mercy to him, and then again turning to Mrs. Meyrick, said with more collectedness in her sweet tones than he had heard before –

'I am a stranger. I am a Jewess. You might have thought I was wicked.'

'No, we are sure you are good,' burst out Mab.

'We think no evil of you, poor child. You shall be safe with us,' said Mrs. Meyrick. 'Come now and sit down. You must have some food, and then go to rest.'

The stranger looked up again at Deronda, who said –

'You will have no more fears with these friends? You will rest to-night?'

'Oh, I should not fear. I should rest. I think these are the ministering angels.'

Mrs. Meyrick wanted to lead her to a seat, but again hanging back gently, the poor weary thing spoke as if with a scruple at being received without a further account of herself:

'My name is Mirah Lapidoth. I am come a long way, all the way from Prague by myself. I made my escape. I ran away from dreadful things. I came to find my mother and brother in London. I had been taken from my mother when I was little, but I thought I could find her again. I had trouble – the houses were all gone – I could not find her. It has been a long while, and I had not much money. That is why I am in distress.'

'Our mother will be good to you,' cried Mab. 'See what a nice little mother she is!'

'Do sit down now,' said Kate, moving a chair forward, while Amy ran to get some tea.

Mirah resisted no longer, but seated herself with perfect grace, crossing her little feet, laying her hands one over the other on her lap, and looking at her friends with placid reverence; whereupon Hafiz, who had been watching the scene restlessly, came forward with tail erect and rubbed himself against her ankles. Deronda felt it time to take his leave.

'Will you allow me to come again and inquire – perhaps at five to-morrow?' he said to Mrs. Meyrick.

'Yes, pray; we shall have had time to make acquaintance then.'

'Good-bye,' said Deronda, looking down at Mirah, and putting out his hand. She rose as she took it, and the moment brought back to them both strongly the other moment when she had first taken that outstretched hand. She lifted her eyes to his and said with reverential fervour, 'The God of our fathers bless you and deliver you from all evil as you have delivered me. I did not believe there was any man so good. None before have thought me worthy of the best. You found me poor and miserable, yet you have given me the best.'

Deronda could not speak, but with silent adieux to the Meyricks, hurried away.

BOOK III
Maidens Choosing

XIX

'I pity the man who can travel from Dan to Beersheba, and say,
"Tis all barren;" and so it is: and so is all the world to him who will
not cultivate the fruits it offers.'
— STERNE: *Sentimental Journey.*

To say that Deronda was romantic would be to misrepres-
ent him; but under his calm and somewhat self-repressed
exterior there was a fervour which made him easily find
poetry and romance among the events of everyday life.
And perhaps poetry and romance are as plentiful as ever in
the world except for those phlegmatic natures who I suspect would in any age have regarded them as a dull form of
erroneous thinking. They exist very easily in the same
room with the microscope and even in railway carriages:
what banishes them is the vacuum in gentlemen and lady
passengers. How should all the apparatus of heaven and
earth, from the farthest firmament to the tender bosom of
the mother who nourished us, make poetry for a mind that
has no movements of awe and tenderness, no sense of
fellowship which thrills from the near to the distant, and
back again from the distant to the near?

To Deronda this event of finding Mirah was as heart-
stirring as anything that befell Orestes or Rinaldo. He sat
up half the night, living again through the moments since
he had first discerned Mirah on the river-brink, with the
fresh and fresh vividness which belongs to emotive memory. When he took up a book to try and dull this urgency of
inward vision, the printed words were no more than a network through which he saw and heard everything as clearly
as before – saw not only the actual events of two hours, but
possibilities of what had been and what might be which
those events were enough to feed with the warm blood of
passionate hope and fear. Something in his own experience

caused Mirah's search after her mother to lay hold with peculiar force on his imagination. The first prompting of sympathy was to aid her in the search: if given persons were extant in London there were ways of finding them, as subtle as scientific experiment, the right machinery being set at work. But here the mixed feelings which belonged to Deronda's kindred experience naturally transfused themselves into his anxiety on behalf of Mirah.

The desire to know his own mother, or to know about her, was constantly haunted with dread; and in imagining what might befall Mirah it quickly occurred to him that finding the mother and brother from whom she had been parted when she was a little one might turn out to be a calamity. When she was in the boat she said that her mother and brother were good; but the goodness might have been chiefly in her own ignorant innocence and yearning memory, and the ten or twelve years since the parting had been time enough for much worsening. Spite of his strong tendency to side with the objects of prejudice, and in general with those who got the worst of it, his interest had never been practically drawn towards existing Jews, and the facts he knew about them, whether they walked conspicuous in fine apparel or lurked in by-streets, were chiefly of the sort most repugnant to him. Of learned and accomplished Jews he took it for granted that they had dropped their religion, and wished to be merged in the people of their native lands. Scorn flung at a Jew as such would have roused all his sympathy in griefs of inheritance; but the indiscriminate scorn of a race will often strike a specimen who has well earned it on his own account, and might fairly be gibbeted as a rascally son of Adam. It appears that the Caribs, who know little of theology, regard thieving as a practice peculiarly connected with Christian tenets, and probably they could allege experimental grounds for this opinion. Deronda could not escape (who can?) knowing ugly stories of Jewish characteristics and occupations; and though one of his favourite protests was against the severance of past

222

and present history, he was like others who shared his
protest, in never having cared to reach any more special
conclusions about actual Jews than that they retained the
virtues and vices of a long-oppressed race. But now that
Mirah's longing roused his mind to a closer survey of
details, very disagreeable images urged themselves of
what it might be to find out this middle-aged Jewess and
her son. To be sure, there was the exquisite refinement
and charm of the creature herself to make a presumption
in favour of her immediate kindred, but – he must wait to
know more: perhaps through Mrs. Meyrick he might
gather some guiding hints from Mirah's own lips. Her
voice, her accent, her looks – all the sweet purity that
clothed her as with a consecrating garment made him
shrink the more from giving her, either ideally or practically, an association with what was hateful or contaminat-
ing. But these fine words with which we fumigate and
becloud unpleasant facts are not the language in which we
think. Deronda's thinking went on in rapid images of what
might be: he saw himself guided by some official scout
into a dingy street; he entered through a dim doorway, and
saw a hawk-eyed woman, rough-headed, and unwashed,
cheapening a hungry girl's last bit of finery; or in some
quarter only the more hideous for being smarter, he found
himself under the breath of a young Jew talkative and
familiar, willing to show his acquaintance with gentlemen's tastes, and not fastidious in any transactions with
which they would favour him – and so on through the brief
chapter of his experience in this kind. Excuse him: his
mind was not apt to run spontaneously into insulting
ideas, or to practise a form of wit which identifies Moses
with the advertisement sheet; but he was just now governed by dread, and if Mirah's parents had been Christian,
the chief difference would have been that his forebodings
would have been fed with wider knowledge. It was the
habit of his mind to connect dread with unknown parentage, and in this case as well as his own there was enough to
make the connection reasonable.

But what was to be done with Mirah? She needed shelter and protection in the fullest sense, and all his chivalrous sentiment roused itself to insist that the sooner and the more fully he could engage for her the interest of others besides himself, the better he should fulfil her claims on him. He had no right to provide for her entirely, though he might be able to do so; the very depth of the impression she had produced made him desire that she should understand herself to be entirely independent of him; and vague visions of the future which he tried to dispel as fantastic left their influence in an anxiety, stronger than any motive he could give for it, that those who saw his actions closely should be acquainted from the first with the history of his relation to Mirah. He had learned to hate secrecy about the grand ties and obligations of his life – to hate it the more because a strong spell of interwoven sensibilities hindered him from breaking such secrecy. Deronda had made a vow to himself that – since the truths which disgrace mortals are not all of their own making – the truth should never be made a disgrace to another by his act. He was not without terror lest he should break this vow, and fall into the apologetic philosophy which explains the world into containing nothing better than one's own conduct.

At one moment he resolved to tell the whole of his adventure to Sir Hugo and Lady Mallinger the next morning at breakfast, but the possibility that something quite new might reveal itself on his next visit to Mrs. Meyrick's checked this impulse, and he finally went to sleep on the conclusion that he would wait until that visit had been made.

XX

'It will hardly be denied that even in this frail and corrupted world, we sometimes meet persons who, in their very mien and aspect, as well as in the whole habit of life, manifest such a signature and stamp of virtue, as to make our judgment of them a matter of intuition rather than the result of continued examination.'

– ALEXANDER KNOX: quoted in Southey's Life of Wesley.

MIRAH said that she had slept well that night; and when she came down in Mab's black dress, her dark hair curling in fresh fibrils as it gradually dried from its plenteous bath, she looked like one who was beginning to take comfort after the long sorrow and watching which had paled her cheek and made deep blue semicircles under her eyes. It was Mab who carried her breakfast and ushered her down – with some pride in the effect produced by a pair of tiny felt slippers which she had rushed out to buy because there were no shoes in the house small enough for Mirah, whose borrowed dress ceased about her ankles and displayed the cheap clothing that moulding itself on her feet seemed an adornment as choice as the sheaths of buds. The farthing buckles were bijoux.

'Oh, if you please, mamma!' cried Mab, clasping her hands and stooping towards Mirah's feet, as she entered the parlour. 'Look at the slippers, how beautifully they fit! I declare she is like the Queen Budoor – "two delicate feet, the work of the protecting and all-recompensing Creator, support her; and I wonder how they can sustain what is above them."'

Mirah looked down at her own feet in a child-like way and then smiled at Mrs. Meyrick, who was saying inwardly, 'One could hardly imagine this creature having an evil thought. But wise people would tell me to be cautious.' She returned Mirah's smile and said, 'I fear the feet have had to sustain their burthen a little too often lately. But to-day she will rest and be my companion.'

'And she will tell you so many things and I shall not hear them,' grumbled Mab, who felt herself in the first volume of a delightful romance and obliged to miss some chapters because she had to go to pupils.

Kate was already gone to make sketches along the river, and Amy was away on business errands. It was what the mother wished, to be alone with this stranger, whose story must be a sorrowful one, yet was needful to be told.

The small front parlour was as good as a temple that morning. The sunlight was on the river and soft air came in through the open window; the walls showed a glorious silent cloud of witnesses – the Virgin soaring amid her cherubic escort; grand Melancholia with her solemn universe; the Prophets and Sibyls; the School of Athens; the Last Supper; mystic groups where far-off ages made one moment; grave Holbein and Rembrandt heads; the Tragic Muse; last-century children at their musings or their play; Italian poets – all were there through the medium of a little black and white. The neat mother who had weathered her troubles, and come out of them with a face still cheerful, was sorting coloured wools for her embroidery. Hafiz purred on the window-ledge, the clock on the mantelpiece ticked without hurry, and the occasional sound of wheels seemed to lie outside the more massive central quiet. Mrs. Meyrick thought that this quiet might be the best invitation to speech on the part of her companion, and chose not to disturb it by remark. Mirah sat opposite in her former attitude, her hands clasped on her lap, her ankles crossed, her eyes at first travelling slowly over the objects around her, but finally resting with a sort of placid reverence on Mrs. Meyrick. At length she began to speak softly.

'I remember my mother's face better than anything; yet I was not seven when I was taken away, and I am nineteen now.'

'I can understand that,' said Mrs. Meyrick. 'There are some earliest things that last the longest.'

'Oh yes, it was the earliest. I think my life began with waking up and loving my mother's face: it was so near to me, and her arms were round me, and she sang to me. One hymn she sang so often, so often: and then she taught me to sing it with her: it was the first I ever sang. They were always Hebrew hymns she sang; and because I never knew the meaning of the words they seemed full of nothing but our love and happiness. When I lay in my little bed and it was all white above me, she used to bend over me between me and the white, and sing in a sweet low voice. I can dream myself back into that time when I am awake, and often it comes back to me in my sleep – my hand is very little, I put it up to her face and she kisses it. Sometimes in my dream I begin to tremble and think that we are both dead; but then I wake up and my hand lies like this, and for a moment I hardly know myself. But if I could see my mother again, I should know her.'

'You must expect some change after twelve years,' said Mrs. Meyrick, gently. 'See my grey hair: ten years ago it was bright brown. The days and the months pace over us like restless little birds, and leave the marks of their feet backwards and forwards; especially when they are like birds with heavy hearts – then they tread heavily.'

'Ah, I am sure her heart has been heavy for want of me. But to feel her joy if we could meet again, and I could make her know how I love her and give her deep comfort after all her mourning! If that could be, I should mind nothing; I should be glad that I have lived through my trouble. I did despair. The world seemed miserable and wicked; none helped me so that I could bear their looks and words; I felt that my mother was dead, and death was the only way to her. But then in the last moment – yesterday, when I longed for the water to close over me – and I thought that death was the best image of mercy – then goodness came to me living, and I felt trust in the living. And – it is strange – but I began to hope that she was living too. And now I am with you – here – this morning, peace and hope have come into me like a flood. I want nothing; I can wait; because I hope and believe and am grateful – oh, so grateful! You have not thought evil of me – you have not despised me.'

Mirah spoke with low-toned fervour, and sat as still as a picture all the while.

'Many others would have felt as we do, my dear,' said Mrs. Meyrick, feeling a mist come over her eyes as she looked at her work.

'But I did not meet them – they did not come to me.'

'How was it that you were taken from your mother?'

'Ah, I am a long while coming to that. It is dreadful to speak of, yet I must tell you – I must tell you everything. My father – it was he who took me away. I thought we were only going on a little journey; and I was pleased. There was a box with all my little things in. But we went on board a ship, and got farther and farther away from the land. Then I was ill; and I thought it would never end – it was the first misery, and it seemed endless. But at last we landed. I knew nothing then, and believed what my father said. He comforted me, and told me I should go back to my mother. But it was America we had reached, and it was long years before we came back to Europe. At first I often asked my father when we were going back; and I tried to learn writing fast, because I wanted to write to my mother; but one day when he found me trying to write a letter, he took me on his knee and told me that my mother and brother were dead; that was why we did not go back. I remember my brother a little; he carried me once; but he was not always at home. I believed my father when he said that they were dead. I saw them under the earth when he said they were there, with their eyes for ever closed. I never thought of its not being true; and I used to cry every night in my bed for a long while. Then when she came so often to me, in my sleep, I thought she must be living about me though I could not always see her, and that comforted me. I was never afraid in the dark, because of that; and very often in the day I used to shut my eyes and bury my face and try to see her and to hear her singing. I came to do that at last without shutting my eyes.'

Mirah paused with a sweet content in her face, as if she were having her happy vision, while she looked out towards the river.

'Still your father was not unkind to you, I hope,' said Mrs. Meyrick, after a minute, anxious to recall her.

'No; he petted me, and took pains to teach me. He was an actor; and I found out, after, that the "Coburg" I used to hear of his going to at home was a theatre. But he had more to do with the theatre than acting. He had not always been an actor; he had been a teacher, and knew many languages. His acting was not very good, I think; but he managed the stage, and wrote and translated plays. An Italian lady, a singer, lived with us a long time. They both taught me; and I had a master besides, who made me learn by heart and recite. I worked quite hard, though I was so little; and I was not nine when I first went on the stage. I could easily learn things, and I was not afraid. But then and ever since I hated our way of life. My father had money, and we had finery about us in a disorderly way; always there were men and women coming and going, there was loud laughing and disputing, strutting, snapping of fingers, jeering, faces I did not like to look at – though many petted and caressed me. But then I remembered my mother. Even at first when I understood nothing, I shrank away from all those things outside me into companionship with thoughts that were not like them; and I gathered thoughts very fast, because I read many things – plays and poetry, Shakespeare and Schiller, and learned evil and good. My father began to believe that I might be a great singer: my voice was considered wonderful for a child; and he had the best teaching for me. But it was painful that he boasted of me, and set me to sing for show at any minute, as if I had been a musical box. Once when I was ten years old, I played the part of a little girl who had been forsaken and did not know it, and sat singing to herself while she played with flowers. I did it without any trouble; but the clapping and all the sounds of the theatre were hateful to me; and I never liked the praise I had, because it seemed all very hard and unloving: I missed the love and the trust I had been born into. I made a life in my own thoughts quite different from everything about me: I chose what seemed to me beautiful out of the plays and everything, and made my world out of it; and it was like a sharp knife always grazing me that we had two sorts of life which jarred so with each other – women looking good and gentle on the stage, and saying good things as if they felt them, and directly after I saw them with coarse, ugly manners. My father sometimes noticed my shrinking ways; and Signora said one day when I had been rehearsing, "She will never be an artist: she has no notion of being anybody but herself. That does very well now, but by-and-by you will see – she will have no more face and action than a singing-bird." My father was angry, and they quarrelled. I sat alone and cried, because what she had said was like a long unhappy future unrolled before me. I did not want to be an artist; but this was what my father expected of me. After a while Signora left us, and a governess used to come and give me lessons in different things, because my father began to be afraid of my singing too much; but I still acted from time to time. Rebellious feelings grew stronger in me, and I wished to get away from this life; but I could not tell where to go, and I dreaded the world. Besides, I felt it would be wrong to leave my father: I dreaded doing wrong, for I thought I might get wicked and hateful to myself, in the same way that many others seemed hateful to me. For so long, so long I had never felt my outside world happy; and if I got wicked I should lose my world of happy thoughts where my mother lived with me. That was my childish notion all through those years. Oh how long they were!'

Mirah fell to musing again.

'Had you no teaching about what was your duty?' said Mrs. Meyrick. She did not like to say 'religion' – finding herself on inspection rather dim as to what the Hebrew religion might have turned into at this date.

'No – only that I ought to do what my father wished. He did not follow our religion at New York, and I think he wanted me not to know much about it. But because my mother used to take me to the synagogue, and I remembered sitting on her knee and looking through the railing and hearing the chanting and singing, I longed to go. One day when I was quite small I slipped out and tried to find the synagogue, but I lost myself a long while till a pedlar questioned me and took me home. My father, missing me, had been in much fear, and was very angry. I too had been so frightened at losing myself that it was long before I thought of venturing out again. But after Signora left us we went to rooms where our landlady was a Jewess and observed her religion. I asked her to take me with her to the synagogue; and I read in her prayer-books and Bible, and when I had money enough I asked her to buy me books of my own, for these books seemed a closer companionship with my mother: I knew that she must have looked at the very words and said them. In that way I have come to know a little of our religion, and the history of our people, besides piecing together what I read in plays and other books about Jews and Jewesses; because I was sure that my mother obeyed her religion. I had left off asking my father about her. It is very dreadful to say it, but I began to disbelieve him. I had found that he did not always tell the truth, and made promises without meaning to keep them; and that raised my suspicion that my mother and brother were still alive though he had told me that they were dead. For in going over the past again and again as I got older and knew more, I felt sure that my mother had been deceived, and had expected to see us back again after a very little while; and my father taking me on his knee and telling me that my mother and brother were both dead seemed to me now nothing but a bit of acting, to set my mind at rest. The cruelty of that falsehood sank into me, and I hated all untruth because of it. I wrote to my mother secretly: I knew the street, Colman Street, where we lived, and that it was near Blackfriars Bridge and the Coburg, and that our name was Cohen then, though my father called us Lapidoth, because, he said, it was a name of his forefathers in Poland. I sent my letter secretly; but no answer came, and I thought there was no hope for me. Our life in America did not last much longer. My father suddenly told me we were to pack up and go to Hamburg, and I was rather glad. I hoped we might get among a different sort of people, and I knew German quite well – some German plays almost all by heart. My father spoke it better than he spoke English. I was thirteen then, and I seemed to myself quite old – I knew so much, and yet so little. I think other children cannot feel as I did. I had often wished that I had been drowned when I was going away from my mother. But I set myself to obey and suffer: what else could I do? One day when we were on our voyage, a new thought came into my mind. I was not very ill that time, and I kept on deck a good deal. My father acted and sang and joked to amuse people on board, and I used often to overhear remarks about him. One day, when I was looking at the sea and nobody took notice of me, I overheard a gentleman say, "Oh, he is one of those clever Jews – a rascal, I shouldn't wonder. There's no race like them for cunning in the men and beauty in the women. I wonder what market he means that daughter for." When I heard this, it darted into my mind that the unhappiness in my life came from my being a Jewess, and that always, to the end the world would think slightly of me and that I must bear it, for I should be judged by that name, and it comforted me to believe that my suffering was part of the affliction of my people, my part in the long song of mourning that has been going on through ages and ages. For if many of our race were wicked and made merry in their wickedness – what was that but part of the affliction borne by the just among them, who were despised for the sins of their brethren? – But you have not rejected me.'

Mirah had changed her tone in this last sentence, having suddenly reflected that at this moment she had reason not for complaint but for gratitude.

'And we will try to save you from being judged unjustly by others, my poor child,' said Mrs. Meyrick, who had now given up all attempt at going on with her work, and sat listening with folded hands and a face hardly less eager than Mab's would have been. 'Go on, go on: tell me all.'

'After that we lived in different towns – Hamburg and Vienna, the longest. I began to study singing again, and my father always got money about the theatres. I think he brought a good deal of money from America: I never knew why we left. For some time he was in great spirits about my singing, and he made me rehearse parts and act continually. He looked forward to my coming out in the opera. But by-and-by it seemed that my voice would never be strong enough – it did not fulfil its promise. My master at Vienna said, "Don't strain it further: it will never do for the public: – it is gold, but a thread of gold dust." My father was bitterly disappointed: we were not so well off at that time. I think I have not quite told you what I felt about my father. I knew he was fond of me and meant to indulge me, and that made me afraid of hurting him; but he always mistook what would please me and give me happiness. It was his nature to take everything lightly; and I soon left off asking him any question about things that I cared for much, because he always turned them off with a joke. He would even ridicule our own people; and once when he had been imitating their movements and their tones in praying, only to make others laugh, I could not restrain myself – for I always had an anger in my heart about my mother – and when we were alone, I said, "Father, you ought not to mimic our own people before Christians who mock them: would it not be bad if I mimicked you, that they might mock you?" But he only shrugged his shoulders and laughed and pinched my chin, and said, "You couldn't do it, my dear." It was this way of turning off everything, that made a great wall between me and my father, and whatever I felt most I took the most care to hide from him. For there were some things – when they were laughed at I could not bear it: the world seemed like a hell to me. Is this world and all the life upon it only like a farce or a vaudeville, where you find no great meanings? Why then are there tragedies and grand operas, where men do difficult things and choose to suffer? I think it is silly to speak of all things as a joke. And I saw that his wishing me to sing the

233

greatest music, and parts in grand operas, was only wishing for what would fetch the greatest price. That hemmed in my gratitude for his affectionateness, and the tenderest feeling I had towards him was pity. Yes, I did sometimes pity him. He had aged and changed. Now he was no longer so lively. I thought he seemed worse – less good to others and to me. Every now and then in the latter years his gaiety went away suddenly, and he would sit at home silent and gloomy; or he would come in and fling himself down and sob, just as I have done myself when I have been in trouble. If I put my hand on his knee and said, "What is the matter, father?" he would make no answer, but would draw my arm round his neck and put his arm round me, and go on crying. There never came any confidence between us; but oh, I was sorry for him. At those moments I knew he must feel his life bitter, and I pressed my cheek against his head and prayed. Those moments were what most bound me to him; and I used to think how much my mother once loved him, else she would not have married him.

'But soon there came the dreadful time. We had been at Pesth and we came back to Vienna. In spite of what my master Leo had said, my father got me an engagement, not at the opera, but to take singing parts at a suburb theatre in Vienna. He had nothing to do with the theatre then; I did not understand what he did, but I think he was continually at a gambling-house, though he was careful always about taking me to the theatre. I was very miserable. The plays I acted in were detestable to me. Men came about us and wanted to talk to me: women and men seemed to look at me with a sneering smile: it was no better than a fiery furnace. Perhaps I make it worse than it was – you don't know that life; but the glare and the faces, and my having to go on and act and sing what I hated, and then see people who came to stare at me behind the scenes – it was all so much worse than when I was a little girl. I went through with it; I did it; I had set my mind to obey my father and work, for I saw nothing better that I could do. But I felt that my voice was getting weaker, and I knew that my acting was not good except when it was not really acting, but the part was one that I could be myself in, and some feeling within me carried me along. That was seldom.

'Then in the midst of all this, the news came to me one morning that my father had been taken to prison, and he had sent for me. He did not tell me the reason why he was there, but he ordered me to go to an address he gave me, to see a Count who would be able to get him released. The address was to some public rooms where I was to ask for the Count, and beg him to come to my father. I found him, and recognized him as a gentleman whom I had seen the other night for the first time behind the scenes. That agitated me, for I remembered his way of looking at me and kissing my hand – I thought it was in mockery. But I delivered my errand and he promised to go immediately to my father, who came home again that very evening, bringing the Count with him. I now began to feel a horrible dread of this man, for he worried me with his attentions, his eyes were always on me: I felt sure that whatever else there might be in his mind towards me, below it all there was scorn for the Jewess and the actress. And when he came to me the next day in the theatre and would put my shawl round me, a terror took hold of me; I saw that my father wanted me to look pleased. The Count was neither very young nor very old: his hair and eyes were pale; he was tall and walked heavily, and his face was heavy and grave except when he looked at me. He smiled at me, and his smile went through me with horror: I could not tell why he was so much worse to me than other men. Some feelings are like our hearing: they come as sounds do, before we know their reason. My father talked to me about him when we were alone, and praised him – said what a good friend he had been. I said nothing, because I supposed he had got my father out of prison. When the Count came again, my father left the room. He asked me if I liked being on the stage. I said No, I only acted in obedience to my father. He always spoke French, and called me "petit ange" and such things, which I felt insulting. I knew he meant to make love to me, and I had it firmly in my mind that a nobleman and one who was not a Jew could have no love for me that was not half contempt. But then he told me that I need not act any longer; he wished me to visit him at his beautiful place, where I might be queen of everything. It was difficult to me to speak, I felt so shaken with anger: I could only say, "I would rather stay on the stage for ever," and I left him there. Hurrying out of the room I saw my father sauntering in the passage. My heart was crushed. I went past him and locked myself up. It had sunk into me that my father was in a conspiracy with that man against me. But the next day he persuaded me to come out: he said that I had mistaken everything, and he would explain: if I did not come out and act and fulfil my engagement, we should be ruined and he must starve. So I went on acting, and for a week or more the Count never came near me. My father changed our lodgings, and kept at home except when he went to the theatre with me. He began one day to speak discouragingly of my acting, and say I could never go on singing in public – I should lose my voice – I ought to think of my future and not put my nonsensical feelings between me and my fortune. He said, "What will you do? You will be brought down to sing and beg at people's doors. You have had a splendid offer and ought to accept it." I could not speak: a horror took possession of me when I thought of my mother and of him. I felt for the first time that I should not do wrong to leave him. But the next day he told me that he had put an end to my engagement at the theatre, and that we were to go to Prague. I was getting suspicious of everything, and my will was hardening to act against him. It took us two days to pack and get ready; and I had it in my mind that I might be obliged to run away from my father, and then I would come to London and try if it were possible to find my mother. I had a little money, and I sold some things to get more. I packed a few clothes in a little bag that I could carry with me, and I kept my mind on the watch. My father's silence – his letting drop that subject of the Count's offer – made me feel sure that there was a plan against me. I felt as if it had been a plan to take me to a madhouse. I once saw a picture of a madhouse, that I could never forget; it seemed to me very much like some of the life I had seen – the people strutting, quarrelling, leering – the faces with cunning and malice in them. It was my will to keep myself from wickedness; and I prayed for help. I had seen what despised women were: and my heart turned against my father, for I saw always behind him that man who made me shudder. You will think I had not enough reason for my suspicions, and perhaps I had not, outside my own feeling; but it seemed to me that my mind had been lit up, and all that might be stood out clear and sharp. If I slept, it was only to see the same sort of things, and I could hardly sleep at all. Through our journey I was everywhere on the watch. I don't know why, but it came before me like a real event, that my father would suddenly leave me and I should find myself with the Count where I could not get away from him. I thought God was warning me: my mother's voice was in my soul. It was dark when we reached Prague, and though the strange bunches of lamps were lit it was difficult to distinguish faces as we drove along the street. My father chose to sit outside – he was always smoking now – and I watched everything in spite of the darkness. I do believe I could see better then than I ever did before: the strange clearness within seemed to have got outside me. It was not my habit to notice faces and figures much in the street; but this night I saw every one; and when we passed before a great hotel I caught sight only of a back that was passing in – the light of the great bunch of lamps a good way off fell on it. I knew it – before the face was turned, as it fell into shadow, I knew who it was. Help came to me. I feel sure help came to me. I did not sleep that night. I put on my plainest things – the cloak and hat I have worn ever since; and I sat watching for the light and the sound of the doors being unbarred. Some one rose early – at four o'clock, to go to the railway. That gave me courage. I slipped out with my little bag under my cloak, and none noticed me. I had been a long while attending to the railway guide that I might learn the way to England; and before the sun had risen I was in the train for Dresden. Then I cried for joy. I did not know whether my money would last out, but I trusted. I could sell the things in my bag, and the little rings in my ears, and I could live on bread only. My only terror was lest my father should follow me. But I never paused. I came on, and on, and on, only eating bread now and then. When I got to Brussels I saw that I should not have enough money, and I sold all that I could sell; but here a strange thing happened. Putting my hand into the pocket of my cloak, I found a half-napoleon. Wondering and wondering how it came there, I remembered that on the way from Cologne there was a young workman sitting against me. I was frightened at every one, and did not like to be spoken to. At first he tried to talk, but when he saw that I did not like it, he left off. It was a long journey; I ate nothing but a bit of bread, and he once offered me some of the food he brought in, but I refused it. I do believe it was he who put that bit of gold in my pocket. Without it I could hardly have got to Dover, and I did walk a good deal of the way from Dover to London. I knew I should look like a miserable beggar-girl. I wanted not to look very miserable, because if I found my mother it would grieve her to see me so. But oh, how vain my hope was that she would be there to see me come! As soon as I set foot in London, I began to ask for Lambeth and Blackfriars Bridge, but they were a long way off, and I went wrong. At last I got to Blackfriars Bridge and asked for Colman Street. People shook their heads. None knew it. I saw it in my mind – our doorsteps, and the white tiles hung in the windows, and the large brick building opposite with wide doors. But there was nothing like it. At last when I asked a tradesman where the Coburg Theatre and Colman Street were, he said, "Oh, my little woman, that's all done away with. The old streets have been pulled down; everything is new." I turned away, and felt as if death had laid a hand on me. He said: "Stop, stop! young woman; what is it you're wanting with Colman Street, eh?"

meaning well, perhaps. But his tone was what I could not bear; and how could I tell him what I wanted? I felt blinded and bewildered with a sudden shock. I suddenly felt that I was very weak and weary, and yet where could I go? for I looked so poor and dusty, and had nothing with me – I looked like a street-beggar. And I was afraid of all places where I could enter. I lost my trust. I thought I was forsaken. It seemed that I had been in a fever of hope – delirious – all the way from Prague: I thought that I was helped, and I did nothing but strain my mind forward and think of finding my mother; and now – there I stood in a strange world. All who saw me would think ill of me, and I must herd with beggars. I stood on the bridge and looked along the river. People were going on to a steamboat. Many of them seemed poor, and I felt as if it would be a refuge to get away from the streets: perhaps the boat would take me where I could soon get into a solitude. I had still some pence left, and I bought a loaf when I went on the boat. I wanted to have a little time and strength to think of life and death. How could I live? And now again it seemed that if ever I were to find my mother again, death was the way to her. I ate, that I might have strength to think. The boat set me down at a place along the river – I don't know where – and it was late in the evening. I found some large trees apart from the road and I sat down under them that I might rest through the night. Sleep must have soon come to me, and when I awoke it was morning. The birds were singing, the dew was white about me, I felt chill and oh so lonely! I got up and walked and followed the river a long way and then turned back again. There was no reason why I should go anywhere. The world about me seemed like a vision that was hurrying by while I stood still with my pain. My thoughts were stronger than I was: they rushed in and forced me to see all my life from the beginning; ever since I was carried away from my mother I had felt myself a lost child taken up and used by strangers, who did not care what my life was to me, but only what I could do for them. It seemed all a weary wandering and heart-loneliness – as if

I had been forced to go to merry-makings without the expectation of joy. And now it was worse. I was lost again, and I dreaded lest any stranger should notice me and speak to me. I had a terror of the world. None knew me; all would mistake me. I had seen so many in my life who made themselves glad with scorning, and laughed at another's shame. What could I do? This life seemed to be closing in upon me with a wall of fire – everywhere there was scorching that made me shrink. The high sunlight made me shrink. And I began to think that my despair was the voice of God telling me to die. But it would take me long to die of hunger. Then I thought of my People, how they had been driven from land to land and been afflicted, and multitudes had died of misery in their wandering – was I the first? And in the wars and troubles when Christians were cruellest, our fathers had sometimes slain their children and afterwards themselves; it was to save them from being false apostates. That seemed to make it right for me to put an end to my life; for calamity had closed me in too, and I saw no pathway but to evil. But my mind got into war with itself, for there were contrary things in it. I knew that some had held it wrong to hasten their own death, though they were in the midst of flames; and while I had some strength left, it was a longing to bear if I ought to bear – else where was the good of all my life? It had not been happy since the first years: when the light came every morning I used to think, "I will bear it." But always before, I had some hope; now it was gone. With these thoughts I wandered and wandered, inwardly crying to the Most High, from whom I should not flee in death more than in life – though I had no strong faith that He cared for me. The strength seemed departing from my soul: deep below all my cries was the feeling that I was alone and forsaken. The more I thought, the wearier I got, till it seemed I was not thinking at all, but only the sky and the river and the Eternal God were in my soul. And what was it whether I died or lived? If I lay down to die in the river, was it more than lying down to sleep? – for there too I committed my soul – I gave myself up. I could not bear memories any more: I could only feel what was present in me – it was all one longing to cease from my weary life, which seemed only a pain outside the great peace that I might enter into. That was how it was. When the evening came and the sun was gone, it seemed as if that was all I had to wait for. And a new strength came into me to will what I would do. You know what I did. I was going to die. You know what happened – did he not tell you? Faith came to me again: I was not forsaken. He told you how he found me?'

Mrs. Meyrick gave no audible answer, but pressed her lips against Mirah's forehead.

'She's just a pearl: the mud has only washed her,' was the fervid little woman's closing commentary when, *tête-à-tête* with Deronda in the back parlour that evening, she had conveyed Mirah's story to him with much vividness.

'What is your feeling about a search for this mother?' said Deronda. 'Have you no fears? I have, I confess.'

'Oh, I believe the mother's good,' said Mrs. Meyrick, with rapid decisiveness. 'Or *was* good. She may be dead – that's my fear. A good woman, you may depend: you may know it by the scoundrel the father is. Where did the child get her goodness from? Wheaten flour has to be accounted for.'

Deronda was rather disappointed at this answer: he had wanted a confirmation of his own judgment, and he began to put in demurrers. The argument about the mother would not apply to the brother; and Mrs. Meyrick admitted that the brother might be an ugly likeness of the father. Then, as to advertising, if the name was Cohen, you might as well advertise for two undescribed terriers: and here Mrs. Meyrick helped him, for the idea of an advertisement, already mentioned to Mirah, had roused the poor child's terror: she was convinced that her father would see it – he saw everything in the papers. Certainly there were safer means than advertising: men might be set to work whose business it was to find missing persons; but Deronda wished Mrs. Meyrick to feel with him that it would be wiser to wait, before seeking a dubious – perhaps a deplorable result; especially as he was engaged to go abroad the next week for a couple of months. If a search were made, he would like to be at hand, so that Mrs. Meyrick might not be unaided in meeting any consequences – supposing that she would generously continue to watch over Mirah.

'We should be very jealous of any one who took the task from us,' said Mrs. Meyrick. 'She will stay under my roof: there is Hans's old room for her.'

'Will she be content to wait?' said Deronda, anxiously.

'No trouble there! It is not her nature to run into planning and devising; only to submit. See how she submitted to that father. It was a wonder to herself how she found the will and contrivance to run away from him. About finding her mother, her only notion now is to trust: since you were sent to save her and we are good to her, she trusts that her mother will be found in the same unsought way. And when she is talking I catch her feeling like a child.'

Mrs. Meyrick hoped that the sum Deronda put into her hands as a provision for Mirah's wants was more than would be needed; after a little while Mirah would perhaps like to occupy herself as the other girls did, and make herself independent. Deronda pleaded that she must need a long rest.

'Oh yes; we will hurry nothing,' said Mrs. Meyrick. 'Rely upon it, she shall be taken tender care of. If you like to give me your address abroad, I will write to let you know how we get on. It is not fair that we should have all the pleasure of her salvation to ourselves. And besides, I want to make believe that I am doing something for you as well as for Mirah.'

'That is no make-believe. What should I have done without you last night? Everything would have gone wrong. I shall tell Hans that the best of having him for a friend is, knowing his mother.'

After that they joined the girls in the other room, where Mirah was seated placidly, while the others were telling

her what they knew about Mr. Deronda – his goodness to
Hans, and all the virtues that Hans had reported of him.

'Kate burns a pastille before his portrait every day,' said
Mab. 'And I carry his signature in a little black-silk bag
round my neck to keep off the cramp. And Amy says the
multiplication-table in his name. We must all do something extra in honour of him, now he has brought you
to us.'

'I suppose he is too great a person to want anything,' said
Mirah, smiling at Mab, and appealing to the graver Amy.
'He is perhaps very high in the world?'

'He is very much above us in rank,' said Amy. 'He is
related to grand people. I dare say he leans on some of the
satin cushions we prick our fingers over.'

'I am glad he is of high rank,' said Mirah, with her usual
quietness.

'Now, why are you glad of that?' said Amy, rather
suspicious of this sentiment, and on the watch for Jewish
peculiarities which had not appeared.

'Because I have always disliked men of high rank
before.'

'Oh, Mr. Deronda is not so very high,' said Kate. 'He
need not hinder us from thinking ill of the whole peerage
and baronetage if we like.'

When he entered, Mirah rose with the same look of
grateful reverence that she had lifted to him the evening
before: impossible to see a creature freer at once from
embarrassment and boldness. Her theatrical training had
left no recognizable trace; probably her manners had not
much changed since she played the forsaken child at nine
years of age; and she had grown up in her simplicity and
truthfulness like a little flower-seed that absorbs the
chance confusion of its surroundings into its own definite
mould of beauty. Deronda felt that he was making
acquaintance with something quite new to him in the
form of womanhood. For Mirah was not childlike from
ignorance: her experience of evil and trouble was deeper
and stranger than his own. He felt inclined to watch her

243

and listen to her as if she had come from a far-off shore inhabited by a race different from our own.

But for that very reason he made his visit brief: with his usual activity of imagination as to how his conduct might affect others, he shrank from what might seem like curiosity, or the assumption of a right to know as much as he pleased of one to whom he had done a service. For example, he would have liked to hear her sing, but he would have felt the expression of such a wish to be a rudeness in him – since she could not refuse, and he would all the while have a sense that she was being treated like one whose accomplishments were to be ready on demand. And whatever reverence could be shown to woman, he was bent on showing to this girl. Why? He gave himself several good reasons; but whatever one does with a strong unhesitating outflow of will, has a store of motive that it would be hard to put into words. Some deeds seem little more than interjections which give vent to the long passion of a life.

So Deronda soon took his farewell for the two months during which he expected to be absent from London, and in a few days he was on his way with Sir Hugo and Lady Mallinger to Leubronn.

He had fulfilled his intention of telling them about Mirah. The baronet was decidedly of opinion that the search for the mother and brother had better be let alone. Lady Mallinger was much interested in the poor girl, observing that there was a Society for the Conversion of the Jews, and that it was to be hoped Mirah would embrace Christianity; but perceiving that Sir Hugo looked at her with amusement, she concluded that she had said something foolish. Lady Mallinger felt apologetically about herself as a woman who had produced nothing but daughters in a case where sons were required, and hence regarded the apparent contradictions of the world as probably due to the weakness of her own understanding. But when she was much puzzled, it was her habit to say to herself, 'I will ask Daniel.' Deronda was altogether a convenience in the family; and Sir Hugo too, after intending to do the best for him, had begun to feel that the pleasantest result would be to have this substitute for a son always ready at his elbow.

This was the history of Deronda, so far as he knew it, up to the time of that visit to Leubronn in which he saw Gwendolen Harleth at the gaming-table.

XXI

It is a common sentence that Knowledge is power; but who hath duly considered or set forth the power of Ignorance? Knowledge slowly builds up what Ignorance in an hour pulls down. Knowledge, through patient and frugal centuries, enlarges discovery and makes record of it; Ignorance, wanting its day's dinner, lights a fire with the record, and gives flavour to its one roast with the burnt souls of many generations. Knowledge, instructing the sense, refining and multiplying needs, transforms itself into skill and makes life various with a new six days' work; comes Ignorance drunk on the seventh, with a firkin of oil and a match and an easy 'Let there not be' – and the many-coloured creation is shrivelled up in blackness. Of a truth, Knowledge is power, but it is a power reined by scruple, having a conscience of what must be and what may be; whereas Ignorance is a blind giant who, let him but wax unbound, would make it a sport to seize the pillars that hold up the long-wrought fabric of human good, and turn all the places of joy dark as a buried Babylon. And looking at life parcel-wise, in the growth of a single lot, who having a practised vision may not see that ignorance of the true bond between events, and false conceit of means whereby sequences may be compelled – like that falsity of eyesight which overlooks the gradations of distance, seeing that which is afar off as if it were within a step or a grasp – precipitates the mistaken soul on destruction?

IT was half-past ten in the morning when Gwendolen Harleth, after her gloomy journey from Leubronn, arrived at the station from which she must drive to Offendene. No carriage or friend was awaiting her, for in the telegram she had sent from Dover she had mentioned a later train, and in her impatience of lingering at a London station she had set off without picturing what it would be to arrive unannounced at half an hour's drive from home – at one of those stations which have been fixed on not as near anywhere but as equidistant from everywhere. Deposited as a *feme sole* with her large trunks, and having to wait while a vehicle was being got from the large-sized lantern called the Railway Inn, Gwendolen felt that the dirty plant in the waiting-room, the dusty decanter of flat water, and the texts in large letters calling on her to repent and be converted, were part of the dreary prospect opened by her family troubles; and she hurried away to the outer door looking towards the lane and fields. But here the very gleams of sunshine seemed melancholy, for the autumnal leaves and grass were shivering, and the wind was turning up the feathers of a cock and two croaking hens which had doubtless parted with their grown-up offspring and did not know what to do with themselves. The railway official also seemed without resources, and his innocent demeanour in observing Gwendolen and her trunks was rendered intolerable by the cast in his eye; especially since, being a new man, he did not know her, and must conclude that she was not very high in the world. The vehicle – a dirty old barouche – was within sight, and was being slowly prepared by an elderly labourer. Contemptible details these, to make part of a history; yet the turn of most lives is hardly to be accounted for without them. They are continually entering with cumulative force into a mood until it gets the mass and momentum of a theory or a motive. Even philosophy is not quite free from such determining influences; and to be dropt solitary at an ugly irrelevant-looking spot with a sense of no income on the mind, might well prompt a man to discouraging speculation on the origin of things and the reason of a world where a subtle thinker found himself so badly off. How much more might such trifles tell on a young lady equipped for society with a fastidious taste, an Indian shawl over her arm, some ten cubic feet of trunks by her side, and a mortal dislike to the new consciousness of poverty which was stimulating her imagination of disagreeables? At any rate they told heavily on poor Gwendolen, and helped to quell her resistant spirit. What was the good of living in the midst of hardships, ugliness, and humiliation? This was the beginning of being at home again, and it was a sample of what she had to expect.

Here was the theme on which her discontent rung its sad changes during her slow drive in the uneasy barouche, with one great trunk squeezing the meek driver, and the other fastened with a rope on the seat in front of her. Her ruling vision all the way from Leubronn had been that the family would go abroad again; for of course there must be some little income left – her mamma did not mean that they would have literally nothing. To go to a dull place abroad and live poorly, was the dismal future that threatened her: she had seen plenty of poor English people abroad, and imagined herself plunged in the despised dullness of their ill-plenished lives, with Alice, Bertha, Fanny, and Isabel all growing up in tediousness around her, while she advanced towards thirty, and her mamma got more and more melancholy. But she did not mean to submit, and let misfortune do what it would with her: she had not yet quite believed in the misfortune; but weariness, and disgust with this wretched arrival, had begun to affect her like an uncomfortable waking, worse than the uneasy dreams which had gone before. The self-delight with which she had kissed her image in the glass had faded before the sense of futility in being anything whatever – charming, clever, resolute – what was the good of it all? Events might turn out anyhow, and men were hateful. Yes, men were hateful. Those few words were filled out with very vivid memories. But in these last hours, a certain change had come over their meaning. It is one thing to hate stolen goods, and another thing to hate them the more because their being stolen hinders us from making use of them. Gwendolen had begun to be angry with Grandcourt for being what had hindered her from marrying him, angry with him as the cause of her present dreary lot.

But the slow drive was nearly at an end, and the lumbering vehicle coming up the avenue was within sight of the windows. A figure appearing under the portico brought a rush of new and less selfish feeling in Gwendolen, and when springing from the carriage she saw the dear beautiful face with fresh lines of sadness in it, she threw her arms round her mother's neck, and for the moment felt all sorrows only in relation to her mother's feeling about them.

Behind, of course, were the sad faces of the four superfluous girls, each, poor thing – like those other many thousand sisters of us all – having her peculiar world which was of no importance to any one else, but all of them feeling Gwendolen's presence to be somehow a relenting of misfortune: where Gwendolen was, something interesting would happen; even her hurried submission to their kisses, and 'Now go away, girls,' carried the sort of comfort which all weakness finds in decision and authoritativeness. Good Miss Merry, whose air of meek depression, hitherto held unaccountable in a governess affectionately attached to the family, was now at the general level of circumstances, did not expect any greeting, but busied herself with the trunks and the coachman's pay; while Mrs. Davilow and Gwendolen hastened upstairs and shut themselves in the black and yellow bedroom.

'Never mind, mamma dear,' said Gwendolen, tenderly pressing her handkerchief against the tears that were rolling down Mrs. Davilow's cheeks. 'Never mind. I don't mind. I will do something. I will be something. Things will come right. It seemed worse because I was away. Come now! you must be glad because I am here.'

Gwendolen felt every word of that speech. A rush of compassionate tenderness stirred all her capability of generous resolution; and the self-confident projects which had vaguely glanced before her during her journey sprang instantaneously into new definiteness. Suddenly she seemed to perceive how she could be 'something.' It was one of her best moments, and the fond mother, forgetting everything below that tide-mark, looked at her with a sort of adoration. She said –

'Bless you, my good, good darling! I can be happy, if you can!'

But later in the day there was an ebb; the old slippery rocks, the old weedy places reappeared. Naturally, there was a shrinking of courage as misfortune ceased to be a mere announcement, and began to disclose itself as a grievous tyrannical inmate. At first – that ugly drive at an end – it was still Offendene that Gwendolen had come home to, and all surroundings of immediate consequence to her were still there to secure her personal ease; the roomy stillness of the large solid house while she rested; all the luxuries of her toilet cared for without trouble to her; and a little tray with her favourite food brought to her in private. For she had said, 'Keep them all away from us to-day, mamma. Let you and me be alone together.'

When Gwendolen came down into the drawing-room, fresh as a newly-dipped swan, and sat leaning against the cushions of the settee beside her mamma, their misfortune had not yet turned its face and breath upon her. She felt prepared to hear everything, and began in a tone of deliberate intention:

'What have you thought of doing exactly, mamma?'

'Oh my dear, the next thing to be done is to move away from this house. Mr. Haynes most fortunately is as glad to have it now as he would have been when we took it. Lord Brackenshaw's agent is to arrange everything with him to the best advantage for us: Bazley, you know; not at all an ill-natured man.'

'I cannot help thinking that Lord Brackenshaw would let you stay here rent-free, mamma,' said Gwendolen, whose talents had not been applied to business so much as to discernment of the admiration excited by her charms.

'My dear child, Lord Brackenshaw is in Scotland, and knows nothing about us. Neither your uncle nor I would choose to apply to him. Besides, what could we do in this house without servants, and without money to warm it? The sooner we are out the better. We have nothing to carry but our clothes, you know.'

'I suppose you mean to go abroad, then?' said Gwendolen. After all, this was what she had familiarized her mind with.

'Oh no, dear, no. How could we travel? You never did learn anything about income and expenses,' said Mrs. Davilow, trying to smile, and putting her hand on Gwendolen's as she added, mournfully, 'that makes it so much harder for you, my pet.'

'But where are we to go?' said Gwendolen, with a trace of sharpness in her tone. She felt a new current of fear passing through her.

'It is all decided. A little furniture is to be got in from the rectory – all that can be spared.' Mrs. Davilow hesitated. She dreaded the reality for herself less than the shock she must give Gwendolen, who looked at her with tense expectancy, but was silent.

'It is Sawyer's Cottage we are to go to.'

At first, Gwendolen remained silent, paling with anger – justifiable anger, in her opinion. Then she said with haughtiness –

'That is impossible. Something else than that ought to have been thought of. My uncle ought not to allow that. I will not submit to it.'

'My sweet child, what else could have been thought of? Your uncle, I am sure, is as kind as he can be; but he is suffering himself: he has his family to bring up. And do you quite understand? You must remember – we have nothing. We shall have absolutely nothing except what he and my sister give us. They have been as wise and active as possible, and we must try to earn something. I and the girls are going to work a table-cloth border for the Ladies' Charity at Wancester, and a communion cloth that the parishioners are to present to Pennicote Church.'

Mrs. Davilow went into these details timidly, but how else was she to bring the fact of their position home to this poor child who, alas! must submit at present, whatever might be in the background for her? and she herself had a superstition that there must be something better in the background.

'But surely somewhere else than Sawyer's Cottage might have been found,' Gwendolen persisted – taken hold of (as if in a nightmare) by the image of this house where an exciseman had lived.

'No, indeed, dear. You know houses are scarce, and we may be thankful to get anything so private. It is not so very bad. There are two little parlours and four bedrooms. You shall sit alone whenever you like.'

The ebb of sympathetic care for her mamma had gone so low just now, that Gwendolen took no notice of these deprecatory words.

'I cannot conceive that all your property is gone at once, mamma. How can you be sure in so short a time? It is not a week since you wrote to me.'

'The first news came much earlier, dear. But I would not spoil your pleasure till it was quite necessary.'

'Oh how vexatious!' said Gwendolen, colouring with fresh anger. 'If I had known, I could have brought home the money I had won; and for want of knowing, I stayed and lost it. I had nearly two hundred pounds, and it would have done for us to live on a little while, till I could carry out some plan.' She paused an instant and then added more impetuously, 'Everything has gone against me. People have come near me only to blight me.'

Among the 'people' she was including Deronda. If he had not interfered in her life she would have gone to the gaming-table again with a few napoleons, and might have won back her losses.

'We must resign ourselves to the will of Providence, my child,' said poor Mrs. Davilow, startled by this revelation of the gambling, but not daring to say more. She felt sure that 'people' meant Grandcourt, about whom her lips were sealed. And Gwendolen answered immediately –

'But I don't resign myself. I shall do what I can against it. What is the good of calling people's wickedness Providence? You said in your letter it was Mr. Lassmann's fault we had lost our money. Has he run away with it all?'

'No, dear, you don't understand. There were great speculations: he meant to gain. It was all about mines and things of that sort. He risked too much.'

'I don't call that Providence: it was his improvidence with our money, and he ought to be punished. Can't we go to law and recover our fortune? My uncle ought to take measures, and not sit down by such wrongs. We ought to go to law.'

'My dear child, law can never bring back money lost in that way. Your uncle says it is milk spilt upon the ground. Besides, one must have a fortune to get any law: there is no law for people who are ruined. And our money has only gone along with other people's. We are not the only sufferers: others have to resign themselves besides us.'

'But I don't resign myself to live at Sawyer's Cottage and see you working for sixpences and shillings because of that. I shall not do it. I shall do what is more befitting our rank and education.'

'I am sure your uncle and all of us will approve of that, dear, and admire you the more for it,' said Mrs. Davilow, glad of an unexpected opening for speaking on a difficult subject. 'I didn't mean that you should resign yourself to worse when anything better offered itself. Both your uncle and aunt have felt that your abilities and education were a fortune for you, and they have already heard of something within your reach.'

'What is that, mamma?' Some of Gwendolen's anger gave way to interest, and she was not without conjectures.

'There are two situations that offer themselves. One is in a bishop's family, where there are three daughters, and the other is in quite a high class of school; and in both your French, and music, and dancing – and then your manners and habits as a lady, are exactly what is wanted. Each is a hundred a-year – and – just for the present' – Mrs. Davilow had become frightened and hesitating – 'to save you from the petty, common way of living that we must go to – you would perhaps accept one of the two.'

'What! be like Miss Graves at Madame Meunier's? No.'

'I think, myself, that Dr. Mompert's would be more suitable. There could be no hardship in a bishop's family.'

'Excuse me, mamma. There are hardships everywhere for a governess. And I don't see that it would be pleasanter to be looked down on in a bishop's family than in any other. Besides, you know very well I hate teaching. Fancy me shut up with three awkward girls something like Alice! I would rather emigrate than be a governess.'

What it precisely was to emigrate, Gwendolen was not called on to explain. Mrs. Davilow was mute, seeing no outlet, and thinking with dread of the collision that might happen when Gwendolen had to meet her uncle and aunt. There was an air of reticence in Gwendolen's haughty resistant speeches, which implied that she had a definite plan in reserve; and her practical ignorance, continually exhibited, could not nullify the mother's belief in the effectiveness of that forcible will and daring which had held the mastery over herself.

'I have some ornaments, mamma, and I could sell them,' said Gwendolen. 'They would make a sum: I want a little sum – just to go on with. I dare say Marshall at Wancester would take them: I know he showed me some bracelets once that he said he had bought from a lady. Jocosa might go and ask him. Jocosa is going to leave us, of course. But she might do that first.'

'She would do anything she could, poor dear soul. I have not told you yet – she wanted me to take all her savings – her three hundred pounds. I tell her to set up a little school. It will be hard for her to go into a new family now she has been so long with us.'

'Oh, recommend her for the bishop's daughters,' said Gwendolen, with a sudden gleam of laughter in her face. 'I am sure she will do better than I should.'

'Do take care not to say such things to your uncle,' said Mrs. Davilow. 'He will be hurt at your despising what he has exerted himself about. But I dare say you have some-thing else in your mind that he might not disapprove, if you consulted him.'

'There is some one else I want to consult first. Are the Arrowpoints at Quetcham still, and is Herr Klesmer there? But I dare say you know nothing about it, poor dear mamma. Can Jeffries go on horseback with a note?'

'Oh, my dear, Jeffries is not here, and the dealer has taken the horses. But some one could go for us from Leek's farm. The Arrowpoints are at Quetcham, I know. Miss Arrowpoint left her card the other day. I could not see her. But I don't know about Herr Klesmer. Do you want to send before to-morrow?'

'Yes, as soon as possible. I will write a note,' said Gwendolen, rising.

'What can you be thinking of, Gwen?' said Mrs. Davilow, relieved in the midst of her wonderment by signs of alacrity and better humour.

'Don't mind what, there's a dear good mamma,' said Gwendolen, reseating herself a moment to give atoning caresses. 'I mean to do something. Never mind what, until it is all settled. And then you shall be comforted. The dear face! – it is ten years older in these three weeks. Now, now, now! don't cry' – Gwendolen, holding her mamma's head with both hands, kissed the trembling eyelids. 'But mind you don't contradict me or put hindrances in my way. I must decide for myself. I cannot be dictated to by my uncle or any one else. My life is my own affair. And I think' – here her tone took an edge of scorn – 'I think I can do better for you than let you live in Sawyer's Cottage.'

In uttering this last sentence Gwendolen again rose, and went to a desk where she wrote the following note to Klesmer: –

'Miss Harleth presents her compliments to Herr Klesmer and ventures to request of him the very great favour that he will call upon her, if possible to-morrow. Her reason for presuming so far on his kindness is of a very serious nature. Unfortunate family circumstances have obliged her to take a course in which she can only turn for advice to the great knowledge and judgment of Herr Klesmer.'

'Pray get this sent to Quetcham at once, mamma,' said Gwendolen, as she addressed the letter. 'The man must be told to wait for an answer. Let no time be lost.'

For the moment, the absorbing purpose was to get the letter dispatched; but when she had been assured on this point, another anxiety arose and kept her in a state of

DANIEL DERONDA

uneasy excitement. If Klesmer happened not to be at
Quetcham, what could she do next? Gwendolen's belief
in her star, so to speak, had had some bruises. Things had
gone against her. A splendid marriage which presented
itself within reach had shown a hideous flaw. The chances
of roulette had not adjusted themselves to her claims; and a
man of whom she knew nothing had thrust himself
between her and her intentions. The conduct of those
uninteresting people who managed the business of the
world had been culpable just in the points most injurious
to her in particular. Gwendolen Harleth, with all her
beauty and conscious force, felt the close threats of humiliation: for the first time the conditions of this world
seemed to her like a hurrying roaring crowd in which she
had got astray, no more cared for and protected than a
myriad of other girls, in spite of its being a peculiar hardship to her. If Klesmer were not at Quetcham – that would
be all of a piece with the rest: the unwelcome negative
urged itself as a probability, and set her brain working at
desperate alternatives which might deliver her from
Sawyer's Cottage or the ultimate necessity of 'taking a
situation,' a phrase that summed up for her the disagreeables most wounding to her pride, most irksome to her
tastes; at least so far as her experience enabled her to
imagine disagreeables.

Still Klesmer might be there, and Gwendolen thought
of the result in that case with a hopefulness which even
cast a satisfactory light over her peculiar troubles, as what
might well enter into the biography of celebrities and
remarkable persons. And if she had heard her immediate
acquaintances cross-examined as to whether they thought
her remarkable, the first who said 'No' would have surprised her.

XXII

We please our fancy with ideal webs
Of innovation, but our life meanwhile
Is in the loom, where busy passion plies
The shuttle to and fro, and gives our deeds
The accustomed pattern.

GWENDOLEN'S note, coming 'pat betwixt too early and too late,' was put into Klesmer's hands just when he was leaving Quetcham, and in order to meet her appeal to his kindness he with some inconvenience to himself spent the night at Wancester. There were reasons why he would not remain at Quetcham.

That magnificent mansion, fitted with regard to the greatest expense, had in fact become too hot for him, its owners having, like some great politicians, been astonished at an insurrection against the established order of things, which we plain people after the event can perceive to have been prepared under their very noses.

There were as usual many guests in the house, and among them one in whom Miss Arrowpoint foresaw a new pretender to her hand: a political man of good family who confidently expected a peerage, and felt on public grounds that he required a larger fortune to support the title properly. Heiresses vary, and persons interested in one of them beforehand are prepared to find that she is too yellow or too red, tall and toppling or short and square, violent and capricious or moony and insipid; but in every case it is taken for granted that she will consider herself an appendage to her fortune, and marry where others think her fortune ought to go. Nature, however, not only accommodates herself ill to our favourite practices by making 'only children' daughters, but also now and then endows the misplaced daughter with a clear head and a strong will. The Arrowpoints had already felt some anxiety owing to these endowments of their Catherine. She would not accept the view of her social duty which required her to marry a needy nobleman or a commoner on the ladder

257

towards nobility; and they were not without uneasiness concerning her persistence in declining suitable offers. As to the possibility of her being in love with Klesmer they were not at all uneasy – a very common sort of blindness. For in general mortals have a great power of being astonished at the presence of an effect towards which they have done everything, and at the absence of an effect towards which they have done nothing but desire it. Parents are astonished at the ignorance of their sons, though they have used the most time-honoured and expensive means of securing it; husbands and wives are mutually astonished at the loss of affection which they have taken no pains to keep; and all of us in our turn are apt to be astonished that our neighbours do not admire us. In this way it happens that the truth seems highly improbable. The truth is something different from the habitual lazy combinations begotten by our wishes. The Arrowpoints' hour of astonishment was come.

When there is a passion between an heiress and a proud independent-spirited man, it is difficult for them to come to an understanding; but the difficulties are likely to be overcome unless the proud man secures himself by a constant *alibi*. Brief meetings after studied absence are potent in disclosure: but more potent still is frequent companionship, with full sympathy in taste, and admirable qualities on both sides; especially where the one is in the position of teacher and the other is delightedly conscious of receptive ability which also gives the teacher delight. The situation is famous in history and has no less charm now than it had in the days of Abelard.

But this kind of comparison had not occurred to the Arrowpoints when they first engaged Klesmer to come down to Quetcham. To have a first-rate musician in your house is a privilege of wealth; Catherine's musical talent demanded every advantage; and she particularly desired to use her quieter time in the country for more thorough study. Klesmer was not yet a Liszt, understood to be adored by ladies of all European countries with the

exception of Lapland: and even with that understanding it
did not follow that he would make proposals to an heiress.
No musician of honour would do so. Still less was it conceivable that Catherine would give him the slightest pretext for such daring. The large cheque that Mr. Arrowpoint
was to draw in Klesmer's name seemed to make him as safe
an inmate as a footman. Where marriage is inconceivable, a
girl's sentiments are safe.

Klesmer was eminently a man of honour, but marriages
rarely begin with formal proposals, and moreover,
Catherine's limit of the conceivable did not exactly correspond with her mother's.

Outsiders might have been more apt to think that
Klesmer's position was dangerous for himself if Miss
Arrowpoint had been an acknowledged beauty; not taking
into account that the most powerful of all beauty is that
which reveals itself after sympathy and not before it.
There is a charm of eye and lip which comes with every
little phrase that certifies delicate perception or fine judgment, with every unostentatious word or smile that shows a
heart awake to others; and no sweep of garment or turn of
figure is more satisfying than that which enters as a restoration of confidence that one person is present on whom no
intention will be lost. What dignity of meaning goes on
gathering in frowns and laughs which are never observed in
the wrong place; what suffused adorableness in a human
frame where there is a mind that can flash out comprehension and hands that can execute finely! The more obvious
beauty, also adorable sometimes – one may say it without
blasphemy – begins by being an apology for folly, and ends
like other apologies in becoming tiresome by iteration; and
that Klesmer, though very susceptible to it, should have a
passionate attachment to Miss Arrowpoint, was no more a
paradox than any other triumph of a manifold sympathy
over a monotonous attraction. We object less to be taxed
with the enslaving excess of our passions than with our
deficiency in wider passion; but if the truth were known,
our reputed intensity is often the dullness of not knowing

what else to do with ourselves. Tannhäuser, one suspects, was a knight of ill-furnished imagination, hardly of larger discourse than a heavy Guardsman; Merlin had certainly seen his best days, and was merely repeating himself, when he fell into that hopeless captivity; and we know that Ulysses felt so manifest an *ennui* under similar circumstances that Calypso herself furthered his departure. There is indeed a report that he afterwards left Penelope; but since she was habitually absorbed in worsted work, and it was probably from her that Telemachus got his mean, pettifogging disposition, always anxious about the property and the daily consumption of meat, no inference can be drawn from this already dubious scandal as to the relation between companionship and constancy.

Klesmer was as versatile and fascinating as a young Ulysses on a sufficient acquaintance – one whom nature seemed to have first made generously and then to have added music as a dominant power using all the abundant rest, and, as in Mendelssohn, finding expression for itself not only in the highest finish of execution, but in that fervour of creative work and theoretic belief which pierces the whole future of a life with the light of congruous, devoted purpose. His foibles of arrogance and vanity did not exceed such as may be found in the best English families; and Catherine Arrowpoint had no corresponding restlessness to clash with his: notwithstanding her native kindliness she was perhaps too coolly firm and self-sustained. But she was one of those satisfactory creatures whose intercourse has the charm of discovery; whose integrity of faculty and expression begets a wish to know what they will say on all subjects, or how they will perform whatever they undertake; so that they end by raising not only a continual expectation but a continual sense of fulfilment – the systole and diastole of blissful companionship. In such cases the outward presentment easily becomes what the image is to the worshipper. It was not long before the two became aware that each was interesting to the other; but the 'how far' remained a matter of doubt.

Klesmer did not conceive that Miss Arrowpoint was likely to think of him as a possible lover, and she was not accustomed to think of herself as likely to stir more than a friendly regard, or to fear the expression of more from any man who was not enamoured of her fortune. Each was content to suffer some unshared sense of denial for the sake of loving the other's society a little too well; and under these conditions no need had been felt to restrict Klesmer's visits for the last year either in country or in town. He knew very well that if Miss Arrowpoint had been poor he would have made ardent love to her instead of sending a storm through the piano, or folding his arms and pouring out a hyperbolical tirade about something as impersonal as the north pole; and she was not less aware that if it had been possible for Klesmer to wish for her hand she would have found overmastering reasons for giving it to him. Here was the safety of full cups, which are as secure from overflow as the half-empty, always supposing no disturbance. Naturally, silent feeling had not remained at the same point any more than the stealthy dial-hand, and in the present visit to Quetcham, Klesmer had begun to think that he would not come again; while Catherine was more sensitive to his frequent *brusquerie*, which she rather resented as a needless effort to assert his footing of superior in every sense except the conventional.

Meanwhile enters the expectant peer, Mr. Bult, an esteemed party man who, rather neutral in private life, had strong opinions concerning the districts of the Niger, was much at home also in the Brazils, spoke with decision of affairs in the South Seas, was studious of his parliamentary and itinerant speeches, and had the general solidity and suffusive pinkness of a healthy Briton on the central table-land of life. Catherine, aware of a tacit understanding that he was an undeniable husband for an heiress, had nothing to say against him but that he was thoroughly tiresome to her. Mr. Bult was amiably confident, and had no idea that his insensibility to counterpoint could ever be reckoned

against him. Klesmer he hardly regarded in the light of a
serious human being who ought to have a vote; and he did
not mind Miss Arrowpoint's addiction to music any more
than her probable expenses in antique lace. He was consequently a little amazed at an after-dinner outburst of
Klesmer's on the lack of idealism in English politics,
which left all mutuality between distant races to be determined simply by the need of a market: the Crusades, to his
mind, had at least this excuse, that they had a banner of
sentiment round which generous feelings could rally: of
course, the scoundrels rallied too, but what then? they rally
in equal force round your advertisement van of 'Buy cheap,
sell dear.' On this theme Klesmer's eloquence, gesticulat-
ory and other, went on for a little while like stray fireworks
accidentally ignited, and then sank into immovable
silence. Mr. Bult was not surprised that Klesmer's opinions
should be flighty, but was astonished at his command of
English idiom and his ability to put a point in a way that
would have told at a constituents' dinner – to be accounted
for probably by his being a Pole, or a Czech, or something
of that fermenting sort, in a state of political refugeeism
which had obliged him to make a profession of his music;
and that evening in the drawing-room he for the first time
went up to Klesmer at the piano, Miss Arrowpoint being
near, and said –

'I had no idea before that you were a political man.'

Klesmer's only answer was to fold his arms, put out his
nether lip, and stare at Mr. Bult.

'You must have been used to public speaking. You speak
uncommonly well, though I don't agree with you. From
what you said about sentiment, I fancy you are a
Panslavist.'

'No; my name is Elijah. I am the Wandering Jew,' said
Klesmer, flashing a smile at Miss Arrowpoint, and suddenly making a mysterious wind-like rush backwards and
forwards on the piano. Mr. Bult felt this buffoonery rather
offensive and Polish, but – Miss Arrowpoint being there –
did not like to move away.

'Herr Klesmer has cosmopolitan ideas,' said Miss Arrowpoint, trying to make the best of the situation. 'He looks forward to a fusion of races.'

'With all my heart,' said Mr. Bult, willing to be gracious. 'I was sure he had too much talent to be a mere musician.'

'Ah, sir, you are under some mistake there,' said Klesmer, firing up. 'No man has too much talent to be a musician. Most men have too little. A creative artist is no more a mere musician than a great statesman is a mere politician. We are not ingenious puppets, sir, who live in a box and look out on the world only when it is gaping for amusement. We help to rule the nations and make the age as much as any other public men. We count ourselves on level benches with legislators. And a man who speaks effectively through music is compelled to something more difficult than parliamentary eloquence.'

With the last word Klesmer wheeled from the piano and walked away.

Miss Arrowpoint coloured, and Mr. Bult observed with his usual phlegmatic solidity, 'Your pianist does not think small beer of himself.'

'Herr Klesmer is something more than a pianist,' said Miss Arrowpoint, apologetically. 'He is a great musician in the fullest sense of the word. He will rank with Schubert and Mendelssohn.'

'Ah, you ladies understand these things,' said Mr. Bult, none the less convinced that these things were frivolous because Klesmer had shown himself a coxcomb.

Catherine, always sorry when Klesmer gave himself airs, found an opportunity the next day in the music-room to say, 'Why were you so heated last night with Mr. Bult? He meant no harm.'

'You wish me to be complaisant to him?' said Klesmer, rather fiercely.

'I think it is hardly worth your while to be other than civil.'

'You find no difficulty in tolerating him, then? – you have a respect for a political platitudinarian as insensible as an ox to everything he can't turn into political capital. You think his monumental obtuseness suited to the dignity of the English gentleman.'

'I did not say that.'

'You mean that I acted without dignity and you are offended with me.'

'Now you are slightly nearer the truth,' said Catherine, smiling.

'Then I had better put my burial-clothes in my portmanteau and set off at once.'

'I don't see that. If I have to bear your criticism of my operetta, you should not mind my criticism of your impatience.'

'But I do mind it. You would have wished me to take his ignorant impertinence about a "mere musician" without letting him know his place. I am to hear my gods blasphemed as well as myself insulted. But I beg pardon. It is impossible you should see the matter as I do. Even you can't understand the wrath of the artist: he is of another caste for you.'

'That is true,' said Catherine, with some betrayal of feeling. 'He is of a caste to which I look up – a caste above mine.'

Klesmer, who had been seated at a table looking over scores, started up and walked to a little distance, from which he said –

'That is finely felt – I am grateful. But I had better go, all the same. I have made up my mind to go, for good and all. You can get on exceedingly well without me: your operetta is on wheels – it will go of itself. And your Mr. Bult's company fits me "wie die Faust ins Auge." I am neglecting my engagements. I must go off to St. Petersburg.'

There was no answer.

'You agree with me that I had better go?' said Klesmer, with some irritation.

'Certainly; if that is what your business and feeling prompt. I have only to wonder that you have consented to give us so much of your time in the last year. There must be treble the interest to you anywhere else. I have never thought of your consenting to come here as anything else than a sacrifice.'

'Why should I make the sacrifice?' said Klesmer, going to seat himself at the piano, and touching the keys so as to give with the delicacy of an echo in the far distance a melody which he had set to Heine's 'Ich hab' dich geliebet und liebe dich noch.'

'That is the mystery,' said Catherine, not wanting to affect anything, but from mere agitation. From the same cause she was tearing a piece of paper into minute morsels, as if at a task of utmost multiplication imposed by a cruel fairy.

'You can conceive no motive?' said Klesmer, folding his arms.

'None that seems in the least probable.'

'Then I shall tell you. It is because you are to me the chief woman in the world – the throned lady whose colours I carry between my heart and my armour.'

Catherine's hands trembled so much that she could no longer tear the paper: still less could her lips utter a word. Klesmer went on –

'This would be the last impertinence in me, if I meant to found anything upon it. That is out of the question. I mean no such thing. But you once said it was your doom to suspect every man who courted you of being an adventurer, and what made you angriest was men's imputing to you the folly of believing that they courted you for your own sake. Did you not say so?'

'Very likely,' was the answer, in a low murmur.

'It was a bitter word. Well, at least one man who has seen women as plenty as flowers in May has lingered about you for your own sake. And since he is one whom you can never marry, you will believe him. That is an argument in favour of some other man. But don't give yourself for a meal to a minotaur like Bult. I shall go now and pack. I shall make my excuses to Mrs. Arrowpoint.' Klesmer rose as he ended, and walked quickly towards the door.

'You must take this heap of manuscript, then,' said Catherine, suddenly making a desperate effort. She had risen to fetch the heap from another table. Klesmer came back, and they had the length of the folio sheets between them.

'Why should I not marry the man who loves me, if I love him?' said Catherine. To her the effort was something like the leap of a woman from the deck into the lifeboat.

'It would be too hard – impossible – you could not carry it through. I am not worth what you would have to encounter. I will not accept the sacrifice. It would be thought a *mésalliance* for you, and I should be liable to the worst accusations.'

'Is it the accusations you are afraid of? I am afraid of nothing but that we should miss the passing of our lives together.'

The decisive word had been spoken: there was no doubt concerning the end willed by each: there only remained the way of arriving at it, and Catherine determined to take the straightest possible. She went to her father and mother in the library, and told them that she had promised to marry Klesmer.

Mrs. Arrowpoint's state of mind was pitiable. Imagine Jean Jacques, after his essay on the corrupting influence of the arts, waking up among children of nature who had no idea of grilling the raw bone they offered him for breakfast with the primitive *couvert* of a flint; or Saint Just, after fervidly denouncing all recognition of pre-eminence, receiving a vote of thanks for the unbroken mediocrity of his speech, which warranted the dullest patriots in delivering themselves at equal length. Something of the same sort befell the authoress of 'Tasso,' when what she had safely demanded of the dead Leonora was enacted by her own Catherine. It is hard for us to live up to our own eloquence, and keep pace with our winged words, while we are treading the solid earth and are liable to heavy dining. Besides, it has long been understood that the proprieties of literature are not those of practical life. Mrs. Arrowpoint naturally wished for the best of everything. She not only liked to feel herself at a higher level of literary sentiment than the ladies with whom she associated; she wished not to be below them in any point of social consideration. While Klesmer was seen in the light of a patronized musician, his peculiarities were picturesque and acceptable; but to see him by a sudden flash in the light of her son-in-law gave her a burning sense of what the world would say. And the poor lady had been used to represent her Catherine as a model of excellence.

Under the first shock she forgot everything but her anger, and snatched at any phrase that would serve as a weapon.

'If Klesmer has presumed to offer himself to you, your father shall horsewhip him off the premises. Pray, speak, Mr. Arrowpoint.'

The father took his cigar from his mouth, and rose to the occasion by saying, 'This will never do, Cath.'

'Do!' cried Mrs. Arrowpoint; 'who in their senses ever thought it would do? You might as well say poisoning and strangling will not do. It is a comedy you have got up, Catherine. Else you are mad.'

'I am quite sane and serious, mamma, and Herr Klesmer is not to blame. He never thought of my marrying him. I found out that he loved me, and loving him, I told him I would marry him.'

'Leave that unsaid, Catherine,' said Mrs. Arrowpoint, bitterly. 'Every one else will say it for you. You will be a public fable. Every one will say that you must have made the offer to a man who has been paid to come to the house – who is nobody knows what – a gypsy, a Jew, a mere bubble of the earth.'

'Never mind, mamma,' said Catherine, indignant in her turn. 'We all know he is a genius – as Tasso was.'

'Those times were not these, nor is Klesmer Tasso,' said Mrs. Arrowpoint, getting more heated. 'There is no sting in *that* sarcasm, except the sting of undutifulness.'

'I am sorry to hurt you, mamma. But I will not give up the happiness of my life to ideas that I don't believe in and customs I have no respect for.'

'You have lost all sense of duty, then? You have forgotten that you are our only child – that it lies with you to place a great property in the right hands?'

'What are the right hands? My grandfather gained the property in trade.'

'Mr. Arrowpoint, *will* you sit by and hear this without speaking?'

'I am a gentleman, Cath. We expect you to marry a gentleman,' said the father, exerting himself.

'And a man connected with the institutions of this country,' said the mother. 'A woman in your position has serious duties. Where duty and inclination clash, she must follow duty.'

'I don't deny that,' said Catherine, getting colder in proportion to her mother's heat. 'But one may say very true things and apply them falsely. People can easily take the sacred word duty as a name for what they desire any one else to do.'

'Your parents' desire makes no duty for you, then?'

'Yes, within reason. But before I give up the happiness of my life—'

'Catherine, Catherine, it will not be your happiness,' said Mrs. Arrowpoint, in her most raven-like tones.

'Well, what seems to me my happiness – before I give it up, I must see some better reason than the wish that I should marry a nobleman, or a man who votes with a party that he may be turned into a nobleman. I feel at liberty to marry the man I love and think worthy, unless some higher duty forbids.'

'And so it does, Catherine, though you are blinded and cannot see it. It is a woman's duty not to lower herself. You are lowering yourself. Mr. Arrowpoint, will you tell your daughter what is her duty?'

'You must see, Catherine, that Klesmer is not the man for you,' said Mr. Arrowpoint. 'He won't do at the head of estates. He has a deuced foreign look – is an unpractical man.'

'I really can't see what that has to do with it, papa. The land of England has often passed into the hands of foreigners – Dutch soldiers, sons of foreign women of bad character: – if our land were sold to-morrow it would very likely pass into the hands of some foreign merchant on 'Change. It is in everybody's mouth that successful swindlers may buy up half the land in the country. How can I stem that tide?'

'It will never do to argue about marriage, Cath,' said Mr. Arrowpoint. 'It's no use getting up the subject like a parliamentary question. We must do as other people do. We must think of the nation and the public good.'

'I can't see any public good concerned here, papa,' said Catherine. 'Why is it to be expected of an heiress that she should carry the property gained in trade into the hands of a certain class? That seems to me a ridiculous mish-mash of superannuated customs and false ambition. I should call it a public evil. People had better make a new sort of public good by changing their ambitions.'

'That is mere sophistry, Catherine,' said Mrs. Arrowpoint. 'Because you don't wish to marry a nobleman, you are not obliged to marry a mountebank or a charlatan.'

'I cannot understand the application of such words, mamma.'

'No, I dare say not,' rejoined Mrs. Arrowpoint, with significant scorn. 'You have got to a pitch at which we are not likely to understand each other.'

'It can't be done, Cath,' said Mr. Arrowpoint, wishing to substitute a better-humoured reasoning for his wife's impetuosity. 'A man like Klesmer can't marry such a property as yours. It can't be done.'

'It certainly will not be done,' said Mrs. Arrowpoint, imperiously. 'Where is the man? Let him be fetched.'

'I cannot fetch him to be insulted,' said Catherine. 'Nothing will be achieved by that.'

'I suppose you would wish him to know that in marrying you he will not marry your fortune,' said Mrs. Arrowpoint.

'Certainly; if it were so, I should wish him to know it.'

'Then you had better fetch him.'

Catherine only went into the music-room and said, 'Come:' she felt no need to prepare Klesmer.

'Herr Klesmer,' said Mrs. Arrowpoint, with a rather contemptuous stateliness, 'it is unnecessary to repeat what has passed between us and our daughter. Mr. Arrowpoint will tell you our resolution.'

'Your marrying is quite out of the question,' said Mr. Arrowpoint, rather too heavily weighted with his task, and standing in an embarrassment unrelieved by a cigar. 'It is a wild scheme altogether. A man has been called out for less.'

'You have taken a base advantage of our confidence,' burst in Mrs. Arrowpoint, unable to carry out her purpose and leave the burthen of speech to her husband.

Klesmer made a low bow in silent irony.

'The pretension is ridiculous. You had better give it up and leave the house at once,' continued Mr. Arrowpoint. He wished to do without mentioning the money.

'I can give up nothing without reference to your daughter's wish,' said Klesmer. 'My engagement is to her.'

'It is useless to discuss the question,' said Mrs. Arrowpoint. 'We shall never consent to the marriage. If Catherine disobeys us we shall disinherit her. You will not marry her fortune. It is right you should know that.'

'Madam, her fortune has been the only thing I have had to regret about her. But I must ask her if she will not think the sacrifice greater than I am worthy of.'

'It is no sacrifice to me,' said Catherine, 'except that I am sorry to hurt my father and mother. I have always felt my fortune to be a wretched fatality of my life.'

'You mean to defy us, then?' said Mrs. Arrowpoint.

'I mean to marry Herr Klesmer,' said Catherine, firmly.

'He had better not count on our relenting,' said Mrs. Arrowpoint, whose manners suffered from that impunity in insult which has been reckoned among the privileges of women.

'Madam,' said Klesmer, 'certain reasons forbid me to retort. But understand that I consider it out of the power either of you or of your fortune to confer on me anything that I value. My rank as an artist is of my own winning, and I would not exchange it for any other. I am able to maintain your daughter, and I ask for no change in my life but her companionship.'

'You will leave the house, however,' said Mrs. Arrowpoint.

'I go at once,' said Klesmer, bowing and quitting the room.

'Let there be no misunderstanding, mamma,' said Catherine; 'I consider myself engaged to Herr Klesmer, and I intend to marry him.'

The mother turned her head away and waved her hand in sign of dismissal.

'It's all very fine,' said Mr. Arrowpoint, when Catherine was gone; 'but what the deuce are we to do with the property?'

'There is Harry Brendall. He can take the name.'

'Harry Brendall will get through it all in no time,' said Mr. Arrowpoint, relighting his cigar.

And thus, with nothing settled but the determination of the lovers, Klesmer had left Quetcham.

XXIII

Among the heirs of Art, as at the division of the promised land, each has to win his portion by hard fighting: the bestowal is after the manner of prophecy, and is a title without possession. To carry the map of an ungotten estate in your pocket is a poor sort of copyhold. And in fancy to cast his shoe over Edom is little warrant that a man shall ever set the sole of his foot on an acre of his own there.

The most obstinate beliefs that mortals entertain about themselves are such as they have no evidence for beyond a constant, spontaneous pulsing of their self-satisfaction – as it were a hidden seed of madness, a confidence that they can move the world without precise notion of standing-place or lever.

'PRAY go to church, mamma,' said Gwendolen the next morning. 'I prefer seeing Herr Klesmer alone.' (He had written in reply to her note that he would be with her at eleven.)

'That is hardly correct, I think,' said Mrs. Davilow, anxiously.

'Our affairs are too serious for us to think of such nonsensical rules,' said Gwendolen, contemptuously. 'They are insulting as well as ridiculous.'

'You would not mind Isabel sitting with you? She would be reading in a corner.'

'No, she could not: she would bite her nails and stare. It would be too irritating. Trust my judgment, mamma. I must be alone. Take them all to church.'

Gwendolen had her way, of course; only that Miss Merry and two of the girls stayed at home, to give the house a look of habitation by sitting at the dining-room windows.

It was a delicious Sunday morning. The melancholy waning sunshine of autumn rested on the leaf-strown grass and came mildly through the windows in slanting bands of brightness over the old furniture, and the glass panel that reflected the furniture; over the tapestried chairs with their faded flower-wreaths, the dark enigmatic pictures, the superannuated organ at which Gwendolen had pleased herself with acting Saint Cecilia on her first joyous arrival, the crowd of pallid, dusty knick-knacks seen through the open doors of the antechamber where she had achieved the wearing of her Greek dress as Hermione. This last memory was just now very busy in her; for had not Klesmer then been struck with admiration of her pose and expression? Whatever he had said, whatever she imagined him to have thought, was at this moment pointed with keenest interest for her: perhaps she had never before in her life felt so inwardly dependent, so consciously in need of another person's opinion. There was a new fluttering of spirit within her, a new element of deliberation in her self-estimate which had hitherto been a blissful gift of intuition. Still it was the recurrent burthen of her inward soliloquy that Klesmer had seen but little of her, and any unfavourable conclusion of his must have too narrow a foundation. She really felt clever enough for anything.

To fill up the time she collected her volumes and pieces of music, and laying them on the top of the piano, set herself to classify them. Then catching the reflection of her movements in the glass panel, she was diverted to the contemplation of the image there and walked towards it. Dressed in black without a single ornament, and with the warm whiteness of her skin set off between her light-brown coronet of hair and her square-cut bodice, she might have tempted an artist to try again the Roman trick of a statue in black, white, and tawny marble. Seeing her image slowly advancing, she thought, 'I *am* beautiful' – not exultingly, but with grave decision. Being beautiful was after all the condition on which she most needed external testimony. If any one objected to the turn of her nose or the form of her neck and chin, she had not the sense that she could presently show her power of attainment in these branches of feminine perfection.

There was not much time to fill up in this way before the sound of wheels, the loud ring, and the opening doors, assured her that she was not by any accident to be disappointed. This slightly increased her inward flutter. In spite of her self-confidence, she dreaded Klesmer as part of that unmanageable world which was independent of her wishes – something vitriolic that would not cease to burn because you smiled or frowned at it. Poor thing! she was at a higher crisis of her woman's fate than in her past experience with Grandcourt. The questioning then, was whether she should take a particular man as a husband. The inmost fold of her questioning now, was whether she need take a husband at all – whether she could not achieve substantiality for herself and know gratified ambition without bondage.

Klesmer made his most deferential bow in the wide doorway of the antechamber – showing also the deference of the finest grey kerseymere trousers and perfect gloves (the 'masters of those who know' are happily altogether human). Gwendolen met him with unusual gravity, and holding out her hand, said, 'It is most kind of you to come, Herr Klesmer. I hope you have not thought me presumptuous.'

'I took your wish as a command that did me honour,' said Klesmer, with answering gravity. He was really putting by his own affairs in order to give his utmost attention to what Gwendolen might have to say; but his temperament was still in a state of excitation from the events of yesterday, likely enough to give his expressions a more than usually biting edge.

Gwendolen for once was under too great a strain of feeling to remember formalities. She continued standing near the piano, and Klesmer took his stand at the other end of it, with his back to the light and his terribly omniscient eyes upon her. No affectation was of use, and she began without delay.

'I wish to consult you, Herr Klesmer. We have lost all our fortune; we have nothing. I must get my own bread, and I desire to provide for my mamma, so as to save her from any hardship. The only way I can think of – and I should like it better than anything – is to be an actress – to go on the stage. But of course I should like to take a high position, and I thought – if you thought I could,' – here Gwendolen became a little more nervous, – 'it would be better for me to be a singer – to study singing also.'

Klesmer put down his hat on the piano, and folded his arms as if to concentrate himself.

'I know,' Gwendolen resumed, turning from pale to pink and back again – 'I know that my method of singing is very defective; but I have been ill taught. I could be better taught; I could study. And you will understand my wish: – to sing and act too, like Grisi, is a much higher position. Naturally, I should wish to take as high a rank as I can. And I can rely on your judgment. I am sure you will tell me the truth.'

Gwendolen somehow had the conviction that now she made this serious appeal the truth would be favourable.

Still Klesmer did not speak. He drew off his gloves quickly, tossed them into his hat, rested his hands on his hips, and walked to the other end of the room. He was filled with compassion for this girl: he wanted to put a guard on his speech. When he turned again, he looked at her with a mild frown of inquiry, and said with gentle though quick utterance, 'You have never seen anything, I think, of artists and their lives? – I mean of musicians, actors, artists of that kind?'

'Oh no,' said Gwendolen, not perturbed by a reference to this obvious fact in the history of a young lady hitherto well provided for.

'You are, – pardon me,' said Klesmer, again pausing near the piano – 'in coming to a conclusion on such a matter as this, everything must be taken into consideration, – you are perhaps twenty?'

'I am twenty-one,' said Gwendolen, a slight fear rising in her. 'Do you think I am too old?'

Klesmer pouted his under lip and shook his long fingers upward in a manner totally enigmatic.

'Many persons begin later than others,' said Gwendolen, betrayed by her habitual consciousness of having valuable information to bestow.

Klesmer took no notice, but said with more studied gentleness than ever, 'You have probably not thought of an artistic career until now: you did not entertain the notion, the longing – what shall I say? – you did not wish yourself an actress, or anything of that sort, till the present trouble?'

'Not exactly; but I was fond of acting. I have acted; you saw me, if you remember – you saw me here in charades, and as Hermione,' said Gwendolen, really fearing that Klesmer had forgotten.

'Yes, yes,' he answered quickly, 'I remember – I remember perfectly,' and again walked to the other end of the room. It was difficult for him to refrain from this kind of movement when he was in any argument either audible or silent.

Gwendolen felt that she was being weighed. The delay was unpleasant. But she did not yet conceive that the scale could dip on the wrong side, and it seemed to her only graceful to say, 'I shall be very much obliged to you for taking the trouble to give me your advice, whatever it may be.'

'Miss Harleth,' said Klesmer, turning towards her and speaking with a slight increase of accent, 'I will veil nothing from you in this matter. I should reckon myself guilty if I put a false visage on things – made them too black or too white. The gods have a curse for him who willingly tells another the wrong road. And if I misled one who is so young, so beautiful – who, I trust, will find her happiness along the right road, I should regard myself as a – *Bösewicht*.' In the last word Klesmer's voice had dropped to a loud whisper.

Gwendolen felt a sinking of heart under this unexpected solemnity, and kept a sort of fascinated gaze on Klesmer's face, while he went on.

'You are a beautiful young lady – you have been brought up in ease – you have done what you would – you have not said to yourself, "I must know this exactly," "I must understand this exactly," "I must do this exactly"' – in uttering

276

these three terrible *musts*, Klesmer lifted up three long fingers in succession. 'In sum, you have not been called upon to be anything but a charming young lady, whom it is an impoliteness to find fault with.'

He paused an instant; then resting his fingers on his hips again, and thrusting out his powerful chin, he said –

'Well, then, with that preparation, you wish to try the life of the artist; you wish to try a life of arduous, unceasing work, and – uncertain praise. Your praise would have to be earned, like your bread; and both would come slowly, scantily – what do I say? – they might hardly come at all.'

This tone of discouragement, which Klesmer half hoped might suffice without anything more unpleasant, roused some resistance in Gwendolen. With a slight turn of her head away from him, and an air of pique, she said –

'I thought that you, being an artist, would consider the life one of the most honourable and delightful. And if I can do nothing better? – I suppose I can put up with the same risks as other people do.'

'Do nothing better?' said Klesmer, a little fired. 'No, my dear Miss Harleth, you could do nothing better – neither man nor woman could do anything better – if you could do what was best or good of its kind. I am not decrying the life of the true artist. I am exalting it. I say, it is out of the reach of any but choice organizations – natures framed to love perfection and to labour for it; ready, like all true lovers, to endure, to wait, to say, I am not yet worthy, but she – Art, my mistress – is worthy, and I will live to merit her. An honourable life? Yes. But the honour comes from the inward vocation and the hard-won achievement: there is no honour in donning the life as a livery.'

Some excitement of yesterday had revived in Klesmer and hurried him into speech a little aloof from his immediate friendly purpose. He had wished as delicately as possible to rouse in Gwendolen a sense of her unfitness for a perilous, difficult course; but it was his wont to be angry with the pretensions of incompetence, and he was in danger of getting chafed. Conscious of this he paused

277

suddenly. But Gwendolen's chief impression was that he had not yet denied her the power of doing what would be good of its kind. Klesmer's fervour seemed to be a sort of glamour such as he was prone to throw over things in general; and what she desired to assure him of was that she was not afraid of some preliminary hardships. The belief that to present herself in public on the stage must produce an effect such as she had been used to feel certain of in private life, was like a bit of her flesh – it was not to be peeled off readily, but must come with blood and pain. She said, in a tone of some insistence –

'I am quite prepared to bear hardships at first. Of course no one can become celebrated all at once. And it is not necessary that every one should be first-rate – either actresses or singers. If you would be so kind as to tell me what steps I should take, I shall have the courage to take them. I don't mind going up hill. It will be easier than the dead level of being a governess. I will take any steps you recommend.'

Klesmer was more convinced now that he must speak plainly.

'I will tell you the steps, not that I recommend, but that will be forced upon you. It is all one, so far, what your goal may be – excellence, celebrity, second, third rateness – it is all one. You must go to town under the protection of your mother. You must put yourself under training – musical, dramatic, theatrical: – whatever you desire to do, you have to learn—' here Gwendolen looked as if she were going to speak, but Klesmer lifted up his hand and said decisively, 'I know. You have exercised your talents – you recite – you sing – from the drawing-room *standpunkt*. My dear Fräulein, you must unlearn all that. You have not yet conceived what excellence is: you must unlearn your mistaken admirations. You must know what you have to strive for, and then you must subdue your mind and body to unbroken discipline. Your mind, I say. For you must not be thinking of celebrity: – put that candle out of your eyes, and look only at excellence. You would of course earn nothing – you could get no engagement for a long while. You would need money for yourself and your family. But that,' here Klesmer frowned and shook his fingers as if to dismiss a triviality – 'that could perhaps be found.'

Gwendolen turned pink and pale during this speech. Her pride had felt a terrible knife-edge, and the last sentence only made the smart keener. She was conscious of appearing moved, and tried to escape from her weakness by suddenly walking to a seat and pointing out a chair to Klesmer. He did not take it, but turned a little in order to face her and leaned against the piano. At that moment she wished that she had not sent for him: this first experience of being taken on some other ground than that of her social rank and her beauty was becoming bitter to her. Klesmer, preoccupied with a serious purpose, went on without change of tone.

'Now, what sort of issue might be fairly expected from all this self-denial? You would ask that. It is right that your eyes should be open to it. I will tell you truthfully. The issue would be uncertain and – most probably – would not be worth much.'

At these relentless words Klesmer put out his lip and looked through his spectacles with the air of a monster impenetrable by beauty.

Gwendolen's eyes began to burn, but the dread of showing weakness urged her to added self-control. She compelled herself to say in a hard tone –

'You think I want talent, or am too old to begin.'

Klesmer made a sort of hum and then descended on an emphatic 'Yes! The desire and the training should have begun seven years ago – or a good deal earlier. A mountebank's child who helps her father to earn shillings when she is six years old – a child that inherits a singing throat from a long line of choristers and learns to sing as it learns to talk, has a likelier beginning. Any great achievement in acting or in music grows with the growth. Whenever an artist has been able to say, "I came, I saw, I conquered," it has been at the end of patient practice. Genius at first is little more than a great capacity for receiving discipline. Singing and acting, like the fine dexterity of the juggler with his cups and balls, require a shaping of the organs towards a finer and finer certainty of effect. Your muscles – your whole frame – must go like a watch, true, true, true, to a hair. That is the work of spring-time, before habits have been determined.'

'I did not pretend to genius,' said Gwendolen, still feeling that she might somehow do what Klesmer wanted to represent as impossible. 'I only supposed that I might have a little talent – enough to improve.'

'I don't deny that,' said Klesmer. 'If you had been put in the right track some years ago and had worked well, you might now have made a public singer, though I don't think your voice would have counted for much in public. For the stage your personal charms and intelligence might then have told without the present drawback of inexperience – lack of discipline – lack of instruction.'

Certainly Klesmer seemed cruel, but his feeling was the reverse of cruel. Our speech even when we are most single-minded can never take its line absolutely from one impulse; but Klesmer's was as far as possible directed by compassion for poor Gwendolen's ignorant eagerness to enter on a course of which he saw all the miserable details with a definiteness which he could not if he would have conveyed to her mind.

Gwendolen, however, was not convinced. Her self-opinion rallied, and since the counsellor whom she had called in gave a decision of such severe peremptoriness, she was tempted to think that his judgment was not only fallible but biased. It occurred to her that a simpler and wiser step for her to have taken would have been to send a letter through the post to the manager of a London theatre, asking him to make an appointment. She would make no further reference to her singing: Klesmer, she saw, had set himself against her singing. But she felt equal to arguing with him about her going on the stage, and she answered in a resistant tone –

'I understand, of course, that no one can be a finished actress at once. It may be impossible to tell beforehand whether I should succeed; but that seems to me a reason why I should try. I should have thought that I might have taken an engagement at a theatre meanwhile, so as to earn money and study at the same time.'

'Can't be done, my dear Miss Harleth – I speak plainly – it can't be done. I must clear your mind of these notions, which have no more resemblance to reality than a panto-mime. Ladies and gentlemen think that when they have made their toilet and drawn on their gloves they are as presentable on the stage as in a drawing-room. No manager thinks that. With all your grace and charm, if you were to present yourself as an aspirant to the stage, a manager would either require you to pay as an amateur for being allowed to perform, or he would tell you to go and be taught – trained to bear yourself on the stage, as a horse, however beautiful, must be trained for the circus; to say nothing of that study which would enable you to personate a character consistently, and animate it with the natural language of face, gesture, and tone. For you to get an engagement fit for you straight away is out of the question.'

'I really cannot understand that,' said Gwendolen, rather haughtily – then, checking herself, she added in another tone – 'I shall be obliged to you if you will explain how it is that such poor actresses get engaged. I have been to the theatre several times, and I am sure there were actresses who seemed to me to act not at all well and who were quite plain.'

'Ah, my dear Miss Harleth, that is the easy criticism of the buyer. We who buy slippers toss away this pair and the other as clumsy; but there went an apprenticeship to the making of them. Excuse me: you could not at present teach one of those actresses; but there is certainly much that she could teach you. For example, she can pitch her voice so as to be heard: ten to one you could not do it till after many trials. Merely to stand and move on the stage is an art – requires practice. It is understood that we are not now talking of a *comparse* in a petty theatre who earns the wages of a needlewoman. That is out of the question for you.'

'Of course I must earn more than that,' said Gwendolen, with a sense of wincing rather than of being refuted; 'but I think I could soon learn to do tolerably well all those little things you have mentioned. I am not so very stupid. And even in Paris I am sure I saw two actresses playing important ladies' parts who were not at all ladies and quite ugly. I suppose I have no particular talent, but I *must* think it is an advantage, even on the stage, to be a lady and not a perfect fright.'

'Ah, let us understand each other,' said Klesmer, with a flash of new meaning. 'I was speaking of what you would have to go through if you aimed at becoming a real artist – if you took music and the drama as a higher vocation in which you would strive after excellence. On that head, what I have said stands fast. You would find – after your education in doing things slackly for one-and-twenty years – great difficulties in study: you would find mortifications in the treatment you would get when you presented yourself on the footing of skill. You would be subjected to tests; people would no longer feign not to see your blunders. You would at first only be accepted on trial. You would have to bear what I may call a glaring insignificance: any success must be won by the utmost patience. You would have to keep your place in a crowd, and after all it is likely you would lose it and get out of sight. If you determine to face these hardships and still try, you will have the dignity of a high purpose, even though you may have chosen unfortunately. You will have some merit, though you may win no prize. You have asked my judgment on your chances of winning. I don't pretend to speak absolutely; but measuring probabilities, my judgment is: – you will hardly achieve more than mediocrity.'

Klesmer had delivered himself with emphatic rapidity, and now paused a moment. Gwendolen was motionless, looking at her hands, which lay over each other on her lap, till the deep-toned, long-drawn '*But*,' with which he resumed, had a startling effect, and made her look at him again.

'But – there are certainly other ideas, other dispositions with which a young lady may take up an art that will bring her before the public. She may rely on the unquestioned power of her beauty as a passport. She may desire to exhibit herself to an admiration which dispenses with skill. This goes a certain way on the stage: not in music: but on the stage, beauty is taken when there is nothing more commanding to be had. Not without some drilling, however: as I have said before, technicalities have in any case to be mastered. But these excepted, we have here nothing to do with art. The woman who takes up this career is not an artist: she is usually one who thinks of entering on a luxurious life by a short and easy road – perhaps by marriage – that is her most brilliant chance, and the rarest. Still, her career will not be luxurious to begin with: she can hardly earn her own poor bread independently at once, and the indignities she will be liable to are such as I will not speak of.'

'I desire to be independent,' said Gwendolen, deeply stung and confusedly apprehending some scorn for herself in Klesmer's words. 'That was my reason for asking whether I could not get an immediate engagement. Of course I cannot know how things go on about theatres. But I thought that I could have made myself independent. I have no money, and I will not accept help from any one.'

Her wounded pride could not rest without making this disclaimer. It was intolerable to her that Klesmer should imagine her to have expected other help from him than advice.

'That is a hard saying for your friends,' said Klesmer, recovering the gentleness of tone with which he had begun the conversation. 'I have given you pain. That was inevitable. I was bound to put the truth, the unvarnished truth before you. I have not said – I will not say – you will do wrong to choose the hard, climbing path of an endeavouring artist. You have to compare its difficulties with those of any less hazardous – any more private course which opens itself to you. If you take that more courageous resolve I will ask leave to shake hands with you on the strength of our free-masonry, where we are all vowed to the service of Art, and to serve her by helping every fellow-servant.'

Gwendolen was silent, again looking at her hands. She felt herself very far away from taking the resolve that would enforce acceptance; and after waiting an instant or two, Klesmer went on with deepened seriousness.

'Where there is the duty of service there must be the duty of accepting it. The question is not one of personal obligation. And in relation to practical matters immedi-ately affecting your future – excuse my permitting myself to mention in confidence an affair of my own. I am expect-ing an event which would make it easy for me to exert myself on your behalf in furthering your opportunities of instruction and residence in London – under the care, that is, of your family – without need for anxiety on your part. If you resolve to take art as a bread-study, you need only undertake the study at first; the bread will be found with-out trouble. The event I mean is my marriage, – in fact – you will receive this as a matter of confidence, – my marriage with Miss Arrowpoint, which will more than double such right as I have to be trusted by you as a friend. Your friendship will have greatly risen in value for *her* by your having adopted that generous labour.'

Gwendolen's face had begun to burn. That Klesmer was about to marry Miss Arrowpoint caused her no surprise, and at another moment she would have amused herself in quickly imagining the scenes that must have occurred at Quetcham. But what engrossed her feeling, what filled her imagination now, was the panorama of her own immediate future that Klesmer's words seemed to have unfolded. The suggestion of Miss Arrowpoint as a patroness was only another detail added to its repulsiveness: Klesmer's pro-posal to help her seemed an additional irritation after the humiliating judgment he had passed on her capabilities.

His words had really bitten into her self-confidence and turned it into the pain of a bleeding wound; and the idea of presenting herself before other judges was now poisoned with the dread that they also might be harsh: they also would not recognize the talent she was conscious of. But she controlled herself, and rose from her seat before she made any answer. It seemed natural that she should pause. She went to the piano and looked absently at leaves of music, pinching up the corners. At last she turned towards Klesmer and said, with almost her usual air of proud equality, which in this interview had not been hitherto perceptible –

'I congratulate you sincerely, Herr Klesmer. I think I never saw any one more admirable than Miss Arrowpoint. And I have to thank you for every sort of kindness this morning. But I can't decide now. If I make the resolve you have spoken of, I will use your permission – I will let you know. But I fear the obstacles are too great. In any case, I am deeply obliged to you. It was very bold of me to ask you to take this trouble.'

Klesmer's inward remark was, 'She will never let me know.' But with the most thorough respect in his manner, he said, 'Command me at any time. There is an address on this card which will always find me with little delay.'

When he had taken up his hat and was going to make his bow, Gwendolen's better self, conscious of an ingratitude which the clear-seeing Klesmer must have penetrated, made a desperate effort to find its way above the stifling layers of egoistic disappointment and irritation. Looking at him with a glance of the old gaiety, she put out her hand, and said with a smile, 'If I take the wrong road, it will not be because of your flattery.'

'God forbid that you should take any road but one where you will find and give happiness!' said Klesmer, fervently. Then, in foreign fashion, he touched her fingers lightly with his lips, and in another minute she heard the sound of his departing wheels getting more distant on the gravel.

DANIEL DERONDA

Gwendolen had never in her life felt so miserable. No
sob came, no passion of tears, to relieve her. Her eyes were
burning; and the noonday only brought into more dreary
clearness the absence of interest from her life. All memories, all objects, the pieces of music displayed, the open
piano – the very reflection of herself in the glass – seemed
no better than the packed-up shows of a departing fair. For
the first time since her consciousness began, she was having a vision of herself on the common level, and had lost
the innate sense that there were reasons why she should
not be slighted, elbowed, jostled – treated like a passenger
with a third-class ticket, in spite of private objections on
her own part. She did not move about; the prospects
begotten by disappointment were too oppressively preoc-
cupying; she threw herself into the shadiest corner of a
settee, and pressed her fingers over her burning eyelids.
Every word that Klesmer had said seemed to have been
branded into her memory, as most words are which bring
with them a new set of impressions and make an epoch for
us. Only a few hours before, the dawning smile of self-
contentment rested on her lips as she vaguely imagined
a future suited to her wishes: it seemed but the affair of a
year or so for her to become the most approved Juliet of the
time; or, if Klesmer encouraged her idea of being a singer,
to proceed by more gradual steps to her place in the opera,
while she won money and applause by occasional performances. Why not? At home, at school, among acquaintances,
she had been used to have her conscious superiority
admitted; and she had moved in a society where everything, from low arithmetic to high art, is of the amateur
kind politely supposed to fall short of perfection only
because gentlemen and ladies are not obliged to do more
than they like – otherwise they would probably give forth
abler writings and show themselves more commanding
artists than any the world is at present obliged to put up
with. The self-confident visions that had beguiled her
were not of a highly exceptional kind; and she had at
least shown some rationality in consulting the person

who knew the most and had flattered her the least. In asking Klesmer's advice, however, she had rather been borne up by a belief in his latent admiration than bent on knowing anything more unfavourable that might have lain behind his slight objections to her singing; and the truth she had asked for with an expectation that it would be agreeable, had come like a lacerating thong.

'Too old – should have begun seven years ago – you will not, at best, achieve more than mediocrity – hard, incessant work, uncertain praise – bread coming slowly, scantily, perhaps not at all – mortifications, people no longer feigning not to see your blunders – glaring insignificance' – all these phrases rankled in her; and even more galling was the hint that she could only be accepted on the stage as a beauty who hoped to get a husband. The 'indignities' that she might be visited with had no very definite form for her, but the mere association of anything called 'indignity' with herself, roused a resentful alarm. And along with the vaguer images which were raised by those biting words, came the more precise conception of disagreeables which her experience enabled her to imagine. How could she take her mamma and the four sisters to London, if it were not possible for her to earn money at once? And as for submitting to be a *protégée*, and asking her mamma to submit with her to the humiliation of being supported by Miss Arrowpoint – that was as bad as being a governess; nay, worse; for suppose the end of all her study to be as worthless as Klesmer clearly expected it to be, the sense of favours received and never repaid, would embitter the miseries of disappointment. Klesmer doubtless had magnificent ideas about helping artists; but how could he know the feelings of ladies in such matters? It was all over: she had entertained a mistaken hope; and there was an end of it.

'An end of it!' said Gwendolen, aloud, starting from her seat as she heard the steps and voices of her mamma and sisters coming in from church. She hurried to the piano and began gathering together her pieces of music with assumed diligence, while the expression on her pale face and in her burning eyes was what would have suited a woman enduring a wrong which she might not resent, but would probably revenge.

'Well, my darling,' said gentle Mrs. Davilow, entering, 'I see by the wheel-marks that Klesmer has been here. Have you been satisfied with the interview?' She had some guesses as to its object, but felt timid about implying them.

'Satisfied, mamma? oh yes,' said Gwendolen, in a high hard tone, for which she must be excused, because she dreaded a scene of emotion. If she did not set herself resolutely to feign proud indifference, she felt that she must fall into a passionate outburst of despair, which would cut her mamma more deeply than all the rest of their calamities.

'Your uncle and aunt were disappointed at not seeing you,' said Mrs. Davilow, coming near the piano, and watching Gwendolen's movements. 'I only said that you wanted rest.'

'Quite right, mamma,' said Gwendolen, in the same tone, turning to put away some music.

'Am I not to know anything now, Gwendolen? Am I always to be in the dark?' said Mrs. Davilow, too keenly sensitive to her daughter's manner and expression not to fear that something painful had occurred.

'There is really nothing to tell now, mamma,' said Gwendolen, in a still higher voice. 'I had a mistaken idea about something I could do. Herr Klesmer has undeceived me. That is all.'

'Don't look and speak in that way, my dear child: I cannot bear it,' said Mrs. Davilow, breaking down. She felt an undefinable terror.

Gwendolen looked at her a moment in silence, biting her inner lip; then she went up to her, and putting her hands on her mamma's shoulders, said with a drop of her voice to the lowest undertone, 'Mamma, don't speak to me now. It is useless to cry and waste our strength over what can't be altered. You will live at Sawyer's Cottage, and I am going to the bishop's daughters. There is no more to be said. Things cannot be altered, and who cares? It makes no difference to any one else what we do. We must try not to care ourselves. We must not give way. I dread giving way. Help me to be quiet.'

Mrs. Davilow was like a frightened child under her daughter's face and voice: her tears were arrested and she went away in silence.

XXIV

'I question things and do not find
One that will answer to my mind;
And all the world appears unkind.'

— WORDSWORTH.

GWENDOLEN was glad that she had got through her interview with Klesmer before meeting her uncle and aunt. She had made up her mind now that there were only disagreeables before her, and she felt able to maintain a dogged calm in the face of any humiliation that might be proposed.

The meeting did not happen until the Monday, when Gwendolen went to the Rectory with her mamma. They had called at Sawyer's Cottage by the way, and had seen every cranny of the narrow rooms in a mid-day light unsoftened by blinds and curtains; for the furnishing to be done by gleanings from the Rectory had not yet begun.

'How *shall* you endure it, mamma?' said Gwendolen, as they walked away. She had not opened her lips while they were looking round at the bare walls and floors, and the little garden with the cabbage-stalks, and the yew arbour all dust and cobwebs within. 'You and the four girls all in that closet of a room, with the green and yellow paper pressing on your eyes? And without me?'

'It will be some comfort that you have not to bear it too, dear.'

'If it were not that I must get some money, I would rather be there than go to be a governess.'

'Don't set yourself against it beforehand, Gwendolen. If you go to the palace you will have every luxury about you. And you know how much you have always cared for that. You will not find it so hard as going up and down those steep narrow stairs, and hearing the crockery rattle through the house, and the dear girls talking.'

'It is like a bad dream,' said Gwendolen, impetuously. 'I cannot believe that my uncle will let you go to such a place. He ought to have taken some other steps.'

'Don't be unreasonable, dear child. What could he have done?'

'That was for him to find out. It seems to me a very extraordinary world if people in our position must sink in this way all at once,' said Gwendolen, the other worlds with which she was conversant being constructed with a sense of fitness that arranged her own future agreeably.

It was her temper that framed her sentences under this entirely new pressure of evils: she could have spoken more suitably on the vicissitudes in other people's lives, though it was never her aspiration to express herself virtuously so much as cleverly – a point to be remembered in extenuation of her words, which were usually worse than she was.

And, notwithstanding the keen sense of her own bruises, she was capable of some compunction when her uncle and aunt received her with a more affectionate kindness than they had ever shown before. She could not but be struck by the dignified cheerfulness with which they talked of the necessary economies in their way of living, and in the education of the boys. Mr. Gascoigne's worth of character, a little obscured by worldly opportunities – as the poetic beauty of women is obscured by the demands of fashionable dressing – showed itself to great advantage under this sudden reduction of fortune. Prompt and methodical, he had set himself not only to put down his carriage, but to reconsider his worn suits of clothes, to leave off meat for breakfast, to do without periodicals, to get Edwy from school and arrange hours of study for all the boys under himself, and to order the whole establishment on the sparest footing possible. For all healthy people economy has its pleasures; and the Rector's spirit had spread through the household. Mrs. Gascoigne and Anna, who always made papa their model, really did not miss anything they cared about for themselves, and in all sincerity felt that the saddest part of the family losses was the change for Mrs. Davilow and her children.

Anna for the first time could merge her resentment on behalf of Rex in her sympathy with Gwendolen; and Mrs.

Gascoigne was disposed to hope that trouble would have a salutary effect on her niece, without thinking it her duty to add any bitters by way of increasing the salutariness. They had both been busy devising how to get blinds and curtains for the cottage out of the household stores; but with delicate feeling they left these matters in the background, and talked at first of Gwendolen's journey, and the comfort it was to her mamma to have her at home again.

In fact there was nothing for Gwendolen to take as a justification for extending her discontent with events to the persons immediately around her, and she felt shaken into a more alert attention, as if by a call to drill that everybody else was obeying, when her uncle began in a voice of firm kindness to talk to her of the efforts he had been making to get her a situation which would offer her as many advantages as possible. Mr. Gascoigne had not forgotten Grandcourt, but the possibility of further advances from that quarter was something too vague for a man of his good sense to be determined by it: uncertainties of that kind must not now slacken his action in doing the best he could for his niece under actual conditions.

'I felt that there was no time to be lost, Gwendolen; – for a position in a good family where you will have some consideration is not to be had at a moment's notice. And however long we waited we could hardly find one where you would be better off than at Bishop Mompert's. I am known to both him and Mrs. Mompert, and that of course is an advantage for you. Our correspondence has gone on favourably; but I cannot be surprised that Mrs. Mompert wishes to see you before making an absolute engagement. She thinks of arranging for you to meet her at Wancester when she is on her way to town. I dare say you will feel the interview rather trying for you, my dear; but you will have a little time to prepare your mind.'

'Do you know *why* she wants to see me, uncle?' said Gwendolen, whose mind had quickly gone over various reasons that an imaginary Mrs. Mompert with three daughters might be supposed to entertain, reasons all of a disagreeable kind to the person presenting herself for inspection.

The Rector smiled. 'Don't be alarmed, my dear. She would like to have a more precise idea of you than my report can give. And a mother is naturally scrupulous about a companion for her daughters. I have told her you are very young. But she herself exercises a close supervision over her daughters' education, and that makes her less anxious as to age. She is a woman of taste and also of strict principle, and objects to having a French person in the house. I feel sure that she will think your manners and accomplishments as good as she is likely to find; and over the religious and moral tone of the education she, and indeed the bishop himself, will preside.'

Gwendolen dared not answer, but the repression of her decided dislike to the whole prospect sent an unusually deep flush over her face and neck, subsiding as quickly as it came. Anna, full of tender fears, put her little hand into her cousin's, and Mr. Gascoigne was too kind a man not to conceive something of the trial which this sudden change must be for a girl like Gwendolen. Bent on giving a cheerful view of things, he went on in an easy tone of remark, not as if answering supposed objections –

'I think so highly of the position, that I should have been tempted to try and get it for Anna, if she had been at all likely to meet Mrs. Mompert's wants. It is really a home, with a continuance of education in the highest sense: "governess" is a misnomer. The bishop's views are of a more decidedly Low Church colour than my own – he is a close friend of Lord Grampian's; but though privately strict, he is not by any means narrow in public matters. Indeed, he has created as little dislike in his diocese as any bishop on the bench. He has always remained friendly to me, though before his promotion, when he was an incumbent of this diocese, we had a little controversy about the Bible Society.'

The Rector's words were too pregnant with satisfactory meaning to himself for him to imagine the effect they produced in the mind of his niece. 'Continuance of education' – 'bishop's views' – 'privately strict' – 'Bible Society,' – it was as if he had introduced a few snakes at large for the instruction of ladies who regarded them as all alike furnished with poison-bags, and biting or stinging according to convenience. To Gwendolen, already shrinking from the prospect opened to her, such phrases came like the growing heat of a burning-glass – not at all as the links of persuasive reflection which they formed for the good uncle. She began desperately to seek an alternative.

'There was another situation, I think, mamma spoke of?' she said, with determined self-mastery.

'Yes,' said the Rector, in rather a depreciatory tone; 'but that is in a school. I should not have the same satisfaction in your taking that. It would be much harder work, you are aware, and not so good in any other respect. Besides, you have not an equal chance of getting it.'

'Oh dear no,' said Mrs. Gascoigne, 'it would be much harder for you, my dear – much less appropriate. You might not have a bedroom to yourself.' And Gwendolen's memories of school suggested other particulars which forced her to admit to herself that this alternative would be no relief. She turned to her uncle again and said, apparently in acceptance of his ideas –

'When is Mrs. Mompert likely to send for me?'

'That is rather uncertain, but she has promised not to entertain any other proposal till she has seen you. She has entered with much feeling into your position. It will be within the next fortnight, probably. But I must be off now. I am going to let part of my glebe uncommonly well.'

The Rector ended very cheerfully, leaving the room with the satisfactory conviction that Gwendolen was going to adapt herself to circumstances like a girl of good sense. Having spoken appropriately, he naturally supposed that the effects would be appropriate; being accustomed as a household and parish authority to be asked to 'speak to' refractory persons, with the understanding that the measure was morally coercive.

'What a stay Henry is to us all!' said Mrs. Gascoigne, when her husband had left the room.

'He is indeed,' said Mrs. Davilow, cordially. 'I think cheerfulness is a fortune in itself. I wish I had it.'

'And Rex is just like him,' said Mrs. Gascoigne. 'I must tell you the comfort we have had in a letter from him. I must read you a little bit,' she added, taking the letter from her pocket, while Anna looked rather frightened – she did not know why, except that it had been a rule with her not to mention Rex before Gwendolen.

The proud mother ran her eyes over the letter, seeking for sentences to read aloud. But apparently she had found it sown with what might seem to be closer allusions than she desired to the recent past, for she looked up, folding the letter, and saying –

'However, he tells us that our trouble has made a man of him; he sees a reason for any amount of work: he means to get a fellowship, to take pupils, to set one of his brothers going, to be everything that is most remarkable. The letter is full of fun – just like him. He says, "Tell mother she has put out an advertisement for a jolly good hard-working son, in time to hinder me from taking ship; and I offer myself for the place." The letter came on Friday. I never saw my husband so much moved by anything since Rex was born. It seemed a gain to balance our loss.'

This letter, in fact, was what had helped both Mrs. Gascoigne and Anna to show Gwendolen an unmixed kindliness; and she herself felt very amiably about it, smiling at Anna and pinching her chin as much as to say, 'Nothing is wrong with you now, is it?' She had no gratuitously ill-natured feeling, or egoistic pleasure in making men miserable. She only had an intense objection to their making her miserable.

But when the talk turned on furniture for the cottage, Gwendolen was not roused to show even a languid interest. She thought that she had done as much as could be expected of her this morning and indeed felt at an heroic pitch in keeping to herself the struggle that was going on within her. The recoil of her mind from the only definite prospect allowed her, was stronger than even she had imagined beforehand. The idea of presenting herself before Mrs. Mompert in the first instance, to be approved or disapproved, came as pressure on an already painful bruise: even as a governess, it appeared, she was to be tested and was liable to rejection. After she had done herself the violence to accept the bishop and his wife, they were still to consider whether they would accept her; it was at her peril that she was to look, speak, or be silent. And even when she had entered on her dismal task of self-constraint in the society of three girls whom she was bound incessantly to edify, the same process of inspection was to go on: there was always to be Mrs. Mompert's supervision; always something or other would be expected of her to which she had not the slightest inclination; and perhaps the bishop would examine her on serious topics. Gwendolen, lately used to the social successes of a handsome girl, whose lively venturesomeness of talk has the effect of wit, and who six weeks before would have pitied the dullness of the bishop rather than have been embarrassed by him, saw the life before her as an entrance into a penitentiary. Wild thoughts of running away to be an actress, in spite of Klesmer, came to her with the lure of freedom; but his words still hung heavily on her soul; they had alarmed her pride and even her maidenly dignity: dimly she conceived herself getting amongst vulgar people who would treat her with rude familiarity – odious men whose grins and smirks would not be seen through the strong grating of polite society. Gwendolen's daring was not in the least that of the adventuress; the demand to be held a lady was in her very marrow; and when she had dreamed that she might be the heroine of the gaming-table, it was with the understanding that no one should treat her with the less consideration, or presume to look at her with irony as Deronda had done. To be protected and petted, and to have her susceptibilities consulted in every detail, had gone along with her food and clothing as

matters of course in her life: even without any such warning as Klesmer's she could not have thought it an attractive
freedom to be thrown in solitary dependence on the doubtful civility of strangers. The endurance of the episcopal
penitentiary was less repulsive than that; though here too
she would certainly never be petted or have her susceptibilities consulted. Her rebellion against this hard necessity which had come just to her of all people in the world –
to her whom all circumstances had concurred in preparing
for something quite different – was exaggerated instead of
diminished as one hour followed another, filled with the
imagination of what she might have expected in her lot and
what it was actually to be. The family troubles, she
thought, were easier for every one than for her – even for
poor dear mamma, because she had always used herself to
not enjoying. As to hoping that if she went to the
Momperts' and was patient a little while, things might
get better – it would be stupid to entertain hopes for
herself after all that had happened: her talents, it appeared,
would never be recognized as anything remarkable, and
there was not a single direction in which probability
seemed to flatter her wishes. Some beautiful girls who,
like her, had read romances where even plain governesses
are centres of attraction and are sought in marriage, might
have solaced themselves a little by transporting such pictures into their own future; but even if Gwendolen's
experience had led her to dwell on love-making and marriage as her elysium, her heart was too much oppressed by
what was near to her, in both the past and the future, for her
to project her anticipations very far off. She had a world-
nausea upon her, and saw no reason all through her life why
she should wish to live. No religious view of trouble helped
her: her troubles had in her opinion all been caused by
other people's disagreeable or wicked conduct; and there
was really nothing pleasant to be counted on in the world:
that was her feeling; everything else she had heard said
about trouble was mere phrase-making not attractive
enough for her to have caught it up and repeated it. As to

the sweetness of labour and fulfilled claims; the interest of inward and outward activity; the impersonal delights of life as a perpetual discovery; the dues of courage, fortitude, industry, which it is mere baseness not to pay towards the common burthen; the supreme worth of the teacher's vocation; – these, even if they had been eloquently preached to her, could have been no more than faintly apprehended doctrines: the fact which wrought upon her was her invariable observation that for a lady to become a governess – to 'take a situation' – was to descend in life and to be treated at best with a compassionate patronage. And poor Gwendolen had never dissociated happiness from personal pre-eminence and *éclat*. That where these threatened to forsake her, she should take life to be hardly worth the having, cannot make her so unlike the rest of us, men or women, that we should cast her out of our compassion; our moments of temptation to a mean opinion of things in general being usually dependent on some susceptibility about ourselves and some dullness to subjects which every one else would consider more important. Surely a young creature is pitiable who has the labyrinth of life before her and no clue – to whom distrust in herself and her good fortune has come as a sudden shock, like a rent across the path that she was treading carelessly.

In spite of her healthy frame, her irreconcilable repugnance affected her even physically: she felt a sort of numbness and could set about nothing; the least urgency, even that she should take her meals, was an irritation to her; the speech of others on any subject seemed unreasonable, because it did not include her feeling and was an ignorant claim on her. It was not in her nature to busy herself with the fancies of suicide to which disappointed young people are prone: what occupied and exasperated her was the sense that there was nothing for her but to live in a way she hated. She avoided going to the Rectory again: it was too intolerable to have to look and talk as if she were compliant; and she could not exert herself to show interest about the furniture of that horrible cottage. Miss Merry was staying on purpose to help, and such people as Jocosa liked that sort of thing. Her mother had to make excuses for her not appearing, even when Anna came to see her. For that calm which Gwendolen had promised herself to maintain had changed into sick motivelessness: she thought, 'I suppose I shall begin to pretend by-and-by, but why should I do it now?'

Her mother watched her with silent distress; and, lapsing into the habit of indulgent tenderness, she began to think what she imagined that Gwendolen was thinking, and to wish that everything should give way to the poss-ibility of making her darling less miserable.

One day when she was in the black and yellow bedroom and her mother was lingering there under the pretext of considering and arranging Gwendolen's articles of dress, she suddenly roused herself to fetch the casket which contained her ornaments.

'Mamma,' she began, glancing over the upper layer, 'I had forgotten these things. Why didn't you remind me of them? Do see about getting them sold. You will not mind about parting with them. You gave them all to me long ago.'

She lifted the upper tray and looked below.

'If we can do without them, darling, I would rather keep them for you,' said Mrs. Davilow, seating herself beside Gwendolen with a feeling of relief that she was beginning to talk about something. The usual relation between them had become reversed. It was now the mother who tried to cheer the daughter. 'Why, how came you to put that pocket-handkerchief in here?'

It was the handkerchief with the corner torn off which Gwendolen had thrust in with the turquoise necklace.

'It happened to be with the necklace – I was in a hurry,' said Gwendolen, taking the handkerchief away and put-ting it in her pocket. 'Don't sell the necklace, mamma,' she added, a new feeling having come over her about that rescue of it which had formerly been so offensive.

'No, dear, no; it was made out of your dear father's chain. And I should prefer not selling the other things. None of them are of any great value. All my best ornaments were taken from me long ago.'

Mrs. Davilow coloured. She usually avoided any reference to such facts about Gwendolen's stepfather as that he had carried off his wife's jewellery and disposed of it. After a moment's pause she went on –

'And these things have not been reckoned on for any expenses. Carry them with you.'

'That would be quite useless, mamma,' said Gwendolen, coldly. 'Governesses don't wear ornaments. You had better get me a grey frieze livery and a straw poke, such as my aunt's charity children wear.'

'No, dear, no; don't take that view of it. I feel sure the Momperts will like you the better for being graceful and elegant.'

'I am not at all sure what the Momperts will like me to be. It is enough that I am expected to be what they like,' said Gwendolen, bitterly.

'If there is anything you would object to less – anything that could be done – instead of your going to the bishop's, do say so, Gwendolen. Tell me what is in your heart. I will try for anything you wish,' said the mother, beseechingly. 'Don't keep things away from me. Let us bear them together.'

'Oh mamma, there is nothing to tell. I can't do anything better. I must think myself fortunate if they will have me. I shall get some money for you. That is the only thing I have to think of. I shall not spend any money this year: you will have all the eighty pounds. I don't know how far that will go in housekeeping; but you need not stitch your poor fingers to the bone, and stare away all the sight that the tears have left in your dear eyes.'

Gwendolen did not give any caresses with her words as she had been used to do. She did not even look at her mother, but was looking at the turquoise necklace as she turned it over her fingers.

'Bless you for your tenderness, my good darling!' said Mrs. Davilow, with tears in her eyes. 'Don't despair because there are clouds now. You are so young. There may be great happiness in store for you yet.'

'I don't see any reason for expecting it, mamma,' said Gwendolen, in a hard tone; and Mrs. Davilow was silent, thinking as she had often thought before – 'What did happen between her and Mr. Grandcourt?'

'I *will* keep this necklace, mamma,' said Gwendolen, laying it apart and then closing the casket. 'But do get the other things sold even if they will not bring much. Ask my uncle what to do with them. I shall certainly not use them again. I am going to take the veil. I wonder if all the poor wretches who have ever taken it felt as I do.'

'Don't exaggerate evils, dear.'

'How can any one know that I exaggerate, when I am speaking of my own feeling? I did not say what any one else felt.'

She took out the torn handkerchief from her pocket again, and wrapt it deliberately round the necklace. Mrs. Davilow observed the action with some surprise, but the tone of the last words discouraged her from asking any question.

The 'feeling' Gwendolen spoke of with an air of tragedy was not to be explained by the mere fact that she was going to be a governess: she was possessed by a spirit of general disappointment. It was not simply that she had a distaste for what she was called on to do: the distaste spread itself over the world outside her penitentiary, since she saw nothing very pleasant in it that seemed attainable by her even if she were free. Naturally her grievances did not seem to her smaller than some of her male contemporaries held theirs to be when they felt a profession too narrow for their powers, and had an *à priori* conviction that it was not worth while to put forth their latent abilities. Because her education had been less expensive than theirs it did not follow that she should have wider emotions or a keener intellectual vision. Her griefs were feminine; but to her as a woman they were not the less hard to bear, and she felt an equal right to the Promethean tone.

But the movement of mind which led her to keep the necklace, to fold it up in the handkerchief, and rise to put it in her *nécessaire*, where she had first placed it when it had been returned to her, was more peculiar, and what would be called less reasonable. It came from that streak of superstition in her which attached itself both to her confidence and her terror – a superstition which lingers in an intense personality even in spite of theory and science; any dread or hope for self being stronger than all reasons for or against it. Why she should suddenly determine not to part with the necklace was not much clearer to her than why she should sometimes have been frightened to find herself in the fields alone: she had a confused state of emotion about Deronda – was it wounded pride and resentment, or a certain awe and exceptional trust? It was something vague and yet mastering, which impelled her to this action about the necklace. There is a great deal of unmapped country within us which would have to be taken into account in an explanation of our gusts and storms.

XXV

How trace the why and wherefore in a mind reduced to the
barrenness of a fastidious egoism, in which all direct desires are
dulled, and have dwindled from motives into a vacillating
expectation of motives: a mind made up of moods, where a fitful
impulse springs here and there conspicuously rank amid the
general weediness? 'Tis a condition apt to befall a life too much
at large, unmoulded by the pressure of obligation. *Nam deteriores
omnes sumus licentiæ*, saith Terence; or, as a more familiar tongue
might deliver it, *'As you like' is a bad finger-post.*

POTENTATES make known their intentions and affect
the funds at a small expense of words. So, when
Grandcourt, after learning that Gwendolen had left
Leubronn, incidentally pronounced that resort of fashion
a beastly hole worse than Baden, the remark was conclus-
ive to Mr. Lush that his patron intended straightway to
return to Diplow. The execution was sure to be slower than
the intention, and in fact Grandcourt did loiter through the
next day without giving any distinct orders about departure – perhaps because he discerned that Lush was expecting them: he lingered over his toilet, and certainly came
down with a faded aspect of perfect distinction which
made fresh complexions, and hands with the blood in
them, seem signs of raw vulgarity; he lingered on the
terrace, in the gambling-rooms, in the reading-room, occupying himself in being indifferent to everybody and everything around him. When he met Lady Mallinger, however,
he took some trouble – raised his hat, paused, and proved
that he listened to her recommendation of the waters by
replying, 'Yes; I heard somebody say how providential it
was that there always happened to be springs at gambling
places.'

'Oh, that was a joke,' said innocent Lady Mallinger,
misled by Grandcourt's languid seriousness, 'in imitation
of the old one about the towns and the rivers, you know.'

'Ah, perhaps,' said Grandcourt, without change of
expression. Lady Mallinger thought this worth telling to

Sir Hugo, who said, 'Oh my dear, he is not a fool. You must not suppose that he can't see a joke. He can play his cards as well as most of us.'

'He has never seemed to me a very sensible man,' said Lady Mallinger, in excuse of herself. She had a secret objection to meeting Grandcourt, who was little else to her than a large living sign of what she felt to be her failure as a wife – the not having presented Sir Hugo with a son. Her constant reflection was that her husband might fairly regret his choice, and if he had not been very good might have treated her with some roughness in consequence, gentlemen naturally disliking to be disappointed.

Deronda, too, had a recognition from Grandcourt, for which he was not grateful, though he took care to return it with perfect civility. No reasoning as to the foundations of custom could do away with the early-rooted feeling that his birth had been attended with injury for which his father was to blame; and seeing that but for this injury Grandcourt's prospect might have been his, he was proudly resolute not to behave in any way that might be inter-preted into irritation on that score. He saw a very easy descent into mean unreasoning rancour and triumph in others' frustration; and being determined not to go down that ugly pit, he turned his back on it, clinging to the kindlier affections within him as a possession. Pride cer-tainly helped him well – the pride of not recognizing a disadvantage for one's self which vulgar minds are dis-posed to exaggerate, such as the shabby equipage of pov-erty: he would not have a man like Grandcourt suppose himself envied by him. But there is no guarding against interpretation. Grandcourt did believe that Deronda, poor devil, who he had no doubt was his cousin by the father's side, inwardly winced under their mutual position; where-fore the presence of that less lucky person was more agree-able to him than it would otherwise have been. An imaginary envy, the idea that others feel their comparative deficiency, is the ordinary *cortège* of egoism; and his pet dogs were not the only beings that Grandcourt liked to feel his power over in making them jealous. Hence he was civil enough to exchange several words with Deronda on the terrace about the hunting round Diplow, and even said, 'You had better come over for a run or two when the season begins.'

Lush, not displeased with delay, amused himself very well, partly in gossiping with Sir Hugo and in answering his questions about Grandcourt's affairs so far as they might affect his willingness to part with his interest in Diplow. Also about Grandcourt's personal entanglements, the baronet knew enough already for Lush to feel released from silence on a sunny autumn day, when there was nothing more agreeable to do in lounging promenades than to speak freely of a tyrannous patron behind his back. Sir Hugo willingly inclined his ear to a little good-humoured scandal, which he was fond of calling *traits de mœurs*; but he was strict in keeping such communications from hearers who might take them too seriously. Whatever knowledge he had of his nephew's secrets, he had never spoken of it to Deronda, who considered Grandcourt a pale-blooded mortal, but was far from wishing to hear how the red corpuscles had been washed out of him. It was Lush's policy and inclination to gratify everybody when he had no reason to the contrary; and the baronet always treated him well, as one of those easy-handled personages who, frequenting the society of gentlemen, without being exactly gentlemen themselves, can be the more serviceable, like the second-best articles of our wardrobe, which we use with a comfortable freedom from anxiety.

'Well, you will let me know the turn of events,' said Sir Hugo, 'if this marriage seems likely to come off after all, or if anything else happens to make the want of money more pressing. My plan would be much better for him than burthening Ryelands.'

'That's true,' said Lush, 'only it must not be urged on him – just placed in his way that the scent may tickle him. Grandcourt is not a man to be always led by what makes for his own interest; especially if you let him see that it makes for your interest too. I'm attached to him, of course. I've given up everything else for the sake of keeping by him, and it has lasted a good fifteen years now. He would not easily get any one else to fill my place. He's a peculiar character, is Henleigh Grandcourt, and it has been growing on him of late years. However, I'm of a constant disposition, and I've been a sort of guardian to him since he was twenty: an uncommonly fascinating fellow he was then, to be sure – and could be now, if he liked. I'm attached to him; and it would be a good deal worse for him if he missed me at his elbow.'

Sir Hugo did not think it needful to express his sympathy or even assent, and perhaps Lush himself did not expect this sketch of his motives to be taken as exact. But how can a man avoid himself as a subject in conversation? And he must make some sort of decent toilet in words, as in cloth and linen. Lush's listener was not severe: a member of Parliament could allow for the necessities of verbal toilet; and the dialogue went on without any change of mutual estimate.

However, Lush's easy prospect of indefinite procrastination was cut off the next morning by Grandcourt's saluting him with the question –

'Are you making all the arrangements for our starting by the Paris train?'

'I didn't know you meant to start,' said Lush, not exactly taken by surprise.

'You might have known,' said Grandcourt, looking at the burnt length of his cigar, and speaking in that lowered tone which was usual with him when he meant to express disgust and be peremptory. 'Just see to everything, will you? and mind no brute gets into the same carriage with us. And leave my P.P.C. at the Mallingers.'

In consequence they were at Paris the next day; but here Lush was gratified by the proposal or command that he should go straight on to Diplow and see that everything was right, while Grandcourt and the valet remained behind; and it was not until several days later that Lush received the telegram ordering the carriage to the Wancester station.

He had used the interim actively, not only in carrying out Grandcourt's orders about the stud and household, but in learning all he could of Gwendolen, and how things were going on at Offendene. What was the probable effect that the news of the family misfortunes would have on Grandcourt's fitful obstinacy he felt to be quite incalculable. So far as the girl's poverty might be an argument that she would accept an offer from him now in spite of any previous coyness, it might remove that bitter objection to risk a repulse which Lush divined to be one of Grandcourt's deterring motives; on the other hand, the certainty of acceptance was just 'the sort of thing' to make him lapse hither and thither with no more apparent will than a moth. Lush had had his patron under close observation for many years, and knew him perhaps better than he knew any other subject; but to know Grandcourt was to doubt what he would do in any particular case. It might happen that he would behave with an apparent magnanimity, like the hero of a modern French drama, whose sudden start into moral splendour after much lying and meanness, leaves you little confidence as to any part of his career that may follow the fall of the curtain. Indeed, what attitude would have been more honourable for a final scene than that of declining to seek an heiress for her money, and determining to marry the attractive girl who had none? But Lush had some general certainties about Grandcourt, and one was, that of all inward movements those of generosity were the least likely to occur in him. Of what use, however, is a general certainty that an insect will not walk with his head hindmost, when what you need to know is the play of inward stimulus that sends him hither and thither in a network of possible paths? Thus Lush was much at fault as to the probable issue between Grandcourt and Gwendolen, when what he desired was a perfect confidence that they would never be married. He would have consented willingly that Grandcourt should marry an heiress, or that he should marry Mrs. Glasher: in the one match there would have been the immediate abundance that prospective heirship could not supply, in the other there would have been the security of the wife's gratitude, for Lush had always been Mrs. Glasher's friend; and that the future Mrs. Grandcourt should not be socially received could not affect his private comfort. He would not have minded, either, that there should be no marriage in question at all; but he felt himself justified in doing his utmost to hinder a marriage with a girl who was likely to bring nothing but trouble to her husband – not to speak of annoyance if not ultimate injury to her husband's old companion, whose future Mr. Lush earnestly wished to make as easy as possible, considering that he had well deserved such compensation for leading a dog's life, though that of a dog who enjoyed many tastes undisturbed, and who profited by a large establishment. He wished for himself what he felt to be good, and was not conscious of wishing harm to any one else; unless perhaps it were just now a little harm to the inconvenient and impertinent Gwendolen. But the easiest-humoured amateur of luxury and music, the toad-eater the least liable to nausea, must be expected to have his susceptibilities. And Mr. Lush was accustomed to be treated by the world in general as an apt, agreeable fellow: he had not made up his mind to be insulted by more than one person.

With this imperfect preparation of a war policy, Lush was awaiting Grandcourt's arrival, doing little more than wondering how the campaign would begin. The first day Grandcourt was much occupied with the stables, and amongst other things he ordered a groom to put a side-saddle on Criterion and let him review the horse's paces. This marked indication of purpose set Lush on considering over again whether he should incur the ticklish consequences of speaking first, while he was still sure that no compromising step had been taken; and he rose the next morning almost resolved that if Grandcourt seemed in as good a humour as yesterday and entered at all into talk, he would let drop the interesting facts about Gwendolen and her family, just to see how they would work, and to get some guidance. But Grandcourt did not enter into talk, and in answer to a question even about his own convenience, no fish could have maintained a more unwinking silence. After he had read his letters he gave various orders to be executed or transmitted by Lush, and then thrust his shoulders towards that useful person, who accordingly rose to leave the room. But before he was out of the door, Grandcourt turned his head slightly and gave a broken languid 'Oh.'

'What is it?' said Lush, who, it must have been observed, did not take his dusty puddings with a respectful air.

'Shut the door, will you? I can't speak into the corridor.'

Lush closed the door, came forward, and chose to sit down.

After a little pause Grandcourt said, 'Is Miss Harleth at Offendene?' He was quite certain that Lush had made it his business to inquire about her, and he had some pleasure in thinking that Lush did not want *him* to inquire.

'Well, I hardly know,' said Lush, carelessly. 'The family's utterly done up. They and the Gascoignes too have lost all their money. It's owing to some rascally banking business. The poor mother hasn't a *sou*, it seems. She and the girls have to huddle themselves into a little cottage like a labourer's.'

'Don't lie to me, if you please,' said Grandcourt, in his lowest audible tone. 'It's not amusing, and it answers no other purpose.'

'What do you mean?' said Lush, more nettled than was common with him – the prospect before him being more than commonly disturbing.

'Just tell me the truth, will you?'

'It's no invention of mine. I have heard the story from several – Bazley, Brackenshaw's man, for one. He is getting a new tenant for Offendene.'

'I don't mean that. Is Miss Harleth there, or is she not?' said Grandcourt, in his former tone.

'Upon my soul, I can't tell,' said Lush, rather sulkily. 'She may have left yesterday. I heard she had taken a situation as governess; she may be gone to it for what I know. But if you wanted to see her, no doubt the mother would send for her back.' This sneer slipped off his tongue without strict intention.

'Send Hutchins to inquire whether she will be there to-morrow.'

Lush did not move. Like many persons who have thought over beforehand what they shall say in given cases, he was impelled by an unexpected irritation to say some of those prearranged things before the cases were given. Grandcourt, in fact, was likely to get into a scrape so tremendous, that it was impossible to let him take the first step towards it without remonstrance. Lush retained enough caution to use a tone of rational friendliness; still he felt his own value to his patron, and was prepared to be daring.

'It would be as well for you to remember, Grandcourt, that you are coming under closer fire now. There can be none of the ordinary flirting done, which may mean every-thing or nothing. You must make up your mind whether you wish to be accepted; and more than that, how you would like being refused. Either one or the other. You can't be philandering after her again for six weeks.'

Grandcourt said nothing, but pressed the newspaper down on his knees and began to light another cigar. Lush took this as a sign that he was willing to listen, and was the more bent on using the opportunity; he wanted if possible to find out which would be the more potent cause of hesitation – probable acceptance or probable refusal.

'Everything has a more serious look now than it had before. There is her family to be provided for. You could not let your wife's mother live in beggary. It will be a confoundedly hampering affair. Marriage will pin you down in a way you haven't been used to; and in point of money you have not too much elbow-room. And after all, what will you get by it? You are master over your estates, present or future, as far as choosing your heir goes; it's a pity to go on encumbering them for a mere whim, which you may repent of in a twelvemonth. I should be sorry to see you making a mess of your life in that way. If there were anything solid to be gained by the marriage, that would be a different affair.'

Lush's tone had gradually become more and more unctuous in its friendliness of remonstrance, and he was almost in danger of forgetting that he was merely gambling in argument. When he left off, Grandcourt took his cigar out of his mouth, and looking steadily at the moist end while he adjusted the leaf with his delicate finger-tips, said,

'I knew before that you had an objection to my marrying Miss Harleth.' Here he made a little pause, before he continued, 'But I never considered that a reason against it.'

'I never supposed you did,' answered Lush, not unctuously, but drily. 'It was not *that* I urged as a reason. I should have thought it might have been a reason against it, after all your experience, that you would be acting like the hero of a ballad, and making yourself absurd – and all for what? You know you couldn't make up your mind before. It's impossible you can care much about her. And as for the tricks she is likely to play, you may judge of that from what you heard at Leubronn. However, what I wished to point out to you was, that there can be no shilly-shally now.'

'Perfectly,' said Grandcourt, looking round at Lush and fixing him with narrow eyes; 'I don't intend that there should be. I dare say it's disagreeable to you. But if you suppose I care a damn for that, you are most stupendously mistaken.'

'Oh, well,' said Lush, rising with his hands in his pockets, and feeling some latent venom stir within him, 'if you have made up your mind! – only there's another aspect of the affair. I have been speaking on the supposition that it was absolutely certain she would accept you, and that destitution would have no choice. But I am not so sure that the young lady is to be counted on. She is kittle cattle to shoe, I think. And she had her reasons for running away before.' Lush had moved a step or two till he stood nearly in front of Grandcourt, though at some distance from him. He did not feel himself much restrained by consequences, being aware that the only strong hold he had on his present position was his serviceableness; and even after a quarrel, the want of him was likely sooner or later to recur. He foresaw that Gwendolen would cause him to be ousted for a time, and his temper at this moment urged him to risk a quarrel.

'She had her reasons,' he repeated, more significantly.

'I had come to that conclusion before,' said Grandcourt, with contemptuous irony.

'Yes, but I hardly think you know what her reasons were.'

'You do, apparently,' said Grandcourt, not betraying by so much as an eyelash that he cared for the reasons.

'Yes, and you had better know too, that you may judge of the influence you have over her, if she swallows her reasons and accepts you. For my own part, I would take odds against it. She saw Lydia in Cardell Chase and heard the whole story.'

Grandcourt made no immediate answer, and only went on smoking. He was so long before he spoke, that Lush moved about and looked out of the windows, unwilling to go away without seeing some effect of his daring move. He had expected that Grandcourt would tax him with having contrived the affair, since Mrs. Glasher was then living at Gadsmere a hundred miles off, and he was prepared to admit the fact: what he cared about was that Grandcourt should be staggered by the sense that his intended advances must be made to a girl who had that knowledge in her mind and had been scared by it. At length Grandcourt, seeing Lush turn towards him, looked at him again and said, contemptuously, 'What follows?'

Here certainly was a 'mate' in answer to Lush's 'check;' and though his exasperation with Grandcourt was perhaps stronger than it had ever been before, it would have been mere idiocy to act as if any further move could be useful. He gave a slight shrug with one shoulder and was going to walk away, when Grandcourt, turning on his seat towards the table, said, as quietly as if nothing had occurred, 'Oblige me by pushing that pen and paper here, will you?'

No thunderous, bullying superior could have exercised the imperious spell that Grandcourt did. Why, instead of being obeyed, he had never been told to go to a warmer place, was perhaps a mystery to several who found themselves obeying him. The pen and paper were pushed to him, and as he took them he said, 'Just wait for this letter.'

He scrawled with ease, and the brief note was quickly addressed. 'Let Hutchins go with it at once, will you?' said Grandcourt, pushing the letter away from him.

As Lush had expected, it was addressed to Miss Harleth, Offendene. When his irritation had cooled down he was glad there had been no explosive quarrel; but he felt sure that there was a notch made against him, and that somehow or other he was intended to pay. It was also clear to him that the immediate effect of his revelation had been to harden Grandcourt's previous determination. But as to the particular movements which made this process in his baffling mind, Lush could only toss up his chin in despair of a theory.

XXVI

He brings white asses laden with the freight
Of Tyrian vessels, purple, gold, and balm,
To bribe my will: I'll bid them chase him forth,
Nor let him breathe the taint of his surmise
On my secure resolve.
                      Ay, 'tis secure;
And therefore let him come to spread his freight.
For firmness hath its appetite and craves
The stronger lure, more strongly to resist;
Would know the touch of gold to fling it off;
Scent wine to feel its lip the soberer;
Behold soft byssus, ivory, and plumes
To say, 'They're fair, but I will none of them,'
And flout Enticement in the very face.

MR. GASCOIGNE one day came to Offendene with what he felt to be the satisfactory news that Mrs. Mompert had fixed Tuesday in the following week for her interview with Gwendolen at Wancester. He said nothing of his having incidentally heard that Mr. Grandcourt had returned to Diplow; knowing no more than she did that Leubronn had been the goal of her admirer's journeying, and feeling that it would be unkind uselessly to revive the memory of a brilliant prospect under the present reverses. In his secret soul he thought of his niece's unintelligible caprice with regret, but he vindicated her to himself by considering that Grandcourt had been the first to behave oddly, in suddenly walking away when there had been the best opportunity for crowning his marked attentions. The Rector's practical judgment told him that his chief duty to his niece now was to encourage her resolutely to face the change in her lot, since there was no manifest promise of any event that would avert it.

'You will find an interest in varied experience, my dear, and I have no doubt you will be a more valuable woman for having sustained such a part as you are called to.'

'I cannot pretend to believe that I shall like it,' said Gwendolen, for the first time showing her uncle some petulance. 'But I am quite aware that I am obliged to bear it.'

She remembered having submitted to his admonition on a different occasion, when she was expected to like a very different prospect.

'And your good sense will teach you to behave suitably under it,' said Mr. Gascoigne, with a shade more gravity. 'I feel sure that Mrs. Mompert will be pleased with you. You will know how to conduct yourself to a woman who holds in all senses the relation of superior to you. This trouble has come on you young, but that makes it in some respects easier, and there is benefit in all chastisement if we adjust our minds to it.'

This was precisely what Gwendolen was unable to do; and after her uncle was gone, the bitter tears, which had rarely come during the late trouble, rose and fell slowly as she sat alone. Her heart denied that the trouble was easier because she was young. When was she to have any happiness, if it did not come while she was young? Not that her visions of possible happiness for herself were as unmixed with necessary evil as they used to be – not that she could still imagine herself plucking the fruits of life without suspicion of their core. But this general disenchantment with the world – nay, with herself, since it appeared that she was not made for easy pre-eminence – only intensified her sense of forlornness: it was a visibly sterile distance enclosing the dreary path at her feet, in which she had no courage to tread. She was in that first crisis of passionate youthful rebellion against what is not fitly called pain, but rather the absence of joy – that first rage of disappointment in life's morning, which we whom the years have subdued are apt to remember but dimly as part of our own experience, and so to be intolerant of its self-enclosed unreasonableness and impiety. What passion seems more absurd, when we have got outside it and looked at calamity as a collective risk, than this amazed anguish that I and not Thou, He, or She, should be just the smitten one? Yet perhaps some who have afterwards made themselves a willing fence before the breast of another, and have carried their own heart-wound in heroic silence – some who have made their latter deeds great, nevertheless began with this angry amazement at their own smart, and on the mere denial of their fantastic desires raged as if under the sting of wasps which reduced the universe for them to an unjust infliction of pain. This was nearly poor Gwendolen's condition. What though such a reverse as hers had often happened to other girls? The one point she had been all her life learning to care for was, that it had happened to *her*: it was what *she* felt under Klesmer's demonstration that she was not remarkable enough to command fortune by force of will and merit; it was what *she* would feel under the rigours of Mrs. Mompert's constant expectation, under the dull demand that she should be cheerful with three Miss Momperts, under the necessity of showing herself entirely submissive, and keeping her thoughts to herself. To be a queen disthroned is not so hard as some other down-stepping: imagine one who had been made to believe in his own divinity finding all homage withdrawn, and himself unable to perform a miracle that would recall the homage and restore his own confidence. Something akin to this illusion and this helplessness had befallen the poor spoiled child, with the lovely lips and eyes and the majestic figure – which seemed now to have no magic in them.

She rose from the low ottoman where she had been sitting purposeless, and walked up and down the drawing-room, resting her elbow on one palm while she leaned down her cheek on the other, and a slow tear fell. She thought, 'I have always, ever since I was little, felt that mamma was not a happy woman; and now I dare say I shall be more unhappy than she has been.' Her mind dwelt for a few moments on the picture of herself losing her youth and ceasing to enjoy – not minding whether she did this or that: but such picturing inevitably brought back the image of her mother. 'Poor mamma! it will be still worse for her now. I can get a little money for her – that is all I shall care about now.' And then with an entirely new movement of her imagination, she saw her mother getting quite old and white, and herself no longer young but faded, and their two faces meeting still with memory and love, and she knowing what was in her mother's mind – 'Poor Gwen too is sad and faded now' – and then for the first time she sobbed, not in anger but with a sort of tender misery.

Her face was towards the door and she saw her mother enter. She barely saw that; for her eyes were large with tears, and she pressed her handkerchief against them hurriedly. Before she took it away she felt her mother's arms round her, and this sensation, which seemed a prolongation of her inward vision, overcame her will to be reticent; she sobbed anew in spite of herself, as they pressed their cheeks together.

Mrs. Davilow had brought something in her hand which had already caused her an agitating anxiety, and she dared not speak until her darling had become calmer. But Gwendolen, with whom weeping had always been a painful manifestation to be resisted if possible, again pressed her handkerchief against her eyes, and with a deep breath drew her head backward and looked at her mother, who was pale and tremulous.

'It was nothing, mamma,' said Gwendolen, thinking that her mother had been moved in this way simply by finding her in distress. 'It is all over now.'

But Mrs. Davilow had withdrawn her arms, and Gwendolen perceived a letter in her hand.

'What is that letter? – worse news still?' she asked, with a touch of bitterness.

'I don't know what you will think it, dear,' said Mrs. Davilow, keeping the letter in her hand. 'You will hardly guess where it comes from.'

'Don't ask me to guess anything,' said Gwendolen, rather impatiently, as if a bruise were being pressed.

'It is addressed to you, dear.'

Gwendolen gave the slightest perceptible toss of the head.

'It comes from Diplow,' said Mrs. Davilow, giving her the letter.

She knew Grandcourt's indistinct handwriting, and her mother was not surprised to see her blush deeply; but watching her as she read, and wondering much what was the purport of the letter, she saw the colour die out. Gwendolen's lips even were pale as she turned the open note towards her mother. The words were few and formal.

'Mr. Grandcourt presents his compliments to Miss Harleth, and begs to know whether he may be permitted to call at Offendene to-morrow after two, and to see her alone. Mr. Grandcourt has just returned from Leubronn, where he had hoped to find Miss Harleth.'

Mrs. Davilow read, and then looked at her daughter inquiringly, leaving the note in her hand. Gwendolen let it fall on the floor, and turned away.

'It must be answered, darling,' said Mrs. Davilow, timidly. 'The man waits.'

Gwendolen sank on the settee, clasped her hands, and looked straight before her, not at her mother. She had the expression of one who had been startled by a sound and was listening to know what would come of it. The sudden change of the situation was bewildering. A few minutes before she was looking along an inescapable path of repulsive monotony, with hopeless inward rebellion against the imperious lot which left her no choice: and lo, now, a moment of choice was come. Yet – was it triumph she felt most or terror? Impossible for Gwendolen not to feel some triumph in a tribute to her power at a time when she was first tasting the bitterness of insignificance: again she seemed to be getting a sort of empire over her own life. But how to use it? Here came the terror. Quick, quick, like pictures in a book beaten open with a sense of hurry, came back vividly, yet in fragments, all that she had gone through in relation to Grandcourt – the allurements, the vacillations, the resolve to accede, the final repulsion;

the incisive face of that dark-eyed lady with the lovely boy; her own pledge (was it a pledge not to marry him?) – the new disbelief in the worth of men and things for which that scene of disclosure had become a symbol. That unalterable experience made a vision at which in the first agitated moment, before tempering reflections could suggest themselves, her native terror shrank.

Where was the good of choice coming again? What did she wish? Anything different? No! and yet in the dark seed-growths of consciousness a new wish was forming itself – 'I wish I had never known it!' Something, anything she wished for that would have saved her from the dread to let Grandcourt come.

It was no long while – yet it seemed long to Mrs. Davilow, before she thought it well to say, gently –

'It will be necessary for you to write, dear. Or shall I write an answer for you – which you will dictate?'

'No, mamma,' said Gwendolen, drawing a deep breath. 'But please lay me out the pen and paper.'

That was gaining time. Was she to decline Grandcourt's visit – close the shutters – not even look out on what would happen? – though with the assurance that she should remain just where she was? The young activity within her made a warm current through her terror and stirred towards something that would be an event – towards an opportunity in which she could look and speak with the former effectiveness. The interest of the morrow was no longer at a dead-lock.

'There is really no reason on earth why you should be so alarmed at the man's waiting a few minutes, mamma,' said Gwendolen, remonstrantly, as Mrs. Davilow, having pre-pared the writing materials, looked towards her expect-antly. 'Servants expect nothing else than to wait. It is not to be supposed that I must write on the instant.'

'No, dear,' said Mrs. Davilow, in the tone of one cor-rected, turning to sit down and take up a bit of work that lay at hand; 'he can wait another quarter of an hour, if you like.'

It was very simple speech and action on her part, but it was what might have been subtly calculated. Gwendolen felt a contradictory desire to be hastened: hurry would save her from deliberate choice.

'I did not mean him to wait long enough for that needle-work to be finished,' she said, lifting her hands to stroke the backward curves of her hair, while she rose from her seat and stood still.

'But if you don't feel able to decide?' said Mrs. Davilow, sympathizingly.

'I *must* decide,' said Gwendolen, walking to the writing-table and seating herself. All the while there was a busy undercurrent in her, like the thought of a man who keeps up a dialogue while he is considering how he can slip away. Why should she not let him come? It bound her to nothing. He had been to Leubronn after her: of course he meant a direct unmistakable renewal of the suit which before had been only implied. What then? She could reject him. Why was she to deny herself the freedom of doing this – which she would like to do?

'If Mr. Grandcourt has only just returned from Leubronn,' said Mrs. Davilow, observing that Gwendolen leaned back in her chair after taking the pen in her hand – 'I wonder whether he has heard of our misfortunes.'

'That could make no difference to a man in his position,' said Gwendolen, rather contemptuously.

'It would, to some men,' said Mrs. Davilow. 'They would not like to take a wife from a family in a state of beggary almost, as we are. Here we are at Offendene with a great shell over us as usual. But just imagine his finding us at Sawyer's Cottage. Most men are afraid of being bored or taxed by a wife's family. If Mr. Grandcourt did know, I think it a strong proof of his attachment to you.'

Mrs. Davilow spoke with unusual emphasis: it was the first time she had ventured to say anything about Grandcourt which would necessarily seem intended as an argument in favour of him, her habitual impression being that such arguments would certainly be useless and might be worse. The effect of her words now was stronger than she could imagine: they raised a new set of possibilities in Gwendolen's mind – a vision of what Grandcourt might do for her mother if she, Gwendolen, did – what she was not going to do. She was so moved by a new rush of ideas, that like one conscious of being urgently called away, she felt that the immediate task must be hastened: the letter must be written, else it might be endlessly deferred. After all, she acted in a hurry as she had wished to do. To act in a hurry was to have a reason for keeping away from an absolute decision, and to leave open as many issues as possible.

She wrote: 'Miss Harleth presents her compliments to Mr. Grandcourt. She will be at home after two o'clock to-morrow.'

Before addressing the note she said, 'Pray ring the bell, mamma, if there is any one to answer it.' She really did not know who did the work of the house.

It was not till after the letter had been taken away and Gwendolen had risen again, stretching out one arm and then resting it on her head, with a long moan which had a sound of relief in it, that Mrs. Davilow ventured to ask –

'What did you say, Gwen?'

'I said that I should be at home,' answered Gwendolen, rather loftily. Then, after a pause, 'You must not expect, because Mr. Grandcourt is coming, that anything is going to happen, mamma.'

'I don't allow myself to expect anything, dear. I desire you to follow your own feeling. You have never told me what that was.'

'What is the use of telling?' said Gwendolen, hearing a reproach in that true statement. 'When I have anything pleasant to tell, you may be sure I will tell you.'

'But Mr. Grandcourt will consider that you have already accepted him, in allowing him to come. His note tells you plainly enough that he is coming to make you an offer.'

'Very well; and I wish to have the pleasure of refusing him.'

Mrs. Davilow looked up in wonderment, but Gwendolen implied her wish not to be questioned further by saying –

'Put down that detestable needlework, and let us walk in the avenue. I am stifled.'

XXVII

Desire has trimmed the sails, and Circumstance
Brings but the breeze to fill them.

WHILE Grandcourt on his beautiful black Yarico, the groom behind him on Criterion, was taking the pleasant ride from Diplow to Offendene, Gwendolen was seated before the mirror while her mother gathered up the lengthy mass of light-brown hair which she had been carefully brushing.

'Only gather it up easily and make a coil, mamma,' said Gwendolen.

'Let me bring you some earrings, Gwen,' said Mrs. Davilow, when the hair was adjusted, and they were both looking at the reflection in the glass. It was impossible for them not to notice that the eyes looked brighter than they had done of late, that there seemed to be a shadow lifted from the face, leaving all the lines once more in their placid youthfulness. The mother drew some inferences that made her voice rather cheerful. 'You do want your earrings?'

'No, mamma; I shall not wear any ornaments, and I shall put on my black silk. Black is the only wear when one is going to refuse an offer,' said Gwendolen, with one of her old smiles at her mother, while she rose to throw off her dressing-gown.

'Suppose the offer is not made after all,' said Mrs. Davilow, not without a sly intention.

'Then that will be because I refuse it beforehand,' said Gwendolen. 'It comes to the same thing.'

There was a proud little toss of her head as she said this; and when she walked down-stairs in her long black robes, there was just that firm poise of head and elasticity of form which had lately been missing, as in a parched plant. Her mother thought, 'She is quite herself again. It must be pleasure in his coming. Can her mind be really made up against him?'

Gwendolen would have been rather angry if that thought had been uttered; perhaps all the more because through the last twenty hours, with a brief interruption of sleep, she had been so occupied with perpetually alternating images and arguments for and against the possibility of her marrying Grandcourt, that the conclusion which she had determined on beforehand ceased to have any hold on her consciousness: the alternate dip of counterbalancing thoughts begotten of counterbalancing desires had brought her into a state in which no conclusion could look fixed to her. She would have expressed her resolve as before; but it was a form out of which the blood had been sucked – no more a part of quivering life than the 'God's will be done' of one who is eagerly watching chances. She did not mean to accept Grandcourt; from the first moment of receiving his letter she had meant to refuse him; still, that could not but prompt her to look the unwelcome reasons full in the face until she had a little less awe of them, could not hinder her imagination from filling out her knowledge in various ways, some of which seemed to change the aspect of what she knew. By dint of looking at a dubious object with a constructive imagination, one can give it twenty different shapes. Her indistinct grounds of hesitation before the interview at the Whispering Stones, at present counted for nothing; they were all merged in the final repulsion. If it had not been for that day in Cardell Chase, she said to herself now, there would have been no obstacle to her marrying Grandcourt. On that day and after it, she had not reasoned and balanced: she had acted with a force of impulse against which all questioning was no more than a voice against a torrent. The impulse had come – not only from her maidenly pride and jealousy, not only from the shock of another woman's calamity thrust close on her vision, but – from her dread of wrong-doing, which was vague, it is true, and aloof from the daily details of her life, but not the less strong. Whatever was accepted as consistent with being a lady she had no scruple about; but from the dim region of what was called disgraceful, wrong, guilty, she shrank with mingled pride and terror; and even apart from shame, her feeling would have made her place any deliberate injury of another in the region of guilt.

But now – did she know exactly what was the state of the case with regard to Mrs. Glasher and her children? She had given a sort of promise – had said, 'I will not interfere with your wishes.' But would another woman who married Grandcourt be in fact the decisive obstacle to her wishes, or be doing her and her boy any real injury? Might it not be just as well, nay better, that Grandcourt should marry? For what could not a woman do when she was married, if she knew how to assert herself? Here all was constructive imagination. Gwendolen had about as accurate a conception of marriage – that is to say, of the mutual influences, demands, duties of man and woman in a state of matrimony – as she had of magnetic currents and the law of storms.

'Mamma managed badly,' was her way of summing up what she had seen of her mother's experience: she herself would manage quite differently. And the trials of matrimony were the last theme into which Mrs. Davilow could choose to enter fully with this daughter.

'I wonder what mamma and my uncle would say if they knew about Mrs. Glasher!' thought Gwendolen, in her inward debating; not that she could imagine herself telling them, even if she had not felt bound to silence. 'I wonder what anybody would say; or what they would say to Mr. Grandcourt's marrying some one else and having other children!' To consider what 'anybody' would say, was to be released from the difficulty of judging where everything was obscure to her when feeling had ceased to be decisive. She had only to collect her memories, which proved to her that 'anybody' regarded illegitimate children as more rightfully to be looked shy on and deprived of social advantages than illegitimate fathers. The verdict of 'anybody' seemed to be that she had no reason to concern herself greatly on behalf of Mrs. Glasher and her children.

DANIEL DERONDA

But there was another way in which they had caused her concern. What others might think, could not do away with a feeling which in the first instance would hardly be too strongly described as indignation and loathing that she should have been expected to unite herself with an out-worn life, full of backward secrets which must have been more keenly felt than any association with *her*. True, the question of love on her own part had occupied her scarcely at all in relation to Grandcourt. The desirability of marriage for her had always seemed due to other feelings than love; and to be enamoured was the part of the man, on whom the advances depended. Gwendolen had found no objection to Grandcourt's way of being enamoured before she had had that glimpse of his past, which she resented as if it had been a deliberate offence against her. His advances to *her* were deliberate, and she felt a retrospective disgust for them. Perhaps other men's lives were of the same kind – full of secrets which made the ignorant suppositions of the woman they wanted to marry a farce at which they were laughing in their sleeves.

These feelings of disgust and indignation had sunk deep; and though other troublous experience in the last weeks had dulled them from passion into remembrance, it was chiefly their reverberating activity which kept her firm to the understanding with herself, that she was not going to accept Grandcourt. She had never meant to form a new determination; she had only been considering what might be thought or said. If anything could have induced her to change, it would have been the prospect of making all things easy for 'poor mamma:' that, she admitted, was a temptation. But no! she was going to refuse him. Meanwhile, the thought that he was coming to be refused was inspiriting: she had the white reins in her hands again; there was a new current in her frame, reviving her from the beaten-down consciousness in which she had been left by the interview with Klesmer. She was not now going to crave an opinion of her capabilities; she was going to exercise her power.

Was this what made her heart palpitate annoyingly when she heard the horses' footsteps on the gravel? – when Miss Merry, who opened the door to Grandcourt, came to tell her that he was in the drawing-room? The hours of preparation and the triumph of the situation were apparently of no use: she might as well have seen Grandcourt coming suddenly on her in the midst of her despondency. While walking into the drawing-room she had to concentrate all her energy in that self-control which made her appear gravely gracious as she gave her hand to him, and answered his hope that she was quite well in a voice as low and languid as his own. A moment afterwards, when they were both of them seated on two of the wreath-painted chairs – Gwendolen upright with downcast eye-lids, Grandcourt about two yards distant, leaning one arm over the back of his chair and looking at her, while he still held his hat in his left hand – any one seeing them as a picture would have concluded that they were in some stage of love-making suspense. And certainly the love-making had begun: she already felt herself being wooed by this silent man seated at an agreeable distance, with the subtlest atmosphere of atta of roses and an attention bent wholly on her. And he also considered himself to be woo-ing: he was not a man to suppose that his presence carried no consequences; and he was exactly the man to feel the utmost piquancy in a girl whom he had not found quite calculable.

'I was disappointed not to find you at Leubronn,' he began, his usual broken drawl having just a shade of amor-ous languor in it. 'The place was intolerable without you. A mere kennel of a place. Don't you think so?'

'I can't judge what it would be without myself,' said Gwendolen, turning her eyes on him, with some recovered sense of mischief. '*With* myself I liked it well enough to have stayed longer, if I could. But I was obliged to come home on account of family troubles.'

'It was very cruel of you to go to Leubronn,' said Grandcourt, taking no notice of the troubles, on which

Gwendolen – she hardly knew why – wished that there should be a clear understanding at once. 'You must have known that it would spoil everything: you knew you were the heart and soul of everything that went on. Are you quite reckless about me?'

It was impossible to say 'yes' in a tone that would be taken seriously; equally impossible to say 'no;' but what else could she say? In her difficulty, she turned down her eyelids again and blushed over face and neck. Grandcourt saw her in a new phase, and believed that she was showing her inclination. But he was determined that she should show it more decidedly.

'Perhaps there is some deeper interest? Some attraction – some engagement – which it would have been only fair to make me aware of? Is there any man who stands between us?'

Inwardly the answer framed itself, 'No; but there is a woman.' Yet how could she utter this? Even if she had not promised that woman to be silent, it would have been impossible for her to enter on the subject with Grandcourt. But how could she arrest this wooing by beginning to make a formal speech – 'I perceive your intention – it is most flattering, &c.' A fish honestly invited to come and be eaten has a clear course in declining, but how if it finds itself swimming against a net? And apart from the network, would she have dared at once to say anything decisive? Gwendolen had not time to be clear on that point. As it was, she felt compelled to silence, and after a pause, Grandcourt said –

'Am I to understand that someone else is preferred?'

Gwendolen, now impatient of her own embarrassment, determined to rush at the difficulty and free herself. She raised her eyes again and said with something of her former clearness and defiance, 'No' – wishing him to understand, 'What then? I may not be ready to take *you*.' There was nothing that Grandcourt could not understand which he perceived likely to affect his *amour propre*.

'The last thing I would do, is to importune you. I should

not hope to win you by making myself a bore. If there were no hope for me, I would ask you to tell me so at once, that I might just ride away to – no matter where.'

Almost to her own astonishment, Gwendolen felt a sudden alarm at the image of Grandcourt finally riding away. What would be left her then? Nothing but the former dreariness. She liked him to be there. She snatched at the subject that would defer any decisive answer.

'I fear you are not aware of what has happened to us. I have lately had to think so much of my mamma's troubles, that other subjects have been quite thrown into the background. She has lost all her fortune, and we are going to leave this place. I must ask you to excuse my seeming preoccupied.'

In eluding a direct appeal Gwendolen recovered some of her self-possession. She spoke with dignity and looked straight at Grandcourt, whose long, narrow, impenetrable eyes met hers, and mysteriously arrested them: mysteriously; for the subtly-varied drama between man and woman is often such as can hardly be rendered in words put together like dominoes, according to obvious fixed marks. The word of all work Love will no more express the myriad modes of mutual attraction, than the word Thought can inform you what is passing through your neighbour's mind. It would be hard to tell on which side – Gwendolen's or Grandcourt's – the influence was more mixed. At that moment his strongest wish was to be completely master of this creature – this piquant combination of maidenliness and mischief: that she knew things which had made her start away from him, spurred him to triumph over that repugnance; and he was believing that he should triumph. And she – ah, piteous equality in the need to dominate! – she was overcome like the thirsty one who is drawn towards the seeming water in the desert, overcome by the suffused sense that here in this man's homage to her lay the rescue from helpless subjection to an oppressive lot.

All the while they were looking at each other; and

Grandcourt said, slowly and languidly, as if it were of no importance, other things having been settled –

'You will tell me now, I hope, that Mrs. Davilow's loss of fortune will not trouble you further. You will trust to me to prevent it from weighing upon her. You will give me the claim to provide against that.'

The little pauses and refined drawlings with which this speech was uttered, gave time for Gwendolen to go through the dream of a life. As the words penetrated her, they had the effect of a draught of wine, which suddenly makes all things easier, desirable things not so wrong, and people in general less disagreeable. She had a momentary phantasmal love for this man who chose his words so well, and who was a mere incarnation of delicate homage. Repugnance, dread, scruples – these were dim as remembered pains, while she was already tasting relief under the immediate pain of hopelessness. She imagined herself already springing to her mother, and being playful again. Yet when Grandcourt had ceased to speak, there was an instant in which she was conscious of being at the turning of the ways.

'You are very generous,' she said, not moving her eyes, and speaking with a gentle intonation.

'You accept what will make such things a matter of course?' said Grandcourt, without any new eagerness. 'You consent to become my wife?'

This time Gwendolen remained quite pale. Something made her rise from her seat in spite of herself, and walk to a little distance. Then she turned and with her hands folded before her stood in silence.

Grandcourt immediately rose too, resting his hat on the chair, but still keeping hold of it. The evident hesitation of this destitute girl to take his splendid offer stung him into a keenness of interest such as he had not known for years. None the less because he attributed her hesitation entirely to her knowledge about Mrs. Glasher. In that attitude of preparation, he said –

'Do you command me to go?' No familiar spirit could have suggested to him more effective words.

'No,' said Gwendolen. She could not let him go: that negative was a clutch. She seemed to herself to be, after all, only drifted towards the tremendous decision: – but drifting depends on something besides the currents, when the sails have been set beforehand.

'You accept my devotion?' said Grandcourt, holding his hat by his side and looking straight into her eyes, without other movement. Their eyes meeting in that way seemed to allow any length of pause; but wait as long as she would, how could she contradict herself? What had she detained him for? He had shut out any explanation.

'Yes,' came as gravely from Gwendolen's lips as if she had been answering to her name in a court of justice. He received it gravely, and they still looked at each other in the same attitude. Was there ever before such a way of accepting the bliss-giving 'Yes'? Grandcourt liked better to be at that distance from her, and to feel under a ceremony imposed by an indefinable prohibition that breathed from Gwendolen's bearing.

But he did at length lay down his hat and advance to take her hand, just pressing his lips upon it and letting it go again. She thought his behaviour perfect, and gained a sense of freedom which made her almost ready to be mischievous. Her 'Yes' entailed so little at this moment, that there was nothing to screen the reversal of her gloomy prospects: her vision was filled by her own release from the Momperts, and her mother's release from Sawyer's Cottage. With a happy curl of the lips, she said –

'Will you not see mamma? I will fetch her.'

'Let us wait a little,' said Grandcourt, in his favourite attitude, having his left fore-finger and thumb in his waist-coat-pocket, and with his right caressing his whisker, while he stood near Gwendolen and looked at her – not unlike a gentleman who has a felicitous introduction at an evening party.

'Have you anything else to say to me?' said Gwendolen, playfully.

'Yes. – I know having things said to you is a great bore,' said Grandcourt, rather sympathetically.

'Not when they are things I like to hear.'

'Will it bother you to be asked how soon we can be married?'

'I think it will, to-day,' said Gwendolen, putting up her chin saucily.

'Not to-day, then. But to-morrow. Think of it before I come to-morrow. In a fortnight – or three weeks – as soon as possible.'

'Ah, you think you will be tired of my company,' said Gwendolen. 'I notice when people are married the husband is not so much with his wife as when they were engaged. But perhaps I shall like that better too.'

She laughed charmingly.

'You shall have whatever you like,' said Grandcourt.

'And nothing that I don't like? – please say that; because I think I dislike what I don't like more than I like what I like,' said Gwendolen, finding herself in the woman's paradise where all her nonsense is adorable.

Grandcourt paused: these were subtilties in which he had much experience of his own. 'I don't know – this is such a brute of a world, things are always turning up that one doesn't like. I can't always hinder your being bored. If you like to hunt Criterion, I can't hinder his coming down by some chance or other.'

'Ah, my friend Criterion, how is he?'

'He is outside: I made the groom ride him, that you might see him. He had the side-saddle on for an hour or two yesterday. Come to the window and look at him.'

They could see the two horses being taken slowly round the sweep, and the beautiful creatures, in their fine grooming, sent a thrill of exultation through Gwendolen. They were the symbols of command and luxury, in delightful contrast with the ugliness of poverty and humiliation at which she had lately been looking close.

'Will you ride Criterion to-morrow?' said Grandcourt. 'If you will, everything shall be arranged.'

'I should like it of all things,' said Gwendolen. 'I want to lose myself in a gallop again. But now I must go and fetch mamma.'

'Take my arm to the door, then,' said Grandcourt, and she accepted. Their faces were very near each other, being almost on a level, and he was looking at her. She thought his manners as a lover more agreeable than any she had seen described. She had no alarm lest he meant to kiss her, and was so much at her ease, that she suddenly paused in the middle of the room and said, half-archly, half-earnestly –

'Oh, while I think of it – there is something I dislike that you can save me from. I do *not* like Mr. Lush's company.'

'You shall not have it. I'll get rid of him.'

'You are not fond of him yourself?'

'Not in the least. I let him hang on me because he has always been a poor devil,' said Grandcourt, in an *adagio* of utter indifference. 'They got him to travel with me when I was a lad. He was always that coarse-haired kind of brute – a sort of class between a hog and a *dilettante*.'

Gwendolen laughed. All that seemed kind and natural enough: Grandcourt's fastidiousness enhanced the kindness. And when they reached the door, his way of opening it for her was the perfection of easy homage. Really, she thought, he was likely to be the least disagreeable of husbands.

Mrs. Davilow was waiting anxiously in her bedroom when Gwendolen entered, stepped towards her quickly, and kissing her on both cheeks said in a low tone, 'Come down, mamma, and see Mr. Grandcourt. I am engaged to him.'

'My darling child!' said Mrs. Davilow, with a surprise that was rather solemn than glad.

'Yes,' said Gwendolen, in the same tone, and with a quickness which implied that it was needless to ask questions. 'Everything is settled. You are not going to Sawyer's Cottage, I am not going to be inspected by Mrs. Mompert, and everything is to be as I like. So come down with me immediately.'

BOOK IV
Gwendolen Gets Her Choice

XXVIII

'Il est plus aisé de connoître l'homme en général que de connoître un homme en particulier.'
— LA ROCHEFOUCAULD.

AN hour after Grandcourt had left, the important news of Gwendolen's engagement was known at the Rectory, and Mr. and Mrs. Gascoigne, with Anna, spent the evening at Offendene.

'My dear, let me congratulate you on having created a strong attachment,' said the Rector. 'You look serious, and I don't wonder at it: a life-long union is a solemn thing. But from the way Mr. Grandcourt has acted and spoken I think we may already see some good arising out of our adversity. It has given you an opportunity of observing your future husband's delicate liberality.'

Mr. Gascoigne referred to Grandcourt's mode of implying that he would provide for Mrs. Davilow – a part of the love-making which Gwendolen had remembered to cite to her mother with perfect accuracy.

'But I have no doubt that Mr. Grandcourt would have behaved quite as handsomely if you had not gone away to Germany, Gwendolen, and had been engaged to him, as you no doubt might have been, more than a month ago,' said Mrs. Gascoigne, feeling that she had to discharge a duty on this occasion. 'But now there is no more room for caprice; indeed, I trust you have no inclination to any. A woman has a great debt of gratitude to a man who perseveres in making her such an offer. But no doubt you feel properly.'

'I am not at all sure that I do, aunt,' said Gwendolen, with saucy gravity. 'I don't know everything it is proper to feel on being engaged.'

DANIEL DERONDA

The Rector patted her shoulder and smiled as at a bit of innocent naughtiness, and his wife took his behaviour as an indication that she was not to be displeased. As for Anna, she kissed Gwendolen and said, 'I do hope you will be happy,' but then sank into the background and tried to keep the tears back too. In the late days she had been imagining a little romance about Rex – how if he still longed for Gwendolen her heart might be softened by trouble into love, so that they could by-and-by be married. And the romance had turned to a prayer that she, Anna, might be able to rejoice like a good sister, and only think of being useful in working for Gwendolen, as long as Rex was not rich. But now she wanted grace to rejoice in something else. Miss Merry and the four girls, Alice with the high shoulders, Bertha and Fanny the whisperers, and Isabel the listener, were all present on this family occasion, when everything seemed appropriately turning to the honour and glory of Gwendolen, and real life was as interesting as 'Sir Charles Grandison.' The evening passed chiefly in decisive remarks from the Rector, in answer to conjectures from the two elder ladies. According to him, the case was not one in which he could think it his duty to mention settlements: everything must, and doubtless would safely be left to Mr. Grandcourt.

'I should like to know exactly what sort of places Ryelands and Gadsmere are,' said Mrs. Davilow.

'Gadsmere, I believe, is a secondary place,' said Mr. Gascoigne; 'but Ryelands I know to be one of our finest seats. The park is extensive and the woods of a very valuable order. The house was built by Inigo Jones, and the ceilings are painted in the Italian style. The estate is said to be worth twelve thousand a-year, and there are two livings, one a rectory, in the gift of the Grandcourts. There may be some burthens on the land. Still, Mr. Grandcourt was an only child.'

'It would be most remarkable,' said Mrs. Gascoigne, 'if he were to become Lord Stannery in addition to everything else. Only think: there is the Grandcourt estate, the

336

Mallinger estate, *and* the baronetcy, *and* the peerage,' – she was marking off the items on her fingers, and paused on the fourth while she added, 'but they say there will be no land coming to him with the peerage.' It seemed a pity there was nothing for the fifth finger.

'The peerage,' said the Rector, judiciously, 'must be regarded as a remote chance. There are two cousins between the present peer and Mr. Grandcourt. It is certainly a serious reflection how death and other causes do sometimes concentrate inheritances on one man. But an excess of that kind is to be deprecated. To be Sir Mallinger Grandcourt Mallinger – I suppose that will be his style – with the corresponding properties, is a valuable talent enough for any man to have committed to him. Let us hope it will be well used.'

'And what a position for the wife, Gwendolen!' said Mrs. Gascoigne; 'a great responsibility indeed. But you must lose no time in writing to Mrs. Mompert, Henry. It is a good thing that you have an engagement of marriage to offer as an excuse, else she might feel offended. She is rather a high woman.'

'I am rid of that horror,' thought Gwendolen, to whom the name of Mompert had become a sort of Mumbo-jumbo. She was very silent through the evening, and that night could hardly sleep at all in her little white bed. It was a rarity in her strong youth to be wakeful; and perhaps a still greater rarity for her to be careful that her mother should not know of her restlessness. But her state of mind was altogether new: she who had been used to feel sure of herself, and ready to manage others, had just taken a decisive step which she had beforehand thought that she would not take – nay, perhaps, was bound not to take. She could not go backward now; she liked a great deal of what lay before her; and there was nothing for her to like if she went back. But her resolution was dogged by the shadow of that previous resolve which had at first come as the undoubting movement of her whole being. While she lay on her pillow with wide-open eyes, 'looking on darkness which the blind do see,' she was appalled by the idea that she was going to do what she had once started away from with repugnance. It was new to her that a question of right or wrong in her conduct should rouse her terror; she had known no compunction that atoning caresses and presents could not lay to rest. But here had come a moment when something like a new consciousness was awaked. She seemed on the edge of adopting deliberately, as a notion for all the rest of her life, what she had rashly said in her bitterness, when her discovery had driven her away to Leubronn: – that it did not signify what she did; she had only to amuse herself as best she could. That lawlessness, that casting away of all care for justification, suddenly frightened her: it came to her with the shadowy array of possible calamity behind it – calamity which had ceased to be a mere name for her; and all the infiltrated influences of disregarded religious teaching, as well as the deeper impressions of something awful and inexorable enveloping her seemed to concentrate themselves in the vague conception of avenging power. The brilliant position she had longed for, the imagined freedom she would create for herself in marriage, the deliverance from the dull insignificance of her girlhood – all were immediately before her; and yet they had come to her hunger like food with the taint of sacrilege upon it, which she must snatch with terror. In the darkness and loneliness of her little bed, her more resistant self could not act against the first onslaught of dread after her irrevocable decision. That unhappy-faced woman and her children – Grandcourt and his relations with her – kept repeating themselves in her imagination like the clinging memory of a disgrace, and gradually obliterated all other thought, leaving only the consciousness that she had taken those scenes into her life. Her long wakefulness seemed a delirium; a faint, faint light penetrated beside the window-curtain; the chillness increased. She could bear it no longer, and cried 'Mamma!'

'Yes, dear,' said Mrs. Davilow, immediately, in a wakeful voice.

'Let me come to you.'

She soon went to sleep on her mother's shoulder, and slept on till late, when, dreaming of a lit-up ball-room, she opened her eyes on her mother standing by the bedside with a small packet in her hand.

'I am sorry to wake you, darling, but I thought it better to give you this at once. The groom has brought Criterion; he has come on another horse, and says he is to stay here.'

Gwendolen sat up in bed and opened the packet. It was a delicate little enamelled casket, and inside was a splendid diamond ring with a letter which contained a folded bit of coloured paper and these words: –

'Pray wear this ring when I come at twelve in sign of our betrothal. I enclose a cheque drawn in the name of Mr. Gascoigne, for immediate expenses. Of course Mrs. Davilow will remain at Offendene, at least for some time. I hope, when I come, you will have granted me an early day, when you may begin to command me at a shorter distance. – Yours devotedly,

'H. M. GRANDCOURT.'

The cheque was for five hundred pounds, and Gwendolen turned it towards her mother, with the letter.

'How very kind and delicate!' said Mrs. Davilow, with much feeling. 'But I really should like better not to be dependent on a son-in-law. I and the girls could get along very well.'

'Mamma, if you say that again, I will not marry him,' said Gwendolen, angrily.

'My dear child, I trust you are not going to marry only for my sake,' said Mrs. Davilow, deprecatingly.

Gwendolen tossed her head on the pillow away from her mother, and let the ring lie. She was irritated at this attempt to take away a motive. Perhaps the deeper cause of her irritation was the consciousness that she was not going to marry solely for her mamma's sake – that she was drawn towards the marriage in ways against which stronger reasons than her mother's renunciation were yet not strong enough to hinder her. She had waked up to the signs that she was irrevocably engaged, and all the ugly visions, the alarms, the arguments of the night, must be met by daylight, in which probably they would show themselves weak.

'What I long for is your happiness, dear,' continued Mrs. Davilow, pleadingly. 'I will not say anything to vex you. Will you not put on the ring?'

For a few moments Gwendolen did not answer, but her thoughts were active. At last she raised herself with a determination to do as she would do if she had started on horseback, and go on with spirit, whatever ideas might be running in her head.

'I thought the lover always put on the betrothal ring himself,' she said, laughingly, slipping the ring on her finger, and looking at it with a charming movement of her head. 'I know why he has sent it,' she added, nodding at her mamma.

'Why?'

'He would rather make me put it on, than ask me to let him do it. Aha! he is very proud. But so am I. We shall match each other. I should hate a man who went down on his knees, and came fawning on me. He really is not disgusting.'

'That is very moderate praise, Gwen.'

'No, it is not, for a man,' said Gwendolen, gaily. 'But now I must get up and dress. Will you come and do my hair, mamma dear,' she went on, drawing down her mamma's face to caress it with her own cheeks, 'and not be so naughty any more as to talk of living in poverty? You must bear to be made comfortable, even if you don't like it. And Mr. Grandcourt behaves perfectly, now, does he not?'

'Certainly he does,' said Mrs. Davilow, encouraged, and persuaded that after all Gwendolen was fond of her betrothed. She herself thought him a man whose attentions were likely to tell on a girl's feeling. Suitors must often be judged as words are, by their standing and the figure they make in polite society: it is difficult to know much else of them. And all the mother's anxiety turned, not on Grandcourt's character, but on Gwendolen's mood in accepting him.

The mood was necessarily passing through a new phase this morning. Even in the hour of making her toilet, she had drawn on all the knowledge she had for grounds to justify her marriage. And what she most dwelt on was the determination, that when she was Grandcourt's wife, she would urge him to the most liberal conduct towards Mrs. Glasher's children.

'Of what use would it be to her that I should not marry him? He could have married her if he had liked; but he did *not* like. Perhaps she is to blame for that. There must be a great deal about her that I know nothing of. And he must have been good to her in many ways, else she would not have wanted to marry him.'

But that last argument at once began to appear doubtful. Mrs. Glasher naturally wished to exclude other children who would stand between Grandcourt and her own; and Gwendolen's comprehension of this feeling prompted another way of reconciling claims.

'Perhaps we shall have no children. I hope we shall not. And he might leave the estate to the pretty little boy. My uncle said that Mr. Grandcourt could do as he liked with the estates. Only when Sir Hugo Mallinger dies there will be enough for two.'

This made Mrs. Glasher appear quite unreasonable in demanding that her boy should be sole heir; and the double property was a security that Grandcourt's marriage would do her no wrong, when the wife was Gwendolen Harleth with all her proud resolution not to be fairly accused. This maiden had been accustomed to think herself blameless: other persons only were faulty.

It was striking, that in the hold which this argument of her doing no wrong to Mrs. Glasher had taken on her mind, her repugnance to the idea of Grandcourt's past had sunk

341

into a subordinate feeling. The terror she had felt in the night watches at overstepping the border of wickedness by doing what she had at first felt to be wrong, had dulled any emotions about his conduct. She was thinking of him, whatever he might be, as a man over whom she was going to have indefinite power; and her loving him having never been a question with her, any agreeableness he had was so much gain. Poor Gwendolen had no awe of unmanageable forces in the state of matrimony, but regarded it as altogether a matter of management, in which she would know how to act. In relation to Grandcourt's past she encouraged new doubts whether he were likely to have differed much from other men; and she devised little schemes for learning what was expected of men in general.

But whatever else might be true in the world, her hair was dressed suitably for riding, and she went down in her riding-habit, to avoid delay before getting on horseback. She wanted to have her blood stirred once more with the intoxication of youth, and to recover the daring with which she had been used to think of her course in life. Already a load was lifted off her; for in daylight and activity it was less oppressive to have doubts about her choice, than to feel that she had no choice but to endure insignificance and servitude.

'Go back and make yourself look like a duchess, mamma,' she said, turning suddenly as she was going down-stairs. 'Put your point-lace over your head. I must have you look like a duchess. You must not take things humbly.'

When Grandcourt raised her left hand gently and looked at the ring, she said gravely, 'It was very good of you to think of everything and send me that packet.'

'You will tell me if there is anything I forget?' he said, keeping the hand softly within his own. 'I will do anything you wish.'

'But I am very unreasonable in my wishes,' said Gwendolen, smiling.

'Yes, I expect that. Women always are.'

'Then I will not be unreasonable,' said Gwendolen, taking away her hand, and tossing her head saucily. 'I will not be told that I am what women always are.'

'I did not say that,' said Grandcourt looking at her with his usual gravity. 'You are what no other woman is.'

'And what is that, pray?' said Gwendolen, moving to a distance with a little air of menace.

Grandcourt made his pause before he answered. 'You are the woman I love.'

'Oh what nice speeches!' said Gwendolen, laughing. The sense of that love which he must once have given to another woman under strange circumstances was getting familiar.

'Give me a nice speech in return. Say when we are to be married.'

'Not yet. Not till we have had a gallop over the downs. I am so thirsty for that, I can think of nothing else. I wish the hunting had begun. Sunday the twentieth, twenty-seventh, Monday, Tuesday.' Gwendolen was counting on her fingers with the prettiest nod while she looked at Grandcourt, and at last swept one palm over the other while she said triumphantly, 'It will begin in ten days!'

'Let us be married in ten days, then,' said Grandcourt, 'and we shall not be bored about the stables.'

'What do women always say in answer to that?' said Gwendolen, mischievously.

'They agree to it,' said the lover, rather off his guard.

'Then I will not!' said Gwendolen, taking up her gauntlets and putting them on, while she kept her eyes on him with gathering fun in them.

The scene was pleasant to both sides. A cruder lover would have lost the view of her pretty ways and attitudes, and spoiled all by stupid attempts at caresses, utterly destructive of drama. Grandcourt preferred the drama; and Gwendolen, left at ease, found her spirits rising continually as she played at reigning. Perhaps if Klesmer had seen more of her in this unconscious kind of acting, instead of when she was trying to be theatrical, he might have rated her chance higher.

When they had had a glorious gallop, however, she was in a state of exhilaration that disposed her to think well of hastening the marriage which would make her life all of a piece with this splendid kind of enjoyment. She would not debate any more about an act to which she had committed herself; and she consented to fix the wedding on that day three weeks, notwithstanding the difficulty of fulfilling the customary laws of the *trousseau*.

Lush, of course, was made aware of the engagement by abundant signs, without being formally told. But he expected some communication as a consequence of it, and after a few days he became rather impatient under Grandcourt's silence, feeling sure that the change would affect his personal prospects, and wishing to know exactly how. His tactics no longer included any opposition – which he did not love for its own sake. He might easily cause Grandcourt a great deal of annoyance, but it would be to his own injury, and to create annoyance was not a motive with him. Miss Gwendolen he would certainly not have been sorry to frustrate a little, but – after all there was no knowing what would come. It was nothing new that Grandcourt should show a perverse wilfulness; yet in his freak about this girl he struck Lush rather newly as something like a man who was *fey* – led on by an ominous fatality; and that one born to his fortune should make a worse business of his life than was necessary, seemed really pitiable. Having protested against the marriage, Lush had a second-sight for its evil consequences. Grandcourt had been taking the pains to write letters and give orders himself instead of employing Lush; and appeared to be ignoring his usefulness, even choosing, against the habit of years, to breakfast alone in his dressing-room. But a *tête-à-tête* was not to be avoided in a house empty of guests; and Lush hastened to use an opportunity of saying – it was one day after dinner, for there were difficulties in Grandcourt's dining at Offendene –

'And when is the marriage to take place?'

Grandcourt, who drank little wine, had left the table and was lounging, while he smoked, in an easy-chair near the hearth, where a fire of oak boughs was gaping to its glowing depths, and edging them with a delicate tint of ashes delightful to behold. The chair of red-brown velvet brocade was a becoming background for his pale-tinted well-cut features and exquisite long hands: omitting the cigar, you might have imagined him a portrait by Moroni, who would have rendered wonderfully the impenetrable gaze and air of distinction; and a portrait by that great master would have been quite as lively a companion as Grandcourt was disposed to be. But he answered without unusual delay.

'On the tenth.'

'I suppose you intend to remain here.'

'We shall go to Ryelands for a little while; but we shall return here for the sake of the hunting.'

After this word there was the languid inarticulate sound frequent with Grandcourt when he meant to continue speaking, and Lush waited for something more. Nothing came, and he was going to put another question, when the inarticulate sound began again and introduced the mildly-uttered suggestion –

'You had better make some new arrangement for yourself.'

'What! I am to cut and run?' said Lush, prepared to be good-tempered on the occasion.

'Something of that kind.'

'The bride objects to me. I hope she will make up to you for the want of my services.'

'I can't help your being so damnably disagreeable to women,' said Grandcourt, in soothing apology.

'To one woman, if you please.'

'It makes no difference, since she is the one in question.'

'I suppose I am not to be turned adrift after fifteen years without some provision.'

'You must have saved something out of me.'

'Deuced little. I have often saved something for you.'

'You can have three hundred a-year. But you must live in town and be ready to look after things for me when I want you. I shall be rather hard up.'

'If you are not going to be at Ryelands this winter, I might run down there and let you know how Swinton goes on.'

'If you like. I don't care a toss where you are, so that you keep out of sight.'

'Much obliged,' said Lush, able to take the affair more easily than he had expected. He was supported by the secret belief that he should by-and-by be wanted as much as ever.

'Perhaps you will not object to packing up as soon as possible,' said Grandcourt. 'The Torringtons are coming, and Miss Harleth will be riding over here.'

'With all my heart. Can't I be of use in going to Gadsmere?'

'No. I am going myself.'

'About your being rather hard up. Have you thought of that plan—'

'Just leave me alone, will you?' said Grandcourt, in his lowest audible tone, tossing his cigar into the fire, and rising to walk away.

He spent the evening in the solitude of the smaller drawing-room, where, with various new publications on the table, of the kind a gentleman may like to have at hand without touching, he employed himself (as a philosopher might have done) in sitting meditatively on a sofa and abstaining from literature – political, comic, cynical, or romantic. In this way hours may pass surprisingly soon, without the arduous invisible chase of philosophy; not from love of thought, but from hatred of effort – from a state of the inward world, something like premature age, where the need for action lapses into a mere image of what has been, is, and may or might be; where impulse is born and dies in a phantasmal world, pausing in rejection even of a shadowy fulfilment. That is a condition which often comes with whitening hair; and sometimes, too, an intense obstinacy and tenacity of rule, like the main trunk of an exorbitant egoism, conspicuous in proportion as the varied susceptibilities of younger years are stripped away.

But Grandcourt's hair, though he had not much of it, was of a fine sunny blond, and his moods were not entirely to be explained as ebbing energy. We mortals have a strange spiritual chemistry going on within us, so that a lazy stagnation or even a cottony milkiness may be preparing one knows not what biting or explosive material. The navvy waking from sleep and without malice heaving a stone to crush the life out of his still sleeping comrade, is understood to lack the trained motive which makes a character fairly calculable in its actions; but by a roundabout course even a gentleman may make of himself a chancy personage, raising an uncertainty as to what he may do next, which sadly spoils companionship.

Grandcourt's thoughts this evening were like the circlets one sees in a dark pool continually dying out and continually started again by some impulse from below the surface. The deeper central impulse came from the image of Gwendolen; but the thoughts it stirred would be imperfectly illustrated by a reference to the amatory poets of all ages. It was characteristic that he got none of his satisfaction from the belief that Gwendolen was in love with him; and that love had overcome the jealous resentment which had made her run away from him. On the contrary, he believed that this girl was rather exceptional in the fact that, in spite of his assiduous attention to her, she was not in love with him; and it seemed to him very likely that if it had not been for the sudden poverty which had come over her family, she would not have accepted him. From the very first there had been an exasperating fascination in the tricksiness with which she had – not met his advances, but – wheeled away from them. She had been brought to accept him in spite of everything – brought to kneel down like a horse under training for the arena, though she might have an objection to it all the while. On the whole, Grandcourt got more pleasure out of this notion than he could have done out of winning a girl of whom he was sure that she had a strong inclination for him personally. And yet this pleasure in mastering reluctance flourished along with the habitual persuasion that no woman whom he favoured could be quite indifferent to his personal influence; and it seemed to him not unlikely that by-and-by Gwendolen might be more enamoured of him than he of her. In any case she would have to submit; and he enjoyed thinking of her as his future wife, whose pride and spirit were suited to command every one but himself. He had no taste for a woman who was all tenderness to him, full of petitioning solicitude and willing obedience. He meant to be master of a woman who would have liked to master him, and who perhaps would have been capable of mastering another man.

Lush, having failed in his attempted reminder to Grandcourt, thought it well to communicate with Sir Hugo, in whom, as a man having perhaps interest enough to command the bestowal of some place where the work was light, gentlemanly, and not ill-paid, he was anxious to cultivate a sense of friendly obligation, not feeling at all secure against the future need of such a place. He wrote the following letter, and addressed it to Park Lane, whither he knew the family had returned from Leubronn: –

'MY DEAR SIR HUGO, – Since we came home the marriage has been absolutely decided on, and is to take place in less than three weeks. It is so far the worse for him that her mother has lately lost all her fortune, and he will have to find supplies. Grandcourt, I know, is feeling the want of cash; and unless some other plan is resorted to, he will be raising money in a foolish way. I am going to leave Diplow immediately, and I shall not be able to start the topic. What I should advise is, that Mr. Deronda, who I know has your confidence, should propose to come and pay a short visit here, according to invitation (there are going to be other people in the house), and that you should put him fully in possession of your wishes and the possible extent of your offer. Then, that he should introduce the subject to Grandcourt so as not to imply that you suspect any particular want of money on his part, but only that there is a strong wish on yours. What I have formerly said to him has been in the way of a conjecture that you might be willing to give a good sum for his chance of Diplow; but if Mr. Deronda came armed with a definite offer, that would take another sort of hold. Ten to one he will not close for some time to come; but the proposal will have got a stronger lodgement in his mind; and though at present he has a great notion of the hunting here, I see a likelihood, under the circumstances, that he will get a distaste for the neighbourhood, and there will be the notion of the money sticking by him without being urged. I would bet on your ultimate success. As I am not to be exiled to Siberia, but am to be within call, it is possible that, by-and-by, I may be of more service to you. But at present I can think of no medium so good as Mr. Deronda. Nothing puts Grandcourt in worse humour than having the lawyers thrust their paper under his nose uninvited.

'Trusting that your visit to Leubronn has put you in excellent condition for the winter, I remain, my dear Sir Hugo, yours very faithfully,

'THOMAS CRANMER LUSH.'

Sir Hugo, having received this letter at breakfast, handed it to Deronda, who, though he had chambers in town, was somehow hardly ever in them, Sir Hugo not being contented without him. The chatty baronet would have liked a young companion even if there had been no peculiar reasons for attachment between them: one with a fine harmonious unspoiled face fitted to keep up a cheerful view of posterity and inheritance generally, notwith-standing particular disappointments; and his affection for Deronda was not diminished by the deep-lying though not obtrusive difference in their notions and tastes. Perhaps it was all the stronger; acting as the same sort of difference does between a man and a woman in giving a piquancy to the attachment which subsists in spite of it. Sir Hugo did not think unapprovingly of himself; but he looked at men and society from a liberal-menagerie point of view, and he had a certain pride in Deronda's differing from him, which, if it had found voice, might have said – 'You see this fine young fellow – not such as you see every day, is he? – he belongs to me in a sort of way, I brought him up from a child; but you would not ticket him off easily, he has notions of his own, and he's as far as the poles asunder from what I was at his age.' This state of feeling was kept up by the mental balance in Deronda, who was moved by an affectionateness such as we are apt to call feminine, disposing him to yield in ordinary details, while he had a certain inflexibility of judgment, an independence of opinion, held to be rightfully masculine.

When he had read the letter, he returned it without speaking, inwardly wincing under Lush's mode of attributing a neutral usefulness to him in the family affairs.

'What do you say, Dan? It would be pleasant enough for you. You have not seen the place for a good many years now, and you might have a famous run with the harriers if you went down next week,' said Sir Hugo.

'I should not go on that account,' said Deronda, buttering his bread attentively. He had an objection to this transparent kind of persuasiveness, which all intelligent animals are seen to treat with indifference. If he went to Diplow he should be doing something disagreeable to oblige Sir Hugo.

'I think Lush's notion is a good one. And it would be a pity to lose the occasion.'

'That is a different matter – if you think my going of importance to your object,' said Deronda, still with that aloofness of manner which implied some suppression. He knew that the baronet had set his heart on the affair.

'Why, you will see the fair gambler, the Leubronn Diana, I shouldn't wonder,' said Sir Hugo, gaily. 'We shall have to invite her to the Abbey, when they are married, Louisa,' he added, turning to Lady Mallinger, as if she too had read the letter.

'I cannot conceive whom you mean,' said Lady Mallinger, who in fact had not been listening, her mind having been taken up with her first sips of coffee, the objectionable cuff of her sleeve, and the necessity of carrying Theresa to the dentist – innocent and partly laudable preoccupations, as the gentle lady's usually were. Should her appearance be inquired after, let it be said that she had reddish blond hair (the hair of the period), a small Roman nose, rather prominent blue eyes and delicate eyelids, with a figure which her thinner friends called fat, her hands showing curves and dimples like a magnified baby's.

'I mean that Grandcourt is going to marry the girl you saw at Leubronn – don't you remember her? – the Miss Harleth who used to play at roulette.'

'Dear me! Is that a good match for him?'

'That depends on the sort of goodness he wants,' said Sir Hugo, smiling. 'However, she and her friends have nothing, and she will bring him expenses. It's a good match for my purposes, because if I am willing to fork out a sum of money, he may be willing to give up his chance of Diplow, so that we shall have it out and out, and when I die you will have the consolation of going to the place you would like to go to – wherever I may go.'

'I wish you would not talk of dying in that light way, dear.'

'It's rather a heavy way, Lou, for I shall have to pay a heavy sum – forty thousand, at least.'

'But why are we to invite them to the Abbey?' said Lady Mallinger. 'I do *not* like women who gamble, like Lady Cragstone.'

'Oh, you will not mind her for a week. Besides, she is not like Lady Cragstone because she gambled a little, any more than I am like a broker because I'm a Whig. I want to keep Grandcourt in good humour, and to let him see plenty of this place, that he may think the less of Diplow. I don't know yet whether I shall get him to meet me in this matter. And if Dan were to go over on a visit there, he might hold out the bait to him. It would be doing me a great service.' This was meant for Deronda.

'Daniel is not fond of Mr. Grandcourt, I think, is he?' said Lady Mallinger, looking at Deronda inquiringly.

'There is no avoiding everybody one doesn't happen to be fond of,' said Deronda. 'I will go to Diplow – I don't know that I have anything better to do – since Sir Hugo wishes it.'

'That's a trump!' said Sir Hugo, well pleased. 'And if you don't find it very pleasant, it's so much experience. Nothing used to come amiss to me when I was young. You must see men and manners.'

'Yes; but I have seen that man, and something of his manners too,' said Deronda.

'Not nice manners, I think,' said Lady Mallinger.

'Well, you see they succeed with your sex,' said Sir Hugo, provokingly. 'And he was an uncommonly good-looking fellow when he was two or three and twenty – like his father. He doesn't take after his father in marrying the heiress, though. If he had got Miss Arrowpoint and my land too, confound him, he would have had a fine principality.'

Deronda, in anticipating the projected visit, felt less disinclination than when consenting to it. The drama of that girl's marriage did interest him: what he had heard through Lush of her having run away from the suit of the man she was now going to take as a husband, had thrown a new sort of light on her gambling; and it was probably the transition from that fevered worldliness into poverty which had urged her acceptance where she must in some way have felt repulsion. All this implied a nature liable to difficulty and struggle – elements of life which had a predominant attraction for his sympathy, due perhaps to his early pain in dwelling on the conjectured story of his own existence. Persons attracted him, as Hans Meyrick had done, in proportion to the possibility of his defending them, rescuing them, telling upon their lives with some sort of redeeming influence; and he had to resist an inclination, easily accounted for, to withdraw coldly from the fortunate. But in the movement which had led him to redeem Gwendolen's necklace for her, and which was at work in him still, there was something beyond his habitual compassionate fervour – something due to the fascination of her womanhood. He was very open to that sort of charm, and mingled it with the consciously Utopian pictures of his own future; yet any one able to trace the folds of his character might have conceived that he would be more likely than many less passionate men to love a woman without telling her of it. Sprinkle food before a delicate-eared bird: there is nothing he would more willingly take, yet he keeps aloof, because of his sensibility to checks which to you are imperceptible. And one man differs from another, as we all differ from the Bosjesman, in a sensibility to checks, that come from variety of needs, spiritual or other. It seemed to foreshadow that capability of reticence in Deronda that his imagination was much occupied with two women, to neither of whom would he have held it possible that he should ever make love. Hans Meyrick had laughed at him for having something of the knight-errant in his disposition; and he would have found his proof if he had known what was just now going on in Deronda's mind about Mirah and Gwendolen.

He wrote without delay to announce the visit to Diplow, and received in reply a polite assurance that his coming would give great pleasure. That was not altogether untrue. Grandcourt thought it probable that the visit was prompted by Sir Hugo's desire to court him for a purpose which he did not make up his mind to resist; and it was not a disagreeable idea to him that this fine fellow, whom he believed to be his cousin under the rose, would witness, perhaps with some jealousy, Henleigh Mallinger Grandcourt play the commanding part of betrothed lover to a splendid girl whom the cousin had already looked at with admiration.

Grandcourt himself was not jealous of anything unless it threatened his mastery – which he did not think himself likely to lose.

XXIX

'Surely whoever speaks to me in the right voice,
   him or her I shall follow,
As the water follows the moon, silently,
   with fluid steps anywhere around the globe.'
                                        – WALT WHITMAN.

'NOW my cousins are at Diplow,' said Grandcourt, 'will you go there? – to-morrow? The carriage shall come for Mrs. Davilow. You can tell me what you would like done in the rooms. Things must be put in decent order while we are away at Ryelands. And to-morrow is the only day.'

He was sitting sideways on a sofa in the drawing-room at Offendene, one hand and elbow resting on the back, and the other hand thrust between his crossed knees – in the attitude of a man who is much interested in watching the person next to him. Gwendolen, who had always disliked needlework, had taken to it with apparent zeal since her engagement, and now held a piece of white embroidery which on examination would have shown many false stitches. During the last eight or nine days their hours had been chiefly spent on horseback, but some margin had always been left for this more difficult sort of companionship, which, however, Gwendolen had not found disagreeable. She was very well satisfied with Grandcourt. His answers to her lively questions about what he had seen and done in his life, bore drawling very well. From the first she had noticed that he knew what to say; and she was constantly feeling not only that he had nothing of the fool in his composition, but that by some subtle means he communicated to her the impression that all the folly lay with other people, who did what he did not care to do. A man who seems to have been able to command the best, has a sovereign power of depreciation. Then Grandcourt's behaviour as a lover had hardly at all passed the limit of an amorous homage which was inobtrusive as a wafted odour of roses, and spent all its effect in a gratified vanity. One

355

day, indeed, he had kissed not her cheek but her neck a little below her ear; and Gwendolen, taken by surprise, had started up with a marked agitation which made him rise too and say, 'I beg your pardon – did I annoy you?' 'Oh, it was nothing,' said Gwendolen, rather afraid of herself, 'only I cannot bear – to be kissed under my ear.' She sat down again with a little playful laugh, but all the while she felt her heart beating with a vague fear: she was no longer at liberty to flout him as she had flouted poor Rex. Her agitation seemed not uncomplimentary, and he had been contented not to transgress again.

To-day a slight rain hindered riding; but to compensate, a package had come from London, and Mrs. Davilow had just left the room after bringing in for admiration the beautiful things (of Grandcourt's ordering) which lay scattered about on the tables. Gwendolen was just then enjoying the scenery of her life. She let her hands fall on her lap and said with a pretty air of perversity –

'Why is to-morrow the only day?'

'Because the next day is the first with the hounds,' said Grandcourt.

'And after that?'

'After that I must go away for a couple of days – it's a bore – but I shall go one day and come back the next.' Grandcourt noticed a change in her face, and releasing his hand from under his knees, he laid it on hers and said, 'You object to my going away?'

'It is no use objecting,' said Gwendolen, coldly. She was resisting to the utmost her temptation to tell him that she suspected to whom he was going – and the temptation to make a clean breast, speaking without restraint.

'Yes, it is,' said Grandcourt, enfolding her hand. 'I will put off going. And I will travel at night, so as only to be away one day.' He thought that he knew the reason of what he inwardly called this bit of temper, and she was particularly fascinating to him at this moment.

'Then don't put off going, but travel at night,' said Gwendolen, feeling that she could command him, and finding in this peremptoriness a small outlet for her irritation.

'Then you will go to Diplow to-morrow?'

'Oh yes, if you wish it,' said Gwendolen, in a high tone of careless assent. Her concentration in other feelings had really hindered her from taking notice that her hand was being held.

'How you treat us poor devils of men,' said Grandcourt, lowering his tone. 'We are always getting the worst of it.'

'*Are* you?' said Gwendolen, in a tone of inquiry, looking at him more naïvely than usual. She longed to believe this commonplace badinage as the serious truth about her lover: in that case, she too was justified. If she knew everything, Mrs. Glasher would appear more blamable than Grandcourt. '*Are* you always getting the worst?'

'Yes. Are you as kind to me as I am to you?' said Grandcourt, looking into her eyes with his narrow gaze.

Gwendolen felt herself stricken. She was conscious of having received so much, that her sense of command was checked, and sank away in the perception that, look around her as she might, she could not turn back: it was as if she had consented to mount a chariot where another held the reins; and it was not in her nature to leap out in the eyes of the world. She had not consented in ignorance, and all she could say now would be a confession that she had not been ignorant. Her right to explanation was gone. All she had to do now was to adjust herself, so that the spikes of that unwilling penance which conscience imposed should not gall her. With a sort of mental shiver, she resolutely changed her mental attitude. There had been a little pause, during which she had not turned away her eyes; and with a sudden break into a smile, she said –

'If I were as kind to you as you are to me, that would spoil your generosity: it would no longer be as great as it could be – and it is that now.'

'Then I am not to ask for one kiss,' said Grandcourt, contented to pay a large price for this new kind of love-making, which introduced marriage by the finest contrast.

'Not one!' said Gwendolen, getting saucy, and nodding at him defiantly.

He lifted her little left hand to his lips, and then released it respectfully. Clearly it was faint praise to say of him that he was not disgusting: he was almost charming; and she felt at this moment that it was not likely she could ever have loved another man better than this one. His reticence gave her some inexplicable, delightful consciousness.

'Apropos,' she said, taking up her work again, 'is there any one besides Captain and Mrs. Torrington at Diplow? – or do you leave them *tête-à-tête*? I suppose he converses in cigars, and she answers with her chignon.'

'She has a sister with her,' said Grandcourt, with his shadow of a smile, 'and there are two men besides – one of them you know, I believe.'

'Ah, then, I have a poor opinion of him,' said Gwendolen, shaking her head.

'You saw him at Leubronn – young Deronda – a young fellow with the Mallingers.'

Gwendolen felt as if her heart were making a sudden gambol, and her fingers, which tried to keep a firm hold on her work, got cold.

'I never spoke to him,' she said, dreading any discernible change in herself. 'Is he not disagreeable?'

'No, not particularly,' said Grandcourt, in his most languid way. 'He thinks a little too much of himself. I thought he had been introduced to you.'

'No. Some one told me his name the evening before I came away. That was all. What is he?'

'A sort of ward of Sir Hugo Mallinger's. Nothing of any consequence.'

'Oh, poor creature! How very unpleasant for him!' said Gwendolen, speaking from the lip, and not meaning any sarcasm. 'I wonder if it has left off raining!' she added, rising and going to look out of the window.

Happily it did not rain the next day, and Gwendolen rode to Diplow on Criterion as she had done on that former day when she returned with her mother in the carriage. She always felt the more daring for being in her riding-dress; besides having the agreeable belief that she looked as well as possible in it – a sustaining consciousness in any meeting which seems formidable. Her anger towards Deronda had changed into a superstitious dread – due, perhaps, to the coercion he had exercised over her thought – lest that first interference of his in her life might foreshadow some future influence. It is of such stuff that superstitions are commonly made: an intense feeling about ourselves which makes the evening star shine at us with a threat, and the blessing of a beggar encourage us. And superstitions carry consequences which often verify their hope or their foreboding.

The time before luncheon was taken up for Gwendolen by going over the rooms with Mrs. Torrington and Mrs. Davilow; and she thought it likely that if she saw Deronda, there would hardly be need for more than a bow between them. She meant to notice him as little as possible.

And after all she found herself under an inward compulsion too strong for her pride. From the first moment of their being in the room together, she seemed to herself to be doing nothing but notice him: everything else was automatic performance of an habitual part.

When he took his place at lunch, Grandcourt had said, 'Deronda, Miss Harleth tells me you were not introduced to her at Leubronn?'

'Miss Harleth hardly remembers me, I imagine,' said Deronda, looking at her quite simply, as they bowed. 'She was intensely occupied when I saw her.'

Now, did he suppose that she had not suspected him of being the person who redeemed her necklace?

'On the contrary. I remember you very well,' said Gwendolen, feeling rather nervous, but governing herself and looking at him in return with new examination. 'You did not approve of my playing at roulette.'

'How did you come to that conclusion?' said Deronda, gravely.

359

'Oh, you cast an evil eye on my play,' said Gwendolen, with a turn of her head and a smile. 'I began to lose as soon as you came to look on. I had always been winning till then.'

'Roulette in such a kennel as Leubronn is a horrid bore,' said Grandcourt.

'*I* found it a bore when I began to lose,' said Gwendolen. Her face was turned towards Grandcourt as she smiled and spoke, but she gave a sidelong glance at Deronda, and saw his eyes fixed on her with a look so gravely penetrating that it had a keener edge for her than his ironical smile at her losses – a keener edge than Klesmer's judgment. She wheeled her neck round as if she wanted to listen to what was being said by the rest, while she was only thinking of Deronda. His face had that disturbing kind of form and expression which threatens to affect opinion – as if one's standard were somehow wrong. (Who has not seen men with faces of this corrective power till they frustrated it by speech or action?) His voice, heard now for the first time, was to Grandcourt's toneless drawl, which had been in her ears every day, as the deep notes of a violoncello to the broken discourse of poultry and other lazy gentry in the afternoon sunshine. Grandcourt, she inwardly conjectured, was perhaps right in saying that Deronda thought too much of himself: – a favourite way of explaining a superiority that humiliates. However, the talk turned on the rinderpest and Jamaica; and no more was said about roulette. Grandcourt held that the Jamaican negro was a beastly sort of baptist Caliban; Deronda said he had always felt a little with Caliban, who naturally had his own point of view and could sing a good song; Mrs. Davilow observed that her father had an estate in Barbadoes, but that she herself had never been in the West Indies; Mrs. Torrington was sure she should never sleep in her bed if she lived among blacks; her husband corrected her by saying that the blacks would be manageable enough if it were not for the half-breeds; and Deronda remarked that the whites had to thank themselves for the half-breeds.

While this polite pea-shooting was going on, Gwendolen trifled with her jelly, and looked at every speaker in turn that she might feel at ease in looking at Deronda.

'I wonder what he thinks of me really? He must have felt interested in me, else he would not have sent me my necklace. I wonder what he thinks of my marriage? What notions has he to make him so grave about things? Why is he come to Diplow?'

These questions ran in her mind as the voice of an uneasy longing to be judged by Deronda with unmixed admiration – a longing which had had its seed in her first resentment at his critical glance. Why did she care so much about the opinion of this man who was 'nothing of any consequence'? She had no time to find the reason – she was too much engaged in caring. In the drawing-room, when something had called Grandcourt away, she went quite unpremeditatedly up to Deronda, who was standing at a table apart, turning over some prints, and said to him –

'Shall you hunt to-morrow, Mr. Deronda?'

'Yes, I believe so.'

'You don't object to hunting, then?'

'I find excuses for it. It is a sin I am inclined to – when I can't get boating or cricketing.'

'Do you object to my hunting?' said Gwendolen, with a saucy movement of the chin.

'I have no right to object to anything you choose to do.'

'You thought you had a right to object to my gambling,' persisted Gwendolen.

'I was sorry for it. I am not aware that I told you of my objection,' said Deronda, with his usual directness of gaze – a large-eyed gravity, innocent of any intention. His eyes had a peculiarity which has drawn many men into trouble: they were of a dark yet mild intensity, which seemed to express a special interest in every one on whom he fixed them, and might easily help to bring on him those claims which ardently sympathetic people are often creating in the minds of those who need help. In mendicant fashion, we make the goodness of others a reason for exorbitant demands on them. That sort of effect was penetrating Gwendolen.

'You hindered me from gambling again,' she answered. But she had no sooner spoken than she blushed over face and neck; and Deronda blushed too, conscious that in the little affair of the necklace he had taken a questionable freedom.

It was impossible to speak further; and she turned away to a window, feeling that she had stupidly said what she had not meant to say, and yet being rather happy that she had plunged into this mutual understanding. Deronda also did not dislike it. Gwendolen seemed more decidedly attractive than before; and certainly there had been changes going on within her since that time at Leubronn: the struggle of mind attending a conscious error had wakened something like a new soul, which had better, but also worse, possibilities than her former poise of crude self-confidence: among the forces she had come to dread was something within her that troubled satisfaction.

That evening Mrs. Davilow said, 'Was it really so, or only a joke of yours, about Mr. Deronda's spoiling your play, Gwen?'

Her curiosity had been excited, and she could venture to ask a question that did not concern Mr. Grandcourt.

'Oh, it merely happened that he was looking on when I began to lose,' said Gwendolen, carelessly. 'I noticed him.'

'I don't wonder at that: he is a striking young man. He puts me in mind of Italian paintings. One would guess, without being told, that there was foreign blood in his veins.'

'Is there?' said Gwendolen.

'Mrs. Torrington says so. I asked particularly who he was, and she told me that his mother was some foreigner of high rank.'

'His mother?' said Gwendolen, rather sharply. 'Then who was his father?'

'Well – every one says he is the son of Sir Hugo Mallinger, who brought him up; though he passes for a ward. She says, if Sir Hugo Mallinger could have done as he liked with his estates, he would have left them to this Mr. Deronda, since he has no legitimate son.'

Gwendolen was silent; but her mother observed so marked an effect in her face that she was angry with herself for having repeated Mrs. Torrington's gossip. It seemed, on reflection, unsuited to the ear of her daughter, for whom Mrs. Davilow disliked what is called knowledge of the world; and indeed she wished that she herself had not had any of it thrust upon her.

An image which had immediately arisen in Gwendolen's mind was that of the unknown mother – no doubt a dark-eyed woman – probably sad. Hardly any face could be less like Deronda's than that represented as Sir Hugo's in a crayon portrait at Diplow. A dark-eyed beautiful woman, no longer young, had become 'stuff o' the conscience' to Gwendolen.

That night when she had got into her little bed, and only a dim light was burning, she said –

'Mamma, have men generally children before they are married?'

'No, dear, no,' said Mrs. Davilow. 'Why do you ask such a question?' (But she began to think that she saw the why.)

'If it were so, I ought to know,' said Gwendolen, with some indignation.

'You are thinking of what I said about Mr. Deronda and Sir Hugo Mallinger. That is a very unusual case, dear.'

'Does Lady Mallinger know?'

'She knows enough to satisfy her. That is quite clear, because Mr. Deronda has lived with them.'

'And people think no worse of him?'

'Well, of course he is under some disadvantage: it is not as if he were Lady Mallinger's son. He does not inherit the property, and he is not of any consequence in the world.

But people are not obliged to know anything about his birth; you see, he is very well received.'

'I wonder whether he knows about it; and whether he is angry with his father?'

'My dear child, why should you think of that?'

'Why?' said Gwendolen, impetuously, sitting up in her bed. 'Haven't children reason to be angry with their parents? How can they help their parents marrying or not marrying?'

But a consciousness rushed upon her, which made her fall back again on her pillow. It was not only what she would have felt months before – that she might seem to be reproaching her mother for that second marriage of hers; – what she chiefly felt now was, that she had been led on to a condemnation which seemed to make her own marriage a forbidden thing.

There was no further talk, and till sleep came over her, Gwendolen lay struggling with the reasons against that marriage – reasons which pressed upon her newly now that they were unexpectedly mirrored in the story of a man whose slight relations with her had, by some hidden affinity, bitten themselves into the most permanent layers of feeling. It was characteristic that, with all her debating, she was never troubled by the question whether the indefensibleness of her marriage did not include the fact that she had accepted Grandcourt solely as the man whom it was convenient for her to marry, not in the least as one to whom she would be binding herself in duty. Gwendolen's ideas were pitiably crude; but many grand difficulties of life are apt to force themselves on us in our crudity. And to judge wisely I suppose we must know how things appear to the unwise; that kind of appearance making the larger part of the world's history.

In the morning, there was a double excitement for her. She was going to hunt, from which scruples about propriety had threatened to hinder her, until it was found that Mrs. Torrington was horsewoman enough to accompany her: – going to hunt for the first time since her escapade with Rex; and she was going again to see Deronda, in whom, since last night, her interest had so gathered that she expected, as people do about revealed celebrities, to see something in his appearance which she had missed before. What was he going to be? What sort of life had he before him – he being nothing of any consequence? And with only a little difference in events he might have been as important as Grandcourt, nay – her imagination inevitably went in that direction – might have held the very estates which Grandcourt was to have. But now, Deronda would probably some day see her mistress of the Abbey at Topping, see her bearing the title which would have been his own wife's. These obvious, futile thoughts of what might have been, made a new epoch for Gwendolen. She, whose unquestioning habit it had been to take the best that came to her for less than her own claim, had now to see the position which tempted her in a new light, as a hard, unfair exclusion of others. What she had now heard about Deronda seemed to her imagination to throw him into one group with Mrs. Glasher and her children; before whom she felt herself in an attitude of apology – she who had hitherto been surrounded by a group that in her opinion had need be apologetic to her. Perhaps Deronda himself was thinking of these things. Could he know of Mrs. Glasher? If he knew that she knew, he would despise her; but he could have no such knowledge. Would he, without that, despise her for marrying Grandcourt? His possible judgment of her actions was telling on her as importunately as Klesmer's judgment of her powers; but she found larger room for resistance to a disapproval of her marriage, because it is easier to make our conduct seem justifiable to ourselves than to make our ability strike others. 'How can I help it?' is not our favourite apology for incompetence. But Gwendolen felt some strength in saying –

'How can I help what other people have done? Things would not come right if I were to turn round now and declare that I would not marry Mr. Grandcourt.' And such turning round was out of the question. The horses in the chariot she had mounted were going at full speed.

This mood of youthful, elated desperation had a tidal recurrence. She could dare anything that lay before her sooner than she could choose to go backward into humiliation; and it was even soothing to think that there would now be as much ill-doing in the one as in the other. But the immediate delightful fact was the hunt, where she would see Deronda, and where he would see her; for always lurking ready to obtrude before other thoughts about him was the impression that he was very much interested in her. But to-day she was resolved not to repeat her folly of yesterday, as if she were anxious to say anything to him. Indeed, the hunt would be too absorbing.

And so it was for a long while. Deronda was there, and within her sight very often; but this only added to the stimulus of a pleasure which Gwendolen had only once before tasted, and which seemed likely always to give a delight independent of any crosses, except such as took away the chance of riding. No accident happened to throw them together; the run took them within convenient reach of home, and in the agreeable sombreness of the grey November afternoon, with a long stratum of yellow light in the west, Gwendolen was returning with the company from Diplow, who were attending her on the way to Offendene. Now that the sense of glorious excitement was over and gone, she was getting irritably disappointed that she had had no opportunity of speaking to Deronda, whom she would not see again, since he was to go away in a couple of days. What was she going to say? That was not quite certain. She wanted to speak to him. Grandcourt was by her side; Mrs. Torrington, her husband, and another gentleman in advance; and Deronda's horse she could hear behind. The wish to speak to him and have him speaking to her was becoming imperious; and there was no chance of it, unless she simply asserted her will and defied everything. Where the order of things could give way to Miss Gwendolen, it must be made to do so. They had lately emerged from a wood of pines and beeches, where the twilight stillness had a repressing effect, which increased her impatience. The horse-hoofs again heard behind at some little distance were a growing irritation. She reined in her horse and looked behind her; Grandcourt, after a few paces, also paused; but she, waving her whip and nodding sideways with playful imperiousness, said, 'Go on! I want to speak to Mr. Deronda.'

Grandcourt hesitated; but that he would have done after any proposition. It was an awkward situation for him. No gentleman, before marriage, could give the emphasis of refusal to a command delivered in this playful way. He rode on slowly, and she waited till Deronda came up. He looked at her with tacit inquiry, and she said at once, letting her horse go alongside of his –

'Mr. Deronda, you must enlighten my ignorance. I want to know why you thought it wrong for me to gamble. Is it because I am a woman?'

'Not altogether; but I regretted it the more because you were a woman,' said Deronda, with an irrepressible smile. Apparently it must be understood between them now that it was he who sent the necklace. 'I think it would be better for men not to gamble. It is a besotting kind of taste, likely to turn into a disease. And, besides, there is something revolting to me in raking a heap of money together, and internally chuckling over it, when others are feeling the loss of it. I should even call it base, if it were more than an exceptional lapse. There are enough inevitable turns of fortune which force us to see that our gain is another's loss: – that is one of the ugly aspects of life. One would like to reduce it as much as one could, not get amusement out of exaggerating it.' Deronda's voice had gathered some indignation while he was speaking.

'But you do admit that we can't help things,' said Gwendolen, with a drop in her tone. The answer had not been anything like what she had expected. 'I mean that things are so in spite of us; we can't always help it that our gain is another's loss.'

'Clearly. Because of that, we should help it where we can.'

Gwendolen, biting her lip inside, paused a moment, and then forcing herself to speak with an air of playfulness again, said –

'But why should you regret it more because I am a woman?'

'Perhaps because we need that you should be better than we are.'

'But suppose *we* need that men should be better than we are,' said Gwendolen, with a little air of 'check!'

'That is rather a difficulty,' said Deronda, smiling. 'I suppose I should have said, we each of us think it would be better for the other to be good.'

'You see, I needed you to be better than I was – and you thought so,' said Gwendolen, nodding and laughing, while she put her horse forward and joined Grandcourt, who made no observation.

'Don't you want to know what I had to say to Mr. Deronda?' said Gwendolen, whose own pride required her to account for her conduct.

'A – no,' said Grandcourt, coldly.

'Now that is the first impolite word you have spoken – that you don't wish to hear what I had to say,' said Gwendolen, playing at a pout.

'I wish to hear what you say to me – not to other men,' said Grandcourt.

'Then you wish to hear this. I wanted to make him tell me why he objected to my gambling, and he gave me a little sermon.'

'Yes – but excuse me the sermon.' If Gwendolen imagined that Grandcourt cared about her speaking to Deronda, he wished her to understand that she was mistaken. But he was not fond of being told to ride on. She saw he was piqued, but did not mind. She had accomplished her object of speaking again to Deronda before he raised his hat and turned with the rest towards Diplow, while her lover attended her to Offendene, where he was to bid farewell before a whole day's absence on the unspecified journey. Grandcourt had spoken truth in calling the journey a bore: he was going by train to Gadsmere.

XXX

No penitence and no confessional:
No priest ordains it, yet they're forced to sit
Amid deep ashes of their vanished years.

IMAGINE a rambling, patchy house, the best part built of
grey stone, and red-tiled, a round tower jutting at one of
the corners, the mellow darkness of its conical roof surmounted by a weather-cock making an agreeable object
either amidst the gleams and greenth of summer or the
low-hanging clouds and snowy branches of winter: the
ground shady with spreading trees: a great cedar flourishing on one side, backward some Scotch firs on a broken
bank where the roots hung naked, and beyond, a rookery:
on the other side a pool overhung with bushes, where the
water-fowl fluttered and screamed: all around, a vast
meadow which might be called a park, bordered by an
old plantation and guarded by stone lodges which looked
like little prisons. Outside the gate the country, once
entirely rural and lovely, now black with coal-mines, was
chiefly peopled by men and brethren with candles stuck in
their hats, and with a diabolic complexion which laid them
peculiarly open to suspicion in the eyes of the children at
Gadsmere – Mrs. Glasher's four beautiful children, who
had dwelt there for about three years. Now, in November,
when the flower-beds were empty, the trees leafless, and
the pool blackly shivering, one might have said that the
place was sombrely in keeping with the black roads and
black mounds which seemed to put the district in mourning; – except when the children were playing on the gravel
with the dogs for their companions. But Mrs. Glasher
under her present circumstances liked Gadsmere as well
as she would have liked any other abode. The complete
seclusion of the place, which the unattractiveness of the
country secured, was exactly to her taste. When she drove
her two ponies with a waggonet full of children, there were
no gentry in carriages to be met, only men of business in

370

gigs; at church there were no eyes she cared to avoid, for the curate's wife and the curate himself were either ignorant of anything to her disadvantage, or ignored it: to them she was simply a widow lady, the tenant of Gadsmere; and the name of Grandcourt was of little interest in that district compared with the names of Fletcher and Gawcome, the lessees of the collieries.

It was full ten years since the elopement of an Irish officer's beautiful wife with young Grandcourt, and a consequent duel where the bullets wounded the air only, had made some little noise. Most of those who remembered the affair now wondered what had become of that Mrs. Glasher whose beauty and brilliancy had made her rather conspicuous to them in foreign places, where she was known to be living with young Grandcourt.

That he should have disentangled himself from that connection seemed only natural and desirable. As to her it was thought that a woman who was understood to have forsaken her child along with her husband had probably sunk lower. Grandcourt had of course got weary of her. He was much given to the pursuit of women; but a man in his position would by this time desire to make a suitable marriage with the fair young daughter of a noble house. No one talked of Mrs. Glasher now, any more than they talked of the victim in a trial for manslaughter ten years before: she was a lost vessel after whom nobody would send out an expedition of search; but Grandcourt was seen in harbour with his colours flying, registered as seaworthy as ever.

Yet in fact Grandcourt had never disentangled himself from Mrs. Glasher. His passion for her had been the strongest and most lasting he had ever known; and though it was now as dead as the music of a cracked flute, it had left a certain dull disposedness, which on the death of her husband three years before had prompted in him a vacillating notion of marrying her, in accordance with the understanding often expressed between them during the days of his first ardour. At that early time Grandcourt would willingly have paid for the freedom to be won by a divorce; but the husband would not oblige him, not wanting to be married again himself, and not wishing to have his domestic habits printed in evidence.

The altered poise which the years had brought in Mrs. Glasher was just the reverse. At first she was comparatively careless about the possibility of marriage. It was enough that she had escaped from a disagreeable husband and found a sort of bliss with a lover who had completely fascinated her – young, handsome, amorous, and living in the best style, with equipage and conversation *en suite*, of the kind to be expected in young men of fortune who have seen everything. She was an impassioned, vivacious woman, fond of adoration, exasperated by five years of marital rudeness; and the sense of release was so strong upon her that it stilled anxiety for more than she actually enjoyed. An equivocal position was of no importance to her then; she had no envy for the honours of a dull, disregarded wife: the one spot which spoiled her vision of her new pleasant world, was the sense that she had left her three-year-old boy, who died two years afterwards, and whose first tones saying 'mamma' retained a difference from those of the children that came after. But now the years had brought many changes besides those in the contour of her cheek and throat; and that Grandcourt should marry her had become her dominant desire. The equivocal position which she had not minded about for herself was now telling upon her through her children, whom she loved with a devotion charged with the added passion of atonement. She had no repentance except in this direction. If Grandcourt married her, the children would be none the worse off for what had passed: they would see their mother in a dignified position, and they would be at no disadvantage with the world: her son would be made his father's heir. It was the yearning for this result which gave the supreme importance to Grandcourt's feeling for her; her love for him had long resolved itself into anxiety that he should give her the unique, permanent claim of a wife, and she expected no other happiness in marriage than the satisfaction of her maternal love and pride – including her pride for herself in the presence of her children. For the sake of that result she was prepared even with a tragic firmness to endure anything quietly in marriage; and she had had acuteness enough to cherish Grandcourt's flickering purpose negatively, by not molesting him with passionate appeals and with scene-making. In her, as in every one else who wanted anything of him, his incalculable turns, and his tendency to harden under beseeching, had created a reasonable dread: – a slow discovery, of which no presentiment had been given in the bearing of a youthful lover with a fine line of face and the softest manners. But reticence had necessarily cost something to this impassioned woman, and she was the bitterer for it. There is no quailing – even that forced on the helpless and injured – which has not an ugly obverse: the withheld sting was gathering venom. She was absolutely dependent on Grandcourt; for though he had been always liberal in expenses for her, he had kept everything voluntary on his part; and with the goal of marriage before her she would ask for nothing less. He had said that he would never settle anything except by will; and when she was thinking of alternatives for the future it often occurred to her that, even if she did not become Grandcourt's wife, he might never have a son who would have a legitimate claim on him, and the end might be that her son would be made heir to the best part of his estates. No son at that early age could promise to have more of his father's *physique*. But her becoming Grandcourt's wife was so far from being an extravagant notion of possibility, that even Lush had entertained it, and had said that he would as soon bet on it as on any other likelihood with regard to his familiar companion. Lush, indeed, on inferring that Grandcourt had a preconception of using his residence at Diplow in order to win Miss Arrowpoint, had thought it well to fan that project, taking it as a tacit renunciation of the marriage with Mrs. Glasher, which had long been a mark for the hovering and wheeling

373

of Grandcourt's caprice. But both prospects had been negatived by Gwendolen's appearance on the scene; and it was natural enough for Mrs. Glasher to enter with eagerness into Lush's plan of hindering that new danger by setting up a barrier in the mind of the girl who was being sought as a bride. She entered into it with an eagerness which had passion in it as well as purpose, some of the stored-up venom delivering itself in that way.

After that, she had heard from Lush of Gwendolen's departure, and the probability that all danger from her was got rid of; but there had been no letter to tell her that the danger had returned and had become a certainty. She had since then written to Grandcourt as she did habitually, and he had been longer than usual in answering. She was inferring that he might intend coming to Gadsmere at the time when he was actually on the way; and she was not without hope – what construction of another's mind is not strong wishing equal to? – that a certain sickening from that frustrated courtship might dispose him to slip the more easily into the old track of intention.

Grandcourt had two grave purposes in coming to Gadsmere: to convey the news of his approaching marriage in person, in order to make this first difficulty final; and to get from Lydia his mother's diamonds, which long ago he had confided to her and wished her to wear. Her person suited diamonds and made them look as if they were worth some of the money given for them. These particular diamonds were not mountains of light – they were mere peas and haricots for the ears, neck, and hair; but they were worth some thousands, and Grandcourt necessarily wished to have them for his wife. Formerly when he had asked Lydia to put them into his keeping again, simply on the ground that they would be safer and ought to be deposited at the bank, she had quietly but absolutely refused, declaring that they were quite safe; and at last had said, 'If you ever marry another woman I will give them up to her: are you going to marry another woman?' At that time Grandcourt had no motive which urged him to persist, and he had this grace in him, that the disposition to exercise power either by cowing or disappointing others or exciting in them a rage which they dared not express – a disposition which was active in him as other propensities became languid – had always been in abeyance before Lydia. A severe interpreter might say that the mere facts of their relation to each other, the melancholy position of this woman who depended on his will, made a standing banquet for his delight in dominating. But there was something else than this in his forbearance towards her: there was the surviving though metamorphosed effect of the power she had had over him; and it was this effect, the fitful dull lapse towards solicitations that once had the zest now missing from life, which had again and again inclined him to espouse a familiar past rather than rouse himself to the expectation of novelty. But now novelty had taken hold of him and urged him to make the most of it.

Mrs. Glasher was seated in the pleasant room where she habitually passed her mornings with her children round her. It had a square projecting window and looked on broad gravel and grass, sloping towards a little brook that entered the pool. The top of a low black cabinet, the old oak table, the chairs in tawny leather, were littered with the children's toys, books, and garden garments, at which a maternal lady in pastel looked down from the walls with smiling indulgence. The children were all there. The three girls seated round their mother near the window, were miniature portraits of her – dark-eyed, delicate-featured brunettes with a rich bloom on their cheeks, their little nostrils and eyebrows singularly finished as if they were tiny women, the eldest being barely nine. The boy was seated on the carpet at some distance, bending his blond head over the animals from a Noah's ark, admonishing them separately in a voice of threatening command, and occasionally licking the spotted ones to see if the colours would hold. Josephine, the eldest, was having her French lesson; and the others, with their dolls on their laps, sate demurely enough for images of the Madonna. Mrs.

Glasher's toilet had been made very carefully – each day now she said to herself that Grandcourt might come in. Her head, which, spite of emaciation, had an ineffaceable beauty in the fine profile, crisp curves of hair, and clearly-marked eyebrows, rose impressively above her bronze-coloured silk and velvet, and the gold necklace which Grandcourt had first clasped round her neck years ago. Not that she had any pleasure in her toilet; her chief thought of herself seen in the glass was, 'How changed!' – but such good in life as remained to her she would keep. If her chief wish were fulfilled, she could imagine herself getting the comeliness of a matron fit for the highest rank. The little faces beside her, almost exact reductions of her own, seemed to tell of the blooming curves which had once been where now was sunken pallor. But the children kissed the pale cheeks and never found them deficient. That love was now the one end of her life.

Suddenly Mrs. Glasher turned away her head from Josephine's book and listened. 'Hush, dear! I think some one is coming.'

Henleigh the boy jumped up and said, 'Mamma, is it the miller with my donkey?'

He got no answer, and going up to his mamma's knee repeated his question in an insistent tone. But the door opened, and the servant announced Mr. Grandcourt. Mrs. Glasher rose in some agitation. Henleigh frowned at him in disgust at his not being the miller, and the three little girls lifted up their dark eyes to him timidly. They had none of them any particular liking for this friend of mamma's – in fact, when he had taken Mrs. Glasher's hand and then turned to put his other hand on Henleigh's head, that energetic scion began to beat the friend's arm away with his fists. The little girls submitted bashfully to be patted under the chin and kissed, but on the whole it seemed better to send them into the garden, where they were presently dancing and chatting with the dogs on the gravel.

'How far are you come?' said Mrs. Glasher, as Grandcourt put away his hat and overcoat.

'From Diplow,' he answered slowly, seating himself opposite her and looking at her with an unnoting gaze which she noted.

'You are tired, then.'

'No, I rested at the Junction – a hideous hole. These railway journeys are always a confounded bore. But I had coffee and smoked.'

Grandcourt drew out his handkerchief, rubbed his face, and in returning the handkerchief to his pocket looked at his crossed knee and blameless boot, as if any stranger were opposite to him, instead of a woman quivering with a suspense which every word and look of his was to incline towards hope or dread. But he was really occupied with their interview and what it was likely to include. Imagine the difference in rate of emotion between this woman whom the years had worn to a more conscious dependence and sharper eagerness, and this man whom they were dulling into a more and more neutral obstinacy.

'I expected to see you – it was so long since I had heard from you. I suppose the weeks seem longer at Gadsmere than they do at Diplow,' said Mrs. Glasher. She had a quick, incisive way of speaking that seemed to go with her features, as the tone and *timbre* of a violin go with its form.

'Yes,' drawled Grandcourt. 'But you found the money paid into the bank.'

'Oh yes,' said Mrs. Glasher, curtly, tingling with impatience. Always before – at least she fancied so – Grandcourt had taken more notice of her and the children than he did to-day.

'Yes,' he resumed, playing with his whisker, and at first not looking at her, 'the time has gone on at rather a rattling pace with me; generally it is slow enough. But there has been a good deal happening, as you know' – here he turned his eyes upon her.

'What do I know?'

He left a pause before he said, without change of manner, 'That I was thinking of marrying. You saw Miss Harleth?'

'*She* told you that?'

The pale cheeks looked even paler, perhaps from the fierce brightness in the eyes above them.

'No. Lush told me,' was the slow answer. It was as if the thumb-screw and the iron-boot were being placed by creeping hands within sight of the expectant victim.

'Good God! say at once that you are going to marry her,' she burst out passionately, her knee shaking and her hands tightly clasped.

'Of course, this kind of thing must happen some time or other, Lydia,' said he; really, now the thumb-screw was on, not wishing to make the pain worse.

'You didn't always see the necessity.'

'Perhaps not. I see it now.'

In those few undertoned words of Grandcourt's she felt as absolute a resistance as if her thin fingers had been pushing at a fast-shut iron door. She knew her helplessness, and shrank from testing it by any appeal – shrank from crying in a dead ear and clinging to dead knees, only to see the immovable face and feel the rigid limbs. She did not weep nor speak: she was too hard pressed by the sudden certainty which had as much of chill sickness in it as of thought and emotion. The defeated clutch of struggling hope gave her in these first moments a horrible sensation. At last she rose with a spasmodic effort, and, unconscious of everything but her wretchedness, pressed her forehead against the hard cold glass of the window. The children, playing on the gravel, took this as a sign that she wanted them, and running forward stood in front of her with their sweet faces upturned expectantly. This roused her: she shook her head at them, waved them off, and overcome with this painful exertion sank back in the nearest chair.

Grandcourt had risen too. He was doubly annoyed – at the scene itself, and at the sense that no imperiousness of his could save him from it; but the task had to be gone through, and there was the administrative necessity of arranging things so that there should be as little annoyance as possible in future. He was leaning against the corner of the fireplace. She looked up at him and said bitterly –

'All this is of no consequence to you. I and the children are importunate creatures. You wish to get away again and be with Miss Harleth.'

'Don't make the affair more disagreeable than it need be, Lydia. It is of no use to harp on things that can't be altered. Of course it's deucedly disagreeable to me to see you making yourself miserable. I've taken this journey to tell you what you must make up your mind to; – you and the children will be provided for as usual; – and there's an end of it.'

Silence. She dared not answer. This woman with the intense eager look had had the iron of the mother's anguish in her soul, and it had made her sometimes capable of a repression harder than shrieking and struggle. But underneath the silence there was an outlash of hatred and vindictiveness: she wished that the marriage might make two others wretched, besides herself. Presently he went on.

'It will be better for you. You may go on living here. But I think of by-and-by settling a good sum on you and the children, and you can live where you like. There will be nothing for you to complain of then. Whatever happens, you will feel secure. Nothing could be done beforehand. Everything has gone on in a hurry.'

Grandcourt ceased his slow delivery of sentences. He did not expect her to thank him, but he considered that she might reasonably be contented; if it were possible for Lydia to be contented. She showed no change, and after a minute he said –

'You have never had any reason to fear that I should be illiberal. I don't care a curse about the money.'

'If you did care about it, I suppose you would not give it us,' said Lydia. The sarcasm was irrepressible.

'That's a devilishly unfair thing to say,' Grandcourt replied, in a lower tone; 'and I advise you not to say that sort of thing again.'

'Should you punish me by leaving the children in beggary?' In spite of herself, the one outlet of venom had brought the other.

'There is no question about leaving the children in beggary,' said Grandcourt, still in his low voice. 'I advise you not to say things that you will repent of.'

'I am used to repenting,' said she, bitterly. 'Perhaps *you* will repent. You have already repented of loving me.'

'All this will only make it uncommonly difficult for us to meet again. What friend have you besides me?'

'Quite true.'

The words came like a low moan. At the same moment there flashed through her the wish that after promising himself a better happiness than that he had had with her, he might feel a misery and loneliness which would drive him back to her to find some memory of a time when he was young, glad, and hopeful. But no! he would go scatheless; it was she who had to suffer.

With this the scorching words were ended. Grandcourt had meant to stay till evening; he wished to curtail his visit, but there was no suitable train earlier than the one he had arranged to go by, and he had still to speak to Lydia on the second object of his visit, which like a second surgical operation seemed to require an interval. The hours had to go by; there was eating to be done; the children came in again – all this mechanism of life had to be gone through with the dreary sense of constraint which is often felt in domestic quarrels of a commoner kind. To Lydia it was some slight relief for her stifled fury to have the children present: she felt a savage glory in their loveliness, as if it would taunt Grandcourt with his indifference to her and them – a secret darting of venom which was strongly imaginative. He acquitted himself with all the advantage of a man whose grace of bearing has long been moulded on an experience of boredom – nursed the little Antonia, who sat with her hands crossed and eyes upturned to his bald head, which struck her as worthy of observation – and propitiated Henleigh by promising him a beautiful saddle and bridle. It was only the two eldest girls who had known him as a continual presence; and the intervening years had overlaid their infantine memories with a bashfulness which Grandcourt's bearing was not likely to dissipate. He and Lydia occasionally, in the presence of the servants, made a conventional remark; otherwise they never spoke; and the stagnant thought in Grandcourt's mind all the while was of his own infatuation in having given her those diamonds, which obliged him to incur the nuisance of speaking about them. He had an ingrained care for what he held to belong to his caste, and about property he liked to be lordly; also he had a consciousness of indignity to himself in having to ask for anything in the world. But however he might assert his independence of Mrs. Glasher's past, he had made a past for himself which was a stronger yoke than any he could impose. He must ask for the diamonds which he had promised to Gwendolen.

At last they were alone again, with the candles above them, face to face with each other. Grandcourt looked at his watch, and then said, in an apparently indifferent drawl, 'There is one thing I had to mention, Lydia. My diamonds – you have them.'

'Yes, I have them,' she answered promptly, rising, and standing with her arms thrust down and her fingers threaded, while Grandcourt sat still. She had expected the topic, and made her resolve about it. But she meant to carry out her resolve, if possible, without exasperating him. During the hours of silence she had longed to recall the words which had only widened the breach between them.

'They are in this house, I suppose?'

'No; not in this house.'

'I thought you said you kept them by you.'

'When I said so it was true. They are in the bank at Dudley.'

'Get them away, will you? I must make an arrangement for your delivering them to some one.'

'Make no arrangement. They shall be delivered to the person you intend them for. *I* will make the arrangement.'

'What do you mean?'

'What I say. I have always told you that I would give them up to your wife. I shall keep my word. She is not your wife yet.'

'This is foolery,' said Grandcourt, with undertoned disgust. It was too irritating that his indulgence of Lydia had given her a sort of mastery over him in spite of her dependent condition.

She did not speak. He also rose now, but stood leaning against the mantelpiece with his side-face towards her.

'The diamonds must be delivered to me before my marriage,' he began again.

'What is your wedding-day?'

'The tenth. There is no time to be lost.'

'And where do you go after the marriage?'

He did not reply except by looking more sullen. Presently he said, 'You must appoint a day before then, to get them from the bank and meet me – or somebody else I will commission: – it's a great nuisance. Mention a day.'

'No; I shall not do that. They shall be delivered to her safely. I shall keep my word.'

'Do you mean to say,' said Grandcourt, just audibly, turning to face her, 'that you will not do as I tell you?'

'Yes, I mean that,' was the answer that leaped out, while her eyes flashed close to him. The poor creature was immediately conscious that if her words had any effect on her own lot, the effect must be mischievous, and might nullify all the remaining advantage of her long patience. But the word had been spoken.

He was in a position the most irritating to him. He could not shake her or touch her hostilely; and if he could, the process would not bring the diamonds. He shrank from the only sort of threat that would frighten her – if she believed it. And in general, there was nothing he hated more than to be forced into anything like violence even in words: his will must impose itself without trouble. After looking at her for a moment, he turned his side-face towards her again, leaning as before, and said –

'Infernal idiots that women are!'

'Why will you not tell me where you are going after the marriage? I could be at the wedding if I liked, and learn in that way,' said Lydia, not shrinking from the one suicidal form of threat within her power.

'Of course, if you like, you can play the mad woman,' said Grandcourt, with *sotto voce* scorn. 'It is not to be supposed that you will wait to think what good will come of it – or what you owe to me.'

He was in a state of disgust and embitterment quite new in the history of their relation to each other. It was undeniable that this woman whose life he had allowed to send such deep suckers into his had a terrible power of annoyance in her; and the rash hurry of his proceedings had left her opportunities open. His pride saw very ugly possibilities threatening it, and he stood for several minutes in silence reviewing the situation – considering how he could act upon her. Unlike himself she was of a direct nature, with certain simple strongly-coloured tendencies, and there was one often-experienced effect which he thought he could count upon now. As Sir Hugo had said of him, Grandcourt knew how to play his cards upon occasion.

He did not speak again, but looked at his watch, rang the bell, and ordered the vehicle to be brought round immediately. Then he removed farther from her, walked as if in expectation of a summons, and remained silent without turning his eyes upon her.

She was suffering the horrible conflict of self-reproach and tenacity. She saw beforehand Grandcourt leaving her without even looking at her again – herself left behind in lonely uncertainty – hearing nothing from him – not knowing whether she had done her children harm – feeling that she had perhaps made him hate her: – all the wretchedness of a creature who had defeated her own motives. And yet she could not bear to give up a purpose which was a sweet

DANIEL DERONDA

morsel to her vindictiveness. If she had not been a mother
she would willingly have sacrificed herself to her revenge –
to what she felt to be the justice of hindering another from
getting happiness by willingly giving her over to misery.
The two dominant passions were at struggle. She must
satisfy them both.

'Don't let us part in anger, Henleigh,' she began, without changing her place or attitude: 'it is a very little thing I
ask. If I were refusing to give anything up that you call
yours, it would be different: that would be a reason for
treating me as if you hated me. But I ask such a little thing.
If you will tell me where you are going on the wedding-day,
I will take care that the diamonds shall be delivered to her
without scandal. Without scandal,' she repeated entreatingly.

'Such preposterous whims make a woman odious,' said
Grandcourt, not giving way in look or movement. 'What is
the use of talking to mad people?'

'Yes, I am foolish – loneliness has made me foolish –
indulge me.' Sobs rose as she spoke. 'If you will indulge me
in this one folly, I will be very meek – I will never trouble
you.' She burst into hysterical crying, and said again almost
with a scream – 'I will be very meek after that.'

There was a strange mixture of acting and reality in this
passion. She kept hold of her purpose as a child might
tighten its hand over a small stolen thing, crying and
denying all the while. Even Grandcourt was wrought
upon by surprise: this capricious wish, this childish violence, was as unlike Lydia's bearing as it was incongruous
with her person. Both had always had a stamp of dignity on
them. Yet she seemed more manageable in this state than
in her former attitude of defiance. He came close up to her
again, and said, in his low imperious tone, 'Be quiet, and
hear what I tell you. I will never forgive you if you present
yourself again and make a scene.'

She pressed her handkerchief against her face, and
when she could speak firmly said, in the muffled voice
that follows sobbing, 'I will not – if you will let me have my

way – I promise you not to thrust myself forward again. I have never broken my word to you – how many have you broken to me? When you gave me the diamonds to wear, you were not thinking of having another wife. And I now give them up – I don't reproach you – I only ask you to let me give them up in my own way. Have I not borne it well? Everything is to be taken from me, and when I ask for a straw, a chip – you deny it me.' She had spoken rapidly, but after a little pause she said more slowly, her voice freed from its muffled tone: 'I will not bear to have it denied me.'

Grandcourt had a baffling sense that he had to deal with something like madness; he could only govern by giving way. The servant came to say the fly was ready. When the door was shut again, Grandcourt said, sullenly, 'We are going to Ryelands, then.'

'They shall be delivered to her there,' said Lydia, with decision.

'Very well, I am going.' He felt no inclination even to take her hand: she had annoyed him too sorely. But now that she had gained her point, she was prepared to humble herself that she might propitiate him.

'Forgive me; I will never vex you again,' she said, with beseeching looks. Her inward voice said distinctly – 'It is only I who have to forgive.' Yet she was obliged to ask forgiveness.

'You had better keep that promise. You have made me feel uncommonly ill with your folly,' said Grandcourt, apparently choosing this statement as the strongest possible use of language.

'Poor thing!' said Lydia, with a faint smile: – was he aware of the minor fact that he had made her feel ill this morning?

But with the quick transition natural to her, she was now ready to coax him if he would let her, that they might part in some degree reconciled. She ventured to lay her hand on his shoulder, and he did not move away from her: she had so far succeeded in alarming him, that he was not sorry for these proofs of returned subjection.

'Light a cigar,' she said, soothingly, taking the case from his breast-pocket and opening it.

Amidst such caressing signs of mutual fear they parted. The effect that clung and gnawed within Grandcourt was a sense of imperfect mastery.

XXXI

'A wild dedication of yourselves
To unpath'd waters, undream'd shores.'
– SHAKESPEARE.

ON the day when Gwendolen Harleth was married and
became Mrs. Grandcourt, the morning was clear and
bright, and while the sun was low a slight frost crisped
the leaves. The bridal party was worth seeing, and half
Pennicote turned out to see it, lining the pathway up to the
church. An old friend of the Rector's performed the marriage ceremony, the Rector himself acting as father, to the
great advantage of the procession. Only two faces, it was
remarked, showed signs of sadness – Mrs. Davilow's and
Anna's. The mother's delicate eyelids were pink, as if she
had been crying half the night; and no one was surprised
that, splendid as the match was, she should feel the parting
from a daughter who was the flower of her children and of
her own life. It was less understood why Anna should be
troubled when she was being so well set off by the bridesmaid's dress. Every one else seemed to reflect the brilliancy of the occasion – the bride most of all. Of her it was
agreed that as to figure and carriage she was worthy to be a
'lady o' title:' as to face, perhaps it might be thought that a
title required something more rosy; but the bridegroom
himself not being fresh-coloured – being indeed, as the
miller's wife observed, very much of her own husband's
complexion – the match was the more complete. Anyhow
he must be very fond of her; and it was to be hoped that he
would never cast it up to her that she had been going out to
service as a governess, and her mother to live at Sawyer's
Cottage – vicissitudes which had been much spoken of in
the village. The miller's daughter of fourteen could not
believe that high gentry behaved badly to their wives, but
her mother instructed her – 'Oh, child, men's men: gentle
or simple, they're much of a muchness. I've heard my
mother say Squire Pelton used to take his dogs and a long

whip into his wife's room, and flog 'em there to frighten her; and my mother was lady's-maid there at the very time.'

'That's unlucky talk for a wedding, Mrs. Girdle,' said the tailor. 'A quarrel may end wi' the whip, but it begins wi' the tongue, and it's the women have got the most o' that.'

'The Lord gave it 'em to use, I suppose,' said Mrs. Girdle; '*He* never meant you to have it all your own way.'

'By what I can make out from the gentleman as attends to the grooming at Offendene,' said the tailor, 'this Mr. Grandcourt has wonderful little tongue. Everything must be done dummy-like without his ordering.'

'Then he's the more whip, I doubt,' said Mrs. Girdle. '*She's* got tongue enough, I warrant her. See, there they come out together!'

'What wonderful long corners she's got to her eyes!' said the tailor. 'She makes you feel comical when she looks at you.'

Gwendolen, in fact, never showed more elasticity in her bearing, more lustre in her long brown glance: she had the brilliancy of strong excitement, which will sometimes come even from pain. It was not pain, however, that she was feeling: she had wrought herself up to much the same condition as that in which she stood at the gambling-table when Deronda was looking at her, and she began to lose. There was enjoyment in it: whatever uneasiness a growing conscience had created, was disregarded as an ailment might have been, amidst the gratification of that ambitious vanity and desire for luxury within her which it would take a great deal of slow poisoning to kill. This morning she could not have said truly that she repented her acceptance of Grandcourt, or that any fears in hazy perspective could hinder the glowing effects of the immediate scene in which she was the central object. That she was doing something wrong – that a punishment might be hanging over her – that the woman to whom she had given a promise and broken it, was thinking of her in bitterness and misery with a just reproach – that Deronda with his way of looking into things very likely despised her for marrying Grandcourt, as he had despised her for gambling – above all, that the cord which united her with this lover and which she had hitherto held by the hand, was now being flung over her neck, – all this yeasty mingling of dimly understood facts with vague but deep impressions, and with images half real, half fantastic, had been disturbing her during the weeks of her engagement. Was that agitating experience nullified this morning? No: it was surmounted and thrust down with a sort of exulting defiance as she felt herself standing at the game of life with many eyes upon her, daring everything to win much – or if to lose, still with *éclat* and a sense of importance. But this morning a losing destiny for herself did not press upon her as a fear: she thought that she was entering on a fuller power of managing circumstance – with all the official strength of marriage, which some women made so poor a use of. That intoxication of youthful egoism out of which she had been shaken by trouble, humiliation, and a new sense of culpability, had returned upon her under the newly-fed strength of the old fumes. She did not in the least present the ideal of the tearful, tremulous bride. Poor Gwendolen, whom some had judged much too forward and instructed in the world's ways! – with her erect head and elastic footstep she was walking amid illusions; and yet, too, there was an under-consciousness in her that she was a little intoxicated.

'Thank God you bear it so well, my darling!' said Mrs. Davilow, when she had helped Gwendolen to doff her bridal white and put on her travelling dress. All the trembling had been done by the poor mother, and her agitation urged Gwendolen doubly to take the morning as if it were a triumph.

'Why, you might have said that, if I had been going to Mrs. Mompert's, you dear, sad, incorrigible mamma!' said Gwendolen, just putting her hands to her mother's cheeks with laughing tenderness – then retreating a little and spreading out her arms as if to exhibit herself. 'Here am

I – Mrs. Grandcourt! What else would you have me, but what I am sure to be? You know you were ready to die with vexation when you thought that I would not be Mrs. Grandcourt.'

'Hush, hush, my child, for heaven's sake!' said Mrs. Davilow, almost in a whisper. 'How can I help feeling it when I am parting from you? But I can bear anything gladly if you are happy.'

'Not gladly, mamma, no!' said Gwendolen, shaking her head, with a bright smile. 'Willingly you would bear it, but always sorrowfully. Sorrowing is your sauce; you can take nothing without it.' Then, clasping her mother's shoulders and raining kisses first on one cheek and then on the other between her words, she said, gaily, 'And you shall sorrow over my having everything at my beck – and enjoying everything gloriously – splendid houses – and horses – and diamonds, I shall have diamonds – and going to court – and being Lady Certainly – and Lady Perhaps – and grand here – and tantivy there – and always loving you better than anybody else in the world.'

'My sweet child! – But I shall not be jealous if you love your husband better; and he will expect to be first.'

Gwendolen thrust out her lips and chin with a pretty grimace, saying, 'Rather a ridiculous expectation. However, I don't mean to treat him ill, unless he deserves it.'

Then the two fell into a clinging embrace, and Gwendolen could not hinder a rising sob when she said, 'I wish you were going with me, mamma.'

But the slight dew on her long eyelashes only made her the more charming when she gave her hand to Grandcourt to be led to the carriage.

The Rector looked in on her to give a final 'Good-bye; God bless you; we shall see you again before long,' and then returned to Mrs. Davilow saying half cheerfully, half solemnly –

'Let us be thankful, Fanny. She is in a position well suited to her, and beyond what I should have dared to hope

390

for. And few women can have been chosen more entirely for their own sake. You should feel yourself a happy mother.'

There was a railway journey of some fifty miles before the new husband and wife reached the station near Ryelands. The sky had veiled itself since the morning, and it was hardly more than twilight when they entered the park-gates, but still Gwendolen, looking out of the carriage-window as they drove rapidly along, could see the grand outlines and the nearer beauties of the scene – the long winding drive bordered with evergreens backed by huge grey stems; then the opening of wide grassy spaces and undulations studded with dark clumps; till at last came a wide level where the white house could be seen, with a hanging wood for a background, and the rising and sinking balustrade of a terrace in front.

Gwendolen had been at her liveliest during the journey, chatting incessantly, ignoring any change in their mutual position since yesterday; and Grandcourt had been rather ecstatically quiescent, while she turned his gentle seizure of her hand into a grasp of his hand by both hers, with an increased vivacity as of a kitten that will not sit quiet to be petted. She was really getting somewhat febrile in her excitement; and now in this drive through the park her usual susceptibility to changes of light and scenery helped to make her heart palpitate newly. Was it at the novelty simply, or the almost incredible fulfilment about to be given to her girlish dreams of being 'somebody' – walking through her own furlong of corridors and under her own ceilings of an out-of-sight loftiness, where her own painted Spring was shedding painted flowers, and her own fore-shortened Zephyrs were blowing their trumpets over her; while her own servants, lackeys in clothing but men in bulk and shape, were as nought in her presence, and revered the propriety of her insolence to them: – being in short the heroine of an admired play without the pains of art? Was it alone the closeness of this fulfilment which made her heart flutter? or was it some dim forecast, the

391

insistent penetration of suppressed experience, mixing the expectation of a triumph with the dread of a crisis? Hers was one of the natures in which exultation inevitably carries an infusion of dread ready to curdle and declare itself.

She fell silent in spite of herself as they approached the gates, and when her husband said, 'Here we are at home!' and for the first time kissed her on the lips, she hardly knew of it: it was no more than the passive acceptance of a greeting in the midst of an absorbing show. Was not all her hurrying life of the last three months a show, in which her consciousness was a wondering spectator? After the half-wilful excitement of the day, a numbness had come over her personality.

But there was a brilliant light in the hall – warmth, matting, carpets, full-length portraits, Olympian statues, assiduous servants. Not many servants, however: only a few from Diplow in addition to those constantly in charge of the house; and Gwendolen's new maid, who had come with her, was taken under guidance by the housekeeper. Gwendolen felt herself being led by Grandcourt along a subtly-scented corridor, then into an anteroom where she saw an open doorway sending out a rich glow of light and colour.

'These are our dens,' said Grandcourt. 'You will like to be quiet here till dinner. We shall dine early.'

He pressed her hand to his lips and moved away, more in love than he had ever expected to be.

Gwendolen, yielding up her hat and mantle, threw herself into a chair by the glowing hearth, and saw herself repeated in glass panels with all her faint-green satin sur-roundings. The housekeeper had passed into this boudoir from the adjoining dressing-room and seemed disposed to linger, Gwendolen thought, in order to look at the new mistress of Ryelands, who however, being impatient for solitude, said to her, 'Will you tell Hudson when she has put out my dress to leave everything? I shall not want her again, unless I ring.'

The housekeeper, coming forward, said, 'Here is a packet, madam, which I was ordered to give into nobody's hands but yours, when you were alone. The person who brought it said it was a present particularly ordered by Mr. Grandcourt; but he was not to know of its arrival till he saw you wear it. Excuse me, madam; I felt it right to obey orders.'

Gwendolen took the packet and let it lie on her lap till she heard the doors close. It came into her mind that the packet might contain the diamonds which Grandcourt had spoken of as being deposited somewhere and to be given to her on her marriage. In this moment of confused feeling and creeping luxurious languor she was glad of this diversion – glad of such an event as having her own diamonds to try on.

Within all the sealed paper coverings was a box, but within the box there *was* a jewel-case; and now she felt no doubt that she had the diamonds. But on opening the case, in the same instant that she saw their gleam she saw a letter lying above them. She knew the handwriting of the address. It was as if an adder had lain on them. Her heart gave a leap which seemed to have spent all her strength; and as she opened the bit of thin paper, it shook with the trembling of her hands. But it was legible as print, and thrust its words upon her.

'These diamonds, which were once given with ardent love to Lydia Glasher, she passes on to you. You have broken your word to her, that you might possess what was hers. Perhaps you think of being happy, as she once was, and of having beautiful children such as hers, who will thrust hers aside. God is too just for that. The man you have married has a withered heart. His best young love was mine; you could not take that from me when you took the rest. It is dead; but I am the grave in which your chance of happiness is buried as well as mine. You had your warning. You have chosen to injure me and my children. He had meant to marry me. He would have married me at last, if

393

you had not broken your word. You will have your punishment. I desire it with all my soul.

'Will you give him this letter to set him against me and ruin us more – me and my children? Shall you like to stand before your husband with these diamonds on you, and these words of mine in his thoughts and yours? Will he think you have any right to complain when he has made you miserable? You took him with your eyes open. The willing wrong you have done me will be your curse.'

It seemed at first as if Gwendolen's eyes were spellbound in reading the horrible words of the letter over and over again as a doom of penance; but suddenly a new spasm of terror made her lean forward and stretch out the paper towards the fire, lest accusation and proof at once should meet all eyes. It flew like a feather from her trembling fingers and was caught up in the great draught of flame. In her movement the casket fell on the floor and the diamonds rolled out. She took no notice, but fell back in her chair again helpless. She could not see the reflections of herself then: they were like so many women petrified white; but coming near herself you might have seen the tremor in her lips and hands. She sat so for a long while, knowing little more than that she was feeling ill, and that those written words kept repeating themselves in her.

Truly here were poisoned gems, and the poison had entered into this poor young creature.

After that long while, there was a tap at the door and Grandcourt entered, dressed for dinner. The sight of him brought a new nervous shock, and Gwendolen screamed again and again with hysterical violence. He had expected to see her dressed and smiling, ready to be led down. He saw her pallid, shrieking as it seemed with terror, the jewels scattered around her on the floor. Was it a fit of madness?

In some form or other the Furies had crossed his threshold.

XXXII

In all ages it hath been a favourite text that a potent love hath the nature of an isolated fatality, whereto the mind's opinions and wonted resolves are altogether alien: as, for example, Daphnis his frenzy, wherein it had little availed him to have been convinced of Heraclitus his doctrine; or the philtre-bred passion of Tristan, who, though he had been as deep as Duns Scotus, would have had his reasoning marred by that cup too much; or Romeo in his sudden taking for Juliet, wherein any objections he might have held against Ptolemy had made little difference to his discourse under the balcony. Yet all love is not such, even though potent; nay, this passion hath as large scope as any for allying itself with every operation of the soul: so that it shall acknowledge an effect from the imagined light of unproven firmaments, and have its scale set to the grander orbits of what hath been and shall be.

DERONDA, on his return to town, could assure Sir Hugo of his having lodged in Grandcourt's mind a distinct understanding that he could get fifty thousand pounds by giving up a prospect which was probably distant, and not absolutely certain; but he had no further sign of Grandcourt's disposition in the matter than that he was evidently inclined to keep up friendly communications.

'And what did you think of the future bride on a nearer survey?' said Sir Hugo.

'I thought better of her than I did at Leubronn. Roulette was not a good setting for her; it brought out something of the demon. At Diplow she seemed much more womanly and attractive – less hard and self-possessed. I thought her mouth and eyes had quite a different expression.'

'Don't flirt with her too much, Dan,' said Sir Hugo, meaning to be agreeably playful. 'If you make Grandcourt savage when they come to the Abbey at Christmas, it will interfere with my affairs.'

'I can stay in town, sir.'

'No, no. Lady Mallinger and the children can't do without you at Christmas. Only don't make mischief – unless you can get up a duel, and manage to shoot Grandcourt, which might be worth a little inconvenience.'

'I don't think you ever saw me flirt,' said Deronda, not amused.

'Oh, haven't I, though?' said Sir Hugo, provokingly. 'You are always looking tenderly at the women, and talking to them in a Jesuitical way. You are a dangerous young fellow – a kind of Lovelace who will make the Clarissas run after you instead of your running after them.'

What was the use of being exasperated at a tasteless joke? – only the exasperation comes before the reflection on utility. Few friendly remarks are more annoying than the information that we are always seeming to do what we never mean to do. Sir Hugo's notion of flirting, it was to be hoped, was rather peculiar; for his own part, Deronda was sure that he had never flirted. But he was glad that the baronet had no knowledge about the redemption of Gwendolen's necklace to feed his taste for this kind of rallying.

He would be on his guard in future; for example, in his behaviour at Mrs. Meyrick's, where he was about to pay his first visit since his arrival from Leubronn. For Mirah was certainly a creature in whom it was difficult not to show a tender kind of interest both by looks and speech.

Mrs. Meyrick had not failed to send Deronda a report of Mirah's well-being in her family. 'We are getting fonder of her every day,' she had written. 'At breakfast-time we all look towards the door with expectation to see her come in; and we watch her and listen to her as if she were a native from a new country. I have not heard a word from her lips that gives me a doubt about her. She is quite contented and full of gratitude. My daughters are learning from her, and they hope to get her other pupils; for she is anxious not to eat the bread of idleness, but to work, like my girls. Mab says our life has become like a fairy tale, and all she is afraid of is that Mirah will turn into a nightingale again and fly away from us. Her voice is just perfect: not loud and strong, but searching and melting, like the thoughts of what has been. That is the way old people like me feel a beautiful voice.'

But Mrs. Meyrick did not enter into particulars which would have required her to say that Amy and Mab, who had accompanied Mirah to the synagogue, found the Jewish faith less reconcilable with their wishes in her case than in that of Scott's Rebecca. They kept silence out of delicacy to Mirah, with whom her religion was too tender a subject to be touched lightly; but after a while, Amy, who was much of a practical reformer, could not restrain a question.

'Excuse me, Mirah, but *does* it seem quite right to you that the women should sit behind rails in a gallery apart?'

'Yes, I never thought of anything else,' said Mirah, with mild surprise.

'And you like better to see the men with their hats on?' said Mab, cautiously proposing the smallest item of difference.

'Oh yes. I like what I have always seen there, because it brings back to me the same feelings – the feelings I would not part with for anything else in the world.'

After this, any criticism, whether of doctrine or of practice, would have seemed to these generous little people an inhospitable cruelty. Mirah's religion was of one fibre with her affections, and had never presented itself to her as a set of propositions.

'She says herself she is a very bad Jewess, and does not half know her people's religion,' said Amy, when Mirah was gone to bed. 'Perhaps it would gradually melt away from her, and she would pass into Christianity like the rest of the world, if she got to love us very much, and never found her mother. It is so strange to be of the Jews' religion now.'

'Oh, oh, oh!' cried Mab. 'I wish I were not such a hideous Christian. How can an ugly Christian, who is always dropping her work, convert a beautiful Jewess, who has not a fault?'

'It may be wicked of me,' said shrewd Kate, 'but I cannot help wishing that her mother may not be found. There might be something unpleasant.'

'I don't think it, my dear,' said Mrs. Meyrick. 'I believe Mirah is cut out after the pattern of her mother. And what a joy it would be to her to have such a daughter brought back again! But a mother's feelings are not worth reckoning, I suppose' (she shot a mischievous glance at her own daughters), 'and a dead mother is worth more than a living one.'

'Well, and so she may be, little mother,' said Kate; 'but we would rather hold you cheaper, and have you alive.'

Not only the Meyricks, whose various knowledge had been acquired by the irregular foraging to which clever girls have usually been reduced, but Deronda himself, with all his masculine instruction, had been roused by this apparition of Mirah to the consciousness of knowing hardly anything about modern Judaism or the inner Jewish history. The Chosen People have been commonly treated as a people chosen for the sake of somebody else; and their thinking as something (no matter exactly what) that ought to have been entirely otherwise; and Deronda, like his neighbours, had regarded Judaism as a sort of eccentric fossilized form, which an accomplished man might dispense with studying, and leave to specialists. But Mirah, with her terrified flight from one parent, and her yearning after the other, had flashed on him the hitherto neglected reality that Judaism was something still throbbing in human lives, still making for them the only conceivable vesture of the world; and in the idling excursion on which he immediately afterwards set out with Sir Hugo he began to look for the outsides of synagogues, and the titles of books about the Jews. This wakening of a new interest – this passing from the supposition that we hold the right opinions on a subject we are careless about, to a sudden care for it, and a sense that our opinions were ignorance – is an effectual remedy for *ennui*, which unhappily cannot be secured on a physician's prescription; but Deronda had carried it with him, and endured his weeks of lounging all the better. It was on this journey that he first entered a Jewish synagogue – at Frankfort – where his party rested on a Friday. In exploring the Juden-gasse, which he had

seen long before, he remembered well enough its picturesque old houses; what his eyes chiefly dwelt on now were
the human types there; and his thought, busily connecting
them with the past phases of their race, stirred that fibre of
historic sympathy which had helped to determine in him
certain traits worth mentioning for those who are interested in his future. True, when a young man has a fine
person, no eccentricity of manners, the education of a
gentleman, and a present income, it is not customary to
feel a prying curiosity about his way of thinking, or his
peculiar tastes. He may very well be settled in life as an
agreeable clever young fellow without passing a special
examination on those heads. Later, when he is getting
rather slovenly and portly, his peculiarities are more distinctly discerned, and it is taken as a mercy if they are not
highly objectionable. But any one wishing to understand
the effect of after-events on Deronda should know a little
more of what he was at five-and-twenty than was evident
in ordinary intercourse.

It happened that the very vividness of his impressions
had often made him the more enigmatic to his friends, and
had contributed to an apparent indefiniteness in his sentiments. His early-wakened sensibility and reflectiveness
had developed into a many-sided sympathy, which
threatened to hinder any persistent course of action: as
soon as he took up any antagonism, though only in thought,
he seemed to himself, like the Sabine warriors in the memorable story – with nothing to meet his spear but flesh of his
flesh, and objects that he loved. His imagination had so
wrought itself to the habit of seeing things as they probably
appeared to others, that a strong partisanship, unless it were
against an immediate oppression, had become an insincerity for him. His plenteous, flexible sympathy had ended by
falling into one current with that reflective analysis
which tends to neutralize sympathy. Few men were able
to keep themselves clearer of vices than he; yet he hated
vices mildly, being used to think of them less in the
abstract than as a part of mixed human natures having an

individual history, which it was the bent of his mind to
trace with understanding and pity. With the same innate
balance he was fervidly democratic in his feeling for the
multitude, and yet, through his affections and imagination, intensely conservative; voracious of speculations
on government and religion, yet loath to part with long-
sanctioned forms which, for him, were quick with memories and sentiments that no argument could lay dead. We
fall on the leaning side; and Deronda suspected himself of
loving too well the losing causes of the world. Martyrdom
changes sides, and he was in danger of changing with it,
having a strong repugnance to taking up that clue of success which the order of the world often forces upon us and
makes it treason against the common weal to reject. And
yet his fear of falling into an unreasoning narrow hatred
made a check for him: he apologized for the heirs of
privilege; he shrank with dislike from the loser's bitterness
and the denunciatory tone of the unaccepted innovator. A
too reflective and diffusive sympathy was in danger of
paralysing in him that indignation against wrong and that
selectness of fellowship which are the conditions of moral
force; and in the last few years of confirmed manhood he
had become so keenly aware of this that what he most
longed for was either some external event, or some inward
light, that would urge him into a definite line of action, and
compress his wandering energy. He was ceasing to care for
knowledge – he had no ambition for practice – unless they
could both be gathered up into one current with his emotions; and he dreaded, as if it were a dwelling-place of lost
souls, that dead anatomy of culture which turns the universe into a mere ceaseless answer to queries, and knows,
not everything, but everything else about everything – as if
one should be ignorant of nothing concerning the scent of
violets except the scent itself for which one had no nostril.
But how and whence was the needed event to come? – the
influence that would justify partiality, and make him what
he longed to be yet was unable to make himself – an
organic part of social life, instead of roaming in it like a

yearning disembodied spirit, stirred with a vague social passion, but without fixed local habitation to render fellowship real? To make a little difference for the better was what he was not contented to live without; but how make it? It is one thing to see your road, another to cut it. He found some of the fault in his birth and the way he had been brought up, which had laid no special demands on him and given him no fixed relationship except one of a doubtful kind; but he did not attempt to hide from himself that he had fallen into a meditative numbness, and was gliding farther and farther from that life of practically energetic sentiment which he would have proclaimed (if he had been inclined to proclaim anything) to be the best of all life, and for himself the only life worth living. He wanted some way of keeping emotion and its progeny of sentiments – which make the savours of life – substantial and strong in the face of a reflectiveness that threatened to nullify all differences. To pound the objects of sentiment into small dust, yet keep sentiment alive and active, was something like the famous recipe for making cannon – to first take a round hole and then enclose it with iron; whatever you do keeping fast hold of your round hole. Yet how distinguish what our will may wisely save in its completeness, from the heaping of cat-mummies and the expensive cult of enshrined putrefactions?

Something like this was the common undercurrent in Deronda's mind, while he was reading law, or imperfectly attending to polite conversation. Meanwhile he had not set about one function in particular with zeal and steadiness. Not an admirable experience, to be proposed as an ideal; but a form of struggle before break of day which some young men since the patriarch have had to pass through, with more or less of bruising if not laming.

I have said that under his calm exterior he had a fervour which made him easily feel the presence of poetry in everyday events; and the forms of the Juden-gasse, rousing the sense of union with what is remote, set him musing on two elements of our historic life which that sense raises into the same region of poetry: – the faint beginnings of faiths and institutions, and their obscure lingering decay; the dust and withered remnants with which they are apt to be covered, only enhancing for the awakened perception the impressiveness either of a sublimely penetrating life, as in the twin green leaves that will become the sheltering tree, or of a pathetic inheritance in which all the grandeur and the glory have become a sorrowing memory.

This imaginative stirring, as he turned out of the Juden-gasse, and continued to saunter in the warm evening air, meaning to find his way to the synagogue, neutralized the repellent effect of certain ugly little incidents on his way. Turning into an old book-shop to ask the exact time of service at the synagogue, he was affectionately directed by a precocious Jewish youth, who entered cordially into his wanting not the fine new building of the Reformed but the old Rabbinical school of the orthodox; and then cheated him like a pure Teuton, only with more amenity, in his charge for a book quite out of request as one 'nicht so leicht zu bekommen.' Meanwhile at the opposite counter a deaf and grisly tradesman was casting a flinty look at certain cards, apparently combining advantages of business with religion, and shoutingly proposed to him in Jew-dialect by a dingy man in a tall coat hanging from neck to heel, a bag in hand, and a broad low hat surmounting his chosen nose – who had no sooner disappeared than another dingy man of the same pattern issued from the backward glooms of the shop and also shouted in the same dialect. In fact, Deronda saw various queer-looking Israelites not altogether with-out guile, and just distinguishable from queer-looking Christians of the same mixed *morale*. In his anxiety about Mirah's relatives, he had lately been thinking of vulgar Jews with a sort of personal alarm. But a little comparison will often diminish our surprise and disgust at the aberra-tions of Jews and other dissidents whose lives do not offer a consistent or lovely pattern of their creed, and this evening Deronda, becoming more conscious that he was falling into unfairness and ridiculous exaggeration, began to use that corrective comparison: he paid his thaler too much, without prejudice to his interest in the Hebrew destiny, or his wish to find the *Rabbinische Schule*, which he arrived at by sunset, and entered with a good congregation of men.

He happened to take his seat in a line with an elderly man from whom he was distant enough to glance at him more than once as rather a noticeable figure – his ordinary clothes, as well as the *talith* or white blue-fringed kind of blanket which is the garment of prayer, being much worn; while his ample white beard and old felt hat framed a profile of that fine contour which may as easily be Italian as Hebrew. He returned Deronda's notice till at last their eyes met: an undesirable chance with unknown persons, and a reason to Deronda for not looking again; but he immediately found an open prayer-book pushed towards him and had to bow his thanks. However, the white *taliths* had mustered, the Reader had mounted to the *almemor* or platform, and the service began. Deronda, having looked enough at the German translation of the Hebrew in the book before him to know that he was chiefly hearing Psalms and Old Testament passages or phrases, gave himself up to that strongest effect of chanted liturgies which is independent of detailed verbal meaning – like the effect of an Allegri's *Miserere* or a Palestrina's *Magnificat*. The most powerful movement of feeling with a liturgy is the prayer which seeks for nothing special, but is a yearning to escape from the limitations of our own weakness and an invocation of all Good to enter and abide with us; or else a self-oblivious lifting up of gladness, a *Gloria in excelsis* that such Good exists; both the yearning and the exultation gathering their utmost force from the sense of communion in a form which has expressed them both, for long generations of struggling fellow-men. The Hebrew liturgy, like others, has its transitions of litany, lyric, proclamation, dry statement and blessing; but this evening all were one for Deronda: the chant of the *Chazan's* or Reader's grand wideranging voice with its passage from monotony to sudden cries, the outburst of sweet boys' voices from the little quire, the devotional swaying of men's bodies backwards and forwards, the very commonness of the building and shabbiness of the scene where a national faith, which had penetrated the thinking of half the world, and moulded the splendid forms of that world's religion, was finding a remote, obscure echo – all were blent for him as one expression of a binding history, tragic and yet glorious. He wondered at the strength of his own feeling; it seemed beyond the occasion – what one might imagine to be a divine influx in the darkness, before there was any vision to interpret. The whole scene was a coherent strain, its burthen a passionate regret, which, if he had known the liturgy for the Day of Reconciliation, he might have clad in its antithetic burthen: 'Happy the eye which saw all these things; but verily to hear only of them afflicts our soul. Happy the eye that saw our temple and the joy of our congregation; but verily to hear only of them afflicts our soul. Happy the eye that saw the fingers when tuning every kind of song; but verily to hear only of them afflicts our soul.'

But with the cessation of the devotional sounds and the movement of many indifferent faces and vulgar figures before him there darted into his mind the frigid idea that he had probably been alone in his feeling, and perhaps the only person in the congregation for whom the service was more than a dull routine. There was just time for this chilling thought before he had bowed to his civil neighbour and was moving away with the rest – when he felt a hand on his arm, and turning with the rather unpleasant sensation which this abrupt sort of claim is apt to bring, he saw close to him the white-bearded face of that neighbour, who said to him in German, 'Excuse me, young gentleman – allow me – what is your parentage – your mother's family – her maiden name?'

Deronda had a strongly resistant feeling: he was inclined to shake off hastily the touch on his arm; but he managed to slip it away and said coldly, 'I am an Englishman.'

The questioner looked at him dubiously still for an instant, then just lifted his hat and turned away – whether under a sense of having made a mistake or of having been repulsed, Deronda was uncertain. In his walk back to the hotel he tried to still any uneasiness on the subject by reflecting that he could not have acted differently. How could he say that he did not know the name of his mother's family to that total stranger? – who indeed had taken an unwarrantable liberty in the abruptness of his question, dictated probably by some fancy of likeness such as often occurs without real significance. The incident, he said to himself, was trivial; but whatever import it might have, his inward shrinking on the occasion was too strong for him to be sorry that he had cut it short. It was a reason however for his not mentioning the synagogue to the Mallingers – in addition to his usual inclination to reticence on anything that the baronet would have been likely to call Quixotic enthusiasm. Hardly any man could be more good-natured than Sir Hugo; indeed in his kindliness, especially to women, he did actions which others would have called romantic; but he never took a romantic view of them, and in general smiled at the introduction of motives on a grand scale, or of reasons that lay very far off. This was the point of strongest difference between him and Deronda, who rarely ate his breakfast without some silent discursive flight after grounds for filling up his day according to the practice of his contemporaries.

This halt at Frankfort was taken on their way home, and its impressions were kept the more actively vibrating in him by the duty of caring for Mirah's welfare. That question about his parentage, which if he had not both inwardly and outwardly shaken it off as trivial, would have seemed a threat rather than a promise of revelation, had reinforced his anxiety as to the effect of finding Mirah's relatives and his resolve to proceed with caution. If he made any unpleasant discovery, was he bound to a disclosure that might cast a new net of trouble around her?

405

He had written to Mrs. Meyrick to announce his visit at four o'clock, and he found Mirah seated at work with only Mrs. Meyrick and Mab, the open piano, and all the glorious company of engravings. The dainty neatness of her hair and dress, the glow of tranquil happiness in a face where a painter need have changed nothing if he had wanted to put it in front of the host singing 'peace on earth and goodwill to men,' made a contrast to his first vision of her that was delightful to Deronda's eyes. Mirah herself was thinking of it, and immediately on their greeting said –

'See how different I am from that miserable creature by the river! – all because you found me and brought me to the very best.'

'It was my good chance to find you,' said Deronda. 'Any other man would have been glad to do what I did.'

'That is not the right way of thinking about it,' said Mirah, shaking her head with decisive gravity. 'I think of what really was. It was you, and not another, who found me, and were good to me.'

'I agree with Mirah,' said Mrs. Meyrick. 'Saint Anybody is a bad saint to pray to.'

'Besides, Anybody could not have brought me to you,' said Mirah, smiling at Mrs. Meyrick. 'And I would rather be with you than with any one else in the world except my mother. I wonder if ever a poor little bird, that was lost and could not fly, was taken and put into a warm nest where there was a mother and sisters who took to it so that everything came naturally, as if it had been always there. I hardly thought before that the world could ever be as happy and without fear as it is to me now.' She looked meditative a moment, and then said, 'Sometimes I am a *little* afraid.'

'What is it you are afraid of?' said Deronda, with anxiety.

'That when I am turning at the corner of a street I may meet my father. It seems dreadful that I should be afraid of meeting him. That is my only sorrow,' said Mirah, plaintively.

'It is surely not very probable,' said Deronda, wishing that it were less so; then, not to let the opportunity escape

– 'Would it be a great grief to you now, if you were never to meet your mother?'

She did not answer immediately, but meditated again, with her eyes fixed on the opposite wall. Then she turned them on Deronda and said firmly, as if she had arrived at the exact truth, 'I want her to know that I have always loved her, and if she is alive I want to comfort her. She may be dead. If she were, I should long to know where she was buried; and to know whether my brother lives to say *Kaddish* in memory of her. But I will try not to grieve. I have thought much for so many years of her being dead. And I shall have her with me in my mind, as I have always had. We can never be really parted. I think I have never sinned against her. I have always tried not to do what would hurt her. Only she might be sorry that I was not a good Jewess.'

'In what way are you not a good Jewess?' said Deronda.

'I am ignorant, and we never observed the laws, but lived among Christians just as they did. But I have heard my father laugh at the strictness of the Jews about their food and all customs, and their not liking Christians. I think my mother was strict; but she could never want me not to like those who are better to me than any of my own people I have ever known. I think I could obey in other things that she wished, but not in that. It is so much easier to me to share in love than in hatred. I remember a play I read in German – since I have been here, it has come into my mind – where the heroine says something like that.'

'Antigone,' said Deronda.

'Ah, you know it. But I do not believe that my mother would wish me not to love my best friends. She would be grateful to them.' Here Mirah had turned to Mrs. Meyrick, and with a sudden lighting up of her whole countenance she said, 'Oh, if we ever do meet and know each other as we are now, so that I could tell what would comfort her – I should be so full of blessedness, my soul would know no want but to love her!'

'God bless you, child!' said Mrs. Meyrick, the words escaping involuntarily from her motherly heart. But to relieve the strain of feeling she looked at Deronda and said, 'It is curious that Mirah, who remembers her mother so well, it is as if she saw her, cannot recall her brother the least bit – except the feeling of having been carried by him when she was tired, and of his being near her when she was in her mother's lap. It must be that he was rarely at home. He was already grown up. It is a pity her brother should be quite a stranger to her.'

'He is good; I feel sure Ezra is good,' said Mirah, eagerly. 'He loved my mother – he would take care of her. I remember more of him than that. I remember my mother's voice once calling, "Ezra!" and then his answering from the distance, "Mother!"' – Mirah had changed her voice a little in each of these words and had given them a loving intonation – 'and then he came close to us. I feel sure he is good. I have always taken comfort from that.'

It was impossible to answer this either with agreement or doubt. Mrs. Meyrick and Deronda exchanged a quick glance: about this brother she felt as painfully dubious as he did. But Mirah went on, absorbed in her memories –

'Is it not wonderful how I remember the voices better than anything else? I think they must go deeper into us than other things. I have often fancied heaven might be made of voices.'

'Like your singing – yes,' said Mab, who had hitherto kept a modest silence, and now spoke bashfully, as was her wont in the presence of Prince Camaralzaman, – 'Ma, do ask Mirah to sing. Mr. Deronda has not heard her.'

'Would it be disagreeable to you to sing now?' said Deronda, with a more deferential gentleness than he had ever been conscious of before.

'Oh, I shall like it,' said Mirah. 'My voice has come back a little with rest.'

Perhaps her ease of manner was due to something more than the simplicity of her nature. The circumstances of her life had made her think of everything she did as work demanded from her, in which affectation had nothing to do; and she had begun her work before self-consciousness was born.

She immediately rose and went to the piano – a somewhat worn instrument that seemed to get the better of its infirmities under the firm touch of her small fingers as she preluded. Deronda placed himself where he could see her while she sang; and she took everything as quietly as if she had been a child going to breakfast.

Imagine her – it is always good to imagine a human creature in whom bodily loveliness seems as properly one with the entire being as the bodily loveliness of those wondrous transparent orbs of life that we find in the sea – imagine her with her dark hair brushed from her temples, but yet showing certain tiny rings there which had cunningly found their own way back, the mass of it hanging behind just to the nape of the little neck in curly fibres, such as renew themselves at their own will after being bathed into straightness like that of water-grasses. Then see the perfect cameo her profile makes, cut in a duskish shell where by some happy fortune there pierced a gem-like darkness for the eye and eyebrow; the delicate nostrils defined enough to be ready for sensitive movements, the finished ear, the firm curves of the chin and neck entering into the expression of a refinement which was not feebleness.

She sang Beethoven's 'Per pietà non dirmi addio,' with a subdued but searching pathos which had that essential of perfect singing, the making one oblivious of art or manner, and only possessing one with the song. It was the sort of voice that gives the impression of being meant like a bird's wooing for an audience near and beloved. Deronda began by looking at her, but felt himself presently covering his eyes with his hand, wanting to seclude the melody in darkness; then he refrained from what might seem oddity, and was ready to meet the look of mute appeal which she turned towards him at the end.

'I think I never enjoyed a song more than that,' he said, gratefully.

'You like my singing? I am so glad,' she said, with a smile of delight. 'It has been a great pain to me, because it failed in what it was wanted for. But now we think I can use it to get my bread. I have really been taught well. And now I have two pupils, that Miss Meyrick found for me. They pay me nearly two crowns for their two lessons.'

'I think I know some ladies who would find you many pupils after Christmas,' said Deronda. 'You would not mind singing before any one who wished to hear you?'

'Oh no, I want to do something to get money. I could teach reading and speaking, Mrs. Meyrick thinks. But if no one would learn of me, that is difficult.' Mirah smiled with a touch of merriment he had not seen in her before. 'I dare say I should find her poor – I mean my mother. I should want to get money for her. And I cannot always live on charity; though' – here she turned so as to take all three of her companions in one glance – 'it is the sweetest charity in all the world.'

'I should think you can get rich,' said Deronda, smiling. 'Great ladies will perhaps like you to teach their daughters. We shall see. But now, do sing again to us.'

She went on willingly, singing with ready memory various things by Gordigiani and Schubert; then, when she had left the piano, Mab said, entreatingly, 'Oh Mirah, if you would not mind singing the little hymn.'

'It is too childish,' said Mirah. 'It is like lisping.'

'What is the hymn?' said Deronda.

'It is the Hebrew hymn she remembers her mother singing over her when she lay in her cot,' said Mrs. Meyrick.

'I should like very much to hear it,' said Deronda, 'if you think I am worthy to hear what is so sacred.'

'I will sing it if you like,' said Mirah, 'but I don't sing real words – only here and there a syllable like hers – the rest is lisping. Do you know Hebrew? because if you do, my singing will seem childish nonsense.'

Deronda shook his head. 'It will be quite good Hebrew to me.'

Mirah crossed her little feet and hands in her easiest attitude, and then lifted up her head at an angle which seemed to be directed to some invisible face bent over her, while she sang a little hymn of quaint melancholy intervals, with syllables that really seemed childish lisping to her audience; but the voice in which she gave it forth had gathered even a sweeter, more cooing tenderness than was heard in her other songs.

'If I were ever to know the real words, I should still go on in my old way with them,' said Mirah, when she had repeated the hymn several times.

'Why not?' said Deronda. 'The lisped syllables are very full of meaning.'

'Yes, indeed,' said Mrs. Meyrick. 'A mother hears something like a lisp in her children's talk to the very last. Their words are not just what everybody else says, though they may be spelt the same. If I were to live till my Hans got old, I should still see the boy in him. A mother's love, I often say, is like a tree that has got all the wood in it, from the very first it made.'

'Is not that the way with friendship, too?' said Deronda, smiling. 'We must not let mothers be too arrogant.'

The bright little woman shook her head over her darning.

'It is easier to find an old mother than an old friend. Friendships begin with liking or gratitude – roots that can be pulled up. Mother's love begins deeper down.'

'Like what you were saying about the influence of voices,' said Deronda, looking at Mirah. 'I don't think your hymn would have had more expression for me if I had known the words. I went to the synagogue at Frankfort before I came home, and the service impressed me just as much as if I had followed the words – perhaps more.'

'Oh, was it great to you? Did it go to your heart?' said Mirah, eagerly. 'I thought none but our people would feel that. I thought it was all shut away like a river in a deep

411

valley, where only heaven saw – I mean – ' she hesitated, feeling that she could not disentangle her thought from its imagery.

'I understand,' said Deronda. 'But there is not really such a separation – deeper down, as Mrs. Meyrick says. Our religion is chiefly a Hebrew religion; and since Jews are men, their religious feelings must have much in common with those of other men – just as their poetry, though in one sense peculiar, has a great deal in common with the poetry of other nations. Still it is to be expected that a Jew would feel the forms of his people's religion more than one of another race – and yet' – here Deronda hesitated in his turn – 'that is perhaps not always so.'

'Ah no,' said Mirah, sadly. 'I have seen that. I have seen them mock. Is it not like mocking your parents? – like rejoicing in your parents' shame?'

'Some minds naturally rebel against whatever they were brought up in, and like the opposite: they see the faults in what is nearest to them,' said Deronda, apologetically.

'But you are not like that,' said Mirah, looking at him with unconscious fixedness.

'No, I think not,' said Deronda; 'but you know I was not brought up as a Jew.'

'Ah, I am always forgetting,' said Mirah, with a look of disappointed recollection, and slightly blushing.

Deronda also felt rather embarrassed, and there was an awkward pause, which he put an end to by saying playfully –

'Whichever way we take it, we have to tolerate each other; for if we all went in opposition to our teaching, we must end in difference, just the same.'

'To be sure. We should go on for ever in zigzags,' said Mrs. Meyrick. 'I think it is very weak-minded to make your creed up by the rule of contrary. Still one may honour one's parents, without following their notions exactly, any more than the exact cut of their clothing. My father was a Scotch Calvinist and my mother was a French Calvinist:

I am neither quite Scotch, nor quite French, nor two Calvinists rolled into one, yet I honour my parents' memory.'

'But I could not make myself not a Jewess,' said Mirah, insistently, 'even if I changed my belief.'

'No, my dear. But if Jews and Jewesses went on changing their religion, and making no difference between themselves and Christians, there would come a time when there would be no Jews to be seen,' said Mrs. Meyrick, taking that consummation very cheerfully.

'Oh please not to say that,' said Mirah, the tears gathering. 'It is the first unkind thing you ever said. I will not begin that. I will never separate myself from my mother's people. I was forced to fly from my father; but if he came back in age and weakness and want, and needed me, should I say, "This is not my father"? If he had shame I must share it. It was he who was given to me for my father, and not another. And so it is with my people. I will always be a Jewess. I will love Christians when they are good, like you. But I will always cling to my people. I will always worship with them.'

As Mirah had gone on speaking she had become possessed with a sorrowful passion – fervent, not violent. Holding her little hands tightly clasped and looking at Mrs. Meyrick with beseeching, she seemed to Deronda a personification of that spirit which impelled men after a long inheritance of professed Catholicism to leave wealth and high place, and risk their lives in flight, that they might join their own people and say, 'I am a Jew.'

'Mirah, Mirah, my dear child, you mistake me!' said Mrs. Meyrick, alarmed. 'God forbid I should want you to do anything against your conscience. I was only saying what might be if the world went on. But I had better have left the world alone, and not wanted to be over-wise. Forgive me, come! we will not try to take you from anybody you feel has more right to you.'

'I would do anything else for you. I owe you my life,' said Mirah, not yet quite calm.

'Hush, hush, now,' said Mrs. Meyrick. 'I have been punished enough for wagging my tongue foolishly – making an almanac for the Millennium, as my husband used to say.'

'But everything in the world must come to an end some time. We must bear to think of that,' said Mab, unable to hold her peace on this point. She had already suffered from a bondage of tongue which threatened to become severe if Mirah were to be too much indulged in this inconvenient susceptibility to innocent remarks.

Deronda smiled at the irregular, blond face, brought into strange contrast by the side of Mirah's – smiled, Mab thought, rather sarcastically as he said, 'That prospect of everything coming to an end will not guide us far in practice. Mirah's feelings, she tells us, are concerned with what is.'

Mab was confused and wished she had not spoken, since Mr. Deronda seemed to think that she had found fault with Mirah; but to have spoken once is a tyrannous reason for speaking again, and she said –

'I only meant that we must have courage to hear things, else there is hardly anything we can talk about.' Mab felt herself unanswerable here, inclining to the opinion of Socrates: 'What motive has a man to live, if not for the pleasures of discourse?'

Deronda took his leave soon after, and when Mrs. Meyrick went outside with him to exchange a few words about Mirah, he said, 'Hans is to share my chambers when he comes at Christmas.'

'You have written to Rome about that?' said Mrs. Meyrick, her face lighting up. 'How very good and thoughtful of you! You mentioned Mirah, then?'

'Yes, I referred to her. I concluded he knew everything from you.'

'I must confess my folly. I have not yet written a word about her. I have always been meaning to do it, and yet have ended my letter without saying a word. And I told the girls to leave it to me. However! – Thank you a thousand times.'

Deronda divined something of what was in the mother's mind, and his divination reinforced a certain anxiety already present in him. His inward colloquy was not soothing. He said to himself that no man could see this exquisite creature without feeling it possible to fall in love with her; but all the fervour of his nature was engaged on the side of precaution. There are personages who feel themselves tragic because they march into a palpable morass, dragging another with them, and then cry out against all the gods. Deronda's mind was strongly set against imitating them.

'I have my hands on the reins now,' he thought, 'and I will not drop them. I shall go there as little as possible.'

He saw the reasons acting themselves out before him. How could he be Mirah's guardian and claim to unite with Mrs. Meyrick, to whose charge he had committed her, if he showed himself as a lover – whom she did not love – whom she would not marry? And if he encouraged any germ of lover's feeling in himself it would lead up to that issue. Mirah's was not a nature that would bear dividing against itself; and even if love won her consent to marry a man who was not of her race and religion, she would never be happy in acting against that strong native bias which would still reign in her conscience as remorse.

Deronda saw these consequences as we see any danger of marring our own work well begun. It was a delight to have rescued this child acquainted with sorrow, and to think of having placed her little feet in protected paths. The creature we help to save, though only a half-reared linnet, bruised and lost by the wayside – how we watch and fence it, and doat on its signs of recovery! Our pride becomes loving, our self is a not-self for whose sake we become virtuous, when we set to some hidden work of reclaiming a life from misery and look for our triumph in the secret joy – 'This one is the better for me.'

'I would as soon hold out my finger to be bitten off as set about spoiling her peace,' said Deronda. 'It was one of the rarest bits of fortune that I should have had friends like the Meyricks to place her with – generous, delicate friends without any loftiness in their ways, so that her dependence on them is not only safety but happiness. There could be no refuge to replace that, if it were broken up. But what is the use of my taking the vows and settling everything as it should be, if that marplot Hans comes and upsets it all?'

Few things were more likely. Hans was made for mishaps: his very limbs seemed more breakable than other people's – his eyes more of a resort for uninvited flies and other irritating guests. But it was impossible to forbid Hans's coming to London. He was intending to get a studio there and make it his chief home; and to propose that he should defer coming on some ostensible ground, concealing the real motive of winning time for Mirah's position to become more confirmed and independent, was impracticable. Having no other resource Deronda tried to believe that both he and Mrs. Meyrick were foolishly troubling themselves about one of those endless things called probabilities, which never occur; but he did not quite succeed in his trying; on the contrary, he found himself going inwardly through a scene where on the first discovery of Hans's inclination, he gave him a very energetic warning – suddenly checked, however, by the suspicion of personal feeling that his warmth might be creating in Hans. He could come to no result, but that the position was peculiar, and that he could make no further provision against dangers until they came nearer. To save an unhappy Jewess from drowning herself, would not have seemed a startling variation among police reports; but to discover in her so rare a creature as Mirah, was an exceptional event which might well bring exceptional consequences. Deronda would not let himself for a moment dwell on any supposition that the consequences might enter deeply into his own life. The image of Mirah had never yet had that penetrating radiation which would have been given to it by the idea of her loving him. When this sort of effluence is absent from the fancy (whether from the fact or not) a man may go far in devotedness without perturbation.

As to the search for Mirah's mother and brother, Deronda took what she had said to-day as a warrant for deferring any immediate measures. His conscience was not quite easy in this desire for delay, any more than it was quite easy in his not attempting to learn the truth about his own mother: in both cases he felt that there might be an unfulfilled duty to a parent, but in both cases there was an overpowering repugnance to the possible truth, which threw a turning weight into the scale of argument.

'At least, I will look about,' was his final determination. 'I may find some special Jewish machinery. I will wait till after Christmas.'

What should we all do without the calendar, when we want to put off a disagreeable duty? The admirable arrangements of the solar system, by which our time is measured, always supply us with a term before which it is hardly worth while to set about anything we are disinclined to.

XXXIII

'No man,' says a Rabbi, by way of indisputable instance, 'may turn the bones of his father and mother into spoons' – sure that his hearers felt the checks against that form of economy. The market for spoons has never expanded enough for anyone to say, 'Why not?' and to argue that human progress lies in such an application of material. The only check to be alleged is a sentiment which will coerce none who do not hold that sentiments are the better part of the world's wealth.

DERONDA meanwhile took to a less fashionable form of exercise than riding in Rotten Row. He went often rambling in those parts of London which are most inhabited by common Jews: he walked to the synagogues at times of service, he looked into shops, he observed faces: – a process not very promising of particular discovery. Why did he not address himself to an influential Rabbi or other member of a Jewish community, to consult on the chances of finding a mother named Cohen, with a son named Ezra, and a lost daughter named Mirah? He thought of doing so – after Christmas. The fact was, notwithstanding all his sense of poetry in common things, Deronda, where a keen personal interest was aroused, could not, more than the rest of us, continuously escape suffering from the pressure of that hard unaccommodating Actual, which has never consulted our taste and is entirely unselect. Enthusiasm, we know, dwells at ease among ideas, tolerates garlic breathed in the middle ages, and sees no shabbiness in the official trappings of classic processions: it gets squeamish when ideals press upon it as something warmly incarnate, and can hardly face them without fainting. Lying dreamily in a boat, imagining oneself in quest of a beautiful maiden's relatives in Cordova elbowed by Jews in the time of Ibn-Gebirol, all the physical incidents can be borne without shock. Or if the scenery of St. Mary Axe and Whitechapel were imaginatively transported to the borders of the Rhine at the end of the eleventh century, when in the ears listening for the signals of the Messiah, the Hep! Hep! Hep! of the Crusaders came like the bay of bloodhounds; and in the presence of those devilish missionaries with sword and firebrand the crouching figure of the reviled Jew turned round erect, heroic, flashing with sublime constancy in the face of torture and death – what would the dingy shops and unbeautiful faces signify to the thrill of contemplative emotion? But the fervour of sympathy with which we contemplate a grandiose martyrdom is feeble compared with the enthusiasm that keeps unslacked where there is no danger, no challenge – nothing but impartial mid-day falling on commonplace, perhaps half-repulsive, objects which are really the beloved ideas made flesh. Here undoubtedly lies the chief poetic energy: – in the force of imagination that pierces or exalts the solid fact, instead of floating among cloud-pictures. To glory in a prophetic vision of knowledge covering the earth, is an easier exercise of believing imagination than to see its beginning in newspaper placards, staring at you from a bridge beyond the corn-fields; and it might well happen to most of us dainty people that we were in the thick of the battle of Armageddon without being aware of anything more than the annoyance of a little explosive smoke and struggling on the ground immediately about us.

It lay in Deronda's nature usually to contemn the feeble, fastidious sympathy which shrinks from the broad life of mankind; but now, with Mirah before him as a living reality whose experience he had to care for, he saw every common Jew and Jewess in the light of comparison with her, and had a presentiment of the collision between her idea of the unknown mother and brother and the discovered fact – a presentiment all the keener in him because of a suppressed consciousness that a not unlike possibility of collision might lie hidden in his own lot. Not that he would have looked with more complacency of expectation at wealthy Jews, outdoing the lords of the Philistines in their sports; but since there was no likelihood of Mirah's friends being found among that class, their habits did not immediately affect him. In this mood he rambled, without

expectation of a more pregnant result than a little preparation of his own mind, perhaps for future theorising as well
as practice – very much as if, Mirah being related to Welsh
miners, he had gone to look more closely at the ways of
those people, not without wishing at the same time to get a
little light of detail on the history of Strikes.

He really did not long to find anybody in particular; and
when, as his habit was, he looked at the name over a shop-
door, he was well content that it was not Ezra Cohen. I
confess, he particularly desired that Ezra Cohen should not
keep a shop. Wishes are held to be ominous; according to
which belief the order of the world is so arranged that if you
have an impious objection to a squint, your offspring is the
more likely to be born with one; also, that if you happened
to desire a squint, you would not get it. This desponding
view of probability the hopeful entirely reject, taking their
wishes as good and sufficient security for all kinds of
fulfilment. Who is absolutely neutral? Deronda happening
one morning to turn into a little side street out of the noise
and obstructions of Holborn, felt the scale dip on the
desponding side.

He was rather tired of the streets and had paused to hail
a hansom cab which he saw coming, when his attention was
caught by some fine old clasps in chased silver displayed in
the window at his right hand. His first thought was that
Lady Mallinger, who had a strictly Protestant taste for such
Catholic spoils, might like to have these missal-clasps
turned into a bracelet; then his eyes travelled over the
other contents of the window, and he saw that the shop
was that kind of pawnbroker's where the lead is given to
jewellery, lace, and all equivocal objects introduced as *bric-
à-brac*. A placard in one corner announced – *Watches and
Jewellery exchanged and repaired*. But his survey had been
noticed from within, and a figure appeared at the door,
looking round at him and saying, in a tone of cordial
encouragement, 'Good day, sir.' The instant was enough
for Deronda to see that the face, unmistakably Jewish,
belonged to a young man about thirty; and wincing from

the shopkeeper's persuasiveness that would probably follow, he had no sooner returned the 'good day,' than he
passed to the other side of the street and beckoned to the
cabman to draw up there. From that station he saw the
name over the shop-window – *Ezra Cohen.*

There might be a hundred Ezra Cohens lettered above
shop-windows, but Deronda had not seen them. Probably
the young man interested in a possible customer was Ezra
himself; and he was about the age to be expected in
Mirah's brother, who was grown up while she was still a
little child. But Deronda's first endeavour as he drove
homewards was to convince himself that there was not
the slightest warrantable presumption of this Ezra being
Mirah's brother; and next, that even if, in spite of good
reasoning, he turned out to be that brother, while on
inquiry the mother was found to be dead, it was not his –
Deronda's – duty to make known the discovery to Mirah.
In inconvenient disturbance of this conclusion there came
his lately acquired knowledge that Mirah would have a
religious desire to know of her mother's death, and also to
learn whether her brother were living. How far was he
justified in determining another life by his own notions?
Was it not his secret complaint against the way in which
others had ordered his own life, that he had not open
daylight on all its relations, so that he had not, like other
men, the full guidance of primary duties?

The immediate relief from this inward debate was the
reflection that he had not yet made any real discovery, and
that by looking into the facts more closely he should be
certified that there was no demand on him for any decision
whatever. He intended to return to that shop as soon as he
could conveniently, and buy the clasps for Lady Mallinger.
But he was hindered for several days by Sir Hugo, who,
about to make an after-dinner speech on a burning topic,
wanted Deronda to forage for him on the legal part of the
question, besides wasting time every day on argument
which always ended in a drawn battle. As on many other
questions, they held different sides; but Sir Hugo did not

mind this, and when Deronda put his point well said, with a mixture of satisfaction and regret –

'Confound it, Dan! why don't you make an opportunity of saying these things in public? You're wrong, you know. You won't succeed. You've got the massive sentiment – the heavy artillery of the country against you. But it's all the better ground for a young man to display himself on. When I was your age, I should have taken it. And it would be quite as well for you to be in opposition to me here and there. It would throw you more into relief. If you would seize an occasion of this sort to make an impression, you might be in Parliament in no time. And you know that would gratify me.'

'I am sorry not to do what would gratify you, sir,' said Deronda. 'But I cannot persuade myself to look at politics as a profession.'

'Why not? If a man is not born into public life by his position in the country, there's no way for him but to embrace it by his own efforts. The business of the country must be done – her Majesty's Government carried on, as the old Duke said. And it never could be, my boy, if everybody looked at politics as if they were prophecy, and demanded an inspired vocation. If you are to get into Parliament, it won't do to sit still and wait for a call either from heaven or constituents.'

'I don't want to make a living out of opinions,' said Deronda; 'especially out of borrowed opinions. Not that I mean to blame other men. I dare say many better fellows than I don't mind getting on to a platform to praise themselves, and giving their word of honour for a party.'

'I'll tell you what, Dan,' said Sir Hugo, 'a man who sets his face against every sort of humbug is simply a three-cornered, impracticable fellow. There's a bad style of humbug, but there is also a good style – one that oils the wheels and makes progress possible. If you are to rule men, you must rule them through their own ideas; and I agree with the Archbishop at Naples who had a St. Januarius procession against the plague. It's no use having an Order in

Council against popular shallowness. There is no action possible without a little acting.'

'One may be obliged to give way to an occasional necessity,' said Deronda. 'But it is one thing to say, "In this particular case I am forced to put on this foolscap and grin," and another to buy a pocket foolscap and practise myself in grinning. I can't see any real public expediency that does not keep an ideal before it which makes a limit of deviation from the direct path. But if I were to set up for a public man I might mistake my own success for public expediency.'

It was after this dialogue, which was rather jarring to him, that Deronda set out on his meditated second visit to Ezra Cohen's. He entered the street at the end opposite to the Holborn entrance, and an inward reluctance slackened his pace, while his thoughts were transferring what he had just been saying about public expediency to the entirely private difficulty which brought him back again into this unattractive thoroughfare. It might soon become an immediate practical question with him how far he could call it a wise expediency to conceal the fact of close kindred. Such questions turning up constantly in life are often decided in a rough and ready way; and to many it will appear an over-refinement in Deronda that he should make any great point of a matter confined to his own knowledge. But we have seen the reasons why he had come to regard concealment as a bane of life, and the necessity of concealment as a mark by which lines of action were to be avoided. The prospect of being urged against the confirmed habit of his mind was naturally grating. He even paused here and there before the most plausible shop-windows for a gentleman to look into, half inclined to decide that he would not increase his knowledge about that modern Ezra, who was certainly not a leader among his people – a hesitation which proved how, in a man much given to reasoning, a bare possibility may weigh more than the best-clad likelihood; for Deronda's reasoning had decided that all likelihood was against this man's being Mirah's brother.

One of the shop-windows he paused before was that of a second-hand book-shop, where, on a narrow table outside, the literature of the ages was represented in judicious mixture, from the immortal verse of Homer to the mortal prose of the railway novel. That the mixture was judicious was apparent from Deronda's finding in it something that he wanted – namely, that wonderful bit of autobiography, the life of the Polish Jew, Salomon Maimon; which, as he could easily slip it into his pocket, he took from its place, and entered the shop to pay for, expecting to see behind the counter a grimy personage showing that *nonchalance* about sales which seems to belong universally to the second-hand book-business. In most other trades you find generous men who are anxious to sell you their wares for your own welfare; but even a Jew will not urge Simson's Euclid on you with an affectionate assurance that you will have pleasure in reading it, and that he wishes he had twenty more of the article, so much is it in request. One is led to fear that a second-hand bookseller may belong to that unhappy class of men who have no belief in the good of what they get their living by, yet keep conscience enough to be morose rather than unctuous in their vocation.

But instead of the ordinary tradesman, he saw, on the dark background of books in the long narrow shop, a figure that was somewhat startling in its unusualness. A man in threadbare clothing, whose age was difficult to guess – from the dead yellowish flatness of the flesh, something like an old ivory carving – was seated on a stool against some book-shelves that projected beyond the short counter, doing nothing more remarkable than reading the yesterday's *Times*; but when he let the paper rest on his lap and looked at the incoming customer, the thought glanced through Deronda that precisely such a physiognomy as that might possibly have been seen in a prophet of the Exile, or in some New Hebrew poet of the mediæval time. It was a finely typical Jewish face, wrought into intensity of expression apparently by a strenuous eager experience in

which all the satisfaction had been indirect and far off, and
perhaps by some bodily suffering also, which involved that
absence of ease in the present. The features were clear-
cut, not large; the brow not high but broad, and fully
defined by the crisp black hair. It might never have been
a particularly handsome face, but it must always have
been forcible; and now with its dark, far-off gaze, and
yellow pallor in relief on the gloom of the backward shop,
one might have imagined one's self coming upon it in some
past prison of the Inquisition, which a mob had suddenly
burst open; while the look fixed on an incidental customer
seemed eager and questioning enough to have been
turned on one who might have been a messenger either
of delivery or of death. The figure was probably familiar
and unexciting enough to the inhabitants of this street; but
to Deronda's mind it brought so strange a blending of the
unwonted with the common, that there was a perceptible
interval of mutual observation before he asked his question: 'What is the price of this book?'

After taking the book and examining the fly-leaves
without rising, the supposed bookseller said, 'There is no
mark, and Mr. Ram is not in now. I am keeping the
shop while he is gone to dinner. What are you disposed to
give for it?' He held the book closed on his lap with
his hand on it and looked examiningly at Deronda,
over whom there came the disagreeable idea, that possibly
this striking personage wanted to see how much could be
got out of a customer's ignorance of prices. But without
further reflection he said, 'Don't you know how much it is
worth?'

'Not its market-price. May I ask, have you read it?'

'No. I have read an account of it, which makes me want
to buy it.'

'You are a man of learning – you are interested in Jewish
history?' This was said in a deepened tone of eager inquiry.

'I am certainly interested in Jewish history,' said
Deronda, quietly, curiosity overcoming his dislike to the
sort of inspection as well as questioning he was under.

But immediately the strange Jew rose from his sitting posture, and Deronda felt a thin hand pressing his arm tightly, while a hoarse, excited voice, not much above a loud whisper, said –

'You are perhaps of our race?'

Deronda coloured deeply, not liking the grasp, and then answered with a slight shake of the head, 'No.' The grasp was relaxed, the hand withdrawn, the eagerness of the face collapsed into uninterested melancholy, as if some possessing spirit which had leaped into the eyes and gestures had sunk back again to the inmost recesses of the frame; and moving further off as he held out the little book, the stranger said in a tone of distant civility, 'I believe Mr. Ram will be satisfied with half-a-crown, sir.'

The effect of this change on Deronda – he afterwards smiled when he recalled it – was oddly embarrassing and humiliating, as if some high dignitary had found him deficient and given him his *congé*. There was nothing further to be said, however: he paid his half-crown and carried off his *Salomon Maimon's Lebensgeschichte* with a mere 'good morning.'

He felt some vexation at the sudden arrest of the interview, and the apparent prohibition that he should know more of this man, who was certainly something out of the common way – as different probably as a Jew could well be from Ezra Cohen, through whose door Deronda was presently entering, and whose flourishing face glistening on the way to fatness was hanging over the counter in negotiation with some one on the other side of the partition, concerning two plated stoppers and three teaspoons, which lay spread before him. Seeing Deronda enter, he called out 'Mother! Mother!' and then with a familiar nod and smile, said, 'Coming, sir – coming directly.'

Deronda could not help looking towards the door from the back with some anxiety, which was not soothed when he saw a vigorous woman beyond fifty enter and approach to serve him. Not that there was anything very repulsive about her: the worst that could be said was that she had that

look of having made her toilet with little water, and by
twilight, which is common to unyouthful people of her
class, and of having presumably slept in her large earrings,
if not in her rings and necklace. In fact, what caused a
sinking of heart in Deronda was, her not being so coarse
and ugly as to exclude the idea of her being Mirah's
mother. Any one who has looked at a face to try and discern
signs of known kinship in it will understand his process of
conjecture – how he tried to think away the fat which had
gradually disguised the outlines of youth, and to discern
what one may call the elementary expressions of the face.
He was sorry to see no absolute negative to his fears. Just as
it was conceivable that this Ezra, brought up to trade,
might resemble the scapegrace father in everything but
his knowledge and talent, so it was not impossible that this
mother might have had a lovely refined daughter whose
type of feature and expression was like Mirah's. The eyebrows had a vexatious similarity of line; and who shall
decide how far a face may be masked when the uncherish-
ing years have thrust it far onward in the ever-new procession of youth and age? The good-humour of the glance
remained and shone out in a motherly way at Deronda, as
she said, in a mild guttural tone –

'How can I serve you, sir?'

'I should like to look at the silver clasps in the window,'
said Deronda; 'the larger ones, please, in the corner there.'

They were not quite easy to get at from the mother's
station, and the son seeing this called out, 'I'll reach 'em,
mother; I'll reach 'em,' running forward with alacrity, and
then handing the clasps to Deronda with the smiling
remark –

'Mother's too proud: she wants to do everything herself.
That's why I called her to wait on you, sir. When there's a
particular gentleman customer, sir, I daren't do any other
than call her. But I can't let her do herself a mischief with
stretching.'

Here Mr. Cohen made way again for his parent, who
gave a little guttural amiable laugh while she looked at

Deronda, as much as to say, 'This boy will be at his jokes, but you see he's the best son in the world;' and evidently the son enjoyed pleasing her, though he also wished to convey an apology to his distinguished customer for not giving him the advantage of his own exclusive attention.

Deronda began to examine the clasps as if he had many points to observe before he could come to a decision.

'They are only three guineas, sir,' said the mother, encouragingly.

'First-rate workmanship, sir – worth twice the money; only I got 'em a bargain from Cologne,' said the son, parenthetically, from a distance.

Meanwhile two new customers entered, and the repeated call, 'Addy!' brought from the back of the shop a group that Deronda turned frankly to stare at, feeling sure that the stare would be held complimentary. The group consisted of a black-eyed young woman who carried a black-eyed little one, its head already well-covered with black curls, and deposited it on the counter, from which station it looked round with even more than the usual intelligence of babies; also a robust boy of six and a younger girl, both with black eyes and black-ringed hair – looking more Semitic than their parents, as the puppy lions show the spots of far-off progenitors. The young woman answering to 'Addy' – a sort of paroquet in a bright blue dress, with coral necklace and earrings, her hair set up in a huge bush – looked as complacently lively and unrefined as her husband; and by a certain difference from the mother deepened in Deronda the unwelcome impression that the latter was not so utterly common a Jewess as to exclude her being the mother of Mirah. While that thought was glancing through his mind, the boy had run forward into the shop with an energetic stamp, and setting himself about four feet from Deronda, with his hands in the pockets of his miniature knickerbockers, looked at him with a precocious air of survey. Perhaps it was chiefly with a diplomatic design to linger and ingratiate himself that Deronda patted the boy's head, saying –

'What is your name, sirrah?'

'Jacob Alexander Cohen,' said the small man, with much ease and distinctness.

'You are not named after your father, then?'

'No; after my grandfather. He sells knives and razors and scissors – my grandfather does,' said Jacob, wishing to impress the stranger with that high connection. 'He gave me this knife.' Here a pocket-knife was drawn forth, and the small fingers, both naturally and artificially dark, opened two blades and a cork-screw with much quickness.

'Is not that a dangerous plaything?' said Deronda, turning to the grandmother.

'*He*'ll never hurt himself, bless you!' said she, contemplating her grandson with placid rapture.

'Have *you* got a knife?' says Jacob, coming closer. His small voice was hoarse in its glibness, as if it belonged to an aged commercial soul, fatigued with bargaining through many generations.

'Yes. Do you want to see it?' said Deronda, taking a small penknife from his waistcoat-pocket.

Jacob seized it immediately and retreated a little, holding the two knives in his palms and bending over them in meditative comparison. By this time the other clients were gone, and the whole family had gathered to the spot, centring their attention on the marvellous Jacob: the father, mother, and grandmother behind the counter, with baby held staggering thereon, and the little girl in front leaning at her brother's elbow to assist him in looking at the knives.

'Mine's the best,' said Jacob, at last, returning Deronda's knife, as if he had been entertaining the idea of exchange and had rejected it.

Father and mother laughed aloud with delight. 'You won't find Jacob choosing the worst,' said Mr. Cohen, winking, with much confidence in the customer's admiration. Deronda, looking at the grandmother, who had only an inward silent laugh, said –

'Are these the only grandchildren you have?'

'All. This is my only son,' she answered, in a communicative tone, Deronda's glance and manner as usual conveying the impression of sympathetic interest – which on this occasion answered his purpose well. It seemed to come naturally enough that he should say –

'And you have no daughter?'

There was an instantaneous change in the mother's face. Her lips closed more firmly, she looked down, swept her hands outward on the counter, and finally turned her back on Deronda to examine some Indian handkerchiefs that hung in pawn behind her. Her son gave a significant glance, set up his shoulders an instant and just put his finger to his lips, – then said quickly, 'I think you're a first-rate gentleman in the city, sir, if I may be allowed to guess.'

'No,' said Deronda, with a preoccupied air, 'I have nothing to do with the city.'

'That's a bad job. I thought you might be the young principal of a first-rate firm,' said Mr. Cohen, wishing to make amends for the check on his customer's natural desire to know more of him and his. 'But you understand silver-work, I see.'

'A little,' said Deronda, taking up the clasps a moment and laying them down again. That unwelcome bit of circumstantial evidence had made his mind busy with a plan which was certainly more like acting than anything he had been aware of in his own conduct before. But the bare possibility that more knowledge might nullify the evidence, now overpowered the inclination to rest in uncertainty.

'To tell you the truth,' he went on, 'my errand is not so much to buy as to borrow. I dare say you go into rather heavy transactions occasionally.'

'Well, sir, I've accommodated gentlemen of distinction – I'm proud to say it. I wouldn't exchange my business with any in the world. There's none more honourable, nor more charitable, nor more necessary for all classes, from the good lady who wants a little of the ready for the baker, to a gentleman like yourself, sir, who may want it for amusement.

I like my business, I like my street, and I like my shop. I wouldn't have it a door further down. And I wouldn't be without a pawn-shop, sir, to be the Lord Mayor. It puts you in connection with the world at large. I say it's like the Government revenue – it embraces the brass as well as the gold of the country. And a man who doesn't get money, sir, can't accommodate. Now what can I do for *you*, sir?'

If an amiable self-satisfaction is the mark of earthly bliss, Solomon in all his glory was a pitiable mortal compared with Mr. Cohen – clearly one of those persons who, being in excellent spirits about themselves, are willing to cheer strangers by letting them know it. While he was delivering himself with lively rapidity, he took the baby from his wife and holding it on his arm presented his features to be explored by its small fists. Deronda, not in a cheerful mood, was rashly pronouncing this Ezra Cohen to be the most unpoetic Jew he had ever met with in books or life: his phraseology was as little as possible like that of the Old Testament; and no shadow of a Suffering Race distinguished his vulgarity of soul from that of a prosperous pink-and-white huckster of the purest English lineage. It is naturally a Christian feeling that a Jew ought not to be conceited. However, this was no reason for not persevering in his project, and he answered at once in adventurous ignorance of technicalities –

'I have a fine diamond ring to offer as security – not with me at this moment, unfortunately, for I am not in the habit of wearing it. But I will come again this evening and bring it with me. Fifty pounds at once would be a convenience to me.'

'Well, you know, this evening is the Sabbath, young gentleman,' said Cohen, 'and I go to the *Shool*. The shop will be closed. But accommodation is a work of charity; if you can't get here before, and are any ways pressed – why, I'll look at your diamond. You're perhaps from the West End – a longish drive?'

'Yes; and your Sabbath begins early at this season. I could be here by five – will that do?' Deronda had not been without hope that by asking to come on a Friday evening he might get a better opportunity of observing points in the family character, and might even be able to put some decisive question.

Cohen assented; but here the marvellous Jacob, whose *physique* supported a precocity that would have shattered a Gentile of his years, showed that he had been listening with much comprehension by saying, 'You are coming again. Have you got any more knives at home?'

'I think I have one,' said Deronda, smiling down at him.

'Has it two blades and a hook – and a white handle like that?' said Jacob, pointing to the waistcoat-pocket.

'I dare say it has.'

'Do you like a cork-screw?' said Jacob, exhibiting that article in his own knife again, and looking up with serious inquiry.

'Yes,' said Deronda, experimentally.

'Bring your knife, then, and we'll shwop,' said Jacob, returning the knife to his pocket, and stamping about with the sense that he had concluded a good transaction.

The grandmother had now recovered her usual manners, and the whole family watched Deronda radiantly when he caressingly lifted the little girl, to whom he had not hitherto given attention, and seating her on the counter, asked for her name also. She looked at him in silence, and put her fingers to her gold earrings, which he did not seem to have noticed.

'Adelaide Rebekah is her name,' said her mother, proudly. 'Speak to the gentleman, lovey.'

'Shlav'm Shabbes fyock on,' said Adelaide Rebekah.

'Her Sabbath frock, she means,' said the father, in explanation. 'She'll have her Sabbath frock on this evening.'

'And will you let me see you in it, Adelaide?' said Deronda, with that gentle intonation which came very easily to him.

'Say yes, lovey – yes, if you please, sir,' said her mother, enchanted with this handsome young gentleman, who appreciated remarkable children.

'And will you give me a kiss this evening?' said Deronda, with a hand on each of her little brown shoulders.

Adelaide Rebekah (her miniature crinoline and monumental features corresponded with the combination of her names) immediately put up her lips to pay the kiss in advance; whereupon her father, rising into still more glowing satisfaction with the general meritoriousness of his circumstances, and with the stranger who was an admiring witness said cordially –

'You see there's somebody will be disappointed if you don't come this evening, sir. You won't mind sitting down in our family place and waiting a bit for me, if I'm not in when you come, sir? I'll stretch a point to accommodate a gent of your sort. Bring the diamond, and I'll see what I can do for you.'

Deronda thus left the most favourable impression behind him as a preparation for more easy intercourse. But for his own part those amenities had been carried on under the heaviest spirits. If these were really Mirah's relatives, he could not imagine that even her fervid filial piety could give the reunion with them any sweetness beyond such as could be found in the strict fulfilment of a painful duty. What did this vaunting brother need? And with the most favourable supposition about the hypothetic mother, Deronda shrank from the image of a first meeting between her and Mirah, and still more from the idea of Mirah's domestication with this family. He took refuge in disbelief. To find an Ezra Cohen when the name was running in your head was no more extraordinary than to find a Josiah Smith under like circumstances; and as to the coincidence about the daughter, it would probably turn out to be a difference. If, however, further knowledge confirmed the more undesirable conclusion, what would be wise expediency? – to try and determine the best consequences by concealment, or to brave other consequences for the sake of that openness which is the sweet fresh air of our moral life?

XXXIV

'Er ist geheissen
Israel. Ihn hat verwandelt
Hexenspruch in einen Hund.

. . . . .

Aber jeden Freitag Abend,
In der Dämmrungstunde, plötzlich
Weicht der Zauber, und der Hund
Wird aufs Neu' ein menschlich Wesen.'
— HEINE: *Prinzessin Sabbath.*

WHEN Deronda arrived at five o'clock, the shop was closed and the door was opened for him by the Christian servant. When she showed him into the room behind the shop he was surprised at the prettiness of the scene. The house was old, and rather extensive at the back: probably the large room he now entered was gloomy by daylight, but now it was agreeably lit by a fine old brass lamp with seven oil-lights hanging above the snow-white cloth spread on the central table. The ceiling and walls were smoky, and all the surroundings were dark enough to throw into relief the human figures, which had a Venetian glow of colouring. The grandmother was arrayed in yellowish brown with a large gold chain in lieu of the necklace, and by this light her yellow face with its darkly-marked eyebrows and framing *rouleau* of grey hair looked as handsome as was necessary for picturesque effect. Young Mrs. Cohen was clad in red and black, with a string of large artificial pearls wound round and round her neck; the baby lay asleep in the cradle under a scarlet counterpane; Adelaide Rebekah was in braided amber; and Jacob Alexander was in black velvet-een with scarlet stockings. As the four pairs of black eyes all glistened a welcome at Deronda, he was almost ashamed of the supercilious dislike these happy-looking creatures had raised in him by daylight. Nothing could be more cordial than the greeting he received, and both mother and grandmother seemed to gather more dignity from being seen on the private hearth, showing hospitality.

He looked round with some wonder at the old furniture: the oaken bureau and high side table must surely be mere matters of chance and economy, and not due to the family taste. A large dish of blue-and-yellow ware was set up on the side table, and flanking it were two old silver vessels; in front of them a large volume in darkened vellum with a deep-ribbed back. In the corner at the farther end was an open door into an inner room, where there was also a light.

Deronda took in these details by parenthetic glances while he met Jacob's pressing solicitude about the knife. He had taken the pains to buy one with the requisites of the hook and white handle, and produced it on demand, saying –

'Is that the sort of thing you want, Jacob?'

It was subjected to a severe scrutiny, the hook and blades were opened, and the article of barter with the cork-screw was drawn forth for comparison.

'Why do you like a hook better than a cork-screw?' said Deronda.

'Caush I can get hold of things with a hook. A cork-screw won't go into anything but corks. But it's better for you, you can draw corks.'

'You agree to change, then?' said Deronda, observing that the grandmother was listening with delight.

'What else have you got in your pockets?' said Jacob, with deliberative seriousness.

'Hush, hush, Jacob, love,' said the grandmother. And Deronda, mindful of discipline, answered –

'I think I must not tell you that. Our business was with the knives.'

Jacob looked up into his face scanningly for a moment or two, and apparently arriving at his conclusions, said gravely –

'I'll shwop,' handing the cork-screw knife to Deronda, who pocketed it with corresponding gravity.

Immediately the small son of Shem ran off into the next room, whence his voice was heard in rapid chat; and then ran back again – when, seeing his father enter, he seized a

435

little velveteen hat which lay on a chair and put it on to approach him. Cohen kept on his own hat, and took no notice of the visitor, but stood still while the two children went up to him and clasped his knees: then he laid his hands on each in turn and uttered his Hebrew benediction; whereupon the wife who had lately taken baby from the cradle brought it up to her husband and held it under his outstretched hands, to be blessed in its sleep. For the moment Deronda thought that this pawnbroker proud of his vocation was not utterly prosaic.

'Well, sir, you found your welcome in my family, I think,' said Cohen, putting down his hat, and becoming his former self. 'And you've been punctual. Nothing like a little stress here,' he added, tapping his side pocket, as he sat down. 'It's good for us all in our turn. I've felt it when I've had to make up payments. I began early – had to turn myself about and put myself into shapes to fit every sort of box. It's bracing to the mind. Now then! let us see, let us see.'

'That is the ring I spoke of,' said Deronda, taking it from his finger. 'I believe it cost a hundred pounds. It will be a sufficient pledge to you for fifty, I think. I shall probably redeem it in a month or so.'

Cohen's glistening eyes seemed to get a little nearer together as he met the ingenuous look of this crude young gentleman, who apparently supposed that redemption was a satisfaction to pawnbrokers. He took the ring, examined and returned it, saying with indifference, 'Good, good. We'll talk of it after our meal. Perhaps you'll join us, if you've no objection. Me and my wife'll feel honoured, and so will mother; won't you, mother?'

The invitation was doubly echoed and Deronda gladly accepted it. All now turned and stood round the table. No dish was at present seen except one covered with a napkin; and Mrs. Cohen had placed a china bowl near her husband that he might wash his hands in it. But after putting on his hat again, he paused, and called in a loud voice, 'Mordecai!'

Can this be part of the religious ceremony? thought Deronda, not knowing what might be expected of the ancient hero. But he heard a 'Yes' from the next room, which made him look towards the open door; and there, to his astonishment, he saw the figure of the enigmatic Jew whom he had this morning met with in the book-shop. Their eyes met, and Mordecai looked as much surprised as Deronda – neither in his surprise making any sign of recognition. But when Mordecai was seating himself at the end of the table, he just bent his head to the guest in a cold and distant manner, as if the disappointment of the morning remained a disagreeable association with this new acquaintance.

Cohen now washed his hands, pronouncing Hebrew words the while: afterwards he took off the napkin covering the dish and disclosed the two long flat loaves besprinkled with seed – the memorial of the manna that fed the wandering forefathers – and breaking off small pieces gave one to each of the family, including Adelaide Rebekah, who stood on the chair with her whole length exhibited in her amber-coloured garment, her little Jewish nose lengthened by compression of the lip in the effort to make a suitable appearance. Cohen then began another Hebrew blessing, in which Jacob put on his hat to join with close imitation. After that, the heads were uncovered, all seated themselves, and the meal went on without any peculiarity that interested Deronda. He was not very conscious of what dishes he ate from, being preoccupied with a desire to turn the conversation in a way that would enable him to ask some leading question; and also with thinking of Mordecai, between whom and himself there was an exchange of fascinated, half-furtive glances. Mordecai had no handsome Sabbath garment, but instead of the threadbare rusty black coat of the morning he wore one of light drab, which looked as if it had once been a handsome loose paletot now shrunk with washing; and this change of clothing gave a still stronger accentuation to his dark-haired, eager face, which might have belonged

437

to the prophet Ezekiel – also probably not modish in the eyes of contemporaries. It was noticeable that the thin tails of the fried fish were given to Mordecai; and in general the sort of share assigned to a poor relation – no doubt a 'survival' of prehistoric practice, not yet generally admitted to be superstitious.

Mr. Cohen kept up the conversation with much liveliness, introducing as subjects always in taste (the Jew is proud of his loyalty) the Queen and the Royal Family, the Emperor and Empress of the French – into which both grandmother and wife entered with zest. Mrs. Cohen the younger showed an accurate memory of distinguished birthdays; and the elder assisted her son in informing the guest of what occurred when the Emperor and Empress were in England and visited the city, ten years before.

'I dare say you know all about it better than we do, sir,' said Cohen, repeatedly, by way of preface to full information; and the interesting statements were kept up in a trio.

'Our baby is named *Eu*genie Esther,' said young Mrs. Cohen, vivaciously.

'It's wonderful how the Emperor's like a cousin of mine in the face,' said the grandmother; 'it struck me like lightning when I caught sight of him. I couldn't have thought it.'

'Mother and me went to see the Emperor and Empress at the Crystal Palace,' said Mr. Cohen. 'I had a fine piece of work to take care of mother; she might have been squeezed flat – though she was pretty near as lusty then as she is now. I said, if I had a hundred mothers I'd never take one of 'em to see the Emperor and Empress at the Crystal Palace again; and you may think a man can't afford it when he's got but one mother – not if he'd ever so big an insurance on her.' He stroked his mother's shoulder affectionately, and chuckled a little at his own humour.

'Your mother has been a widow a long while, perhaps,' said Deronda, seizing his opportunity. 'That has made your care for her the more needful.'

'Ay, ay, it's a good many *yore-zeit* since I had to manage for her and myself,' said Cohen, quickly. 'I went early to it. It's that makes you a sharp knife.'

'What does – what makes a sharp knife, father?' said Jacob, his cheek very much swollen with sweet-cake.

The father winked at his guest and said, 'Having your nose put on the grindstone.'

Jacob slipped from his chair with the piece of sweet-cake in his hand, and going close up to Mordecai, who had been totally silent hitherto, said, 'What does that mean – putting my nose to the grindstone?'

'It means that you are to bear being hurt without making a noise,' said Mordecai, turning his eyes benignantly on the small face close to his. Jacob put the corner of the cake into Mordecai's mouth as an invitation to bite, saying meanwhile, 'I shan't though,' and keeping his eyes on the cake to observe how much of it went in this act of generosity. Mordecai took a bite and smiled, evidently meaning to please the lad, and the little incident made them both look more lovable. Deronda, however, felt with some vexation that he had taken little by his question.

'I fancy that is the right quarter for learning,' said he, carrying on the subject that he might have an excuse for addressing Mordecai, to whom he turned and said, 'You have been a great student, I imagine.'

'I have studied,' was the quiet answer. 'And you? – you know German, by the book you were buying.'

'Yes, I have studied in Germany. Are you generally engaged in bookselling?' said Deronda.

'No; I only go to Mr. Ram's shop every day to keep it while he goes to meals,' said Mordecai, who was now looking at Deronda with what seemed a revival of his original interest: it seemed as if the face had some attractive indication for him which now neutralized the former disappointment. After a slight pause, he said, 'Perhaps you know Hebrew?'

'I am sorry to say, not at all.'

Mordecai's countenance fell: he cast down his eyelids, looking at his hands, which lay crossed before him,
and said no more. Deronda had now noticed more
decisively than in their former interview a difficulty of
breathing, which he thought must be a sign of consumption.

'I've had something else to do than to get book-
learning,' said Mr. Cohen, – 'I've had to make myself
knowing about useful things. I know stones well,' – here
he pointed to Deronda's ring. 'I'm not afraid of taking that
ring of yours at my own valuation. But now,' he added, with
a certain drop in his voice to a lower, more familiar nasal,
'what do you want for it?'

'Fifty or sixty pounds,' Deronda answered, rather too
carelessly.

Cohen paused a little, thrust his hands into his pockets,
fixed on Deronda a pair of glistening eyes that suggested a
miraculous guinea-pig, and said, 'Couldn't do you that.
Happy to oblige, but couldn't go that lengths. Forty
pound – say forty – I'll let you have forty on it.'

Deronda was aware that Mordecai had looked up again
at the words implying a monetary affair, and was now
examining him again, while he said, 'Very well; I shall
redeem it in a month or so.'

'Good. I'll make you out the ticket by-and-by,' said
Cohen, indifferently. Then he held up his finger as a sign
that conversation must be deferred. He, Mordecai, and
Jacob put on their hats, and Cohen opened a thanksgiving,
which was carried on by responses, till Mordecai delivered
himself alone at some length, in a solemn chanting tone,
with his chin slightly uplifted and his thin hands clasped
easily before him. Not only in his accent and tone, but in
his freedom from the self-consciousness which has reference to others' approbation, there could hardly have been a
stronger contrast to the Jew at the other end of the table. It
was an unaccountable conjunction – the presence among
these common, prosperous, shopkeeping types, of a man
who, in an emaciated threadbare condition, imposed a

certain awe on Deronda, and an embarrassment at not meeting his expectations.

No sooner had Mordecai finished his devotional strain, than rising, with a slight bend of his head to the stranger, he walked back into his room, and shut the door behind him.

'That seems to be rather a remarkable man,' said Deronda, turning to Cohen, who immediately set up his shoulders, put out his tongue slightly, and tapped his own brow. It was clearly to be understood that Mordecai did not come up to the standard of sanity which was set by Mr. Cohen's view of men and things.

'Does he belong to your family?' said Deronda.

This idea appeared to be rather ludicrous to the ladies as well as to Cohen, and the family interchanged looks of amusement.

'No, no,' said Cohen. 'Charity! charity! He worked for me, and when he got weaker and weaker I took him in. He's an encumbrance; but he brings a blessing down, and he teaches the boy. Besides, he does the repairing at the watches and jewellery.'

Deronda hardly abstained from smiling at this mixture of kindliness and the desire to justify it in the light of a calculation; but his willingness to speak further of Mordecai, whose character was made the more enigmatically striking by these new details, was baffled. Mr. Cohen immediately dismissed the subject by reverting to the 'accommodation,' which was also an act of charity, and proceeded to make out the ticket, get the forty pounds, and present them both in exchange for the diamond ring. Deronda, feeling that it would be hardly delicate to protract his visit beyond the settlement of the business which was its pretext, had to take his leave, with no more decided result than the advance of forty pounds and the pawn-ticket in his breast-pocket, to make a reason for returning when he came up to town after Christmas. He was resolved that he would then endeavour to gain a little more insight into the character and history of Mordecai; from whom also he might gather something decisive about the Cohens – for example, the reason why it was forbidden to ask Mrs. Cohen the elder whether she had a daughter.

BOOK V
Mordecai

XXXV

Were uneasiness of conscience measured by extent of crime,
human history had been different, and one should look to see
the contrivers of greedy wars and the mighty marauders of the
money-market in one troop of self-lacerating penitents with the
meaner robber and cut-purse and the murderer that doth his
butchery in small with his own hand. No doubt wickedness
hath its rewards to distribute; but whoso wins in this devil's
game must needs be baser, more cruel, more brutal than the
order of this planet will allow for the multitude born of woman,
the most of these carrying a form of conscience – a fear which is
the shadow of justice, a pity which is the shadow of love – that
hindereth from the prize of serene wickedness, itself difficult of
maintenance in our composite flesh.

ON the 29th of December Deronda knew that the
Grandcourts had arrived at the Abbey, but he had no
glimpse of them before he went to dress for dinner.
There had been a splendid fall of snow, allowing the
party of children the rare pleasures of snow-balling and
snow-building, and in the Christmas holidays the
Mallinger girls were content with no amusement unless it
were joined in and managed by 'cousin,' as they had always
called Deronda. After that outdoor exertion he had been
playing billiards, and thus the hours had passed without his
dwelling at all on the prospect of meeting Gwendolen at
dinner. Nevertheless that prospect was interesting to him,
and when, a little tired and heated with working at amusement, he went to his room before the half-hour bell had
rung, he began to think of it with some speculation on the
sort of influence her marriage with Grandcourt would have
on her, and on the probability that there would be some
discernible shades of change in her manner since he
saw her at Diplow, just as there had been since his first
vision of her at Leubronn.

'I fancy there are some natures one could see growing or degenerating every day, if one watched them,' was his thought. 'I suppose some of us go on faster than others; and I am sure she is a creature who keeps strong traces of anything that has once impressed her. That little affair of the necklace, and the idea that somebody thought her gambling wrong, had evidently bitten into her. But such impressibility tells both ways: it may drive one to desperation as soon as to anything better. And whatever fascinations Grandcourt may have for capricious tastes – good heavens! who can believe that he would call out the tender affections in daily companionship? One might be tempted to horsewhip him for the sake of getting some show of passion into his face and speech. I'm afraid she married him out of ambition – to escape poverty. But why did she run out of his way at first? The poverty came after, though. Poor thing! she may have been urged into it. How can one feel anything else than pity for a young creature like that – full of unused life – ignorantly rash – hanging all her blind expectations on that remnant of a human being!'

Doubtless the phrases which Deronda's meditation applied to the bridegroom were the less complimentary for the excuses and pity in which it clad the bride. His notion of Grandcourt as a 'remnant' was founded on no particular knowledge, but simply on the impression which ordinary polite intercourse had given him that Grandcourt had worn out all his natural healthy interest in things.

In general, one may be sure that whenever a marriage of any mark takes place, male acquaintances are likely to pity the bride, female acquaintances the bridegroom: each, it is thought, might have done better; and especially where the bride is charming, young gentlemen on the scene are apt to conclude that she can have no real attachment to a fellow so uninteresting to themselves as her husband, but has married him on other grounds. Who under such circumstances pities the husband? Even his female friends are apt to think his position retributive: he should have chosen some one else. But perhaps Deronda may be excused that he did not prepare any pity for Grandcourt, who had never struck acquaintances as likely to come out of his experiences with more suffering than he inflicted; whereas for Gwendolen, young, headlong, eager for pleasure, fed with the flattery which makes a lovely girl believe in her divine right to rule – how quickly life might turn from expectancy to a bitter sense of the irremediable! After what he had seen of her he must have had rather dull feelings not to have looked forward with some interest to her entrance into the room. Still, since the honeymoon was already three weeks in the distance, and Gwendolen had been enthroned not only at Ryelands but at Diplow, she was likely to have composed her countenance with suitable manifestation or concealment, not being one who would indulge the curious by a helpless exposure of her feelings.

A various party had been invited to meet the new couple: the old aristocracy was represented by Lord and Lady Pentreath; the old gentry by young Mr. and Mrs. Fitzadam of the Worcestershire branch of the Fitzadams; politics and the public good, as specialized in the cider interest, by Mr. Fenn, member for West Orchards, accompanied by his two daughters; Lady Mallinger's family, by her brother, Mr. Raymond, and his wife; the useful bachelor element by Mr. Sinker, the eminent counsel, and by Mr. Vandernoodt, whose acquaintance Sir Hugo had found pleasant enough at Leubronn to be adopted in England.

All had assembled in the drawing-room before the new couple appeared. Meanwhile the time was being passed chiefly in noticing the children – various little Raymonds, nephews and nieces of Lady Mallinger's, with her own three girls, who were always allowed to appear at this hour. The scene was really delightful – enlarged by full-length portraits with deep backgrounds, inserted in the cedar panelling – surmounted by a ceiling that glowed with the rich colours of the coats of arms ranged between the sockets – illuminated almost as much by the red fire of oak-boughs as by the pale wax-lights – stilled by the deep-piled carpet and by the high English breeding that subdues all voices; while the mixture of ages, from the white-haired Lord and Lady Pentreath to the four-year-old Edgar Raymond, gave a varied charm to the living groups. Lady Mallinger, with fair matronly roundness and mildly prominent blue eyes, moved about in her black velvet, carrying a tiny white dog on her arm as a sort of finish to her costume; the children were scattered among the ladies, while most of the gentlemen were standing rather aloof conversing with that very moderate vivacity observable during the long minutes before dinner. Deronda was a little out of the circle in a dialogue fixed upon him by Mr. Vandernoodt, a man of the best Dutch blood imported at the revolution: for the rest, one of those commodious persons in society who are nothing particular themselves, but are understood to be acquainted with the best in every department; close-clipped, pale-eyed, *nonchalant*, as good a foil as could well be found to the intense colouring and vivid gravity of Deronda.

He was talking of the bride and bridegroom, whose appearance was being waited for. Mr. Vandernoodt was an industrious gleaner of personal details, and could probably tell everything about a great philosopher or physicist except his theories or discoveries: he was now implying that he had learned many facts about Grandcourt since meeting him at Leubronn.

'Men who have seen a good deal of life don't always end by choosing their wives so well. He has had rather an anecdotic history – gone rather deep into pleasures, I fancy, lazy as he is. But, of course, you know all about him.'

'No, really,' said Deronda, in an indifferent tone. 'I know little more of him than that he is Sir Hugo's nephew.'

But now the door opened and deferred any satisfaction of Mr. Vandernoodt's communicativeness.

The scene was one to set off any figure of distinction that entered on it, and certainly when Mr. and Mrs. Grandcourt entered, no beholder could deny that their figures had distinction. The bridegroom had neither more nor less easy perfection of costume, neither more nor less well-cut impassibility of face, than before his marriage. It was to be supposed of him that he would put up with nothing less than the best in outward equipment, wife included; and the wife on his arm was what he might have been expected to choose. 'By George, I think she's handsomer if anything!' said Mr. Vandernoodt. And Deronda was of the same opinion, but he said nothing. The white silk and diamonds – it may seem strange, but she did wear the diamonds on her neck, in her ears, in her hair – might have something to do with the new imposing-ness of her beauty, which flashed on him as more unques-tionable if not more thoroughly satisfactory than when he had first seen her at the gaming-table. Some faces which are peculiar in their beauty are like original works of art: for the first time they are almost always met with question. But in seeing Gwendolen at Diplow, Deronda had dis-cerned in her more than he had expected of that tender appealing charm which we call womanly. Was there any new change since then? He distrusted his impressions; but as he saw her receiving greetings with what seemed a proud cold quietude and a superficial smile, there seemed to be at work within her the same demonic force that had possessed her when she took him in her resolute glance and turned away a loser from the gaming-table. There was no time for more of a conclusion – no time even for him to give his greeting before the summons to dinner.

He sat not far from opposite to her at table, and could sometimes hear what she said in answer to Sir Hugo, who was at his liveliest in conversation with her; but though he looked towards her with the intention of bowing, she gave him no opportunity of doing so for some time. At last Sir Hugo, who might have imagined that they had already spoken to each other, said, 'Deronda, you will like to hear what Mrs. Grandcourt tells me about your favourite Klesmer.'

Gwendolen's eyelids had been lowered, and Deronda, already looking at her, thought he discerned a quivering reluctance as she was obliged to raise them and return his unembarrassed bow and smile, her own smile being one of the lip merely. It was but an instant, and Sir Hugo continued without pause –

'The Arrowpoints have condoned the marriage, and he is spending the Christmas with his bride at Quetcham.'

'I suppose he will be glad of it for the sake of his wife, else I dare say he would not have minded keeping at a distance,' said Deronda.

'It's a sort of troubadour story,' said Lady Pentreath, an easy, deep-voiced old lady; 'I'm glad to find a little romance left among us. I think our young people now are getting too worldly wise.'

'It shows the Arrowpoints' good sense, however, to have adopted the affair, after the fuss in the papers,' said Sir Hugo. 'And disowning your only child because of a *mésalliance* is something like disowning your one eye: everybody knows it's yours, and you have no other to make an appearance with.'

'As to *mésalliance*, there's no blood on any side,' said Lady Pentreath. 'Old Admiral Arrowpoint was one of Nelson's men, you know – a doctor's son. And we all know how the mother's money came.'

'If there were any *mésalliance* in the case, I should say it was on Klesmer's side,' said Deronda.

'Ah, you think it is a case of the immortal marrying the mortal. What is your opinion?' said Sir Hugo, looking at Gwendolen.

'I have no doubt that Herr Klesmer thinks himself immortal. But I dare say his wife will burn as much incense before him as he requires,' said Gwendolen. She had recovered any composure that she might have lost.

'Don't you approve of a wife burning incense before her husband?' said Sir Hugo, with an air of jocoseness.

'Oh yes,' said Gwendolen, 'if it were only to make others believe in him.' She paused a moment and then said with more gaiety, 'When Herr Klesmer adores his own genius, it will take off some of the absurdity if his wife says Amen.'

'Klesmer is no favourite of yours, I see,' said Sir Hugo.
'I think very highly of him, I assure you,' said
Gwendolen. 'His genius is quite above my judgment,
and I know him to be exceedingly generous.'

She spoke with the sudden seriousness which is often
meant to correct an unfair or indiscreet sally, having a
bitterness against Klesmer in her secret soul which she
knew herself unable to justify. Deronda was wondering
what he should have thought of her if he had never heard
of her before: probably that she put on a little hardness and
defiance by way of concealing some painful consciousness
– if, indeed, he could imagine her manners otherwise than
in the light of his suspicion. But why did she not recognize
him with more friendliness?

Sir Hugo, by way of changing the subject, said to her, 'Is
not this a beautiful room? It was part of the refectory of the
Abbey. There was a division made by those pillars and the
three arches, and afterwards they were built up. Else it was
half as large again originally. There used to be rows of
Benedictines sitting where we are sitting. Suppose we
were suddenly to see the lights burning low and the ghosts
of the old monks rising behind all our chairs!'

'Please don't!' said Gwendolen, with a playful shudder.
'It is very nice to come after ancestors and monks, but they
should know their places and keep underground. I should
be rather frightened to go about this house all alone. I
suppose the old generations must be angry with us because
we have altered things so much.'

'Oh, the ghosts must be of all political parties,' said Sir
Hugo. 'And those fellows who wanted to change things
while they lived and couldn't do it, must be on our side.
But if you would not like to go over the house alone, you
will like to go in company, I hope. You and Grandcourt
ought to see it all. And we will ask Deronda to go round
with us. He is more learned about it than I am.' The
baronet was in the most complaisant of humours.

Gwendolen stole a glance at Deronda, who must have
heard what Sir Hugo said, for he had his face turned

towards them helping himself to an *entrée*; but he looked as impassive as a picture. At the notion of Deronda's showing her and Grandcourt the place which was to be theirs, and which she with painful emphasis remembered might have been his (perhaps, if others had acted differently), certain thoughts had rushed in – thoughts often repeated within her, but now returning on an occasion embarrassingly new; and she was conscious of something furtive and awkward in her glance, which Sir Hugo must have noticed. With her usual readiness of resource against betrayal, she said playfully, 'You don't know how much I am afraid of Mr. Deronda.'

'How's that? Because you think him too learned?' said Sir Hugo, whom the peculiarity of her glance had not escaped.

'No. It is ever since I first saw him at Leubronn. Because when he came to look on at the roulette-table, I began to lose. He cast an evil eye on my play. He didn't approve it. He has told me so. And now whatever I do before him, I am afraid he will cast an evil eye upon it.'

'Gad! I'm rather afraid of him myself when he doesn't approve,' said Sir Hugo, glancing at Deronda; and then turning his face towards Gwendolen, he said less audibly, 'I don't think ladies generally object to have his eyes upon them.' The baronet's small chronic complaint of facetiousness was at this moment almost as annoying to Gwendolen as it often was to Deronda.

'I object to any eyes that are critical,' she said, in a cool high voice, with a turn of her neck. 'Are there many of these old rooms left in the Abbey?'

'Not many. There is a fine cloistered court with a long gallery above it. But the finest bit of all is turned into stables. It is part of the old church. When I improved the place I made the most of every other bit; but it was out of my reach to change the stables, so the horses have the benefit of the fine old choir. You must go and see it.'

'I shall like to see the horses as well as the building,' said Gwendolen.

'Oh, I have no stud to speak of. Grandcourt will look with contempt at my horses,' said Sir Hugo. 'I've given up hunting, and go on in a jog-trot way, as becomes an old gentleman with daughters. The fact is, I went in for doing too much at this place. We all lived at Diplow for two years while the alterations were going on. Do you like Diplow?'

'Not particularly,' said Gwendolen, with indifference. One would have thought that the young lady had all her life had more family seats than she cared to go to.

'Ah! it will not do after Ryelands,' said Sir Hugo, well pleased. 'Grandcourt, I know, took it for the sake of the hunting. But he found something so much better there,' added the baronet, lowering his voice, 'that he might well prefer it to any other place in the world.'

'It has one attraction for me,' said Gwendolen, passing over this compliment with a chill smile, 'that it is within reach of Offendene.'

'I understand that,' said Sir Hugo, and then let the subject drop.

What amiable baronet can escape the effect of a strong desire for a particular possession? Sir Hugo would have been glad that Grandcourt with or without reason, should prefer any other place to Diplow; but inasmuch as in the pure process of wishing we can always make the conditions of our gratification benevolent, he did wish that Grandcourt's convenient disgust for Diplow should not be associated with his marriage of this very charming bride. Gwendolen was much to the baronet's taste, but as he observed afterwards to Lady Mallinger, he should never have taken her for a young girl who had married beyond her expectations.

Deronda had not heard much of this conversation, having given his attention elsewhere, but the glimpses he had of Gwendolen's manner deepened the impression that it had something newly artificial.

Later in the drawing-room, Deronda, at somebody's request, sat down to the piano and sang. Afterwards Mrs. Raymond took his place; and on rising he observed that

Gwendolen had left her seat, and had come to this end of the room, as if to listen more fully, but was now standing with her back to every one, apparently contemplating a fine cowled head carved in ivory which hung over a small table. He longed to go to her and speak. Why should he not obey such an impulse, as he would have done towards any other lady in the room? Yet he hesitated some moments, observing the graceful lines of her back, but not moving.

If you have any reason for not indulging a wish to speak to a fair woman, it is a bad plan to look long at her back: the wish to see what it screens becomes the stronger. There may be a very sweet smile on the other side. Deronda ended by going to the end of the small table, at right angles to Gwendolen's position, but before he could speak she had turned on him no smile, but such an appealing look of sadness, so utterly different from the chill effort of her recognition at table, that his speech was checked. For what was an appreciable space of time to both, though the observation of others could not have measured it, they looked at each other – she seeming to take the deep rest of confession, he with an answering depth of sympathy that neutralized other feelings.

'Will you not join in the music?' he said, by way of meeting the necessity for speech.

That her look of confession had been involuntary was shown by that just perceptible shake and change of countenance with which she roused herself to reply calmly, 'I join in it by listening. I am fond of music.'

'Are you not a musician?'

'I have given a great deal of time to music. But I have not talent enough to make it worth while. I shall never sing again.'

'But if you are fond of music, it will always be worth while in private, for your own delight. I make it a virtue to be content with my middlingness,' said Deronda, smiling; 'it is always pardonable, so that one does not ask others to take it for superiority.'

'I cannot imitate you,' said Gwendolen, recovering her tone of artificial vivacity. 'To be middling with me is another phrase for being dull. And the worst fault I have to find with the world is, that it is dull. Do you know, I am going to justify gambling in spite of you. It is a refuge from dullness.'

'I don't admit the justification,' said Deronda. 'I think what we call the dullness of things is a disease in ourselves. Else how could any one find an intense interest in life? And many do.'

'Ah, I see! The fault I find in the world is my own fault,' said Gwendolen, smiling at him. Then after a moment, looking up at the ivory again, she said, 'Do *you* never find fault with the world or with others?'

'Oh yes. When I am in a grumbling mood.'

'And hate people? Confess you hate them when they stand in your way – when their gain is your loss? That is your own phrase, you know.'

'We are often standing in each other's way when we can't help it. I think it is stupid to hate people on that ground.'

'But if they injure you and could have helped it?' said Gwendolen, with a hard intensity unaccountable in incidental talk like this.

Deronda wondered at her choice of subjects. A painful impression arrested his answer a moment, but at last he said, with a graver, deeper intonation, 'Why then, after all, I prefer my place to theirs.'

'There I believe you are right,' said Gwendolen, with a sudden little laugh, and turned to join the group at the piano.

Deronda looked round for Grandcourt, wondering whether he followed his bride's movements with any attention; but it was rather undiscerning in him to suppose that he could find out the fact. Grandcourt had a delusive mode of observing whatever had an interest for him, which could be surpassed by no sleepy-eyed animal on the watch for prey. At that moment he was plunged in the depth of an easy-chair, being talked to by Mr. Vandernoodt, who apparently thought the acquaintance of such a bridegroom worth cultivating; and an incautious person might have supposed it safe to telegraph secrets in front of him, the common prejudice being that your quick observer is one whose eyes have quick movements. Not at all. If you want a respectable witness who will see nothing inconvenient, choose a vivacious gentleman, very much on the alert, with two eyes wide open, a glass in one of them, and an entire impartiality as to the purpose of looking. If Grandcourt cared to keep any one under his power he saw them out of the corners of his long narrow eyes, and if they went behind him, he had a constructive process by which he knew what they were doing there. He knew perfectly well where his wife was, and how she was behaving. Was he going to be a jealous husband? Deronda imagined that to be likely; but his imagination was as much astray about Grandcourt as it would have been about an unexplored continent where all the species were peculiar. He did not conceive that he himself was a likely object of jealousy, or that he should give any pretext for it; but the suspicion that a wife is not happy naturally leads one to speculate on the husband's private deportment; and Deronda found himself after one o'clock in the morning in the rather ludicrous position of sitting up severely holding a Hebrew grammar in his hands (for somehow, in deference to Mordecai, he had begun to study Hebrew), with the consciousness that he had been in that attitude nearly an hour, and had thought of nothing but Gwendolen and her husband. To be an unusual young man means for the most part to get a difficult mastery over the usual, which is often like the sprite of ill-luck you pack up your goods to escape from, and see grinning at you from the top of your luggage-van. The peculiarities of Deronda's nature had been acutely touched by the brief incidents and words which made the history of his intercourse with Gwendolen; and this evening's slight addition had given them an importunate recurrence. It was not vanity – it was ready sympathy that had made him alive to a certain appealingness in her behaviour towards him; and the difficulty with which she had seemed to raise her eyes to bow to him, in the first instance, was to be interpreted now by that unmistakable look of involuntary confidence which she had afterwards turned on him under the consciousness of his approach.

'What is the use of it all?' thought Deronda, as he threw down his grammar, and began to undress. 'I can't do anything to help her – nobody can, if she has found out her mistake already. And it seems to me that she has a dreary lack of the ideas that might help her. Strange and piteous to think what a centre of wretchedness a delicate piece of human flesh like that might be, wrapped round with fine raiment, her ears pierced for gems, her head held loftily, her mouth all smiling pretence, the poor soul within her sitting in sick distaste of all things! But what do I know of her? There may be a demon in her to match the worst husband, for what I can tell. She was clearly an ill-educated, worldly girl: perhaps she is a coquette.'

This last reflection, not much believed in, was a self-administered dose of caution, prompted partly by Sir Hugo's much-contemned joking on the subject of flirtation. Deronda resolved not to volunteer any *tête-à-tête* with Gwendolen during the few days of her stay at the Abbey; and he was capable of keeping a resolve in spite of much inclination to the contrary.

But a man cannot resolve about a woman's actions, least of all about those of a woman like Gwendolen, in whose nature there was a combination of proud reserve with rashness, of perilously-poised terror with defiance, which might alternately flatter and disappoint control. Few words could less represent her than 'coquette.' She had a native love of homage, and belief in her own power; but no cold artifice for the sake of enslaving. And the poor thing's belief in her power, with her other dreams before marriage, had often to be thrust aside now like the toys of a sick child, which it looks at with dull eyes, and has no heart to play with, however it may try.

The next day at lunch Sir Hugo said to her, 'The thaw has gone on like magic, and it's so pleasant out of doors just now – shall we go and see the stables and the other old bits about the place?'

'Yes, pray,' said Gwendolen. 'You will like to see the stables, Henleigh?' she added, looking at her husband.

'Uncommonly,' said Grandcourt, with an indifference which seemed to give irony to the word, as he returned her look. It was the first time Deronda had seen them speak to each other since their arrival, and he thought their exchange of looks as cold and official as if it had been a ceremony to keep up a charter. Still, the English fondness for reserve will account for much negation; and Grandcourt's manners with an extra veil of reserve over them might be expected to present the extreme type of the national taste.

'Who else is inclined to make the tour of the house and premises?' said Sir Hugo. 'The ladies must muffle themselves: there is only just about time to do it well before sunset. You will go, Dan, won't you?'

'Oh yes,' said Deronda, carelessly, knowing that Sir Hugo would think any excuse disobliging.

'All meet in the library, then, when they are ready – say in half an hour,' said the baronet. Gwendolen made herself ready with wonderful quickness, and in ten minutes came down into the library in her sables, plume, and little thick boots. As soon as she entered the room she was aware that someone else was there: it was precisely what she had hoped for. Deronda was standing with his back towards her at the far end of the room, and was looking over a newspaper. How could little thick boots make any noise on an Axminster carpet? And to cough would have seemed an intended signalling which her pride could not condescend to; also, she felt bashful about walking up to him and letting him know that she was there, though it was her hunger to speak to him which had set her imagination on constructing this chance of finding him, and had made her hurry down, as birds hover near the water which they dare not drink. Always uneasily dubious about his opinion of her, she felt a peculiar anxiety to-day, lest he might think of her with contempt, as one triumphantly conscious of being Grandcourt's wife, the future lady of this domain. It was her habitual effort now to magnify the satisfactions of her pride, on which she nourished her strength; but somehow Deronda's being there disturbed them all. There was not the faintest touch of coquetry in the attitude of her mind towards him: he was unique to her among men, because he had impressed her as being not her admirer but her superior: in some mysterious way he was becoming a part of her conscience, as one woman whose nature is an object of reverential belief may become a new conscience to a man.

And now he would not look round and find out that she was there! The paper crackled in his hand, his head rose and sank, exploring those stupid columns, and he was evidently stroking his beard, as if this world were a very easy affair to her. Of course all the rest of the company would soon be down, and the opportunity of her saying something to efface her flippancy of the evening before, would be quite gone. She felt sick with irritation – so fast do young creatures like her absorb misery through invisible suckers of their own fancies – and her face had gathered that peculiar expression which comes with a mortification to which tears are forbidden.

At last he threw down the paper and turned round.

'Oh, you are there already,' he said, coming forward a step or two; 'I must go and put on my coat.'

He turned aside and walked out of the room. This was behaving quite badly. Mere politeness would have made him stay to exchange some words before leaving her alone. It was true that Grandcourt came in with Sir Hugo immediately after, so that the words must have been too few to be worth anything. As it was, they saw him walking from the library door.

'A – you look rather ill,' said Grandcourt, going straight up to her, standing in front of her, and looking into her eyes. 'Do you feel equal to the walk?'

'Yes, I shall like it,' said Gwendolen, without the slight-est movement except this of the lips.

'We could put off going over the house, you know, and only go out of doors,' said Sir Hugo, kindly, while Grandcourt turned aside.

'Oh dear no!' said Gwendolen, speaking with deter-mination; 'let us put off nothing. I want a long walk.'

The rest of the walking party – two ladies and two gentlemen besides Deronda – had now assembled; and Gwendolen, rallying, went with due cheerfulness by the side of Sir Hugo, paying apparently an equal attention to the commentaries Deronda was called upon to give on the various architectural fragments, and to Sir Hugo's reasons for not attempting to remedy the mixture of the undisguised modern with the antique – which in his opinion only made the place the more truly historical. On their way to the buttery and kitchen, they took the outside of the house and paused before a beautiful pointed doorway, which was the only old remnant in the east front.

'Well, now, to my mind,' said Sir Hugo, 'that is more interesting standing as it is in the middle of what is frankly four centuries later, than if the whole front had been dressed up in a pretence of the thirteenth century. Additions ought to smack of the time when they are made and carry the stamp of their period. I wouldn't destroy any old bits, but that notion of reproducing the old is a mis-take, I think. At least, if a man likes to do it he must pay for his whistle. Besides, where are you to stop along that road – making loopholes where you don't want to peep, and so on? You may as well ask me to wear out the stones with kneeling; eh, Grandcourt?'

'A confounded nuisance,' drawled Grandcourt. 'I hate fellows wanting to howl litanies – acting the greatest bores that have ever existed.'

'Well, yes, that's what their romanticism must come to,' said Sir Hugo, in a tone of confidential assent – 'that is, if they carry it out logically.'

'I think that way of arguing against a course because it may be ridden down to an absurdity would soon bring life to a standstill,' said Deronda. 'It is not the logic of human action, but of a roasting-jack, that must go on to the last turn when it has been once wound up. We can do nothing safely without some judgment as to where we are to stop.'

'I find the rule of the pocket the best guide,' said Sir Hugo, laughingly. 'And as for most of your new-old building, you had need hire men to scratch and chip it all over artistically to give it an elderly-looking surface; which at the present rate of labour would not answer.'

'Do you want to keep up the old fashions, then, Mr. Deronda?' said Gwendolen, taking advantage of the freedom of grouping to fall back a little, while Sir Hugo and Grandcourt went on.

'Some of them. I don't see why we should not use our choice there as we do elsewhere – or why either age or novelty by itself is an argument for or against. To delight in doing things because our fathers did them is good if it shuts out nothing better; it enlarges the range of affection – and affection is the broadest basis of good in life.'

'Do you think so?' said Gwendolen, with a little surprise. 'I should have thought you cared most about ideas, knowledge, wisdom, and all that.'

'But to care about *them* is a sort of affection,' said Deronda, smiling at her sudden *naïveté*. 'Call it attachment, interest, willingness to bear a great deal for the sake of being with them and saving them from injury. Of course it makes a difference if the objects of interest are human beings; but generally in all deep affections the objects are a mixture – half persons and half ideas – sentiments and affections flow in together.'

'I wonder whether I understand that,' said Gwendolen, putting up her chin in her old saucy manner. 'I believe I am not very affectionate; perhaps you mean to tell me, that is the reason why I don't see much good in life.'

'No, I did *not* mean to tell you that; but I admit that I should think it true if I believed what you say of yourself,' said Deronda, gravely.

Here Sir Hugo and Grandcourt turned round and paused.

'I never can get Mr. Deronda to pay me a compliment,' said Gwendolen. 'I have quite a curiosity to see whether a little flattery can be extracted from him.'

'Ah!' said Sir Hugo, glancing at Deronda, 'the fact is, it is hopeless to flatter a bride. We give it up in despair. She has been so fed on sweet speeches that everything we say seems tasteless.'

'Quite true,' said Gwendolen, bending her head and smiling. 'Mr. Grandcourt won me by neatly-turned compliments. If there had been one word out of place it would have been fatal.'

'Do you hear that?' said Sir Hugo, looking at the husband.

'Yes,' said Grandcourt, without change of countenance. 'It is a deucedly hard thing to keep up, though.'

All this seemed to Sir Hugo a natural playfulness between such a husband and wife; but Deronda wondered at the misleading alternations in Gwendolen's manner, which at one moment seemed to invite sympathy by child-like indiscretion, at another to repel it by proud conceal-ment. He tried to keep out of her way by devoting himself to Miss Juliet Fenn, a young lady whose profile had been so unfavourably decided by circumstances over which she had no control, that Gwendolen some months ago had felt it impossible to be jealous of her. Nevertheless when they were seeing the kitchen – a part of the original building in perfect preservation – the depth of shadow in the niches of the stone walls and groined vault, the play of light from the huge glowing fire on polished tin, brass, and copper, the fine resonance that came with every sound of voice or metal, were all spoiled for Gwendolen, and Sir Hugo's speech about them was made rather importunate, because Deronda was discoursing to the other ladies and kept at a

distance from her. It did not signify that the other gentlemen took the opportunity of being near her: of what use in
the world was their admiration while she had an uneasy
sense that there was some standard in Deronda's mind
which measured her into littleness? Mr. Vandernoodt,
who had the mania of always describing one thing while
you were looking at another, was quite intolerable with his
insistence on Lord Blough's kitchen, which he had seen in
the north.

'Pray don't ask us to see two kitchens at once. It makes
the heat double. I must really go out of it,' she cried at last,
marching resolutely into the open air, and leaving the
others in the rear. Grandcourt was already out, and as she
joined him, he said –

'I wondered how long you meant to stay in that damned
place' – one of the freedoms he had assumed as a husband
being the use of his strongest epithets. Gwendolen, turning to see the rest of the party approach, said –

'It was certainly rather too warm in one's wraps.'

They walked on the gravel across a green court, where
the snow still lay in islets on the grass, and in masses on the
boughs of the great cedar and the crenellated coping of the
stone walls, and then into a larger court, where there was
another cedar, to find the beautiful choir long ago turned
into stables, in the first instance perhaps after an
impromptu fashion by troopers, who had a pious satisfaction in insulting the priests of Baal and the images of
Ashtoreth, the queen of heaven. The exterior – its west
end, save for the stable door, walled in with brick and
covered with ivy – was much defaced, maimed of finial
and gurgoyle, the friable limestone broken and fretted, and
lending its soft grey to a powdery dark lichen; the long
windows, too, were filled in with brick as far as the springing of the arches, the broad clerestory windows with wire or
ventilating blinds. With the low wintry afternoon sun upon
it, sending shadows from the cedar boughs, and lighting up
the touches of snow remaining on every ledge, it had still a
scarcely disturbed aspect of antique solemnity, which gave

the scene in the interior rather a startling effect; though, ecclesiastical or reverential indignation apart, the eyes could hardly help dwelling with pleasure on its piquant picturesqueness. Each finely-arched chapel was turned into a stall, where in the dusty glazing of the windows there still gleamed patches of crimson, orange, blue, and palest violet; for the rest, the choir had been gutted, the floor levelled, paved, and drained according to the most approved fashion, and a line of loose-boxes erected in the middle: a soft light fell from the upper windows on sleek brown or grey flanks and haunches, on mild equine faces looking out with active nostrils over the varnished brown boarding; on the hay hanging from racks where the saints once looked down from the altar-pieces, and on the pale-golden straw scattered or in heaps; on a little white-and-liver-coloured spaniel making his bed on the back of an elderly hackney, and on four ancient angels, still showing signs of devotion like mutilated martyrs – while over all, the grand pointed roof, untouched by reforming wash, showed its lines and colours mysteriously through veiling shadow and cobweb, and a hoof now and then striking against the boards seemed to fill the vault with thunder, while outside there was the answering bay of the blood-hounds.

'Oh, this is glorious!' Gwendolen burst forth, in forget-fulness of everything but the immediate impression: there had been a little intoxication for her in the grand spaces of courts and building, and the fact of her being an important person among them. 'This *is* glorious! Only I wish there were a horse in every one of the boxes. I would ten times rather have these stables than those at Diplow.'

But she had no sooner said this than some consciousness arrested her, and involuntarily she turned her eyes towards Deronda, who oddly enough had taken off his felt hat and stood holding it before him as if they had entered a room or an actual church. He, like others, happened to be looking at her, and their eyes met – to her intense vexation, for it seemed to her that by looking at him she had betrayed the reference of her thoughts, and she felt herself blushing: she exaggerated the impression that even Sir Hugo as well as Deronda would have of her bad taste in referring to the possession of anything at the Abbey: as for Deronda, she had probably made him despise her. Her annoyance at what she imagined to be the obviousness of her confusion robbed her of her usual facility in carrying it off by playful speech, and turning up her face to look at the roof, she wheeled away in that attitude. If any had noticed her blush as significant, they had certainly not interpreted it by the secret windings and recesses of her feeling. A blush is no language: only a dubious flag-signal which may mean either of two contradictories. Deronda alone had a faint guess at some part of her feeling; but while he was observing her he was himself under observation.

'Do you take off your hat to the horses?' said Grandcourt with a slight sneer.

'Why not?' said Deronda, covering himself. He had really taken off the hat automatically, and if he had been an ugly man might doubtless have done so with impunity: ugliness having naturally the air of involuntary exposure, and beauty, of display.

Gwendolen's confusion was soon merged in the survey of the horses, which Grandcourt politely abstained from appraising, languidly assenting to Sir Hugo's alternate depreciation and eulogy of the same animal, as one that he should not have bought when he was younger, and piqued himself on his horses, but yet one that had better qualities than many more expensive brutes.

'The fact is, stables dive deeper and deeper into the pocket nowadays, and I am very glad to have got rid of that *démangeaison*,' said Sir Hugo as they were coming out.

'What is a man to do, though?' said Grandcourt. 'He must ride. I don't see what else there is to do. And I don't call it riding to sit astride a set of brutes with every deformity under the sun.'

This delicate diplomatic way of characterizing Sir Hugo's stud did not require direct notice; and the baronet feeling that the conversation had worn rather thin, said to the party generally, 'Now we are going to see the cloister – the finest bit of all – in perfect preservation: the monks might have been walking there yesterday.'

But Gwendolen had lingered behind to look at the kennelled blood-hounds, perhaps because she felt a little dispirited; and Grandcourt waited for her.

'You had better take my arm,' he said, in his low tone of command; and she took it.

'It's a great bore being dragged about in this way, and no cigar,' said Grandcourt.

'I thought you would like it.'

'Like it? – one eternal chatter. And encouraging those ugly girls – inviting one to meet such monsters. How that *fat* Deronda can bear looking at her— '

'Why do you call him a *fat*? Do you object to him so much?'

'Object? no. What do I care about his being a *fat*? It's of no consequence to me. I'll invite him to Diplow again if you like.'

'I don't think he would come. He is too clever and learned to care about *us*,' said Gwendolen, thinking it useful for her husband to be told (privately) that it was possible for him to be looked down upon.

'I never saw that make much difference in a man. Either he is a gentleman, or he is not,' said Grandcourt.

That a new husband and wife should snatch a moment's *tête-à-tête* was what could be understood and indulged; and the rest of the party left them in the rear till, re-entering the garden, they all paused in that cloistered court where, among the falling rose-petals thirteen years before, we saw a boy becoming acquainted with his first sorrow. This cloister was built of harder stone than the church, and had been in greater safety from the wearing weather. It was a rare example of a northern cloister with arched and pillared openings not intended for glazing, and the delicately-wrought foliage of the capitals seemed still to carry the very touches of the chisel. Gwendolen had dropped her husband's arm and joined the other ladies, to whom Deronda was noticing the delicate sense which had combined freedom with accuracy in the imitation of natural forms.

'I wonder whether one oftener learns to love real objects through their representations, or the representations through the real objects,' he said, after pointing out a lovely capital made by the curled leaves of greens, showing their reticulated under-side with the firm gradual swell of its central rib. 'When I was a little fellow these capitals taught me to observe, and delight in, the structure of leaves.'

'I suppose you can see every line of them with your eyes shut,' said Juliet Fenn.

'Yes. I was always repeating them, because for a good many years this court stood for me as my only image of a convent, and whenever I read of monks and monasteries, this was my scenery for them.'

'You must love this place very much,' said Miss Fenn, innocently, not thinking of inheritance. 'So many homes are like twenty others. But this is unique, and you seem to know every cranny of it. I dare say you could never love another home so well.'

'Oh, I carry it with me,' said Deronda, quietly, being used to all possible thoughts of this kind. 'To most men their early home is no more than a memory of their early years, and I'm not sure but they have the best of it. The image is never marred. There's no disappointment in memory, and one's exaggerations are always on the good side.'

Gwendolen felt sure that he spoke in that way out of delicacy to her and Grandcourt – because he knew they must hear him; and that he probably thought of her as a selfish creature who only cared about possessing things in her own person. But whatever he might say, it must have been a secret hardship to him that any circumstances of his birth had shut him out from the inheritance of his father's position; and if he supposed that she exulted in her

DANIEL DERONDA

husband's taking it, what could he feel for her but scornful pity? Indeed it seemed clear to her that he was avoiding her, and preferred talking to others – which nevertheless was not kind in him.

With these thoughts in her mind she was prevented by a mixture of pride and timidity from addressing him again, and when they were looking at the rows of quaint portraits in the gallery above the cloisters, she kept up her air of interest and made her vivacious remarks without any direct appeal to Deronda. But at the end she was very weary of her assumed spirits, and as Grandcourt turned into the billiard-room, she went to the pretty boudoir which had been assigned to her, and shut herself up to look melancholy at her ease. No chemical process shows a more wonderful activity than the transforming influence of the thoughts we imagine to be going on in another. Changes in theory, religion, admirations, may begin with a suspicion of dissent or disapproval, even when the grounds of disapproval are but matter of searching conjecture.

Poor Gwendolen was conscious of an uneasy, transforming process – all the old nature shaken to its depths, its hopes spoiled, its pleasures perturbed, but still showing wholeness and strength in the will to reassert itself. After every new shock of humiliation she tried to adjust herself and seize her old supports – proud concealment, trust in new excitements that would make life go by without much thinking; trust in some deed of reparation to nullify her self-blame and shield her from a vague, ever-visiting dread of some horrible calamity; trust in the hardening effect of use and wont that would make her indifferent to her miseries.

Yes – miseries. This beautiful, healthy young creature, with her two-and-twenty years and her gratified ambition, no longer felt inclined to kiss her fortunate image in the glass; she looked at it with wonder that she could be so miserable. One belief which had accompanied her through her unmarried life as a self-cajoling superstition, encouraged by the subordination of every one about her – the belief in her own power of dominating – was utterly gone. Already, in seven short weeks, which seemed half her life, her husband had gained a mastery which she could no more resist than she could have resisted the benumbing effect from the touch of a torpedo. Gwendolen's will had seemed imperious in its small girlish sway; but it was the will of a creature with a large discourse of imaginative fears: a shadow would have been enough to relax its hold. And she had found a will like that of a crab or a boa-constrictor which goes on pinching or crushing without alarm at thunder. Not that Grandcourt was without calculation of the intangible effects which were the chief means of mastery; indeed he had a surprising acuteness in detecting that situation of feeling in Gwendolen which made her proud and rebellious spirit dumb and helpless before him.

She had burnt Lydia Glasher's letter with an instantaneous terror lest other eyes should see it, and had tenaciously concealed from Grandcourt that there was any other cause of her violent hysterics than the excitement and fatigue of the day: she had been urged into an implied falsehood. 'Don't ask me – it was my feeling about everything – it was the sudden change from home.' The words of that letter kept repeating themselves, and hung on her consciousness with the weight of a prophetic doom. 'I am the grave in which your chance of happiness is buried as well as mine. You had your warning. You have chosen to injure me and my children. He had meant to marry me. He would have married me at last, if you had not broken your word. You will have your punishment. I desire it with all my soul. Will you give him this letter to set him against me and ruin us more – me and my children? Shall you like to stand before your husband with these diamonds on you, and these words of mine in his thoughts and yours? Will he think you have any right to complain when he has made you miserable? You took him with your eyes open. The willing wrong you have done me will be your curse.'

The words had nestled their venomous life within her, and stirred continually the vision of the scene at the Whispering Stones. That scene was now like an accusing apparition: she dreaded that Grandcourt should know of it – so far out of her sight now was that possibility she had once satisfied herself with, of speaking to him about Mrs. Glasher and her children, and making them rich amends. Any endurance seemed easier than the mortal humiliation of confessing that she knew all before she married him, and in marrying him had broken her word. For the reasons by which she had justified herself when the marriage tempted her, and all her easy arrangement of her future power over her husband to make him do better than he might be inclined to do, were now as futile as the burnt-out lights which set off a child's pageant. Her sense of being blame-worthy was exaggerated by a dread both definite and vague. The definite dread was lest the veil of secrecy should fall between her and Grandcourt, and give him the right to taunt her. With the reading of that letter had begun her husband's empire of fear.

And her husband all the while knew it. He had not, indeed, any distinct knowledge of her broken promise, and would not have rated highly the effect of that breach on her conscience; but he was aware not only of what Lush had told him about the meeting at the Whispering Stones, but also of Gwendolen's concealment as to the cause of her sudden illness. He felt sure that Lydia had enclosed some-thing with the diamonds, and that this something, what-ever it was, had at once created in Gwendolen a new repulsion for him and a reason for not daring to manifest it. He did not greatly mind, or feel as many men might have felt, that his hopes in marriage were blighted: he had wanted to marry Gwendolen, and he was not a man to repent. Why should a gentleman whose other relations in life are carried on without the luxury of sympathetic feel-ing, be supposed to require that kind of condiment in domestic life? What he chiefly felt was that a change had come over the conditions of his mastery, which, far from shaking it, might establish it the more thoroughly. And it was established. He judged that he had not married a simpleton unable to perceive the impossibility of escape, or to see alternative evils: he had married a girl who had spirit and pride enough not to make a fool of herself by forfeiting all the advantages of a position which had attracted her; and if she wanted pregnant hints to help her in making up her mind properly, he would take care not to withhold them.

Gwendolen, indeed, with all that gnawing trouble in her consciousness, had hardly for a moment dropped the sense that it was her part to bear herself with dignity, and appear what is called happy. In disclosure of disappointment or sorrow she saw nothing but a humiliation which would have been vinegar to her wounds. Whatever her husband might come at last to be to her, she meant to wear the yoke so as not to be pitied. For she did think of the coming years with presentiment: she was frightened at Grandcourt. The poor thing had passed from her girlish sauciness of superiority over this inert specimen of personal distinction into an amazed perception of her former ignorance about the possible mental attitude of a man towards the woman he sought in marriage – of her present ignorance as to what their life with each other might turn into. For novelty gives immeasurableness to fear, and fills the early time of all sad changes with phantoms of the future. Her little coquetries, voluntary or involuntary, had told on Grandcourt during courtship, and formed a medium of communication between them, showing him in the light of a creature such as she could understand and manage: but marriage had nullified all such interchange, and Grandcourt had become a blank uncertainty to her in everything but this, that he would do just what he willed, and that she had neither devices at her command to determine his will, nor any rational means of escaping it.

What had occurred between them about her wearing the diamonds was typical. One evening, shortly before they came to the Abbey, they were going to dine at

Brackenshaw Castle. Gwendolen had said to herself that she would never wear those diamonds: they had horrible words clinging and crawling about them, as from some bad dream, whose images lingered on the perturbed sense. She came down dressed in her white, with only a streak of gold and a pendant of emeralds, which Grandcourt had given her, round her neck, and little emerald stars in her ears.

Grandcourt stood with his back to the fire and looked at her as she entered.

'Am I altogether as you like?' she said, speaking rather gaily. She was not without enjoyment in this occasion of going to Brackenshaw Castle with her new dignities upon her, as men whose affairs are sadly involved will enjoy dining out among persons likely to be under a pleasant mistake about them.

'No,' said Grandcourt.

Gwendolen felt suddenly uncomfortable, wondering what was to come. She was not unprepared for some struggle about the diamonds; but suppose he were going to say, in low contemptuous tones, 'You are not in any way what I like.' It was very bad for her to be secretly hating him; but it would be much worse when he gave the first sign of hating her.

'Oh, mercy!' she exclaimed, the pause lasting till she could bear it no longer. 'How am I to alter myself?'

'Put on the diamonds,' said Grandcourt, looking straight at her with his narrow glance.

Gwendolen paused in her turn, afraid of showing any emotion, and feeling that nevertheless there was some change in her eyes as they met his. But she was obliged to answer, and said as indifferently as she could, 'Oh, please not. I don't think diamonds suit me.'

'What you think has nothing to do with it,' said Grandcourt, his *sotto voce* imperiousness seeming to have an evening quietude and finish, like his toilet. 'I wish you to wear the diamonds.'

'Pray excuse me; I like these emeralds,' said Gwendolen, frightened in spite of her preparation. That white hand of his which was touching his whisker was capable, she fancied, of clinging round her neck and threatening to throttle her; for her fear of him, mingling with the vague foreboding of some retributive calamity which hung about her life, had reached a superstitious point.

'Oblige me by telling me your reason for not wearing the diamonds when I desire it,' said Grandcourt. His eyes were still fixed upon her, and she felt her own eyes narrowing under them as if to shut out an entering pain.

Of what use was the rebellion within her? She could say nothing that would not hurt her worse than submission. Turning slowly and covering herself again, she went to her dressing-room. As she reached out the diamonds it occurred to her that her unwillingness to wear them might have already raised a suspicion in Grandcourt that she had some knowledge about them which he had not given her. She fancied that his eyes showed a delight in torturing her. How could she be defiant? She had nothing to say that would touch him – nothing but what would give him a more painful grasp on her consciousness.

'He delights in making the dogs and horses quail: that is half his pleasure in calling them his,' she said to herself, as she opened the jewel-case with a shivering sensation. 'It will come to be so with me; and I shall quail. What else is there for me? I will not say to the world, "Pity me."'

She was about to ring for her maid when she heard the door open behind her. It was Grandcourt who came in.

'You want some one to fasten them,' he said, coming towards her.

She did not answer, but simply stood still, leaving him to take out the ornaments and fasten them as he would. Doubtless he had been used to fasten them on some one else. With a bitter sort of sarcasm against herself, Gwendolen thought, 'What a privilege this is, to have robbed another woman of!'

'What makes you so cold?' said Grandcourt, when he had fastened the last ear-ring. 'Pray put plenty of furs on. I hate to see a woman come into a room looking frozen. If you are to appear as a bride at all, appear decently.'

This marital speech was not exactly persuasive, but it touched the quick of Gwendolen's pride and forced her to rally. The words of the bad dream crawled about the diamonds still, but only for her: to others they were brilliants that suited her perfectly, and Grandcourt inwardly observed that she answered to the rein.

'Oh yes, mamma, quite happy,' Gwendolen had said on her return to Diplow. 'Not at all disappointed in Ryelands. It is a much finer place than this – larger in every way. But don't you want some more money?'

'Did you not know that Mr. Grandcourt left me a letter on your wedding-day? I am to have eight hundred a-year. He wishes me to keep Offendene for the present, while you are at Diplow. But if there were some pretty cottage near the park at Ryelands we might live there without much expense, and I should have you most of the year, perhaps.'

'We must leave that to Mr. Grandcourt, mamma.'

'Oh, certainly. It is exceedingly handsome of him to say that he will pay the rent for Offendene till June. And we can go on very well – without any man-servant except Crane, just for out of doors. Our good Merry will stay with us and help me to manage everything. It is natural that Mr. Grandcourt should wish me to live in a good style of house in your neighbourhood, and I cannot decline. So he said nothing about it to you?'

'No; he wished me to hear it from you, I suppose.'

Gwendolen in fact had been very anxious to have some definite knowledge of what would be done for her mother, but at no moment since her marriage had she been able to overcome the difficulty of mentioning the subject to Grandcourt. Now, however, she had a sense of obligation which would not let her rest without saying to him, 'It is very good of you to provide for mamma. You took a great deal on yourself in marrying a girl who had nothing but relations belonging to her.'

Grandcourt was smoking, and only said carelessly, 'Of course I was not going to let her live like a gamekeeper's mother.'

'At least he is not mean about money,' thought Gwendolen, 'and mamma is the better off for my marriage.'

She often pursued the comparison between what might have been, if she had not married Grandcourt, and what actually was, trying to persuade herself that life generally was barren of satisfaction, and that if she had chosen differently she might now have been looking back with a regret as bitter as the feeling she was trying to argue away. Her mother's dullness, which used to irritate her, she was at present inclined to explain as the ordinary result of women's experience. True, she still said that she would 'manage differently from mamma;' but her management now only meant that she would carry her troubles with spirit, and let none suspect them. By-and-by she promised herself that she should get used to her heart-sores, and find excitements that would carry her through life, as a hard gallop carried her through some of the morning hours. There was gambling: she had heard stories at Leubronn of fashionable women who gambled in all sorts of ways. It seemed very flat to her at this distance, but perhaps if she began to gamble again, the passion might awake. Then there was the pleasure of producing an effect by her appearance in society: what did celebrated beauties do in town when their husbands could afford display? All men were fascinated by them: they had a perfect equipage and toilet, walked into public places, and bowed, and made the usual answers, and walked out again: perhaps they bought china, and practised accomplishments. If she could only feel a keen appetite for those pleasures – could only believe in pleasure as she used to do! Accomplishments had ceased to have the exciting quality of promising any pre-eminence to her; and as for fascinated gentlemen – adorers who might hover round her with languishment, and diversify married life with the romantic stir of mystery, passion, and danger which her French reading had given her some girlish notion of – they presented themselves to her imagination with the fatal circumstance that, instead of fascinating her in return, they were clad in her own weariness and disgust. The admiring male, rashly adjusting the expression of his features and the turn of his conversation to her supposed tastes, had always been an absurd object to her, and at present seemed rather detestable. Many courses are actually pursued – follies and sins both convenient and inconvenient – without pleasure or hope of pleasure; but to solace ourselves with imagining any course beforehand, there must be some foretaste of pleasure in the shape of appetite; and Gwendolen's appetite had sickened. Let her wander over the possibilities of her life as she would, an uncertain shadow dogged her. Her confidence in herself and her destiny had turned into remorse and dread; she trusted neither herself nor her future.

This hidden helplessness gave fresh force to the hold Deronda had from the first taken on her mind, as one who had an unknown standard by which he judged her. Had he some way of looking at things which might be a new footing for her – an inward safeguard against possible events which she dreaded as stored-up retribution? It is one of the secrets in that change of mental poise which has been fitly named conversion, that to many among us neither heaven nor earth has any revelation till some personality touches theirs with a peculiar influence, subduing them into receptiveness. It had been Gwendolen's habit to think of the persons around her as stale books, too familiar to be interesting. Deronda had lit up her attention with a sense of novelty: not by words only, but by imagined facts, his influence had entered into the current of that self-suspicion and self-blame which awakens a new consciousness.

'I wish he could know everything about me without my telling him,' was one of her thoughts, as she sat leaning over the end of a couch, supporting her head with her hand, and looking at herself in a mirror – not in admiration, but in a sad kind of companionship. 'I wish he knew that I am not so contemptible as he thinks me – that I am in deep trouble, and want to be something better if I could.' Without the aid of sacred ceremony or costume, her feelings had turned this man, only a few years older than herself, into a priest; a sort of trust less rare than the fidelity that guards it. Young reverence for one who is also young is the most coercive of all: there is the same level of temptation, and the higher motive is believed in as a fuller force – not suspected to be a mere residue from weary experience.

But the coercion is often stronger on the one who takes the reverence. Those who trust us educate us. And perhaps in that ideal consecration of Gwendolen's, some education was being prepared for Deronda.

XXXVI

'Rien ne pèse tant qu'un secret,
Le porter loin est difficile aux dames:
Et je sçais mesme sur ce fait
Bon nombre d'hommes qui sont femmes.'
— LA FONTAINE.

MEANWHILE Deronda had been fastened and led off by Mr. Vandernoodt, who wished for a brisker walk, a cigar, and a little gossip. Since we cannot tell a man his own secrets, the restraint of being in his company often breeds a desire to pair off in conversation with some more ignorant person, and Mr. Vandernoodt presently said –

'What a washed-out piece of cambric Grandcourt is! But if he is a favourite of yours, I withdraw the remark.'

'Not the least in the world,' said Deronda.

'I thought not. One wonders how he came to have a great passion again; and he must have had – to marry in this way. Though Lush, his old chum, hints that he married this girl out of obstinacy. By George! it was a very account-able obstinacy. A man might make up his mind to marry her without the stimulus of contradiction. But he must have made himself a pretty large drain of money, eh?'

'I know nothing of his affairs.'

'What! not of the other establishment he keeps up?'

'Diplow? Of course. He took that of Sir Hugo. But merely for the year.'

'No, no: not Diplow: Gadsmere. Sir Hugo knows, I'll answer for it.'

Deronda said nothing. He really began to feel some curiosity, but he foresaw that he should hear what Mr. Vandernoodt had to tell, without the condescension of asking.

'Lush would not altogether own to it, of course. He's a confidant and go-between of Grandcourt's. But I have it on the best authority. The fact is, there's another lady with four children at Gadsmere. She has had the upper hand of

him these ten years and more, and by what I can understand has it still – left her husband for him, and used to
travel with him everywhere. Her husband's dead now: I
found a fellow who was in the same regiment with him, and
knew this Mrs. Glasher before she took wing. A fiery dark-
eyed woman – a noted beauty at that time – he thought she
was dead. They say she has Grandcourt under her thumb
still, and it's a wonder he didn't marry her, for there's a very
fine boy, and I understand Grandcourt can do absolutely as
he pleases with the estates. Lush told me as much as that.'

'What right had he to marry this girl?' said Deronda,
with disgust.

Mr. Vandernoodt, adjusting the end of his cigar,
shrugged his shoulders and put out his lips.

'*She* can know nothing of it,' said Deronda, emphatically. But that positive statement was immediately followed by an inward query – 'Could she have known
anything of it?'

'It's rather a piquant picture,' said Mr. Vandernoodt –
'Grandcourt between two fiery women. For depend upon
it this light-haired one has plenty of devil in her. I formed
that opinion of her at Leubronn. It's a sort of Medea and
Creüsa business. Fancy the two meeting! Grandcourt is a
new kind of Jason: I wonder what sort of a part he'll make
of it. It's a dog's part at best. I think I hear Ristori now,
saying, "Jasone! Jasone!" These fine women generally get
hold of a stick.'

'Grandcourt can bite, I fancy,' said Deronda. 'He is no
stick.'

'No, no; I meant Jason. I can't quite make out
Grandcourt. But he's a keen fellow enough – uncommonly
well built too. And if he comes into all this property, the
estates will bear dividing. This girl, whose friends had
come to beggary, I understand, may think herself lucky
to get him. I don't want to be hard on a man because he gets
involved in an affair of that sort. But he might make
himself more agreeable. I was telling him a capital story
last night, and he got up and walked away in the middle. I

felt inclined to kick him. Do you suppose that is inattention or insolence, now?'

'Oh, a mixture. He generally observes the forms; but he doesn't listen much,' said Deronda. Then, after a moment's pause, he went on, 'I should think there must be some exaggeration or inaccuracy in what you have heard about this lady at Gadsmere.'

'Not a bit, depend upon it; it has all lain snug of late years. People have forgotten all about it. But there the nest is, and the birds are in it. And I know Grandcourt goes there. I have good evidence that he goes there. However, that's nobody's business but his own. The affair has sunk below the surface.'

'I wonder you could have learned so much about it,' said Deronda, rather drily.

'Oh, there are plenty of people who knew all about it; but such stories get packed away like old letters. They interest me. I like to know the manners of my time – contemporary gossip, not antediluvian. These Dryasdust fellows get a reputation by raking up some small scandal about Semiramis or Nitocris, and then we have a thousand and one poems written upon it by all the warblers big and little. But I don't care a straw about the *faux pas* of the mummies. You do, though. You are one of the historical men – more interested in a lady when she's got a rag face and skeleton toes peeping out. Does that flatter your imagination?'

'Well, if she had any woes in her love, one has the satisfaction of knowing that she's well out of them.'

'Ah, you are thinking of the Medea, I see.'

Deronda then chose to point to some giant oaks worth looking at in their bareness. He also felt an interest in this piece of contemporary gossip, but he was satisfied that Mr. Vandernoodt had no more to tell about it.

Since the early days when he tried to construct the hidden story of his own birth, his mind had perhaps never been so active in weaving probabilities about any private affair as it had now begun to be about Gwendolen's marriage. This unavowed relation of Grandcourt's, – could she have gained some knowledge of it, which caused her to shrink from the match – a shrinking finally overcome by the urgence of poverty? He could recall almost every word she had said to him, and in certain of these words he seemed to discern that she was conscious of having done some wrong – inflicted some injury. His own acute experience made him alive to the form of injury which might affect the unavowed children and their mother. Was Mrs. Grandcourt, under all her determined show of satisfaction, gnawed by a double, a treble-headed grief – self-reproach, disappointment, jealousy? He dwelt especially on all the slight signs of self-reproach: he was inclined to judge her tenderly, to excuse, to pity. He thought he had found a key now by which to interpret her more clearly: what magnifying of her misery might not a young creature get into who had wedded her fresh hopes to old secrets! He thought he saw clearly enough now why Sir Hugo had never dropped any hint of this affair to him; and immediately the image of this Mrs. Glasher became painfully associated with his own hidden birth. Gwendolen knowing of that woman and her children, marrying Grandcourt, and showing herself contented, would have been among the most repulsive of beings to him; but Gwendolen tasting the bitterness of remorse for having contributed to their injury was brought very near to his fellow-feeling. If it were so, she had got to a common plane of understanding with him on some difficulties of life which a woman is rarely able to judge of with any justice or generosity; for, according to precedent, Gwendolen's view of her position might easily have been no other than that her husband's marriage with her was his entrance on the path of virtue, while Mrs. Glasher represented his forsaken sin. And Deronda had naturally some resentment on behalf of the Hagars and Ishmaels.

Undeniably Deronda's growing solicitude about Gwendolen depended chiefly on her peculiar manner towards him; and I suppose neither man nor woman would be the better for an utter insensibility to such appeals. One sign

that his interest in her had changed its footing was that he
dismissed any caution against her being a coquette setting
snares to involve him in a vulgar flirtation, and determined
that he would not again evade any opportunity of talking
with her. He had shaken off Mr. Vandernoodt, and got into
a solitary corner in the twilight; but half an hour was long
enough to think of those possibilities in Gwendolen's position and state of mind; and on forming the determination
not to avoid her, he remembered that she was likely to be
at tea with the other ladies in the drawing-room. The
conjecture was true; for Gwendolen, after resolving not to
go down again for the next four hours, began to feel, at the
end of one, that in shutting herself up she missed all
chances of seeing and hearing, and that her visit would
only last two days more. She adjusted herself, put on her
little air of self-possession, and going down, made herself
resolutely agreeable. Only ladies were assembled, and
Lady Pentreath was amusing them with a description of a
drawing-room under the Regency, and the figure that was
cut by ladies and gentlemen in 1819, the year she was
presented – when Deronda entered.

'Shall I be acceptable?' he said. 'Perhaps I had better go
back and look for the others. I suppose they are in the
billiard-room.'

'No, no; stay where you are,' said Lady Pentreath. 'They
were all getting tired of me; let us hear what *you* have to
say.'

'That is rather an embarrassing appeal,' said Deronda,
drawing up a chair near Lady Mallinger's elbow at the
tea-table. 'I think I had better take the opportunity of
mentioning our songstress,' he added, looking at Lady
Mallinger, – 'unless you have done so.'

'Oh, the little Jewess!' said Lady Mallinger. 'No, I have
not mentioned her. It never entered my head that any one
here wanted singing lessons.'

'All ladies know some one else who wants singing lessons,' said Deronda. 'I have happened to find an exquisite
singer;' – here he turned to Lady Pentreath. 'She is living

with some ladies who are friends of mine – the mother and sisters of a man who was my chum at Cambridge. She was on the stage at Vienna; but she wants to leave that life, and maintain herself by teaching.'

'There are swarms of those people, aren't there?' said the old lady. 'Are her lessons to be very cheap or very expensive? Those are the two baits I know of.'

'There is another bait for those who hear her,' said Deronda. 'Her singing is something quite exceptional, I think. She has had such first-rate teaching – or rather first-rate instinct with her teaching – that you might imagine her singing all came by nature.'

'Why did she leave the stage, then?' said Lady Pentreath. 'I'm too old to believe in first-rate people giving up first-rate chances.'

'Her voice was too weak. It is a delicious voice for a room. You who put up with my singing of Schubert would be enchanted with hers,' said Deronda, looking at Mrs. Raymond. 'And I imagine she would not object to sing at private parties or concerts. Her voice is quite equal to that.'

'I am to have her in my drawing-room when we go up to town,' said Lady Mallinger. 'You shall hear her then. I have not heard her myself yet; but I trust Daniel's recommendation. I mean my girls to have lessons of her.'

'Is it a charitable affair?' said Lady Pentreath. 'I can't bear charitable music.'

Lady Mallinger, who was rather helpless in conversation, and felt herself under an engagement not to tell anything of Mirah's story, had an embarrassed smile on her face, and glanced at Deronda.

'It is a charity to those who want to have a good model of feminine singing,' said Deronda. 'I think everybody who has ears would benefit by a little improvement on the ordinary style. If you heard Miss Lapidoth' – here he looked at Gwendolen – 'perhaps you would revoke your resolution to give up singing.'

'I should rather think my resolution would be

confirmed,' said Gwendolen. 'I don't feel able to follow your advice of enjoying my own middlingness.'

'For my part,' said Deronda, 'people who do anything finely always inspirit me to try. I don't mean that they make me believe I can do it as well. But they make the thing, whatever it may be, seem worthy to be done. I can bear to think my own music not good for much, but the world would be more dismal if I thought music itself not good for much. Excellence encourages one about life generally; it shows the spiritual wealth of the world.'

'But then if we can't imitate it? – it only makes our own life seem the tamer,' said Gwendolen, in a mood to resent encouragement founded on her own insignificance.

'That depends on the point of view, I think,' said Deronda. 'We should have a poor life of it if we were reduced for all our pleasure to our own performances. A little private imitation of what is good is a sort of private devotion to it, and most of us ought to practise art only in the light of private study – preparation to understand and enjoy what the few can do for us. I think Miss Lapidoth is one of the few.'

'She must be a very happy person, don't you think?' said Gwendolen, with a touch of sarcasm, and a turn of her neck towards Mrs. Raymond.

'I don't know,' answered the independent lady; 'I must hear more of her before I said that.'

'It may have been a bitter disappointment to her that her voice failed her for the stage,' said Juliet Fenn, sympathetically.

'I suppose she's past her best, though,' said the deep voice of Lady Pentreath.

'On the contrary, she has not reached it,' said Deronda. 'She is barely twenty.'

'And very pretty,' interposed Lady Mallinger, with an amiable wish to help Deronda. 'And she has very good manners. I'm sorry she is a bigoted Jewess; I should not like it for anything else, but it doesn't matter in singing.'

'Well, since her voice is too weak for her to scream

much, I'll tell Lady Clementina to set her on my nine granddaughters,' said Lady Pentreath; 'and I hope she'll convince eight of them that they have not voice enough to sing anywhere but at church. My notion is, that many of our girls nowadays want lessons not to sing.'

'I have had my lessons in that,' said Gwendolen, looking at Deronda. 'You see Lady Pentreath is on my side.'

While she was speaking, Sir Hugo entered with some of the other gentlemen, including Grandcourt, and standing against the group at the low tea-table said –

'What imposition is Deronda putting on you ladies – slipping in among you by himself?'

'Wanting to pass off an obscurity on us as better than any celebrity,' said Lady Pentreath – 'a pretty singing Jewess who is to astonish these young people. You and I, who heard Catalani in her prime, are not so easily astonished.'

Sir Hugo listened with his good-humoured smile as he took a cup of tea from his wife, and then said, 'Well, you know, a Liberal is bound to think that there have been singers since Catalani's time.'

'Ah, you are younger than I am. I dare say you are one of the men who ran after Alcharisi. But she married off and left you all in the lurch.'

'Yes, yes; it's rather too bad when these great singers marry themselves into silence before they have a crack in their voices. And the husband is a public robber. I remember Leroux saying, "A man might as well take down a fine peal of church bells and carry them off to the steppes,"' said Sir Hugo, setting down his cup and turning away, while Deronda, who had moved from his place to make room for others, and felt that he was not in request, sat down a little apart. Presently he became aware that, in the general dispersion of the group, Gwendolen had extricated herself from the attentions of Mr. Vandernoodt and had walked to the piano, where she stood apparently examining the music which lay on the desk. Will any one be surprised at Deronda's concluding that she wished him to join her? Perhaps she wanted to make amends for the unpleasant tone of resistance with which she had met his recommendation of Mirah, for he had noticed that her first impulse often was to say what she afterwards wished to retract. He went to her side and said –

'Are you relenting about the music and looking for something to play or sing?'

'I am not looking for anything, but I *am* relenting,' said Gwendolen, speaking in a submissive tone.

'May I know the reason?'

'I should like to hear Miss Lapidoth and have lessons from her, since you admire her so much – that is, of course, when we go to town. I mean lessons in rejoicing at her excellence and my own deficiency,' said Gwendolen, turning on him a sweet open smile.

'I shall be really glad for you to see and hear her,' said Deronda, returning the smile in kind.

'Is she as perfect in everything else as in her music?'

'I can't vouch for that exactly. I have not seen enough of her. But I have seen nothing in her that I could wish to be different. She has had an unhappy life. Her troubles began in early childhood, and she has grown up among very painful surroundings. But I think you will say that no advantages could have given her more grace and truer refinement.'

'I wonder what sort of troubles hers were?'

'I have not any very precise knowledge. But I know that she was on the brink of drowning herself in despair.'

'And what hindered her?' said Gwendolen, quickly, looking at Deronda.

'Some ray or other came – which made her feel that she ought to live – that it was good to live,' he answered, quietly. 'She is full of piety and seems capable of submitting to anything when it takes the form of duty.'

'Those people are not to be pitied,' said Gwendolen, impatiently. 'I have no sympathy with women who are always doing right. I don't believe in their great sufferings.' Her fingers moved quickly among the edges of the music.

'It is true,' said Deronda, 'that the consciousness of

having done wrong is something deeper, more bitter. I suppose we faulty creatures can never feel so much for the irreproachable as for those who are bruised in the struggle with their own faults. It is a very ancient story, that of the lost sheep – but it comes up afresh every day.'

'That is a way of speaking – it is not acted on, it is not real,' said Gwendolen, bitterly. 'You admire Miss Lapidoth because you think her blameless, perfect. And you know you would despise a woman who had done something you thought very wrong.'

'That would depend entirely on her own view of what she had done,' said Deronda.

'You would be satisfied if she were very wretched, I suppose?' said Gwendolen, impetuously.

'No, not satisfied – full of sorrow for her. It was not a mere way of speaking. I did not mean to say that the finer nature is not more adorable; I meant that those who would be comparatively uninteresting beforehand may become worthier of sympathy when they do something that awakens in them a keen remorse. Lives are enlarged in different ways. I dare say some would never get their eyes opened if it were not for a violent shock from the consequences of their own actions. And when they are suffering in that way one must care for them more than for the comfortably self-satisfied.' Deronda forgot everything but his vision of what Gwendolen's experience had probably been, and urged by compassion let his eyes and voice express as much interest as they would.

Gwendolen had slipped on to the music-stool, and looked up at him with pain in her long eyes, like a wounded animal asking help.

'Are you persuading Mrs. Grandcourt to play to us, Dan?' said Sir Hugo, coming up and putting his hand on Deronda's shoulder with a gentle admonitory pinch.

'I cannot persuade myself,' said Gwendolen, rising.

Others had followed Sir Hugo's lead, and there was an end of any liability to confidences for that day. But the next was New Year's Eve; and a grand dance, to which the chief tenants were invited, was to be held in the picture-gallery above the cloister – the sort of entertainment in which numbers and general movement may create privacy. When Gwendolen was dressing, she longed, in remembrance of Leubronn, to put on the old turquoise necklace for her sole ornament; but she dared not offend her husband by appearing in that shabby way on an occasion when he would demand her utmost splendour. Determined to wear the memorial necklace somehow, she wound it thrice round her wrist and made a bracelet of it – having gone to her room to put it on just before the time of entering the ball-room.

It was always a beautiful scene, this dance on New Year's Eve, which had been kept up by family tradition as nearly in the old fashion as inexorable change would allow. Red carpet was laid down for the occasion; hothouse plants and evergreens were arranged in bowers at the extremities and in every recess of the gallery; and the old portraits stretching back through generations even to the pre-portraying period, made a piquant line of spectators. Some neighbouring gentry, major and minor, were invited; and it was certainly an occasion when a prospective master and mistress of Abbot's and King's Topping might see their future glory in an agreeable light, as a picturesque provincial supremacy with a rent-roll personified by the most prosperous looking tenants. Sir Hugo expected Grandcourt to feel flattered by being asked to the Abbey at a time which included this festival in honour of the family estate; but he also hoped that his own hale appearance might impress his successor with the probable length of time that would elapse before the succession came, and with the wisdom of preferring a good actual sum to a minor property that must be waited for. All present, down to the least important farmer's daughter, knew that they were to see 'young Grandcourt,' Sir Hugo's nephew, the presumptive heir and future baronet, now visiting the Abbey with his bride after an absence of many years; any coolness between uncle and nephew having, it was understood, given way to a friendly warmth. The bride opening the ball with Sir Hugo was necessarily the cynosure of all eyes; and less than a year before, if some magic mirror could have shown Gwendolen her actual position, she would have imagined herself moving in it with a glow of triumphant pleasure, conscious that she held in her hands a life full of favourable chances which her cleverness and spirit would enable her to make the best of. And now she was wondering that she could get so little joy out of the exaltation to which she had been suddenly lifted, away from the distasteful petty empire of her girlhood with its irksome lack of distinction and superfluity of sisters. She would have been glad to be even unreasonably elated, and to forget everything but the flattery of the moment; but she was like one courting sleep, in whom thoughts insist like wilful tormentors.

Wondering in this way at her own dullness, and all the while longing for an excitement that would deaden importunate aches, she was passing through files of admiring beholders in the country-dance with which it was traditional to open the ball, and was being generally regarded by her own sex as an enviable woman. It was remarked that she carried herself with a wonderful air, considering that she had been nobody in particular, and without a farthing to her fortune: if she had been a duke's daughter, or one of the royal princesses, she could not have taken the honours of the evening more as a matter of course. Poor Gwendolen! It would by-and-by become a sort of skill in which she was automatically practised, to bear this last great gambling loss with an air of perfect self-possession.

The next couple that passed were also worth looking at. Lady Pentreath had said, 'I shall stand up for one dance, but I shall choose my partner. Mr. Deronda, you are the youngest man; I mean to dance with you. Nobody is old enough to make a good pair with me. I must have a contrast.' And the contrast certainly set off the old lady to the utmost. She was one of those women who are never handsome till they are old, and she had had the wisdom to embrace the beauty of age as early as possible. What might have seemed harshness in her features when she was young, had turned now into a satisfactory strength of form and expression which defied wrinkles, and was set off by a crown of white hair; her well-built figure was well covered with black drapery, her ears and neck comfortably caressed with lace, showing none of those withered spaces which one would think it a pitiable condition of poverty to expose. She glided along gracefully enough, her dark eyes still with a mischievous smile in them as she observed the company. Her partner's young richness of tint against the flattened hues and rougher forms of her aged head had an effect something like that of a fine flower against a lichen-ous branch. Perhaps the tenants hardly appreciated this pair. Lady Pentreath was nothing more than a straight, active old lady: Mr. Deronda was a familiar figure regarded with friendliness; but if he had been the heir, it would have been regretted that his face was not as unmistakably English as Sir Hugo's.

Grandcourt's appearance when he came up with Lady Mallinger was not impeached with foreignness: still the satisfaction in it was not complete. It would have been matter of congratulation if one who had the luck to inherit two old family estates had had more hair, a fresher colour, and a look of greater animation; but that fine families dwindled off into females, and estates ran together into the single heirship of a mealy-complexioned male, was a tendency in things which seemed to be accounted for by a citation of other instances. It was agreed that Mr. Grandcourt could never be taken for anything but what he was – a born gentleman; and that, in fact, he looked like an heir. Perhaps the person least complacently disposed towards him at that moment was Lady Mallinger, to whom going in procession up this country-dance with Grandcourt was a blazonment of herself as the infelicitous wife who had produced nothing but daughters, little better than no children, poor dear things, except for her own fondness and for Sir Hugo's wonderful goodness to them. But such inward discomfort could not prevent the gentle lady from looking fair and stout to admiration, or her full blue eyes from glancing mildly at her neighbours. All the mothers and fathers held it a thousand pities that she had not had a fine boy, or even several – which might have been expected, to look at her when she was first married.

The gallery included only three sides of the quadrangle, the fourth being shut off as a lobby or corridor: one side was used for dancing, and the opposite side for the supper-table, while the intermediate part was less brilliantly lit, and fitted with comfortable seats. Later in the evening Gwendolen was in one of these seats, and Grandcourt was standing near her. They were not talking to each other: she was leaning backward in her chair, and he against the wall; and Deronda, happening to observe this, went up to ask her if she had resolved not to dance any more. Having himself been doing hard duty in this way among the guests, he thought he had earned the right to sink for a little while into the background, and he had spoken little to Gwendolen since their conversation at the piano the day before. Grandcourt's presence would only make it the easier to show that pleasure in talking to her even about trivialities which would be a sign of friend-liness; and he fancied that her face looked blank. A smile beamed over it as she saw him coming, and she raised herself from her leaning posture. Grandcourt had been grumbling at the ennui of staying so long in this stupid dance, and proposing that they should vanish: she had resisted on the ground of politeness – not without being a little frightened at the probability that he was silently angry with her. She had her reason for staying, though she had begun to despair of the opportunity for the sake of which she had put the old necklace on her wrist. But now at last Deronda had come.

'Yes; I shall not dance any more. Are you not glad?' she said, with some gaiety. 'You might have felt obliged humbly to offer yourself as a partner, and I feel sure you have danced more than you like already.'

'I will not deny that,' said Deronda, 'since you have danced as much as you like.'

'But will you take trouble for me in another way, and fetch me a glass of that fresh water?'

It was but a few steps that Deronda had to go for the water. Gwendolen was wrapped in the lightest, softest of white woollen burnouses, under which her hands were hidden. While he was gone she had drawn off her glove, which was finished with a lace ruffle, and when she put up her hand to take the glass and lifted it to her mouth, the necklace-bracelet, which in its triple winding adapted itself clumsily to her wrist, was necessarily conspicuous. Grandcourt saw it, and saw that it was attracting Deronda's notice.

'What is that hideous thing you have got on your wrist?' said the husband.

'That?' said Gwendolen, composedly, pointing to the turquoises, while she still held the glass; 'it is an old necklace that I like to wear. I lost it once, and some one found it for me.'

With that she gave the glass again to Deronda, who immediately carried it away, and on returning said, in order to banish any consciousness about the necklace –

'It is worth while for you to go and look out at one of the windows on that side. You can see the finest possible moonlight on the stone pillars and carving, and shadows waving across it in the wind.'

'I should like to see it. Will you go?' said Gwendolen, looking up at her husband.

He cast his eyes down at her, and saying, 'No, Deronda will take you,' slowly moved from his leaning attitude, and slowly walked away.

Gwendolen's face for a moment showed a fleeting vexation: she resented this show of indifference towards her. Deronda felt annoyed, chiefly for her sake; and with a quick sense that it would relieve her most to behave as if nothing peculiar had occurred, he said, 'Will you take my arm and go, while only servants are there?' He thought that he understood well her action in drawing his attention to the necklace: she wished him to infer that she had submitted her mind to rebuke – her speech and manner had from the first fluctuated towards that submission – and that she felt no lingering resentment. Her evident confidence in his interpretation of her appealed to him as a peculiar claim.

When they were walking together, Gwendolen felt as if the annoyance which had just happened had removed another film of reserve from between them, and she had more right than before to be as open as she wished. She did not speak, being filled with the sense of silent confidence, until they were in front of the window looking out on the moonlit court. A sort of bower had been made round the window, turning it into a recess. Quitting his arm, she folded her hands in her burnous, and pressed her brow against the glass. He moved slightly away, and held the lapels of his coat with his thumbs under the collar as his manner was: he had a wonderful power of standing perfectly still, and in that position reminded one sometimes of Dante's *spiriti magni con occhi tardi e gravi*. (Doubtless some of these danced in their youth, doubted of their own vocation, and found their own times too modern.) He abstained from remarking on the scene before them, fearing that any indifferent words might jar on her: already the calm light and shadow, the ancient steadfast forms, had aloofness enough from those inward troubles which he felt sure were agitating her. And he judged aright: she would have been impatient of polite conversation. The incidents of the last minute or two had receded behind former thoughts which she had imagined herself uttering to Deronda, and which now urged themselves to her lips. In a subdued voice, she said –

'Suppose I had gambled again, and lost the necklace again, what should you have thought of me?'

'Worse than I do now.'

'Then you are mistaken about me. You wanted me not to do that – not to make my gain out of another's loss in that way – and I have done a great deal worse.'

'I can imagine temptations,' said Deronda. 'Perhaps I am able to understand what you mean. At least I understand self-reproach.' In spite of preparation he was almost alarmed at Gwendolen's precipitancy of confidence towards him, in contrast with her habitual resolute concealment.

'What should you do if you were like me – feeling that you were wrong and miserable, and dreading everything to come?' It seemed that she was hurrying to make the utmost use of this opportunity to speak as she would.

'That is not to be amended by doing one thing only – but many,' said Deronda, decisively.

'What?' said Gwendolen, hastily, moving her brow from the glass and looking at him.

He looked full at her in return, with what she thought was severity. He felt that it was not a moment in which he must let himself be tender, and flinch from implying a hard opinion.

'I mean there are many thoughts and habits that may help us to bear inevitable sorrow. Multitudes have to bear it.'

She turned her brow to the window again, and said impatiently, 'You must tell me then what to think and what to do; else why did you not let me go on doing as I liked, and not minding? If I had gone on gambling I might have won again, and I might have got not to care for anything else. You would not let me do that. Why shouldn't I do as I like, and not mind? Other people do.' Poor Gwendolen's speech expressed nothing very clearly except her irritation.

'I don't believe you would ever get not to mind,' said Deronda, with deep-toned decision. 'If it were true that baseness and cruelty made an escape from pain, what difference would that make to people who can't be quite base or cruel? Idiots escape some pain; but you can't be an idiot. Some may do wrong to another without remorse; but suppose one does feel remorse? I believe you could never lead an injurious life – all reckless lives are injurious, pestilential – without feeling remorse.' Deronda's unconscious fervour had gathered as he went on: he was uttering thoughts which he had used for himself in moments of painful meditation.

'Then tell me what better I can do,' said Gwendolen, insistently.

'Many things. Look on other lives besides your own. See what their troubles are, and how they are borne. Try to care about something in this vast world besides the gratification of small selfish desires. Try to care for what is best in thought and action – something that is good apart from the accidents of your own lot.'

For an instant or two Gwendolen was mute. Then, again moving her brow from the glass, she said –

'You mean that I am selfish and ignorant.'

He met her fixed look in silence before he answered firmly –

'You will not go on being selfish and ignorant.'

She did not turn away her glance or let her eyelids fall, but a change came over her face – that subtle change in nerve and muscle which will sometimes give a childlike expression even to the elderly: it is the subsidence of self-assertion.

'Shall I lead you back?' said Deronda, gently, turning and offering her his arm again. She took it silently, and in that way they came in sight of Grandcourt, who was walking slowly near their former place. Gwendolen went up to him and said, 'I am ready to go now. Mr. Deronda will excuse us to Lady Mallinger.'

'Certainly,' said Deronda. 'Lord and Lady Pentreath disappeared some time ago.'

Grandcourt gave his arm in silent compliance, nodding over his shoulder to Deronda, and Gwendolen too only half turned to bow and say, 'Thanks.' The husband and wife left the gallery and paced the corridors in silence. When the door had closed on them in the boudoir Grandcourt threw himself into a chair and said, with undertoned peremptoriness, 'Sit down.' She, already in the expectation of something unpleasant, had thrown off her burnous with nervous unconsciousness, and immediately obeyed. Turning his eyes towards her, he began:

'Oblige me in future by not showing whims like a mad woman in a play.'

'What do you mean?' said Gwendolen.

'I suppose there is some understanding between you and Deronda about that thing you have on your wrist. If you have anything to say to him, say it. But don't carry on a telegraphing which other people are supposed not to see. It's damnably vulgar.'

'You can know all about the necklace,' said Gwendolen, her angry pride resisting the nightmare of fear.

'I don't want to know. Keep to yourself whatever you like.' Grandcourt paused between each sentence, and in each his speech seemed to become more preternaturally distinct in its inward tones. 'What I care to know, I shall know without your telling me. Only you will please to behave as becomes my wife. And not make a spectacle of yourself.'

'Do you object to my talking to Mr. Deronda?'

'I don't care two straws about Deronda, or any other conceited hanger-on. You may talk to him as much as you like. He is not going to take my place. You are my wife. And you will either fill your place properly – to the world and to me – or you will go to the devil.'

'I never intended anything but to fill my place properly,' said Gwendolen, with bitterest mortification in her soul.

'You put that thing on your wrist, and hid it from me till you wanted him to see it. Only fools go into that deaf and dumb talk, and think they're secret. You will understand that you are not to compromise yourself. Behave with dignity. That's all I have to say.'

With that last word Grandcourt rose, turned his back to the fire and looked down on her. She was mute. There was no reproach that she dared to fling at him in return for these insulting admonitions, and the very reason she felt them to be insulting was that their purport went with the most absolute dictate of her pride. What she would least like to incur was the making a fool of herself and being compromised. It was futile and irrelevant to try and explain that Deronda too had only been a monitor – the strongest of all monitors. Grandcourt was contemptuous, not jealous; contemptuously certain of all the subjection he cared for. Why could she not rebel, and defy him? She longed to do it. But she might as well have tried to defy the texture of her nerves and the palpitation of her heart. Her husband had a ghostly army at his back, that could close round her wherever she might turn. She sat in her splendid attire, like a white image of helplessness, and he seemed to gratify himself with looking at her. She could not even make a passionate exclamation, or throw up her arms, as she would have done in her maiden days. The sense of his scorn kept her still.

'Shall I ring?' he said, after what seemed to her a long while. She moved her head in assent, and after ringing he went to his dressing-room.

Certain words were gnawing within her. 'The wrong you have done me will be your own curse.' As he closed the door, the bitter tears rose, and the gnawing words provoked an answer: 'Why did you put your fangs into me and not into him?' It was uttered in a whisper, as the tears came up silently. But immediately she pressed her handkerchief against her eyes, and checked her tendency to sob.

The next day, recovered from the shuddering fit of this evening scene, she determined to use the charter which Grandcourt had scornfully given her, and to talk as much as she liked with Deronda; but no opportunities occurred, and any little devices she could imagine for creating them were rejected by her pride, which was now doubly active. Not towards Deronda himself – she was curiously free from alarm lest he should think her openness wanting

in dignity: it was part of his power over her that she
believed him free from all misunderstanding as to the
way in which she appealed to him: or rather, that he should
misunderstand her had never entered into her mind. But
the last morning came, and still she had never been able to
take up the dropped thread of their talk, and she was
without devices. She and Grandcourt were to leave at
three o'clock. It was too irritating that after a walk in the
grounds had been planned in Deronda's hearing, he did
not present himself to join in it. Grandcourt was gone with
Sir Hugo to King's Topping, to see the old manor-house;
others of the gentlemen were shooting; she was condemned to go and see the decoy and the water-fowl, and
everything else that she least wanted to see, with the
ladies, with old Lord Pentreath and his anecdotes, with
Mr. Vandernoodt and his admiring manners. The irritation
became too strong for her: without premeditation, she took
advantage of the winding road to linger a little out of sight,
and then set off back to the house, almost running when
she was safe from observation. She entered by a side door,
and the library was on her left hand; Deronda, she knew,
was often there; why might she not turn in there as well as
into any other room in the house? She had been taken
there expressly to see the illuminated family tree, and
other remarkable things – what more natural than that
she should like to look in again? The thing most to be
feared was that the room would be empty of Deronda, for
the door was ajar. She pushed it gently, and looked round
it. He was there, writing busily at a distant table, with his
back towards the door (in fact, Sir Hugo had asked him to
answer some constituents' letters which had become
pressing). An enormous log-fire, with the scent of russia
from the books, made the great room as warmly odorous as
a private chapel in which the censers have been swinging.
It seemed too daring to go in – too rude to speak and
interrupt him; yet she went in on the noiseless carpet,
and stood still for two or three minutes, till Deronda,
having finished a letter, pushed it aside for signature, and

threw himself back to consider whether there were any-thing else for him to do, or whether he could walk out for the chance of meeting the party which included Gwendolen, when he heard her voice saying, 'Mr Deronda.'

It was certainly startling. He rose hastily, turned round, and pushed away his chair with a strong expression of surprise.

'Am I wrong to come in?' said Gwendolen.

'I thought you were far on your walk,' said Deronda.

'I turned back,' said Gwendolen.

'Do you not intend to go out again? I could join you now, if you would allow me.'

'No; I want to say something, and I can't stay long,' said Gwendolen, speaking quickly in a subdued tone, while she walked forward and rested her arms and muff on the back of the chair he had pushed away from him. 'I want to tell you that it is really so – I can't help feeling remorse for having injured others. That was what I meant when I said that I had done worse than gamble again and pawn the necklace again – something more injurious, as you called it. And I can't alter it. I am punished, but I can't alter it. You said I could do many things. Tell me again. What should you do – what should you feel, if you were in my place?'

The hurried directness with which she spoke – the absence of all her little airs, as if she were only concerned to use the time in getting an answer that would guide her, made her appeal unspeakably touching.

Deronda said, – 'I should feel something of what you feel – deep sorrow.'

'But what would you try to do?' said Gwendolen, with urgent quickness.

'Order my life so as to make any possible amends, and keep away from doing any sort of injury again,' said Deronda, catching her sense that the time for speech was brief.

'But I can't – I can't; I must go on,' said Gwendolen, in a passionate loud whisper. 'I have thrust out others – I have

497

made my gain out of their loss – tried to make it – tried. And I must go on. I can't alter it.'

It was impossible to answer this instantaneously. Her words had confirmed his conjecture, and the situation of all concerned rose in swift images before him. His feeling for those who had been 'thrust out' sanctioned her remorse; he could not try to nullify it, yet his heart was full of pity for her. But as soon as he could he answered – taking up her last words –

'That is the bitterest of all – to wear the yoke of our own wrong-doing. But if you submitted to that, as men submit to maiming or a lifelong incurable disease? – and made the unalterable wrong a reason for more effort towards a good that may do something to counterbalance the evil? One who has committed irremediable errors may be scourged by that consciousness into a higher course than is common. There are many examples. Feeling what it is to have spoiled one life may well make us long to save other lives from being spoiled.'

'But you have not wronged any one, or spoiled their lives,' said Gwendolen, hastily. 'It is only others who have wronged *you*.'

Deronda coloured slightly, but said immediately – 'I suppose our keen feeling for ourselves might end in giving us a keen feeling for others, if, when we are suffering acutely, we were to consider that others go through the same sharp experience. That is a sort of remorse before commission. Can't you understand that?'

'I think I do – now,' said Gwendolen. 'But you were right – I *am* selfish. I have never thought much of any one's feelings, except my mother's. I have not been fond of people. – But what can I do?' she went on, more quickly. 'I must get up in the morning and do what every one else does. It is all like a dance set beforehand. I seem to see all that can be – and I am tired and sick of it. And the world is all confusion to me' – she made a gesture of disgust. 'You say I am ignorant. But what is the good of trying to know more, unless life were worth more?'

'This good,' said Deronda promptly, with a touch of indignant severity, which he was inclined to encourage as his own safeguard; 'life *would* be worth more to you: some real knowledge would give you an interest in the world beyond the small drama of personal desires. It is the curse of your life – forgive me – of so many lives, that all passion is spent in that narrow round, for want of ideas and sympathies to make a larger home for it. Is there any single occupation of mind that you care about with passionate delight or even independent interest?'

Deronda paused, but Gwendolen, looking startled and thrilled as by an electric shock, said nothing, and he went on more insistently –

'I take what you said of music for a small example – it answers for all larger things – you will not cultivate it for the sake of a private joy in it. What sort of earth or heaven would hold any spiritual wealth in it for souls pauperized by inaction? If one firmament has no stimulus for our attention and awe, I don't see how four would have it. We should stamp every possible world with the flatness of our own inanity – which is necessarily impious, without faith or fellowship. The refuge you are needing from personal trouble is the higher, the religious life, which holds an enthusiasm for something more than our own appetites and vanities. The few may find themselves in it simply by an elevation of feeling; but for us who have to struggle for our wisdom, the higher life must be a region in which the affections are clad with knowledge.'

The half-indignant remonstrance that vibrated in Deronda's voice came, as often happens, from the habit of inward argument with himself rather than from severity towards Gwendolen; but it had a more beneficent effect on her than any soothings. Nothing is feebler than the indolent rebellion of complaint; and to be roused into self-judgment is comparative activity. For the moment she felt like a shaken child – shaken out of its wailings into awe, and she said humbly –

'I will try. I will think.'

They both stood silent for a minute, as if some third presence had arrested them, – for Deronda, too, was under that sense of pressure which is apt to come when our own winged words seem to be hovering around us, – till Gwendolen began again –

'You said affection was the best thing, and I have hardly any – none about me. If I could, I would have mamma; but that is impossible. Things have changed to me so – in such a short time. What I used not to like, I long for now. I think I am almost getting fond of the old things now they are gone.' Her lip trembled.

'Take the present suffering as a painful letting in of light,' said Deronda, more gently. 'You are conscious of more beyond the round of your own inclinations – you know more of the way in which your life presses on others, and their life on yours. I don't think you could have escaped the painful process in some form or other.'

'But it is a very cruel form,' said Gwendolen, beating her foot on the ground with returning agitation. 'I am frightened at everything. I am frightened at myself. When my blood is fired I can do daring things – take any leap; but that makes me frightened at myself.' She was looking at nothing outside her; but her eyes were directed toward the window, away from Deronda, who, with quick comprehension, said –

'Turn your fear into a safeguard. Keep your dread fixed on the idea of increasing that remorse which is so bitter to you. Fixed meditation may do a great deal towards defining our longing or dread. We are not always in a state of strong emotion, and when we are calm we can use our memories and gradually change the bias of our fear, as we do our tastes. Take your fear as a safeguard. It is like quickness of hearing. It may make consequences passionately present to you. Try to take hold of your sensibility, and use it as if it were a faculty, like vision.' Deronda uttered each sentence more urgently; he felt as if he were seizing a faint chance of rescuing her from some indefinite danger.

'Yes, I know; I understand what you mean,' said Gwendolen, in her loud whisper, not turning her eyes, but lifting up her small gloved hand and waving it in deprecation of the notion that it was easy to obey that advice. 'But if feelings rose – there are some feelings – hatred and anger – how can I be good when they keep rising? And if there came a moment when I felt stifled and could bear it no longer—' She broke off, and with agitated lips looked at Deronda, but the expression on his face pierced her with an entirely new feeling. He was under the baffling difficulty of discerning, that what he had been urging on her was thrown into the pallid distance of mere thought before the outburst of her habitual emotion. It was as if he saw her drowning while his limbs were bound. The pained compassion which was spread over his features as he watched her, affected her with a compunction unlike any she had felt before, and in a changed imploring tone she said –

'I am grieving you. I am ungrateful. You *can* help me. I will think of everything. I will try. Tell me – it will not be a pain to you that I have dared to speak of my trouble to you? You began it, you know, when you rebuked me.' There was a melancholy smile on her lips as she said that, but she added more entreatingly, 'It will not be a pain to you?'

'Not if it does anything to save you from an evil to come,' said Deronda, with strong emphasis; 'otherwise, it will be a lasting pain.'

'No – no – it shall not be. It may be – it shall be better with me because I have known you.' She turned immediately, and quitted the room.

When she was on the first landing of the staircase, Sir Hugo passed across the hall on his way to the library, and saw her. Grandcourt was not with him.

Deronda, when the baronet entered, was standing in his ordinary attitude, grasping his coat collar, with his back to the table, and with that indefinable expression by which we judge that a man is still in the shadow of a scene

501

which he has just gone through. He moved, however, and began to arrange the letters.

'Has Mrs. Grandcourt been in here?' said Sir Hugo.

'Yes, she has.'

'Where are the others?'

'I believe she left them somewhere in the grounds.'

After a moment's silence, in which Sir Hugo looked at a letter without reading it, he said, 'I hope you are not playing with fire, Dan – you understand me.'

'I believe I do, sir,' said Deronda, after a slight hesitation, which had some repressed anger in it. 'But there is nothing answering to your metaphor – no fire, and therefore no chance of scorching.'

Sir Hugo looked searchingly at him, and then said, 'So much the better. For between ourselves, I fancy there may be some hidden gunpowder in that establishment.'

Aspern.	Pardon, my lord – I speak for Sigismund.
Fronsberg.	For him? Oh, ay – for him I always hold
	A pardon safe in bank, sure he will draw
	Sooner or later on me. What his need?
	Mad project broken? fine mechanic wings
	That would not fly? durance, assault on watch,
	Bill for Epernay, not a crust to eat?
Aspern.	Oh, none of these, my lord; he has escaped
	From Circe's herd, and seeks to win the love
	Of your fair ward Cecilia; but would win
	First your consent. You frown.
Fronsberg.	Distinguish words.
	I said I held a pardon, not consent.

IN spite of Deronda's reasons for wishing to be in town again – reasons in which his anxiety for Mirah was blent with curiosity to know more of the enigmatic Mordecai – he did not manage to go up before Sir Hugo, who preceded his family that he might be ready for the opening of Parliament on the 6th of February. Deronda took up his quarters in Park Lane, aware that his chambers were sufficiently tenanted by Hans Meyrick. This was what he expected; but he found other things not altogether according to his expectations.

Most of us remember Retzsch's drawing of destiny in the shape of Mephistopheles playing at chess with man for his soul, a game in which we may imagine the clever adversary making a feint of unintended moves so as to set the beguiled mortal on carrying his defensive pieces away from the true point of attack. The fiend makes preparation his favourite object of mockery, that he may fatally persuade us against our best safeguard: he even meddles so far as to suggest our taking out waterproofs when he is well aware the sky is going to clear, foreseeing that the imbecile will turn this delusion into a prejudice against waterproofs instead of giving a closer study to the weather-signs. It is a peculiar test of a man's metal when, after he has painfully adjusted himself to what seems a wise provision, he finds all his mental precaution a little beside the mark, and his excellent intentions no better than miscalculated dovetails, accurately cut from a wrong starting-point. His magnanimity has got itself ready to meet misbehaviour, and finds quite a different call upon it. Something of this kind happened to Deronda.

His first impression was one of pure pleasure and amusement at finding his sitting-room transformed into an *atelier* strewed with miscellaneous drawings and with the contents of two chests from Rome, the lower half of the windows darkened with baize, and the blond Hans in his weird youth as the presiding genius of the littered place – his hair longer than of old, his face more whimsically creased, and his high voice as usual getting higher under the excitement of rapid talk. The friendship of the two had been kept up warmly since the memorable Cambridge time, not only by correspondence but by little episodes of companionship abroad and in England, and the original relation of confidence on one side and indulgence on the other had been developed in practice, as is wont to be the case where such spiritual borrowing and lending has been well begun.

'I knew you would like to see my casts and antiquities,' said Hans, after the first hearty greetings and inquiries, 'so I didn't scruple to unlade my chests here. But I've found two rooms at Chelsea not many hundred yards from my mother and sisters, and I shall soon be ready to hang out there – when they've scraped the walls and put in some new lights. That's all I'm waiting for. But you see I don't wait to begin work: you can't conceive what a great fellow I'm going to be. The seed of immortality has sprouted within me.'

'Only a fungoid growth, I dare say – a crowing disease in the lungs,' said Deronda, accustomed to treat Hans in brotherly fashion. He was walking towards some drawings propped on the ledge of his bookcases; five rapidly-sketched heads – different aspects of the same face. He stood at a convenient distance from them, without making any remark. Hans, too, was silent for a minute, took up his palette and began touching the picture on his easel.

'What do you think of them?' he said at last.

'The full face looks too massive; otherwise the like-nesses are good,' said Deronda, more coldly than was usual with him.

'No, it is not too massive,' said Hans, decisively. 'I have noted that. There is always a little surprise when one passes from the profile to the full face. But I shall enlarge her scale for Berenice. I am making a Berenice series – look at the sketches along there – and now I think of it, you are just the model I want for the Agrippa.' Hans, still with pencil and palette in hand, had moved to Deronda's side while he said this, but he added hastily, as if conscious of a mistake, 'No, no, I forgot; you don't like sitting for your portrait, confound you! However, I've picked up a capital Titus. There are to be five in the series. The first is Berenice clasping the knees of Gessius Florus and beseeching him to spare her people; I've got that on the easel. Then this, where she is standing on the Xystus with Agrippa, entreating the people not to injure themselves by resistance.'

'Agrippa's legs will never do,' said Deronda.

'The legs are good realistically,' said Hans, his face creasing drolly; 'public men are often shaky about the legs – "Their legs, the emblem of their various thought," as somebody says in the *Rehearsal*.'

'But these are as impossible as the legs of Raphael's Alcibiades,' said Deronda.

'Then they are good ideally,' said Hans. 'Agrippa's legs were possibly bad; I idealize that and make them imposs-ibly bad. Art, my Eugenius, must intensify. But never mind the legs now: the third sketch in the series is Berenice exulting in the prospect of being Empress of Rome, when the news has come that Vespasian is declared Emperor and her lover Titus his successor.'

'You must put a scroll in her mouth, else people will not understand that. You can't tell that in a picture.'

'It will make them feel their ignorance then – an excellent æsthetic effect. The fourth is, Titus sending Berenice away from Rome after she has shared his palace for ten years – both reluctant, both sad – *invitus invitam*, as Suetonius hath it. I've found a model for the Roman brute.'

'Shall you make Berenice look fifty? She must have been that.'

'No, no; a few mature touches to show the lapse of time. Dark-eyed beauty wears well, hers particularly. But now, here is the fifth: Berenice seated lonely on the ruins of Jerusalem. That is pure imagination. That is what ought to have been – perhaps was. Now, see how I tell a pathetic negative. Nobody knows what became of her: – that is finely indicated by the series coming to a close. There is no sixth picture.' Here Hans pretended to speak with a gasping sense of sublimity, and drew back his head with a frown, as if looking for a like impression on Deronda. 'I break off in the Homeric style. The story is chipped off, so to speak, and passes with a ragged edge into nothing – *le néant*; can anything be more sublime, especially in French? The vulgar would desire to see her corpse and burial – perhaps her will read and her linen distributed. But now come and look at this on the easel. I have made some way there.'

'That beseeching attitude is really good,' said Deronda, after a moment's contemplation. 'You have been very industrious in the Christmas holidays; for I suppose you have taken up the subject since you came to London.' Neither of them had yet mentioned Mirah.

'No,' said Hans, putting touches to his picture, 'I made up my mind to the subject before. I take that lucky chance for an augury that I am going to burst on the world as a great painter. I saw a splendid woman in the Trastevere – the grandest women there are half Jewesses – and she set me hunting for a fine situation of a Jewess at Rome. Like other men of vast learning, I ended by taking what lay on the surface. I'll show you a sketch of the Trasteverina's head when I can lay my hands on it.'

'I should think she would be a more suitable model for Berenice,' said Deronda, not knowing exactly how to express his discontent.

'Not a bit of it. The model ought to be the most beautiful Jewess in the world, and I have found her.'

'Have you made yourself sure that she would like to figure in that character? I should think no woman would be more abhorrent to her. Does she quite know what you are doing?'

'Certainly. I got her to throw herself precisely into this attitude. Little mother sat for Gessius Florus, and Mirah clasped her knees.' – Here Hans went a little way off and looked at the effect of his touches.

'I dare say she knows nothing about Berenice's history,' said Deronda, feeling more indignation than he would have been able to justify.

'Oh yes, she does – ladies' edition. Berenice was a fervid patriot, but was beguiled by love and ambition into attaching herself to the arch enemy of her people. Whence the Nemesis. Mirah takes it as a tragic parable, and cries to think what the penitent Berenice suffered as she wandered back to Jerusalem and sat desolate amidst desolation. That was her own phrase. I couldn't find in my heart to tell her I invented that part of the story.'

'Show me your Trasteverina,' said Deronda, chiefly in order to hinder himself from saying something else.

'Shall you mind turning over that folio?' said Hans. 'My studies of heads are all there. But they are in confusion. You will perhaps find her next to a crop-eared undergraduate.'

After Deronda had been turning over the drawings a minute or two, he said –

'These seem to be all Cambridge heads and bits of country. Perhaps I had better begin at the other end.'

'No; you'll find her about the middle. I emptied one folio into another.'

'Is this one of your undergraduates?' said Deronda, holding up a drawing. 'It's an unusually agreeable face.'

'That? Oh, that's a man named Gascoigne – Rex Gascoigne. An uncommonly good fellow; his upper lip, too, is good. I coached him before he got his scholarship. He ought to have taken honours last Easter. But he was ill, and has had to stay up another year. I must look him up. I want to know how he's going on.'

'Here she is, I suppose,' said Deronda, holding up the sketch of the Trasteverina.

'Ah,' said Hans, looking at it rather contemptuously, 'too coarse. I was unregenerate then.'

Deronda was silent while he closed the folio, leaving the Trasteverina outside. Then grasping his coat collar, and turning towards Hans, he said, 'I dare say my scruples are excessive, Meyrick, but I must ask you to oblige me by giving up this notion.'

Hans threw himself into a tragic attitude, and screamed, 'What! my series – my immortal Berenice series? Think of what you are saying, man – destroying, as Milton says, not a life but an immortality. Wait before you answer, that I may deposit the implements of my art and be ready to uproot my hair.'

Here Hans laid down his pencil and palette, threw himself backward into a great chair, and hanging limply over the side, shook his long hair half over his face, lifted his hooked fingers on each side his head, and looked up with comic terror at Deronda, who was obliged to smile as he said –

'Paint as many Berenices as you like, but I wish you could feel with me – perhaps you will, on reflection – that you should choose another model.'

'Why?' said Hans, standing up, and looking serious again.

'Because she may get into such a position that her face is likely to be recognized. Mrs. Meyrick and I are anxious for her that she should be known as an admirable singer. It is right, and she wishes it, that she should make herself independent. And she has excellent chances. One good introduction is secured already. And I am going to speak to

Klesmer. Her face may come to be very well known, and –
well, it is useless to attempt to explain, unless you feel as
I do. I believe that if Mirah saw the circumstances clearly,
she would strongly object to being exhibited in this way –
to allowing herself to be used as a model for a heroine of
this sort.'

As Hans stood with his thumbs in the belt of his blouse
listening to this speech, his face showed a growing surprise
melting into amusement, that at last would have its way in
an explosive laugh; but seeing that Deronda looked
gravely offended, he checked himself to say, 'Excuse my
laughing, Deronda. You never gave me an advantage over
you before. If it had been about anything but my own
pictures, I should have swallowed every word, because
you said it. And so you actually believe that I should get
my five pictures hung on the line in a conspicuous position,
and carefully studied by the public? Zounds, man! cider-
cup and conceit never gave me half such a beautiful dream.
My pictures are likely to remain as private as the utmost
hypersensitiveness could desire.'

Hans turned to paint again as a way of filling up awkward pauses. Deronda stood perfectly still, recognizing his
mistake as to publicity, but also conscious that his repugnance was not much diminished. He was the reverse of
satisfied either with himself or with Hans; but the power of
being quiet carries a man well through moments of embarrassment. Hans had a reverence for his friend which made
him feel a sort of shyness at Deronda's being in the wrong;
but it was not in his nature to give up anything readily,
though it were only a whim – or rather, especially if it were
a whim, and he presently went on, painting the while –

'But even supposing I had a public rushing after my
pictures as if they were a railway series including nurses,
babies, and bonnet-boxes, I can't see any justice in your
objection. Every painter worth remembering has painted
the face he admired most, as often as he could. It is a part
of his soul that goes out into his pictures. He diffuses
its influence in that way. He puts what he hates into a

caricature. He puts what he adores into some sacred, heroic form. If a man could paint the woman he loves a thousand times as the *Stella Maris* to put courage into the sailors on board a thousand ships, so much the more honour to her. Isn't that better than painting a piece of staring immodesty and calling it by a worshipful name?'

'Every objection can be answered if you take broad ground enough, Hans: no special question of conduct can be properly settled in that way,' said Deronda, with a touch of peremptoriness. 'I might admit all your generalities, and yet be right in saying you ought not to publish Mirah's face as a model for Berenice. But I give up the question of publicity. I was unreasonable there.' Deronda hesitated a moment. 'Still, even as a private affair, there might be good reasons for your not indulging yourself too much in painting her from the point of view you mention. You must feel that her situation at present is a very delicate one; and until she is in more independence, she should be kept as carefully as a bit of Venetian glass, for fear of shaking her out of the safe place she is lodged in. Are you quite sure of your own discretion? Excuse me, Hans. My having found her binds me to watch over her. Do you understand me?'

'Perfectly,' said Hans, turning his face into a good-humoured smile. 'You have the very justifiable opinion of me that I am likely to shatter all the glass in my way, and break my own skull into the bargain. Quite fair. Since I got into the scrape of being born, everything I have liked best has been a scrape either for myself or somebody else. Everything I have taken to heartily has somehow turned into a scrape. My painting is the last scrape; and I shall be all my life getting out of it. You think now I shall get into a scrape at home. No; I am regenerate. You think I must be over head and ears in love with Mirah. Quite right; so I am. But you think I shall scream and plunge and spoil everything. There you are mistaken – excusably, but transcendently mistaken. I have undergone baptism by immersion. Awe takes care of me. Ask the little mother.'

'You don't reckon a hopeless love among your scrapes, then?' said Deronda, whose voice seemed to get deeper as Hans's went higher.

'I don't mean to call mine hopeless,' said Hans, with provoking coolness, laying down his tools, thrusting his thumbs into his belt, and moving away a little, as if to contemplate his picture more deliberately.

'My dear fellow, you are only preparing misery for yourself,' said Deronda, decisively. 'She would not marry a Christian, even if she loved him. Have you heard her – of course you have – heard her speak of her people and her religion?'

'That can't last,' said Hans. 'She will see no Jew who is tolerable. Every male of that race is insupportable, – "insupportably advancing" – his nose.'

'She may rejoin her family. That is what she longs for. Her mother and brother are probably strict Jews.'

'I'll turn proselyte if she wishes it,' said Hans, with a shrug and a laugh.

'Don't talk nonsense, Hans. I thought you professed a serious love for her,' said Deronda, getting heated.

'So I do. You think it desperate, but I don't.'

'I know nothing; I can't tell what has happened. We must be prepared for surprises. But I can hardly imagine a greater surprise to me than that there should have seemed to be anything in Mirah's sentiments for you to found a romantic hope on.' Deronda felt that he was too contemptuous.

'I don't found my romantic hopes on a woman's sentiments,' said Hans, perversely inclined to be the merrier when he was addressed with gravity. 'I go to science and philosophy for my romance. Nature designed Mirah to fall in love with me. The amalgamation of races demands it – the mitigation of human ugliness demands it – the affinity of contrasts assures it. I am the utmost contrast to Mirah – a bleached Christian, who can't sing two notes in tune. Who has a chance against me?'

'I see now; it was all *persiflage*. You don't mean a word of what you say, Meyrick,' said Deronda, laying his hand on Meyrick's shoulder, and speaking in a tone of cordial relief. 'I was a wiseacre to answer you seriously.'

'Upon my honour I do mean it, though,' said Hans, facing round and laying his left hand on Deronda's shoulder, so that their eyes fronted each other closely. 'I am at the confessional. I meant to tell you as soon as you came. My mother says you are Mirah's guardian, and she thinks herself responsible to you for every breath that falls on Mirah in her house. Well, I love her – I worship her – I won't despair – I mean to deserve her.'

'My dear fellow, you can't do it,' said Deronda, quickly.

'I should have said, I mean to try.'

'You can't keep your resolve, Hans. You used to resolve what you would do for your mother and sisters.'

'You have a right to reproach me, old fellow,' said Hans, gently.

'Perhaps I am ungenerous,' said Deronda, not apologetically, however. 'Yet it can't be ungenerous to warn you that you are indulging mad quixotic expectations.'

'Who will be hurt but myself, then?' said Hans, putting out his lip. 'I am not going to say anything to her unless I felt sure of the answer. I dare not ask the oracles: I prefer a cheerful caliginosity, as Sir Thomas Browne might say. I would rather run my chance there and lose, than be sure of winning anywhere else. And I don't mean to swallow the poison of despair, though you are disposed to thrust it on me. I am giving up wine, so let me get a little drunk on hope and vanity.'

'With all my heart, if it will do you any good,' said Deronda, loosing Hans's shoulder, with a little push. He made his tone kindly, but his words were from the lip only. As to his real feeling he was silenced.

He was conscious of that peculiar irritation which will sometimes befall the man whom others are inclined to trust as a mentor – the irritation of perceiving that he is supposed to be entirely off the same plane of desire and temptation as those who confess to him. Our guides, we pretend, must be sinless: as if those were not often the best teachers who only yesterday got corrected for their mistakes. Throughout their friendship Deronda had been used to Hans's egotism, but he had never before felt intolerant of it: when Hans, habitually pouring out his own feelings and affairs, had never cared for any detail in return, and, if he chanced to know any, had soon forgotten it, Deronda had been inwardly as well as outwardly indulgent – nay, satisfied. But now he noted with some indignation, all the stronger because it must not be betrayed, Hans's evident assumption that for any danger of rivalry or jealousy in relation to Mirah, Deronda was as much out of the question as the angel Gabriel. It is one thing to be resolute in placing oneself out of the question, and another to endure that others should perform that exclusion for us. He had expected that Hans would give him trouble: what he had not expected was that the trouble would have a strong element of personal feeling. And he was rather ashamed that Hans's hopes caused him uneasiness in spite of his well-warranted conviction that they would never be fulfilled. They had raised an image of Mirah changing; and however he might protest that the change would not happen, the protest kept up the unpleasant image. Altogether, poor Hans seemed to be entering into Deronda's experience in a disproportionate manner – going beyond his part of rescued prodigal, and rousing a feeling quite distinct from compassionate affection.

When Deronda went to Chelsea he was not made as comfortable as he ought to have been by Mrs. Meyrick's evident release from anxiety about the beloved but incalculable son. Mirah seemed livelier than before, and for the first time he saw her laugh. It was when they were talking of Hans, he being naturally the mother's first topic. Mirah wished to know if Deronda had seen Mr. Hans going through a sort of character piece without changing his dress.

'He passes from one figure to another as if he were a bit of flame, where you fancied the figures without seeing them,' said Mirah, full of her subject; 'he is so wonderfully quick. I used never to like comic things on the stage – they were dwelt on too long; but all in one minute Mr. Hans makes himself a blind bard, and then Rienzi addressing the Romans, and then an opera-dancer, and then a desponding young gentleman – I am sorry for them all, and yet I laugh, all in one' – here Mirah gave a little laugh that might have entered into a song.

'We hardly thought that Mirah could laugh till Hans came,' said Mrs. Meyrick, seeing that Deronda, like herself, was observing the pretty picture.

'Hans seems in great force just now,' said Deronda, in a tone of congratulation. 'I don't wonder at his enlivening you.'

'He's been just perfect ever since he came back,' said Mrs. Meyrick, keeping to herself the next clause – 'if it will but last.'

'It is a great happiness,' said Mirah, 'to see the son and brother come into this dear home. And I hear them all talk about what they did together when they were little. That seems like heaven, to have a mother and brother who talk in that way. I have never had it.'

'Nor I,' said Deronda, involuntarily.

'No?' said Mirah, regretfully. 'I wish you had. I wish you had had every good.' The last words were uttered with a serious ardour as if they had been part of a litany, while her eyes were fixed on Deronda, who with his elbow on the back of his chair was contemplating her by the new light of the impression she had made on Hans, and the possibility of her being attracted by that extraordinary contrast. It was no more than what had happened on each former visit of his, that Mirah appeared to enjoy speaking of what she felt very much as a little girl fresh from school pours forth spontaneously all the long-repressed chat for which she has found willing ears. For the first time in her life Mirah was among those whom she entirely trusted, and her original visionary impression that Deronda was a divinely-sent messenger hung about his image still, stirring always anew the disposition to reliance and openness. It was in this way she took what might have been the injurious flattery of admiring attention into which her helpless dependence had been suddenly transformed: every one around her watched for her looks and words, and the effect on her was simply that of having passed from a stifling imprisonment into an exhilarating air which made speech and action a delight. To her mind it was all a gift from others' goodness. But that word of Deronda's implying that there had been some lack in his life which might be compared with anything she had known in hers, was an entirely new inlet of thought about him. After her first impression of sorrowful surprise she went on –

'But Mr. Hans said yesterday that you thought so much of others you hardly wanted anything for yourself. He told us a wonderful story of Bouddha giving himself to the famished tigress to save her and her little ones from starving. And he said you were like Bouddha. That is what we all imagine of you.'

'Pray don't imagine that,' said Deronda, who had lately been finding such suppositions rather exasperating. 'Even if it were true that I thought so much of others, it would not follow that I had no wants for myself. When Bouddha let the tigress eat him he might have been very hungry himself.'

'Perhaps if he was starved he would not mind so much about being eaten,' said Mab, shyly.

'Please don't think that, Mab; it takes away the beauty of the action,' said Mirah.

'But if it were true, Mirah?' said the rational Amy, having a half-holiday from her teaching; 'you always take what is beautiful as if it were true.'

'So it is,' said Mirah, gently. 'If people have thought what is the most beautiful and the best thing, it must be true. It is always there.'

'Now, Mirah, what *do* you mean?' said Amy.

'I understand her,' said Deronda, coming to the rescue. 'It is a truth in thought though it may never have been carried out in action. It lives as an idea. Is that it?' He turned to Mirah, who was listening with a blind look in her lovely eyes.

'It must be that, because you understand me, but I cannot quite explain,' said Mirah, rather abstractedly – still searching for some expression.

'But *was* it beautiful for Bouddha to let the tiger eat him?' said Amy, changing her ground. 'It would be a bad pattern.'

'The world would get full of fat tigers,' said Mab.

Deronda laughed, but defended the myth. 'It is like a passionate word,' he said; 'the exaggeration is a flash of fervour. It is an extreme image of what is happening every day – the transmutation of self.'

'I think I can say what I mean, now,' said Mirah, who had not heard the intermediate talk. 'When the best thing comes into our thoughts, it is like what my mother has been to me. She has been just as really with me as all the other people about me – often more really with me.'

Deronda, inwardly wincing under this illustration, which brought other possible realities about that mother vividly before him, presently turned the conversation by saying, 'But we must not get too far away from practical matters. I came for one thing, to tell of an interview I had yesterday, which I hope Mirah will find to have been useful to her. It was with Klesmer, the great pianist.'

'Ah?' said Mrs. Meyrick, with satisfaction. 'You think he will help her?'

'I hope so. He is very much occupied, but has promised to fix a time for receiving and hearing Miss Lapidoth, as we must learn to call her' – here Deronda smiled at Mirah – 'if she consents to go to him.'

'I shall be very grateful,' said Mirah, calmly. 'He wants to hear me sing, before he can judge whether I ought to be helped.'

Deronda was struck with her plain sense about these matters of practical concern.

'It will not be at all trying to you, I hope, if Mrs. Meyrick will kindly go with you to Klesmer's house.'

'Oh no, not at all trying. I have been doing that all my life – I mean, told to do things that others may judge of me. And I have gone through a bad trial of that sort. I am prepared to bear it, and do some very small thing. Is Klesmer a severe man?'

'He is peculiar, but I have not had experience enough of him to know whether he would be what you would call severe. I know he is kind-hearted – kind in action, if not in speech.'

'I have been used to be frowned at and not praised,' said Mirah.

'By the by, Klesmer frowns a good deal,' said Deronda, 'but there is often a sort of smile in his eyes all the while. Unhappily he wears spectacles, so you must catch him in the right light to see the smile.'

'I shall not be frightened,' said Mirah. 'If he were like a roaring lion, he only wants me to sing. I shall do what I can.'

'Then I feel sure you will not mind being invited to sing in Lady Mallinger's drawing-room,' said Deronda. 'She intends to ask you next month, and will invite many ladies to hear you, who are likely to want lessons from you for their daughters.'

'How fast we are mounting!' said Mrs. Meyrick, with delight. 'You never thought of getting grand so quickly, Mirah.'

'I am a little frightened at being called Miss Lapidoth,' said Mirah, colouring with a new uneasiness. 'Might I be called Cohen?'

'I understand you,' said Deronda, promptly. 'But, I assure you, you must not be called Cohen. The name is inadmissible for a singer. This is one of the trifles in which we must conform to vulgar prejudice. We could choose some other name, however – such as singers ordinarily choose – an Italian or Spanish name, which would suit your *physique.*' To Deronda just now the name Cohen was equivalent to the ugliest of yellow badges.

Mirah reflected a little, anxiously, then said, 'No. If Cohen will not do, I will keep the name I have been called by. I will not hide myself. I have friends to protect me. And now – if my father were very miserable and wanted help – no,' she said, looking at Mrs. Meyrick, 'I should think then, that he was perhaps crying as I used to see him, and had nobody to pity him, and I had hidden myself from him. He had none belonging to him but me. Others that made friends with him always left him.'

'Keep to what you feel right, my dear child,' said Mrs. Meyrick. '*I* would not persuade you to the contrary.' For her own part she had no patience or pity for that father, and would have left him to his crying.

Deronda was saying to himself, 'I am rather base to be angry with Hans. How can he help being in love with her? But it is too absurdly presumptuous for him even to frame the idea of appropriating her, and a sort of blasphemy to suppose that she could possibly give herself to him.'

What would it be for Daniel Deronda to entertain such thoughts? He was not one who could quite naïvely introduce himself where he had just excluded his friend, yet it was undeniable that what had just happened made a new stage in his feeling towards Mirah. But apart from other grounds for self-repression, reasons both definite and vague made him shut away that question as he might have shut up a half-opened writing that would have carried his imagination too far and given too much shape to presentiments. Might there not come a disclosure which would hold the missing determination of his course? What did he really know about his origin? Strangely in these latter months when it seemed right that he should exert his will in the choice of a destination, the passion of his nature had got more and more locked by this uncertainty. The disclosure might bring its pain, indeed the likelihood seemed to him to be all on that side; but if it helped him to make his life a sequence which would take the form of duty – if it saved him from having to make an arbitrary selection where he felt no preponderance of desire? Still more he wanted to escape standing as a critic outside the activities of men, stiffened into the ridiculous attitude of self-assigned superiority. His chief tether was his early inwrought affection for Sir Hugo, making him gratefully deferential to wishes with which he had little agreement; but gratitude had been sometimes disturbed by doubts which were near reducing it to a fear of being ungrateful. Many of us complain that half our birthright is sharp duty: Deronda was more inclined to complain that he was robbed of this half; yet he accused himself, as he would have accused another, of being weakly self-conscious and wanting in resolve. He was the reverse of that type painted for us in Faulconbridge and Edmund of Gloster, whose coarse ambition for personal success is inflamed by a defiance of accidental disadvantages. To Daniel the words Father and Mother had the altar-fire in them; and the thought of all closest relations of our nature held still something of the mystic power which had made his neck and ears burn in boyhood. The average man may regard this sensibility on the question of birth as preposterous and hardly credible; but with the utmost respect for his knowledge as the rock from which all other knowledge is hewn, it must be admitted that many well-proved facts are dark to the average man, even concerning the action of his own heart and the structure of his own retina. A century ago he and all his forefathers had not had the slightest notion of that electric discharge by means of which they had all wagged their tongues mistakenly; any more than they were awake to the secluded anguish of exceptional sensitiveness into which many a carelessly-begotten child of man is born.

Perhaps the ferment was all the stronger in Deronda's mind because he had never had a confidant to whom he could open himself on these delicate subjects. He had always been leaned on instead of being invited to lean. Sometimes he had longed for the sort of friend to whom he might possibly unfold his experience: a young man like himself who sustained a private grief and was not too confident about his own career; speculative enough to understand every moral difficulty, yet socially susceptible, as he himself was, and having every outward sign of equality either in bodily or in spiritual wrestling; – for he had found it impossible to reciprocate confidences with one who looked up to him. But he had no expectation of meeting the friend he imagined. Deronda's was not one of those quiveringly-poised natures that lend themselves to second-sight.

XXXVIII

There be who hold that the deeper tragedy were a Prometheus
Bound not *after* but *before* he had well got the celestial fire into the
νάρθηξ whereby it might be conveyed to mortals: thrust by the
Kratos and Bia of instituted methods into a solitude of despised
ideas, fastened in throbbing helplessness by the fatal pressure of
poverty and disease – a solitude where many pass by, but none
regard.

'SECOND-SIGHT' is a flag over disputed ground. But it is
matter of knowledge that there are persons whose yearnings, conceptions – nay, travelled conclusions – continually
take the form of images which have a foreshadowing
power: the deed they would do starts up before them in
complete shape, making a coercive type; the event they
hunger for or dread rises into vision with a seed-like
growth, feeding itself fast on unnumbered impressions.
They are not always the less capable of the argumentative
process, or less sane than the commonplace calculators of
the market: sometimes it may be that their natures have
manifold openings, like the hundred-gated Thebes, where
there may naturally be a greater and more miscellaneous
inrush than through a narrow beadle-watched portal. No
doubt there are abject specimens of the visionary, as there
is a minim mammal which you might imprison in the finger
of your glove. That small relative of the elephant has no
harm in him; but what great mental or social type is free
from specimens whose insignificance is both ugly and
noxious? One is afraid to think of all that the genus
'patriot' embraces; or of the elbowing there might be at
the day of judgment for those who ranked as authors, and
brought volumes either in their hands or on trucks.

This apology for inevitable kinship is meant to usher in
some facts about Mordecai, whose figure had bitten itself
into Deronda's mind as a new question which he felt an
interest in getting answered. But the interest was no
more than a vaguely expectant suspense: the consump-
tive-looking Jew, apparently a fervid student of some kind,

getting his crust by a quiet handicraft, like Spinoza, fitted into none of Deronda's anticipations.

It was otherwise with the effect of their meeting on Mordecai. For many winters, while he had been conscious of an ebbing physical life, and a widening spiritual lone-liness, all his passionate desire had concentred itself in the yearning for some young ear into which he could pour his mind as a testament, some soul kindred enough to accept the spiritual product of his own brief, painful life, as a mission to be executed. It was remarkable that the hope-fulness which is often the beneficent illusion of consump-tive patients, was in Mordecai wholly diverted from the prospect of bodily recovery and carried into the current of this yearning for transmission. The yearning, which had panted upward from out of overwhelming discourage-ments, had grown into a hope – the hope into a confident belief, which, instead of being checked by the clear con-ception he had of his hastening decline, took rather the intensity of expectant faith in a prophecy which has only brief space to get fulfilled in.

Some years had now gone since he had first begun to measure men with a keen glance, searching for a possibility which became more and more a distinct conception. Such distinctness as it had at first was reached chiefly by a method of contrast: he wanted to find a man who differed from himself. Tracing reasons in that self for the rebuffs he had met with and the hindrances that beset him, he ima-gined a man who would have all the elements necessary for sympathy with him, but in an embodiment unlike his own: he must be a Jew, intellectually cultured, morally fervid – in all this a nature ready to be plenished from Mordecai's; but his face and frame must be beautiful and strong, he must have been used to all the refinements of social life, his voice must flow with a full and easy current, his circum-stances be free from sordid need: he must glorify the possibilities of the Jew, not sit and wander as Mordecai did, bearing the stamp of his people amid the signs of poverty and waning breath. Sensitive to physical characteristics, he had, both abroad and in England, looked at pictures as well as men, and in a vacant hour he had sometimes lingered in the National Gallery in search of paintings which might feed his hopefulness with grave and noble types of the human form, such as might well belong to men of his own race. But he returned in disappointment. The instances are scattered but thinly over the galleries of Europe, in which the fortune or selection even of the chief masters has given to Art a face at once young, grand, and beautiful, where, if there is any melancholy, it is no feeble passivity, but enters into the foreshadowed capability of heroism.

Some observant persons may perhaps remember his emaciated figure, and dark eyes deep in their sockets, as he stood in front of a picture that had touched him either to new or habitual meditation: he commonly wore a cloth cap with black fur round it, which no painter would have asked him to take off. But spectators would be likely to think of him as an odd-looking Jew, who probably got money out of pictures; and Mordecai, when he noticed them, was perfectly aware of the impression he made. Experience had rendered him morbidly alive to the effect of a man's poverty and other physical disadvantages in cheapening his ideas, unless they are those of a Peter the Hermit who has a tocsin for the rabble. But he was too sane and generous to attribute his spiritual banishment solely to the excusable prejudices of others: certain incapacities of his own had made the sentence of exclusion; and hence it was that his imagination had constructed another man who would be something more ample than the second soul bestowed, according to the notion of the Cabbalists, to help out the insufficient first – who would be a blooming human life, ready to incorporate all that was worthiest in an existence whose visible, palpable part was burning itself fast away. His inward need for the conception of this expanded, prolonged self was reflected as an outward necessity. The thoughts of his heart (that ancient phrase best shadows the truth) seemed to him too precious, too closely inwoven with the growth of things not to have a further destiny. And as the more beautiful, the stronger, the more-executive self took shape in his mind, he loved it beforehand with an affection half identifying, half contemplative and grateful.

Mordecai's mind wrought so constantly in images, that his coherent trains of thought often resembled the significant dreams attributed to sleepers by waking persons in their most inventive moments; nay, they often resembled genuine dreams in their way of breaking off the passage from the known to the unknown. Thus, for a long while, he habitually thought of the Being answering to his need as one distantly approaching or turning his back towards him, darkly painted against a golden sky. The reason of the golden sky lay in one of Mordecai's habits. He was keenly alive to some poetic aspects of London; and a favourite resort of his, when strength and leisure allowed, was to some one of the bridges, especially about sunrise or sunset. Even when he was bending over watch-wheels and trinkets, or seated in a small upper room looking out on dingy bricks and dingy cracked windows, his imagination spontaneously planted him on some spot where he had a far-stretching scene; his thought went on in wide spaces; and whenever he could, he tried to have in reality the influences of a large sky. Leaning on the parapet of Blackfriars Bridge, and gazing meditatively, the breadth and calm of the river, with its long vista half hazy, half luminous, the grand dim masses or tall forms of buildings which were the signs of world-commerce, the oncoming of boats and barges from the still distance into sound and colour, entered into his mood and blent themselves indistinguishably with his thinking, as a fine symphony to which we can hardly be said to listen makes a medium that bears up our spiritual wings. Thus it happened that the figure representative of Mordecai's longing was mentally seen darkened by the excess of light in the aerial background. But in the inevitable progress of his imagination towards fuller detail, he ceased to see the figure with its back towards him. It began to advance, and a face became discernible; the words youth, beauty, refinement, Jewish birth, noble gravity, turned into hardly individual but typical form and colour: gathered from his memory of faces seen among the Jews of Holland and Bohemia, and from the paintings which revived that memory. Reverently let it be said of this mature spiritual need that it was akin to the boy's and girl's picturing of the future beloved; but the stirrings of such young desire are feeble compared with the passionate current of an ideal life straining to embody itself, made intense by resistance to imminent dissolution. The visionary form became a companion and auditor; keeping a place not only in the waking imagination, but in those dreams of lighter slumber of which it is truest to say, 'I sleep, but my heart is awake' – when the disturbing trivial story of yesterday is charged with the impassioned purpose of years.

Of late the urgency of irredeemable time, measured by the gradual choking of life, had turned Mordecai's trust into an agitated watch for the fulfilment that must be at hand. Was the bell on the verge of tolling, the sentence about to be executed? The deliverer's footstep must be near – the deliverer who was to rescue Mordecai's spiritual travail from oblivion, and give it an abiding place in the best heritage of his people. An insane exaggeration of his own value, even if his ideas had been as true and precious as those of Columbus or Newton, many would have counted this yearning, taking it as the sublimer part for a man to say, 'If not I, then another,' and to hold cheap the meaning of his own life. But the fuller nature desires to be an agent, to create, and not merely to look on: strong love hungers to bless, and not merely to behold blessing. And while there is warmth enough in the sun to feed an energetic life, there will still be men to feel, 'I am lord of this moment's change, and will charge it with my soul.'

But with that mingling of inconsequence which belongs to us all, and not unhappily, since it saves us from many effects of mistake, Mordecai's confidence in the friend to come did not suffice to make him passive, and he tried expedients, pathetically humble, such as happened to be within his reach, for communicating something of himself. It was now two years since he had taken up his abode under Ezra Cohen's roof, where he was regarded with much goodwill as a compound of workman, dominie, vessel of charity, inspired idiot, man of piety, and (if he were inquired into) dangerous heretic. During that time little Jacob had advanced into knickerbockers, and into that quickness of apprehension which has been already made manifest in relation to hardware and exchange. He had also advanced in attachment to Mordecai, regarding him as an inferior, but liking him none the worse, and taking his helpful cleverness as he might have taken the services of an enslaved Djinn. As for Mordecai, he had given Jacob his first lessons, and his habitual tenderness easily turned into the teacher's fatherhood. Though he was fully conscious of the spiritual distance between the parents and himself, and would never have attempted any communication to them from his peculiar world, the boy moved him with that idealizing affection which merges the qualities of the individual child in the glory of childhood and the possibilities of a long future. And this feeling had drawn him on, at first without premeditation, and afterwards with conscious purpose, to a sort of outpouring in the ear of the boy which might have seemed wild enough to any excellent man of business who overheard it. But none overheard when Jacob went up to Mordecai's room on a day, for example, in which there was little work to be done, or at an hour when the work was ended, and after a brief lesson in English reading or in numeration, was induced to remain standing at his teacher's knees, or chose to jump astride them, often to the patient fatigue of the wasted limbs. The inducement was perhaps the mending of a toy, or some little mechanical device in which Mordecai's well-practised finger-tips had an exceptional skill; and with the boy thus tethered, he would begin to repeat a Hebrew poem of his own, into which years before he had poured his first youthful ardours for that conception of a blended past and future which was the mistress of his soul, telling Jacob to say the words after him.

'The boy will get them engraved within him,' thought Mordecai; 'it is a way of printing.'

None readier than Jacob at this fascinating game of imitating unintelligible words; and if no opposing diversion occurred, he would sometimes carry on his share in it as long as the teacher's breath would last out. For Mordecai threw into each repetition the fervour befitting a sacred occasion. In such instances, Jacob would show no other distraction than reaching out and surveying the contents of his pockets; or drawing down the skin of his cheeks to make his eyes look awful, and rolling his head to complete the effect; or alternately handling his own nose and Mordecai's as if to test the relation of their masses. Under all this the fervid reciter would not pause, satisfied if the young organs of speech would submit themselves. But most commonly a sudden impulse sent Jacob leaping away into some antic or active amusement, when, instead of following the recitation, he would return upon the foregoing words most ready to his tongue, and mouth or gabble, with a see-saw suited to the action of his limbs, a verse on which Mordecai had spent some of his too scanty heart's blood. Yet he waited with such patience as a prophet needs, and began his strange printing again undiscouraged on the morrow, saying inwardly –

'My words may rule him some day. Their meaning may flash out on him. It is so with a nation – after many days.'

Meanwhile Jacob's sense of power was increased and his time enlivened by a store of magical articulation with which he made the baby crow, or drove the large cat into a dark corner, or promised himself to frighten any incidental Christian of his own years. One week he had unfortunately seen a street mountebank, and this carried off his muscular imitativeness in sad divergence from New Hebrew poetry after the model of Jehuda ha-Levi. Mordecai had arrived at a fresh passage in his poem; for as soon as Jacob had got well used to one portion, he was led on to another, and a fresh combination of sounds generally answered better in keeping him fast for a few minutes. The consumptive voice, originally a strong high baritone, with its variously mingling hoarseness, like a haze amidst illuminations, and its occasional incipient gasp, had more than the usual excitement, while it gave forth Hebrew verses with a meaning something like this: –

> 'Away from me the garment of forgetfulness,
> Withering the heart;
> The oil and wine from presses of the Goyim,
> Poisoned with scorn.
> Solitude is on the sides of Mount Nebo,
> In its heart a tomb:
> There the buried ark and golden cherubim
> Make hidden light:
> There the solemn faces gaze unchanged,
> The wings are spread unbroken:
> Shut beneath in silent awful speech
> The Law lies graven.
> Solitude and darkness are my covering,
> And my heart a tomb;
> Smite and shatter it, O Gabriel!
> Shatter it as the clay of the founder
> Around the golden image.'

In the absorbing enthusiasm with which Mordecai had intoned rather than spoken this last invocation, he was unconscious that Jacob had ceased to follow him and had started away from his knees; but pausing he saw, as by a sudden flash, that the lad had thrown himself on his hands with his feet in the air, mountebank fashion, and was picking up with his lips a bright farthing which was a favourite among his pocket treasures. This might have been reckoned among the tricks Mordecai was used to, but at this moment it jarred him horribly, as if it had been a Satanic grin upon his prayer.

'Child! child!' he called out with a strange cry that startled Jacob to his feet, and then he sank backward with a shudder, closing his eyes.

'What?' said Jacob, quickly. Then, not getting an immediate answer, he pressed Mordecai's knees with a shaking movement, in order to rouse him. Mordecai opened his eyes with a fierce expression in them, leaned forward, grasped the little shoulders, and said in a quick, hoarse whisper –

'A curse is on your generation, child. They will open the mountain and drag forth the golden wings and coin them into money, and the solemn faces they will break up into ear-rings for wanton women! And they shall get themselves a new name, but the angel of ignominy, with a fiery brand, shall know them, and their heart shall be the tomb of dead desires that turn their life to rotten-ness.'

The aspect and action of Mordecai were so new and mysterious to Jacob – they carried such a burthen of obscure threat – it was as if the patient, indulgent companion had turned into something unknown and terrific: the sunken dark eyes and hoarse accents close to him, the thin grappling fingers, shook Jacob's little frame into awe, and while Mordecai was speaking he stood trembling with a sense that the house was tumbling in and they were not going to have dinner any more. But when the terrible speech had ended and the pinch was relaxed, the shock resolved itself into tears; Jacob lifted up his small patriarchal countenance and wept aloud. This sign of childish grief at once recalled Mordecai to his usual gentle self: he was not able to speak again at present, but with a maternal action he drew the curly head towards him and pressed it tenderly against his breast. On this Jacob, feeling the danger wellnigh over, howled at ease, beginning to imitate his own performance and improve upon it – a sort of transition from impulse into art often observable. Indeed, the next day he undertook to terrify Adelaide Rebekah in like manner, and succeeded very well.

But Mordecai suffered a check which lasted long, from the consciousness of a misapplied agitation; sane as well as excitable, he judged severely his moments of aberration into futile eagerness, and felt discredited with himself. All the more his mind was strained towards the discernment of that friend to come, with whom he would have a calm certainty of fellowship and understanding.

It was just then that, in his usual mid-day guardianship of the old book-shop, he was struck by the appearance of Deronda, and it is perhaps comprehensible now why Mordecai's glance took on a sudden eager interest as he looked at the new-comer: he saw a face and frame which seemed to him to realize the long-conceived type. But the disclaimer of Jewish birth was for the moment a backward thrust of double severity, the particular disappointment tending to shake his confidence in the more indefinite expectation. Nevertheless, when he found Deronda seated at the Cohens' table, the disclaimer was for the moment nullified: the first impression returned with added force, seeming to be guaranteed by this second meeting under circumstances more peculiar than the former; and in asking Deronda if he knew Hebrew, Mordecai was so possessed by the new inrush of belief, that he had forgotten the absence of any other condition to the fulfilment of his hopes. But the answering 'No' struck them all down again, and the frustration was more painful than before. After turning his back on the visitor that Sabbath evening, Mordecai went through days of a deep discouragement, like that of men on a doomed ship who, having strained their eyes after a sail, and beheld it with rejoicing, behold it never advance, and say, 'Our sick eyes make it.' But the long-contemplated figure had come as an emotional sequence of Mordecai's firmest theoretic convictions; it had been wrought from the imagery of his most passionate life; and it inevitably reappeared – reappeared in a more specific self-asserting form than ever. Deronda had that sort of resemblance to the preconceived type which a finely individual bust or portrait has to the more generalized copy left in our minds after a long interval: we renew our memory with delight, but we hardly know with how much correction. And now, his face met Mordecai's inward gaze as if it had always belonged to the awaited friend, raying out, moreover, some of that influence which belongs to breathing flesh; till by-and-by it seemed that discouragement had turned into a new obstinacy of resistance, and the ever-recurrent vision had the force of an outward call to disregard counter-evidence, and keep expectation awake. It was Deronda now who was seen in the often painful night-watches, when we are all liable to be held with the clutch of a single thought – whose figure, never with its back turned, was seen in moments of soothed reverie or soothed dozing, painted on that golden sky which was the doubly blessed symbol of advancing day and of approaching rest.

Mordecai knew that the nameless stranger was to come and redeem his ring; and, in spite of contrary chances, the wish to see him again was growing into a belief that he should see him. In the January weeks, he felt an increasing agitation of that subdued hidden quality which hinders nervous people from any steady occupation on the eve of an anticipated change. He could not go on with his printing of Hebrew on little Jacob's mind; or with his attendance at a weekly club, which was another effort of the same forlorn hope: something else was coming. The one thing he longed for was to get as far as the river, which he could do but seldom and with difficulty. He yearned with a poet's yearning for the wide sky, the far-reaching vista of bridges, the tender and fluctuating lights on the water which seems to breathe with a life that can shiver and mourn, be comforted and rejoice.

XXXIX

'Vor den Wissenden sich stellen
Sicher ist's in allen Fällen!
Wenn du lange dich gequälet
Weiss er gleich wo dir es fehlet;
Auch auf Beifall darfst du hoffen,
Denn er weiss wo du's getroffen.'
– GOETHE: *West-östlicher Divan*.

MOMENTOUS things happened to Deronda the very evening of that visit to the small house at Chelsea, when there was the discussion about Mirah's public name. But for the family group there, what appeared to be the chief sequence connected with it occurred two days afterwards. About four o'clock wheels paused before the door, and there came one of those knocks with an accompanying ring which serve to magnify the sense of social existence in a region where the most enlivening signals are usually those of the muffin-man. All the girls were at home, and the two rooms were thrown together to make space for Kate's drawing, as well as a great length of embroidery which had taken the place of the satin cushions – a sort of *pièce de résistance* in the courses of needlework, taken up by any clever fingers that happened to be at liberty. It stretched across the front room picturesquely enough, Mrs. Meyrick bending over it at one corner, Mab in the middle, and Amy at the other end. Mirah, whose performances in point of sewing were on the makeshift level of the tailor-bird's, her education in that branch having been much neglected, was acting as reader to the party, seated on a camp-stool; in which position she also served Kate as model for a title-page vignette, symbolizing a fair public absorbed in the successive volumes of the Family Tea-table. She was giving forth with charming distinctness the delightful Essay of Elia, *The Praise of Chimney-Sweeps*, and all were smiling over the 'innocent blacknesses,' when the imposing knock and ring called their thoughts to loftier spheres, and they looked up in wonderment.

'Dear me!' said Mrs. Meyrick; 'can it be Lady Mallinger? Is there a grand carriage, Amy?'

'No – only a hansom cab. It must be a gentleman.'

'The Prime Minister, I should think,' said Kate, drily. 'Hans says the greatest man in London may get into a hansom cab.'

'Oh, oh, oh!' cried Mab. 'Suppose it should be Lord Russell!'

The five bright faces were all looking amused when the old maid-servant bringing in a card distractedly left the parlour-door open, and there was seen bowing towards Mrs. Meyrick a figure quite unlike that of the respected Premier – tall and physically impressive even in his kid and kerseymere, with massive face, flamboyant hair, and gold spectacles: in fact, as Mrs. Meyrick saw from the card, *Julius Klesmer.*

Even embarrassment could hardly have made the 'little mother' awkward, but quick in her perceptions she was at once aware of the situation, and felt well satisfied that the great personage had come to Mirah instead of requiring her to come to him; taking it as a sign of active interest. But when he entered, the rooms shrank into closets, the cottage piano, Mab thought, seemed a ridiculous toy, and the entire family existence as petty and private as an establishment of mice in the Tuileries. Klesmer's personality, especially his way of glancing round him, immediately suggested vast areas and a multitudinous audience, and probably they made the usual scenery of his consciousness, for we all of us carry on our thinking in some habitual *locus* where there is a presence of other souls, and those who take in a larger sweep than their neighbours are apt to seem mightily vain and affected. Klesmer was vain, but not more so than many contemporaries of heavy aspect, whose vanity leaps out and startles one like a spear out of a walking-stick; as to his carriage and gestures, these were as natural to him as the length of his fingers; and the rankest affectation he could have shown would have been to look diffident and demure. While his grandiose air was making Mab feel herself a ridiculous toy to match the cottage piano, he was taking in the details around him with a keen and thoroughly kind sensibility. He remembered a home no larger than this on the outskirts of Bohemia; and in the figurative Bohemia too he had had large acquaintance with the variety and romance which belong to small incomes. He addressed Mrs. Meyrick with the utmost deference.

'I hope I have not taken too great a freedom. Being in the neighbourhood, I ventured to save time by calling. Our friend Mr. Deronda mentioned to me an understanding that I was to have the honour of becoming acquainted with a young lady here – Miss Lapidoth.'

Klesmer had really discerned Mirah in the first moment of entering, but with subtle politeness he looked round bowingly at the three sisters as if he were uncertain which was the young lady in question.

'Those are my daughters: this is Miss Lapidoth,' said Mrs. Meyrick, waving her hand towards Mirah.

'Ah,' said Klesmer, in a tone of gratified expectation, turning a radiant smile and deep bow to Mirah, who, instead of being in the least taken by surprise, had a calm pleasure in her face. She liked the look of Klesmer, feeling sure that he would scold her, like a great musician and a kind man.

'You will not object to beginning our acquaintance by singing to me,' he added, aware that they would all be relieved by getting rid of preliminaries.

'I shall be very glad. It is good of you to be willing to listen to me,' said Mirah, moving to the piano. 'Shall I accompany myself?'

'By all means,' said Klesmer, seating himself, at Mrs. Meyrick's invitation, where he could have a good view of the singer. The acute little mother would not have acknowledged the weakness, but she really said to herself, 'He will like her singing better if he sees her.'

All the feminine hearts except Mirah's were beating fast with anxiety, thinking Klesmer terrific as he sat with his

listening frown on, and only daring to look at him furtively.
If he did say anything severe it would be so hard for them
all. They could only comfort themselves with thinking that
Prince Camaralzaman, who had heard the finest things,
preferred Mirah's singing to any other: – also she appeared
to be doing her very best, as if she were more instead of less
at ease than usual.

The song she had chosen was a fine setting of some
words selected from Leopardi's grand Ode to Italy: –

> *'O patria mia, vedo le mura e gli archi*
> *E le colonne e i simulacri e l'erme*
> *Torri degli avi nostri'* –

This was recitative: then followed –

> *'Ma la gloria non vedo'* –

a mournful melody, a rhythmic plaint. After this came a
climax of devout triumph – passing from the subdued
adoration of a happy Andante in the words –

> *'Beatissimi voi,*
> *Che offriste il petto alle nemiche lance*
> *Per amor di costei che al sol vi diede'* –

to the joyous outburst of an exultant Allegro in –

> *'Oh viva, oh viva:*
> *Beatissimi voi*
> *Mentre nel mondo si favelli o scriva.'*

When she had ended, Klesmer said after a moment –
'That is old Leo's music.'

'Yes, he was my last master – at Vienna: so fierce and so
good,' said Mirah, with a melancholy smile. 'He proph-
esied that my voice would not do for the stage. And he was
right.'

'*Con*tinue, if you please,' said Klesmer, putting out his
lips and shaking his long fingers, while he went on with a
smothered articulation quite unintelligible to the audience.

The three girls detested him unanimously for not saying
one word of praise. Mrs. Meyrick was a little alarmed.

Mirah, simply bent on doing what Klesmer desired, and imagining that he would now like to hear her sing some German, went through Prince Radzivill's music to Gretchen's songs in the Faust, one after the other, without any interrogatory pause. When she had finished he rose and walked to the extremity of the small space at command, then walked back to the piano, where Mirah had risen from her seat and stood looking towards him with her little hands crossed before her, meekly awaiting judgment; then with a sudden unknitting of his brow and with beaming eyes, he put out his hand and said abruptly, 'Let us shake hands: you are a musician.'

Mab felt herself beginning to cry, and all the three girls held Klesmer adorable. Mrs. Meyrick took a long breath.

But straightway the frown came again, the long hand, back uppermost, was stretched out in quite a different sense to touch with finger-tip the back of Mirah's, and with protruded lip he said –

'Not for great tasks. No high roofs. We are no skylarks. We must be modest.' Klesmer paused here. And Mab ceased to think him adorable: 'as if Mirah had shown the least sign of conceit!'

Mirah was silent, knowing that there was a specific opinion to be waited for, and Klesmer presently went on –

'I would not advise – I would not further your singing in any larger space than a private drawing-room. But you will do there. And here in London that is one of the best careers open. Lessons will follow. Will you come and sing at a private concert at my house on Wednesday?'

'Oh, I shall be grateful,' said Mirah, putting her hands together devoutly. 'I would rather get my bread in that way than by anything more public. I will try to improve. What should I work at most?'

Klesmer made a preliminary answer in noises which sounded like words bitten in two and swallowed before they were half out, shaking his fingers the while, before he said, quite distinctly, 'I shall introduce you to Astorga: he is the foster-father of good singing and will give you advice.' Then addressing Mrs. Meyrick, he added, 'Mrs. Klesmer will call before Wednesday, with your permission.'

'We shall feel that to be a great kindness,' said Mrs. Meyrick.

'You will sing to her,' said Klesmer, turning again to Mirah. 'She is a thorough musician, and has a soul with more ears to it than you will often get in a musician. Your singing will satisfy her: –

"Vor den Wissenden sich stellen" –

you know the rest?'

' "Sicher ist's in allen Fällen," '

said Mirah, promptly. And Klesmer saying, 'Schön!' put out his hand again as a good-bye.

He had certainly chosen the most delicate way of praising Mirah, and the Meyrick girls had now given him all their esteem. But imagine Mab's feeling when, suddenly fixing his eyes on her, he said decisively, 'That young lady is musical, I see!' She was a mere blush and sense of scorching.

'Yes,' said Mirah on her behalf. 'And she has a touch.'

'Oh please, Mirah – a scramble, not a touch,' said Mab, in anguish, with a horrible fear of what the next thing might be: this dreadfully divining personage – evidently Satan in grey trousers – might order her to sit down to the piano, and her heart was like molten wax in the midst of her. But this was cheap payment for her amazed joy when Klesmer said benignantly, turning to Mrs. Meyrick, 'Will she like to accompany Miss Lapidoth and hear the music on Wednesday?'

'There could hardly be a greater pleasure for her,' said Mrs. Meyrick. 'She will be most glad and grateful.'

Thereupon Klesmer bowed round to the three sisters more grandly than they had ever been bowed to before. Altogether it was an amusing picture – the little room with so much of its diagonal taken up in Klesmer's magnificent bend to the small feminine figures like images a little less than life-size, the grave Holbein faces on the walls, as many as were not otherwise occupied, looking hard at this stranger who by his face seemed a dignified contemporary of their own, but whose garments seemed a deplorable mockery of the human form.

Mrs. Meyrick could not help going out of the room with Klesmer and closing the door behind her. He understood her and said with a frowning nod –

'She will do: if she doesn't attempt too much and her voice holds out, she can make an income. I know that is the great point: Deronda told me. You are taking care of her. She looks like a good girl.'

'She is an angel,' said the warm-hearted woman.

'No,' said Klesmer, with a playful nod; 'she is a pretty Jewess: the angels must not get the credit of her. But I think she has found a guardian angel,' he ended, bowing himself out in this amiable way.

The four young creatures had looked at each other mutely till the door banged and Mrs. Meyrick re-entered. Then there was an explosion. Mab clapped her hands and danced everywhere inconveniently; Mrs. Meyrick kissed Mirah and blessed her; Amy said emphatically, 'We can never get her a new dress before Wednesday!' and Kate exclaimed, 'Thank heaven my table is not knocked over!'

Mirah had reseated herself on the music-stool without speaking, and the tears were rolling down her cheeks as she looked at her friends.

'Now, now, Mab!' said Mrs. Meyrick; 'come and sit down reasonably and let us talk.'

'Yes, let us talk,' said Mab, cordially, coming back to her low seat and caressing her knees. 'I am beginning to feel large again. Hans said he was coming this afternoon. I wish he had been here – only there would have been no room for him. Mirah, what are you looking sad for?'

'I am too happy,' said Mirah. 'I feel so full of gratitude to you all; and he was so very kind.'

'Yes, at last,' said Mab, sharply. 'But he might have said something encouraging sooner. I thought him dreadfully ugly when he sat frowning, and only said, "*Con*tinue." I hated him all the long way from the top of his hair to the toe of his polished boot.'

'Nonsense, Mab; he has a splendid profile,' said Kate.

'*Now*, but not *then*. I cannot bear people to keep their minds bottled up for the sake of letting them off with a pop. They seem to grudge making you happy unless they can make you miserable beforehand. However, I forgive him everything,' said Mab, with a magnanimous air, 'because he has invited me. I wonder why he fixed on me as the musical one? Was it because I have a bulging forehead, ma, and peep from under it like a newt from under a stone?'

'It was your way of listening to the singing, child,' said Mrs. Meyrick. 'He has magic spectacles and sees everything through them, depend upon it. But what was that German quotation you were so ready with, Mirah – you learned puss?'

'Oh, that was not learning,' said Mirah, her tearful face breaking into an amused smile. 'I said it so many times for a lesson. It means that it is safer to do anything – singing or anything else – before those who know and understand all about it.'

'That was why you were not one bit frightened, I suppose,' said Amy. 'But now, what we have to talk about is a dress for you on Wednesday.'

'I don't want anything better than this black merino,' said Mirah, rising to show the effect. 'Some white gloves and some new *bottines*.' She put out her little foot, clad in the famous felt slipper.

'There comes Hans,' said Mrs. Meyrick. 'Stand still, and let us hear what he says about the dress. Artists are the best people to consult about such things.'

'You don't consult me, ma,' said Kate, lifting up her eyebrow with a playful complainingness. 'I notice mothers are like the people I deal with – the girls' doings are always priced low.'

'My dear child, the boys are such a trouble – we could never put up with them, if we didn't make believe they were worth more,' said Mrs. Meyrick, just as her boy entered. 'Hans, we want your opinion about Mirah's dress. A great event has happened. Klesmer has been here, and she is going to sing at his house on Wednesday among grand people. She thinks this dress will do.'

'Let me see,' said Hans. Mirah in her child-like way turned towards him to be looked at; and he, going to a little further distance, knelt with one knee on a hassock to survey her.

'This would be thought a very good stage-dress for me,' she said, pleadingly, 'in a part where I was to come on as a poor Jewess and sing to fashionable Christians.'

'It would be effective,' said Hans, with a considering air; 'it would stand out well among the fashionable *chiffons*.'

'But you ought not to claim all the poverty on your side, Mirah,' said Amy. 'There are plenty of poor Christians and dreadfully rich Jews and fashionable Jewesses.'

'I didn't mean any harm,' said Mirah. 'Only I have been used to thinking about my dress for parts in plays. And I almost always had a part with a plain dress.'

'That makes me think it questionable,' said Hans, who had suddenly become as fastidious and conventional on this occasion as he had thought Deronda was, apropos of the Berenice-pictures. 'It looks a little too theatrical. We must not make you a *rôle* of the poor Jewess – or of being a Jewess at all.' Hans had a secret desire to neutralize the Jewess in private life, which he was in danger of not keeping secret.

'But it is what I am really. I am not pretending anything. I shall never be anything else,' said Mirah. 'I always feel myself a Jewess.'

'But we can't feel that about you,' said Hans, with a devout look. 'What does it signify whether a perfect woman is a Jewess or not?'

'That is your kind way of praising me; I never was praised so before,' said Mirah, with a smile, which was

540

rather maddening to Hans and made him feel still more of a cosmopolitan.

'People don't think of me as a British Christian,' he said, his face creasing merrily. 'They think of me as an imperfectly handsome young man and an unpromising painter.'

'But you are wandering from the dress,' said Amy. 'If that will not do, how are we to get another before Wednesday? and to-morrow Sunday?'

'Indeed this will do,' said Mirah, entreatingly. 'It is all real, you know,' here she looked at Hans – 'even if it seemed theatrical. Poor Berenice sitting on the ruins – any one might say that was theatrical, but I know that is just what she would do.'

'I am a scoundrel,' said Hans, overcome by this misplaced trust. 'That is my invention. Nobody knows that she did that. Shall you forgive me for not saying so before?'

'Oh yes,' said Mirah, after a momentary pause of surprise. 'You knew it was what she would be sure to do – a Jewess who had not been faithful – who had done what she did and was penitent. She could have no joy but to afflict herself; and where else would she go? I think it is very beautiful that you should enter so into what a Jewess would feel.'

'The Jewesses of that time sat on ruins,' said Hans, starting up with a sense of being checkmated. 'That makes them convenient for pictures.'

'But the dress – the dress,' said Amy; 'is it settled?'

'Yes; is it not?' said Mirah, looking doubtfully at Mrs. Meyrick, who in her turn looked up at her son, and said, 'What do you think, Hans?'

'That dress will not do,' said Hans, decisively. 'She is not going to sit on ruins. You must jump into a cab with her, little mother, and go to Regent Street. It's plenty of time to get anything you like – a black silk dress such as ladies wear. She must not be taken for an object of charity. She has talents to make people indebted to her.'

'I think it is what Mr. Deronda would like – for her to have a handsome dress,' said Mrs. Meyrick, deliberating.

'Of course it is,' said Hans, with some sharpness. 'You may take my word for what a gentleman would feel.'

'I wish to do what Mr. Deronda would like me to do,' said Mirah, gravely, seeing that Mrs. Meyrick looked towards her; and Hans, turning on his heel, went to Kate's table and took up one of her drawings as if his interest needed a new direction.

'Shouldn't you like to make a study of Klesmer's head, Hans?' said Kate. 'I suppose you have often seen him?'

'Seen him!' exclaimed Hans, immediately throwing back his head and mane, seating himself at the piano and looking round him as if he were surveying an amphi-theatre, while he held his fingers down perpendicularly towards the keys. But then in another instant he wheeled round on the stool, looked at Mirah and said, half timidly – 'Perhaps you don't like this mimicry; you must always stop my nonsense when you don't like it.'

Mirah had been smiling at the swiftly-made image, and she smiled still, but with a touch of something else than amusement, as she said – 'Thank you. But you have never done anything I did not like. I hardly think he could, belonging to you,' she added, looking at Mrs. Meyrick.

In this way Hans got food for his hope. How could the rose help it when several bees in succession took its sweet odour as a sign of personal attachment?

XL

'Within the soul a faculty abides,
That with interpositions, which would hide
And darken, so can deal, that they become
Contingencies of pomp; and serve to exalt
Her native brightness, as the ample moon,
In the deep stillness of a summer even,
Rising behind a thick and lofty grove,
Burns, like an unconsuming fire of light,
In the green trees; and, kindling on all sides
Their leafy umbrage, turns the dusky veil
Into a substance glorious as her own,
Yea, with her own incorporated, by power
Capacious and serene.'
— WORDSWORTH: *Excursion*, B. IV.

DERONDA came out of the narrow house at Chelsea in a
frame of mind that made him long for some good bodily
exercise to carry off what he was himself inclined to call the
fumes of his temper. He was going towards the city, and the
sight of the Chelsea Stairs with the waiting boats at once
determined him to avoid the irritating inaction of being
driven in a cab, by calling a wherry and taking an oar.

His errand was to go to Ram's book-shop, where he had
yesterday arrived too late for Mordecai's mid-day watch,
and had been told that he invariably came there again
between five and six. Some further acquaintance with
this remarkable inmate of the Cohens was particularly
desired by Deronda as a preliminary to redeeming his
ring: he wished that their conversation should not again
end speedily with that drop of Mordecai's interest which
was like the removal of a drawbridge, and threatened to
shut out any easy communication in future. As he got
warmed with the use of the oar, fixing his mind on the
errand before him and the ends he wanted to achieve on
Mirah's account, he experienced, as was wont with him, a
quick change of mental light, shifting his point of view to
that of the person whom he had been thinking of hitherto
chiefly as serviceable to his own purposes, and was

inclined to taunt himself with being not much better than an enlisting sergeant, who never troubles himself with the drama that brings him the needful recruits.

'I suppose if I got from this man the information I am most anxious about,' thought Deronda, 'I should be contented enough if he felt no disposition to tell me more of himself, or why he seemed to have some expectation from me which was disappointed. The sort of curiosity he stirs would die out; and yet it might be that we had neared and parted as one can imagine two ships doing, each freighted with an exile who would have recognized the other if the two could have looked out face to face. Not that there is any likelihood of a peculiar tie between me and this poor fellow, whose voyage, I fancy, must soon be over. But I wonder whether there is much of that momentous mutual missing between people who interchange blank looks, or even long for one another's absence in a crowded place. However, one makes one's self chances of missing by going on the recruiting-sergeant's plan.'

When the wherry was approaching Blackfriars Bridge, where Deronda meant to land, it was half-past four, and the grey day was dying gloriously, its western clouds all broken into narrowing purple strata before a wide-spreading saffron clearness, which in the sky had a monumental calm, but on the river, with its changing objects, was reflected as a luminous movement, the alternate flash of ripples or currents, the sudden glow of the brown sail, the passage of laden barges from blackness into colour, making an active response to that brooding glory.

Feeling well heated by this time, Deronda gave up the oar and drew over him again his Inverness cape. As he lifted up his head while fastening the topmost button, his eyes caught a well-remembered face looking towards him over the parapet of the bridge – brought out by the western light into startling distinctness and brilliancy – an illuminated type of bodily emaciation and spiritual eagerness. It was the face of Mordecai, who also, in his watch towards the west, had caught sight of the advancing boat, and had kept it fast within his gaze, at first simply because it was advancing, then with a recovery of impressions that made him quiver as with a presentiment, till at last the nearing figure lifted up its face towards him – the face of his visions – and then immediately, with white uplifted hand, beckoned again and again.

For Deronda, anxious that Mordecai should recognize and await him, had lost no time before signalling, and the answer came straightway. Mordecai lifted his cap and waved it – feeling in that moment that his inward prophecy was fulfilled. Obstacles, incongruities, all melted into the sense of completion with which his soul was flooded by this outward satisfaction of his longing. His exultation was not widely different from that of the experimenter, bending over the first stirrings of change that correspond to what in the fervour of concentrated prevision his thought has foreshadowed. The prefigured friend had come from the golden background, and had signalled to him: this actually was: the rest was to be.

In three minutes Deronda had landed, had paid his boatman, and was joining Mordecai, whose instinct it was to stand perfectly still and wait for him.

'I was very glad to see you standing here,' said Deronda, 'for I was intending to go on to the book-shop and look for you again. I was there yesterday – perhaps they mentioned it to you?'

'Yes,' said Mordecai; 'that was the reason I came to the bridge.'

This answer, made with simple gravity, was startlingly mysterious to Deronda. Were the peculiarities of this man really associated with any sort of mental alienation, according to Cohen's hint?

'You knew nothing of my being at Chelsea?' he said after a moment.

'No: but I expected you to come down the river. I have been waiting for you these five years.' Mordecai's deep-sunk eyes were fixed on those of the friend who had at last arrived, with a look of affectionate dependence, at once

545

pathetic and solemn. Deronda's sensitiveness was not the less responsive because he could not but believe that this strangely-disclosed relation was founded on an illusion.

'It will be a satisfaction to me if I can be of any real use to you,' he answered very earnestly. 'Shall we get into a cab and drive to – wherever you wish to go? You have probably had walking enough with your short breath.'

'Let us go to the book-shop. It will soon be time for me to be there. But now look up the river,' said Mordecai, turning again towards it and speaking in undertones of what may be called an excited calm – so absorbed by a sense of fulfilment that he was conscious of no barrier to a complete understanding between him and Deronda. 'See the sky, how it is slowly fading. I have always loved this bridge: I stood on it when I was a little boy. It is a meeting-place for the spiritual messengers. It is true – what the Masters said – that each order of things has its angel: that means the full message of each from what is afar. Here I have listened to the messages of earth and sky; when I was stronger I used to stay and watch for the stars in the deep heavens. But this time just about sunset was always what I loved best. It has sunk into me and dwelt with me – fading, slowly fading: it was my own decline: it paused – it waited, till at last it brought me my new life – my new self – who will live when this breath is all breathed out.'

Deronda did not speak. He felt himself strangely wrought upon. The first-prompted suspicion that Mordecai might be liable to hallucinations of thought – might have become a monomaniac on some subject which had given too severe a strain to his diseased organism – gave way to a more submissive expectancy. His nature was too large, too ready to conceive regions beyond his own experience, to rest at once in the easy explanation, 'madness,' whenever a consciousness showed some full-ness and conviction where his own was blank. It accorded with his habitual disposition that he should meet rather than resist any claim on him in the shape of another's need; and this claim brought with it a sense of solemnity which seemed a radiation from Mordecai, as utterly nullifying his outward poverty and lifting him into authority as if he had been that preternatural guide seen in the universal legend, who suddenly drops his mean disguise and stands a manifest Power. That impression was the more sanctioned by a sort of resolved quietude which the persuasion of fulfilment had produced in Mordecai's manner. After they had stood a moment in silence he said, 'Let us go now;' and when they were walking he added, 'We will get down at the end of the street and walk to the shop. You can look at the books, and Mr. Ram will be going away directly and leave us alone.'

It seemed that this enthusiast was just as cautious, just as much alive to judgments in other minds as if he had been that antipole of all enthusiasm called 'a man of the world.'

While they were rattling along in the cab, Mirah was still present with Deronda in the midst of this strange experience, but he foresaw that the course of conversation would be determined by Mordecai, not by himself: he was no longer confident what questions he should be able to ask; and with a reaction on his own mood, he inwardly said, 'I suppose I am in a state of complete superstition, just as if I were awaiting the destiny that could interpret the oracle. But some strong relation there must be between me and this man, since he feels it strongly. Great heaven! what relation has proved itself more potent in the world than faith even when mistaken – than expectation even when perpetually disappointed? Is my side of the relation to be disappointing or fulfilling? – well, if it is ever possible for me to fulfil, I will not disappoint.'

In ten minutes the two men, with as intense a consciousness as if they had been two undeclared lovers, felt themselves alone in the small gas-lit book-shop and turned face to face, each baring his head from an instinctive feeling that they wished to see each other fully. Mordecai came forward to lean his back against the little counter, while Deronda stood against the opposite wall hardly more than four feet off. I wish I could perpetuate those two faces, as Titian's 'Tribute Money' has perpetuated two types presenting another sort of contrast. Imagine – we all of us can – the pathetic stamp of consumption with its brilliancy of glance to which the sharply-defined structure of features, reminding one of a forsaken temple, give already a far-off look as of one getting unwillingly out of reach; and imagine it on a Jewish face naturally accentuated for the expression of an eager mind – the face of a man little above thirty, but with that age upon it which belongs to time lengthened by suffering, the hair and beard still black throwing out the yellow pallor of the skin, the difficult breathing giving more decided marking to the mobile nostril, the wasted yellow hands conspicuous on the folded arms: then give to the yearning consumptive glance something of the slowly dying mother's look when her one loved son visits her bedside, and the flickering power of gladness leaps out as she says, 'My boy!' – for the sense of spiritual perpetuation in another resembles that maternal transference of self.

Seeing such a portrait you would see Mordecai. And opposite to him was a face not more distinctively oriental than many a type seen among what we call the Latin races: rich in youthful health, and with a forcible masculine gravity in its repose, that gave the value of judgment to the reverence with which he met the gaze of this mysterious son of poverty who claimed him as a long-expected friend. The more exquisite quality of Deronda's nature – that keenly perceptive sympathetic emotiveness which ran along with his speculative tendency – was never more thoroughly tested. He felt nothing that could be called belief in the validity of Mordecai's impressions concerning him or in the probability of any greatly effective issue: what he felt was a profound sensibility to a cry from the depths of another soul; and accompanying that, the summons to be receptive instead of superciliously prejudging. Receptiveness is a rare and massive power, like fortitude; and this state of mind now gave Deronda's face its utmost expression of calm benignant force – an expression which nourished Mordecai's confidence and made an open way before him. He began to speak.

'You cannot know what has guided me to you and brought us together at this moment. You are wondering.'

'I am not impatient,' said Deronda. 'I am ready to listen to whatever you may wish to disclose.'

'You see some of the reasons why I needed you,' said Mordecai, speaking quietly, as if he wished to reserve his strength. 'You see that I am dying. You see that I am as one shut up behind bars by the wayside, who if he spoke to any would be met only by head-shaking and pity. The day is closing – the light is fading – soon we should not have been able to discern each other. But you have come in time.'

'I rejoice that I am come in time,' said Deronda, feelingly. He would not say, 'I hope you are not mistaken in me,' – the very word 'mistaken,' he thought, would be a cruelty at that moment.

'But the hidden reasons why I need you began afar off,' said Mordecai; 'began in my early years when I was studying in another land. Then ideas, beloved ideas, came to me, because I was a Jew. They were a trust to fulfil, because I was a Jew. They were an inspiration, because I was a Jew, and felt the heart of my race beating within me. They were my life; I was not fully born till then. I counted this heart, and this breath, and this right hand' – Mordecai had pathetically pressed his hand against his breast, and then stretched its wasted fingers out before him – 'I counted my sleep and my waking, and the work I fed my body with, and the sights that fed my eyes – I counted them but as fuel to the divine flame. But I had done as one who wanders and engraves his thought in rocky solitudes, and before I could change my course came care and labour and disease, and blocked the way before me, and bound me with the iron that eats itself into the soul. Then I said, "How shall I save the life within me from being stifled with this stifled breath?"'

Mordecai paused to rest that poor breath which had been taxed by the rising excitement of his speech. And also he wished to check that excitement. Deronda dared not speak: the very silence in the narrow space seemed alive with mingled awe and compassion before this struggling fervour. And presently Mordecai went on –

'But you may misunderstand me. I speak not as an ignorant dreamer – as one bred up in the inland valleys, thinking ancient thoughts anew and not knowing them ancient, never having stood by the great waters where the world's knowledge passes to and fro. English is my mother-tongue, England is the native land of this body, which is but as a breaking pot of earth around the fruit-bearing tree, whose seed might make the desert rejoice. But my true life was nourished in Holland, at the feet of my mother's brother, a Rabbi skilled in special learning; and when he died I went to Hamburg to study, and afterwards to Göttingen, that I might take a larger outlook on my people, and on the Gentile world, and drink knowledge at all sources. I was a youth: I felt free; I saw our chief seats in Germany; I was not then in utter poverty. And I had possessed myself of a handicraft. For I said, I care not if my lot be as that of Joshua ben Chananja: after the last destruction he earned his bread by making needles, but in his youth he had been a singer on the steps of the Temple, and had a memory of what was, before the glory departed. I said, let my body dwell in poverty, and my hands be as the hands of the toiler; but let my soul be as a temple of remembrance where the treasures of knowledge enter and the inner sanctuary is hope. I knew what I chose. They said, "He feeds himself on visions," and I denied not; for visions are the creators and feeders of the world. I see, I measure the world as it is, which the vision will create anew. You are not listening to one who raves aloof from the lives of his fellows.'

Mordecai paused, and Deronda, feeling that the pause was expectant, said, 'Do me the justice to believe that I was not inclined to call your words raving. I listen that I may know, without prejudgment. I have had experience which gives me a keen interest in the story of a spiritual destiny embraced willingly, and embraced in youth.'

'A spiritual destiny embraced willingly – in youth?' Mordecai repeated in a corrective tone. 'It was the soul fully born within me, and it came in my boyhood. It brought its own world – a mediæval world, where there were men who made the ancient language live again in new psalms of exile. They had absorbed the philosophy of the Gentile into the faith of the Jew, and they still yearned toward a centre for our race. One of their souls was born again within me, and awaked amid the memories of their world. It travelled into Spain and Provence; it debated with Aben-Ezra; it took ship with Jehuda ha-Levi; it heard the roar of the Crusaders and the shrieks of tortured Israel. And when its dumb tongue was loosed, it spoke the speech they had made alive with the new blood of their ardour, their sorrow, and their martyred trust: it sang with the cadence of their strain.'

Mordecai paused again, and then said in a loud, hoarse whisper –

'While it is imprisoned in me, it will never learn another.'

'Have you written entirely in Hebrew, then?' said Deronda, remembering with some anxiety the former question as to his own knowledge of that tongue.

'Yes – yes,' said Mordecai, in a tone of deep sadness; 'in my youth I wandered toward that solitude, not feeling that it was a solitude. I had the ranks of the great dead around me; the martyrs gathered and listened. But soon I found that the living were deaf to me. At first I saw my life spread as a long future: I said, part of my Jewish heritage is an unbreaking patience; part is skill to seek divers methods and find a rooting-place where the planters despair. But there came new messengers from the Eternal. I had to bow under the yoke that presses on the great multitude born of woman: family troubles called me – I had to work, to care, not for myself alone. I was left solitary again; but already the angel of death had turned to me and beckoned, and I felt his skirts continually on my path. I loosed not my effort. I besought hearing and help. I spoke; I went to men of our people – to the rich in influence or knowledge, to the rich in other wealth. But I found none to listen with under-standing. I was rebuked for error; I was offered a small sum in charity. No wonder. I looked poor; I carried a bundle of Hebrew manuscript with me; I said, our chief teachers are misleading the hope of our race. Scholar and merchant were both too busy to listen. Scorn stood as interpreter between me and them. One said, "The Book of Mormon would never have answered in Hebrew; and if you mean to address our learned men, it is not likely you can teach them anything." He touched a truth there.'

The last words had a perceptible irony in their hoarsened tone.

'But though you had accustomed yourself to write in Hebrew, few, surely, can use English better,' said Deronda, wanting to hint consolation in a new effort for which he could smooth the way.

Mordecai shook his head slowly, and answered,

'Too late – too late. I can write no more. My writing would be like this gasping breath. But the breath may wake the fount of pity – the writing not. If I could write now and used English, I should be as one who beats a board to summon those who have been used to no signal but a bell. My soul has an ear to hear the faults of its own speech. New writing of mine would be like this body' – Mordecai spread his arms – 'within it there might be the Ruach-ha-kodesh – the breath of divine thought – but men would smile at it and say, "A poor Jew!" – and the chief smilers would be of my own people.'

Mordecai let his hands fall, and his head sink in melan-choly: for the moment he had lost hold of his hope. Despondency, conjured up by his own words, had floated in and hovered above him with eclipsing wings. He had sunk into momentary darkness.

'I feel with you – I feel strongly with you,' said Deronda, in a clear deep voice which was itself a cordial, apart from the words of sympathy. 'But – forgive me if I speak hastily – for what you have actually written there need be no utter

552

burial. The means of publication are within reach. If you will rely on me, I can assure you of all that is necessary to that end.'

'That is not enough,' said Mordecai, quickly, looking up again with the flash of recovered memory and confidence. 'That is not all my trust in you. You must be not only a hand to me, but a soul – believing my beliefs – being moved by my reasons – hoping my hopes – seeing the vision I point to – beholding a glory where I behold it!' – Mordecai had taken a step nearer as he spoke, and now laid his hand on Deronda's arm with a tight grasp; his face little more than a foot off had something like a pale flame in it – an intensity of reliance that acted as a peremptory claim, while he went on – 'You will be my life: it will be planted afresh; it will grow. You shall take the inheritance; it has been gathering for ages. The generations are crowding on my narrow life as a bridge: what has been and what is to be are meeting there; and the bridge is breaking. But I have found you. You have come in time. You will take the inheritance which the base son refuses because of the tombs which the plough and harrow may not pass over or the gold-seeker disturb: you will take the sacred inheritance of the Jew.'

Deronda had become as pallid as Mordecai. Quick as an alarm of flood or fire, there spread within him not only a compassionate dread of discouraging this fellow-man who urged a prayer as of one in the last agony, but also the opposing dread of fatally feeding an illusion, and being hurried on to a self-committal which might turn into a falsity. The peculiar appeal to his tenderness overcame the repulsion that most of us experience under a grasp and speech which assume to dominate. The difficulty to him was to inflict the accents of hesitation and doubt on this ardent suffering creature, who was crowding too much of his brief being into a moment of perhaps extravagant trust. With exquisite instinct, Deronda, before he opened his lips, placed his palm gently on Mordecai's straining hand – an act just then equal to many speeches. And after that he said, without haste, as if conscious that he might be wrong –

'Do you forget what I told you when we first saw each other? Do you remember that I said I was not of your race?'

'It can't be true,' Mordecai whispered immediately, with no sign of shock. The sympathetic hand still upon him had fortified the feeling which was stronger than those words of denial. There was a perceptible pause, Deronda feeling it impossible to answer, conscious indeed that the assertion, 'It can't be true' – had the pressure of argument for him. Mordecai, too entirely possessed by the supreme importance of the relation between himself and Deronda to have any other care in his speech, followed up that assertion by a second, which came to his lips as a mere sequence of his long-cherished conviction –

'You are not sure of your own origin.'

'How do you know that?' said Daniel, with an habitual shrinking which made him remove his hand from Mordecai's, who also relaxed his hold, and fell back into his former leaning position.

'I know it – I know it; what is my life else?' said Mordecai, with a low cry of impatience. 'Tell me everything: tell me why you deny.'

He could have no conception what that demand was to the hearer – how probingly it touched the hidden sensibility, the vividly conscious reticence of years; how the uncertainty he was insisting on as part of his own hope had always for Daniel been a threatening possibility of painful revelation about his mother. But the moment had influences which were not only new but solemn to Deronda: any evasion here might turn out to be a hateful refusal of some task that belonged to him, some act of due fellowship; in any case it would be a cruel rebuff to a being who was appealing to him as a forlorn hope under the shadow of a coming doom. After a few moments, he said, with a great effort over himself – determined to tell all the truth briefly –

'I have never known my mother. I have no knowledge about her. I have never called any man father. But I am convinced that my father is an Englishman.'

Deronda's deep tones had a tremor in them as he uttered this confession; and all the while there was an under-current of amazement in him at the strange circumstances under which he uttered it. It seemed as if Mordecai were hardly overrating his own power to determine the action of the friend whom he had mysteriously chosen.

'It will be seen – it will be declared,' said Mordecai, triumphantly. 'The world grows, and its frame is knit together by the growing soul; dim, dim at first, then clearer and more clear, the consciousness discerns remote stirrings. As thoughts move within us darkly, and shake us before they are fully discerned – so events – so beings: they are knit with us in the growth of the world. You have risen within me like a thought not fully spelled: my soul is shaken before the words are all there. The rest will come – it will come.'

'We must not lose sight of the fact that the outward event has not always been a fulfilment of the firmest faith,' said Deronda, in a tone that was made hesitating by the painfully conflicting desires, not to give any severe blow to Mordecai, and not to give his confidence a sanction which might have the severest of blows in reserve.

Mordecai's face, which had been illuminated to the utmost in that last declaration of his confidence, changed under Deronda's words, but not into any show of collapsed trust: the force did not disappear from the expression, but passed from the triumphant into the firmly resistant.

'You would remind me that I may be under an illusion – that the history of our people's trust has been full of illusion. I face it all.' Here Mordecai paused a moment. Then bending his head a little forward, he said, in his hoarse whisper, '*So it might be with my trust, if you would make it an illusion. But you will not.*'

The very sharpness with which these words penetrated Deronda, made him feel the more that here was a crisis in which he must be firm.

'What my birth was does not lie in my will,' he answered. 'My sense of claims on me cannot be independent of my knowledge there. And I cannot promise you that I will try to hasten a disclosure. Feelings which have struck root through half my life may still hinder me from doing what I have never yet been able to do. Everything must be waited for. I must know more of the truth about my own life, and I must know more of what it would become if it were made a part of yours.'

Mordecai had folded his arms again while Deronda was speaking, and now answered with equal firmness, though with difficult breathing –

'You *shall* know. What are we met for, but that you should know? Your doubts lie as light as dust on my belief. I know the philosophies of this time and of other times: if I chose I could answer a summons before their tribunals. I could silence the beliefs which are the mother-tongue of my soul and speak with the rote-learned language of a system, that gives you the spelling of all things, sure of its alphabet covering them all. I could silence them: may not a man silence his awe or his love and take to finding reasons, which others demand? But if his love lies deeper than any reasons to be found? Man finds his pathways: at first they were foot-tracks, as those of the beast in the wilderness; now they are swift and invisible: his thought dives through the ocean, and his wishes thread the air: has he found all the pathways yet? What reaches him, stays with him, rules him: he must accept it, not knowing its pathway. Say, my expectation of you has grown but as false hopes grow. That doubt is in your mind? Well, my expectation was there, and you are come. Men have died of thirst. But I was thirsty, and the water is on my lips. What are doubts to me? In the hour when you come to me and say, "I reject your soul: I know that I am not a Jew: we have no lot in common" – I shall not doubt. I shall be certain – certain that I have been deluded. That hour will never come!'

Deronda felt a new chord sounding in this speech: it was rather imperious than appealing – had more of conscious power than of the yearning need which had acted as a beseeching grasp on him before. And usually, though he was the reverse of pugnacious, such a change of attitude towards him would have weakened his inclination to admit a claim. But here there was something that balanced his resistance and kept it aloof. This strong man whose gaze was sustainedly calm and his finger-nails pink with health, who was exercised in all questioning, and accused of excessive mental independence, still felt a subduing influence over him in the tenacious certitude of the fragile creature before him, whose pallid yellow nostril was tense with effort as his breath laboured under the burthen of eager speech. The influence seemed to strengthen the bond of sympathetic obligation. In Deronda at this moment the desire to escape what might turn into a trying embarrassment was no more likely to determine action than the solicitations of indolence are likely to determine it in one with whom industry is a daily law. He answered simply –

'It is my wish to meet and satisfy your wishes wherever that is possible to me. It is certain to me at least that I desire not to undervalue your toil and your suffering. Let me know your thoughts. But where can we meet?'

'I have thought of that,' said Mordecai. 'It is not hard for you to come into this neighbourhood later in the evening? You did so once.'

'I can manage it very well occasionally,' said Deronda. 'You live under the same roof with the Cohens, I think?'

Before Mordecai could answer, Mr. Ram re-entered to take his place behind the counter. He was an elderly son of Abraham, whose childhood had fallen on the evil times at the beginning of this century, and who remained amid this smart and instructed generation as a preserved specimen, soaked through and through with the effect of the poverty and contempt which were the common heritage of most English Jews seventy years ago. He had none of the oily cheerfulness observable in Mr. Cohen's aspect: his very features – broad and chubby – showed that tendency to look mongrel without due cause which, in a miscellaneous London neighbourhood, may perhaps be compared with the marvels of imitation in insects, and may have been nature's imperfect effort on behalf of the purer Caucasian to shield him from the shame and spitting to which purer features would have been exposed in the times of zeal. Mr. Ram dealt ably in books in the same way that he would have dealt in tins of meat and other commodities – without knowledge or responsibility as to the proportion of rottenness or nourishment they might contain. But he believed in Mordecai's learning as something marvellous, and was not sorry that his conversation should be sought by a bookish gentleman, whose visits had twice ended in a purchase. He greeted Deronda with a crabbed goodwill, and, putting on large silver spectacles, appeared at once to abstract himself in the daily accounts.

But Deronda and Mordecai were soon in the street together, and, without any explicit agreement as to their direction, were walking towards Ezra Cohen's.

'We can't meet there: my room is too narrow,' said Mordecai, taking up the thread of talk where they had dropped it. 'But there is a tavern not far from here where I sometimes go to a club. It is the *Hand and Banner*, in the street at the next turning, five doors down. We can have the parlour there any evening.'

'We can try that for once,' said Deronda. 'But you will perhaps let me provide you with some lodging, which would give you more freedom and comfort than where you are.'

'No; I need nothing. My outer life is as nought. I will take nothing less precious from you than your soul's brotherhood. I will think of nothing else yet. But I am glad you are rich. You did not need money on that diamond ring. You had some other motive for bringing it.'

Deronda was a little startled by this clear-sightedness; but before he could reply, Mordecai added – 'It is all one. Had you been in need of the money, the great end would have been that we should meet again. But you are rich?' he ended, in a tone of interrogation.

'Not rich, except in the sense that every one is rich who has more than he needs for himself.'

'I desired that your life should be free,' said Mordecai, dreamily – 'mine has been a bondage.'

It was clear that he had no interest in the fact of Deronda's appearance at the Cohens' beyond its relation to his own ideal purpose. Despairing of leading easily up to the question he wished to ask, Deronda determined to put it abruptly, and said –

'Can you tell me why Mrs. Cohen, the mother, must not be spoken to about her daughter?'

There was no immediate answer, and he thought that he should have to repeat the question. The fact was that Mordecai had heard the words, but had to drag his mind to a new subject away from his passionate preoccupation. After a few moments, he replied, with a careful effort such as he would have used if he had been asked the road to Holborn –

'I know the reason. But I will not speak even of trivial family affairs which I have heard in the privacy of the family. I dwell in their tent as in a sanctuary. Their history, so far as they injure none other, is their own possession.'

Deronda felt the blood mounting to his cheeks at a sort of rebuke he was little used to, and he also found himself painfully baffled where he had reckoned with some confidence on getting decisive knowledge. He became the more conscious of emotional strain from the excitements of the day; and although he had the money in his pocket to redeem his ring, he recoiled from the further task of a visit to the Cohens', which must be made not only under the former uncertainty, but under a new disappointment as to the possibility of its removal.

'I will part from you now,' he said, just before they could reach Cohen's door; and Mordecai paused, looking up at him with an anxious fatigued face under the gaslight.

'When will you come back?' he said, with slow emphasis.

'May I leave that unfixed? May I ask for you at the Cohens' any evening after your hour at the book-shop?

There is no objection, I suppose, to their knowing that you and I meet in private?'

'None,' said Mordecai. 'But the days I wait now are longer than the years of my strength. Life shrinks: what was but a tithe is now the half. My hope abides in you.'

'I will be faithful,' said Deronda – he could not have left those words unuttered. 'I will come the first evening I can after seven: on Saturday or Monday, if possible. Trust me.'

He put out his ungloved hand. Mordecai, clasping it eagerly, seemed to feel a new instreaming of confidence, and he said with some recovered energy – 'This is come to pass, and the rest will come.'

That was their good-bye.

BOOK VI
Revelations

XLI

'This, too, is probable, according to that saying of Agathon: "It is a part of probability that many improbable things will happen."'
— ARISTOTLE: *Poetics*.

IMAGINE the conflict in a mind like Deronda's, given not only to feel strongly but to question actively, on the evening after that interview with Mordecai. To a young man of much duller susceptibilities the adventure might have seemed enough out of the common way to divide his thoughts; but it had stirred Deronda so deeply, that with the usual reaction of his intellect he began to examine the grounds of his emotion, and consider how far he must resist its guidance. The consciousness that he was half dominated by Mordecai's energetic certitude, and still more by his fervent trust, roused his alarm. It was his characteristic bias to shrink from the moral stupidity of valuing lightly what had come close to him, and of missing blindly in his own life of today the crises which he recognized as momentous and sacred in the historic life of men. If he had read of this incident as having happened centuries ago in Rome, Greece, Asia Minor, Palestine, Cairo, to some man young as himself, dissatisfied with his neutral life, and wanting some closer fellowship, some more special duty to give him ardour for the possible consequences of his work, it would have appeared to him quite natural that the incident should have created a deep impression on that far-off man, whose clothing and action would have been seen in his imagination as part of an age chiefly known to us through its more serious effects. Why should he be ashamed of his own agitated feeling merely because he dressed for dinner, wore a white tie, and lived among people who might laugh at his owning any conscience in the matter as the solemn folly of taking himself too seriously? – that bugbear of circles in which the lack of grave emotion passes for wit. From such cowardice before modish ignorance and obtuseness, Deronda shrank. But he also shrank from having his course determined by mere contagion, without consent of reason; or from allowing a reverential pity for spiritual struggle to hurry him along a dimly-seen path.

What, after all, had really happened? He knew quite accurately the answer Sir Hugo would have given: 'A consumptive Jew, possessed by a fanaticism which obstacles and hastening death intensified, had fixed on Deronda as the antitype of some visionary image, the offspring of wedded hope and despair: despair of his own life, irrepressible hope in the propagation of his fanatical beliefs. The instance was perhaps odd, exceptional in its form, but substantially it was not rare. Fanaticism was not so common as bankruptcy, but taken in all its aspects it was abundant enough. While Mordecai was waiting on the bridge for the fulfilment of his visions, another man was convinced that he had the mathematical key of the universe which would supersede Newton, and regarded all known physicists as conspiring to stifle his discovery and keep the universe locked; another, that he had the metaphysical key, with just that hair's-breadth of difference from the old wards which would make it fit exactly. Scattered here and there in every direction you might find a terrible person, with more or less power of speech, and with an eye either glittering or preternaturally dull, on the look-out for the man who must hear him; and in most cases he had volumes which it was difficult to get printed, or if printed to get read. This Mordecai happened to have a more pathetic aspect, a more passionate, penetrative speech than was usual with such monomaniacs: he was more poetical than a social reformer with coloured views of the new moral world in parallelograms, or than an enthusiast in sewage; still he came under the same class. It would be only right and kind to indulge him a little, to comfort him with such help as was practicable; but what likelihood was there that his notions had the sort of value he ascribed to them? In such cases a man of the world knows what to think beforehand. And as to Mordecai's conviction that he had found a new executive self, it might be preparing for him the worst of disappointments – that which presents itself as final.'

Deronda's ear caught all these negative whisperings; nay, he repeated them distinctly to himself. It was not the first but it was the most pressing occasion on which he had had to face this question of the family likeness among the heirs of enthusiasm, whether prophets or dreamers of dreams, whether the

'Great benefactors of mankind, deliverers,'

or the devotees of phantasmal discovery – from the first believer in his own unmanifested inspiration, down to the last inventor of an ideal machine that will achieve per-petual motion. The kinship of human passion, the same-ness of mortal scenery, inevitably fill fact with burlesque and parody. Error and folly have had their hecatombs of martyrs. Reduce the grandest type of man hitherto known to an abstract statement of his qualities and efforts, and he appears in dangerous company: say that, like Copernicus and Galileo, he was immovably convinced in the face of hissing incredulity; but so is the contriver of perpetual motion. We cannot fairly try the spirits by this sort of test. If we want to avoid giving the dose of hemlock or the sentence of banishment in the wrong case, nothing will do but a capacity to understand the subject-matter on which the immovable man is convinced, and fellowship with human travail, both near and afar, to hinder us from scanning any deep experience lightly. Shall we say, 'Let the ages try the spirits, and see what they are worth'? Why, we are the beginning of the ages, which can only be just by virtue of just judgments in separate human breasts – separ-ate yet combined. Even steam-engines could not have got made without that condition, but must have stayed in the mind of James Watt.

This track of thinking was familiar enough to Deronda to have saved him from any contemptuous prejudgment of Mordecai, even if their communication had been free from that peculiar claim on himself strangely ushered in by some long-growing preparation in the Jew's agitated mind. This claim, indeed, considered in what is called a rational way, might seem justifiably dismissed as illusory and even preposterous; but it was precisely what turned Mordecai's hold on him from an appeal to his ready sympathy into a clutch on his struggling conscience. Our consciences are not all of the same pattern, an inner deliverance of fixed laws: they are the voice of sensibilities as various as our memories (which also have their kinship and likeness). And Deronda's conscience included sensibilities beyond the common, enlarged by his early habit of thinking himself imaginatively into the experience of others.

What was the claim this eager soul made upon him? – 'You must believe my beliefs – be moved by my reasons – hope my hopes – see the vision I point to – behold a glory where I behold it!' To take such a demand in the light of an obligation in any direct sense would have been preposterous – to have seemed to admit it would have been dishonesty; and Deronda, looking on the agitation of those moments, felt thankful that in the midst of his compassion he had preserved himself from the bondage of false concessions. The claim hung, too, on a supposition which might be – nay, probably was – in discordance with the full fact: the supposition that he, Deronda, was of Jewish blood. Was there ever a more hypothetic appeal?

But since the age of thirteen Deronda had associated the deepest experience of his affections with what was a pure supposition, namely, that Sir Hugo was his father: that was a hypothesis which had been the source of passionate struggle within him; by its light he had been accustomed to subdue feelings and to cherish them. He had been well used to find a motive in a conception which might be disproved; and he had been also used to think of some revelation that might influence his view of the particular duties belonging to him. To be in a state of suspense which was also one of emotive activity and scruple, was a familiar attitude of his conscience.

And now, suppose that wish-begotten belief in his Jewish birth, and that extravagant demand of discipleship, to be the foreshadowing of an actual discovery and a genuine spiritual result: suppose that Mordecai's ideas made a real conquest over Deronda's conviction? Nay, it was conceivable that as Mordecai needed and believed that he had found an active replenishment of himself, so Deronda might receive from Mordecai's mind the complete ideal shape of that personal duty and citizenship which lay in his own thought like sculptured fragments certifying some beauty yearned after but not traceable by divination.

As that possibility presented itself in his meditations, he was aware that it would be called dreamy, and began to defend it. If the influence he imagined himself submitting to had been that of some honoured professor, some authority in a seat of learning, some philosopher who had been accepted as a voice of the age, would a thorough receptiveness towards direction have been ridiculed? Only by those who hold it a sign of weakness to be obliged for an idea, and prefer to hint that they have implicitly held in a more correct form whatever others have stated with a sadly short-coming explicitness. After all, what was there but vulgarity in taking the fact that Mordecai was a poor Jewish workman, and that he was to be met perhaps on a sanded floor in the parlour of the *Hand and Banner*, as a reason for determining beforehand that there was not some spiritual force within him that might have a determining effect on a white-handed gentleman? There is a legend told of the Emperor Domitian, that having heard of a Jewish family, of the house of David, whence the ruler of the world was to spring, he sent for its members in alarm, but quickly released them on observing that they had the hands of work-people – being of just the opposite opinion with that Rabbi who stood waiting at the gate of Rome in confidence that the Messiah would be found among the destitute who entered there. Both Emperor and Rabbi were wrong in their trust of outward signs: poverty and poor clothes are no sign of inspiration, said Deronda to his inward objector, but they have gone with it in some remarkable cases. And to regard discipleship as out of the question because of them, would be mere dullness of imagination.

A more plausible reason for putting discipleship out of the question was the strain of visionary excitement in Mordecai, which turned his wishes into overmastering impressions, and made him read outward facts as fulfilment. Was such a temper of mind likely to accompany that wise estimate of consequences which is the only safeguard from fatal error, even to ennobling motive? But it remained to be seen whether that rare conjunction existed or not in Mordecai: perhaps his might be one of the natures where a wise estimate of consequences is fused in the fires of that passionate belief which determines the consequences it believes in. The inspirations of the world have come in that way too: even strictly-measuring science could hardly have got on without that forecasting ardour which feels the agitations of discovery beforehand, and has a faith in its preconception that surmounts many failures of experiment. And in relation to human motives and actions, passionate belief has a fuller efficacy. Here enthusiasm may have the validity of proof, and, happening in one soul, give the type of what will one day be general.

At least, Deronda argued, Mordecai's visionary excitability was hardly a reason for concluding beforehand that he was not worth listening to except for pity's sake. Suppose he had introduced himself as one of the strictest reasoners: do they form a body of men hitherto free from false conclusions and illusory speculations? The driest argument has its hallucinations, too hastily concluding that its net will now at last be large enough to hold the universe. Men may dream in demonstrations, and cut out an illusory world in the shape of axioms, definitions, and propositions, with a final exclusion of fact signed Q.E.D. No formulas for thinking will save us mortals from mistake in our imperfect apprehension of the matter to be thought about. And since the unemotional intellect may carry us into a mathematical dreamland where nothing is but what is not, perhaps an emotional intellect may have absorbed into its passionate vision of possibilities some truth of what will be – the more comprehensive massive life feeding theory with new material, as the sensibility of the artist seizes combinations which science explains and justifies. At any rate, presumptions to the contrary are not to be trusted. We must be patient with the inevitable makeshift of our human thinking, whether in its sum total or in the separate minds that have made the sum. Columbus had some impressions about himself which we call superstitions, and used some arguments which we disapprove; but he had also some true physical conceptions, and he had the passionate patience of genius to make them tell on mankind. The world has made up its mind rather contemptuously about those who were deaf to Columbus.

'My contempt for them binds me to see that I don't adopt their mistake on a small scale,' said Deronda, 'and make myself deaf with the assumption that there cannot be any momentous relation between this Jew and me, simply because he has clad it in illusory notions. What I can be to him, or he to me, may not at all depend on his persuasion about the way we came together. To me the way seems made up of plainly discernible links. If I had not found Mirah, it is probable that I should not have begun to be specially interested in the Jews, and certainly I should not have gone on that loitering search after an Ezra Cohen which made me pause at Ram's book-shop and ask the price of *Maimon*. Mordecai, on his side, had his visions of a disciple, and he saw me by their light; I corresponded well enough with the image his longing had created. He took me for one of his race. Suppose that his impression – the elderly Jew at Frankfort seemed to have something like it – suppose, in spite of all presumptions to the contrary, that his impression should somehow be proved true, and that I should come actually to share any of the ideas he is devoted to? This is the only question which really concerns the effect of our meeting on my life.

'But if the issue should be quite different? – well, there will be something painful to go through. I shall almost inevitably have to be an active cause of that poor fellow's crushing disappointment. Perhaps this issue is the one I had need prepare myself for. I fear that no tenderness of mine can make his suffering lighter. Would the alternative – that I should not disappoint him – be less painful to me?'

Here Deronda wavered. Feelings had lately been at work within him which had very much modified the reluctance he would formerly have had to think of himself as probably a Jew. And, if you like, he was romantic. That young energy and spirit of adventure which have helped to create the world-wide legends of youthful heroes going to seek the hidden tokens of their birth and its inheritance of tasks, gave him a certain quivering interest in the bare possibility that he was entering on a like track – all the more because the track was one of thought as well as action.

'The bare possibility.' He could not admit it to be more. The belief that his father was an Englishman only grew firmer under the weak assaults of unwarranted doubt. And that a moment should ever come in which that belief was declared an illusion, was something of which Deronda would not say, 'I should be glad.' His lifelong affection for Sir Hugo, stronger than all his resentment, made him shrink from admitting that wish.

Which way soever the truth might lie, he repeated to himself what he had said to Mordecai – that he could not without farther reason undertake to hasten its discovery. Nay, he was tempted now to regard his uncertainty as a condition to be cherished for the present. If further inter- course revealed nothing but illusions as what he was expected to share in, the want of any valid evidence that he was a Jew might save Mordecai the worst shock in the refusal of fraternity. It might even be justifiable to use the uncertainty on this point in keeping up a suspense which would induce Mordecai to accept those offices of friendship that Deronda longed to urge on him.

These were the meditations that busied Deronda in the interval of four days before he could fulfil his promise to call for Mordecai at Ezra Cohen's, Sir Hugo's demands on him often lasting to an hour so late as to put the evening expedition to Holborn out of the question.

XLII

'Wenn es eine Stufenleiter von Leiden giebt, so hat Israel die
höchste Staffel erstiegen; wenn die Dauer der Schmerzen und
die Geduld, mit welcher sie ertragen werden, adeln, so nehmen
es die Juden mit den Hochgeborenen aller Länder auf; wenn eine
Literatur reich genannt wird, die wenige klassische Trauerspiele
besitzt, welcher Platz gebührt dann einer Tragödie die
anderthalb Jahrtausende währt, gedichtet und dargestellt von
den Helden selber?'

– ZUNZ: *Die Synagogale Poesie des Mittelalters*.

'IF there are ranks in suffering, Israel takes precedence of
all the nations – if the duration of sorrows and the patience
with which they are borne ennoble, the Jews are among the
aristocracy of every land – if a literature is called rich in the
possession of a few classic tragedies, what shall we say to a
National Tragedy lasting for fifteen hundred years, in
which the poets and actors were also the heroes?'

Deronda had lately been reading that passage of Zunz,
and it occurred to him by way of contrast when he was
going to the Cohens, who certainly bore no obvious stamp
of distinction in sorrow or in any other form of aristocracy.
Ezra Cohen was not clad in the sublime pathos of the
martyr, and his taste for money-getting seemed to be
favoured with that success which has been the most exasperating difference in the greed of Jews during all the ages
of their dispersion. This Jeshurun of a pawnbroker was not
a symbol of the great Jewish tragedy; and yet, was there not
something typical in the fact that a life like Mordecai's – a
frail incorporation of the national consciousness, breathing
with difficult breath – was nested in the self-gratulating
ignorant prosperity of the Cohens?

Glistening was the gladness in their faces when
Deronda reappeared among them. Cohen himself took
occasion to intimate that although the diamond ring, let
alone a little longer, would have bred more money, he did
not mind *that* – not a sixpence – when compared with the
pleasure of the women and children in seeing a young

gentleman whose first visit had been so agreeable that they had 'done nothing but talk of it ever since.' Young Mrs. Cohen was very sorry that baby was asleep, and then very glad that Adelaide was not yet gone to bed, entreating Deronda not to stay in the shop but to go forthwith into the parlour to see 'mother and the children.' He willingly accepted the invitation, having provided himself with portable presents; a set of paper figures for Adelaide, and an ivory cup and ball for Jacob.

The grandmother had a pack of cards before her and was making 'plates' with the children. A plate had just been thrown down and kept itself whole.

'Stop!' said Jacob, running up to Deronda as he entered. 'Don't tread on my plate. Stop and see me throw it up again.'

Deronda complied, exchanging a smile of understanding with the grandmother, and the plate bore several tossings before it came to pieces; then the visitor was allowed to come forward and seat himself. He observed that the door from which Mordecai had issued on the former visit was now closed, but he wished to show his interest in the Cohens before disclosing a yet stronger interest in their singular inmate.

It was not until he had Adelaide on his knee, and was setting up the paper figures in their dance on the table, while Jacob was already practising with the cup and ball, that Deronda said –

'Is Mordecai in just now?'

'Where is he, Addy?' said Cohen, who had seized an interval of business to come and look on.

'In the workroom there,' said his wife, nodding towards the closed door.

'The fact is, sir,' said Cohen, 'we don't know what's come to him this last day or two. He's always what I may call a little touched, you know' – here Cohen pointed to his own forehead – 'not quite to say rational in all things, like you and me; but he's mostly wonderful regular and industrious as far as a poor creature can be, and takes as much delight in the boy as anybody could. But this last day or two he's been moving about like a sleep-walker, or else sitting as still as a wax figure.'

'It's the disease, poor dear creature,' said the grand-mother, tenderly. 'I doubt whether he can stand long against it.'

'No; I think it's only something he's got in his head,' said Mrs. Cohen the younger. 'He's been turning over writing continually, and when I speak to him it takes him ever so long to hear and answer.'

'You may think us a little weak ourselves,' said Cohen, apologetically. 'But my wife and mother wouldn't part with him if he was a still worse encumbrance. It isn't that we don't know the long and short of matters, but it's our principle. There's fools do business at a loss and don't know it. I'm not one of 'em.'

'Oh, Mordecai carries a blessing inside him,' said the grandmother.

'He's got something the matter inside him,' said Jacob, coming up to correct this erratum of his grandmother's. 'He said he couldn't talk to me, and he wouldn't have a bit o' bun.'

'So far from wondering at your feeling for him,' said Deronda, 'I already feel something of the same sort myself. I have lately talked to him at Ram's book-shop – in fact, I promised to call for him here, that we might go out together.'

'That's it, then!' said Cohen, slapping his knee. 'He's been expecting you, and it's taken hold of him. I suppose he talks about his learning to you. It's uncommonly kind of *you*, sir; for I don't suppose there's much to be got out of it, else it wouldn't have left him where he is. But there's the shop.' Cohen hurried out, and Jacob, who had been listening inconveniently near to Deronda's elbow, said to him with obliging familiarity, 'I'll call Mordecai for you, if you like.'

'No, Jacob,' said his mother; 'open the door for the gentleman, and let him go in himself. Hush! Don't make a noise.'

Skilful Jacob seemed to enter into the play, and turned the handle of the door as noiselessly as possible, while Deronda went behind him and stood on the threshold. The small room was lit only by a dying fire and one candle with a shade over it. On the board fixed under the window, various objects of jewellery were scattered: some books were heaped in the corner beyond them. Mordecai was seated on a high chair at the board with his back to the door, his hands resting on each other and on the board, a watch propped on a stand before him. He was in a state of expectation as sickening as that of a prisoner listening for the delayed deliverance – when he heard Deronda's voice saying, 'I am come for you. Are you ready?'

Immediately he turned without speaking, seized his furred cap which lay near, and moved to join Deronda. It was but a moment before they were both in the sitting-room, and Jacob, noticing the change in his friend's air and expression, seized him by the arm and said, 'See my cup and ball!' sending the ball up close to Mordecai's face, as something likely to cheer a convalescent. It was a sign of the relieved tension in Mordecai's mind that he could smile and say, 'Fine, fine!'

'You have forgotten your greatcoat and comforter,' said young Mrs. Cohen, and he went back into the workroom and got them.

'He's come to life again, do you see?' said Cohen, who had re-entered – speaking in an undertone. 'I told you so: I'm mostly right.' Then in his usual voice, 'Well, sir, we mustn't detain you now, I suppose; but I hope this isn't the last time we shall see you.'

'Shall you come again?' said Jacob, advancing. 'See, I can catch the ball; I'll bet I catch it without stopping, if you come again.'

'He has clever hands,' said Deronda, looking at the grandmother. 'Which side of the family does he get them from?'

But the grandmother only nodded towards her son, who said promptly, 'My side. My wife's family are not in that

573

line. But, bless your soul! ours is a sort of cleverness as good as gutta percha; you can twist it which way you like. There's nothing some old gentlemen won't do if you set 'em to it.' Here Cohen winked down at Jacob's back, but it was doubtful whether this judicious allusiveness answered its purpose, for its subject gave a nasal whinnying laugh and stamped about singing 'Old gentlemen, old gentlemen,' in chiming cadence.

Deronda thought, 'I shall never know anything decisive about these people until I ask Cohen point-blank whether he lost a sister named Mirah when she was six years old.' The decisive moment did not yet seem easy for him to face. Still his first sense of repulsion at the commonness of these people was beginning to be tempered with kindlier feeling. However unrefined their airs and speech might be, he was forced to admit some moral refinement in their treatment of the consumptive workman, whose mental distinction impressed them chiefly as a harmless, silent raving.

'The Cohens seem to have an affection for you,' said Deronda, as soon as he and Mordecai were off the doorstep.

'And I for them,' was the immediate answer. 'They have the heart of the Israelite within them, though they are as the horse and the mule, without understanding beyond the narrow path they tread.'

'I have caused you some uneasiness, I fear,' said Deronda, 'by my slowness in fulfilling my promise. I wished to come yesterday, but I found it impossible.'

'Yes – yes, I trusted you. But it is true I have been uneasy, for the spirit of my youth has been stirred within me, and this body is not strong enough to bear the beating of its wings. I am as a man bound and imprisoned through long years: behold him brought to speech of his fellow and his limbs set free: he weeps, he totters, the joy within him threatens to break and overthrow the tabernacle of flesh.'

'You must not speak too much in this evening air,' said Deronda, feeling Mordecai's words of reliance like so many cords binding him painfully. 'Cover your mouth with the woollen scarf. We are going to the *Hand and Banner*, I suppose, and shall be in private there?'

'No, that is my trouble that you did not come yesterday. For this is the evening of the club I spoke of, and we might not have any minutes alone until late, when all the rest are gone. Perhaps we had better seek another place. But I am used to that only. In new places the outer world presses on me and narrows the inward vision. And the people there are familiar with my face.'

'I don't mind the club if I am allowed to go in,' said Deronda. 'It is enough that you like this place best. If we have not enough time, I will come again. What sort of club is it?'

'It is called, "The Philosophers." They are few – like the cedars of Lebanon – poor men given to thought. But none so poor as I am: and sometimes visitors of higher worldly rank have been brought. We are allowed to introduce a friend, who is interested in our topics. Each orders beer or some other kind of drink, in payment for the room. Most of them smoke. I have gone when I could, for there are other men of my race who come, and sometimes I have broken silence. I have pleased myself with a faint likeness between these poor philosophers and the Masters who handed down the thought of our race – the great Transmitters, who laboured with their hands for scant bread, but preserved and enlarged for us the heritage of memory, and saved the soul of Israel alive as a seed among the tombs. The heart pleases itself with faint resemblances.'

'I shall be very glad to go and sit among them, if that will suit you. It is a sort of meeting I should like to join in,' said Deronda, not without relief in the prospect of an interval before he went through the strain of his next private conversation with Mordecai.

In three minutes they had opened the glazed door with the red curtain, and were in the little parlour, hardly much more than fifteen feet square, where the gaslight shone through a slight haze of smoke on what to Deronda was a new and striking scene. Half-a-dozen men of various ages, from between twenty and thirty to fifty, all shabbily dressed, most of them with clay pipes in their mouths, were listening with a look of concentrated intelligence to a man in a pepper-and-salt dress, with blond hair, short nose, broad forehead and general breadth, who, holding his pipe slightly uplifted in the left hand, and beating his knee with the right, was just finishing a quotation from Shelley (the comparison of the avalanche in his 'Prometheus Unbound') –

> 'As thought by thought is piled, till some great truth
> Is loosened, and the nations echo round.'

The entrance of the new-comers broke the fixity of attention, and called for a rearrangement of seats in the too narrow semicircle round the fireplace and the table holding the glasses, spare pipes, and tobacco. This was the soberest of clubs; but sobriety is no reason why smoking and 'taking something' should be less imperiously needed as a means of getting a decent status in company and debate. Mordecai was received with welcoming voices which had a slight cadence of compassion in them, but naturally all glances passed immediately to his companion.

'I have brought a friend who is interested in our subjects,' said Mordecai. 'He has travelled and studied much.'

'Is the gentleman anonymous? Is he a Great Unknown?' said the broad-chested quoter of Shelley, with a humorous air.

'My name is Daniel Deronda. I am unknown, but not in any sense great.' The smile breaking over the stranger's grave face as he said this was so agreeable, that there was a general indistinct murmur, equivalent to a 'Hear, hear,' and the broad man said –

'You recommend the name, sir, and are welcome. Here, Mordecai, come to this corner against me,' he added, evidently wishing to give the cosiest place to the one who most needed it.

Deronda was well satisfied to get a seat on the opposite side, where his general survey of the party easily included Mordecai, who remained an eminently striking object in this group of sharply-characterized figures, more than one of whom, even to Daniel's little exercised discrimination, seemed probably of Jewish descent.

In fact, pure English blood (if leech or lancet can furnish us with the precise product) did not declare itself predominantly in the party at present assembled. Miller, the broad man, an exceptional second-hand bookseller who knew the insides of books, had at least grandparents who called themselves German, and possibly far-away ancestors who denied themselves to be Jews; Buchan, the saddler, was Scotch; Pash, the watch-maker, was a small, dark, vivacious, triple-baked Jew; Gideon, the optical instrument maker, was a Jew of the red-haired, generous-featured type easily passing for Englishmen of unusually cordial manners; and Croop, the dark-eyed shoe-maker, was probably more Celtic than he knew. Only three would have been discernible everywhere as Englishmen: the wood-inlayer Goodwin, well-built, open-faced, pleasant-voiced; the florid laboratory assistant Marrables; and Lilly, the pale, neat-faced copying clerk, whose light-brown hair was set up in a small parallelogram above his well-filled forehead, and whose shirt, taken with an otherwise seedy costume, had a freshness that might be called insular, and perhaps even something narrower.

Certainly a company select of the select among poor men, being drawn together by a taste not prevalent even among the privileged heirs of learning and its institutions; and not likely to amuse any gentleman in search of crime or low comedy as the ground of interest in people whose weekly income is only divisible into shillings. Deronda, even if he had not been more than usually inclined to gravity under the influence of what was pending between him and Mordecai, would not have set himself to find food for laughter in the various shades of departure from the tone of polished society sure to be observable in the air and

577

DANIEL DERONDA

talk of these men who had probably snatched knowledge
as most of us snatch indulgences, making the utmost of
scant opportunity. He looked around him with the quiet air
of respect habitual to him among equals, ordered whisky
and water, and offered the contents of his cigar-case,
which, characteristically enough, he always carried and
hardly ever used for his own behoof, having reasons for
not smoking himself, but liking to indulge others. Perhaps
it was his weakness to be afraid of seeming strait-laced, and
turning himself into a sort of diagram instead of a growth
which can exercise the guiding attraction of fellowship.
That he made a decidedly winning impression on the
company was proved by their showing themselves no less
at ease than before, and desirous of quickly resuming their
interrupted talk.

'This is what I call one of our touch and go nights, sir,'
said Miller, who was implicitly accepted as a sort of mod-
erator – addressing Deronda by way of explanation, and
nodding toward each person whose name he mentioned.
'Sometimes we stick pretty close to the point. But to-night
our friend Pash, there, brought up the law of progress, and
we got on statistics; then Lilly, there, saying we knew well
enough before counting that in the same state of society
the same sort of things would happen, and it was no more
wonder that quantities should remain the same than that
qualities should remain the same, for in relation to society
numbers are qualities – the number of drunkards is a
quality in society – the numbers are an index to the qualities, and give us no instruction, only setting us to consider
the causes of difference between different social states –
Lilly saying this, we went off on the causes of social
change, and when you came in I was going upon the
power of ideas, which I hold to be the main transforming
cause.'

'I don't hold with you there, Miller,' said Goodwin, the
inlayer, more concerned to carry on the subject than to wait
for a word from the new guest. 'For either you mean so
many sorts of things by ideas that I get no knowledge by

what you say, any more than if you said light was a cause; or else you mean a particular sort of ideas, and then I go against your meaning as too narrow. For, look at it in one way, all actions men put a bit of thought into are ideas – say, sowing seed, or making a canoe, or baking clay; and such ideas as these work themselves into life and go on growing with it, but they can't go apart from the material that set them to work and makes a medium for them. It's the nature of wood and stone yielding to the knife that raises the idea of shaping them, and with plenty of wood and stone the shaping will go on. I look at it, that such ideas as are mixed straight away with all the other elements of life are powerful along with 'em. The slower the mixing, the less power they have. And as to the causes of social change, I look at it in this way – ideas are a sort of parliament, but there's a commonwealth outside, and a good deal of the commonwealth is working at change without knowing what the parliament is doing.'

'But if you take ready mixing as your test of power,' said Pash, 'some of the least practical ideas beat everything. They spread without being understood, and enter into the language without being thought of.'

'They may act by changing the distribution of gases,' said Marrables; 'instruments are getting so fine now, men may come to register the spread of a theory by observed changes in the atmosphere and corresponding changes in the nerves.'

'Yes,' said Pash, his dark face lighting up rather impishly, 'there is the idea of nationalities; I dare say the wild asses are snuffing it, and getting more gregarious.'

'You don't share that idea?' said Deronda, finding a piquant incongruity between Pash's sarcasm and the strong stamp of race on his features.

'Say rather, he does not share that spirit,' said Mordecai, who had turned a melancholy glance on Pash. 'Unless nationality is a feeling, what force can it have as an idea?'

'Granted, Mordecai,' said Pash, quite good-humouredly. 'And as the feeling of nationality is dying, I take the idea to be no better than a ghost, already walking to announce the death.'

'A sentiment may seem to be dying and yet revive into strong life,' said Deronda. 'Nations have revived. We may live to see a great outburst of force in the Arabs, who are being inspired with a new zeal.'

'Amen, amen,' said Mordecai, looking at Deronda with a delight which was the beginning of recovered energy: his attitude was more upright, his face was less worn.

'That may hold with backward nations,' said Pash, 'but with us in Europe the sentiment of nationality is destined to die out. It will last a little longer in the quarters where oppression lasts, but nowhere else. The whole current of progress is setting against it.'

'Ay,' said Buchan, in a rapid thin Scotch tone which was like the letting in of a little cool air on the conversation, 'ye've done well to bring us round to the point. Ye're all agreed that societies change – not always and everywhere – but on the whole and in the long-run. Now, with all defer-ence, I would beg t'observe that we have got to examine the nature of changes before we have a warrant to call them progress, which word is supposed to include a bettering, though I apprehend it to be ill chosen for that purpose, since mere motion onward may carry us to a bog or a precipice. And the questions I would put are three: Is all change in the direction of progress? if not, how shall we discern which change is progress and which not? and thirdly, how far and in what ways can we act upon the course of change so as to promote it where it is beneficial, and divert it where it is injurious?'

But Buchan's attempt to impose his method on the talk was a failure. Lilly immediately said –

'Change and progress are merged in the idea of development. The laws of development are being dis-covered, and changes taking place according to them are necessarily progressive; that is to say, if we have any notion of progress or improvement opposed to them, the notion is a mistake.'

'I really can't see how you arrive at that sort of certitude about changes by calling them development,' said Deronda. 'There will still remain the degrees of inevitableness in relation to our own will and acts, and the degrees of wisdom in hastening or retarding; there will still remain the danger of mistaking a tendency which should be resisted for an inevitable law that we must adjust ourselves to, – which seems to me as bad a superstition or false god as any that has been set up without the ceremonies of philosophizing.'

'That is a truth,' said Mordecai. 'Woe to the men who see no place for resistance in this generation! I believe in a growth, a passage, and a new unfolding of life whereof the seed is more perfect, more charged with the elements that are pregnant with diviner form. The life of a people grows, it is knit together and yet expanded, in joy and sorrow, in thought and action; it absorbs the thought of other nations into its own forms, and gives back the thought as new wealth to the world; it is a power and an organ in the great body of the nations. But there may come a check, an arrest; memories may be stifled, and love may be faint for the lack of them; or memories may shrink into withered relics – the soul of a people, whereby they know themselves to be one, may seem to be dying for want of common action. But who shall say, "The fountain of their life is dried up, they shall for ever cease to be a nation"? Who shall say it? Not he who feels the life of his people stirring within his own. Shall he say, "That way events are wending, I will not resist"? His very soul is resistance, and is as a seed of fire that may enkindle the souls of multitudes, and make a new pathway for events.'

'I don't deny patriotism,' said Gideon, 'but we all know you have a particular meaning, Mordecai. You know Mordecai's way of thinking, I suppose.' Here Gideon had turned to Deronda, who sat next to him; but without waiting for an answer, he went on. 'I'm a rational Jew myself. I stand by my people as a sort of family relations, and I am for keeping up our worship in a rational way. I don't approve of

our people getting baptized, because I don't believe in a
Jew's conversion to the Gentile part of Christianity. And
now we have political equality, there's no excuse for a
pretence of that sort. But I am for getting rid of all our
superstitions and exclusiveness. There's no reason now
why we shouldn't melt gradually into the populations we
live among. That's the order of the day in point of progress.
I would as soon my children married Christians as Jews.
And I'm for the old maxim, "A man's country is where he's
well off."'

'That country's not so easy to find, Gideon,' said the
rapid Pash, with a shrug and grimace. 'You get ten shillings
a-week more than I do, and have only half the number of
children. If somebody will introduce a brisk trade in
watches among the "Jerusalem wares," I'll go – eh,
Mordecai, what do you say?'

Deronda, all ear for these hints of Mordecai's opinion,
was inwardly wondering at his persistence in coming to this
club. For an enthusiastic spirit to meet continually the
fixed indifference of men familiar with the object of his
enthusiasm is the acceptance of a slow martyrdom, beside
which the fate of a missionary tomahawked without any
considerate rejection of his doctrines seems hardly worthy
of compassion. But Mordecai gave no sign of shrinking:
this was a moment of spiritual fullness, and he cared more
for the utterance of his faith than for its immediate reception. With a fervour which had no temper in it, but seemed
rather the rush of feeling in the opportunity of speech, he
answered Pash: –

'What I say is, let every man keep far away from the
brotherhood and the inheritance he despises. Thousands
on thousands of our race have mixed with the Gentile as
Celt with Saxon, and they may inherit the blessing that
belongs to the Gentile. You cannot follow them. You are
one of the multitudes over this globe who must walk
among the nations and be known as Jews, and with words
on their lips which mean, "I wish I had not been born a Jew,
I disown any bond with the long travail of my race, I will

outdo the Gentile in mocking at our separateness," they all the while feel breathing on them the breath of contempt because they are Jews, and they will breathe it back poisonously. Can a fresh-made garment of citizenship weave itself straightway into the flesh and change the slow deposit of eighteen centuries? What is the citizenship of him who walks among a people he has no hearty kindred and fellowship with, and has lost the sense of brotherhood with his own race? It is a charter of selfish ambition and rivalry in low greed. He is an alien in spirit, whatever he may be in form; he sucks the blood of mankind, he is not a man. Sharing in no love, sharing in no subjection of the soul, he mocks at all. Is it not truth I speak, Pash?'

'Not exactly, Mordecai,' said Pash, 'if you mean that I think the worse of myself for being a Jew. What I thank our fathers for is that there are fewer blockheads among us than among other races. But perhaps you are right in thinking the Christians don't like me so well for it.'

'Catholics and Protestants have not liked each other much better,' said the genial Gideon. 'We must wait patiently for prejudices to die out. Many of our people are on a footing with the best, and there's been a good filtering of our blood into high families. I am for making our expectations rational.'

'And so am I!' said Mordecai, quickly, leaning forward with the eagerness of one who pleads in some decisive crisis, his long thin hands clasped together on his lap. 'I too claim to be a rational Jew. But what is it to be rational – what is it to feel the light of the divine reason growing stronger within and without? It is to see more and more of the hidden bonds that bind and consecrate change as a dependent growth – yea, consecrate it with kinship: the past becomes my parent, and the future stretches towards me the appealing arms of children. Is it rational to drain away the sap of special kindred that makes the families of man rich in interchanged wealth, and various as the forests are various with the glory of the cedar and the palm? When it is rational to say, "I know not my father or my mother, let my children be aliens to me, that no prayer of mine may touch them," then it will be rational for the Jew to say, "I will seek to know no difference between me and the Gentile, I will not cherish the prophetic consciousness of our nationality – let the Hebrew cease to be, and let all his memorials be antiquarian trifles, dead as the wall-paintings of a conjectured race. Yet let his child learn by rote the speech of the Greek, where he adjures his fellow-citizens by the bravery of those who fought foremost at Marathon – let him learn to say, that was noble in the Greek, that is the spirit of an immortal nation! But the Jew has no memories that bind him to action; let him laugh that his nation is degraded from a nation; let him hold the monuments of his law which carried within its frame the breath of social justice, of charity, and of household sanctities – let him hold the energy of the prophets, the patient care of the Masters, the fortitude of martyred generations, as mere stuff for a professorship. The business of the Jew in all things is to be even as the rich Gentile."'

Mordecai threw himself back in his chair, and there was a moment's silence. Not one member of the club shared his point of view or his emotion; but his whole personality and speech had on them the effect of a dramatic representation which had some pathos in it, though no practical consequences; and usually he was at once indulged and contradicted. Deronda's mind went back on what must have been the tragic pressure of outward conditions hindering this man, whose force he felt to be telling on himself, from making any world for his thought in the minds of others – like a poet among people of a strange speech, who may have a poetry of their own, but have no ear for his cadence, no answering thrill to his discovery of latent virtues in his mother tongue.

The cool Buchan was the first to speak, and hint the loss of time. 'I submit,' said he, 'that ye're travelling away from the questions I put concerning progress.'

'Say they're levanting, Buchan,' said Miller, who liked his joke, and would not have objected to be called

Voltairian. 'Never mind. Let us have a Jewish night; we've not had one for a long while. Let us take the discussion on Jewish ground. I suppose we've no prejudice here; we're all philosophers; and we like our friends Mordecai, Pash, and Gideon, as well if they were no more kin to Abraham than the rest of us. We're all related through Adam, until further showing to the contrary, and if you look into history we've all got some discreditable forefathers. So I mean no offence when I say I don't think any great things of the part the Jewish people have played in the world. What then? I think they were iniquitously dealt by in past times. And I suppose we don't want any men to be maltreated, white, black, brown, or yellow – I know I've just given my half-crown to the contrary. And that reminds me, I've a curious old German book – I can't read it myself, but a friend was reading out of it to me the other day – about the prejudices against the Jews, and the stories used to be told against 'em, and what do you think one was? Why, that they're punished with a bad odour in their bodies; and *that*, says the author, date 1715 (I've just been pricing and marking the book this very morning) – that is true, for the ancients spoke of it. But then, he says, the other things are fables, such as that the odour goes away all at once when they're baptized, and that every one of the ten tribes, mind you, all the ten being concerned in the crucifixion, has got a particular punishment over and above the smell: – Asher, I remember, has the right arm a handbreadth shorter than the left, and Naphthali has pigs' ears and a smell of live pork. What do you think of that? There's been a good deal of fun made of rabbinical fables, but in point of fables my opinion is, that all over the world it's six of one and half-a-dozen of the other. However, as I said before, I hold with the philosophers of the last century that the Jews have played no great part as a people, though Pash will have it they're clever enough to beat all the rest of the world. But if so, I ask, why haven't they done it?'

'For the same reason that the cleverest men in the country don't get themselves or their ideas into

Parliament,' said the ready Pash; 'because the blockheads are too many for 'em.'

'That is a vain question,' said Mordecai, 'whether our people would beat the rest of the world. Each nation has its own work, and is a member of the world, enriched by the work of each. But it is true, as Jehuda-ha-Levi first said, that Israel is the heart of mankind, if we mean by heart the core of affection which binds a race and its families in dutiful love, and the reverence for the human body which lifts the needs of our animal life into religion, and the tenderness which is merciful to the poor and weak and to the dumb creature that wears the yoke for us.'

'They're not behind any nation in arrogance,' said Lilly; 'and if they have got in the rear, it has not been because they were over-modest.'

'Oh, every nation brags in its turn,' said Miller.

'Yes,' said Pash, 'and some of them in the Hebrew text.'

'Well, whatever the Jews contributed at one time, they are a standstill people,' said Lilly. 'They are the type of obstinate adherence to the superannuated. They may show good abilities when they take up liberal ideas, but as a race they have no development in them.'

'That is false!' said Mordecai, leaning forward again with his former eagerness. 'Let their history be known and examined; let the seed be sifted, let its beginning be traced to the weed of the wilderness – the more glorious will be the energy that transformed it. Where else is there a nation of whom it may be as truly said that their religion and law and moral life mingled as the stream of blood in the heart and made one growth – where else a people who kept and enlarged their spiritual store at the very time when they were hunted with a hatred as fierce as the forest-fires that chase the wild beast from his covert? There is a fable of the Roman, that swimming to save his life he held the roll of his writings between his teeth and saved them from the waters. But how much more than that is true of our race? They struggled to keep their place among the nations like heroes – yea, when the hand was hacked off, they clung with the teeth; but when the plough and the harrow had passed over the last visible signs of their national covenant, and the fruitfulness of their land was stifled with the blood of the sowers and planters, they said, "The spirit is alive, let us make it a lasting habitation – lasting because movable – so that it may be carried from generation to generation, and our sons unborn may be rich in the things that have been, and possess a hope built on an unchangeable foundation." They said it and they wrought it, though often breathing with scant life, as in a coffin, or as lying wounded amid a heap of slain. Hooted and scared like the unowned dog, the Hebrew made himself envied for his wealth and wisdom, and was bled of them to fill the bath of Gentile luxury; he absorbed knowledge, he diffused it; his dispersed race was a new Phœnicia working the mines of Greece and carrying their products to the world. The native spirit of our tradition was not to stand still, but to use records as a seed, and draw out the compressed virtues of law and prophecy; and while the Gentile, who had said, "What is yours is ours, and no longer yours," was reading the letter of our law as a dark inscription, or was turning its parchments into shoe-soles for an army rabid with lust and cruelty, our Masters were still enlarging and illuminating with fresh-fed interpretation. But the dispersion was wide, the yoke of oppression was a spiked torture as well as a load; the exile was forced afar among brutish people, where the consciousness of his race was no clearer to him than the light of the sun to our fathers in the Roman persecution, who had their hiding-place in a cave, and knew not that it was day save by the dimmer burning of their candles. What wonder that multitudes of our people are ignorant, narrow, superstitious? What wonder?'

Here Mordecai, whose seat was next the fireplace, rose and leaned his arm on the little shelf; his excitement had risen, though his voice, which had begun with unusual strength, was getting hoarser.

'What wonder? The night is unto them, that they have no vision; in their darkness they are unable to divine; the sun is gone down over the prophets, and the day is dark above them; their observances are as nameless relics. But which among the chief of the Gentile nations has not an ignorant multitude? They scorn our people's ignorant observance; but the most accursed ignorance is that which has no observance – sunk to the cunning greed of the fox, to which all law is no more than a trap or the cry of the worrying hound. There is a degradation deep down below the memory that has withered into superstition. In the multitudes of the ignorant on three continents who observe our rites and make the confession of the divine Unity, the soul of Judaism is not dead. Revive the organic centre: let the unity of Israel which has made the growth and form of its religion be an outward reality. Looking towards a land and a polity, our dispersed people in all the ends of the earth may share the dignity of a national life which has a voice among the peoples of the East and the West – which will plant the wisdom and skill of our race so that it may be, as of old, a medium of transmission and understanding. Let that come to pass, and the living warmth will spread to the weak extremities of Israel, and superstition will vanish, not in the lawlessness of the renegade, but in the illumination of great facts which widen feeling, and make all knowledge alive as the young offspring of beloved memories.'

Mordecai's voice had sunk, but with the hectic brilliancy of his gaze it was not the less impressive. His extraordinary excitement was certainly due to Deronda's presence: it was to Deronda that he was speaking, and the moment had a testamentary solemnity for him which rallied all his powers. Yet the presence of those other familiar men promoted expression, for they embodied the indifference which gave a resistant energy to his speech. Not that he looked at Deronda: he seemed to see nothing immediately around him, and if any one had grasped him he would probably not have known it. Again the former words came back to Deronda's mind, – 'You must hope my hopes – see the vision I point to – behold a glory where I behold it.' They came now with gathered pathos. Before him stood, as a living, suffering reality, what hitherto he had only seen as an effort of imagination, which, in its comparative faintness, yet carried a suspicion of being exaggerated: a man steeped in poverty and obscurity, weakened by disease, consciously within the shadow of advancing death, but living an intense life in an invisible past and future, careless of his personal lot, except for its possibly making some obstruction to a conceived good which he would never share except as a brief inward vision – a day afar off, whose sun would never warm him, but into which he threw his soul's desire, with a passion often wanting to the personal motives of healthy youth. It was something more than a grandiose transfiguration of the parental love that toils, renounces, endures, resists the suicidal promptings of despair – all because of the little ones, whose future becomes present to the yearning gaze of anxiety.

All eyes were fixed on Mordecai as he sat down again, and none with unkindness; but it happened that the one who felt the most kindly was the most prompted to speak in opposition. This was the genial and rational Gideon, who also was not without a sense that he was addressing the guest of the evening. He said –

'You have your own way of looking at things, Mordecai, and, as you say, your own way seems to you rational. I know you don't hold with the restoration to Judæa by miracle, and so on; but you are as well aware as I am that the subject has been mixed with a heap of nonsense both by Jews and Christians. And as to the connection of our race with Palestine, it has been perverted by superstition till it's as demoralizing as the old poor-law. The raff and scum go there to be maintained like able-bodied paupers, and to be taken special care of by the angel Gabriel when they die. It's no use fighting against facts. We must look where they point; that's what I call rationality. The most learned and liberal men among us who are attached to our religion are for clearing our liturgy of all such notions as a literal fulfilment of the prophecies about restoration, and so on. Prune it of a few useless rites and literal interpretations of that sort, and our religion is the simplest of all religions, and makes no barrier, but a union, between us and the rest of the world.'

'As plain as a pike-staff,' said Pash, with an ironical laugh. 'You pluck it up by the roots, strip off the leaves and bark, shave off the knots, and smooth it at top and bottom; put it where you will, it will do no harm, it will never sprout. You may make a handle of it, or you may throw it on the bonfire of scoured rubbish. I don't see why our rubbish is to be held sacred any more than the rubbish of Brahmanism or Bouddhism.'

'No,' said Mordecai, 'no, Pash, because you have lost the heart of the Jew. Community was felt before it was called good. I praise no superstition, I praise the living fountains of enlarging belief. What is growth, completion, development? You began with that question, I apply it to the history of our people. I say that the effect of our separateness will not be completed and have its highest transformation unless our race takes on again the character of a nationality. That is the fulfilment of the religious trust that moulded them into a people, whose life has made half the inspiration of the world. What is it to me that the ten tribes are lost untraceably, or that multitudes of the children of Judah have mixed themselves with the Gentile populations as a river with rivers? Behold our people still! Their skirts spread afar; they are torn and soiled and trodden on; but there is a jewelled breastplate. Let the wealthy men, the monarchs of commerce, the learned in all knowledge, the skilful in all arts, the speakers, the political counsellors, who carry in their veins the Hebrew blood which has maintained its vigour in all climates, and the pliancy of the Hebrew genius for which difficulty means new device – let them say, "we will lift up a standard, we will unite in a labour hard but glorious like that of Moses and Ezra, a labour which shall be a worthy fruit of the long anguish whereby our fathers maintained their separateness, refusing the ease of falsehood." They have wealth enough to redeem the soil from debauched and paupered conquerors; they have the skill of the statesman to devise, the tongue of the orator to persuade. And is there no prophet or poet among us to make the ears of Christian Europe tingle with shame at the hideous obloquy of Christian strife which the Turk gazes at as at the fighting of beasts to which he has lent an arena? There is store of wisdom among us to found a new Jewish polity, grand, simple, like the old – a republic where there is equality of protection, an equality which shone like a star on the forehead of our ancient community, and gave it more than the brightness of Western freedom amid the despotisms of the East. Then our race shall have an organic centre, a heart and brain to watch and guide and execute; the outraged Jew shall have a defence in the court of nations, as the outraged Englishman or American. And the world will gain as Israel gains. For there will be a community in the van of the East which carries the culture and the sympathies of every great nation in its bosom; there will be a land set for a halting-place of enmities, a neutral ground for the East as Belgium is for the West. Difficulties? I know there are difficulties. But let the spirit of sublime achievement move in the great among our people, and the work will begin.'

'Ay, we may safely admit that, Mordecai,' said Pash. 'When there are great men on 'Change, and high-flying professors converted to your doctrine, difficulties will vanish like smoke.'

Deronda, inclined by nature to take the side of those on whom the arrows of scorn were falling, could not help replying to Pash's outfling, and said –

'If we look back to the history of efforts which have made great changes, it is astonishing how many of them seemed hopeless to those who looked on in the beginning. Take what we have all heard and seen something of – the effort after the unity of Italy, which we are sure soon to see accomplished to the very last boundary. Look into Mazzini's account of his first yearning, when he was a boy, after a restored greatness, and a new freedom to Italy, and of his first efforts as a young man to rouse the same feelings in other young men, and get them to work towards a united nationality. Almost everything seemed against him: his countrymen were ignorant or indifferent, governments hostile, Europe incredulous. Of course the scorners often seemed wise. Yet you see the prophecy lay with him. As long as there is a remnant of national consciousness, I suppose nobody will deny that there may be a new stirring of memories and hopes which may inspire arduous action.'

'Amen,' said Mordecai, to whom Deronda's words were a cordial. 'What is needed is the leaven – what is needed is the seed of fire. The heritage of Israel is beating in the pulses of millions; it lives in their veins as a power without understanding, like the morning exultation of herds; it is the inborn half of memory, moving as in a dream among writings on the walls, which it sees dimly but cannot divide into speech. Let the torch of visible community be lit! Let the reason of Israel disclose itself in a great outward deed, and let there be another great migration, another choosing of Israel to be a nationality whose members may still stretch to the ends of the earth, even as the sons of England and Germany, whom enterprise carries afar, but who still have a national hearth and a tribunal of national opinion. Will any say "It cannot be"? Baruch Spinoza had not a faithful Jewish heart, though he had sucked the life of his intellect at the breasts of Jewish tradition. He laid bare his father's nakedness and said, "They who scorn him have the higher wisdom." Yet Baruch Spinoza confessed, he saw not why Israel should not again be a chosen nation. Who says that the history and literature of our race are dead? Are they not as living as the history and literature of Greece and Rome, which have inspired revolutions, enkindled the thought of Europe, and made the unrighteous powers tremble? These were an inheritance dug from the tomb. Ours is an inheritance that has never ceased to quiver in millions of human frames.'

Mordecai had stretched his arms upward, and his long thin hands quivered in the air for a moment after he had ceased to speak. Gideon was certainly a little moved, for though there was no long pause before he made a remark in objection, his tone was more mild and deprecatory than before; Pash, meanwhile, pressing his lips together, rubbing his black head with both hands and wrinkling his brow horizontally, with the expression of one who differs from every speaker, but does not think it worth while to say so. There is a sort of human paste that when it comes near the fire of enthusiasm is only baked into harder shape.

'It may seem well enough on one side to make so much of our memories and inheritance as you do, Mordecai,' said Gideon; 'but there's another side. It isn't all gratitude and harmless glory. Our people have inherited a good deal of hatred. There's a pretty lot of curses still flying about, and stiff settled rancour inherited from the times of persecution. How will you justify keeping one sort of memory and throwing away the other? There are ugly debts standing on both sides.'

'I justify the choice as all other choice is justified,' said Mordecai. 'I cherish nothing for the Jewish nation, I seek nothing for them, but the good which promises good to all the nations. The spirit of our religious life, which is one with our national life, is not hatred of aught but wrong. The Masters have said, an offence against man is worse than an offence against God. But what wonder if there is hatred in the breasts of Jews, who are children of the ignorant and oppressed – what wonder, since there is hatred in the breasts of Christians? Our national life was a growing light. Let the central fire be kindled again, and the light will reach afar. The degraded and scorned of our race will learn to think of their sacred land, not as a place for saintly beggary to await death in loathsome idleness, but as a republic where the Jewish spirit manifests itself in a new order founded on the old, purified, enriched by the experience our greatest sons have gathered from the life of the ages. How long is it? – only two centuries since a vessel carried over the ocean the beginning of the great North American nation. The people grew like meeting waters – they were various in habit and sect – there came a time, a century ago, when they needed a polity, and there were heroes of peace among them. What had they to form a polity with but memories of Europe, corrected by the vision of a better? Let our wise and wealthy show themselves heroes. They have the memories of the East and West, and they have the full vision of a better. A new Persia with a purified religion magnified itself in art and wisdom. So will a new Judæa, poised between East and West – a covenant of reconciliation. Will any say, the prophetic vision of your race has been hopelessly mixed with folly and bigotry; the angel of progress has no message for Judaism – it is a half-buried city for the paid workers to lay open – the waters are rushing by it as a forsaken field? I say that the strongest principle of growth lies in human choice. The sons of Judah have to choose that God may again choose them. The Messianic time is the time when Israel shall will the planting of the national ensign. The Nile overflowed and rushed onward: the Egyptian could not choose the overflow, but he chose to work and make channels for the fructifying waters, and Egypt became the land of corn. Shall man, whose soul is set in the royalty of discernment and resolve, deny his rank and say, I am an onlooker, ask no choice or purpose of me? That is the blasphemy of this time. The divine principle of our race is action, choice, resolved memory. Let us contradict the blasphemy, and help to will our own better future and the better future of the world – not renounce our higher gift and say, "Let us be as if we were not among the populations;" but choose our full heritage, claim the brotherhood of our nation, and carry into it a new brotherhood with the nations of the Gentiles. The vision is there; it will be fulfilled.'

With the last sentence, which was no more than a loud whisper, Mordecai let his chin sink on his breast and his eyelids fall. No one spoke. It was not the first time that he had insisted on the same ideas, but he was seen to-night in a new phase. The quiet tenacity of his ordinary self differed as much from his present exaltation of mood as a man in private talk, giving reasons for a revolution of which no sign is discernible, differs from one who feels himself an agent in a revolution begun. The dawn of fulfilment brought to his hope by Deronda's presence had wrought Mordecai's conception into a state of impassioned conviction, and he had found strength in his excitement to pour forth the unlocked floods of emotive argument, with a sense of haste as at a crisis which must be seized. But now there had come with the quiescence of fatigue a sort of thankful wonder that he had spoken – a contemplation of his life as a journey which had come at last to this bourne. After a great excitement, the ebbing strength of impulse is apt to leave us in this aloofness from our active self. And in the moments after Mordecai had sunk his head, his mind was wandering along the paths of his youth, and all the hopes which had ended in bringing him hither.

Every one felt that the talk was ended, and the tone of phlegmatic discussion made unreasonable by Mordecai's high-pitched solemnity. It was as if they had come together to hear the blowing of the *shophar*, and had nothing to do now but to disperse. The movement was unusually general, and in less than ten minutes the room was empty of all except Mordecai and Deronda. 'Goodnights' had been given to Mordecai, but it was evident he had not heard them, for he remained rapt and motionless. Deronda would not disturb this needful rest, but waited for a spontaneous movement.

XLIII

'My spirit is too weak; mortality
Weighs heavily on me like unwilling sleep,
And each imagined pinnacle and steep
Of godlike hardship tells me I must die
Like a sick eagle looking at the sky.'

— KEATS.

AFTER a few minutes the unwonted stillness had penetrated Mordecai's consciousness, and he looked up at
Deronda, not in the least with bewilderment and surprise,
but with a gaze full of reposing satisfaction. Deronda rose
and placed his chair nearer, where there could be no imagined need for raising the voice. Mordecai felt the action as
a patient feels the gentleness that eases his pillow. He
began to speak in a low tone, as if he were only thinking
articulately, not trying to reach an audience.

'In the doctrine of the Cabbala, souls are born again and
again in new bodies till they are perfected and purified,
and a soul liberated from a worn-out body may join the
fellow-soul that needs it, that they may be perfected
together, and their earthly work accomplished. Then
they will depart from the mortal region, and leave place
for new souls to be born out of the store in the eternal
bosom. It is the lingering imperfection of the souls already
born into the mortal region that hinders the birth of new
souls and the preparation of the Messianic time: – thus the
mind has given shape to what is hidden, as the shadow of
what is known, and has spoken truth, though it were only
in parable. When my long-wandering soul is liberated from
this weary body, it will join yours, and its work will be
perfected.'

Mordecai's pause seemed an appeal which Deronda's
feeling would not let him leave unanswered. He tried to
make it truthful; but for Mordecai's ear it was inevitably
filled with unspoken meanings. He only said –

'Everything I can in conscience do to make your life
effective I will do.'

'I know it,' said Mordecai, in the tone of quiet certainty which dispenses with further assurance. 'I heard it. You see it all – you are by my side on the mount of vision, and behold the paths of fulfilment which others deny.'

He was silent a moment or two, and then went on meditatively –

'You will take up my life where it was broken. I feel myself back in that day when my life was broken. The bright morning sun was on the quay – it was at Trieste – the garments of men from all nations shone like jewels – the boats were pushing off – the Greek vessel that would land us at Beyrout was to start in an hour. I was going with a merchant as his clerk and companion. I said, I shall behold the lands and people of the East, and I shall speak with a fuller vision. I breathed then as you do, without labour; I had the light step and the endurance of youth; I could fast, I could sleep on the hard ground. I had wedded poverty, and I loved my bride – for poverty to me was freedom. My heart exulted as if it had been the heart of Moses ben Maimon, strong with the strength of threescore years, and knowing the work that was to fill them. It was the first time I had been south: the soul within me felt its former sun; and standing on the quay, where the ground I stood on seemed to send forth light, and the shadows had an azure glory as of spirits become visible, I felt myself in the flood of a glorious life, wherein my own small year-counted existence seemed to melt, so that I knew it not; and a great sob arose within me as at the rush of waters that were too strong a bliss. So I stood there awaiting my companion; and I saw him not till he said: "Ezra, I have been to the post, and there is your letter."'

'Ezra!' exclaimed Deronda, unable to contain himself.

'Ezra,' repeated Mordecai, affirmatively, engrossed in memory. 'I was expecting a letter; for I wrote continually to my mother. And that sound of my name was like the touch of a wand that recalled me to the body wherefrom I had been released as it were to mingle with the ocean of human existence, free from the pressure of individual bondage. I opened the letter; and the name came again as a cry that would have disturbed me in the bosom of heaven, and made me yearn to reach where that sorrow was. – "Ezra, my son!"'

Mordecai paused again, his imagination arrested by the grasp of that long-past moment. Deronda's mind was almost breathlessly suspended on what was coming. A strange possibility had suddenly presented itself. Mordecai's eyes were cast down in abstracted contemplation, and in a few moments he went on –

'She was a mother of whom it might have come – yea, might have come to be said, "Her children arise up and call her blessed." In her I understood the meaning of that Master who, perceiving the footsteps of his mother, rose up and said, "The majesty of the Eternal cometh near!" And that letter was her cry from the depths of anguish and desolation – the cry of a mother robbed of her little one. I was her eldest. Death had taken four babes, one after the other. Then came late my little sister, who was more than all the rest the desire of her mother's eyes; and the letter was a piercing cry to me – "Ezra, my son, I am robbed of her. He has taken her away, and left disgrace behind. They will never come again."' – Here Mordecai lifted his eyes suddenly, laid his hand on Deronda's arm, and said, 'Mine was the lot of Israel. For the sin of the father my soul must go into exile. For the sin of the father the work was broken, and the day of fulfilment delayed. She who bore me was desolate, disgraced, destitute. I turned back. On the instant I turned – her spirit, and the spirit of her fathers, who had worthy Jewish hearts, moved within me, and drew me. God, in whom dwells the universe, was within me as the strength of obedience. I turned and travelled with hardship – to save the scant money which she would need. I left the sunshine, and travelled into freezing cold. In the last stage I spent a night in exposure to cold and snow. And that was the beginning of this slow death.'

Mordecai let his eyes wander again and removed his hand. Deronda resolutely repressed the questions which urged themselves within him. While Mordecai was in this state of emotion, no other confidence must be sought than what came spontaneously: nay, he himself felt a kindred emotion which made him dread his own speech as too momentous.

'But I worked. We were destitute – everything had been seized. And she was ill: the clutch of anguish was too strong for her, and wrought with some lurking disease. At times she could not stand for the beating of her heart, and the images in her brain became as chambers of terror, where she beheld my sister reared in evil. In the dead of night I heard her crying for her child. Then I rose, and we stretched forth our arms together and prayed. We poured forth our souls in desire that Mirah might be delivered from evil.'

'Mirah?' Deronda repeated, wishing to assure himself that his ears had not been deceived by a forecasting imagination. 'Did you say Mirah?'

'That was my little sister's name. After we had prayed for her my mother would rest awhile. It lasted hardly four years, and in the minutes before she died, we were praying the same prayer – I aloud, she silently. Her soul went out upon its wings.'

'Have you never since heard of your sister?' said Deronda, as quietly as he could.

'Never. Never have I heard whether she was delivered according to our prayer. I know not, I know not. Who shall say where the pathways lie? The poisonous will of the wicked is strong. It poisoned my life – it is slowly stifling this breath. Death delivered my mother, and I felt it a blessedness that I was alone in the winters of suffering. But what are the winters now? – they are far off' – here Mordecai again rested his hand on Deronda's arm, and looked at him with that joy of the hectic patient which pierces us to sadness – 'there is nothing to wail in the withering of my body. The work will be the better done. Once I said, the work of this beginning is mine, I am born to do it. Well, I shall do it. I shall live in you. I shall live in you.'

His grasp had become convulsive in its force, and Deronda, agitated as he had never been before – the certainty that this was Mirah's brother suffusing his own strange relation to Mordecai with a new solemnity and tenderness – felt his strong young heart beating faster and his lips paling. He shrank from speech. He feared, in Mordecai's present state of exaltation (already an alarming strain on his feeble frame) to utter a word of revelation about Mirah. He feared to make an answer below that high pitch of expectation which resembled a flash from a dying fire, making watchers fear to see it dying the faster. His dominant impulse was to do as he had once done before: he laid his firm gentle hand on the hand that grasped him. Mordecai's, as if it had a soul of its own – for he was not distinctly willing to do what he did – relaxed its grasp, and turned upward under Deronda's. As the two palms met and pressed each other, Mordecai recovered some sense of his surroundings, and said –

'Let us go now. I cannot talk any longer.'

And in fact they parted at Cohen's door without having spoken to each other again – merely with another pressure of the hands.

Deronda felt a weight on him which was half joy, half anxiety. The joy of finding in Mirah's brother a nature even more than worthy of that relation to her, had the weight of solemnity and sadness: the reunion of brother and sister was in reality the first stage of a supreme parting – like that farewell kiss which resembles greeting, that last glance of love which becomes the sharpest pang of sorrow. Then there was the weight of anxiety about the revelation of the fact on both sides, and the arrangements it would be desirable to make beforehand. I suppose we should all have felt as Deronda did, without sinking into snobbishness or the notion that the primal duties of life demand a morning and an evening suit, that it was an admissible desire to free Mirah's first meeting with her brother from all jarring outward conditions. His own sense of deliverance from the dreaded relationship of the other Cohens, notwithstanding their good-nature, made him resolve if possible to keep them in the background for Mirah, until her acquaintance with them would be an unmarred rendering of gratitude for any kindness they had shown towards her brother. On all accounts he wished to give Mordecai surroundings not only more suited to his frail bodily condition, but less of a hindrance to easy intercourse, even apart from the decisive prospect of Mirah's taking up her abode with her brother, and tending him through the precious remnant of his life. In the heroic drama, great recognitions are not encumbered with these details; and certainly Deronda had as reverential an interest in Mordecai and Mirah as he could have had in the offspring of Agamemnon; but he was caring for destinies still moving in the dim streets of our earthly life, not yet lifted among the constellations, and his task presented itself to him as difficult and delicate, especially in persuading Mordecai to change his abode and habits. Concerning Mirah's feeling and resolve he had no doubt: there would be a complete union of sentiment towards the departed mother, and Mirah would understand her brother's greatness. Yes, greatness: that was the word which Deronda now deliberately chose to signify the impression that Mordecai made on him. He said to himself, perhaps rather defiantly towards the more negative spirit within him, that this man, however erratic some of his interpretations might be – this consumptive Jewish workman in threadbare clothing, lodged by charity, delivering himself to hearers who took his thoughts without attaching more consequences to them than the Flemings to the ethereal chimes ringing above their market-places – had the chief elements of greatness: a mind consciously, energetically moving with the larger march of human destinies, but not the less full of conscience and tender heart for the footsteps that tread near and need a leaning-place; capable of conceiving and choosing a life's task with far-off issues, yet capable of the unapplauded heroism which turns off the road of achievement at the call of the nearer duty whose

DANIEL DERONDA

effect lies within the beatings of the hearts that are close to us, as the hunger of the unfledged bird to the breast of its parent.

Deronda to-night was stirred with the feeling that the brief remnant of this fervid life had become his charge. He had been peculiarly wrought on by what he had seen at the club of the friendly indifference which Mordecai must have gone on encountering. His own experience of the small room that ardour can make for itself in ordinary minds had had the effect of increasing his reserve; and while tolerance was the easiest attitude to him, there was another bent in him also capable of becoming a weakness – the dislike to appear exceptional or to risk an ineffective insistence on his own opinion. But such caution appeared contemptible to him just now, when he for the first time saw in a complete picture and felt as a reality the lives that burn themselves out in solitary enthusiasm: martyrs of obscure circumstance, exiled in the rarity of their own minds, whose deliverances in other ears are no more than a long passionate soliloquy – unless perhaps at last, when they are nearing the invisible shores, signs of recognition and fulfilment may penetrate the cloud of loneliness; or perhaps it may be with them as with the dying Copernicus made to touch the first printed copy of his book when the sense of touch was gone, seeing it only as a dim object through the deepening dusk.

Deronda had been brought near to one of those spiritual exiles, and it was in his nature to feel the relation as a strong claim, nay, to feel his imagination moving without repugnance in the direction of Mordecai's desires. With all his latent objection to schemes only definite in their generality and nebulous in detail – in the poise of his sentiments he felt at one with this man who had made a visionary selection of him: the lines of what may be called their emotional theory touched. He had not the Jewish consciousness, but he had a yearning, grown the stronger for the denial which had been his grievance, after the obligation of avowed filial and social ties. His feeling was ready for difficult obedience. In this way it came that he set about his new task ungrudgingly; and again he thought of Mrs. Meyrick as his chief helper. To her first he must make known the discovery of Mirah's brother, and with her he must consult on all preliminaries of bringing the mutually lost together. Happily the best quarter for a consumptive patient did not lie too far off the small house at Chelsea, and the first office Deronda had to perform for this Hebrew prophet who claimed him as a spiritual inheritor, was to get him a healthy lodging. Such is the irony of earthly mixtures, that the heroes have not always had carpets and tea-cups of their own; and, seen through the open window by the mackerel-vendor, may have been invited with some hopefulness to pay three hundred per cent in the form of fourpence. However, Deronda's mind was busy with a prospective arrangement for giving a furnished lodging some faint likeness to a refined home by dismantling his own chambers of his best old books in vellum, his easiest chair, and the bas-reliefs of Milton and Dante.

But was not Mirah to be there? What furniture can give such finish to a room as a tender woman's face? – and is there any harmony of tints that has such stirrings of delight as the sweet modulations of her voice? Here is one good, at least, thought Deronda, that comes to Mordecai from his having fixed his imagination on me. He has recovered a perfect sister, whose affection is waiting for him.

XLIV

Fairy folk a-listening
Hear the seed sprout in the spring,
And for music to their dance
Hear the hedgerows wake from trance,
Sap that trembles into buds
Sending little rhythmic floods
Of fairy sound in fairy ears.
Thus all beauty that appears
Has birth as sound to finer sense
And lighter-clad intelligence.

AND Gwendolen? – She was thinking of Deronda much more than he was thinking of her – often wondering what were his ideas 'about things,' and how his life was occupied. But a lap-dog would be necessarily at a loss in framing to itself the motives and adventures of doghood at large; and it was as far from Gwendolen's conception that Deronda's life could be determined by the historical destiny of the Jews, as that he could rise into the air on a brazen horse, and so vanish from her horizon in the form of a twinkling star.

With all the sense of inferiority that had been forced upon her, it was inevitable that she should imagine a larger place for herself in his thoughts than she actually possessed. They must be rather old and wise persons who are not apt to see their own anxiety or elation about themselves reflected in other minds; and Gwendolen, with her youth and inward solitude, may be excused for dwelling on signs of special interest in her shown by the one person who had impressed her with the feeling of submission, and for mistaking the colour and proportion of those signs in the mind of Deronda.

Meanwhile, what would he tell her that she ought to do? 'He said, I must get more interest in others, and more knowledge, and that I must care about the best things – but how am I to begin?' She wondered what books he would tell her to take up to her own room, and recalled the famous writers that she had either not looked into or had found the most unreadable, with a half-smiling wish that she could mischievously ask Deronda if they were not the books called 'medicine for the mind.' Then she repented of her sauciness, and when she was safe from observation carried up a miscellaneous selection – Descartes, Bacon, Locke, Butler, Burke, Guizot – knowing, as a clever young lady of education, that these authors were ornaments of mankind, feeling sure that Deronda had read them, and hoping that by dipping into them all in succession, with her rapid understanding she might get a point of view nearer to his level.

But it was astonishing how little time she found for these vast mental excursions. Constantly she had to be on the scene as Mrs. Grandcourt, and to feel herself watched in that part by the exacting eyes of a husband who had found a motive to exercise his tenacity – that of making his marriage answer all the ends he chose, and with the more completeness the more he discerned any opposing will in her. And she herself, whatever rebellion might be going on within her, could not have made up her mind to failure in her representation. No feeling had yet reconciled her for a moment to any act, word, or look that would be a confession to the world; and what she most dreaded in herself was any violent impulse that would make an involuntary confession: it was the will to be silent in every other direction that had thrown the more impetuosity into her confidences towards Deronda, to whom her thought continually turned as a help against herself. Her riding, her hunting, her visiting and receiving of visits, were all performed in a spirit of achievement which served instead of zest and young gladness, so that all round Diplow, in those weeks of the New Year, Mrs. Grandcourt was regarded as wearing her honours with triumph.

'She disguises it under an air of taking everything as a matter of course,' said Mrs. Arrowpoint. 'A stranger might suppose that she had condescended rather than risen. I always noticed that doubleness in her.'

To her mother most of all Gwendolen was bent on acting complete satisfaction, and poor Mrs. Davilow was so far deceived that she took the unexpected distance at which she was kept, in spite of what she felt to be Grandcourt's handsome behaviour in providing for her, as a comparative indifference in her daughter, now that marriage had created new interests. To be fetched to lunch and then to dinner along with the Gascoignes, to be driven back soon after breakfast the next morning, and to have brief calls from Gwendolen in which her husband waited for her outside either on horseback or sitting in the carriage, was all the intercourse allowed to the mother.

The truth was, that the second time Gwendolen proposed to invite her mother with Mr. and Mrs. Gascoigne, Grandcourt had at first been silent, and then drawled, 'We can't be having *those people* always. Gascoigne talks too much. Country clergy are always bores – with their confounded fuss about everything.'

That speech was full of foreboding for Gwendolen. To have her mother classed under 'those people' was enough to confirm the previous dread of bringing her too near. Still, she could not give the true reasons – she could not say to her mother, 'Mr. Grandcourt wants to recognize you as little as possible; and besides, it is better you should not see much of my married life, else you might find out that I am miserable.' So she waived as lightly as she could every allusion to the subject; and when Mrs. Davilow again hinted the possibility of her having a house close to Ryelands, Gwendolen said, 'It would not be so nice for you as being near the Rectory here, mamma. We shall perhaps be very little at Ryelands. You would miss my aunt and uncle.'

And all the while this contemptuous veto of her husband's on any intimacy with her family, making her proudly shrink from giving them the aspect of troublesome pensioners, was rousing more inward inclination towards them. She had never felt so kindly towards her uncle, so much disposed to look back on his cheerful, complacent activity and spirit of kind management, even when mistaken, as more of a comfort than the neutral loftiness which was every day chilling her. And here perhaps she was unconsciously finding some of that mental enlargement which it was hard to get from her occasional dashes into difficult authors, who instead of blending themselves with her daily agitations required her to dismiss them.

It was a delightful surprise one day when Mr. and Mrs. Gascoigne were at Offendene to see Gwendolen ride up without her husband – with the groom only. All, including the four girls and Miss Merry, seated in the dining-room at lunch, could see the welcome approach; and even the elder ones were not without something of Isabel's romantic sense that the beautiful sister on the splendid chestnut, which held its head as if proud to bear her, was a sort of Harriet Byron or Miss Wardour reappearing out of her 'happiness ever after.'

Her uncle went to the door to give her his hand, and she sprang from her horse with an air of alacrity which might well encourage that notion of guaranteed happiness; for Gwendolen was particularly bent to-day on setting her mother's heart at rest, and her unusual sense of freedom in being able to make this visit alone enabled her to bear up under the pressure of painful facts which were urging themselves anew. The seven family kisses were not so tiresome as they used to be.

'Mr. Grandcourt is gone out, so I determined to fill up the time by coming to you, mamma,' said Gwendolen, as she laid down her hat and seated herself next to her mother; and then looking at her with a playfully monitory air, 'That is a punishment to you for not wearing better lace on your head. You didn't think I should come and detect you – you dreadfully careless-about-yourself mamma!' She gave a caressing touch to the dear head.

'Scold me, dear,' said Mrs. Davilow, her delicate worn face flushing with delight. 'But I wish there were something you could eat after your ride – instead of these scraps.

Let Jocosa make you a cup of chocolate in your old way. You used to like that.'

Miss Merry immediately rose and went out, though Gwendolen said, 'Oh no, a piece of bread, or one of those hard biscuits. I can't think about eating. I am come to say good-bye.'

'What! going to Ryelands again?' said Mr. Gascoigne.

'No, we are going to town,' said Gwendolen, beginning to break up a piece of bread, but putting no morsel into her mouth.

'It is rather early to go to town,' said Mrs. Gascoigne, 'and Mr. Grandcourt not in Parliament.'

'Oh, there is only one more day's hunting to be had, and Henleigh has some business in town with lawyers, I think,' said Gwendolen. 'I am very glad. I shall like to go to town.'

'You will see your house in Grosvenor Square,' said Mrs. Davilow. She and the girls were devouring with their eyes every movement of their goddess, soon to vanish.

'Yes,' said Gwendolen, in a tone of assent to the interest of that expectation. 'And there is so much to be seen and done in town.'

'I wish, my dear Gwendolen,' said Mr. Gascoigne, in a tone of cordial advice, 'that you would use your influence with Mr. Grandcourt to induce him to enter Parliament. A man of his position should make his weight felt in politics. The best judges are confident that the Ministry will have to appeal to the country on this question of further Reform, and Mr. Grandcourt should be ready for the opportunity. I am not quite sure that his opinions and mine accord entirely; I have not heard him express himself very fully. But I don't look at the matter from that point of view. I am thinking of your husband's standing in the country. And he is now come to that stage of life when a man like him should enter into public affairs. A wife has great influence with her husband. Use yours in that direction, my dear.'

The Rector felt that he was acquitting himself of a duty here, and giving something like the aspect of a public benefit to his niece's match. To Gwendolen the whole speech had the flavour of bitter comedy. If she had been merry, she must have laughed at her uncle's explanation to her that he had not heard Grandcourt express himself very fully on politics. And the wife's great influence! General maxims about husbands and wives seemed now of a precarious usefulness. Gwendolen herself had once believed in her future influence as an omnipotence in managing – she did not know exactly what. But her chief concern at present was to give an answer that would be felt appropriate.

'I should be very glad, uncle. But I think Mr. Grandcourt would not like the trouble of an election – at least, unless it could be without his making speeches. I thought candidates always made speeches.'

'Not necessarily – to any great extent,' said Mr. Gascoigne. 'A man of position and weight can get on without much of it. A county member need have very little trouble in that way, and both out of the House and in it is liked the better for not being a speechifier. Tell Mr. Grandcourt that I say so.'

'Here comes Jocosa with my chocolate after all,' said Gwendolen, escaping from a promise to give information that would certainly have been received in a way inconceivable to the good Rector, who, pushing his chair a little aside from the table and crossing his leg, looked as well as felt like a worthy specimen of a clergyman and magistrate giving experienced advice. Mr. Gascoigne had come to the conclusion that Grandcourt was a proud man, but his own self-love, calmed through life by the consciousness of his general value and personal advantages, was not irritable enough to prevent him from hoping the best about his niece's husband because her uncle was kept rather haughtily at a distance. A certain aloofness must be allowed to the representative of an old family; you would not expect him to be on intimate terms even with abstractions. But Mrs. Gascoigne was less dispassionate on her husband's account, and felt Grandcourt's haughtiness as something a little blameable in Gwendolen.

'Your uncle and Anna will very likely be in town about Easter,' she said, with a vague sense of expressing a slight discontent. 'Dear Rex hopes to come out with honours and a fellowship, and he wants his father and Anna to meet him in London, that they may be jolly together, as he says. I shouldn't wonder if Lord Brackenshaw invited them, he has been so very kind since he came back to the Castle.'

'I hope my uncle will bring Anna to stay in Grosvenor Square,' said Gwendolen, risking herself so far, for the sake of the present moment, but in reality wishing that she might never be obliged to bring any of her family near Grandcourt again. 'I am very glad of Rex's good fortune.'

'We must not be premature, and rejoice too much beforehand,' said the Rector, to whom this topic was the happiest in the world, and altogether allowable, now that the issue of that little affair about Gwendolen had been so satisfactory. 'Not but that I am in correspondence with impartial judges, who have the highest hopes about my son, as a singularly clear-headed young man. And of his excellent disposition and principle I have had the best evidence.'

'We shall have him a great lawyer some time,' said Mrs. Gascoigne.

'How very nice!' said Gwendolen, with a concealed scepticism as to niceness in general, which made the word quite applicable to lawyers.

'Talking of Lord Brackenshaw's kindness,' said Mrs. Davilow, 'you don't know how delightful he has been, Gwendolen. He has begged me to consider myself his guest in this house till I can get another that I like – he did it in the most graceful way. But now a house has turned up. Old Mr. Jodson is dead, and we can have his house. It is just what I want; small, but with nothing hideous to make you miserable thinking about it. And it is only a mile from the Rectory. You remember the low white house nearly hidden by the trees, as we turn up the lane to the church?'

'Yes, but you have no furniture, poor mamma,' said Gwendolen, in a melancholy tone.

'Oh, I am saving money for that. You know who has made me rather rich, dear,' said Mrs. Davilow, laying her hand on Gwendolen's. 'And Jocosa really makes so little do for housekeeping – it is quite wonderful.'

'Oh, please let me go up-stairs with you and arrange my hat, mamma,' said Gwendolen, suddenly putting up her hand to her hair, and perhaps creating a desired disarrangement. Her heart was swelling, and she was ready to cry. Her mother *must* have been worse off, if it had not been for Grandcourt. 'I suppose I shall never see all this again,' said Gwendolen, looking round her, as they entered the black and yellow bedroom, and then throwing herself into a chair in front of the glass with a little groan as of bodily fatigue. In the resolve not to cry she had become very pale.

'You are not well, dear?' said Mrs. Davilow.

'No; that chocolate has made me sick,' said Gwendolen, putting up her hand to be taken.

'I should be allowed to come to you if you were ill, darling,' said Mrs. Davilow, rather timidly, as she pressed the hand to her bosom. Something had made her sure to-day that her child loved her – needed her as much as ever.

'Oh yes,' said Gwendolen, leaning her head against her mother, though speaking as lightly as she could. 'But you know I never am ill. I am as strong as possible; and you must not take to fretting about me, but make yourself as happy as you can with the girls. They are better children to you than I have been, you know.' She turned up her face with a smile.

'You have always been good, my darling. I remember nothing else.'

'Why, what did I ever do that was good to you, except marry Mr. Grandcourt?' said Gwendolen, starting up with a desperate resolve to be playful, and keep no more on the perilous edge of agitation. 'And I should not have done *that* unless it had pleased myself.' She tossed up her chin, and reached her hat.

'God forbid, child! I would not have had you marry for my sake. Your happiness by itself is half mine.'

'Very well,' said Gwendolen, arranging her hat fastidiously, 'then you will please to consider that you are half happy, which is more than I am used to seeing you.' With the last words she again turned with her old playful smile to her mother. 'Now I am ready; but oh, mamma, Mr. Grandcourt gives me a quantity of money, and expects me to spend it, and I can't spend it; and you know I can't bear charity children and all that; and here are thirty pounds. I wish the girls would spend it for me on little things for themselves when you go to the new house. Tell them so.' Gwendolen put the notes into her mother's hand and looked away hastily, moving towards the door.

'God bless you, dear,' said Mrs. Davilow. 'It will please them so that you should have thought of *them* in particular.'

'Oh, they are troublesome things; but they don't trouble me now,' said Gwendolen, turning and nodding playfully. She hardly understood her own feeling in this act towards her sisters, but at any rate she did not wish it to be taken as anything serious. She was glad to have got out of the bedroom without showing more signs of emotion, and she went through the rest of her visit and all the good-byes with a quiet propriety that made her say to herself sarcastically as she rode away, 'I think I am making a very good Mrs. Grandcourt.'

She believed that her husband was gone to Gadsmere that day – had inferred this, as she had long ago inferred who were the inmates of what he had described as 'a dog-hutch of a place in a black country;' and the strange conflict of feeling within her had had the characteristic effect of sending her to Offendene with a tightened resolve – a form of excitement which was native to her.

She wondered at her own contradictions. Why should she feel it bitter to her that Grandcourt showed concern for the beings on whose account she herself was undergoing remorse? Had she not before her marriage inwardly determined to speak and act on their behalf? – and since he had lately implied that he wanted to be in town because he was making arrangements about his will, she ought to have been glad of any sign that he kept a conscience awake towards those at Gadsmere; and yet, now that she was a wife, the sense that Grandcourt was gone to Gadsmere was like red heat near a burn. She had brought on herself this indignity in her own eyes – this humiliation of being doomed to a terrified silence lest her husband should discover with what sort of consciousness she had married him; and as she had said to Deronda, she 'must go on.' After the intensest moments of secret hatred towards this husband who from the very first had cowed her, there always came back the spiritual pressure which made submission inevitable. There was no effort at freedom that would not bring fresh and worse humiliation. Gwendolen could dare nothing except in impulsive action – least of all could she dare premeditatedly a vague future in which the only certain condition was indignity. In spite of remorse, it still seemed the worst result of her marriage that she should in any way make a spectacle of herself; and her humiliation was lightened by her thinking that only Mrs. Glasher was aware of the fact which caused it. For Gwendolen had never referred the interview at the Whispering Stones to Lush's agency; her disposition to vague terror investing with shadowy omnipresence any threat of fatal power over her, and so hindering her from imagining plans and channels by which news had been conveyed to the woman who had the poisoning skill of a sorceress. To Gwendolen's mind the secret lay with Mrs. Glasher, and there were words in the horrible letter which implied that Mrs. Glasher would dread disclosure to the husband, as much as the usurping Mrs. Grandcourt.

Something else, too, she thought of as more of a secret from her husband than it really was – namely, that suppressed struggle of desperate rebellion which she herself dreaded. Grandcourt could not indeed fully imagine how things affected Gwendolen: he had no imagination of anything in her but what affected the gratification of his own will; but on this point he had the sensibility which seems like divination. What we see exclusively we are apt to see

DANIEL DERONDA

with some mistake of proportions; and Grandcourt was not
likely to be infallible in his judgments concerning this wife
who was governed by many shadowy powers, to him non-
existent. He magnified her inward resistance, but that did
not lessen his satisfaction in the mastery of it.

XLV

Behold my lady's carriage stop the way,
With powdered lackey and with champing bay:
She sweeps the matting, treads the crimson stair,
Her arduous function solely 'to be there.'
Like Sirius rising o'er the silent sea,
She hides her heart in lustre loftily.

SO the Grandcourts were in Grosvenor Square in time to receive a card for the musical party at Lady Mallinger's, there being reasons of business which made Sir Hugo know beforehand that his ill-beloved nephew was coming up. It was only the third evening after their arrival, and Gwendolen made rather an absent-minded acquaintance with her new ceilings and furniture, preoccupied with the certainty that she was going to speak to Deronda again, and also to see the Miss Lapidoth who had gone through so much, and was 'capable of submitting to anything in the form of duty.' For Gwendolen had remembered nearly every word that Deronda had said about Mirah, and especially that phrase, which she repeated to herself bitterly, having an ill-defined consciousness that her own submission was something very different. She would have been obliged to allow, if any one had said it to her, that what she submitted to could not take the shape of duty, but was submission to a yoke drawn on her by an action she was ashamed of, and worn with a strength of selfish motives that left no weight for duty to carry.

The drawing-rooms in Park Lane, all white, gold, and pale crimson, were agreeably furnished, and not crowded with guests, before Mr. and Mrs. Grandcourt entered; and more than half an hour of instrumental music was being followed by an interval of movement and chat. Klesmer was there with his wife, and in his generous interest for Mirah he proposed to accompany her singing of Leo's 'O patria mia,' which he had before recommended her to choose, as more distinctive of her than better known music. He was already at the piano, and Mirah was

standing there conspicuously, when Gwendolen, magnificent in her pale green velvet and poisoned diamonds, was
ushered to a seat of honour well in view of them. With her
long sight and self-command she had the rare power of
quickly distinguishing persons and objects on entering a
full room, and while turning her glance towards Mirah she
did not neglect to exchange a bow and smile with Klesmer
as she passed. The smile seemed to each a lightning-flash
back on that morning when it had been her ambition to
stand as the 'little Jewess' was standing, and survey a grand
audience from the higher rank of her talent – instead of
which she was one of the ordinary crowd in silk and gems,
whose utmost performance it must be to admire or find
fault. 'He thinks I am in the right road now,' said the
lurking resentment within her.

Gwendolen had not caught sight of Deronda in her
passage, and while she was seated acquitting herself in
chat with Sir Hugo, she glanced round her with careful
ease, bowing a recognition here and there, and fearful lest
an anxious-looking exploration in search of Deronda might
be observed by her husband, and afterwards rebuked as
something 'damnably vulgar.' But all travelling, even that
of a slow gradual glance round a room, brings a liability to
undesired encounters, and amongst the eyes that met
Gwendolen's, forcing her into a slight bow, were those of
the 'amateur too fond of Meyerbeer,' Mr. Lush, whom Sir
Hugo continued to find useful as a half-caste among
gentlemen. He was standing near her husband, who, however, turned a shoulder towards him, and was being understood to listen to Lord Pentreath. How was it that at this
moment, for the first time, there darted through
Gwendolen, like a disagreeable sensation, the idea that
this man knew all about her husband's life? He had been
banished from her sight, according to her will, and she had
been satisfied; he had sunk entirely into the background of
her thoughts, screened away from her by the agitating
figures that kept up an inward drama in which Lush had
no place. Here suddenly he reappeared at her husband's

elbow, and there sprang up in her, like an instantaneously fabricated memory in a dream, the sense of his being connected with the secrets that made her wretched. She was conscious of effort in turning her head away from him, trying to continue her wandering survey as if she had seen nothing of more consequence than the picture on the wall, till she discovered Deronda. But he was not looking towards her, and she withdrew her eyes from him, without having got any recognition, consoling herself with the assurance that he must have seen her come in. In fact, he was standing not far from the door with Hans Meyrick, whom he had been careful to bring into Lady Mallinger's list. They were both a little more anxious than was comfortable lest Mirah should not be heard to advantage. Deronda even felt himself on the brink of betraying emotion, Mirah's presence now being linked with crowding images of what had gone before and was to come after – all centring in the brother whom he was soon to reveal to her; and he had escaped as soon as he could from the side of Lady Pentreath, who had said in her violoncello voice –

'Well, your Jewess is pretty – there's no denying that. But where is her Jewish impudence? She looks as demure as a nun. I suppose she learned that on the stage.'

He was beginning to feel on Mirah's behalf something of what he had felt for himself in his seraphic boyish time, when Sir Hugo asked him if he would like to be a great singer – an indignant dislike to her being remarked on in a free and easy way, as if she were an imported commodity disdainfully paid for by the fashionable public; and he winced the more because Mordecai, he knew, would feel that the name 'Jewess' was taken as a sort of stamp like the lettering of Chinese silk. In this susceptible mood he saw the Grandcourts enter, and was immediately appealed to by Hans about 'that Vandyke duchess of a beauty.' Pray excuse Deronda that in this moment he felt a transient renewal of his first repulsion from Gwendolen, as if she and her beauty and her failings were to blame for the undervaluing of Mirah as a woman – a feeling something like class animosity, which affection for what is not fully recognized by others, whether in persons or in poetry, rarely allows us to escape. To Hans admiring Gwendolen with his habitual hyperbole, he answered, with a sarcasm that was not quite good-humoured –

'I thought you could admire no style of woman but your Berenice.'

'That is the style I worship – not admire,' said Hans. 'Other styles of woman I might make myself wicked for, but for Berenice I could make myself – well, pretty good, which is something much more difficult.'

'Hush!' said Deronda, under the pretext that the singing was going to begin. He was not so delighted with the answer as might have been expected, and was relieved by Hans's movement to a more advanced spot.

Deronda had never before heard Mirah sing '*O patria mia.*' He knew well Leopardi's fine Ode to Italy (when Italy sat like a disconsolate mother in chains, hiding her face on her knees and weeping), and the few selected words were filled for him with the grandeur of the whole, which seemed to breathe as inspiration through the music. Mirah singing this, made Mordecai more than ever one presence with her. Certain words not included in the song nevertheless rang within Deronda as harmonies from one invisible –

> *'Non ti difende*
> *Nessun de' tuoi? L'armi, qua l'armi: io solo*
> *Combatterò, procomberò sol io'* –

they seemed the very voice of that heroic passion which is falsely said to devote itself in vain when it achieves the godlike end of manifesting unselfish love. And that passion was present to Deronda now as the vivid image of a man dying helplessly away from the possibility of battle.

Mirah was equal to his wishes. While the general applause was sounding, Klesmer gave a more valued testimony, audible to her only – 'Good, good – the crescendo better than before.' But her chief anxiety was to know that she had satisfied Mr. Deronda: any failure on her part this evening would have pained her as an especial injury to him. Of course all her prospects were due to what he had done for her; still this occasion of singing in the house that was his home brought a peculiar demand. She looked towards him in the distance, and he could see that she did; but he remained where he was, and watched the stream of emulous admirers closing round her, till presently they parted to make way for Gwendolen, who was taken up to be introduced by Mrs. Klesmer. Easier now about 'the little Jewess,' Daniel relented towards poor Gwendolen in her splendour, and his memory went back, with some penitence for his momentary hardness, over all the signs and confessions that she too needed a rescue, and one much more difficult than that of the wanderer by the river – a rescue for which he felt himself helpless. The silent question – 'But is it not cowardly to make that a reason for turning away?' was the form in which he framed his resolve to go near her on the first opportunity, and show his regard for her past confidence, in spite of Sir Hugo's unwelcome hints.

Klesmer, having risen to Gwendolen as she approached, and being included by her in the opening conversation with Mirah, continued near them a little while, looking down with a smile, which was rather in his eyes than on his lips, at the piquant contrast of the two charming young creatures seated on the red divan. The solicitude seemed to be all on the side of the splendid one.

'You must let me say how much I am obliged to you,' said Gwendolen. 'I had heard from Mr. Deronda that I should have a great treat in your singing, but I was too ignorant to imagine how great.'

'You are very good to say so,' answered Mirah, her mind chiefly occupied in contemplating Gwendolen. It was like a new kind of stage-experience to her to be close to genuine grand ladies with genuine brilliants and complexions, and they impressed her vaguely as coming out of some unknown drama, in which their parts perhaps got more tragic as they went on.

'We shall all want to learn of you – I, at least,' said Gwendolen. 'I sing very badly, as Herr Klesmer will tell you' – here she glanced upward to that higher power rather archly, and continued – 'but I have been rebuked for not liking to be middling, since I can be nothing more. I think that is a different doctrine from yours?' She was still looking at Klesmer, who said quickly –

'Not if it means that it would be worth while for you to study further, and for Miss Lapidoth to have the pleasure of helping you.' With that he moved away, and Mirah, taking everything with *naïve* seriousness, said –

'If you think I could teach you, I shall be very glad. I am anxious to teach, but I have only just begun. If I do it well, it must be by remembering how my master taught me.'

Gwendolen was in reality too uncertain about herself to be prepared for this simple promptitude of Mirah's, and in her wish to change the subject said, with some lapse from the good taste of her first address –

'You have not been long in London, I think? – but you were perhaps introduced to Mr. Deronda abroad?'

'No,' said Mirah; 'I never saw him before I came to England in the summer.'

'But he has seen you often and heard you sing a great deal, has he not?' said Gwendolen, led on partly by the wish to hear anything about Deronda, and partly by the awkwardness which besets the readiest person in carrying on a dialogue when empty of matter. 'He spoke of you to me with the highest praise. He seemed to know you quite well.'

'Oh, I was poor, and needed help,' said Mirah, in a new tone of feeling, 'and Mr. Deronda has given me the best friends in the world. That is the only way he came to know anything about me – because he was sorry for me. I had no friends when I came. I was in distress. I owe everything to him.'

Poor Gwendolen, who had wanted to be a struggling artist herself, could nevertheless not escape the impression that a mode of inquiry which would have been rather rude towards herself was an amiable condescension to this Jewess who was ready to give her lessons. The only effect on Mirah, as always on any mention of Deronda, was to stir reverential gratitude and anxiety that she should be understood to have the deepest obligation to him.

But both he and Hans, who were noticing the pair from a distance, would have felt rather indignant if they had known that the conversation had led up to Mirah's representation of herself in this light of neediness. In the movement that prompted her, however, there was an exquisite delicacy, which perhaps she could not have stated explicitly – the feeling that she ought not to allow any one to assume in Deronda a relation of more equality or less generous interest towards her than actually existed. Her answer was delightful to Gwendolen: she thought of nothing but the ready compassion, which in another form she had trusted in and found for herself; and on the signals that Klesmer was about to play she moved away in much content, entirely without presentiment that this Jewish *protégée* would ever make a more important difference in her life than the possible improvement of her singing – if the leisure and spirits of a Mrs. Grandcourt would allow of other lessons than such as the world was giving her at rather a high charge.

With her wonted alternation from resolute care of appearances to some rash indulgence of an impulse, she chose, under the pretext of getting farther from the instrument, not to go again to her former seat, but placed herself on a settee where she could only have one neighbour. She was nearer to Deronda than before: was it surprising that he came up in time to shake hands before the music began – then, that after he had stood a little while by the elbow of the settee at the empty end, the torrent-like confluences of bass and treble seemed, like a convulsion of nature, to cast the conduct of petty mortals into insignificance, and to warrant his sitting down?

But when at the end of Klesmer's playing there came the outburst of talk under which Gwendolen had hoped to speak as she would to Deronda, she observed that Mr. Lush was within hearing, leaning against the wall close by them. She could not help her flush of anger, but she tried to have only an air of polite indifference in saying –

'Miss Lapidoth is everything you described her to be.'

'You have been very quick in discovering that,' said Deronda, ironically.

'I have not found out all the excellences you spoke of – I don't mean that,' said Gwendolen; 'but I think her singing is charming, and herself too. Her face is lovely – not in the least common; and she is such a complete little person. I should think she will be a great success.'

This speech was grating to Deronda, and he would not answer it, but looked gravely before him. She knew that he was displeased with her, and she was getting so impatient under the neighbourhood of Mr. Lush, which prevented her from saying any word she wanted to say, that she meditated some desperate step to get rid of it, and remained silent too. That constraint seemed to last a long while, neither Gwendolen nor Deronda looking at the other, till Lush slowly relieved the wall of his weight, and joined some one at a distance.

Gwendolen immediately said, 'You despise me for talking artificially.'

'No,' said Deronda, looking at her coolly; 'I think that is quite excusable sometimes. But I did not think what you were last saying was altogether artificial.'

'There was something in it that displeased you,' said Gwendolen. 'What was it?'

'It is impossible to explain such things,' said Deronda. 'One can never communicate niceties of feeling about words and manner.'

'You think I am shut out from understanding them,' said Gwendolen, with a slight tremor in her voice, which she was trying to conquer. 'Have I shown myself so very dense to everything you have said?' There was an indescribable look of suppressed tears in her eyes, which were turned on him.

'Not at all,' said Deronda, with some softening of voice. 'But experience differs for different people. We don't all wince at the same things. I have had plenty of proof that you are not dense.' He smiled at her.

'But one may feel things and not be able to do anything better for all that,' said Gwendolen, not smiling in return – the distance to which Deronda's words seemed to throw her chilling her too much. 'I begin to think we can only get better by having people about us who raise good feelings. You must not be surprised at anything in me. I think it is too late for me to alter. I don't know how to set about being wise, as you told me to be.'

'I seldom find I do any good by my preaching. I might as well have kept from meddling,' said Deronda, thinking rather sadly that his interference about that unfortunate necklace might end in nothing but an added pain to him in seeing her after all hardened to another sort of gambling than roulette.

'Don't say that,' said Gwendolen, hurriedly, feeling that this might be her only chance of getting the words uttered, and dreading the increase of her own agitation. 'If you despair of me, I shall despair. Your saying that I should not go on being selfish and ignorant has been some strength to me. If you say you wish you had not meddled – that means, you despair of me and forsake me. And then you will decide for me that I shall not be good. It is you who will decide; because you might have made me different by keeping as near to me as you could, and believing in me.'

She had not been looking at him as she spoke, but at the handle of the fan which she held closed. With the last words she rose and left him, returning to her former place, which had been left vacant; while every one was settling into quietude in expectation of Mirah's voice, which presently, with that wonderful, searching quality of subdued song in which the melody seems simply an effect of the emotion, gave forth, *Per pietà non dirmi addio*.

In Deronda's ear the strain was for the moment a continuance of Gwendolen's pleading – a painful urging of something vague and difficult, irreconcilable with pressing conditions, and yet cruel to resist. However strange the mixture in her of a resolute pride and a precocious air of knowing the world, with a precipitate, guileless indiscretion, he was quite sure now that the mixture existed. Sir Hugo's hints had made him alive to dangers that his own disposition might have neglected; but that Gwendolen's reliance on him was unvisited by any dream of his being a man who could misinterpret her was as manifest as morning, and made an appeal which wrestled with his sense of present dangers, and with his foreboding of a growing incompatible claim on him in her mind. There was a foreshadowing of some painful collision: on the one side the grasp of Mordecai's dying hand on him, with all the ideals and prospects it aroused; on the other this fair creature in silk and gems, with her hidden wound and her self-dread, making a trustful effort to lean and find herself sustained. It was as if he had a vision of himself besought with outstretched arms and cries, while he was caught by the waves and compelled to mount the vessel bound for a far-off coast. That was the strain of excited feeling in him that went along with the notes of Mirah's song; but when it ceased he moved from his seat with the reflection that he had been falling into an exaggeration of his own importance, and a ridiculous readiness to accept Gwendolen's view of himself, as if he could really have any decisive power over her.

'What an enviable fellow you are,' said Hans to him, 'sitting on a sofa with that young duchess, and having an interesting quarrel with her!'

'Quarrel with her?' repeated Deronda, rather uncomfortably.

'Oh, about theology, of course; nothing personal. But she told you what you ought to think, and then left you with a grand air which was admirable. Is she an Antinomian? – if so, tell her I am an Antinomian painter, and introduce me. I should like to paint her and her husband. He has the sort of handsome *physique* that the Duke ought to have in *Lucrezia Borgia* – if it could go with a fine baritone, which it can't.'

Deronda devoutly hoped that Hans's account of the impression his dialogue with Gwendolen had made on a distant beholder was no more than a bit of fantastic representation, such as was common with him.

And Gwendolen was not without her afterthoughts that her husband's eyes might have been on her, extracting something to reprove – some offence against her dignity as his wife; her consciousness telling her that she had not kept up the perfect air of equability in public which was her own ideal. But Grandcourt made no observation on her behaviour. All he said as they were driving home was –

'Lush will dine with us among the other people to-morrow. You will treat him civilly.'

Gwendolen's heart began to beat violently. The words that she wanted to utter, as one wants to return a blow, were, 'You are breaking your promise to me – the first promise you made me.' But she dared not utter them. She was as frightened at a quarrel as if she had foreseen that it would end with throttling fingers on her neck. After a pause, she said in the tone rather of defeat than resentment –

'I thought you did not intend him to frequent the house again.'

'I want him just now. He is useful to me; and he must be treated civilly.'

Silence. There may come a moment when even an excellent husband who has dropt smoking under more or less of a pledge during courtship, for the first time will introduce his cigar-smoke between himself and his wife, with the tacit understanding that she will have to put up with it. Mr. Lush was, so to speak, a very large cigar.

If these are the sort of lovers' vows at which Jove laughs, he must have a merry time of it.

XLVI

'If any one should importune me to give a reason why I loved him,
I feel it could no otherwise be expressed than by making answer,
"Because it was he; because it was I." There is, beyond what I am
able to say, I know not what inexplicable and inevitable power
that brought on this union.'

— MONTAIGNE: *On Friendship*.

THE time had come to prepare Mordecai for the revelation of the restored sister and for the change of abode
which was desirable before Mirah's meeting with her
brother. Mrs. Meyrick, to whom Deronda had confided
everything except Mordecai's peculiar relation to himself,
had been active in helping him to find a suitable lodging in
Brompton, not many minutes' walk from her own house, so
that the brother and sister would be within reach of her
motherly care. Her happy mixture of Scottish caution with
her Scottish fervour and Gallic liveliness had enabled her
to keep the secret close from the girls as well as from Hans,
any betrayal to them being likely to reach Mirah in some
way that would raise an agitating suspicion, and spoil the
important opening of that work which was to secure her
independence, as we rather arbitrarily call one of the more
arduous and dignified forms of our dependence. And both
Mrs. Meyrick and Deronda had more reasons than they
could have expressed for desiring that Mirah should be
able to maintain herself. Perhaps 'the little mother' was
rather helped in her secrecy by some dubiousness in her
sentiment about the remarkable brother described to her;
and certainly if she felt any joy and anticipatory admiration, it was due to her faith in Deronda's judgment. The
consumption was a sorrowful fact that appealed to her
tenderness; but how was she to be very glad of an enthusiasm which, to tell the truth, she could only contemplate
as Jewish pertinacity, and as rather an undesirable introduction among them all of a man whose conversation
would not be more modern and encouraging than that of
Scott's Covenanters? Her mind was anything but prosaic,

and she had her soberer share of Mab's delight in the romance of Mirah's story and of her abode with them; but the romantic or unusual in real life requires some adaptation. We sit up at night to read about Çakya-Mouni, Saint Francis, or Oliver Cromwell; but whether we should be glad for any one at all like them to call on us the next morning, still more, to reveal himself as a new relation, is quite another affair. Besides, Mrs. Meyrick had hoped, as her children did, that the intensity of Mirah's feeling about Judaism would slowly subside, and be merged in the gradually deepening current of loving interchange with her new friends. In fact, her secret favourite continuation of the romance had been no discovery of Jewish relations, but something much more favourable to the hopes she discerned in Hans. And now – here was a brother who would dip Mirah's mind over again in the deepest dye of Jewish sentiment. She could not help saying to Deronda –

'I am as glad as you are that the pawnbroker is not her brother: there are Ezras and Ezras in the world; and really it is a comfort to think that all Jews are not like those shopkeepers who *will not* let you get out of their shops; and besides, what he said to you about his mother and sister makes me bless him. I am sure he's good. But I never did like anything fanatical. I suppose I heard a little too much preaching in my youth, and lost my palate for it.'

'I don't think you will find that Mordecai obtrudes any preaching,' said Deronda. 'He is not what I should call fanatical. I call a man fanatical when his enthusiasm is narrow and hoodwinked, so that he has no sense of proportions, and becomes unjust and unsympathetic to men who are out of his own track. Mordecai is an enthusiast: I should like to keep that word for the highest order of minds – those who care supremely for grand and general benefits to mankind. He is not a strictly orthodox Jew, and is full of allowances for others: his conformity in many things is an allowance for the condition of other Jews. The people he lives with are as fond of him as possible, and they can't in the least understand his ideas.'

'Oh, well, I can live up to the level of the pawnbroker's mother, and like him for what I see to be good in him; and for what I don't see the merits of, I will take your word. According to your definition, I suppose one might be fanatical in worshipping common-sense; for my husband used to say the world would be a poor place if there were nothing but common-sense in it. However, Mirah's brother will have good bedding – that I have taken care of; and I shall have this extra window pasted up with paper to prevent draughts.' (The conversation was taking place in the destined lodging.) 'It is a comfort to think that the people of the house are no strangers to me – no hypocritical harpies. And when the children know, we shall be able to make the rooms much prettier.'

'The next stage of the affair is to tell all to Mordecai, and get him to move – which may be a more difficult business,' said Deronda.

'And will you tell Mirah before I say anything to the children?' said Mrs. Meyrick. But Deronda hesitated, and she went on in a tone of persuasive deliberation – 'No, I think not. Let me tell Hans and the girls the evening before, and they will be away the next morning.'

'Yes, that will be best. But do justice to my account of Mordecai – or Ezra, as I suppose Mirah will wish to call him; don't assist their imagination by referring to Habakkuk Mucklewrath,' said Deronda, smiling, – Mrs. Meyrick herself having used the comparison of the Covenanters.

'Trust me, trust me,' said the little mother. 'I shall have to persuade them so hard to be glad, that I shall convert myself. When I am frightened I find it a good thing to have somebody to be angry with for not being brave: it warms the blood.'

Deronda might have been more argumentative or persuasive about the view to be taken of Mirah's brother, if he had been less anxiously preoccupied with the more important task immediately before him, which he desired to acquit himself of without wounding the Cohens.

Mordecai, by a memorable answer, had made it evident that he would be keenly alive to any inadvertence in relation to their feelings. In the interval, he had been meeting Mordecai at the *Hand and Banner*, but now after due reflection he wrote to him saying that he had particular reasons for wishing to see him in his own home the next evening, and would beg to sit with him in his workroom for an hour, if the Cohens would not regard it as an intrusion. He would call with the understanding that if there were any objection, Mordecai would accompany him elsewhere. Deronda hoped in this way to create a little expectation that would have a preparatory effect.

He was received with the usual friendliness, some additional costume in the women and children, and in all the elders a slight air of wondering which even in Cohen was not allowed to pass the bounds of silence – the guest's transactions with Mordecai being a sort of mystery which he was rather proud to think lay outside the sphere of light which enclosed his own understanding. But when Deronda said, 'I suppose Mordecai is at home and expecting me,' Jacob, who had profited by the family remarks, went up to his knee and said, 'What do you want to talk to Mordecai about?'

'Something that is very interesting to him,' said Deronda, pinching the lad's ear, 'but that you can't understand.'

'Can you say this?' said Jacob, immediately giving forth a string of his rote-learned Hebrew verses with a wonderful mixture of the throaty and the nasal, and nodding his small head at his hearer, with a sense of giving formidable evidence which might rather alter their mutual position.

'No, really,' said Deronda, keeping grave; 'I can't say anything like it.'

'I thought not,' said Jacob, performing a dance of triumph with his small scarlet legs, while he took various objects out of the deep pockets of his knickerbockers and returned them thither, as a slight hint of his resources; after which running to the door of the workroom, he opened it wide, set his back against it, and said, 'Mordecai, here's the young swell' – a copying of his father's phrase which seemed to him well fitted to cap the recitation of Hebrew.

He was called back with hushes by mother and grand-mother, and Deronda, entering and closing the door behind him, saw that a bit of carpet had been laid down, a chair placed, and the fire and lights attended to, in sign of the Cohens' respect. As Mordecai rose to greet him, Deronda was struck with the air of solemn expectation in his face, such as would have seemed perfectly natural if his letter had declared that some revelation was to be made about the lost sister. Neither of them spoke till Deronda, with his usual tenderness of manner, had drawn the vacant chair from the opposite side of the hearth and had seated himself near to Mordecai, who then said, in a tone of fervid certainty –

'You are come to tell me something that my soul longs for.'

'It is true that I have something very weighty to tell you – something, I trust, that you will rejoice in,' said Deronda, on his guard against the probability that Mordecai had been preparing himself for something quite different from the fact.

'It is all revealed – it is made clear to you,' said Mordecai, more eagerly, leaning forward with clasped hands. 'You are even as my brother that sucked the breasts of my mother – the heritage is yours – there is no doubt to divide us.'

'I have learned nothing new about myself,' said Deronda. The disappointment was inevitable: it was bet-ter not to let the feeling be strained longer in a mistaken hope.

Mordecai sank back in his chair, unable for the moment to care what was really coming. The whole day his mind had been in a state of tension towards one fulfilment. The reaction was sickening, and he closed his eyes.

'Except,' Deronda went on gently after a pause, – 'except that I had really some time ago come into another

sort of hidden connection with you, besides what you have
spoken of as existing in your own feeling.'

The eyes were not opened, but there was a fluttering in
the lids.

'I had made the acquaintance of one in whom you are
interested.'

Mordecai opened his eyes and fixed them in a quiet
gaze on Deronda: the former painful check repressed all
activity of conjecture.

'One who is closely related to your departed mother,'
Deronda went on, wishing to make the disclosure gradual;
but noticing a shrinking movement in Mordecai, he added
– 'whom she and you held dear above all others.'

Mordecai, with a sudden start, laid a spasmodic grasp
on Deronda's wrist: there was a great terror in him. And
Deronda divined it. A tremor was perceptible in his clear
tones as he said –

'What was prayed for has come to pass: Mirah has been
delivered from evil.'

Mordecai's grasp relaxed a little, but he was panting
with a sort of tearless sob.

Deronda went on: 'Your sister is worthy of the mother
you honoured.'

He waited there, and Mordecai, throwing himself backward in his chair, again closed his eyes, uttering himself
almost inaudibly for some minutes in Hebrew, and then
subsiding into a happy-looking silence. Deronda, watching
the expression in his uplifted face, could have imagined
that he was speaking with some beloved object: there was a
new suffused sweetness, something like that on the faces
of the beautiful dead. For the first time Deronda thought
he discerned a family resemblance to Mirah.

Presently, when Mordecai was ready to listen, the rest
was told. But in accounting for Mirah's flight he made the
statements about the father's conduct as vague as he could,
and threw the emphasis on her yearning to come to
England as the place where she might find her mother.
Also he kept back the fact of Mirah's intention to drown

herself, and his own part in rescuing her; merely describing the home she had found with friends of his, whose interest in her and efforts for her he had shared. What he dwelt on finally was Mirah's feeling about her mother and brother; and in relation to this he tried to give every detail.

'It was in search of them,' said Deronda, smiling, 'that I turned into this house: the name Ezra Cohen was just then the most interesting name in the world to me. I confess I had a fear for a long while. Perhaps you will forgive me now for having asked you that question about the elder Mrs. Cohen's daughter. I cared very much what I should find Mirah's friends to be. But I had found a brother worthy of her when I knew that her Ezra was disguised under the name of Mordecai.'

'Mordecai is really my name – Ezra Mordecai Cohen.'

'Is there any kinship between this family and yours?' said Deronda.

'Only the kinship of Israel. My soul clings to these people, who have sheltered me and given me succour out of the affection that abides in Jewish hearts, as a sweet odour in things long crushed and hidden from the outer air. It is good for me to bear with their ignorance and be bound to them in gratitude, that I may keep in mind the spiritual poverty of the Jewish millions, and not put impatient knowledge in the stead of loving wisdom.'

'But you don't feel bound to continue with them now there is a closer tie to draw you?' said Deronda, not without fear that he might find an obstacle to overcome. 'It seems to me right now – is it not? – that you should live with your sister; and I have prepared a home to take you to in the neighbourhood of her friends, that she may join you there. Pray grant me this wish. It will enable me to be with you often in the hours when Mirah is obliged to leave you. That is my selfish reason. But the chief reason is, that Mirah will desire to watch over you, and that you ought to give to her the guardianship of a brother's presence. You shall have books about you. I shall want to learn of you, and to take you out to see the river and trees. And you will have the rest and comfort that you will be more and more in need of – nay, that I need for you. This is the claim I make on you, now that we have found each other.'

Deronda, grasping his own coat-collar rather nervously, spoke in a tone of earnest affectionate pleading, such as he might have used to a venerated elder brother. Mordecai's eyes were fixed on him with a listening contemplation, and he was silent for a little while after Deronda had ceased to speak. Then he said, with an almost reproachful emphasis –

'And you would have me hold it doubtful whether you were born a Jew! Have we not from the first touched each other with invisible fibres – have we not quivered together like the leaves from a common stem with stirrings from a common root? I know what I am outwardly – I am one among the crowd of poor – I am stricken, I am dying. But our souls know each other. They gazed in silence as those who have long been parted and meet again, but when they found voice they were assured, and all their speech is understanding. The life of Israel is in your veins.'

Deronda sat perfectly still, but felt his face tingling. It was impossible either to deny or assent. He waited, hoping that Mordecai would presently give him a more direct answer. And after a pause of meditation he did say firmly –

'What you wish of me I will do. And our mother – may the blessing of the Eternal be with her in our souls! – would have wished it too. I will accept what your loving-kindness has prepared, and Mirah's home shall be mine.' He paused a moment, and then added in a more melancholy tone, 'But I shall grieve to part from these parents and the little ones. You must tell them, for my heart would fail me.'

'I felt that you would want me to tell them. Shall we go now at once?' said Deronda, much relieved by this unwavering compliance.

'Yes; let us not defer it. It must be done,' said Mordecai, rising with the air of a man who has to perform a painful duty. Then came, as an afterthought, 'But do not dwell on my sister more than is needful.'

When they entered the parlour he said to the alert Jacob, 'Ask your father to come, and tell Sarah to mind the shop. My friend has something to say,' he continued, turning to the elder Mrs. Cohen. It seemed part of Mordecai's eccentricity that he should call this gentleman his friend; and the two women tried to show their better manners by warm politeness in begging Deronda to seat himself in the best place.

When Cohen entered with a pen behind his ear, he rubbed his hands and said with loud satisfaction, 'Well, sir! I'm glad you're doing us the honour to join our family party again. We are pretty comfortable, I think.'

He looked round with shiny gladness. And when all were seated on the hearth the scene was worth peeping in upon: on one side Baby under her scarlet quilt in the corner being rocked by the young mother, and Adelaide Rebekah seated on the grandmother's knee; on the other, Jacob between his father's legs; while the two markedly different figures of Deronda and Mordecai were in the middle – Mordecai a little backward in the shade, anxious to conceal his agitated susceptibility to what was going on around him. The chief light came from the fire, which brought out the rich colour on a depth of shadow, and seemed to turn into speech the dark gems of eyes that looked at each other kindly.

'I have just been telling Mordecai of an event that makes a great change in his life,' Deronda began, 'but I hope you will agree with me that it is a joyful one. Since he thinks of you as his best friends, he wishes me to tell you for him at once.'

'Relations with money, sir?' burst in Cohen, feeling a power of divination which it was a pity to nullify by waiting for the fact.

'No; not exactly,' said Deronda, smiling. 'But a very precious relation wishes to be reunited to him – a very good and lovely young sister, who will care for his comfort in every way.'

'Married, sir?'

'No, not married.'

'But with a maintenance?'

'With talents which will secure her a maintenance. A home is already provided for Mordecai.'

There was silence for a moment or two before the grandmother said in a wailing tone –

'Well, well! and so you're going away from us, Mordecai.'

'And where there's no children as there is here,' said the mother, catching the wail.

'No Jacob, and no Adelaide, and no Eugenie!' wailed the grandmother again.

'Ay, ay, Jacob's learning 'ill all wear out of him. He must go to school. It'll be hard times for Jacob,' said Cohen, in a tone of decision.

In the wide-open ears of Jacob his father's words sounded like a doom, giving an awful finish to the dirge-like effect of the whole announcement. His face had been gathering a wondering incredulous sorrow at the notion of Mordecai's going away: he was unable to imagine the change as anything lasting; but at the mention of 'hard times for Jacob' there was no further suspense of feeling, and he broke forth in loud lamentation. Adelaide Rebekah always cried when her brother cried, and now began to howl with astonishing suddenness, whereupon baby awaking contributed angry screams, and required to be taken out of the cradle. A great deal of hushing was necessary, and Mordecai, feeling the cries pierce him, put out his arms to Jacob, who in the midst of his tears and sobs was turning his head right and left for general observation. His father, who had been saying, 'Never mind, old man; you shall go to the riders,' now released him, and he went to Mordecai, who clasped him, and laid his cheek on the little black head without speaking. But Cohen, sensible that the master of the family must make some apology for all this weakness, and that the occasion called for a speech, addressed Deronda with some elevation of pitch, squaring his elbows and resting a hand on each knee: –

'It's not as we're the people to grudge anybody's good luck, sir, or the portion of their cup being made fuller, as I may say. I'm not an envious man, and if anybody offered to set up Mordecai in a shop of my sort two doors lower down, *I* shouldn't make wry faces about it. I'm not one of them that had need have a poor opinion of themselves, and be frightened at anybody else getting a chance. If I'm offal, let a wise man come and tell me, for I've never heard it yet. And in point of business, I'm not a class of goods to be in danger. If anybody takes to rolling me, I can pack myself up like a caterpillar, and find my feet when I'm let alone. And though, as I may say, you're taking some of our good works from us, which is a property bearing interest, I'm not saying but we can afford that, though my mother and my wife had the good will to wish and do for Mordecai to the last; and a Jew must not be like a servant who works for reward – though I see nothing against a reward if I can get it. And as to the extra outlay in schooling, I'm neither poor nor greedy – I wouldn't hang myself for sixpence, nor half a crown neither. But the truth of it is, the women and children are fond of Mordecai. You may partly see how it is, sir, by your own sense. A man is bound to thank God, as we do every Sabbath, that he was not made a woman; but a woman has to thank God that He has made her according to His will. And we all know what He has made her – a child-bearing, tender-hearted thing is the woman of our people. Her children are mostly stout, as I think you'll say Addy's are, and she's not mushy, but her heart is tender. So you must excuse present company, sir, for not being glad all at once. And as to this young lady – for by what you say "young lady" is the proper term' – Cohen here threw some additional emphasis into his look and tone – 'we shall all be glad for Mordecai's sake by-and-by, when we cast up our accounts and see where we are.'

Before Deronda could summon any answer to this oddly mixed speech, Mordecai exclaimed –

'Friends, friends! For food and raiment and shelter I would not have sought better than you have given me. You have sweetened the morsel with love; and what I thought of as a joy that would be left to me even in the last months of my waning strength was to go on teaching the lad. But now I am as one who had clad himself beforehand in his shroud, and used himself to make the grave his bed, and the divine command came, "Arise, and go forth; the night is not yet come." For no light matter would I have turned away from your kindness to take another's. But it has been taught us, as you know, that *the reward of one duty is the power to fulfil another* – so said Ben Azai. You have made your duty to one of the poor among your brethren a joy to you and me; and your reward shall be that you will not rest without the joy of like deeds in the time to come. And may not Jacob come and visit me?'

Mordecai had turned with this question to Deronda, who said –

'Surely that can be managed. It is no further than Brompton.'

Jacob, who had been gradually calmed by the need to hear what was going forward, began now to see some day-light on the future, the word 'visit' having the lively charm of cakes and general relaxation at his grandfather's, the dealer in knives. He danced away from Mordecai, and took up a station of survey in the middle of the hearth with his hands in his knickerbockers.

'Well,' said the grandmother, with a sigh of resignation, 'I hope there'll be nothing in the way of your getting *kosher* meat, Mordecai. For you'll have to trust to those you live with.'

'That's all right, that's all right, you may be sure, mother,' said Cohen, as if anxious to cut off inquiry on matters in which he was uncertain of the guest's position. 'So, sir,' he added, turning with a look of amused enlightenment to Deronda, 'it was better than learning you had to talk to Mordecai about! I wondered to myself at the time. I thought somehow there was a something.'

'Mordecai will perhaps explain to you how it was that I was seeking him,' said Deronda, feeling that he had better go, and rising as he spoke.

It was agreed that he should come again and the final move be made on the next day but one; but when he was going Mordecai begged to walk with him to the end of the street, and wrapped himself in coat and comforter. It was a March evening, and Deronda did not mean to let him go far, but he understood the wish to be outside the house with him in communicative silence, after the exciting speech that had been filling the last hour. No word was spoken until Deronda had proposed parting, when he said –

'Mirah would wish to thank the Cohens for their goodness. You would wish her to do so – to come and see them, would you not?'

Mordecai did not answer immediately, but at length said –

'I cannot tell. I fear not. There is a family sorrow, and the sight of my sister might be to them as the fresh bleeding of wounds. There is a daughter and sister who will never be restored as Mirah is. But who knows the pathways? We are all of us denying or fulfilling prayers – and men in their careless deeds walk amidst invisible outstretched arms and pleadings made in vain. In my ears I have the prayers of generations past and to come. My life is nothing to me but the beginning of fulfilment. And yet I am only another prayer – which you will fulfil.'

Deronda pressed his hand, and they parted.

XLVII

'And you must love him ere to you
He will seem worthy of your love.'
– WORDSWORTH.

ONE might be tempted to envy Deronda providing new clothes for Mordecai, and pleasing himself as if he were sketching a picture in imagining the effect of the fine grey flannel shirts and a dressing-gown very much like a Franciscan's brown frock, with Mordecai's head and neck above them. Half his pleasure was the sense of seeing Mirah's brother through her eyes, and securing her fervid joy from any perturbing impression. And yet, after he had made all things ready, he was visited with a doubt whether he were not mistaking her, and putting the lower effect for the higher: was she not just as capable as he himself had been of feeling the impressive distinction in her brother all the more for that aspect of poverty which was among the memorials of his past? But there were the Meyricks to be propitiated towards this too Judaic brother; and Deronda detected himself piqued into getting out of sight everything that might feed the ready repugnance in minds unblessed with that 'precious seeing,' that bathing of all objects in a solemnity as of sunset-glow, which is begotten of a loving reverential emotion.

And his inclination would have been the more confirmed if he had heard the dialogue round Mrs. Meyrick's fire late in the evening, after Mirah had gone to her room. Hans, settled now in his Chelsea rooms, had stayed late, and Mrs. Meyrick, poking the fire into a blaze, said –

'Now, Kate, put out your candle, and all come round the fire cosily. Hans, dear, do leave off laughing at those poems for the ninety-ninth time, and come too. I have something wonderful to tell you.'

'As if I didn't know that, ma. I have seen it in the corner of your eye ever so long, and in your pretences of errands,' said Kate, while the girls came to put their feet on the fender, and Hans, pushing his chair near them, sat astride it, resting his fists and chin on the back.

'Well, then, if you are so wise, perhaps you know that Mirah's brother is found!' said Mrs. Meyrick, in her clearest accents.

'Oh, confound it!' said Hans, in the same moment.

'Hans, that is wicked,' said Mab. 'Suppose we had lost you.'

'I *can not* help being rather sorry,' said Kate. 'And her mother? – where is she?'

'Her mother is dead.'

'I hope the brother is not a bad man,' said Amy.

'Nor a fellow all smiles and jewellery – a Crystal Palace Assyrian with a hat on,' said Hans, in the worst humour.

'Were there ever such unfeeling children?' said Mrs. Meyrick, a little strengthened by the need for opposition. 'You don't think the least bit of Mirah's joy in the matter.'

'You know, ma, Mirah hardly remembers her brother,' said Kate.

'People who are lost for twelve years should never come back again,' said Hans. 'They are always in the way.'

'Hans!' said Mrs. Meyrick, reproachfully. 'If you had lost me for *twenty* years, I should have thought —'

'I said twelve years,' Hans broke in. 'Anywhere about twelve years is the time at which lost relations should keep out of the way.'

'Well, but it's nice finding people – there is something to tell,' said Mab, clasping her knees. 'Did Prince Camaralzaman find him?'

Then Mrs. Meyrick, in her neat narrative way, told all she knew without interruption. 'Mr. Deronda has the highest admiration for him,' she ended – 'seems quite to look up to him. And he says Mirah is just the sister to understand this brother.'

'Deronda is getting perfectly preposterous about those Jews,' said Hans with disgust, rising and setting his chair away with a bang. 'He wants to do everything he can to encourage Mirah in her prejudices.'

'Oh, for shame, Hans! – to speak in that way of Mr. Deronda,' said Mab. And Mrs. Meyrick's face showed something like an undercurrent of expression, not allowed to get to the surface.

'And now we shall never be all together,' Hans went on, walking about with his hands thrust into the pockets of his brown velveteen coat, 'but we must have this prophet Elijah to tea with us, and Mirah will think of nothing but sitting on the ruins of Jerusalem. She will be spoiled as an artist – mind that – she will get as narrow as a nun. Everything will be spoiled – our home and everything. I shall take to drinking.'

'Oh, really, Hans,' said Kate, impatiently, 'I do think men are the most contemptible animals in all creation. Every one of them must have everything to his mind, else he is unbearable.'

'Oh, oh, oh, it's very dreadful!' cried Mab. 'I feel as if ancient Nineveh were come again.'

'I should like to know what is the good of having gone to the university and knowing everything, if you are so childish, Hans,' said Amy. 'You ought to put up with a man that Providence sends you to be kind to. *We* shall have to put up with him.'

'I hope you will all of you like the new Lamentations of Jeremiah – "to be continued in our next" – that's all,' said Hans, seizing his wide-awake. 'It's no use being one thing more than another if one has to endure the company of those men with a fixed idea – staring blankly at you, and requiring all your remarks to be small footnotes to their text. If you're to be under a petrifying well, you'd better be an old boot. I don't feel myself an old boot.' Then abruptly, 'Good-night, little mother,' bending to kiss her brow in a hasty, desperate manner, and condescendingly, on his way to the door, 'Good-night, girls.'

'Suppose Mirah knew how you are behaving,' said Kate. But her answer was a slam of the door. 'I *should* like to see Mirah when Mr. Deronda tells her,' she went on, to her mother. 'I know she will look *so* beautiful.'

But Deronda on second thoughts had written a letter which Mrs. Meyrick received the next morning, begging her to make the revelation instead of waiting for him, not giving the real reason – that he shrank from going again through a narrative in which he seemed to be making himself important, and giving himself a character of general beneficence – but saying that he wished to remain with Mordecai while Mrs. Meyrick would bring Mirah on what was to be understood as a visit, so that there might be a little interval before that change of abode which he expected that Mirah herself would propose.

Deronda secretly felt some wondering anxiety how far Mordecai, after years of solitary preoccupation with ideas likely to have become the more exclusive from continual diminution of bodily strength, would allow him to feel a tender interest in his sister over and above the rendering of pious duties. His feeling for the Cohens, and especially for little Jacob, showed a persistent activity of affection; but those objects had entered into his daily life for years; and Deronda felt it noticeable that Mordecai asked no new questions about Mirah, maintaining, indeed, an unusual silence on all subjects, and appearing simply to submit to the changes that were coming over his personal life. He donned his new clothes obediently, but said afterwards to Deronda, with a faint smile, 'I must keep my old garments by me for a remembrance.' And when they were seated awaiting Mirah, he uttered no word, keeping his eyelids closed, but yet showing restless feeling in his face and hands. In fact, Mordecai was undergoing that peculiar nervous perturbation only known to those whose minds, long and habitually moving with strong impetus in one current, are suddenly compelled into a new or reopened channel. Susceptible people whose strength has been long absorbed by a dominant bias dread an interview that imperiously revives the past as they would dread a threatening illness. Joy may be there, but joy, too, is terrible.

Deronda felt the infection of excitement, and when he heard the ring at the door, he went out not knowing exactly

why, that he might see and greet Mirah beforehand. He
was startled to find that she had on the hat and cloak in
which he had first seen her – the memorable cloak that had
once been wetted for a winding-sheet. She had come
down-stairs equipped in this way, and when Mrs.
Meyrick said, in a tone of question, 'You like to go in that
dress, dear?' she answered, 'My brother is poor, and I want
to look as much like him as I can, else he may feel distant
from me' – imagining that she should meet him in the
workman's dress. Deronda could not make any remark,
but felt secretly rather ashamed of his own fastidious
arrangements. They shook hands silently, for Mirah
looked pale and awed.

When Deronda opened the door for her, Mordecai had
risen, and had his eyes turned towards it with an eager
gaze. Mirah took only two or three steps, and then stood
still. They looked at each other, motionless. It was less
their own presence that they felt than another's; they were
meeting first in memories, compared with which touch was
no union. Mirah was the first to break the silence, standing
where she was.

'Ezra,' she said, in exactly the same tone as when she
was telling of her mother's call to him.

Mordecai with a sudden movement advanced and laid
his hands on her shoulders. He was the head taller, and
looked down at her tenderly while he said, 'That was our
mother's voice. You remember her calling me?'

'Yes, and how you answered her – "Mother!" – and I
knew you loved her.' Mirah threw her arms round her
brother's neck, clasped her little hands behind it, and
drew down his face, kissing it with childlike lavishness.
Her hat fell backward on the ground and disclosed all her
curls.

'Ah, the dear head, the dear head!' said Mordecai,
in a low loving tone, laying his thin hand gently on the
curls.

'You are very ill, Ezra,' said Mirah, sadly looking at him
with more observation.

'Yes, dear child, I shall not be long with you in the body,' was the quiet answer.

'Oh, I will love you and we will talk to each other,' said Mirah, with a sweet outpouring of her words, as spontaneous as bird-notes. 'I will tell you everything, and you will teach me: – you will teach me to be a good Jewess – what she would have liked me to be. I shall always be with you when I am not working. For I work now. I shall get money to keep us. Oh, I have had such good friends.'

Mirah until now had quite forgotten that any one was by, but here she turned with the prettiest attitude, keeping one hand on her brother's arm while she looked at Mrs. Meyrick and Deronda. The little mother's happy emotion in witnessing this meeting of brother and sister had already won her to Mordecai, who seemed to her really to have more dignity and refinement than she had felt obliged to believe in from Deronda's account.

'See this dear lady!' said Mirah. 'I was a stranger, a poor wanderer, and she believed in me, and has treated me as a daughter. Please give my brother your hand,' she added, beseechingly, taking Mrs. Meyrick's hand and putting it in Mordecai's, then pressing them both with her own and lifting them to her lips.

'The Eternal Goodness has been with you,' said Mordecai. 'You have helped to fulfil our mother's prayer.'

'I think we will go now, shall we? – and return later,' said Deronda, laying a gentle pressure on Mrs. Meyrick's arm, and she immediately complied. He was afraid of any reference to the facts about himself which he had kept back from Mordecai, and he felt no uneasiness now in the thought of the brother and sister being alone together.

XLVIII

'Tis a hard and ill-paid task to order all things beforehand by the rule of our own security, as is well hinted by Machiavelli concerning Cæsar Borgia, who, saith he, had thought of all that might occur on his father's death, and had provided against every evil chance save only one: it had never come into his mind that when his father died, his own death would quickly follow.

GRANDCOURT'S importance as a subject of this realm was of the grandly passive kind which consists in the inheritance of land. Political and social movements touched him only through the wire of his rental, and his most careful biographer need not have read up on Schleswig-Holstein, the policy of Bismarck, trade-unions, household suffrage, or even the last commercial panic. He glanced over the best newspaper columns on these topics, and his views on them can hardly be said to have wanted breadth, since he embraced all Germans, all commercial men, and all voters liable to use the wrong kind of soap, under the general epithet of 'brutes;' but he took no action on these much agitated questions beyond looking from under his eyelids at any man who mentioned them, and retaining a silence which served to shake the opinions of timid thinkers.

But Grandcourt within his own sphere of interest showed some of the qualities which have entered into triumphal diplomacy of the widest continental sort.

No movement of Gwendolen in relation to Deronda escaped him. He would have denied that he was jealous; because jealousy would have implied some doubt of his own power to hinder what he had determined against. That his wife should have more inclination to another man's society than to his own would not pain him: what he required was that she should be as fully aware as she would have been of a locked hand-cuff, that her inclination was helpless to decide anything in contradiction with his resolve. However much of vacillating whim there might have been in his entrance on matrimony, there was no vacillating in his interpretation of the bond. He had not repented of his marriage; it had really brought more of aim into his life, new objects to exert his will upon; and he had not repented of his choice. His taste was fastidious, and Gwendolen satisfied it: he would not have liked a wife who had not received some elevation of rank from him; nor one who did not command admiration by her mien and beauty; nor one whose nails were not of the right shape; nor one the lobe of whose ear was at all too large and red; nor one who, even if her nails and ears were right, was at the same time a ninny, unable to make spirited answers. These requirements may not seem too exacting to refined contemporaries whose own ability to fall in love has been held in suspense for lack of indispensable details; but fewer perhaps may follow him in his contentment that his wife should be in a temper which would dispose her to fly out if she dared, and that she should have been urged into marrying him by other feelings than passionate attachment. Still, for those who prefer command to love, one does not see why the habit of mind should change precisely at the point of matrimony.

Grandcourt did not feel that he had chosen the wrong wife; and having taken on himself the part of husband, he was not going in any way to be fooled, or allow himself to be seen in a light that could be regarded as pitiable. This was his state of mind – not jealousy; still, his behaviour in some respects was as like jealousy as yellow is to yellow, which colour we know may be the effect of very different causes.

He had come up to town earlier than usual because he wished to be on the spot for legal consultation as to the arrangements of his will, the transference of mortgages, and that transaction with his uncle about the succession to Diplow, which the bait of ready money, adroitly dangled without importunity, had finally won him to agree upon. But another acceptable accompaniment of his being in town was the presentation of himself with the beautiful bride whom he had chosen to marry in spite of what other people might have expected of him. It is true that Grandcourt went about with the sense that he did not care a languid curse for any one's admiration; but this state of not-caring, just as much as desire, required its related object – namely, a world of admiring or envying spectators: for if you are fond of looking stonily at smiling persons, the persons must be there and they must smile – a rudimentary truth which is surely forgotten by those who complain of mankind as generally contemptible, since any other aspect of the race must disappoint the voracity of their contempt. Grandcourt, in town for the first time with his wife, had his non-caring abstinence from curses enlarged and diversified by splendid receptions, by conspicuous rides and drives, by presentations of himself with her on all distinguished occasions. He wished her to be sought after; he liked that 'fellows' should be eager to talk with her and escort her within his observation; there was even a kind of lofty coquetry on her part that he would not have objected to. But what he did not like were her ways in relation to Deronda.

After the musical party at Lady Mallinger's, when Grandcourt had observed the dialogue on the settee as keenly as Hans had done, it was characteristic of him that he named Deronda for invitation along with the Mallingers, tenaciously avoiding the possible suggestion to anybody concerned that Deronda's presence or absence could be of the least importance to him; and he made no direct observation to Gwendolen on her behaviour that evening, lest the expression of his disgust should be a little too strong to satisfy his own pride. But a few days afterwards he remarked without being careful of the *à propos* –

'Nothing makes a woman more of a gawky than looking out after people and showing tempers in public. A woman ought to have fine manners. Else it's intolerable to appear with her.'

Gwendolen made the expected application, and was not without alarm at the notion of being a gawky. For she, too, with her melancholy distaste for things, preferred that her distaste should include admirers. But the sense of over-hanging rebuke only intensified the strain of expectation towards any meeting with Deronda. The novelty and excitement of her town life was like the hurry and constant change of foreign travel: whatever might be the inward despondency, there was a programme to be fulfilled, not without gratification to many-sided self. But, as always happens with a deep interest, the comparatively rare occasions on which she could exchange any words with Deronda had a diffusive effect in her consciousness, magnifying their communication with each other, and therefore enlarging the place she imagined it to have in his mind. How could Deronda help this? He certainly did not avoid her; rather he wished to convince her by every delicate indirect means that her confidence in him had not been indiscreet, since it had not lowered his respect. Moreover, he liked being near her – how could it be otherwise? She was something more than a problem: she was a lovely woman, for the turn of whose mind and fate he had a care which, however futile it might be, kept soliciting him as a responsibility, perhaps all the more that, when he dared to think of his own future, he saw it lying far away from this splendid sad-hearted creature, who, because he had once been impelled to arrest her attention momentarily, as he might have seized her arm with warning to hinder her from stepping where there was danger, had turned to him with a beseeching persistent need.

One instance in which Grandcourt stimulated a feeling in Gwendolen that he would have liked to suppress without seeming to care about it, had relation to Mirah. Gwendolen's inclination lingered over the project of the singing lessons as a sort of obedience to Deronda's advice, but day followed day with that want of perceived leisure which belongs to lives where there is no work to mark off intervals; and the continual liability to Grandcourt's presence and surveillance seemed to flatten every effort to the level of the boredom which his manner expressed:

his negative mind was as diffusive as fog, clinging to all objects, and spoiling all contact.

But one morning when they were breakfasting, Gwendolen, in a recurrent fit of determination to exercise her old spirit, said, dallying prettily over her prawns without eating them –

'I think of making myself accomplished while we are in town, and having singing lessons.'

'Why?' said Grandcourt, languidly.

'Why?' echoed Gwendolen, playing at sauciness; 'because I can't eat *pâté de foie gras* to make me sleepy, and I can't smoke, and I can't go to the club to make me like to come away again – I want a variety of *ennui*. What would be the most convenient time, when you are busy with your lawyers and people, for me to have lessons from that little Jewess, whose singing is getting all the rage?'

'Whenever you like,' said Grandcourt, pushing away his plate, and leaning back in his chair while he looked at her with his most lizard-like expression, and played with the ears of the tiny spaniel on his lap (Gwendolen had taken a dislike to the dogs because they fawned on him).

Then he said, languidly, 'I don't see why a lady should sing. Amateurs make fools of themselves. A lady can't risk herself in that way in company. And one doesn't want to hear squalling in private.'

'I like frankness: that seems to me a husband's great charm,' said Gwendolen, with her little upward movement of her chin, as she turned her eyes away from his, and lifting a prawn before her, looked at the boiled ingenuousness of its eyes as preferable to the lizard's. 'But,' she added, having devoured her mortification, 'I suppose you don't object to Miss Lapidoth's singing at our party on the 4th? I thought of engaging her. Lady Brackenshaw had her, you know; and the Raymonds, who are very particular about their music. And Mr. Deronda, who is a musician himself, and a first-rate judge, says that there is no singing in such good taste as hers for a drawing-room. I think his opinion is an authority.'

She meant to sling a small stone at her husband in that way.

'It's very indecent of Deronda to go about praising that girl,' said Grandcourt, in a tone of indifference.

'Indecent!' exclaimed Gwendolen, reddening and looking at him again, overcome by startled wonder, and unable to reflect on the probable falsity of the phrase – 'to go about praising.'

'Yes; and especially when she is patronized by Lady Mallinger. He ought to hold his tongue about her. Men can see what is his relation to her.'

'Men who judge of others by themselves,' said Gwendolen, turning white after her redness, and immediately smitten with a dread of her own words.

'Of course. And a woman should take their judgment – else she is likely to run her head into the wrong place,' said Grandcourt, conscious of using pincers on that white creature. 'I suppose you take Deronda for a saint.'

'Oh dear no!' said Gwendolen, summoning desperately her almost miraculous power of self-control, and speaking in a high hard tone. 'Only a little less of a monster.'

She rose, pushed her chair away without hurry, and walked out of the room with something like the care of a man who is afraid of showing that he has taken more wine than usual. She turned the keys inside her dressing-room doors, and sat down, for some time looking as pale and quiet as when she was leaving the breakfast-room. Even in the moments after reading the poisonous letter she had hardly had more cruel sensations than now; for emotion was at the acute point, where it is not distinguishable from sensation. Deronda unlike what she had believed him to be, was an image which affected her as a hideous apparition would have done, quite apart from the way in which it was produced. It had taken hold of her as pain before she could consider whether it were fiction or truth; and further to hinder her power of resistance came the sudden perception, how very slight were the grounds of her faith in Deronda – how little she knew of his life – how childish she had been in her confidence. His rebukes and his severity to her began to seem odious, along with all the poetry and lofty doctrine in the world, whatever it might be; and the grave beauty of his face seemed the most unpleasant mask that the common habits of men could put on.

All this went on in her with the rapidity of a sick dream; and her start into resistance was very much like a waking. Suddenly from out the grey sombre morning there came a stream of sunshine, wrapping her in warmth and light where she sat in stony stillness. She moved gently and looked round her – there was a world outside this bad dream, and the dream proved nothing; she rose, stretching her arms upward and clasping her hands with her habitual attitude when she was seeking relief from oppressive feeling, and walked about the room in this flood of sunbeams.

'It is not true! What does it matter whether *he* believes it or not?' This was what she repeated to herself – but this was not her faith come back again; it was only the desperate cry of faith, finding suffocation intolerable. And how could she go on through the day in this state? With one of her impetuous alternations, her imagination flew to wild actions, by which she would convince herself of what she wished: she would go to Lady Mallinger and question her about Mirah; she would write to Deronda and upbraid him with making the world all false and wicked and hopeless to her – to him she dared pour out all the bitter indignation of her heart. No; she would go to Mirah. This last form taken by her need was more definitely practicable, and quickly became imperious. No matter what came of it. She had the pretext of asking Mirah to sing at her party on the 4th. What was she going to say besides? How satisfy herself? She did not foresee – she could not wait to foresee. If that idea which was maddening her had been a living thing, she would have wanted to throttle it without waiting to foresee what would come of the act. She rang her bell and asked if Mr. Grandcourt were gone out: finding that he was, she ordered the carriage, and began to dress for the drive; then she went down, and walked about the large drawing-room like an imprisoned dumb creature, not recognizing herself in the glass panels, not noting any object around her in the painted gilded prison. Her husband would probably find out where she had been, and punish her in some way or other – no matter – she could neither desire nor fear anything just now but the assurance that she had not been deluding herself in her trust.

She was provided with Mirah's address. Soon she was on the way with all the fine equipage necessary to carry about her poor uneasy heart, depending in its palpitations on some answer or other to questioning which she did not know how she should put. She was as heedless of what happened before she found that Miss Lapidoth was at home, as one is of lobbies and passages on the way to a court of justice – heedless of everything till she was in a room where there were folding-doors, and she heard Deronda's voice behind it. Doubtless the identification was helped by forecast, but she was as certain of it as if she had seen him. She was frightened at her own agitation, and began to unbutton her gloves that she might button them again, and bite her lips over the pretended difficulty, while the door opened, and Mirah presented herself with perfect quietude and a sweet smile of recognition. There was relief in the sight of her face, and Gwendolen was able to smile in return, while she put out her hand in silence; and as she seated herself, all the while hearing the voice, she felt some reflux of energy in the confused sense that the truth could not be anything that she dreaded. Mirah drew her chair very near, as if she felt that the sound of the conversation should be subdued, and looked at her visitor with placid expectation, while Gwendolen began in a low tone, with something that seemed like bashfulness –

'Perhaps you wonder to see me – perhaps I ought to have written – but I wished to make a particular request.'

'I am glad to see you instead of having a letter,' said Mirah, wondering at the changed expression and manner of the 'Vandyke duchess,' as Hans had taught her to call

Gwendolen. The rich colour and the calmness of her own face were in strong contrast with the pale agitated beauty under the plumed hat.

'I thought,' Gwendolen went on – 'at least, I hoped you would not object to sing at our house on the 4th – in the evening – at a party like Lady Brackenshaw's. I should be so much obliged.'

'I shall be very happy to sing for you. At half-past-nine or ten?' said Mirah, while Gwendolen seemed to get more instead of less embarrassed.

'At half-past-nine, please,' she answered; then paused, and felt that she had nothing more to say. She could not go. It was impossible to rise and say good-bye. Deronda's voice was in her ears. She must say it – she could contrive no other sentence –

'Mr. Deronda is in the next room.'

'Yes,' said Mirah, in her former tone. 'He is reading Hebrew with my brother.'

'You have a brother?' said Gwendolen, who had heard this from Lady Mallinger, but had not minded it then.

'Yes, a dear brother who is ill – consumptive, and Mr. Deronda is the best of friends to him, as he has been to me,' said Mirah, with the impulse that will not let us pass the mention of a precious person indifferently.

'Tell me,' said Gwendolen, putting her hand on Mirah's, and speaking hardly above a whisper – 'tell me – tell me the truth. You are sure he is quite good. You know no evil of him. Any evil that people say of him is false.'

Could the proud-spirited woman have behaved more like a child? But the strange words penetrated Mirah with nothing but a sense of solemnity and indignation. With a sudden light in her eyes and a tremor in her voice, she said –

'Who are the people that say evil of him? I would not believe any evil of him, if an angel came to tell it me. He found me when I was so miserable – I was going to drown myself – I looked so poor and forsaken – you would have thought I was a beggar by the wayside. And he treated me

as if I had been a king's daughter. He took me to the best of
women. He found my brother for me. And he honours my
brother – though he too was poor – oh, almost as poor as he
could be. And my brother honours him. That is no light
thing to say' – here Mirah's tone changed to one of proud
emphasis, and she shook her head backward – 'for my
brother is very learned and great-minded. And Mr.
Deronda says there are few men equal to him.' Some
Jewish defiance had flamed into her indignant gratitude,
and her anger could not help including Gwendolen, since
she seemed to have doubted Deronda's goodness.

But Gwendolen was like one parched with thirst, drinking the fresh water that spreads through the frame as a
sufficient bliss. She did not notice that Mirah was angry
with her; she was not distinctly conscious of anything but
of the penetrating sense that Deronda and his life were no
more like her husband's conception than the morning in
the horizon was like the morning mixed with street gas:
even Mirah's words seemed to melt into the indefiniteness
of her relief. She could hardly have repeated them, or said
how her whole state of feeling was changed. She pressed
Mirah's hand, and said, 'Thank you, thank you,' in a
hurried whisper – then rose, and added, with only a hazy
consciousness, 'I must go, I shall see you – on the 4th – I am
so much obliged' – bowing herself out automatically; while
Mirah, opening the door for her, wondered at what seemed
a sudden retreat into chill loftiness.

Gwendolen, indeed, had no feeling to spare in any
effusiveness towards the creature who had brought
her relief. The passionate need of contradiction to
Grandcourt's estimate of Deronda, a need which had
blunted her sensibility to everything else, was no sooner
satisfied than she wanted to be gone: she began to be aware
that she was out of place, and to dread Deronda's seeing
her. And once in the carriage again, she had the vision of
what awaited her at home. When she drew up before the
door in Grosvenor Square, her husband was arriving with a
cigar between his fingers. He threw it away and handed her

out, accompanying her upstairs. She turned into the drawing-room, lest he should follow her farther and give her no place to retreat to; then sat down with a weary air, taking off her gloves, rubbing her hand over her forehead, and making his presence as much of a cipher as possible. But he sat too, and not far from her – just in front, where to avoid looking at him must have the emphasis of effort.

'May I ask where you have been at this extraordinary hour?' said Grandcourt.

'Oh yes; I have been to Miss Lapidoth's to ask her to come and sing for us,' said Gwendolen, laying her gloves on the little table beside her, and looking down at them.

'And to ask her about her relations with Deronda?' said Grandcourt, with the coldest possible sneer in his low voice, which in poor Gwendolen's ear was diabolical.

For the first time since their marriage she flashed out upon him without inward check. Turning her eyes full on his she said, in a biting tone –

'Yes; and what you said is false – a low, wicked false-hood.'

'She told you so – did she?' returned Grandcourt, with a more thoroughly distilled sneer.

Gwendolen was mute. The daring anger within her was turned into the rage of dumbness. What reasons for her belief could she give? All the reasons that seemed so strong and living within her – she saw them suffocated and shrivelled up under her husband's breath. There was no proof to give, but her own impression, which would seem to him her own folly. She turned her head quickly away from him and looked angrily towards the end of the room: she would have risen, but he was in her way.

Grandcourt saw his advantage. 'It's of no consequence so far as her singing goes,' he said, in his superficial drawl. 'You can have her to sing, if you like.' Then, after a pause, he added in his lowest imperious tone, 'But you will please to observe that you are not to go near that house again. As my wife, you must take my word about what is proper for you. When you undertook to be Mrs. Grandcourt, you undertook not to make a fool of yourself. You have been making a fool of yourself this morning; and if you were to go on as you have begun, you might soon get yourself talked of at the clubs in a way you would not like. What do *you* know about the world? You have married *me*, and must be guided by my opinion.'

Every slow sentence of that speech had a terrific mastery in it for Gwendolen's nature. If the low tones had come from a physician telling her that her symptoms were those of a fatal disease, and prognosticating its course, she could not have been more helpless against the argument that lay in it. But she was permitted to move now, and her husband never again made any reference to what had occurred this morning. He knew the force of his own words. If this white-handed man with the perpendicular profile had been sent to govern a difficult colony, he might have won reputation among his contemporaries. He had certainly ability, would have understood that it was safer to exterminate than to cajole superseded proprietors, and would not have flinched from making things safe in that way.

Gwendolen did not, for all this, part with her recovered faith; – rather, she kept it with a more anxious tenacity, as a Protestant of old kept his Bible hidden or a Catholic his crucifix, according to the side favoured by the civil arm; and it was characteristic of her that apart from the impression gained concerning Deronda in that visit, her imagination was little occupied with Mirah or the eulogized brother. The one result established for her was, that Deronda had acted simply as a generous benefactor, and the phrase 'reading Hebrew' had fleeted unimpressively across her sense of hearing, as a stray stork might have made its peculiar flight across her landscape without rousing any surprised reflection on its natural history.

But the issue of that visit, as it regarded her husband, took a strongly active part in the process which made an habitual conflict within her, and was the cause of some external change perhaps not observed by any one except

Deronda. As the weeks went on bringing occasional transient interviews with her, he thought that he perceived in
her an intensifying of her superficial hardness and resolute
display, which made her abrupt betrayals of agitation the
more marked and disturbing to him.

In fact, she was undergoing a sort of discipline for the
refractory which, as little as possible like conversion, bends
half the self with a terrible strain, and exasperates the
unwillingness of the other half. Grandcourt had an active
divination rather than discernment of refractoriness in her,
and what had happened about Mirah quickened his suspicion that there was an increase of it dependent on the
occasions when she happened to see Deronda: there was
some 'confounded nonsense' between them: he did not
imagine it exactly as flirtation, and his imagination in other
branches was rather restricted; but it was nonsense that
evidently kept up a kind of simmering in her mind – an
inward action which might become disagreeably outward.
Husbands in the old time are known to have suffered from
a threatening devoutness in their wives, presenting itself
first indistinctly as oddity, and ending in that mild form of
lunatic asylum, a nunnery: Grandcourt had a vague perception of threatening moods in Gwendolen which the unity
between them in his views of marriage required him peremptorily to check. Among the means he chose, one was
peculiar, and was less ably calculated than the speeches we
have just heard.

He determined that she should know the main purport
of the will he was making, but he could not communicate
this himself, because it involved the fact of his relation to
Mrs. Glasher and her children; and that there should be
any overt recognition of this between Gwendolen and
himself was supremely repugnant to him. Like all proud,
closely-wrapped natures, he shrank from explicitness and
detail, even on trivialities, if they were personal: a valet
must maintain a strict reserve with him on the subject of
shoes and stockings. And clashing was intolerable to him:
his habitual want was to put collision out of the question by

the quiet massive pressure of his rule. But he wished Gwendolen to know that before he made her an offer it was no secret to him that she was aware of his relations with Lydia, her previous knowledge being the apology for bringing the subject before her now. Some men in his place might have thought of writing what he wanted her to know, in the form of a letter. But Grandcourt hated writing: even writing a note was a bore to him, and he had long been accustomed to have all his writing done by Lush. We know that there are persons who will forego their own obvious interest rather than do anything so disagreeable as to write letters; and it is not probable that these imperfect utilitarians would rush into manuscript and syntax on a difficult subject in order to save another's feelings. To Grandcourt it did not even occur that he should, would, or could write to Gwendolen the information in question; and the only medium of communication he could use was Lush, who, to his mind, was as much of an implement as pen and paper. But here too Grandcourt had his reserves, and would not have uttered a word likely to encourage Lush in an impudent sympathy with any supposed grievance in a marriage which had been discommended by him. Who that has a confidant escapes believing too little in his penetration, and too much in his discretion? Grandcourt had always allowed Lush to know his external affairs indiscriminately, irregularities, debts, want of ready money; he had only used discrimination about what he would allow his confidant to say to him; and he had been so accustomed to this human tool, that the having him at call in London was a recovery of lost ease. It followed that Lush knew all the provisions of the will more exactly than they were known to the testator himself.

Grandcourt did not doubt that Gwendolen, since she was a woman who could put two and two together, knew or suspected Lush to be the contriver of her interview with Lydia, and that this was the reason why her first request was for his banishment. But the bent of a woman's inferences on mixed subjects which excite mixed passions is not determined by her capacity for simple addition; and here Grandcourt lacked the only organ of thinking that could have saved him from mistake – namely, some experience of the mixed passions concerned. He had correctly divined one half of Gwendolen's dread – all that related to her personal pride, and her perception that his will must conquer hers; but the remorseful half, even if he had known of her broken promise, was as much out of his imagination as the other side of the moon. What he believed her to feel about Lydia was solely a tongue-tied jealousy, and what he believed Lydia to have written with the jewels was the fact that she had once been used to wearing them, with other amenities such as he imputed to the intercourse of jealous women. He had the triumphant certainty that he could aggravate the jealousy and yet smite it with a more absolute dumbness. His object was to engage all his wife's egoism on the same side as his own, and in his employment of Lush he did not intend an insult to her: she ought to understand that he was the only possible envoy. Grandcourt's view of things was considerably fenced in by his general sense, that what suited him, others must put up with. There is no escaping the fact that want of sympathy condemns us to a corresponding stupidity. Mephistopheles thrown upon real life, and obliged to manage his own plots, would inevitably make blunders.

One morning he went to Gwendolen in the boudoir beyond the back drawing-room, hat and gloves in hand, and said with his best-tempered, most persuasive drawl, standing before her and looking down on her as she sat with a book on her lap –

'A – Gwendolen, there's some business about property to be explained. I have told Lush to come and explain it to you. He knows all about these things. I am going out. He can come up now. He's the only person who can explain. I suppose you'll not mind.'

'You know that I do mind,' said Gwendolen, angrily, starting up. 'I shall not see him.' She showed the intention to dart away to the door. Grandcourt was before her, with his back towards it. He was prepared for her anger, and showed none in return, saying, with the same sort of remonstrant tone that he might have used about an objection to dining out –

'It's no use making a fuss. There are plenty of brutes in the world that one has to talk to. People with any *savoir vivre* don't make a fuss about such things. Some business must be done. You don't expect agreeable people to do it. If I employ Lush, the proper thing for you is to take it as a matter of course. Not to make a fuss about it. Not to toss your head and bite your lips about people of that sort.'

The drawling and the pauses with which this speech was uttered gave time for crowding reflections in Gwendolen, quelling her resistance. What was there to be told her about property? This word had certain dominant associations for her, first with her mother, then with Mrs. Glasher and her children. What would be the use if she refused to see Lush? Could she ask Grandcourt to tell her himself? That might be intolerable, even if he consented, which it was certain he would not, if he had made up his mind to the contrary. The humiliation of standing an obvious prisoner, with her husband barring the door, was not to be borne any longer, and she turned away to lean against a cabinet, while Grandcourt again moved towards her.

'I have arranged with Lush to come up now, while I am out,' he said, after a long organ stop, during which Gwendolen made no sign. 'Shall I tell him he may come?'

Yet another pause before she could say 'Yes' – her face turned obliquely and her eyes cast down.

'I shall come back in time to ride, if you like to get ready,' said Grandcourt. No answer. 'She is in a desperate rage,' thought he. But the rage was silent, and therefore not disagreeable to him. It followed that he turned her chin and kissed her, while she still kept her eyelids down, and she did not move them until he was on the other side of the door.

What was she to do? Search where she would in her consciousness, she found no plea to justify a plaint. Any romantic illusions she had had in marrying this man had turned on her power of using him as she liked. He was using her as he liked.

She sat awaiting the announcement of Lush as a sort of searing operation that she had to go through. The facts that galled her gathered a burning power when she thought of their lying in his mind. It was all a part of that new gambling in which the losing was not simply a *minus* but a terrible *plus* that had never entered into her reckoning.

Lush was neither quite pleased nor quite displeased with his task. Grandcourt had said to him by way of conclusion, 'Don't make yourself more disagreeable than nature obliges you.'

'That depends,' thought Lush. But he said, 'I will write a brief abstract for Mrs. Grandcourt to read.' He did not suggest that he should make the whole communication in writing, which was a proof that the interview did not wholly displease him.

Some provision was being made for himself in the will, and he had no reason to be in a bad humour, even if a bad humour had been common with him. He was perfectly convinced that he had penetrated all the secrets of the situation; but he had no diabolic delight in it. He had only the small movements of gratified self-loving resentment in discerning that this marriage fulfilled his own foresight in not being as satisfactory as the supercilious young lady had expected it to be, and as Grandcourt wished to feign that it was. He had no persistent spite much stronger than what gives the seasoning of ordinary scandal to those who repeat it and exaggerate it by their conjectures. With no active compassion or good-will, he had just as little active malevolence, being chiefly occupied in liking his particular pleasures, and not disliking anything but what hindered those pleasures – everything else ranking with the last murder and the last *opera buffa*, under the head of things to talk about. Nevertheless, he was not indifferent to the prospect of being treated uncivilly by a beautiful woman, or to the counterbalancing fact that his present commission put into his hands an official power of humiliating her. He did not mean to use it needlessly; but there are some persons so gifted in relation to us that their 'How do you do?' seems charged with offence.

By the time that Mr. Lush was announced, Gwendolen had braced herself to a bitter resolve that he should not witness the slightest betrayal of her feeling, whatever he might have to tell. She invited him to sit down with stately quietude. After all, what was this man to her? He was not in the least like her husband. Her power of hating a coarse, familiar-mannered man, with clumsy hands, was now relaxed by the intensity with which she hated his contrast.

He held a small paper folded in his hand while he spoke.

'I need hardly say that I should not have presented myself if Mr. Grandcourt had not expressed a strong wish to that effect – as no doubt he has mentioned to you.'

From some voices that speech might have sounded entirely reverential, and even timidly apologetic. Lush had no intention to the contrary, but to Gwendolen's ear his words had as much insolence in them as his prominent eyes, and the pronoun 'you' was too familiar. He ought to have addressed the folding-screen, and spoken of her as Mrs. Grandcourt. She gave the smallest sign of a bow, and Lush went on, with a little awkwardness, getting entangled in what is elegantly called tautology.

'My having been in Mr. Grandcourt's confidence for fifteen years or more – since he was a youth, in fact – of course gives me a peculiar position. He can speak to me of affairs that he could not mention to any one else; and, in fact, he could not have employed any one else in this affair. I have accepted the task out of friendship for him. Which is my apology for accepting the task – if you would have preferred some one else.'

He paused, but she made no sign, and Lush, to give himself a countenance in an apology which met no acceptance, opened the folded paper, and looked at it vaguely before he began to speak again.

'This paper contains some information about Mr. Grandcourt's will, an abstract of a part he wished you to know – if you'll be good enough to cast your eyes over it. But there is something I had to say by way of introduction – which I hope you'll pardon me for, if it's not quite agreeable.' Lush found that he was behaving better than he had expected, and had no idea how insulting he made himself with his 'not quite agreeable.'

'Say what you have to say without apologizing, please,' said Gwendolen, with the air she might have bestowed on a dog-stealer come to claim a reward for finding the dog he had stolen.

'I have only to remind you of something that occurred before your engagement to Mr. Grandcourt,' said Lush, not without the rise of some willing insolence in exchange for her scorn. 'You met a lady in Cardell Chase, if you remember, who spoke to you of her position with regard to Mr. Grandcourt. She had children with her – one a very fine boy.'

Gwendolen's lips were almost as pale as her cheeks: her passion had no weapons – words were no better than chips. This man's speech was like a sharp knife-edge drawn across her skin; but even her indignation at the employment of Lush was getting merged in a crowd of other feelings, dim and alarming as a crowd of ghosts.

'Mr. Grandcourt was aware that you were acquainted with this unfortunate affair beforehand, and he thinks it only right that his position and intentions should be made quite clear to you. It is an affair of property and prospects; and if there were any objection you had to make, if you would mention it to me – it is a subject which of course he would rather not speak about himself – if you will be good enough just to read this.' With the last words Lush rose and presented the paper to her.

When Gwendolen resolved that she would betray no feeling in the presence of this man, she had not prepared

herself to hear that her husband knew the silent consciousness, the silently accepted terms on which she had married
him. She dared not raise her hand to take the paper, lest it
should visibly tremble. For a moment Lush stood holding
it towards her, and she felt his gaze on her as ignominy,
before she could say even with low-toned haughtiness –

'Lay it on the table. And go into the next room, please.'

Lush obeyed, thinking as he took an easy-chair in
the back drawing-room, 'My lady winces considerably.
She didn't know what would be the charge for that
superfine article, Henleigh Grandcourt.' But it seemed to
him that a penniless girl had done better than she had
any right to expect, and that she had been uncommonly
knowing for her years and opportunities: her words to
Lydia meant nothing, and her running away had probably
been part of her adroitness. It had turned out a master-
stroke.

Meanwhile Gwendolen was rallying her nerves to the
reading of the paper. She must read it. Her whole being –
pride, longing for rebellion, dreams of freedom, remorseful
conscience, dread of fresh visitation – all made one need to
know what the paper contained. But at first it was not easy
to take in the meaning of the words. When she had succeeded, she found that in the case of there being no son as
issue of her marriage, Grandcourt had made the small
Henleigh his heir; – that was all she cared to extract from
the paper with any distinctness. The other statements as to
what provision would be made for her in the same case, she
hurried over, getting only a confused perception of thousands and Gadsmere. It was enough. She could dismiss the
man in the next room with the defiant energy which had
revived in her at the idea that this question of property and
inheritance was meant as a finish to her humiliations and
her thraldom.

She thrust the paper between the leaves of her book,
which she took in her hand, and walked with her stateliest
air into the next room, where Lush immediately rose,
awaiting her approach. When she was four yards from

him, it was hardly an instant that she paused to say in a high tone, while she swept him with her eyelashes –

'Tell Mr. Grandcourt that his arrangements are just what I desired' – passing on without haste, and leaving Lush time to mingle some admiration of her graceful back with that half-amused sense of her spirit and impertinence, which he expressed by raising his eyebrows and just thrusting his tongue between his teeth. He really did not want her to be worse punished, and he was glad to think that it was time to go and lunch at the club, where he meant to have a lobster salad.

What did Gwendolen look forward to? When her husband returned he found her equipped in her riding-dress, ready to ride out with him. She was not again going to be hysterical, or take to her bed and say she was ill. That was the implicit resolve adjusting her muscles before she could have framed it in words, as she walked out of the room, leaving Lush behind her. She was going to act in the spirit of her message, and not to give herself time to reflect. She rang the bell for her maid, and went with the usual care through her change of toilet. Doubtless her husband had meant to produce a great effect on her: by-and-by perhaps she would let him see in effect the very opposite of what he intended; but at present all that she could show was a defiant satisfaction in what had been presumed to be disagreeable. It came as an instinct rather than a thought, that to show any sign which could be interpreted as jealousy, when she had just been insultingly reminded that the conditions were what she had accepted with her eyes open, would be the worst self-humiliation. She said to herself that she had not time to-day to be clear about her future actions; all she could be clear about was that she would match her husband in ignoring any ground for excitement. She not only rode, but went out with him to dine, contributing nothing to alter their mutual manner, which was never that of rapid interchange in discourse; and curiously enough she rejected a handkerchief on which her maid had by mistake put the wrong scent – a scent that

Grandcourt had once objected to. Gwendolen would not have liked to be an object of disgust to this husband whom she hated: she liked all disgust to be on her side.

But to defer thought in this way was something like trying to talk down the singing in her own ears. The thought that is bound up with our passion is as penetrative as air – everything is porous to it; bows, smiles, conversation, repartee, are mere honeycombs where such thought rushes freely, not always with a taste of honey. And without shutting herself up in any solitude, Gwendolen seemed at the end of nine or ten hours to have gone through a labyrinth of reflection, in which already the same succession of prospects had been repeated, the same fallacious outlets rejected, the same shrinking from the necessities of every course. Already she was undergoing some hardening effect from feeling that she was under eyes which saw her past actions solely in the light of her lowest motives. She lived back in the scenes of her courtship, with the new bitter consciousness of what had been in Grandcourt's mind – certain now, with her present experience of him, that he had had a peculiar triumph in conquering her dumb repugnance, and that ever since their marriage he had had a cold exultation in knowing her fancied secret. Her imagination exaggerated every tyrannical impulse he was capable of. 'I will insist on being separated from him' – was her first darting determination: then, 'I will leave him, whether he consents or not. If this boy becomes his heir, I have made an atonement.' But neither in darkness nor in daylight could she imagine the scenes which must carry out those determinations with the courage to feel them endurable. How could she run away to her own family – carry distress among them, and render herself an object of scandal in the society she had left behind her? What future lay before her as Mrs. Grandcourt gone back to her mother, who would be made destitute again by the rupture of the marriage for which one chief excuse had been that it had brought that mother a maintenance? She had lately been seeing her uncle and Anna in London, and though she had been saved from any difficulty about inviting them to stay in Grosvenor Square by their wish to be with Rex, who would not risk a meeting with her, the transient visits she had had from them helped now in giving stronger colour to the picture of what it would be for her to take refuge in her own family. What could she say to justify her flight? Her uncle would tell her to go back. Her mother would cry. Her aunt and Anna would look at her with wondering alarm. Her husband would have power to compel her. She had absolutely nothing that she could allege against him in judicious or judicial ears. And to 'insist on separation!' That was an easy combination of words; but considered as an action to be executed against Grandcourt, it would be about as practicable as to give him a pliant disposition and a dread of other people's unwillingness. How was she to begin? What was she to say that would not be a condemnation of herself? 'If I am to have misery anyhow,' was the bitter refrain of her rebellious dreams, 'I had better have the misery that I can keep to myself.' Moreover, her capability of rectitude told her again and again that she had no right to complain of her contract, or to withdraw from it.

And always among the images that drove her back to submission was Deronda. The idea of herself separated from her husband, gave Deronda a changed, perturbing, painful place in her consciousness: instinctively she felt that the separation would be from him too, and in the prospective vision of herself as a solitary, dubiously regarded woman, she felt some tingling bashfulness at the remembrance of her behaviour towards him. The association of Deronda with a dubious position for herself was intolerable. And what would he say if he knew everything? Probably that she ought to bear what she had brought on herself, unless she were sure that she could make herself a better woman by taking any other course. And what sort of woman was she to be – solitary, sickened of life, looked at with a suspicious kind of pity? – even if she could dream of success in getting that dreary freedom. Mrs. Grandcourt 'run away' would be a more pitiable creature than

Gwendolen Harleth condemned to teach the bishop's daughters, and to be inspected by Mrs. Mompert.

One characteristic trait in her conduct is worth mentioning. She would not look a second time at the paper Lush had given her; and before ringing for her maid she locked it up in a travelling-desk which was at hand, proudly resolved against curiosity about what was allotted to herself in connection with Gadsmere – feeling herself branded in the minds of her husband and his confidant with the meanness that would accept marriage and wealth on any conditions, however dishonourable and humiliating.

Day after day the same pattern of thinking was repeated. There came nothing to change the situation – no new elements in the sketch – only a recurrence which engraved it. The May weeks went on into June, and still Mrs. Grandcourt was outwardly in the same place, presenting herself as she was expected to do in the accustomed scenes, with the accustomed grace, beauty, and costume; from church at one end of the week, through all the scale of desirable receptions, to opera at the other. Church was not markedly distinguished in her mind from the other forms of self-presentation, for marriage had included no instruction that enabled her to connect liturgy and sermon with any larger order of the world than that of unexplained and perhaps inexplicable social fashions. While a laudable zeal was labouring to carry the light of spiritual law up the alleys where law is chiefly known as the policeman, the brilliant Mrs. Grandcourt, condescending a little to a fashionable Rector and conscious of a feminine advantage over a learned Dean, was, so far as pastoral care and religious fellowship were concerned, in as complete a solitude as a man in a lighthouse.

Can we wonder at the practical submission which hid her constructive rebellion? The combination is common enough, as we know from the number of persons who make us aware of it in their own case by a clamorous unwearied statement of the reasons against their submitting to a situation which, on inquiry, we discover to be the least disagreeable within their reach. Poor Gwendolen had both too much and too little mental power and dignity to make herself exceptional. No wonder that Deronda now marked some hardening in a look and manner which were schooled daily to the suppression of feeling.

For example. One morning, riding in Rotten Row with Grandcourt by her side, she saw standing against the railing at the turn, just facing them, a dark-eyed lady with a little girl and a blond boy, whom she at once recognized as the beings in all the world the most painful for her to behold. She and Grandcourt had just slackened their pace to a walk; he being on the outer side was the nearer to the unwelcome vision, and Gwendolen had not presence of mind to do anything but glance away from the dark eyes that met hers piercingly towards Grandcourt, who wheeled past the group with an unmoved face, giving no sign of recognition.

Immediately she felt a rising rage against him mingling with her shame for herself, and the words, 'You might at least have raised your hat to her,' flew impetuously to her lips – but did not pass them. If as her husband, in her company, he chose to ignore these creatures whom she herself had excluded from the place she was filling, how could she be the person to reproach him? She was dumb.

It was not chance, but her own design, that had brought Mrs. Glasher there with her boy. She had come to town under the pretext of making purchases – really wanting educational apparatus for the children, and had had interviews with Lush in which he had not refused to soothe her uneasy mind by representing the probabilities as all on the side of her ultimate triumph. Let her keep quiet, and she might live to see the marriage dissolve itself in one way or other – Lush hinted at several ways – leaving the succession assured to her boy. She had had an interview with Grandcourt too, who had as usual told her to behave like a reasonable woman, and threatened punishment if she were troublesome; but had, also as usual, vindicated himself from any wish to be stingy, the money he was receiving from Sir Hugo on account of Diplow encouraging his disposition to be lavish. Lydia, feeding on the probabilities in her favour, devoured her helpless wrath along with that pleasanter nourishment; but she could not let her discretion go entirely without the reward of making a Medusa-apparition before Gwendolen, vindictiveness and jealousy finding relief in an outlet of venom, though it were as futile as that of a viper already flung to the other side of the hedge. Hence each day, after finding out from Lush the likely time for Gwendolen to be riding, she had watched at that post, daring Grandcourt so far. Why should she not take little Henleigh into the Park?

The Medusa-apparition was made effective beyond Lydia's conception by the shock it gave Gwendolen actually to see Grandcourt ignoring this woman who had once been the nearest in the world to him, along with the children she had borne him. And all the while the dark shadow thus cast on the lot of a woman destitute of acknowledged social dignity, spread itself over her visions of a future that might be her own, and made part of her dread on her own behalf. She shrank all the more from any lonely action. What possible release could there be for her from this hated vantage-ground, which yet she dared not quit, any more than if fire had been raining outside it? What release, but death? Not her own death. Gwendolen was not a woman who could easily think of her own death as a near reality, or front for herself the dark entrance on the untried and invisible. It seemed more possible that Grandcourt should die: – and yet not likely. The power of tyranny in him seemed a power of living in the presence of any wish that he should die. The thought that his death was the only possible deliverance for her was one with the thought that deliverance would never come – the double deliverance from the injury with which other beings might reproach her and from the yoke she had brought on her own neck. No! she foresaw him always living, and her own life dominated by him; the 'always' of her young experience not stretching beyond the few immediate years that seemed immeasurably long with her passionate weariness. The thought of his dying would not subsist: it turned as with a dream-change into the terror that she should die with his throttling fingers on her neck avenging that thought. Fantasies moved within her like ghosts, making no break in her more acknowledged consciousness and finding no obstruction in it: dark rays doing their work invisibly in the broad light.

Only an evening or two after that encounter in the Park, there was a grand concert at Klesmer's, who was living rather magnificently now in one of the large houses in Grosvenor Place, a patron and prince among musical professors. Gwendolen had looked forward to this occasion as one on which she was sure to meet Deronda, and she had been meditating how to put a question to him which, without containing a word that she would feel a dislike to utter, would yet be explicit enough for him to understand it. The struggle of opposite feelings would not let her abide by her instinct that the very idea of Deronda's relation to her was a discouragement to any desperate step towards freedom. The next wave of emotion was a longing for some word of his to enforce a resolve. The fact that her opportunities of conversation with him had always to be snatched in the doubtful privacy of large parties, caused her to live through them many times beforehand, imagining how they would take place and what she would say. The irritation was proportionate when no opportunity came; and this evening at Klesmer's she included Deronda in her anger, because he looked as calm as possible at a distance from her, while she was in danger of betraying her impatience to every one who spoke to her. She found her only safety in a chill haughtiness which made Mr. Vandernoodt remark that Mrs. Grandcourt was becoming a perfect match for her husband. When at last the chances of the evening brought Deronda near her, Sir Hugo and Mrs. Raymond were close by and could hear every word she said. No matter: her husband was not near, and her irritation passed without check into a fit of daring which restored the security of her self-possession. Deronda was there at last, and she would compel him to do what she pleased. Already and without effort rather queenly in her air as she stood in her white lace and green leaves, she threw a royal permissiveness into her way of saying; 'I wish you would come and see me tomorrow between five and six, Mr. Deronda.'

There could be but one answer at that moment: 'Certainly,' with a bow of obedience.

Afterwards it occurred to Deronda that he would write a note to excuse himself. He had always avoided making a call at Grandcourt's. But he could not persuade himself to any step that might hurt her, and whether his excuse were taken for indifference or for the affectation of indifference it would be equally wounding. He kept his promise. Gwendolen had declined to ride out on the plea of not feeling well enough, having left her refusal to the last moment when the horses were soon to be at the door – not without alarm lest her husband should say that he too would stay at home. Become almost superstitious about his power of suspicious divination, she had a glancing forethought of what she would do in that case – namely, have herself denied as not well. But Grandcourt accepted her excuse without remark, and rode off.

Nevertheless when Gwendolen found herself alone, and had sent down the order that only Mr. Deronda was to be admitted, she began to be alarmed at what she had done, and to feel a growing agitation in the thought that he would soon appear, and she should soon be obliged to speak: not of trivialities, as if she had had no serious motive in asking him to come; and yet what she had been for hours determining to say began to seem impossible. For the first time the impulse of appeal to him was being checked by timidity; and now that it was too late she was shaken by the possibility that he might think her invitation unbecoming. If so, she would have sunk in his esteem. But immediately she resisted this intolerable fear as an infection from her husband's way of thinking. That *he* would say she was making a fool of herself was rather a reason why such a judgment would be remote from Deronda's mind. But that she could not rid herself from this sudden invasion of womanly reticence was manifest in a kind of action which had never occurred to her before. In her struggle between agitation and the effort to suppress it, she was walking up and down the length of two drawing-rooms, where at one end a long mirror reflected her in her black dress, chosen in the early morning with a half-admitted reference to this hour. But above this black dress her head on its white pillar of a neck showed to advantage. Some consciousness of this made her turn hastily and hurry to the boudoir, where again there was glass, but also, tossed over a chair, a large piece of black lace which she snatched and tied over her crown of hair so as completely to conceal her neck, and leave only her face looking out from the black frame. In this manifest contempt of appearance, she thought it possible to be freer from nervousness, but the black lace did not take away the uneasiness from her eyes and lips.

She was standing in the middle of the room when Deronda was announced, and as he approached her she perceived that he too for some reason was not his usual self. She could not have defined the change except by saying that he looked less happy than usual, and appeared to be under some effort in speaking to her. And yet the speaking was the slightest possible. They both said, 'How do you do?' quite curtly; and Gwendolen, instead of sitting down, moved to a little distance, resting her arm slightly on the tall back of a chair, while Deronda stood where he was, holding his hat in one hand and his coat-collar with the other – both feeling it difficult to say anything more, though the preoccupation in his mind could hardly have been more remote than it was from Gwendolen's conception. She naturally saw in his embarrassment some reflection of her own. Forced to speak, she found all her training in concealment and self-command of no use to her, and began with timid awkwardness –

'You will wonder why I begged you to come. I wanted to ask you something. You said I was ignorant. That is true. And what can I do but ask you?'

And at this moment she was feeling it utterly impossible to put the questions she had intended. Something new in her nervous manner roused Deronda's anxiety lest there might be a new crisis. He said with the sadness of affection in his voice –

'My only regret is, that I can be of so little use to you.' The words and the tone touched a new spring in her, and she went on with more sense of freedom, yet still not saying anything she had designed to say, and beginning to hurry, that she might somehow arrive at the right words.

'I wanted to tell you that I have always been thinking of your advice, but is it any use? – I can't make myself different, because things about me raise bad feelings – and I must go on – I can alter nothing – it is no use.'

She paused an instant, with the consciousness that she was not finding the right words, but began again as hurriedly, 'But if I go on, I shall get worse. I want not to get worse. I should like to be what you wish. There are people who are good and enjoy great things – I know there are. I am a contemptible creature. I feel as if I should get wicked with hating people. I have tried to think that I would go away from everybody. But I can't. There are so many things to hinder me. You think, perhaps, that I don't mind. But I do mind. I am afraid of everything. I am afraid of getting wicked. Tell me what I can do.'

She had forgotten everything but that image of her helpless misery which she was trying to make present to Deronda in broken allusive speech – wishing to convey but not express all her need. Her eyes were tearless, and had a look of smarting in their dilated brilliancy; there was a subdued sob in her voice which was more and more veiled, till it was hardly above a whisper. She was hurting herself with the jewels that glittered on her tightly-clasped fingers pressed against her heart.

The feeling Deronda endured in these moments he afterwards called horrible. Words seemed to have no more rescue in them than if he had been beholding a vessel in peril of wreck – the poor ship with its many-lived anguish beaten by the inescapable storm. How could he grasp the long-growing process of this young creature's wretchedness? – how arrest and change it with a sentence? He was afraid of his own voice. The words that rushed into his mind seemed in their feebleness nothing better than despair made audible, or than that insensibility to another's hardship which applies precept to soothe pain. He felt himself holding a crowd of words imprisoned within his lips, as if the letting them escape would be a violation of awe before the mysteries of our human lot. The thought that urged itself foremost was – 'Confess everything to your husband; leave nothing concealed:' – the words carried in his mind a vision of reasons which would have needed much fuller expression for Gwendolen to apprehend them, but before he had begun to utter those brief sentences, the door opened and the husband entered.

Grandcourt had deliberately gone out and turned back to satisfy a suspicion. What he saw was Gwendolen's face of anguish framed black like a nun's, and Deronda standing three yards from her with a look of sorrow such as he might have bent on the last struggle of life in a beloved object. Without any show of surprise, Grandcourt nodded to Deronda, gave a second look at Gwendolen, passed on, and seated himself easily at a little distance, crossing his legs, taking out his handkerchief and trifling with it elegantly.

Gwendolen had shrunk and changed her attitude on seeing him, but she did not turn or move from her place. It was not a moment in which she could feign anything, or manifest any strong revulsion of feeling: the passionate movement of her last speech was still too strong within her. What she felt besides was a dull despairing sense that her interview with Deronda was at an end: a curtain had fallen. But he, naturally, was urged into self-possession and effort by susceptibility to what might follow for her from being seen by her husband in this betrayal of agitation; and feeling that any pretence of ease in prolonging his visit would only exaggerate Grandcourt's possible conjectures of duplicity, he merely said –

'I will not stay longer now. Good-bye.'

He put out his hand, and she let him press her poor little chill fingers; but she said no good-bye.

When he had left the room, Gwendolen threw herself into a seat, with an expectation as dull as her despair – the expectation that she was going to be punished. But Grandcourt took no notice; he was satisfied to have let her know that she had not deceived him, and to keep a silence which was formidable with omniscience. He went out that evening, and her plea of feeling ill was accepted without even a sneer.

The next morning at breakfast he said, 'I am going yachting to the Mediterranean.'

'When?' said Gwendolen, with a leap of heart which had hope in it.

'The day after to-morrow. The yacht is at Marseilles. Lush is gone to get everything ready.'

'Shall I have mamma to stay with me, then?' said Gwendolen, the new sudden possibility of peace and affection filling her mind like a burst of morning light.

'No; you will go with me.'

XLIX

Ever in his soul
That larger justice which makes gratitude
Triumphed above resentment. 'Tis the mark
Of regal natures, with the wider life,
And fuller capability of joy: –
Not wits exultant in the strongest lens
To show you goodness vanished into pulp
Never worth 'thank you' – they're the devil's friars,
Vowed to be poor as he in love and trust,
Yet must go begging of a world that keeps
Some human property.

DERONDA, in parting from Gwendolen, had abstained from saying, 'I shall not see you again for a long while: I am going away,' lest Grandcourt should understand him to imply that the fact was of importance to her.

He was actually going away under circumstances so momentous to himself that when he set out to fulfil his promise of calling on her, he was already under the shadow of a solemn emotion which revived the deepest experience of his life.

Sir Hugo had sent for him to his chambers with the note – 'Come immediately. Something has happened:' a preparation that caused him some relief when, on entering the baronet's study, he was received with grave affection instead of the distress which he had apprehended.

'It is nothing to grieve you, sir?' said Deronda, in a tone rather of restored confidence than question, as he took the hand held out to him. There was an unusual meaning in Sir Hugo's look, and a subdued emotion in his voice, as he said –

'No, Dan, no. Sit down. I have something to say.'

Deronda obeyed, not without presentiment. It was extremely rare for Sir Hugo to show so much serious feeling.

'Not to grieve me, my boy, no. At least, if there is nothing in it that will grieve you too much. But I hardly expected that this – just this – would ever happen. There have been reasons why I have never prepared you for it. There have been reasons why I have never told you anything about your parentage. But I have striven in every way not to make that an injury to you.'

Sir Hugo paused, but Deronda could not speak. He could not say, 'I have never felt it an injury.' Even if that had been true, he could not have trusted his voice to say anything. Far more than any one but himself could know of was hanging on this moment when the secrecy was to be broken. Sir Hugo had never seen the grand face he delighted in so pale – the lips pressed together with such a look of pain. He went on with a more anxious tenderness, as if he had a new fear of wounding.

'I have acted in obedience to your mother's wishes. The secrecy was her wish. But now she desires to remove it. She desires to see you. I will put this letter into your hands, which you can look at by-and-by. It will merely tell you what she wishes you to do, and where you will find her.'

Sir Hugo held out a letter written on foreign paper, which Deronda thrust into his breast-pocket, with a sense of relief that he was not called on to read anything immediately. The emotion in Daniel's face had gained on the baronet, and was visibly shaking his composure. Sir Hugo found it difficult to say more. And Deronda's whole soul was possessed by a question which was the hardest in the world to utter. Yet he could not bear to delay it. This was a sacramental moment. If he let it pass, he could not recover the influences under which it was possible to utter the words and meet the answer. For some moments his eyes were cast down, and it seemed to both as if thoughts were in the air between them. But at last Deronda looked at Sir Hugo, and said, with a tremulous reverence in his voice – dreading to convey indirectly the reproach that affection had for years been stifling –

'Is my father also living?'

The answer came immediately in a low emphatic tone – 'No.'

In the mingled emotions which followed that answer it was impossible to distinguish joy from pain.

Some new light had fallen on the past for Sir Hugo too in this interview. After a silence in which Deronda felt like one whose creed is gone before he has religiously embraced another, the baronet said, in a tone of confession –

'Perhaps I was wrong, Dan, to undertake what I did. And perhaps I liked it a little too well – having you all to myself. But if you have had any pain which I might have helped, I ask you to forgive me.'

'The forgiveness has long been there,' said Deronda. 'The chief pain has always been on account of some one else – whom I never knew – whom I am now to know. It has not hindered me from feeling an affection for you which has made a large part of all the life I remember.'

It seemed one impulse that made the two men clasp each other's hand for a moment.

BOOK VII
The Mother and the Son

L

'If some mortal, born too soon,
Were laid away in some great trance – the ages
Coming and going all the while – till dawned
His true time's advent; and could then record
The words they spoke who kept watch by his bed, –
Then I might tell more of the breath so light
Upon my eyelids, and the fingers warm
Among my hair. Youth is confused; yet never
So dull was I but, when that spirit passed,
I turned to him, scarce consciously, as turns
A water-snake when fairies cross his sleep.'
BROWNING: *Paracelsus*.

THIS was the letter which Sir Hugo put into Deronda's hands:–

TO MY SON, DANIEL DERONDA.

My good friend and yours, Sir Hugo Mallinger, will have told you that I wish to see you. My health is shaken, and I desire there should be no time lost before I deliver to you what I have long withheld. Let nothing hinder you from being at the *Albergo dell' Italia* in Genoa by the fourteenth of this month. Wait for me there. I am uncertain when I shall be able to make the journey from Spezia, where I shall be staying. That will depend on several things. Wait for me – the Princess Halm-Eberstein. Bring with you the diamond ring that Sir Hugo gave you. I shall like to see it again. – Your unknown mother,
LEONORA HALM-EBERSTEIN.

This letter with its colourless wording gave Deronda no clue to what was in reserve for him; he could not do otherwise than accept Sir Hugo's reticence, which seemed to imply some pledge not to anticipate the mother's disclosures; and the discovery that his lifelong conjectures had been mistaken checked further surmise. Deronda could not hinder his imagination from taking a quick flight over what seemed possibilities, but he refused to contemplate any one of them as more likely than another, lest he should be nursing it into a dominant desire or repugnance, instead of simply preparing himself with resolve to meet the fact bravely, whatever it might turn out to be.

In this state of mind he could not have communicated to any one the reason for the absence which in some quarters he was obliged to mention beforehand, least of all to Mordecai, whom it would affect as powerfully as it did himself, only in rather a different way. If he were to say, 'I am going to learn the truth about my birth,' Mordecai's hope would gather what might prove a painful, dangerous excitement. To exclude suppositions, he spoke of his journey as being undertaken by Sir Hugo's wish, and threw as much indifference as he could into his manner of announcing it, saying he was uncertain of its duration, but it would perhaps be very short.

'I will ask to have the child Jacob to stay with me,' said Mordecai, comforting himself in this way, after the first mournful glances.

'I will drive round and ask Mrs. Cohen to let him come,' said Mirah.

'The grandmother will deny you nothing,' said Deronda. 'I'm glad you were a little wrong as well as I,' he added, smiling at Mordecai. 'You thought that old Mrs. Cohen would not bear to see Mirah.'

'I undervalued her heart,' said Mordecai. 'She is capable of rejoicing that another's plant blooms though her own be withered.'

'Oh, they are dear good people; I feel as if we all belonged to each other,' said Mirah, with a tinge of merriment in her smile.

'What should you have felt if that Ezra had been your brother?' said Deronda, mischievously – a little provoked that she had taken kindly at once to people who had caused him so much prospective annoyance on her account.

Mirah looked at him with a slight surprise for a moment, and then said, 'He is not a bad man – I think he would never forsake any one.' But when she had uttered the words she blushed deeply, and glancing timidly at Mordecai, turned away to some occupation. Her father was in her mind, and this was a subject on which she and her brother had a painful mutual consciousness. 'If he should come and find us!' was a thought which to Mirah sometimes made the street daylight as shadowy as a haunted forest where each turn screened for her an imaginary apparition.

Deronda felt what was her involuntary allusion, and understood the blush. How could he be slow to understand feelings which now seemed nearer than ever to his own? for the words of his mother's letter implied that his filial relation was not to be freed from painful conditions; indeed, singularly enough that letter which had brought his mother nearer as a living reality had thrown her into more remoteness for his affections. The tender yearning after a being whose life might have been the worse for not having his care and love, the image of a mother who had not had all her dues whether of reverence or compassion, had long been secretly present with him in his observation of all the women he had come near. But it seemed now that this picturing of his mother might fit the facts no better than his former conceptions about Sir Hugo. He wondered to find that when this mother's very handwriting had come to him with words holding her actual feeling, his affections had suddenly shrunk into a state of comparative neutrality towards her. A veiled figure with enigmatic speech had thrust away that image which, in spite of uncertainty, his clinging thought had gradually modelled and made the possessor of his tenderness and duteous longing. When he set off to Genoa, the interest really uppermost in his mind had hardly so much relation to his mother as to Mordecai and Mirah.

'God bless you, Dan!' Sir Hugo had said, when they shook hands. 'Whatever else changes for you, it can't change my being the oldest friend you have known, and the one who has all along felt the most for you. I couldn't have loved you better if you'd been my own – only I should have been better pleased with thinking of you always as the future master of the Abbey instead of my fine nephew; and then you would have seen it necessary for you to take a political line. However – things must be as they may.' It was a defensive measure of the baronet's to mingle purposeless remarks with the expression of serious feeling.

When Deronda arrived at the *Italia* in Genoa, no Princess Halm-Eberstein was there; but on the second day there was a letter for him, saying that her arrival might happen within a week, or might be deferred a fortnight and more: she was under circumstances which made it impossible for her to fix her journey more precisely, and she entreated him to wait as patiently as he could.

With this indefinite prospect of suspense on matters of supreme moment to him, Deronda set about the difficult task of seeking amusement on philosophic grounds, as a means of quieting excited feeling and giving patience a lift over a weary road. His former visit to the superb city had been only cursory, and left him much to learn beyond the prescribed round of sight-seeing, by spending the cooler hours in observant wandering about the streets, the quay, and the environs; and he often took a boat that he might enjoy the magnificent view of the city and harbour from the sea. All sights, all subjects, even the expected meeting with his mother, found a central union in Mordecai and Mirah, and the ideas immediately associated with them; and among the thoughts that most filled his mind while his boat was pushing about within view of the grand harbour was that of the multitudinous Spanish Jews centuries ago driven destitute from their Spanish homes, suffered to land from the crowded ships only for brief rest on this grand quay of Genoa, overspreading it with a pall of famine and plague – dying mothers with dying children at their

683

breasts – fathers and sons agaze at each other's haggardness, like groups from a hundred Hunger-towers turned out beneath the mid-day sun. Inevitably, dreamy constructions of a possible ancestry for himself would weave themselves with historic memories which had begun to have a new interest for him on his discovery of Mirah, and now, under the influence of Mordecai, had become irresistibly dominant. He would have sealed his mind against such constructions if it had been possible, and he had never yet fully admitted to himself that he wished the facts to verify Mordecai's conviction: he inwardly repeated that he had no choice in the matter, and that wishing was folly – nay, on the question of parentage, wishing seemed part of that meanness which disowns kinship: it was a disowning by anticipation. What he had to do was simply to accept the fact; and he had really no strong presumption to go upon, now that he was assured of his mistake about Sir Hugo. There had been a resolved concealment which made all inference untrustworthy, and the very name he bore might be a false one. If Mordecai were wrong – if he, the so-called Daniel Deronda, were held by ties entirely aloof from any such course as his friend's pathetic hope had marked out? – he would not say 'I wish;' but he could not help feeling on which side the sacrifice lay.

Across these two importunate thoughts, which he resisted as much as one can resist anything in that unstrung condition which belongs to suspense, there came continually an anxiety which he made no effort to banish – dwelling on it rather with a mournfulness, which often seems to us the best atonement we can make to one whose need we have been unable to meet. The anxiety was for Gwendolen. In the wonderful mixtures of our nature there is a feeling distinct from that exclusive passionate love of which some men and women (by no means all) are capable, which yet is not the same with friendship, nor with a merely benevolent regard, whether admiring or compassionate: a man, say – for it is a man who is here concerned – hardly represents to himself this shade of feeling towards a woman more nearly than in the words, 'I should have loved her, if—:' the 'if' covering some prior growth in the inclinations, or else some circumstances which have made an inward prohibitory law as a stay against the emotions ready to quiver out of balance. The 'if' in Deronda's case carried reasons of both kinds; yet he had never throughout his relations with Gwendolen been free from the nervous consciousness that there was something to guard against not only on her account but on his own – some precipitancy in the manifestation of impulsive feeling – some ruinous inroad of what is but momentary on the permanent chosen treasure of the heart – some spoiling of her trust, which wrought upon him now as if it had been the retreating cry of a creature snatched and carried out of his reach by swift horsemen or swifter waves, while his own strength was only a stronger sense of weakness. How could his feeling for Gwendolen ever be exactly like his feeling for other women, even when there was one by whose side he desired to stand apart from them? Strangely her figure entered into the pictures of his present and future; strangely (and now it seemed sadly) their two lots had come in contact, hers narrowly personal, his charged with far-reaching sensibilities, perhaps with durable purposes, which were hardly more present to her than the reasons why men migrate are present to the birds that come as usual for the crumbs and find them no more. Not that Deronda was too ready to imagine himself of supreme importance to a woman; but her words of insistence that he 'must remain near her – must not forsake her' – continually recurred to him with the clearness and importunity of imagined sounds, such as Dante has said pierce us like arrows whose points carry the sharpness of pity:–

> *'Lamenti saettaron me diversi*
> *Che di pietà ferrati avean gli strali.'*

Day after day passed, and the very air of Italy seemed to carry the consciousness that war had been declared against

Austria, and every day was a hurrying march of crowded Time towards the world-changing battle of Sadowa. Meanwhile, in Genoa, the noons were getting hotter, the converging outer roads getting deeper with white dust, the oleanders in the tubs along the wayside gardens looking more and more like fatigued holidaymakers, and the sweet evening changing her office – scattering abroad those whom the mid-day had sent under shelter, and sowing all paths with happy social sounds, little tinklings of mule-bells and whirrings of thrummed strings, light footsteps and voices, if not leisurely, then with the hurry of pleasure in them; while the encircling heights, crowned with forts, skirted with fine dwellings and gardens, seemed also to come forth and gaze in fullness of beauty after their long siesta, till all strong colour melted in the stream of moon-light which made the streets a new spectacle with shadows, both still and moving, on cathedral steps and against the façades of massive palaces; and then slowly with the des-cending moon all sank in deep night and silence, and nothing shone but the port lights of the great Lanterna in the blackness below, and the glimmering stars in the black-ness above. Deronda, in his suspense, watched this revol-ving of the days as he might have watched a wonderful clock where the striking of the hours was made solemn with antique figures advancing and retreating in monitory pro-cession, while he still kept his ear open for another kind of signal which would have its solemnity too. He was begin-ning to sicken of occupation, and found himself contem-plating all activity with the aloofness of a prisoner awaiting ransom. In his letters to Mordecai and Hans, he had avoided writing about himself, but he was really getting into that state of mind to which all subjects become perso-nal; and the few books he had brought to make him a refuge in study were becoming unreadable, because the point of view that life would make for him was in that agitating moment of uncertainty which is close upon decision.

Many nights were watched through by him in gazing from the open window of his room on the double, faintly pierced darkness of the sea and the heavens: often in struggling under the oppressive scepticism which represented his particular lot, with all the importance he was allowing Mordecai to give it, as of no more lasting effect than a dream – a set of changes which made passion to him, but beyond his consciousness were no more than an imperceptible difference of mass or shadow; sometimes with a reaction of emotive force which gave even to sustained disappointment, even to the fulfilled demand of sacrifice, the nature of a satisfied energy, and spread over his young future, whatever it might be, the attraction of devoted service; sometimes with a sweet irresistible hopefulness that the very best of human possibilities might befall him – the blending of a complete personal love in one current with a larger duty; and sometimes again in a mood of rebellion (what human creature escapes it?) against things in general because they are thus and not otherwise, a mood in which Gwendolen and her equivocal fate moved as busy images of what was amiss in the world along with the concealments which he had felt as a hardship in his own life, and which were acting in him now under the form of an afflicting doubtfulness about the mother who had announced herself coldly and still kept away.

But at last she was come. One morning in his third week of waiting there was a new kind of knock at the door. A servant in chasseur's livery entered and delivered in French the verbal message that the Princess Halm-Eberstein had arrived, that she was going to rest during the day, but would be obliged if Monsieur would dine early, so as to be at liberty at seven, when she would be able to receive him.

LI

She held the spindle as she sat,
Erinna with the thick-coiled mat
Of raven hair and deepest agate eyes,
Gazing with a sad surprise
At surging visions of her destiny –
To spin the byssus drearily
In insect-labour, while the throng
Of gods and men wrought deeds that poets wrought in song.

WHEN Deronda presented himself at the door of his mother's apartment in the *Italia*, he felt some revival of his boyhood with its premature agitations. The two servants in the antechamber looked at him markedly, a little surprised that the doctor their lady had come to consult was this striking young gentleman whose appearance gave even the severe lines of an evening dress the credit of adornment. But Deronda could notice nothing until, the second door being opened, he found himself in the presence of a figure which at the other end of the large room stood awaiting his approach.

She was covered, except as to her face and part of her arms, with black lace hanging loosely from the summit of her whitening hair to the long train stretching from her tall figure. Her arms, naked from the elbow, except for some rich bracelets, were folded before her, and the fine poise of her head made it look handsomer than it really was. But Deronda felt no interval of observation before he was close in front of her, holding the hand she had put out and then raising it to his lips. She still kept her hand in his and looked at him examiningly; while his chief consciousness was that her eyes were piercing and her face so mobile that the next moment she might look like a different person. For even while she was examining him there was a play of the brow and nostril which made a tacit language. Deronda dared no movement, not able to conceive what sort of manifestation her feeling demanded; but he felt himself changing colour like a girl, and yet wondering at his own

lack of emotion: he had lived through so many ideal meetings with his mother, and they had seemed more real than
this! He could not even conjecture in what language she
would speak to him. He imagined it would not be English.
Suddenly, she let fall his hand, and placed both hers on his
shoulders, while her face gave out a flash of admiration in
which every worn line disappeared and seemed to leave a
restored youth.

'You are a beautiful creature!' she said, in a low melodious voice, with syllables which had what might be
called a foreign but agreeable outline. 'I knew you would
be.' Then she kissed him on each cheek, and he returned
her kisses. But it was something like a greeting between
royalties.

She paused a moment, while the lines were coming
back into her face, and then said in a colder tone, 'I am
your mother. But you can have no love for me.'

'I have thought of you more than of any other being in
the world,' said Deronda, his voice trembling nervously.

'I am not like what you thought I was,' said the mother,
decisively, withdrawing her hands from his shoulders and
folding her arms as before, looking at him as if she invited
him to observe her. He had often pictured her face in his
imagination as one which had a likeness to his own: he saw
some of the likeness now, but amidst more striking differences. She was a remarkable-looking being. What was it
that gave her son a painful sense of aloofness? – Her worn
beauty had a strangeness in it as if she were not quite a
human mother, but a Melusina, who had ties with some
world which is independent of ours.

'I used to think that you might be suffering,' said
Deronda, anxious above all not to wound her. 'I used to
wish that I could be a comfort to you.'

'I *am* suffering. But with a suffering that you can't
comfort,' said the Princess, in a harder voice than before,
moving to a sofa where cushions had been carefully
arranged for her. 'Sit down.' She pointed to a seat near
her; and then discerning some distress in Deronda's face,

she added, more gently, 'I am not suffering at this moment. I am at ease now. I am able to talk.'

Deronda seated himself and waited for her to speak again. It seemed as if he were in the presence of a mysterious Fate rather than of the longed-for mother. He was beginning to watch her with wonder, from the spiritual distance to which she had thrown him.

'No,' she began; 'I did not send for you to comfort me. I could not know beforehand – I don't know now – what you will feel towards me. I have not the foolish notion that you can love me merely because I am your mother, when you have never seen or heard of me all your life. But I thought I chose something better for you than being with me. I did not think that I deprived you of anything worth having.'

'You cannot wish me to believe that your affection would not have been worth having,' said Deronda, finding that she paused as if she expected him to make some answer.

'I don't mean to speak ill of myself,' said the Princess, with proud impetuosity, 'but I had not much affection to give you. I did not want affection. I had been stifled with it. I wanted to live out the life that was in me, and not to be hampered with other lives. You wonder what I was. I was no princess then.' She rose with a sudden movement, and stood as she had done before. Deronda immediately rose too: he felt breathless.

'No princess in this tame life that I live in now. I was a great singer, and I acted as well as I sang. All the rest were poor beside me. Men followed me from one country to another. I was living a myriad lives in one. I did not want a child.'

There was a passionate self-defence in her tone. She had cast all precedent out of her mind. Precedent had no excuse for her, and she could only seek a justification in the intensest words she could find for her experience. She seemed to fling out the last words against some possible reproach in the mind of her son, who had to stand and hear them – clutching his coat-collar as if he were keeping himself above water by it, and feeling his blood in the sort of commotion that might have been excited if he had seen her going through some strange rite of a religion which gave a sacredness to crime. What else had she to tell him? She went on with the same intensity and a sort of pale illumination in her face.

'I did not want to marry. I was forced into marrying your father – forced, I mean, by my father's wishes and commands; and besides, it was my best way of getting some freedom. I could rule my husband, but not my father. I had a right to be free. I had a right to seek my freedom from a bondage that I hated.'

She seated herself again, while there was that subtle movement in her eyes and closed lips which is like the suppressed continuation of speech. Deronda continued standing, and after a moment or two she looked up at him with a less defiant pleading as she said –

'And the bondage I hated for myself I wanted to keep you from. What better could the most loving mother have done? I relieved you from the bondage of having been born a Jew.'

'Then I *am* a Jew?' Deronda burst out with a deep-voiced energy that made his mother shrink a little backward against her cushions. 'My father was a Jew, and you are a Jewess?'

'Yes, your father was my cousin,' said the mother, watching him with a change in her look, as if she saw something that she might have to be afraid of.

'I am glad of it,' said Deronda, impetuously, in the veiled voice of passion. He could not have imagined beforehand how he would come to say that which he had never hitherto admitted. He could not have dreamed that it would be in impulsive opposition to his mother. He was shaken by a mixed anger which no reflection could come soon enough to check, against this mother who it seemed had borne him unwillingly, had willingly made herself a stranger to him, and – perhaps – was now making herself known unwillingly. This last suspicion seemed to flash some explanation over her speech.

But the mother was equally shaken by an anger differently mixed, and her frame was less equal to any repression. The shaking with her was visibly physical, and her eyes looked the larger for her pallid excitement as she said violently –

'Why do you say you are glad? You are an English gentleman. I secured you that.'

'You did not know *what* you secured me. How could you choose my birthright for me?' said Deronda, throwing himself sideways into his chair again, almost unconsciously, and leaning his arm over the back while he looked away from his mother.

He was fired with an intolerance that seemed foreign to him. But he was now trying hard to master himself and keep silence. A horror had swept in upon his anger lest he should say something too hard in this moment which made an epoch never to be recalled. There was a pause before his mother spoke again, and when she spoke her voice had become more firmly resistant in its finely-varied tones:

'I chose for you what I would have chosen for myself. How could I know that you would have the spirit of my father in you? How could I know that you would love what I hated? – if you really love to be a Jew.' The last words had such bitterness in them that any one overhearing might have supposed some hatred had arisen between the mother and son.

But Deronda had recovered his fuller self. He was recalling his sensibilities to what life had been and actually was for her whose best years were gone, and who with the signs of suffering in her frame was now exerting herself to tell him of a past which was not his alone but also hers. His habitual shame at the acceptance of events as if they were his only, helped him even here. As he looked at his mother silently after her last words, his face regained some of its penetrative calm; yet it seemed to have a strangely agitating influence over her: her eyes were fixed on him with a sort of fascination, but not with any repose of maternal delight.

'Forgive me if I speak hastily,' he said, with diffident gravity. 'Why have you resolved now on disclosing to me what you took care to have me brought up in ignorance of? Why – since you seem angry that I should be glad?'

'Oh – the reasons of our actions!' said the Princess, with a ring of something like sarcastic scorn. 'When you are as old as I am, it will not seem so simple a question – "Why did you do this?" People talk of their motives in a cut and dried way. Every woman is supposed to have the same set of motives, or else to be a monster. I am not a monster, but I have not felt exactly what other women feel – or say they feel, for fear of being thought unlike others. When you reproach me in your heart for sending you away from me, you mean that I ought to say I felt about you as other women say they feel about their children. I did *not* feel that. I was glad to be freed from you. But I did well for you, and I gave you your father's fortune. Do I seem now to be revoking everything? – Well, there are reasons. I feel many things that I can't understand. A fatal illness has been growing in me for a year. I shall very likely not live another year. I will not deny anything I have done. I will not pretend to love where I have no love. But shadows are rising round me. Sickness makes them. If I have wronged the dead – I have but little time to do what I left undone.'

The varied transitions of tone with which this speech was delivered were as perfect as the most accomplished actress could have made them. The speech was in fact a piece of what may be called sincere acting: this woman's nature was one in which all feeling – and all the more when it was tragic as well as real – immediately became matter of conscious representation: experience immediately passed into drama, and she acted her own emotions. In a minor degree this is nothing uncommon, but in the Princess the acting had a rare perfection of physiognomy, voice, and gesture. It would not be true to say that she felt less because of this double consciousness: she felt – that is,

her mind went through – all the more, but with a difference: each nucleus of pain or pleasure had a deep atmosphere of the excitement or spiritual intoxication which at
once exalts and deadens. But Deronda made no reflection
of this kind. All his thoughts hung on the purport of what
his mother was saying; her tones and her wonderful face
entered into his agitation without being noted. What he
longed for with an awed desire was to know as much as she
would tell him of the strange mental conflict under which
it seemed that he had been brought into the world: what
his compassionate nature made the controlling idea within
him were the suffering and the confession that breathed
through her later words, and these forbade any further
question, when she paused and remained silent, with her
brow knit, her head turned a little away from him, and her
large eyes fixed as if on something incorporeal. He must
wait for her to speak again. She did so with strange abruptness, turning her eyes upon him suddenly, and saying more
quickly –

'Sir Hugo has written much about you. He tells me you
have a wonderful mind – you comprehend everything –
you are wiser than he is with all his sixty years. You say you
are glad to know that you were born a Jew. I am not going to
tell you that I have changed my mind about that. Your
feelings are against mine. You don't thank me for what
I did. Shall you comprehend your mother – or only blame
her?'

'There is not a fibre within me but makes me wish to
comprehend her,' said Deronda, meeting her sharp gaze
solemnly. 'It is a bitter reversal of my longing to think of
blaming her. What I have been most trying to do for fifteen
years is to have some understanding of those who differ
from myself.'

'Then you have become unlike your grandfather in
that,' said the mother, 'though you are a young copy of
him in your face. He never comprehended me, or if he did,
he only thought of fettering me into obedience. I was to be
what he called "the Jewish woman" under pain of his curse.

I was to feel everything I did not feel, and believe everything I did not believe. I was to feel awe for the bit of parchment in the *mezuza* over the door; to dread lest a bit of butter should touch a bit of meat; to think it beautiful that men should bind the *tephillin* on them, and women not, – to adore the wisdom of such laws, however silly they might seem to me. I was to love the long prayers in the ugly synagogue, and the howling, and the gabbling, and the dreadful fasts, and the tiresome feasts, and my father's endless discoursing about Our People, which was a thunder without meaning in my ears. I was to care for ever about what Israel had been; and I did not care at all. I cared for the wide world, and all that I could represent in it. I hated living under the shadow of my father's strictness. Teaching, teaching for everlasting – "this you must be," "that you must not be" – pressed on me like a frame that got tighter and tighter as I grew. I wanted to live a large life, with freedom to do what every one else did, and be carried along in a great current, not obliged to care. Ah!' – here her tone changed to one of a more bitter incisiveness – 'you are glad to have been born a Jew. You say so. That is because you have not been brought up as a Jew. That separateness seems sweet to you because I saved you from it.'

'When you resolved on that, you meant that I should never know my origin?' said Deronda, impulsively. 'You have at least changed in your feeling on that point.'

'Yes, that was what I meant. That is what I persevered in. And it is not true to say that I have changed. Things have changed in spite of me. I am still the same Leonora' – she pointed with her forefinger to her breast – 'here within me is the same desire, the same will, the same choice, *but*' – she spread out her hands, palm upwards, on each side of her, as she paused with a bitter compression of her lip, then let her voice fall into muffled, rapid utterance – 'events come upon us like evil enchantments: and thoughts, feelings, apparitions in the darkness are events – are they not? I don't consent. We only consent to what we love. I obey something tyrannic' – she spread out her hands again –

'I am forced to be withered, to feel pain, to be dying slowly. Do I love that? Well, I have been forced to obey my dead father. I have been forced to tell you that you are a Jew, and deliver to you what he commanded me to deliver.'

'I beseech you to tell me what moved you – when you were young, I mean – to take the course you did,' said Deronda, trying by this reference to the past to escape from what to him was the heart-rending piteousness of this mingled suffering and defiance. 'I gather that my grandfather opposed your bent to be an artist. Though my own experience has been quite different, I enter into the painfulness of your struggle. I can imagine the hardship of an enforced renunciation.'

'No,' said the Princess, shaking her head, and folding her arms with an air of decision. 'You are not a woman. You may try – but you can never imagine what it is to have a man's force of genius in you, and yet to suffer the slavery of being a girl. To have a pattern cut out – "this is the Jewish woman; this is what you must be; this is what you are wanted for; a woman's heart must be of such a size and no larger, else it must be pressed small, like Chinese feet; her happiness is to be made as cakes are, by a fixed receipt." That was what my father wanted. He wished I had been a son; he cared for me as a makeshift link. His heart was set on his Judaism. He hated that Jewish women should be thought of by the Christian world as a sort of ware to make public singers and actresses of. As if we were not the more enviable for that! That is a chance of escaping from bondage.'

'Was my grandfather a learned man?' said Deronda, eager to know particulars that he feared his mother might not think of.

She answered impatiently, putting up her hand, 'Oh yes, – and a clever physician – and good: I don't deny that he was good. A man to be admired in a play – grand, with an iron will. Like the old Foscari before he pardons. But such men turn their wives and daughters into slaves. They would rule the world if they could; but not ruling the world, they throw all the weight of their will on the necks and souls of women. But nature sometimes thwarts them. My father had no other child than his daughter, and she was like himself.'

She had folded her arms again, and looked as if she were ready to face some impending attempt at mastery.

'Your father was different. Unlike me – all lovingness and affection. I knew I could rule him; and I made him secretly promise me, before I married him, that he would put no hindrance in the way of my being an artist. My father was on his deathbed when we were married: from the first he had fixed his mind on my marrying my cousin Ephraim. And when a woman's will is as strong as the man's who wants to govern her, half her strength must be concealment. I meant to have my will in the end, but I could only have it by seeming to obey. I had an awe of my father – always I had had an awe of him: it was impossible to help it. I hated to feel awed – I wished I could have defied him openly; but I never could. It was what I could not imagine: I could not act it to myself that I should begin to defy my father openly and succeed. And I never would risk failure.'

That last sentence was uttered with an abrupt emphasis, and she paused after it as if the words had raised a crowd of remembrances which obstructed speech. Her son was listening to her with feelings more and more highly mixed: the first sense of being repelled by the frank coldness which had replaced all his preconceptions of a mother's tender joy in the sight of him; the first impulses of indignation at what shocked his most cherished emotions and principles – all these busy elements of collision between them were subsiding for a time, and making more and more room for that effort at just allowance and that admiration of a forcible nature whose errors lay along high pathways, which he would have felt if, instead of being his mother, she had been a stranger who had appealed to his sympathy. Still it was impossible to be dispassionate: he trembled lest the next thing she had to say would be more repugnant to him than what had gone before: he was afraid of the strange coercion she seemed to be under to lay her mind bare: he almost wished he could say, 'Tell me only what is necessary,' and then again he felt the fascination that made him watch her and listen to her eagerly. He tried to recall her to particulars by asking –

'Where was my grandfather's home?'

'Here in Genoa, when I was married; and his family had lived here generations ago. But my father had been in various countries.'

'You must surely have lived in England?'

'My mother was English – a Jewess of Portuguese descent. My father married her in England. Certain circumstances of that marriage made all the difference in my life: through that marriage, my father thwarted his own plans. My mother's sister was a singer, and afterwards she married the English partner of a merchant's house here in Genoa, and they came and lived here eleven years. My mother died when I was eight years old, and then my father allowed me to be continually with my aunt Leonora and be taught under her eyes, as if he had not minded the danger of her encouraging my wish to be a singer, as she had been. But this was it – I saw it again and again in my father: – he did not guard against consequences, because he felt sure he could hinder them if he liked. Before my aunt left Genoa, I had had enough teaching to bring out the born singer and actress within me: my father did not know everything that was done; but he knew that I was taught music and singing – he knew my inclination. That was nothing to him: he meant that I should obey his will. And he was resolved that I should marry my cousin Ephraim, the only one left of my father's family that he knew. I wanted not to marry. I thought of all plans to resist it, but at last I found that I could rule my cousin, and I consented. My father died three weeks after we were married, and then I had my way!' She uttered these words almost exultantly; but after a little pause her face changed, and she said in a biting tone, 'It has not lasted, though. My father is getting his way now.'

She began to look more contemplatively again at her son, and presently said –

'You are like him – but milder – there is something of your own father in you; and he made it the labour of his life to devote himself to me: wound up his money-changing and banking, and lived to wait upon me – he went against his conscience for me. As I loved the life of my art, so he loved me. Let me look at your hand again: the hand with the ring on. It was your father's ring.'

He drew his chair nearer to her and gave her his hand. We know what kind of hand it was: her own, very much smaller, was of the same type. As he felt the smaller hand holding his, as he saw nearer to him the face that held a likeness of his own, aged not by time but by intensity, the strong bent of his nature towards a reverential tenderness asserted itself above every other impression, and in his most fervent tone he said –

'Mother! take us all into your heart – the living and the dead. Forgive everything that hurts you in the past. Take my affection.'

She looked at him admiringly rather than lovingly, then kissed him on the brow, and saying sadly, 'I reject nothing, but I have nothing to give,' she released his hand and sank back on her cushions. Deronda turned pale with what seems always more of a sensation than an emotion – the pain of repulsed tenderness. She noticed the expression of pain, and said, still with melodious melancholy in her tones –

'It is better so. We must part again soon, and you owe me no duties. I did not wish you to be born. I parted with you willingly. When your father died, I resolved that I would have no more ties, but such as I could free myself from. I was the Alcharisi you have heard of: the name had magic wherever it was carried. Men courted me. Sir Hugo Mallinger was one who wished to marry me. He was madly in love with me. One day I asked him, "Is there a man capable of doing something for love of me, and expecting nothing in return?" He said, "What is it you want done?" I said, "Take my boy and bring him up as an Englishman, and let him never know anything about his parents." You were little more than two years old, and were sitting on his foot. He declared that he would pay money to have such a boy. I had not meditated much on the plan beforehand, but as soon as I had spoken about it, it took possession of me as something I could not rest without doing. At first he thought I was not serious, but I convinced him, and he was never surprised at anything. He agreed that it would be for your good, and the finest thing for you. A great singer and actress is a queen, but she gives no royalty to her son. – All that happened at Naples. And afterwards I made Sir Hugo the trustee of your fortune. That is what I did; and I had a joy in doing it. My father had tyrannized over me – he cared more about a grandson to come than he did about me: I counted as nothing. You were to be such a Jew as he; you were to be what he wanted. But you were my son, and it was my turn to say what you should be. I said you should not know you were a Jew.'

'And for months events have been preparing me to be glad that I am a Jew,' said Deronda, his opposition roused again. The point touched the quick of his experience. 'It would always have been better that I should have known the truth. I have always been rebelling against the secrecy that looked like shame. It is no shame to have Jewish parents – the shame is to disown it.'

'You say it was a shame to me, then, that I used that secrecy,' said his mother, with a flash of new anger. 'There is no shame attaching to me. I have no reason to be ashamed. I rid myself of the Jewish tatters and gibberish that make people nudge each other at sight of us, as if we were tattooed under our clothes, though our faces are as whole as theirs. I delivered you from the pelting contempt that pursues Jewish separateness. I am not ashamed that I did it. It was the better for you.'

'Then why have you now undone the secrecy? – no, not undone it – the effects will never be undone. But why have you now sent for me to tell me that I am a Jew?' said

Deronda, with an intensity of opposition in feeling that was almost bitter. It seemed as if her words had called out a latent obstinacy of race in him.

'Why? – ah, why?' said the Princess, rising quickly and walking to the other side of the room, where she turned round and slowly approached him, as he, too, stood up. Then she began to speak again in a more veiled voice. 'I can't explain; I can only say what is. I don't love my father's religion now any more than I did then. Before I married the second time, I was baptized; I made myself like the people I lived among. I had a right to do it; I was not, like a brute, obliged to go with my own herd. I have not repented; I will not say that I have repented. But yet,' – here she had come near to her son, and paused; then again retreated a little and stood still, as if resolute not to give way utterly to an imperious influence; but, as she went on speaking, she became more and more unconscious of anything but the awe that subdued her voice. 'It is illness, I don't doubt that it has been gathering illness, – my mind has gone back; more than a year ago it began. You see my grey hair, my worn look: it has all come fast. Sometimes I am in an agony of pain – I dare say I shall be to-night. Then it is as if all the life I have chosen to live, all thoughts, all will, forsook me and left me alone in spots of memory, and I can't get away: my pain seems to keep me there. My childhood – my girlhood – the day of my marriage – the day of my father's death – there seems to be nothing since. Then a great horror comes over me: what do I know of life or death? and what my father called "right" may be a power that is laying hold of me – that is clutching me now. Well, I will satisfy him. I cannot go into the darkness without satisfying him. I have hidden what was his. I thought once I would burn it. I have not burnt it. I thank God I have not burnt it!'

She threw herself on her cushions again, visibly fatigued. Deronda, moved too strongly by her suffering for other impulses to act within him, drew near her, and said, entreatingly –

'Will you not spare yourself this evening? Let us leave the rest till to-morrow.'

'No,' she said, decisively. 'I will confess it all, now that I have come up to it. Often when I am at ease it all fades away; my whole self comes quite back; but I know it will sink away again, and the other will come – the poor, solitary, forsaken remains of self, that can resist nothing. It was my nature to resist, and say, "I have a right to resist." Well, I say so still when I have any strength in me. You have heard me say it, and I don't withdraw it. But when my strength goes, some other right forces itself upon me like iron in an inexorable hand; and even when I am at ease, it is beginning to make ghosts upon the daylight. And now you have made it worse for me,' she said, with a sudden return of impetuosity; 'but I shall have told you everything. And what reproach is there against me,' she added, bitterly, 'since I have made you glad to be a Jew? Joseph Kalonymos reproached me: he said you had been turned into a proud Englishman, who resented being touched by a Jew. I wish you had!' she ended, with a new marvellous alternation. It was as if her mind were breaking into several, one jarring the other into impulsive action.

'Who is Joseph Kalonymos?' said Deronda, with a darting recollection of that Jew who touched his arm in the Frankfort synagogue.

'Ah! some vengeance sent him back from the East, that he might see you and come to reproach me. He was my father's friend. He knew of your birth: he knew of my husband's death, and once, twenty years ago, after he had been away in the Levant, he came to see me and inquire about you. I told him that you were dead: I meant you to be dead to all the world of my childhood. If I had said you were living, he would have interfered with my plans: he would have taken on him to represent my father, and have tried to make me recall what I had done. What could I do but say you were dead? The act was done. If I had told him of it, there would have been trouble and scandal – and all to conquer me, who would not have been conquered. I was strong then, and I would have had my will, though there might have been a hard fight against me. I took the way to have it without any fight. I felt then that I was not really deceiving: it would have come to the same in the end; or if not to the same, to something worse. He believed me, and begged that I would give up to him the chest that my father had charged me and my husband to deliver to our eldest son. I knew what was in the chest – things that had been dinned in my ears since I had had any understanding – things that were thrust on my mind that I might feel them like a wall around my life – my life that was growing like a tree. Once, after my husband died, I was going to burn the chest. But it was difficult to burn; and burning a chest and papers looks like a shameful act. I have committed no shameful act – except what Jews would call shameful. I had kept the chest, and I gave it to Joseph Kalonymos. He went away mournful, and said, "If you marry again, and if another grandson is born to him who is departed, I will deliver up the chest to him." I bowed in silence. I meant not to marry again – no more than I meant to be the shattered woman that I am now.'

She ceased speaking, and her head sank back while she looked vaguely before her. Her thought was travelling through the years, and when she began to speak again her voice had lost its argumentative spirit, and had fallen into a veiled tone of distress.

'But months ago this Kalonymos saw you in the synagogue at Frankfort. He saw you enter the hotel, and he went to ask your name. There was nobody else in the world to whom the name would have told anything about me.'

'Then it is not my real name?' said Deronda, with a dislike even to this trifling part of the disguise which had been thrown round him.

'Oh, as real as another,' said his mother, indifferently. 'The Jews have always been changing their names. My father's family had kept the name of Charisi: my husband was a Charisi. When I came out as a singer, we made it Alcharisi. But there had been a branch of the family my father had lost sight of who called themselves Deronda, and when I wanted a name for you, and Sir Hugo said, "Let it be a foreign name," I thought of Deronda. But Joseph Kalonymos had heard my father speak of the Deronda branch, and the name confirmed his suspicion. He began to suspect what had been done. It was as if everything had been whispered to him in the air. He found out where I was. He took a journey into Russia to see me; he found me weak and shattered. He had come back again, with his white hair, and with rage in his soul against me. He said I was going down to the grave clad in falsehood and robbery – falsehood to my father and robbery of my own child. He accused me of having kept the knowledge of your birth from you, and having brought you up as if you had been the son of an English gentleman. Well, it was true; and twenty years before I would have maintained that I had a right to do it. But I can maintain nothing now. No faith is strong within me. My father may have God on his side. This man's words were like lion's teeth upon me. My father's threats eat into me with my pain. If I tell everything – if I deliver up everything – what else can be demanded of me? I cannot make myself love the people I have never loved – is it not enough that I lost the life I did love?'

She had leaned forward a little in her low-toned pleading, that seemed like a smothered cry: her arms and hands were stretched out at full length, as if strained in beseeching. Deronda's soul was absorbed in the anguish of compassion. He could not mind now that he had been repulsed before. His pity made a flood of forgiveness within him. His single impulse was to kneel by her and take her hand gently between his palms, while he said in that exquisite voice of soothing which expresses oneness with the sufferer –

'Mother, take comfort!'

She did not seem inclined to repulse him now, but looked down at him and let him take both her hands to fold between his. Gradually tears gathered, but she pressed her handkerchief against her eyes and then leaned her cheek against his brow, as if she wished that they should not look at each other.

'Is it not possible that I could be near you often and comfort you?' said Deronda. He was under that stress of pity that propels us on sacrifices.

'No, not possible,' she answered, lifting up her head again and withdrawing her hand as if she wished him to move away. 'I have a husband and five children. None of them know of your existence.'

Deronda felt painfully silenced. He rose and stood at a little distance.

'You wonder why I married,' she went on presently, under the influence of a newly-recurring thought. 'I meant never to marry again. I meant to be free, and to live for my art. I had parted with you. I had no bonds. For nine years I was a queen. I enjoyed the life I had longed for. But something befell me. It was like a fit of forgetfulness. I began to sing out of tune. They told me of it. Another woman was thrusting herself in my place. I could not endure the prospect of failure and decline. It was horrible to me.' She started up again, with a shudder, and lifted screening hands like one who dreads missiles. 'It drove me to marry. I made believe that I preferred being the wife of a Russian noble to being the greatest lyric actress of Europe; I made believe – I acted that part. It was because I felt my greatness sinking away from me, as I feel my life sinking now. I would not wait till men said, "She had better go."'

She sank into her seat again and looked at the evening sky as she went on: 'I repented. It was a resolve taken in desperation. That singing out of tune was only like a fit of illness; it went away. I repented; but it was too late. I could not go back. All things hindered me – all things.'

A new haggardness had come in her face, but her son refrained from again urging her to leave further speech till the morrow; there was evidently some mental relief for her in an outpouring such as she could never have allowed herself before. He stood still while she maintained silence longer than she knew, and the light was perceptibly fading. At last she turned to him and said –

'I can bear no more now.' She put out her hand, but then quickly withdrew it saying, 'Stay. How do I know that I can see you again? I cannot bear to be seen when I am in pain.'

She drew forth a pocket-book, and taking out a letter said, 'This is addressed to the banking-house in Mainz, where you are to go for your grandfather's chest. It is a letter written by Joseph Kalonymos: if he is not there himself, this order of his will be obeyed.'

When Deronda had taken the letter, she said, with effort, but more gently than before, 'Kneel again, and let me kiss you.'

He obeyed, and holding his head between her hands she kissed him solemnly on the brow. 'You see I had no life left to love you with,' she said, in a low murmur. 'But there is more fortune for you. Sir Hugo was to keep it in reserve. I gave you all your father's fortune. They can never accuse me of robbery there.'

'If you had needed anything I would have worked for you,' said Deronda, conscious of a disappointed yearning – a shutting out for ever from long early vistas of affectionate imagination.

'I need nothing that the skill of man can give me,' said his mother, still holding his head, and perusing his features. 'But perhaps now I have satisfied my father's will, your face will come instead of his – your young, loving face.'

'But you will see me again?' said Deronda, anxiously.

'Yes – perhaps. Wait, wait. Leave me now.'

LII

'La même fermeté qui sert à résister à l'amour sert aussi à le
rendre violent et durable; et les personnes foibles qui sont tou-
jours agitées des passions n'en sont presque jamais véritablement
remplies.'

             – LA ROCHEFOUCAULD.

AMONG Deronda's letters the next morning was one from
Hans Meyrick of four quarto pages in the small beautiful
handwriting which ran in the Meyrick family.

MY DEAR DERONDA, – In return for your sketch of
Italian movements and your view of the world's affairs
generally, I may say that here at home the most judicious
opinion going as to the effects of present causes is that
'time will show.' As to the present causes of past effects, it
is now seen that the late swindling telegrams account for
the last year's cattle plague – which is a refutation of
philosophy falsely so called, and justifies the compensation to the farmers. My own idea that a murrain will shortly
break out in the commercial class, and that the cause will
subsequently disclose itself in the ready sale of all rejected
pictures, has been called an unsound use of analogy; but
there are minds that will not hesitate to rob even the
neglected painter of his solace. To my feeling there is
great beauty in the conception that some bad judge
might give a high price for my Berenice series, and that
the men in the city would have already been punished for
my ill-merited luck.

Meanwhile I am consoling myself for your absence by
finding my advantage in it – shining like Hesperus when
Hyperion has departed – sitting with our Hebrew prophet,
and making a study of his head, in the hours when he used
to be occupied with you – getting credit with him as a
learned young Gentile, who would have been a Jew if he
could – and agreeing with him in the general principle, that
whatever is best is for that reason Jewish. I never held it my
forte to be a severe reasoner, but I can see that if whatever is

best is A and B happens to be best, B must be A, however
little you might have expected it beforehand. On that
principle, I could see the force of a pamphlet I once read
to prove that all good art was Protestant. However, our
prophet is an uncommonly interesting sitter – a better
model than Rembrandt had for his Rabbi – and I never
come away from him without a new discovery. For one
thing, it is a constant wonder to me that, with all his fiery
feeling for his race and their traditions, he is no strait-laced
Jew, spitting after the word Christian, and enjoying the
prospect that the Gentile mouth will water in vain for a
slice of the roasted Leviathan, while Israel will be sending
up plates for more, *ad libitum*. (You perceive that my
studies had taught me what to expect from the orthodox
Jew.) I confess that I have always held lightly by your
account of Mordecai, as apologetic, and merely part of
your disposition to take an antediluvian point of view,
lest you should do injustice to the megatherium. But now
I have given ear to him in his proper person, I find him
really a sort of philosophical-allegorical-mystical believer,
and yet with a sharp dialectic point, so that any argumentative rattler of peas in a bladder might soon be pricked
into silence by him. The mixture may be one of the Jewish
prerogatives, for what I know. In fact, his mind seems so
broad that I find my own correct opinions lying in it quite
commodiously, and how they are to be brought into agreement with the vast remainder is his affair, not mine. I leave
it to him to settle our basis, never yet having seen a basis
which is not a world-supporting elephant, more or less
powerful and expensive to keep. My means will not
allow me to keep a private elephant. I go into mystery
instead, as cheaper and more lasting – a sort of gas which
is likely to be continually supplied by the decomposition
of the elephants. And if I like the look of an opinion, I treat
it civilly, without suspicious inquiries. I have quite a
friendly feeling towards Mordecai's notion that a whole
Christian is three-fourths a Jew, and that from the
Alexandrian time downward, the most comprehensive

minds have been Jewish; for I think of pointing out to Mirah that, Arabic and other accidents of life apart, there is really little difference between me and – Maimonides. But I have lately been finding out that it is your shallow lover who can't help making a declaration. If Mirah's ways were less distracting, and it were less of a heaven to be in her presence and watch her, I must long ago have flung myself at her feet, and requested her to tell me, with less indirectness, whether she wished me to blow my brains out. I have a knack of hoping, which is as good as an estate in reversion, if one can keep from the temptation of turning it into certainty, which may spoil all. My Hope wanders among the orchard-blossoms, feels the warm snow falling on it through the sunshine, and is in doubt of nothing; but, catching sight of Certainty in the distance, sees an ugly Janus-faced deity, with a dubious wink on the hither side of him, and turns quickly away. But you, with your supreme reasonableness, and self-nullification, and preparation for the worst – you know nothing about the drama of Hope, that immortal delicious maiden, for ever courted, for ever propitious, whom fools have called deceitful, as if it were Hope that carried the cup of disappointment, whereas it is her deadly enemy Certainty, whom she only escapes by transformation. (You observe my new vein of allegory?) Seriously, however, I must be permitted to allege that truth will prevail, that prejudice will melt before it, that diversity, accompanied by merit, will make itself felt as fascination, and that no virtuous aspiration will be frustrated – all which, if I mistake not, are doctrines of the schools, and all imply that the Jewess I prefer will prefer me. Any blockhead can cite generalities, but the mastermind discerns the particular cases they represent.

I am less convinced that my society makes amends to Mordecai for your absence, but another substitute occasionally comes in the form of Jacob Cohen. It is worth while to catch our prophet's expression when he has that remarkable type of young Israel on his knee, and pours forth some Semitic inspiration with a sublime look of melancholy patience and devoutness. Sometimes it occurs to Jacob that Hebrew will be more edifying to him if he stops his ears with his palms, and imitates the venerable sounds as heard through that muffling medium. When Mordecai gently draws down the little fists and holds them fast, Jacob's features all take on an extraordinary activity, very much as if he were walking through a menagerie and trying to imitate every animal in turn, succeeding best with the owl and the peccary. But I dare say you have seen something of this. He treats me with the easiest familiarity, and seems in general to look at me as a second-hand Christian commodity, likely to come down in price; remarking on my disadvantages with a frankness which seems to imply some thoughts of future purchase. It is pretty, though, to see the change in him if Mirah happens to come in. He turns child suddenly – his age usually strikes one as being like the Israelitish garments in the desert, perhaps near forty, yet with an air of recent production. But, with Mirah, he reminds me of the dogs that have been brought up by women, and remain manageable by them only. Still, the dog is fond of Mordecai too, and brings sugar-plums to share with him, filling his own mouth to rather an embarrassing extent, and watching how Mordecai deals with a smaller supply. Judging from this modern Jacob at the age of six, my astonishment is that his race has not bought us all up long ago, and pocketed our feebler generations in the form of stock and scrip, as so much slave property. There is one Jewess I should not mind being slave to. But I wish I did not imagine that Mirah gets a little sadder, and tries all the while to hide it. It is natural enough, of course, while she has to watch the slow death of this brother, whom she has taken to worshipping with such looks of loving devoutness that I am ready to wish myself in his place.

For the rest, we are a little merrier than usual. Rex Gascoigne – you remember a head you admired among my sketches, a fellow with a good upper lip, reading law – has got some rooms in town now not far off us, and has had a neat sister (upper lip also good) staying with him the last fortnight. I have introduced them both to my mother and the girls, who have found out from Miss Gascoigne that she is cousin to your Vandyke duchess!!! I put the notes of exclamation to mark the surprise that the information at first produced on my feeble understanding. On reflection I discovered that there was not the least ground for surprise, unless I had beforehand believed that nobody could be anybody's cousin without my knowing it. This sort of surprise, I take it, depends on a liveliness of the spine, with a more or less constant nullity of brain. There was a fellow I used to meet at Rome who was in an effervescence of surprise at contact with the simplest information. Tell him what you would – that you were fond of easy boots – he would always say, 'No! *are* you?' with the same energy of wonder: the very fellow of whom pastoral Browne wrote prophetically –

> 'A wretch so empty that if e'er there be
> In nature found the least vacuity
> 'Twill be in him.'

I have accounted for it all – he had a lively spine.

However, this cousinship with the duchess came out by chance one day that Mirah was with them at home and they were talking about the Mallingers. *Apropos*; I am getting so important that I have rival invitations. Gascoigne wants me to go down with him to his father's rectory in August and see the country round there. But I think self-interest well understood will take me to Topping Abbey, for Sir Hugo has invited me and proposes – God bless him for his rashness! – that I should make a picture of his three daughters sitting on a bank – as he says, in the Gainsborough style. He came to my studio the other day and recommended me to apply myself to portrait. Of course I know what that means. – 'My good fellow, your attempts at the historic and poetic are simply pitiable. Your brush is just that of a successful portrait-painter – it has a little truth and a great facility in falsehood – your idealism will never do for gods and goddesses and heroic story, but it may fetch a high price as flattery. Fate, my friend, has made you the hinder wheel – *rota posterior curras, et in axe secundo* – run behind, because you can't help it.' – What great effort it evidently costs our friends to give us these candid opinions! I have even known a man take the trouble to call, in order to tell me that I had irretrievably exposed my want of judgment in treating my subject, and that if I had asked him he would have lent me his own judgment. Such was my ingratitude and my readiness at composition, that even while he was speaking I inwardly sketched a Last Judgment with that candid friend's physiognomy on the left. But all this is away from Sir Hugo, whose manner of implying that one's gifts are not of the highest order is so exceedingly good-natured and comfortable that I begin to feel it an advantage not to be among those poor fellows at the tip-top. And his kindness to me tastes all the better because it comes out of his love for you, old boy. His chat is uncommonly amusing. By the way, he told me that your Vandyke duchess is gone with her husband yachting to the Mediterranean. I bethink me that it is possible to land from a yacht, or to be taken on to a yacht from the land. Shall you by chance have an opportunity of continuing your theological discussion with the fair Supralapsarian – I think you said her tenets were of that complexion? Is Duke Alphonso also theological? – perhaps an Arian who objects to triplicity. (Stage direction. While D. is reading, a profound scorn gathers in his face till at the last word he flings down the letter, grasps his coat-collar in a statuesque attitude and so remains, with a look generally tremendous, throughout the following soliloquy, 'O night, O blackness, &c. &c.')

Excuse the brevity of this letter. You are not used to more from me than a bare statement of facts without comment or digression. One fact I have omitted – that the Klesmers on the eve of departure have behaved magnificently, shining forth as might be expected from the planets of genius and fortune in conjunction. Mirah is rich with their oriental gifts.

What luck it will be if you come back and present yourself at the Abbey while I am there! I am going to behave with consummate discretion and win golden opinions. But I shall run up to town now and then, just for a peep into Gan Eden. You see how far I have got in Hebrew lore – up with my Lord Bolingbroke, who knew no Hebrew, but 'understood that sort of learning and what is writ about it.' If Mirah commanded, I would go to a depth below the tri-literal roots. Already it makes no difference to me whether the points are there or not. But while her brother's life lasts I suspect she would not listen to a lover, even one whose 'hair is like a flock of goats on Mount Gilead' – and I flatter myself that few heads would bear that trying comparison better than mine. So I stay with my hope among the orchard-blossoms. – Your devoted

HANS MEYRICK.

Some months before, this letter from Hans would have divided Deronda's thoughts irritatingly: its romancing about Mirah would have had an unpleasant edge, scarcely anointed with any commiseration for his friend's probable disappointment. But things had altered since March. Mirah was no longer so critically placed with regard to the Meyricks, and Deronda's own position had been undergoing a change which had just been crowned by the revelation of his birth. The new opening towards the future, though he would not trust in any definite visions, inevitably shed new lights, and influenced his mood towards past and present; hence, what Hans called his hope now seemed to Deronda, not a mischievous unreasonableness which roused his indignation, but an unusually persistent bird-dance of an extravagant fancy, and he would have felt quite able to pity any consequent suffering of his friend's, if he had believed in the suffering as probable. But some of the busy thought filling that long day, which passed without his receiving any new summons from his mother, was given to the argument that Hans

Meyrick's nature was not one in which love could strike the deep roots that turn disappointment into sorrow: it was too restless, too readily excitable by novelty, too ready to turn itself into imaginative material, and wear its grief as a fantastic costume. 'Already he is beginning to play at love: he is taking the whole affair as a comedy,' said Deronda to himself; 'he knows very well that there is no chance for him. Just like him – never opening his eyes on any possible objection I could have to receive his outpourings about Mirah. Poor old Hans! If we were under a fiery hail together he would howl like a Greek, and if I did not howl too it would never occur to him that I was as badly off as he. And yet he is tender-hearted and affectionate in intention, and I can't say that he is not active in imagining what goes on in other people – but then he always imagines it to fit his own inclination.'

With this touch of causticity Deronda got rid of the slight heat at present raised by Hans's *naïve* expansiveness. The nonsense about Gwendolen, conveying the fact that she was gone yachting with her husband, only suggested a disturbing sequel to his own strange parting with her. But there was one sentence in the letter which raised a more immediate, active anxiety. Hans's suspicion of a hidden sadness in Mirah was not in the direction of his wishes, and hence, instead of distrusting his observation here, Deronda began to conceive a cause for the sadness. Was it some event that had occurred during his absence, or only the growing fear of some event? Was it something, perhaps alterable, in the new position which had been made for her? Or – had Mordecai, against his habitual resolve, communicated to her those peculiar cherished hopes about him, Deronda, and had her quickly sensitive nature been hurt by the discovery that her brother's will or tenacity of visionary conviction had acted coercively on their friendship – been hurt by the fear that there was more of pitying self-suppression than of equal regard in Deronda's relation to him? For amidst all Mirah's quiet renunciation, the evident thirst of soul with which she received the tribute of equality implied a corresponding pain if she found that what she had taken for a purely reverential regard towards her brother had its mixture of condescension.

In this last conjecture of Deronda's he was not wrong as to the quality in Mirah's nature on which he was founding – the latent protest against the treatment she had all her life been subject to until she met him. For that gratitude which would not let her pass by any notice of their acquaintance without insisting on the depth of her debt to him, took half its fervour from the keen comparison with what others had thought enough to render to her. Deronda's affinity in feeling enabled him to penetrate such secrets. But he was not near the truth in admitting the idea that Mordecai had broken his characteristic reticence. To no soul but Deronda himself had he yet breathed the history of their relation to each other, or his confidence about his friend's origin: it was not only that these subjects were for him too sacred to be spoken of without weighty reason, but that he had discerned Deronda's shrinking at any mention of his birth; and the severity of reserve which had hindered Mordecai from answering a question on a private affair of the Cohen family told yet more strongly here.

'Ezra, how is it?' Mirah one day said to him – 'I am continually going to speak to Mr. Deronda as if he were a Jew?'

He smiled at her quietly, and said, 'I suppose it is because he treats us as if he were our brother. But he loves not to have the difference of birth dwelt upon.'

'He has never lived with his parents, Mr. Hans says,' continued Mirah, to whom this was necessarily a question of interest about every one for whom she had a regard.

'Seek not to know such things from Mr. Hans,' said Mordecai, gravely, laying his hand on her curls, as he was wont. 'What Daniel Deronda wishes us to know about himself is for him to tell us.'

And Mirah felt herself rebuked, as Deronda had done. But to be rebuked in this way by Mordecai made her rather proud.

'I see no one so great as my brother,' she said to Mrs. Meyrick one day that she called at the Chelsea house on her way home, and, according to her hope found the little mother alone. 'It is difficult to think that he belongs to the same world as those people I used to live amongst. I told you once that they made life seem like a madhouse; but when I am with Ezra he makes me feel that his life is a great good, though he has suffered so much; not like me, who wanted to die because I had suffered a little, and only for a little while. His soul is so full, it is impossible for him to wish for death as I did. I get the same sort of feeling from him that I got yesterday, when I was tired, and came home through the park after the sweet rain had fallen and the sunshine lay on the grass and flowers. Everything in the sky and under the sky looked so pure and beautiful that the weariness and trouble and folly seemed only a small part of what is, and I became more patient and hopeful.'

A dove-like note of melancholy in this speech caused Mrs. Meyrick to look at Mirah with new examination. After laying down her hat and pushing her curls flat, with an air of fatigue, she had placed herself on a chair opposite her friend in her habitual attitude, her feet and hands just crossed: and at a distance she might have seemed a coloured statue of serenity. But Mrs. Meyrick discerned a new look of suppressed suffering in her face, which corresponded to the hint that to be patient and hopeful required some extra influence.

'Is there any fresh trouble on your mind, my dear?' said Mrs. Meyrick, giving up her needlework as a sign of concentrated attention.

Mirah hesitated before she said, 'I am too ready to speak of troubles, I think. It seems unkind to put anything painful into other people's minds, unless one were sure it would hinder something worse. And perhaps I am too hasty and fearful.'

'Oh, my dear, mothers are made to like pain and trouble for the sake of their children. Is it because the singing lessons are so few, and are likely to fall off when the season comes to an end? Success in these things can't come all at once.' Mrs. Meyrick did not believe that she was touching the real grief; but a guess that could be corrected would make an easier channel for confidence.

'No, not that,' said Mirah, shaking her head gently. 'I have been a little disappointed because so many ladies said they wanted me to give them or their daughters lessons, and then I never heard of them again. But perhaps after the holidays I shall teach in some schools. Besides, you know, I am as rich as a princess now. I have not touched the hundred pounds that Mrs. Klesmer gave me; and I should never be afraid that Ezra would be in want of anything, because there is Mr. Deronda, and he said, "It is the chief honour of my life that your brother will share anything with me." Oh no! Ezra and I can have no fears for each other about such things as food and clothing.'

'But there is some other fear on your mind,' said Mrs. Meyrick, not without divination – 'a fear of something that may disturb your peace? Don't be forecasting evil, dear child, unless it is what you can guard against. Anxiety is good for nothing if we can't turn it into a defence. But there's no defence against all the things that might be. Have you any more reason for being anxious now than you had a month ago?'

'Yes, I have,' said Mirah. 'I have kept it from Ezra. I have not dared to tell him. Pray forgive me that I can't do without telling you. I *have* more reason for being anxious. It is five days ago now. I am quite sure I saw my father.'

Mrs. Meyrick shrank into smaller space, packing her arms across her chest and leaning forward – to hinder herself from pelting that father with her worst epithets.

'The year has changed him,' Mirah went on. 'He had already been much altered and worn in the time before I left him. You remember I said how he used sometimes to cry. He was always excited one way or the other. I have told Ezra everything that I told you, and he says that my father had taken to gambling, which makes people easily distressed, and then again exalted. And now – it was only a moment that I saw him – his face was more haggard, and his clothes were shabby. He was with a much worse-looking man, who carried something, and they were hurrying along after an omnibus.'

'Well, child, he did not see you, I hope?'

'No. I had just come from Mrs. Raymond's, and I was waiting to cross near the Marble Arch. Soon he was on the omnibus and gone out of sight. It was a dreadful moment. My old life seemed to have come back again, and it was worse than it had ever been before. And I could not help feeling it a new deliverance that he was gone out of sight without knowing that I was there. And yet it hurt me that I was feeling so – it seemed hateful in me – almost like words I once had to speak in a play, that "I had warmed my hands in the blood of my kindred." For where might my father be going? What may become of him? And his having a daughter who would own him in spite of all, might have hindered the worst. Is there any pain like seeing what ought to be the best things in life turned into the worst? All those opposite feelings were meeting and pressing against each other, and took up all my strength. No one could act that. Acting is slow and poor to what we go through within. I don't know how I called a cab. I only remember that I was in it when I began to think, "I cannot tell Ezra; he must not know."'

'You are afraid of grieving him?' Mrs. Meyrick asked, when Mirah had paused a little.

'Yes – and there is something more,' said Mirah, hesitatingly, as if she were examining her feeling before she would venture to speak of it. 'I want to tell you; I could not tell any one else. I could not have told my own mother; I should have closed it up before her. I feel shame for my father, and it is perhaps strange – but the shame is greater before Ezra than before any one else in the world. He desired me to tell him all about my life, and I obeyed him. But it is always like a smart to me to know that those things about my father are in Ezra's mind. And – can you believe it? – when the thought haunts me how it would be if my father were to come and show himself before us both, what seems as if it would scorch me most is seeing my father shrinking before Ezra. That is the truth. I don't know whether it is a right feeling. But I can't help thinking that I would rather try to maintain my father in secret, and bear a great deal in that way, if I could hinder him from meeting my brother.'

'You must not encourage that feeling, Mirah,' said Mrs. Meyrick, hastily. 'It would be very dangerous; it would be wrong. You must not have concealments of that sort.'

'But ought I now to tell Ezra that I have seen my father?' said Mirah, with deprecation in her tone.

'No,' Mrs. Meyrick answered, dubitatively. 'I don't know that it is necessary to do that. Your father may go away with the birds. It is not clear that he came after you; you may never see him again. And then your brother will have been spared a useless anxiety. But promise me that if your father sees you – gets hold of you in any way again – you will let us all know. Promise me that solemnly, Mirah. I have a right to ask it.'

Mirah reflected a little, then leaned forward to put her hands in Mrs. Meyrick's, and said, 'Since you ask it, I do promise. I will bear this feeling of shame. I have been so long used to think that I must bear that sort of inward pain. But the shame for my father burns me more when I think of his meeting Ezra.' She was silent a moment or two, and then said, in a new tone of yearning compassion, 'And we are his children – and he was once young like us – and my mother loved him. Oh! I cannot help seeing it all close, and it hurts me like a cruelty.'

Mirah shed no tears: the discipline of her whole life had been against indulgence in such manifestation, which soon falls under the control of strong motives; but it seemed that the more intense expression of sorrow had entered into her voice. Mrs. Meyrick, with all her quickness and loving insight, did not quite understand that filial feeling in Mirah which had active roots deep below her indignation for the worst offences. She could conceive that a mother would have a clinging pity and shame for a reprobate son, but she was out of patience with what she held an exaggerated susceptibility on behalf of this father, whose reappearance inclined her to wish him under the care of a turnkey. Mirah's promise, however, was some security against her weakness.

That incident was the only reason that Mirah herself could have stated for the hidden sadness which Hans had divined. Of one element in her changed mood she could have given no definite account: it was something as dim as the sense of approaching weather-change, and had extremely slight external promptings, such as we are often ashamed to find all we can allege in support of the busy constructions that go on within us, not only without effort but even against it, under the influence of any blind emotional stirring. Perhaps the first leaven of uneasiness was laid by Gwendolen's behaviour on that visit which was entirely superfluous as a means of engaging Mirah to sing, and could have no other motive than the excited and strange questioning about Deronda. Mirah had instinctively kept the visit a secret, but the active remembrance of it had raised a new susceptibility in her, and made her alive as she had never been before to the relations Deronda must have with that society which she herself was getting frequent glimpses of without belonging to it. Her peculiar life and education had produced in her an extraordinary mixture of unworldliness, with knowledge of the world's evil, and even this knowledge was a strange blending of direct observation with the effects of reading and theatrical study. Her memory was furnished with abundant passionate situation and intrigue, which she never made emotionally her own, but felt a repelled aloofness from, as she had done from the actual life around her. Some of that imaginative knowledge began now to weave itself around Mrs. Grandcourt; and though Mirah would admit no position likely to affect her reverence for Deronda, she could not avoid a new painfully vivid association of his general life with a world away from her own, where there might be some involvement of his feeling and action with a woman like Gwendolen, who was increasingly repugnant to her – increasingly, even after she had ceased to see her; for liking and disliking can grow in meditation as fast as in the more immediate kind of presence. Any disquietude consciously due to the idea that Deronda's deepest care might be for something remote not only from herself but even from his friendship for her brother, she would have checked with rebuking questions: – What was she but one who had shared his generous kindness with many others? and his attachment to her brother, was it not begun late to be soon ended? Other ties had come before, and others would remain after this had been cut by swift-coming death. But her uneasiness had not reached that point of self-recognition in which she would have been ashamed of it as an indirect, presumptuous claim on Deronda's feeling. That she or any one else should think of him as her possible lover was a conception which had never entered her mind; indeed it was equally out of the question with Mrs. Meyrick and the girls, who with Mirah herself regarded his intervention in her life as something exceptional, and were so impressed by his mission as her deliverer and guardian that they would have held it an offence to hint at his holding any other relation towards her: a point of view which Hans also had readily adopted. It is a little hard upon some men that they appear to sink for us in becoming lovers. But precisely to this innocence of the Meyricks was owing the disturbance of Mirah's unconsciousness. The first occasion could hardly have been more trivial, but it prepared her emotive nature for a deeper effect from what happened afterwards.

It was when Anna Gascoigne, visiting the Meyricks, was led to speak of her cousinship with Gwendolen. The visit had been arranged that Anna might see Mirah; the three girls were at home with their mother, and there was naturally a flux of talk among six feminine creatures, free from the presence of a distorting male standard. Anna

Gascoigne felt herself much at home with the Meyrick girls, who knew what it was to have a brother, and to be generally regarded as of minor importance in the world; and she had told Rex that she thought the University very nice, because brothers made friends there whose families were not rich and grand, and yet (like the University) were very nice. The Meyricks seemed to her almost alarmingly clever, and she consulted them much on the best mode of teaching Lotta, confiding to them that she herself was the least clever of her family. Mirah had lately come in, and there was a complete bouquet of young faces round the tea-table – Hafiz, seated a little aloft with large eyes on the alert, regarding the whole scene as an apparatus for supplying his allowance of milk.

'Think of our surprise, Mirah,' said Kate. 'We were speaking of Mr. Deronda and the Mallingers, and it turns out that Miss Gascoigne knows them.'

'I only know about them,' said Anna, a little flushed with excitement, what she had heard and now saw of the lovely Jewess being an almost startling novelty to her. 'I have not even seen them. But some months ago, my cousin married Sir Hugo Mallinger's nephew, Mr. Grandcourt, who lived in Sir Hugo's place at Diplow, near us.'

'There!' exclaimed Mab, clasping her hands. 'Something must come of that. Mrs. Grandcourt, the Vandyke duchess, is your cousin?'

'Oh yes; I was her bridesmaid,' said Anna. 'Her mamma and mine are sisters. My aunt was much richer before last year, but then she and mamma lost all their fortune. Papa is a clergyman, you know, so it makes very little difference to us, except that we keep no carriage, and have no dinner-parties – and I like it better. But it was very sad for poor Aunt Davilow, for she could not live with us, because she has four daughters besides Gwendolen; but then, when she married Mr. Grandcourt, it did not signify so much, because of his being so rich.'

'Oh, this finding out relationships is delightful!' said Mab. 'It is like a Chinese puzzle that one has to fit together. I feel sure something wonderful may be made of it, but I can't tell what.'

'Dear me, Mab!' said Amy, 'relationships must branch out. The only difference is, that we happen to know some of the people concerned. Such things are going on every day.'

'And pray, Amy, why do you insist on the number nine being so wonderful?' said Mab. 'I am sure that is happening every day. Never mind, Miss Gascoigne; please go on. And Mr. Deronda? – have you never seen Mr. Deronda? You *must* bring him in.'

'No, I have not seen him,' said Anna; 'but he was at Diplow before my cousin was married, and I have heard my aunt speaking of him to papa. She said what you have been saying about him – only, not so much: I mean, about Mr. Deronda living with Sir Hugo Mallinger, and being so nice, she thought. We talk a great deal about every one who comes near Pennicote, because it is so seldom there is any one new. But I remember, when I asked Gwendolen what she thought of Mr. Deronda, she said, "Don't mention it, Anna; but I think his hair is dark." That was her droll way of answering; she was always so lively. It is really rather wonderful that I should come to hear so much about him, all through Mr. Hans knowing Rex, and then my having the pleasure of knowing you,' Anna ended, looking at Mrs. Meyrick, with a shy grace.

'The pleasure is on our side too; but the wonder would have been, if you had come to this house without hearing of Mr. Deronda – wouldn't it, Mirah?' said Mrs. Meyrick.

Mirah smiled acquiescently, but had nothing to say. A confused discontent took possession of her at the mingling of names and images to which she had been listening.

'My son calls Mrs. Grandcourt the Vandyke duchess,' continued Mrs. Meyrick, turning again to Anna; 'he thinks her so striking and picturesque.'

'Yes,' said Anna. 'Gwendolen was always so beautiful – people fell dreadfully in love with her. I thought it a pity, because it made them unhappy.'

'And how do you like Mr. Grandcourt, the happy lover?' said Mrs. Meyrick, who, in her way, was as much interested as Mab in the hints she had been hearing of vicissitude in the life of a widow with daughters.

'Papa approved of Gwendolen's accepting him, and my aunt says he is very generous,' said Anna, beginning with a virtuous intention of repressing her own sentiments; but then, unable to resist a rare occasion for speaking them freely, she went on – 'else I should have thought he was not very nice – rather proud, and not at all lively, like Gwendolen. I should have thought some one younger and more lively would have suited her better. But, perhaps, having a brother who seems to us better than any one makes us think worse of others.'

'Wait till you see Mr. Deronda,' said Mab, nodding significantly. 'Nobody's brother will do after him.'

'Our brothers *must* do for people's husbands,' said Kate, curtly, 'because they will not get Mr. Deronda. No woman will do for him to marry.'

'No woman ought to want to marry him,' said Mab, with indignation. '*I* never should. Fancy finding out that he had a tailor's bill, and used boot-hooks, like Hans. Who ever thought of his marrying?'

'I have,' said Kate. 'When I drew a wedding for a frontispiece to "Hearts and Diamonds," I made a sort of likeness of him for the bridegroom, and I went about looking for a grand woman who would do for his countess, but I saw none that would not be poor creatures by the side of him.'

'You should have seen this Mrs. Grandcourt then,' said Mrs. Meyrick. 'Hans said that she and Mr. Deronda set each other off when they are side by side. She is tall and fair. But you know her, Mirah – you can always say something descriptive. What do *you* think of Mrs. Grandcourt?'

'I think she is like the *Princess of Eboli* in *Don Carlos*,' said Mirah, with a quick intensity. She was pursuing an association in her own mind not intelligible to her hearers – an association with a certain actress as well as the part she represented.

724

'Your comparison is a riddle for me, my dear,' said Mrs. Meyrick, smiling.

'You said that Mrs. Grandcourt was tall and fair,' continued Mirah, slightly paler. 'That is quite true.'

Mrs. Meyrick's quick eye and ear detected something unusual, but immediately explained it to herself. Fine ladies had often wounded Mirah by caprices of manner and intention.

'Mrs. Grandcourt had thought of having lessons from Mirah,' she said, turning to Anna. 'But many have talked of having lessons, and then have found no time. Fashionable ladies have too much work to do.'

And the chat went on without further insistence on the *Princess of Eboli*. That comparison escaped Mirah's lips under the urgency of a pang unlike anything she had felt before. The conversation from the beginning had revived unpleasant impressions, and Mrs. Meyrick's suggestion of Gwendolen's figure by the side of Deronda's had the stinging effect of a voice outside her, confirming her secret conviction that this tall and fair woman had some hold on his lot. For a long while afterwards she felt as if she had had a jarring shock through her frame.

In the evening, putting her cheek against her brother's shoulder as she was sitting by him, while he sat propped up in bed under a new difficulty of breathing, she said –

'Ezra, does it ever hurt your love for Mr. Deronda that so much of his life was all hidden away from you, – that he is amongst persons and cares about persons who are all so unlike us – I mean, unlike you?'

'No, assuredly no,' said Mordecai. 'Rather, it is a precious thought to me that he has a preparation which I lacked, and is an accomplished Egyptian.' Then, recollecting that his words had a reference which his sister must not yet understand, he added, 'I have the more to give him, since his treasure differs from mine. That is a blessedness in friendship.'

Mirah mused a little.

725

'Still,' she said, 'it would be a trial to your love for him if that other part of his life were like a crowd in which he had got entangled, so that he was carried away from you – I mean in his thoughts, and not merely carried out of sight as he is now – and not merely for a little while, but continually. How should you bear that? Our religion commands us to bear. But how should you bear it?'

'Not well, my sister – not well; but it will never happen,' said Mordecai, looking at her with a tender smile. He thought that her heart needed comfort on his account.

Mirah said no more. She mused over the difference between her own state of mind and her brother's, and felt her comparative pettiness. Why could she not be completely satisfied with what satisfied his larger judgment? She gave herself no fuller reason than a painful sense of unfitness – in what? Airy possibilities to which she could give no outline, but to which one name and one figure gave the wandering persistency of a blot in her vision. Here lay the vaguer source of the hidden sadness rendered noticeable to Hans by some diminution of that sweet ease, that ready joyousness of response in her speech and smile, which had come with the new sense of freedom and safety, and had made her presence like the freshly-opened daisies and clear bird-notes after the rain. She herself regarded her uneasiness as a sort of ingratitude and dullness of sensibility towards the great things that had been given her in her new life; and whenever she threw more energy than usual into her singing, it was the energy of indignation against the shallowness of her own content. In that mood she once said, 'Shall I tell you what is the difference between you and me, Ezra? You are a spring in the drought, and I am an acorn-cup; the waters of heaven fill me, but the least little shake leaves me empty.'

'Why, what has shaken thee?' said Mordecai. He fell into this antique form of speech habitually in talking to his sister and to the Cohen children.

'Thoughts,' said Mirah; 'thoughts that come like the breeze and shake me – bad people, wrong things, misery – and how they might touch our life.'

'We must take our portion, Mirah. It is there. On whose shoulders would we lay it, that we might be free?'

The one voluntary sign that she made of her inward care was this distant allusion.

LIII

'My desolation does begin to make
A better life.'
– SHAKESPEARE: *Antony and Cleopatra*.

BEFORE Deronda was summoned to a second interview
with his mother, a day had passed in which she had only
sent him a message to say that she was not yet well enough
to receive him again; but on the third morning he had a
note saying, 'I leave to-day. Come and see me at once.'

He was shown into the same room as before; but it was
much darkened with blinds and curtains. The Princess was
not there, but she presently entered, dressed in a loose
wrap of some soft silk, in colour a dusky orange, her head
again with black lace floating about it, her arms showing
themselves bare from under her wide sleeves. Her face
seemed even more impressive in the sombre light, the
eyes larger, the lines more vigorous. You might have
imagined her a sorceress who would stretch forth her
wonderful hand and arm to mix youth-potions for others,
but scorned to mix them for herself, having had enough of
youth.

She put her arms on her son's shoulders at once, and
kissed him on both cheeks, then seated herself among her
cushions with an air of assured firmness and dignity unlike
her fitfulness in their first interview, and told Deronda to
sit down by her. He obeyed, saying, 'You are quite relieved
now, I trust?'

'Yes, I am at ease again. Is there anything more that you
would like to ask me?' she said, with the manner of a queen
rather than of a mother.

'Can I find the house in Genoa where you used to live
with my grandfather?' said Deronda.

'No,' she answered, with a deprecating movement of
her arm, 'it is pulled down – not to be found. But about our
family, and where my father lived at various times – you
will find all that among the papers in the chest, better than

I can tell you. My father, I told you, was a physician. My mother was a Morteira. I used to hear all those things without listening. You will find them all. I was born amongst them without my will. I banished them as soon as I could.'

Deronda tried to hide his pained feeling, and said, 'Anything else that I should desire to know from you could only be what it is some satisfaction to your own feeling to tell me.'

'I think I have told you everything that could be demanded of me,' said the Princess, looking coldly meditative. It seemed as if she had exhausted her emotion in their former interview. The fact was, she had said to herself, 'I have done it all. I have confessed all. I will not go through it again. I will save myself from agitation.' And she was acting out that theme.

But to Deronda's nature the moment was cruel: it made the filial yearning of his life a disappointed pilgrimage to a shrine where there were no longer the symbols of sacredness. It seemed that all the woman lacking in her was present in him as he said, with some tremor in his voice –

'Then are we to part, and I never be anything to you?'

'It is better so,' said the Princess, in a softer, mellower voice. 'There could be nothing but hard duty for you, even if it were possible for you to take the place of my son. You would not love me. Don't deny it,' she said, abruptly, putting up her hand. 'I know what is the truth. You don't like what I did. You are angry with me. You think I robbed you of something. You are on your grandfather's side, and you will always have a condemnation of me in your heart.'

Deronda felt himself under a ban of silence. He rose from his seat by her, preferring to stand if he had to obey that imperious prohibition of any tenderness. But his mother now looked up at him with a new admiration in her glance, saying –

'You are wrong to be angry with me. You are the better for what I did.' After pausing a little, she added, abruptly, 'And now tell me what you shall do.'

'Do you mean now, immediately,' said Deronda; 'or as to the course of my future life?'

'I mean in the future. What difference will it make to you that I have told you about your birth?'

'A very great difference,' said Deronda, emphatically. 'I can hardly think of anything that would make a greater difference.'

'What shall you do, then?' said the Princess, with more sharpness. 'Make yourself just like your grandfather – be what he wished you – turn yourself into a Jew like him?'

'That is impossible. The effect of my education can never be done away with. The Christian sympathies in which my mind was reared can never die out of me,' said Deronda, with increasing tenacity of tone. 'But I consider it my duty – it is the impulse of my feeling – to identify myself, as far as possible, with my hereditary people, and if I can see any work to be done for them that I can give my soul and hand to, I shall choose to do it.'

His mother had her eyes fixed on him with a wondering speculation, examining his face as if she thought that by close attention she could read a difficult language there. He bore her gaze very firmly, sustained by a resolute opposition, which was the expression of his fullest self. She bent towards him a little, and said, with a decisive emphasis –

'You are in love with a Jewess.'

Deronda coloured and said, 'My reasons would be independent of any such fact.'

'I know better. I have seen what men are,' said the Princess, peremptorily. 'Tell me the truth. She is a Jewess who will not accept any one but a Jew. There *are* a few such,' she added, with a touch of scorn.

Deronda had that objection to answer which we all have known in speaking to those who are too certain of their own fixed interpretations to be enlightened by anything we may say. But besides this, the point immediately in question was one on which he felt a repugnance either to deny or affirm. He remained silent, and she presently said –

'You love her as your father loved me, and she draws you after her as I drew him.'

Those words touched Deronda's filial imagination, and some tenderness in his glance was taken by his mother as an assent. She went on with rising passion. 'But I was leading him the other way. And now your grandfather is getting his revenge.'

'Mother,' said Deronda, remonstrantly, 'don't let us think of it in that way. I will admit that there may come some benefit from the education you chose for me. I prefer cherishing the benefit with gratitude, to dwelling with resentment on the injury. I think it would have been right that I should have been brought up with the consciousness that I was a Jew, but it must always have been a good to me to have as wide an instruction and sympathy as possible. And now, you have restored me my inheritance – events have brought a fuller restitution than you could have made – you have been saved from robbing my people of my service and me of my duty: can you not bring your whole soul to consent to this?'

Deronda paused in his pleading: his mother looked at him listeningly, as if the cadence of his voice were taking her ear, yet she shook her head slowly. He began again even more urgently.

'You have told me that you sought what you held the best for me: open your heart to relenting and love towards my grandfather, who sought what he held the best for you.'

'Not for me, no,' she said, shaking her head with more absolute denial, and folding her arms tightly. 'I tell you, he never thought of his daughter except as an instrument. Because I had wants outside his purpose, I was to be put in a frame and tortured. If that is the right law for the world, I will not say that I love it. If my acts were wrong – if it is God who is exacting from me that I should deliver up what I withheld – who is punishing me because I deceived my father and did not warn him that I should contradict his trust – well, I have told everything. I have done what I could. And *your* soul consents. That is enough. I have after

731

all been the instrument my father wanted. – "I desire a grandson who shall have a true Jewish heart. Every Jew should rear his family as if he hoped that a Deliverer might spring from it."'

In uttering these last sentences the Princess narrowed her eyes, waved her head up and down, and spoke slowly with a new kind of chest-voice, as if she were quoting unwillingly.

'Were those my grandfather's words?' said Deronda.

'Yes, yes; and you will find them written. I wanted to thwart him,' said the Princess, with a sudden outburst of the passion she had shown in the former interview. Then she added more slowly, 'You would have me love what I have hated from the time I was so high' – here she held her left hand a yard from the floor. – 'That can never be. But what does it matter? His yoke has been on me, whether I loved it or not. You are the grandson he wanted. You speak as men do – as if you felt yourself wise. What does it all mean?'

Her tone was abrupt and scornful. Deronda, in his pained feeling, and under the solemn urgency of the moment, had to keep a clutching remembrance of their relationship, lest his words should become cruel. He began in a deep, entreating tone.

'Mother, don't say that I feel myself wise. We are set in the midst of difficulties. I see no other way to get any clearness than by being truthful – not by keeping back facts which may – which should carry obligation within them – which should make the only guidance towards duty. No wonder if such facts come to reveal themselves in spite of concealments. The effects prepared by generations are likely to triumph over a contrivance which would bend them all to the satisfaction of self. Your will was strong, but my grandfather's trust which you accepted and did not fulfil – what you call his yoke – is the expression of something stronger, with deeper, farther-spreading roots, knit into the foundations of sacredness for all men. You renounced me – you still banish me – as a son' – there was an involuntary movement of indignation in Deronda's voice – 'But that stronger Something has determined that I shall be all the more the grandson whom also you willed to annihilate.'

His mother was watching him fixedly, and again her face gathered admiration. After a moment's silence she said, in a low persuasive tone –

'Sit down again,' and he obeyed, placing himself beside her. She laid her hand on his shoulder and went on.

'You rebuke me. Well – I am the loser. And you are angry because I banish you. What could you do for me but weary your own patience? Your mother is a shattered woman. My sense of life is little more than a sense of what was – except when the pain is present. You reproach me that I parted with you. I had joy enough without you then. Now you are come back to me, and I cannot make you a joy. Have you the cursing spirit of the Jew in you? Are you not able to forgive me? Shall you be glad to think that I am punished because I was not a Jewish mother to you?'

'How can you ask me that?' said Deronda remonstrantly. 'Have I not besought you that I might now at last be a son to you? My grief is that you have declared me helpless to comfort you. I would give up much that is dear for the sake of soothing your anguish.'

'You shall give up nothing,' said his mother, with the hurry of agitation. 'You shall be happy. You shall let me think of you as happy. I shall have done you no harm. You have no reason to curse me. You shall feel for me as they feel for the dead whom they say prayers for – you shall long that I may be freed from all suffering – from all punishment. And I shall see you instead of always seeing your grandfather. Is any harm come to him because the eleven years went by with no wretched *Kaddish* said for him? I cannot tell: – if you think *Kaddish* will help me – say it, say it. You will come between me and the dead. When I am in your mind, you will look as you do now – always as if you were a tender son, – always – as if I had been a tender mother.'

She seemed resolved that her agitation should not conquer her, but he felt her hand trembling on his shoulder. Deep, deep compassion hemmed in all words. With a face of beseeching he put his arm round her and pressed her head tenderly under his. They sat so for some moments. Then she lifted her head again and rose from her seat with a great sigh, as if in that breath she were dismissing a weight of thoughts. Deronda, standing in front of her, felt that the parting was near. But one of her swift alternations had come upon his mother.

'Is she beautiful?' she said, abruptly.

'Who?' said Deronda, changing colour.

'The woman you love.'

It was not a moment for deliberate explanation. He was obliged to say, 'Yes.'

'Not ambitious?'

'No, I think not.'

'Not one who must have a path of her own?'

'I think her nature is not given to make great claims.'

'She is not like that?' said the Princess, taking from her wallet a miniature with jewels round it, and holding it before her son. It was her own in all the fire of youth, and as Deronda looked at it with admiring sadness, she said, 'Had I not a rightful claim to be something more than a mere daughter and mother? The voice and the genius matched the face. Whatever else was wrong, acknowledge that I had a right to be an artist, though my father's will was against it. My nature gave me a charter.'

'I do acknowledge that,' said Deronda, looking from the miniature to her face, which even in its worn pallor had an expression of living force beyond anything that the pencil could show.

'Will you take the portrait?' said the Princess, more gently. 'If she is a kind woman, teach her to think of me kindly.'

'I shall be grateful for the portrait,' said Deronda, 'but – I ought to say, I have no assurance that she whom I love will have any love for me. I have kept silence.'

'Who and what is she?' said the mother. The question seemed a command.

'She was brought up as a singer for the stage,' said Deronda, with inward reluctance. 'Her father took her away early from her mother, and her life has been unhappy. She is very young – only twenty. Her father wished to bring her up in disregard – even in dislike of her Jewish origin, but she has clung with all her affection to the memory of her mother and the fellowship of her people.'

'Ah! like you. She is attached to the Judaism she knows nothing of,' said the Princess, peremptorily. 'That is poetry – fit to last through an opera night. Is she fond of her artist's life – is her singing worth anything?'

'Her singing is exquisite. But her voice is not suited to the stage. I think that the artist's life has been made repugnant to her.'

'Why, she is made for you, then. Sir Hugo said you were bitterly against being a singer, and I can see that you would never have let yourself be merged in a wife, as your father was.'

'I repeat,' said Deronda, emphatically – 'I repeat that I have no assurance of her love for me, of the possibility that we can ever be united. Other things – painful issues may lie before me. I have always felt that I should prepare myself to renounce, not cherish that prospect. But I suppose I might feel so of happiness in general. Whether it may come or not, one should try and prepare oneself to do without it.'

'Do you feel in that way?' said his mother, laying her hands on his shoulders, and perusing his face, while she spoke in a low meditative tone, pausing between her sentences. 'Poor boy!... I wonder how it would have been if I had kept you with me... whether you would have turned your heart to the old things... against mine... and we should have quarrelled... your grandfather would have been in you... and you would have hampered my life with your young growth from the old root.'

'I think my affection might have lasted through all our quarrelling,' said Deronda, saddened more and more, 'and that would not have hampered – surely it would have enriched your life.'

'Not then, not then . . . I did not want it then . . . I might have been glad of it now,' said the mother, with a bitter melancholy, 'if I could have been glad of anything.'

'But you love your other children, and they love you?' said Deronda, anxiously.

'Oh yes,' she answered, as to a question about a matter of course, while she folded her arms again. 'But,' . . . she added in a deeper tone, . . . 'I am not a loving woman. That is the truth. It is a talent to love – I lacked it. Others have loved me – and I have acted their love. I know very well what love makes of men and women – it is subjection. It takes another for a larger self, enclosing this one,' – she pointed to her own bosom. 'I was never willingly subject to any man. Men have been subject to me.'

'Perhaps the man who was subject was the happier of the two,' said Deronda – not with a smile, but with a grave, sad sense of his mother's privation.

'Perhaps – but I *was* happy – for a few years I was happy. If I had not been afraid of defeat and failure, I might have gone on. I miscalculated. What then? It is all over. Another life! Men talk of "another life," as if it only began on the other side of the grave. I have long entered on another life.' With the last words she raised her arms till they were bare to the elbow, her brow was contracted in one deep fold, her eyes were closed, her voice was smothered: in her dusky flame-coloured garment, she looked like a dreamed visitant from some region of departed mortals.

Deronda's feeling was wrought to a pitch of acuteness in which he was no longer quite master of himself. He gave an audible sob. His mother, opening her eyes, and letting her hands again rest on his shoulders, said –

'Good-bye, my son, good-bye. We shall hear no more of each other. Kiss me.'

He clasped his arms round her neck, and they kissed each other.

Deronda did not know how he got out of the room. He felt an older man. All his boyish yearnings and anxieties about his mother had vanished. He had gone through a tragic experience which must for ever solemnize his life, and deepen the significance of the acts by which he bound himself to others.

LIV

'The unwilling brain
Feigns often what it would not; and we trust
Imagination with such phantasies
As the tongue dares not fashion into words:
Which have no words, their horror makes them dim
To the mind's eye.'

— SHELLEY.

MADONNA PIA, whose husband, feeling himself injured by her, took her to his castle amid the swampy flats of the Maremma and got rid of her there, makes a pathetic figure in Dante's Purgatory, among the sinners who repented at the last and desire to be remembered compassionately by their fellow-countrymen. We know little about the grounds of mutual discontent between the Siennese couple, but we may infer with some confidence that the husband had never been a very delightful companion, and that on the flats of the Maremma his disagreeable manners had a background which threw them out remarkably; whence in his desire to punish his wife to the uttermost, the nature of things was so far against him that in relieving himself of her he could not avoid making the relief mutual. And thus, without any hardness to the poor Tuscan lady who had her deliverance long ago, one may feel warranted in thinking of her with a less sympathetic interest than of the better known Gwendolen who, instead of being delivered from her errors on earth and cleansed from their effect in purgatory, is at the very height of her entanglement in those fatal meshes which are woven within more closely than without, and often make the inward torture disproportionate to what is discernible as outward cause.

In taking his wife with him on a yachting expedition, Grandcourt had no intention to get rid of her; on the contrary, he wanted to feel more securely that she was his to do as he liked with, and to make her feel it also. Moreover, he was himself very fond of yachting: its dreamy do-nothing absolutism, unmolested by social demands, suited his disposition, and he did not in the least regard it as an equivalent for the dreariness of the Maremma. He had his reasons for carrying Gwendolen out of reach, but they were not reasons that can seem black in the mere statement. He suspected a growing spirit of opposition in her, and his feeling about the sentimental inclination she betrayed for Deronda was what in another man he would have called jealousy. In himself it seemed merely a resolution to put an end to such foolery as must have been going on in that prearranged visit of Deronda's which he had divined and interrupted.

And Grandcourt might have pleaded that he was perfectly justified in taking care that his wife should fulfil the obligations she had accepted. Their marriage was a contract where all the ostensible advantages were on her side, and it was only one of those advantages that her husband should use his power to hinder her from any injurious self-committal or unsuitable behaviour. He knew quite well that she had not married him – had not overcome her repugnance to certain facts – out of love to him personally; he had won her by the rank and luxuries he had to give her, and these she had got: he had fulfilled his side of the contract.

And Gwendolen, we know, was thoroughly aware of the situation. She could not excuse herself by saying that there had been a tacit part of the contract on her side – namely, that she meant to rule and have her own way. With all her early indulgence in the disposition to dominate, she was not one of the narrow-brained women who through life regard all their own selfish demands as rights, and every claim upon themselves as an injury. She had a root of conscience in her, and the process of purgatory had begun for her on the green earth: she knew that she had been wrong.

But now enter into the soul of this young creature as she found herself, with the blue Mediterranean dividing her from the world on the tiny plank-island of a yacht, the domain of the husband to whom she felt that she had sold herself, and had been paid the strict price – nay, paid more than she had dared to ask in the handsome maintenance of her mother: – the husband to whom she had sold her truthfulness and sense of justice, so that he held them throttled into silence, collared and dragged behind him to witness what he would, without remonstrance.

What had she to complain of? The yacht was of the prettiest; the cabin fitted up to perfection, smelling of cedar, soft-cushioned, hung with silk, expanded with mirrors; the crew such as suited an elegant toy, one of them having even ringlets, as well as a bronze complexion and fine teeth; and Mr. Lush was not there, for he had taken his way back to England as soon as he had seen all and everything on board. Moreover, Gwendolen herself liked the sea: it did not make her ill; and to observe the rigging of the vessel and forecast the necessary adjustments was a sort of amusement that might have gratified her activity and enjoyment of imaginary rule; the weather was fine, and they were coasting southward, where even the rain-furrowed, heat-cracked clay becomes gem-like with purple shadows, and where one may float between blue and blue in an open-eyed dream that the world has done with sorrow.

But what can still that hunger of the heart which sickens the eye for beauty, and makes sweet-scented ease an oppression? What sort of Moslem paradise would quiet the terrible fury of moral repulsion and cowed resistance which, like an eating pain intensifying into torture, concentrates the mind in that poisonous misery? While Gwendolen, throned on her cushions at evening, and beholding the glory of sea and sky softening as if with boundless love around her, was hoping that Grandcourt in his march up and down was not going to pause near her, not going to look at her or speak to her, some woman under a smoky sky, obliged to consider the price of eggs in arranging her dinner, was listening for the music of a footstep that would remove all risk from her foretaste of joy; some couple, bending, cheek by cheek, over a bit of work done by the one and delighted in by the other, were reckoning the earnings that would make them rich enough for a holiday among the furze and heather.

Had Grandcourt the least conception of what was going on in the breast of this wife? He conceived that she did not love him: but was that necessary? She was under his power, and he was not accustomed to soothe himself, as some cheerfully-disposed persons are, with the conviction that he was very generally and justly beloved. But what lay quite away from his conception was, that she could have any special repulsion for him personally. How could she? He himself knew what personal repulsion was – nobody better: his mind was much furnished with a sense of what brutes his fellow-creatures were, both masculine and feminine; what odious familiarities they had, what smirks, what modes of flourishing their handkerchiefs, what costume, what lavender-water, what bulging eyes, and what foolish notions of making themselves agreeable by remarks which were not wanted. In this critical view of mankind there was an affinity between him and Gwendolen before their marriage, and we know that she had been attractingly wrought upon by the refined negations he presented to her. Hence he understood her repulsion for Lush. But how was he to understand or conceive her present repulsion for Henleigh Grandcourt? Some men bring themselves to believe, and not merely maintain, the non-existence of an external world; a few others believe themselves objects of repulsion to a woman without being told so in plain language. But Grandcourt did not belong to this eccentric body of thinkers. He had all his life had reason to take a flattering view of his own attractiveness, and to place himself in fine antithesis to the men who, he saw at once, must be revolting to a woman of taste. He had no idea of a moral repulsion, and could not have believed, if he had been told, that there may be a resentment and disgust which will gradually make beauty more detestable than ugliness, through exasperation at that outward virtue in which hateful things can flaunt themselves or find a supercilious advantage.

How, then, could Grandcourt divine what was going on in Gwendolen's breast?

For their behaviour to each other scandalized no observer – not even the foreign maid warranted against seasickness; nor Grandcourt's own experienced valet; still less the picturesque crew, who regarded them as a model couple in high life. Their companionship consisted chiefly in a well-bred silence. Grandcourt had no humorous observations at which Gwendolen could refuse to smile, no chitchat to make small occasions of dispute. He was perfectly polite in arranging an additional garment over her when needful, and in handing her any object that he perceived her to need, and she could not fall into the vulgarity of accepting or rejecting such politeness rudely.

Grandcourt put up his telescope and said, 'There's a plantation of sugar-canes at the foot of that rock: should you like to look?'

Gwendolen said, 'Yes, please,' remembering that she must try and interest herself in sugar-canes as something outside her personal affairs. Then Grandcourt would walk up and down and smoke for a long while, pausing occasionally to point out a sail on the horizon, and at last would seat himself and look at Gwendolen with his narrow, immovable gaze, as if she were part of the complete yacht; while she, conscious of being looked at, was exerting her ingenuity not to meet his eyes. At dinner he would remark that the fruit was getting stale, and they must put in somewhere for more; or, observing that she did not drink the wine, he asked her if she would like any other kind better. A lady was obliged to respond to these things suitably; and even if she had not shrunk from quarrelling on other grounds, quarrelling with Grandcourt was impossible: she might as well have made angry remarks to a dangerous serpent ornamentally coiled in her cabin without invitation. And what sort of dispute could a woman of any pride and dignity begin on a yacht?

Grandcourt had an intense satisfaction in leading his wife captive after this fashion: it gave their life on a small scale a royal representation and publicity in which everything familiar was got rid of and everybody must do what was expected of them whatever might be their private protest – the protest (kept strictly private) adding to the piquancy of despotism.

To Gwendolen, who even in the freedom of her maiden time had had very faint glimpses of any heroism or sublimity, the medium that now thrust itself everywhere before her view was this husband and her relation to him. The beings closest to us, whether in love or hate, are often virtually our interpreters of the world, and some feather-headed gentleman or lady whom in passing we regret to take as legal tender for a human being may be acting as a melancholy theory of life in the minds of those who live with them – like a piece of yellow and wavy glass that distorts form and makes colour an affliction. Their trivial sentences, their petty standards, their low suspicions, their loveless *ennui*, may be making somebody else's life no better than a promenade through a pantheon of ugly idols. Gwendolen had that kind of window before her, affecting the distant equally with the near. Some unhappy wives are soothed by the possibility that they may become mothers; but Gwendolen felt that to desire a child for herself would have been a consenting to the completion of the injury she had been guilty of. She was reduced to dread lest she should become a mother. It was not the image of a new sweetly-budding life that came as a vision of deliverance from the monotony of distaste: it was an image of another sort. In the irritable, fluctuating stages of despair, gleams of hope came in the form of some possible accident. To dwell on the benignity of accident was a refuge from worse temptation.

The embitterment of hatred is often as unaccountable to onlookers as the growth of devoted love, and it not only seems but is really out of direct relation with any outward causes to be alleged. Passion is of the nature of seed, and finds nourishment within, tending to a predominance which determines all currents towards itself, and makes the whole life its tributary. And the intensest form of hatred is that rooted in fear, which compels to silence and drives vehemence into a constructive vindictiveness, an imaginary annihilation of the detested object, something like the hidden rites of vengeance with which the persecuted have made a dark vent for their rage, and soothed their suffering into dumbness. Such hidden rites went on in the secrecy of Gwendolen's mind, but not with soothing effect – rather with the effect of a struggling terror. Side by side with the dread of her husband had grown the self-dread which urged her to flee from the pursuing images wrought by her pent-up impulse. The vision of her past wrong-doing, and what it had brought on her, came with a pale ghastly illumination over every imagined deed that was a rash effort at freedom, such as she had made in her marriage. Moreover, she had learned to see all her acts through the impression they would make on Deronda: whatever relief might come to her, she could not sever it from the judgment of her that would be created in his mind. Not one word of flattery, of indulgence, of dependence on her favour, could be fastened on by her in all their intercourse, to weaken his restraining power over her (in this way Deronda's effort over himself was repaid); and amid the dreary uncertainties of her spoiled life the possible remedies that lay in his mind, nay, the remedy that lay in her feeling for him, made her only hope. He seemed to her a terrible-browed angel from whom she could not think of concealing any deed so as to win an ignorant regard from him: it belonged to the nature of their relation that she should be truthful, for his power over her had begun in the raising of a self-discontent which could be satisfied only by genuine change. But in no concealment had she now any confidence: her vision of what she had to dread took more decidedly than ever the form of some fiercely impulsive deed, committed as in a dream that she would instantaneously wake from to find the effects real though the images had been false: to find death under her hands, but instead of darkness, daylight; instead of satisfied hatred, the dismay of guilt; instead of freedom, the palsy of a new terror – a white dead face from which she was for ever trying to flee and for ever held back. She remembered Deronda's words: they were continually recurring in her thought –

'Turn your fear into a safeguard. Keep your dread fixed on the idea of increasing your remorse. . . . Take your fear as a safeguard. It is like quickness of hearing. It may make consequences passionately present to you.'

And so it was. In Gwendolen's consciousness Temptation and Dread met and stared like two pale phantoms, each seeing itself in the other – each obstructed by its own image; and all the while her fuller self beheld the apparitions and sobbed for deliverance from them.

Inarticulate prayers, no more definite than a cry, often swept out from her into the vast silence, unbroken except by her husband's breathing or the plash of the wave or the creaking of the masts; but if ever she thought of definite help, it took the form of Deronda's presence and words, of the sympathy he might have for her, of the direction he might give her. It was sometimes after a white-lipped, fierce-eyed temptation with murdering fingers had made its demon-visit that these best moments of inward crying and clinging for rescue would come to her, and she would lie with wide-open eyes in which the rising tears seemed a blessing, and the thought, 'I will not mind if I can keep from getting wicked,' seemed an answer to the indefinite prayer.

So the days passed, taking them with light breezes beyond and about the Balearic Isles, and then to Sardinia, and then with gentle change persuading them northward again towards Corsica. But this floating, gently-wafted existence, with its apparently peaceful influences, was becoming as bad as a nightmare to Gwendolen.

'How long are we to be yachting?' she ventured to ask one day after they had been touching at Ajaccio, and the

DANIEL DERONDA

mere fact of change in going ashore had given her a relief from some of the thoughts which seemed now to cling about the very rigging of the vessel, mix with the air in the red silk cabin below, and make the smell of the sea odious.

'What else should we do?' said Grandcourt. 'I'm not tired of it. I don't see why we shouldn't stay out any length of time. There's less to bore one in this way. And where would you go to? I'm sick of foreign places. And we shall have enough of Ryelands. Would you rather be at Ryelands?'

'Oh no,' said Gwendolen, indifferently, finding all places alike undesirable as soon as she imagined herself and her husband in them. 'I only wondered how long you would like this.'

'I like yachting longer than I like anything else,' said Grandcourt; 'and I had none last year. I suppose you are beginning to tire of it. Women are so confoundedly whimsical. They expect everything to give way to them.'

'Oh dear, no!' said Gwendolen, letting out her scorn in a flute-like tone. 'I never expect you to give way.'

'Why should I?' said Grandcourt, with his inward voice, looking at her, and then choosing an orange – for they were at table.

She made up her mind to a length of yachting that she could not see beyond; but the next day, after a squall which had made her rather ill for the first time, he came down to her and said –

'There's been the devil's own work in the night. The skipper says we shall have to stay at Genoa for a week while things are set right.'

'Do you mind that?' said Gwendolen, who lay looking very white amidst her white drapery.

'I should think so. Who wants to be broiling at Genoa?'

'It will be a change,' said Gwendolen, made a little incautious by her languor.

'*I* don't want any change. Besides, the place is intolerable; and one can't move along the roads. I shall go out in a boat, as I used to do, and manage it myself. One can get rid of a few hours every day in that way, instead of stiving in a damnable hotel.'

Here was a prospect which held hope in it. Gwendolen thought of hours when she would be alone, since Grandcourt would not want to take her in the said boat, and in her exultation at this unlooked-for relief, she had wild, contradictory fancies of what she might do with her freedom – that 'running away' which she had already innumerable times seen to be a worse evil than any actual endurance, now finding new arguments as an escape from her worst self. Also, visionary relief on a par with the fancy of a prisoner that the night wind may blow down the wall of his prison and save him from desperate devices, insinuated itself as a better alternative, lawful to wish for.

The fresh current of expectation revived her energies, and enabled her to take all things with an air of cheerfulness and alacrity that made a change marked enough to be noticed by her husband. She watched through the evening lights to the sinking of the moon with less of awed loneliness than was habitual to her – nay, with a vague impression that in this mighty frame of things there might be some preparation of rescue for her. Why not? – since the weather had just been on her side. This possibility of hoping, after her long fluctuation amid fears, was like a first return of hunger to the long-languishing patient.

She was waked the next morning by the casting of the anchor in the port of Genoa – waked from a strangely-mixed dream in which she felt herself escaping over the Mont Cenis, and wondering to find it warmer even in the moonlight on the snow, till suddenly she met Deronda, who told her to go back.

In an hour or so from that dream she actually met Deronda. But it was on the palatial staircase of the *Italia*, where she was feeling warm in her light woollen dress and straw hat; and her husband was by her side.

There was a start of surprise in Deronda before he could raise his hat and pass on. The moment did not seem to favour any closer greeting, and the circumstances under which they had last parted made him doubtful whether Grandcourt would be civilly inclined to him.

The doubt might certainly have been changed into a disagreeable certainty, for Grandcourt on this unaccountable appearance of Deronda at Genoa of all places, immediately tried to conceive how there could have been an arrangement between him and Gwendolen. It is true that before they were well in their rooms, he had seen how difficult it was to shape such an arrangement with any probability, being too cool-headed to find it at once easily credible that Gwendolen had not only while in London hastened to inform Deronda of the yachting project, but had posted a letter to him from Marseilles or Barcelona, advising him to travel to Genoa in time for the chance of meeting her there, or of receiving a letter from her telling of some other destination – all which must have implied a miraculous foreknowledge in her, and in Deronda a bird-like facility in flying about and perching idly. Still he was there, and though Grandcourt would not make a fool of himself by fabrications that others might call preposterous, he was not, for all that, disposed to admit fully that Deronda's presence was so far as Gwendolen was concerned a mere accident. It was a disgusting fact; that was enough; and no doubt she was well pleased. A man out of temper does not wait for proofs before feeling towards all things animate and inanimate as if they were in conspiracy against him, but at once thrashes his horse or kicks his dog in consequence. Grandcourt felt towards Gwendolen and Deronda as if he knew them to be in a conspiracy against him, and here was an event in league with them. What he took for clearly certain – and so far he divined the truth – was that Gwendolen was now counting on an interview with Deronda whenever her husband's back was turned.

As he sat taking his coffee at a convenient angle for observing her, he discerned something which he felt sure was the effect of a secret delight – some fresh ease in moving and speaking, some peculiar meaning in her eyes, whatever she looked on. Certainly her troubles had not marred her beauty. Mrs. Grandcourt was handsomer than Gwendolen Harleth: her grace and expression were informed by a greater variety of inward experience, giving new play to the facial muscles, new attitudes in movement and repose; her whole person and air had the nameless something which often makes a woman more interesting after marriage than before, less confident that all things are according to her opinion, and yet with less of deer-like shyness – more fully a human being.

This morning the benefits of the voyage seemed to be suddenly revealing themselves in a new elasticity of mien. As she rose from the table and put her two heavily-jewelled hands on each side of her neck, according to her wont, she had no art to conceal that sort of joyous expectation which makes the present more bearable than usual, just as when a man means to go out he finds it easier to be amiable to the family for a quarter of an hour beforehand. It is not impossible that a terrier whose pleasure was concerned would perceive those amiable signs and know their meaning – know why his master stood in a peculiar way, talked with alacrity, and even had a peculiar gleam in his eye, so that on the least movement towards the door, the terrier would scuttle to be in time. And, in dog fashion, Grandcourt discerned the signs of Gwendolen's expectation, interpreting them with the narrow correctness which leaves a world of unknown feeling behind.

'A – just ring, please, and tell Gibbs to order some dinner for us at three,' said Grandcourt, as he too rose, took out a cigar, and then stretched his hand towards the hat that lay near. 'I'm going to send Angus to find me a little sailing-boat for us to go out in; one that I can manage, with you at the tiller. It's uncommonly pleasant these fine evenings – the least boring of anything we can do.'

Gwendolen turned cold: there was not only the cruel disappointment – there was the immediate conviction that her husband had determined to take her because he would not leave her out of his sight; and probably this dual solitude in a boat was the more attractive to him because it would be wearisome to her. They were not on the plank-island; she felt it the more possible to begin a contest. But the gleaming content had died out of her. There was a change in her like that of a glacier after sunset.

'I would rather not go in the boat,' she said. 'Take some one else with you.'

'Very well; if you don't go, I shall not go,' said Grandcourt. 'We shall stay suffocating here, that's all.'

'I can't bear going in a boat,' said Gwendolen, angrily.

'That is a sudden change,' said Grandcourt, with a slight sneer. 'But since you decline, we shall stay indoors.'

He laid down his hat again, lit his cigar, and walked up and down the room, pausing now and then to look out of the windows. Gwendolen's temper told her to persist. She knew very well now that Grandcourt would not go without her; but if he must tyrannize over her, he should not do it precisely in the way he would choose. She would oblige him to stay in the hotel. Without speaking again she passed into the adjoining bedroom and threw herself into a chair with her anger, seeing no purpose or issue – only feeling that the wave of evil had rushed back upon her, and dragged her away from her momentary breathing-place.

Presently Grandcourt came in with his hat on, but threw it off and sat down sideways on a chair nearly in front of her, saying, in his superficial drawl –

'Have you come round yet? or do you find it agreeable to be out of temper? You make things uncommonly pleasant for me.'

'Why do you want to make them unpleasant for *me*?' said Gwendolen, getting helpless again, and feeling the hot tears rise.

'Now, will you be good enough to say what it is you have to complain of?' said Grandcourt, looking into her eyes, and using his most inward voice. 'Is it that I stay indoors when you stay?'

She could give no answer. The sort of truth that made any excuse for her anger could not be uttered. In the conflict of despair and humiliation she began to sob, and the tears rolled down her cheeks – a form of agitation which she had never shown before in her husband's presence.

'I hope this is useful,' said Grandcourt, after a moment or two. 'All I can say is, it's most confoundedly unpleasant. What the devil women can see in this kind of thing, I don't know. *You* see something to be got by it, of course. All I can see is, that we shall be shut up here when we might have been having a pleasant sail.'

'Let us go, then,' said Gwendolen, impetuously, 'Perhaps we shall be drowned.' She began to sob again.

This extraordinary behaviour, which had evidently some relation to Deronda, gave more definiteness to Grandcourt's conclusions. He drew his chair quite close in front of her, and said, in a low tone, 'Just be quiet and listen, will you?'

There seemed to be a magical effect in this close vicinity. Gwendolen shrank and ceased to sob. She kept her eyelids down, and clasped her hands tightly.

'Let us understand each other,' said Grandcourt, in the same tone. 'I know very well what this nonsense means. But if you suppose I am going to let you make a fool of me, just dismiss that notion from your mind. What are you looking forward to, if you can't behave properly as my wife? There is disgrace for you, if you like to have it, but I don't know anything else; and as to Deronda, it's quite clear that he hangs back from you.'

'It is all false!' said Gwendolen, bitterly. 'You don't in the least imagine what is in my mind. I have seen enough of the disgrace that comes in that way. And you had better leave me at liberty to speak with any one I like. It would be better for you.'

'You will allow me to judge of that,' said Grandcourt, rising and moving to a little distance towards the window, but standing there playing with his whiskers as if he were awaiting something.

Gwendolen's words had so clear and tremendous a meaning for herself, that she thought they must have expressed it to Grandcourt, and had no sooner uttered them than she dreaded their effect. But his soul was garrisoned against presentiments and fears: he had the courage and confidence that belong to domination, and he was at that moment feeling perfectly satisfied that he held his wife with bit and bridle. By the time they had been married a year she would cease to be restive. He continued standing with his air of indifference, till she felt her habitual stifling consciousness of having an immovable obstruction in her life, like the nightmare of beholding a single form that serves to arrest all passage though the wide country lies open.

'What decision have you come to?' he said, presently, looking at her. 'What orders shall I give?'

'Oh, let us go,' said Gwendolen. The walls had begun to be an imprisonment, and while there was breath in this man he would have the mastery over her. His words had the power of thumbscrews and the cold touch of the rack. To resist was to act like a stupid animal unable to measure results.

So the boat was ordered. She even went down to the quay again with him to see it before mid-day. Grandcourt had recovered perfect quietude of temper, and had a scornful satisfaction in the attention given by the nautical groups to the *milord*, owner of the handsome yacht which had just put in for repairs, and who being an Englishman was naturally so at home on the sea, that he could manage a sail with the same ease that he could manage a horse. The sort of exultation he had discerned in Gwendolen this morning she now thought that she discerned in him; and it was true that he had set his mind on this boating, and carried out his purpose as something that people might not expect him to do, with the gratified impulse of a strong will which had nothing better to exert itself upon. He had remarkable physical courage, and was proud of it – or rather he had a great contempt for the coarser, bulkier men who generally had less. Moreover, he was ruling that Gwendolen should go with him.

And when they came down again at five o'clock, equipped for their boating, the scene was as good as a theatrical representation for all beholders. This handsome, fair-skinned English couple manifesting the usual eccentricity of their nation, both of them proud, pale, and calm, without a smile on their faces, moving like creatures who were fulfilling a supernatural destiny – it was a thing to go out and see, a thing to paint. The husband's chest, back, and arms, showed very well in his close-fitting dress, and the wife was declared to be like a statue.

Some suggestions were proffered concerning a possible change in the breeze, and the necessary care in putting about, but Grandcourt's manner made the speakers understand that they were too officious, and that he knew better than they.

Gwendolen, keeping her impassible air, as they moved away from the strand, felt her imagination obstinately at work. She was not afraid of any outward dangers – she was afraid of her own wishes, which were taking shapes possible and impossible, like a cloud of demon-faces. She was afraid of her own hatred, which under the cold iron touch that had compelled her to-day had gathered a fierce intensity. As she sat guiding the tiller under her husband's eyes, doing just what he told her, the strife within her seemed like her own effort to escape from herself. She clung to the thought of Deronda: she persuaded herself that he would not go away while she was there – he knew that she needed help. The sense that he was there would save her from acting out the evil within. And yet quick, quick, came images, plans of evil that would come again and seize her in the night, like furies preparing the deed that they would straightway avenge.

They were taken out of the port and carried eastward by a gentle breeze. Some clouds tempered the sunlight, and the hour was always deepening towards the supreme beauty of evening. Sails larger and smaller changed their aspect like sensitive things, and made a cheerful companionship, alternately near and far. The grand city shone more vaguely, the mountains looked out above it, and there was stillness as in an island sanctuary. Yet suddenly Gwendolen let her hands fall, and said in a scarcely audible tone, 'God help me!'

'What is the matter?' said Grandcourt, not distinguishing the words.

'Oh, nothing,' said Gwendolen, rousing herself from her momentary forgetfulness and resuming the ropes.

'Don't you find this pleasant?' said Grandcourt.

'Very.'

'You admit now we couldn't have done anything better?'

'No – I see nothing better. I think we shall go on always, like the Flying Dutchman,' said Gwendolen, wildly.

Grandcourt gave her one of his narrow, examining glances, and then said, 'If you like, we can go to Spezia in the morning, and let them take us up there.'

'No; I shall like nothing better than this.'

'Very well; we'll do the same to-morrow. But we must be turning in soon. I shall put about.'

LV

'Ritorna a tua scienza
Che vuol, quanto la cosa è più perfetta
Più senta il bene, e così la doglienza.'
— DANTE.

WHEN Deronda met Gwendolen and Grandcourt on the staircase, his mind was seriously preoccupied. He had just been summoned to the second interview with his mother.

In two hours after his parting from her he knew that the Princess Halm-Eberstein had left the hotel, and so far as the purpose of his journey to Genoa was concerned he might himself have set off on his way to Mainz, to deliver the letter from Joseph Kalonymos, and get possession of the family chest. But mixed mental conditions, which did not resolve themselves into definite reasons, hindered him from departure. Long after the farewell he was kept passive by a weight of retrospective feeling. He lived again, with the new keenness of emotive memory, through the exciting scenes which seemed past only in the sense of preparation for their actual presence in his soul. He allowed himself in his solitude to sob, with perhaps more than a woman's acuteness of compassion, over that woman's life, so near to his, and yet so remote. He beheld the world changed for him by the certitude of ties that altered the poise of hopes and fears, and gave him a new sense of fellowship, as if under cover of the night he had joined the wrong band of wanderers, and found with the rise of morning that the tents of his kindred were grouped far off. He had a quivering imaginative sense of close relation to the grandfather who had been animated by strong impulses and beloved thoughts, which were now perhaps being roused from their slumber within himself. And through all this passionate meditation Mordecai and Mirah were always present, as beings who clasped hands with him in sympathetic silence.

Of such quick, responsive fibre was Deronda made, under that mantle of self-controlled reserve into which early experience had thrown so much of his young strength.

When the persistent ringing of a bell as a signal reminded him of the hour, he thought of looking into *Bradshaw*, and making the brief necessary preparations for starting by the next train – thought of it, but made no movement in consequence. Wishes went to Mainz and what he was to get possession of there – to London and the beings there who made the strongest attachments of his life; but there were other wishes that clung in these moments to Genoa, and they kept him where he was, by that force which urges us to linger over an interview that carries a presentiment of final farewell or of overshadowing sorrow. Deronda did not formally say, 'I will stay over to-night, because it is Friday, and I should like to go to the evening service at the synagogue where they must all have gone; and besides, I may see the Grandcourts again.' But simply, instead of packing and ringing for his bill, he sat doing nothing at all, while his mind went to the synagogue and saw faces there probably little different from those of his grandfather's time, and heard the Spanish-Hebrew liturgy which had lasted through the seasons of wandering generations like a plant with wandering seed, that gives the far-off lands a kinship to the exile's home – while, also, his mind went towards Gwendolen, with anxious remembrance of what had been, and with a half-admitted impression that it would be hardness in him willingly to go away at once without making some effort, in spite of Grandcourt's probable dislike, to manifest the continuance of his sympathy with her since their abrupt parting.

In this state of mind he deferred departure, ate his dinner without sense of flavour, rose from it quickly to find the synagogue, and in passing the porter asked if Mr. and Mrs. Grandcourt were still in the hotel, and what was the number of their apartment. The porter gave him the number, but added that they were gone out boating. That information had somehow power enough over Deronda to divide his thoughts with the memories wakened among the sparse *taliths* and keen dark faces of worshippers whose way of taking awful prayers and invocations with the easy familiarity which might be called Hebrew dyed Italian, made him reflect that his grandfather, according to the Princess's hints of his character, must have been almost as exceptional a Jew as Mordecai. But were not men of ardent zeal and far-reaching hope everywhere exceptional? – the men who had the visions which, as Mordecai said, were the creators and feeders of the world – moulding and feeding the more passive life which without them would dwindle and shrivel into the narrow tenacity of insects, unshaken by thoughts beyond the reaches of their antennæ. Something of a mournful impatience perhaps added itself to the solicitude about Gwendolen (a solicitude that had room to grow in his present release from immediate cares) as an incitement to hasten from the synagogue and choose to take his evening walk towards the quay, always a favourite haunt with him, and just now attractive with the possibility that he might be in time to see the Grandcourts come in from their boating. In this case, he resolved that he would advance to greet them deliberately, and ignore any grounds that the husband might have for wishing him elsewhere.

The sun had set behind a bank of cloud, and only a faint yellow light was giving its farewell kisses to the waves, which were agitated by an active breeze. Deronda, sauntering slowly within sight of what took place on the strand, observed the groups there concentrating their attention on a sailing boat which was advancing swiftly landward, being rowed by two men. Amidst the clamorous talk in various languages, Deronda held it the surer means of getting information not to ask questions, but to elbow his way to the foreground and be an unobstructed witness of what was occurring. Telescopes were being used, and loud statements made that the boat held somebody who had been drowned. One said it was the *milord* who had gone out in a

DANIEL DERONDA

sailing boat; another maintained that the prostrate figure he discerned was *miladi*; a Frenchman who had no glass would rather say that it was *milord* who had probably taken his wife out to drown her, according to the national practice – a remark which an English skipper immediately commented on in our native idiom (as nonsense which – had undergone a mining operation), and further dismissed by the decision that the reclining figure was a woman. For Deronda, terribly excited by fluctuating fears, the strokes of the oars as he watched them were divided by swift visions of events, possible and impossible, which might have brought about this issue, or this broken-off fragment of an issue, with a worse half undisclosed – if this woman apparently snatched from the waters were really Mrs. Grandcourt.

But soon there was no longer any doubt: the boat was being pulled to land and he saw Gwendolen half raising herself on her hands, by her own effort, under her heavy covering of tarpaulin and pea-jackets – pale as one of the sheeted dead, shivering, with wet hair streaming, a wild amazed consciousness in her eyes, as if she had waked up in a world where some judgment was impending, and the beings she saw around were coming to seize her. The first rower who jumped to land was also wet through, and ran off; the sailors, close about the boat, hindered Deronda from advancing, and he could only look on while Gwendolen gave scared glances, and seemed to shrink with terror as she was carefully, tenderly helped out, and led on by the strong arms of those rough, bronzed men, her wet clothes clinging about her limbs, and adding to the impediment of her weakness. Suddenly her wandering eyes fell on Deronda, standing before her, and immediately, as if she had been expecting him and looking for him, she tried to stretch out her arms, which were held back by her supporters, saying in a muffled voice –

'It is come, it is come! He is dead!'

'Hush, hush!' said Deronda, in a tone of authority; 'quiet yourself.' Then, to the men who were assisting

758

her, 'I am a connection of this lady's husband. If you will get her on to the *Italia* as quickly as possible, I will undertake everything else.'

He stayed behind to hear from the remaining boatman that her husband had gone down irrecoverably, and that his boat was left floating empty. He and his comrade had heard a cry, had come up in time to see the lady jump in after her husband, and had got her out fast enough to save her from much damage.

After this, Deronda hastened to the hotel, to assure himself that the best medical help would be provided; and being satisfied on this point, he telegraphed the event to Sir Hugo, begging him to come forthwith, and also to Mr. Gascoigne, whose address at the Rectory made his nearest known way of getting the information to Gwendolen's mother. Certain words of Gwendolen's in the past had come back to him with the effectiveness of an inspiration: in moments of agitated confession she had spoken of her mother's presence as a possible help, if she could have had it.

LVI

'The pang, the curse with which they died,
    Had never passed away;
I could not draw my eyes from theirs,
    Nor lift them up to pray.'
                    – COLERIDGE.

DERONDA did not take off his clothes that night. Gwendolen, after insisting on seeing him again before she would consent to be undrest, had been perfectly quiet, and had only asked him, with a whispering, repressed eagerness, to promise that he would come to her when she sent for him in the morning. Still, the possibility that a change might come over her, the danger of a supervening feverish condition, and the suspicion that something in the late catastrophe was having an effect which might betray itself in excited words, acted as a foreboding within him. He mentioned to her attendant that he should keep himself ready to be called if there were any alarming change of symptoms, making it understood by all concerned that he was in communication with her friends in England, and felt bound meanwhile to take all care on her behalf – a position which it was the easier for him to assume, because he was well known to Grandcourt's valet, the only old servant who had come on the late voyage.

But when fatigue from the strangely various emotion of the day at last sent Deronda to sleep, he remained undisturbed except by the morning dreams which came as a tangled web of yesterday's events, and finally waked him with an image drawn by his pressing anxiety.

Still, it was morning, and there had been no summons – an augury which cheered him while he made his toilet, and reflected that it was too early to send inquiries. Later, he learned that she had passed a too wakeful night, but had shown no violent signs of agitation, and was at last sleeping. He wondered at the force that dwelt in this creature, so alive to dread; for he had an irresistible impression that even under the effects of a severe physical shock she was mastering herself with a determination of concealment. For his own part, he thought that his sensibilities had been blunted by what he had been going through in the meeting with his mother: he seemed to himself now to be only fulfilling claims, and his more passionate sympathy was in abeyance. He had lately been living so keenly in an experience quite apart from Gwendolen's lot, that his present cares for her were like a revisiting of scenes famil-iar in the past, and there was not yet a complete revival of the inward response to them.

Meanwhile he employed himself in getting a formal, legally-recognized statement from the fishermen who had rescued Gwendolen. Few details came to light. The boat in which Grandcourt had gone out had been found drifting with its sail loose, and had been towed in. The fishermen thought it likely that he had been knocked overboard by the flapping of the sail while putting about, and that he had not known how to swim; but, though they were near, their attention had been first arrested by a cry which seemed like that of a man in distress, and while they were hasten-ing with their oars, they heard a shriek from the lady, and saw her jump in.

On re-entering the hotel, Deronda was told that Gwendolen had risen, and was desiring to see him. He was shown into a room darkened by blinds and curtains, where she was seated with a white shawl wrapped round her, looking towards the opening door like one waiting uneasily. But her long hair was gathered up and coiled carefully, and, through all, the blue stars in her ears had kept their place: as she started impulsively to her full height, sheathed in her white shawl, her face and neck not less white, except for a purple line under her eyes, her lips a little apart with the peculiar expression of one accused and helpless, she looked like the unhappy ghost of that Gwendolen Harleth whom Deronda had seen turn-ing with firm lips and proud self-possession from her losses at the gaming-table. The sight pierced him with pity, and the effects of all their past relation began to revive within him.

'I beseech you to rest – not to stand,' said Deronda, as he approached her; and she obeyed, falling back into her chair again.

'Will you sit down near me?' she said. 'I want to speak very low.'

She was in a large arm-chair, and he drew a small one near to her side. The action seemed to touch her peculiarly: turning her pale face full upon his, which was very near, she said, in the lowest audible tone, 'You know I am a guilty woman?'

Deronda himself turned paler as he said, 'I know nothing.' He did not dare to say more.

'He is dead.' She uttered this with the same undertoned decision.

'Yes,' said Deronda, in a mournful suspense which made him reluctant to speak.

'His face will not be seen above the water again,' said Gwendolen, in a tone that was not louder, but of a suppressed eagerness, while she held both her hands clenched.

'No.'

'Not by any one else – only by me – a dead face – I shall never get away from it.'

It was with an inward voice of desperate self-repression that she spoke these last words, while she looked away from Deronda towards something at a distance from her on the floor. Was she seeing the whole event – her own acts included – through an exaggerating medium of excitement and horror? Was she in a state of delirium into which there entered a sense of concealment and necessity for self-repression? Such thoughts glanced through Deronda as a sort of hope. But imagine the conflict of feeling that kept him silent. She was bent on confession, and he dreaded hearing her confession. Against his better will, he shrank from the task that was laid on him: he wished, and yet rebuked the wish as cowardly, that she could bury her secrets in her own bosom. He was not a priest. He dreaded the weight of this woman's soul flung upon his own with imploring dependence. But she spoke again, hurriedly, looking at him –

'You will not say that I ought to tell the world? you will not say that I ought to be disgraced? I could not do it. I could not bear it. I cannot have my mother know. Not if I were dead. I could not have her know. I must tell you; but you will not say that any one else should know.'

'I can say nothing in my ignorance,' said Deronda, mournfully, 'except that I desire to help you.'

'I told you from the beginning – as soon as I could – I told you I was afraid of myself.' There was a piteous pleading in the low murmur to which Deronda turned his ear only. Her face afflicted him too much. 'I felt a hatred in me that was always working like an evil spirit – contriving things. Everything I could do to free myself came into my mind; and it got worse – all things got worse. That was why I asked you to come to me in town. I thought then I would tell you the worst about myself. I tried. But I could not tell everything. And *he* came in.'

She paused, while a shudder passed through her; but soon went on.

'I will tell you everything now. Do you think a woman who cried, and prayed, and struggled to be saved from herself, could be a murderess?'

'Great God!' said Deronda, in a deep, shaken voice, 'don't torture me needlessly. You have not murdered him. You threw yourself into the water with the impulse to save him. Tell me the rest afterwards. This death was an accident that you could not have hindered.'

'Don't be impatient with me.' The tremor, the childlike beseeching in these words compelled Deronda to turn his head and look at her face. The poor quivering lips went on. 'You said – you used to say – you felt more for those who had done something wicked and were miserable; you said they might get better – they might be scourged into something better. If you had not spoken in that way, everything would have been worse. I *did* remember all you said to me. It came to me always. It came to me at the very last – that was the reason why I— But now, if you cannot bear with me when I tell you everything – if you turn away from me and forsake me, what shall I do? Am I worse than I was when you found me and wanted to make me better? All the wrong I have done was in me then – and more – and more—if you had not come and been patient with me. And now – will you forsake me?'

Her hands which had been so tightly clenched some minutes before, were now helplessly relaxed and trembling on the arm of her chair. Her quivering lips remained parted as she ceased speaking. Deronda could not answer; he was obliged to look away. He took one of her hands, and clasped it as if they were going to walk together like two children: it was the only way in which he could answer, 'I will not forsake you.' And all the while he felt as if he were putting his name to a blank paper which might be filled up terribly. Their attitude, his averted face with its expression of a suffering which he was solemnly resolved to undergo, might have told half the truth of the situation to a beholder who had suddenly entered.

That grasp was an entirely new experience to Gwendolen: she had never before had from any man a sign of tenderness which her own being had needed, and she interpreted its powerful effect on her into a promise of inexhaustible patience and constancy. The stream of renewed strength made it possible for her to go on as she had begun – with that fitful, wandering confession where the sameness of experience seems to nullify the sense of time or of order in events. She began again in a fragmentary way –

'All sorts of contrivances in my mind – but all so difficult. And I fought against them – I was terrified at them – I saw his dead face' – here her voice sank almost to a whisper close to Deronda's ear – 'ever so long ago I saw it; and I wished him to be dead. And yet it terrified me. I was like two creatures. I could not speak – I wanted to kill – it was as strong as thirst – and then directly – I felt beforehand I had done something dreadful, unalterable – that would make me like an evil spirit. And it came – it came.'

She was silent a moment or two, as if her memory had lost itself in a web where each mesh drew all the rest.

'It had all been in my mind when I first spoke to you – when we were at the Abbey. I had done something then. I could not tell you that. It was the only thing I did towards carrying out my thoughts. They went about over everything; but they all remained like dreadful dreams – all but one. I did one act – and I never undid it – it is there still – as long ago as when we were at Ryelands. There it was – something my fingers longed for among the beautiful toys in the cabinet in my boudoir – small and sharp, like a long willow leaf in a silver sheath. I locked it in the drawer of my dressing-case. I was continually haunted with it, and how I should use it. I fancied myself putting it under my pillow. But I never did. I never looked at it again. I dared not unlock the drawer: it had a key all to itself; and not long ago, when we were in the yacht, I dropped the key into the deep water. It was my wish to drop it and deliver myself. After that I began to think how I could open the drawer without the key; and when I found we were to stay in Genoa, it came into my mind that I could get it opened privately at the hotel. But then, when we were going up the stairs, I met you; and I thought I should talk to you alone and tell you this – everything I could not tell you in town; and then I was forced to go out in the boat.'

A sob had for the first time risen with the last words, and she sank back in her chair. The memory of that acute disappointment seemed for the moment to efface what had come since. Deronda did not look at her, but he said, insistently –

'And it has all remained in your imagination. It has gone on only in your thought. To the last the evil temptation has been resisted?'

There was silence. The tears had rolled down her cheeks. She pressed her handkerchief against them and sat upright. She was summoning her resolution; and again, leaning a little towards Deronda's ear, she began in a whisper –

'No, no; I will tell you everything as God knows it. I will tell you no falsehood; I will tell you the exact truth. What should I do else? I used to think I could never be wicked. I thought of wicked people as if they were a long way off me. Since then I have been wicked. I have felt wicked. And everything has been a punishment to me – all the things I used to wish for – it is as if they had been made red-hot. The very daylight has often been a punishment to me. Because – you know – I ought not to have married. That was the beginning of it. I wronged some one else. I broke my promise. I meant to get pleasure for myself, and it all turned to misery. I wanted to make my gain out of another's loss – you remember? – it was like roulette – and the money burnt into me. And I could not complain. It was as if I had prayed that another should lose and I should win. And I had won. I knew it all – I knew I was guilty. When we were on the sea, and I lay awake at night in the cabin, I sometimes felt that everything I had done lay open with-out excuse – nothing was hidden – how could anything be known to me only? – it was not my own knowledge, it was God's that had entered into me; and even the stillness – everything held a punishment for me – everything but you. I always thought that you would not want me to be pun-ished – you would have tried and helped me to be better. And only thinking of that helped me. You will not change – you will not want to punish me now?'

Again a sob had risen.

'God forbid!' groaned Deronda. But he sat motionless.

This long wandering with the poor conscience-stricken one over her past was difficult to bear, but he dared not again urge her with a question. He must let her mind follow its own need. She unconsciously left intervals in her retrospect, not clearly distinguishing between what she said and what she had only an inward vision of. Her next words came after such an interval.

'That all made it so hard when I was forced to go in the boat. Because when I saw you it was an unexpected joy, and I thought I could tell you everything – about the locked-up drawer and what I had not told you before. And if I had told you, and knew it was in your mind, it would have less power over me. I hoped and trusted in that. For after all my struggles and my crying, the hatred and rage, the temptation that frightened me, the longing, the thirst for what I dreaded, always came back. And that disappointment – when I was quite shut out from speaking to you, and I was driven to go in the boat – brought all the evil back, as if I had been locked in a prison with it and no escape. Oh, it seems so long ago now since I stepped into that boat! I could have given up everything in that moment, to have the forked lightning for a weapon to strike him dead.'

Some of the compressed fierceness that she was recalling seemed to find its way into her undertoned utterance. After a little silence she said, with agitated hurry –

'If he were here again, what should I do? I cannot wish him here – and yet I cannot bear his dead face. I was a coward. I ought to have borne contempt. I ought to have gone away – gone and wandered like a beggar rather than stay to feel like a fiend. But turn where I would there was something I could not bear. Sometimes I thought he would kill *me* if I resisted his will. But now – his dead face is there, and I cannot bear it.'

Suddenly loosing Deronda's hand, she started up, stretching her arms to their full length upward, and said with a sort of moan –

'I have been a cruel woman! What can *I* do but cry for help? *I* am sinking. Die – die – you are forsaken – go down, go down into darkness. Forsaken – no pity – *I* shall be forsaken.'

She sank in her chair again and broke into sobs. Even Deronda had no place in her consciousness at that moment. He was completely unmanned. Instead of finding, as he had imagined, that his late experience had dulled

767

his susceptibility to fresh emotion, it seemed that the lot of this young creature, whose swift travel from her bright rash girlhood into this agony of remorse he had had to behold in helplessness, pierced him the deeper because it came close upon another sad revelation of spiritual conflict: he was in one of those moments when the very anguish of passionate pity makes us ready to choose that we will know pleasure no more, and live only for the stricken and afflicted. He had risen from his seat while he watched that terrible outburst – which seemed the more awful to him because, even in this supreme agitation, she kept the suppressed voice of one who confesses in secret. At last he felt impelled to turn his back towards her and walk to a distance.

But presently there was stillness. Her mind had opened to the sense that he had gone away from her. When Deronda turned round to approach her again, he saw her face bent towards him, her eyes dilated, her lips parted. She was an image of timid forlorn beseeching – too timid to entreat in words while he kept himself aloof from her. Was she forsaken by him – now – already? But his eyes met hers sorrowfully – met hers for the first time fully since she had said, 'You know I am a guilty woman;' and that full glance in its intense mournfulness seemed to say, 'I know it, but I shall all the less forsake you.' He sat down by her side again in the same attitude – without turning his face towards her and without again taking her hand.

Once more Gwendolen was pierced, as she had been by his face of sorrow at the Abbey, with a compunction less egoistic than that which urged her to confess, and she said, in a tone of loving regret –

'I make you very unhappy.'

Deronda gave an indistinct 'Oh,' just shrinking together and changing his attitude a little. Then he had gathered resolution enough to say clearly, 'There is no question of being happy or unhappy. What I most desire at this moment is what will most help you. Tell me all you feel it a relief to tell.'

Devoted as these words were, they widened his spiritual distance from her, and she felt it more difficult to speak: she had a vague need of getting nearer to that compassion which seemed to be regarding her from a halo of superiority, and the need turned into an impulse to humble herself more. She was ready to throw herself on her knees before him; but no – her wonderfully mixed consciousness held checks on that impulse, and she was kept silent and motionless by the pressure of opposing needs. Her stillness made Deronda at last say –

'Perhaps you are too weary. Shall I go away, and come again whenever you wish it?'

'No, no,' said Gwendolen – the dread of his leaving her bringing back her power of speech. She went on with her low-toned eagerness, 'I want to tell you what it was that came over me in that boat. I was full of rage at being obliged to go – full of rage – and I could do nothing but sit there like a galley-slave. And then we got away – out of the port – into the deep – and everything was still – and we never looked at each other, only he spoke to order me – and the very light about me seemed to hold me a prisoner and force me to sit as I did. It came over me that when I was a child I used to fancy sailing away into a world where people were not forced to live with any one they did not like – I did not like my father-in-law to come home. And now, I thought just the opposite had come to me. I had stept into a boat, and my life was a sailing and sailing away – gliding on and no help – always into solitude with *him*, away from deliverance. And because I felt more helpless than ever, my thoughts went out over worse things – I longed for worse things – I had cruel wishes – I fancied impossible ways of— I did not want to die myself; I was afraid of our being drowned together. If it had been any use I should have prayed – that something might befall him. I should have prayed that he might sink out of my sight and leave me alone. I knew no way of killing him there, but I did, I did kill him in my thoughts.'

She sank into silence for a minute, submerged by the weight of memory which no words could represent.

'But yet all the while I felt that I was getting more wicked. And what had been with me so much, came to me just then – what you once said – about dreading to increase my wrong-doing and my remorse – I should hope for nothing then. It was all like a writing of fire within me. Getting wicked was misery – being shut out for ever from knowing what you – what better lives were. That had always been coming back to me in the midst of bad thoughts – it came back to me then – but yet with a despair – a feeling that it was no use – evil wishes were too strong. I remember then letting go the tiller and saying "God help me!" But then I was forced to take it again and go on; and the evil longings, the evil prayers came again and blotted everything else dim, till, in the midst of them – I don't know how it was – he was turning the sail – there was a gust – he was struck – I know nothing – I only know that I saw my wish outside me.'

She began to speak more hurriedly, and in more of a whisper.

'I saw him sink, and my heart gave a leap as if it were going out of me. I think I did not move. I kept my hands tight. It was long enough for me to be glad, and yet to think it was no use – he would come up again. And he *was* come – farther off – the boat had moved. It was all like lightning. "The rope!" he called out in a voice – not his own – I hear it now – and I stooped for the rope – I felt I must – I felt sure he could swim, and he would come back whether or not, and I dreaded him. That was in my mind – he would come back. But he was gone down again, and I had the rope in my hand – no, there he was again – his face above the water – and he cried again – and I held my hand, and my heart said, "Die!" – and he sank; and I felt "It is done – I am wicked, I am lost!" – and I had the rope in my hand – I don't know what I thought – I was leaping away from myself – I would have saved him then. I was leaping from my crime, and there it was – close to me as I fell –

there was the dead face – dead, dead. It can never be altered. That was what happened. That was what I did. You know it all. It can never be altered.'

She sank back in her chair, exhausted with the agitation of memory and speech. Deronda felt the burden on his spirit less heavy than the foregoing dread. The word 'guilty' had held a possibility of interpretations worse than the fact; and Gwendolen's confession, for the very reason that her conscience made her dwell on the determining power of her evil thoughts, convinced him the more that there had been throughout a counterbalancing struggle of her better will. It seemed almost certain that her murderous thought had had no outward effect – that quite apart from it, the death was inevitable. Still, a question as to the outward effectiveness of a criminal desire dominant enough to impel even a momentary act, cannot alter our judgment of the desire; and Deronda shrank from putting that question forward in the first instance. He held it likely that Gwendolen's remorse aggravated her inward guilt, and that she gave the character of decisive action to what had been an inappreciably instantaneous glance of desire. But her remorse was the precious sign of a recoverable nature; it was the culmination of that self-disapproval which had been the awakening of a new life within her; it marked her off from the criminals whose only regret is failure in securing their evil wish. Deronda could not utter one word to diminish that sacred aversion to her worse self – that thorn-pressure which must come with the crowning of the sorrowful Better, suffering because of the Worse. All this mingled thought and feeling kept him silent: speech was too momentous to be ventured on rashly. There were no words of comfort that did not carry some sacrilege. If he had opened his lips to speak, he could only have echoed, 'It can never be altered – it remains unaltered, to alter other things.' But he was silent and motionless – he did not know how long – before he turned to look at her, and saw her sunk back with closed eyes, like a lost, weary, storm-beaten white doe, unable to rise and pursue its unguided way. He rose and stood before her. The movement touched her consciousness, and she opened her eyes with a slight quivering that seemed like fear.

'You must rest now. Try to rest: try to sleep. And may I see you again this evening – to-morrow – when you have had some rest? Let us say no more now.'

The tears came, and she could not answer except by a slight movement of the head. Deronda rang for attendance, spoke urgently of the necessity that she should be got to rest, and then left her.

LVII

'The unripe grape, the ripe, and the dried. All things are changes,
not into nothing, but into that which is not at present.'
                                    – MARCUS AURELIUS.

Deeds are the pulse of Time, his beating life,
And righteous or unrighteous, being done,
Must throb in after-throbs till Time itself
Be laid in stillness, and the universe
Quiver and breathe upon no mirror more.

IN the evening she sent for him again. It was already near the hour at which she had been brought in from the sea the evening before, and the light was subdued enough with blinds drawn up and windows open. She was seated gazing fixedly on the sea, resting her cheek on her hand, looking less shattered than when he had left her, but with a deep melancholy in her expression which as Deronda approached her passed into an anxious timidity. She did not put out her hand, but said, 'How long ago it is!' Then, 'Will you sit near me again a little while?'

He placed himself by her side as he had done before, and seeing that she turned to him with that indefinable expression which implies a wish to say something, he waited for her to speak. But again she looked towards the window silently, and again turned with the same expression, which yet did not issue in speech. There was some fear hindering her, and Deronda, wishing to relieve her timidity, averted his face. Presently he heard her cry imploringly –

'You will not say that any one else should know?'

'Most decidedly not,' said Deronda. 'There is no action that ought to be taken in consequence. There is no injury that could be righted in that way. There is no retribution that any mortal could apportion justly.'

She was so still during a pause, that she seemed to be holding her breath before she said –

'But if I had not had that murderous will – that moment – if I had thrown the rope on the instant – perhaps it would have hindered death?'

'No – I think not,' said Deronda, slowly. 'If it were true that he could swim, he must have been seized with cramp. With your quickest, utmost effort, it seems impossible that you could have done anything to save him. That momentary murderous will cannot, I think, have altered the course of events. Its effect is confined to the motives in your own breast. Within ourselves our evil will is momentous, and sooner or later it works its way outside us – it may be in the vitiation that breeds evil acts, but also it may be in the self-abhorrence that stings us into better striving.'

'I am saved from robbing others – there are others – they will have everything – they will have what they ought to have. I knew that some time before I left town. You do not suspect me of wrong desires about those things?' She spoke hesitatingly.

'I had not thought of them,' said Deronda; 'I was thinking too much of the other things.'

'Perhaps you don't quite know the beginning of it all,' said Gwendolen, slowly, as if she were overcoming her reluctance. 'There was some one else he ought to have married. And I knew it, and I told her I would not hinder it. And I went away – that was when you first saw me. But then we became poor all at once, and I was very miserable, and I was tempted. I thought, "I shall do as I like and make everything right." I persuaded myself. And it was all different. It was all dreadful. Then came hatred and wicked thoughts. That was how it all came. I told you I was afraid of myself. And I did what you told me – I did try to make my fear a safeguard. I thought of what would be if I— I felt what would come – how I should dread the morning – wishing it would be always night – and yet in the darkness always seeing something – seeing death. If you did not know how miserable I was, you might—but now it has all been no use. I can care for nothing but saving the rest from knowing – poor mamma, who has never been happy.'

There was silence again before she said with a repressed sob – 'You cannot bear to look at me any more. You think I am too wicked. You do not believe that I can become any better – worth anything – worthy enough – I shall always be too wicked to—' The voice broke off helpless.

Deronda's heart was pierced. He turned his eyes on her poor beseeching face and said, 'I believe that you may become worthier than you have ever yet been – worthy to lead a life that may be a blessing. No evil dooms us hopelessly except the evil we love, and desire to continue in, and make no effort to escape from. You *have* made efforts – you will go on making them.'

'But you were the beginning of them. You must not forsake me,' said Gwendolen, leaning with her clasped hands on the arm of her chair and looking at him, while her face bore piteous traces of the life-experience concentrated in the twenty-four hours – that new terrible life lying on the other side of the deed which fulfils a criminal desire. 'I will bear any penance. I will lead any life you tell me. But you must not forsake me. You must be near. If you had been near me – if I could have said everything to you, I should have been different. You will not forsake me?'

'It could never be my impulse to forsake you,' said Deronda promptly, with that voice which, like his eyes, had the unintentional effect of making his ready sympathy seem more personal and special than it really was. And in that moment he was not himself quite free from a foreboding of some such self-committing effect. His strong feeling for this stricken creature could not hinder rushing images of future difficulty. He continued to meet her appealing eyes as he spoke, but it was with the painful consciousness that to her ear his words might carry a promise which one day would seem unfulfilled: he was making an indefinite promise to an indefinite hope. Anxieties, both immediate and distant, crowded on his thought, and it was under their influence that, after a moment's silence, he said –

'I expect Sir Hugo Mallinger to arrive by to-morrow night at least; and I am not without hope that Mrs.

775

Davilow may shortly follow him. Her presence will be the greatest comfort to you – it will give you a motive, to save her from unnecessary pain?'

'Yes, yes – I will try. And you will not go away?'

'Not till after Sir Hugo has come.'

'But we shall all go to England?'

'As soon as possible,' said Deronda, not wishing to enter into particulars.

Gwendolen looked toward the window again with an expression which seemed like a gradual awakening to new thoughts. The twilight was perceptibly deepening, but Deronda could see a movement in her eyes and hands such as accompanies a return of perception in one who has been stunned.

'You will always be with Sir Hugo now?' she said presently, looking at him. 'You will always live at the Abbey – or else at Diplow?'

'I am quite uncertain where I shall live,' said Deronda, colouring.

She was warned by his changed colour that she had spoken too rashly, and fell silent. After a little while she began, again looking away –

'It is impossible to think how my life will go on. I think now it would be better for me to be poor and obliged to work.'

'New promptings will come as the days pass. When you are among your friends again, you will discern new duties,' said Deronda. 'Make it a task now to get as well and calm – as much like yourself as you can, before—' He hesitated.

'Before my mother comes,' said Gwendolen. 'Ah! I must be changed. I have not looked at myself. Should you have known me,' she added, turning towards him, 'if you had met me now? – should you have known me for the one you saw at Leubronn?'

'Yes, I should have known you,' said Deronda, mournfully. 'The outside change is not great. I should have seen at once that it was you, and that you had gone through some great sorrow.'

'Don't wish now that you had never seen me – don't wish that,' said Gwendolen, imploringly, while the tears gathered.

'I should despise myself for wishing it,' said Deronda. 'How could I know what I was wishing? We must find our duties in what comes to us, not in what we imagine might have been. If I look to foolish wishing of that sort, I should wish – not that I had never seen you, but that I had been able to save you from this.'

'You have saved me from worse,' said Gwendolen, in a sobbing voice. 'I should have been worse, if it had not been for you. If you had not been good, I should have been more wicked than I am.'

'It will be better for me to go now,' said Deronda, worn in spirit by the perpetual strain of this scene. 'Remember what we said of your task – to get well and calm before other friends come.'

He rose as he spoke, and she gave him her hand submissively. But when he had left her she sank on her knees, in hysterical crying. The distance between them was too great. She was a banished soul – beholding a possible life which she had sinned herself away from.

She was found in this way, crushed on the floor. Such grief seemed natural in a poor lady whose husband had been drowned in her presence.

BOOK VIII
Fruit and Seed

LVIII

'Much adoe there was, God wot:
He wold love and she wold not.'
– NICHOLAS BRETON.

EXTENSION, we know, is a very imperfect measure of
things; and the length of the sun's journeying can no more
tell us how far life has advanced than the acreage of a field
can tell us what growths may be active within it. A man
may go south, and, stumbling over a bone, may meditate
upon it till he has found a new starting-point for anatomy;
or eastward, and discover a new key to language telling a
new story of races; or he may head an expedition that opens
new continental pathways, get himself maimed in body,
and go through a whole heroic poem of resolve and endurance; and at the end of a few months he may come back to
find his neighbours grumbling at the same parish grievance
as before, or to see the same elderly gentleman treading
the pavement in discourse with himself, shaking his head
after the same percussive butcher's boy, and pausing at the
same shop-window to look at the same prints. If the swift-
est thinking has about the pace of a greyhound, the slowest
must be supposed to move, like the limpet, by an apparent
sticking, which after a good while is discerned to be a slight
progression. Such differences are manifest in the variable
intensity which we call human experience, from the revolutionary rush of change which makes a new inner and outer
life, to that quiet recurrence of the familiar, which has no
other epochs than those of hunger and the heavens.

Something of this contrast was seen in the year's experience which had turned the brilliant, self-confident
Gwendolen Harleth of the Archery Meeting into the
crushed penitent impelled to confess her unworthiness

where it would have been her happiness to be held worthy; while it had left her family in Pennicote without deeper change than that of some outward habits, and some adjustment of prospects and intentions to reduced income, fewer visits, and fainter compliments. The Rectory was as pleasant a home as before: the red and pink peonies on the lawn, the rows of hollyhocks by the hedges, had bloomed as well this year as last; the Rector maintained his cheerful confidence in the goodwill of patrons and his resolution to deserve it by diligence in the fulfilment of his duties, whether patrons were likely to hear of it or not; doing nothing solely with an eye to promotion except, perhaps, the writing of two ecclesiastical articles, which, having no signature, were attributed to some one else, except by the patrons who had a special copy sent them, and these certainly knew the author but did not read the articles. The Rector, however, chewed no poisonous cud of suspicion on this point: he made marginal notes on his own copies to render them a more interesting loan, and was gratified that the Archdeacon and other authorities had nothing to say against the general tenor of his argument. Peaceful authorship! – living in the air of the fields and downs, and not in the thrice-breathed breath of criticism – bringing no Dantesque leanness; rather, assisting nutrition by complacency, and perhaps giving a more suffusive sense of achievement than the production of a whole *Divina Commedia*. Then there was the father's recovered delight in his favourite son, which was a happiness outweighing the loss of eighteen hundred a-year. Of whatever nature might be the hidden change wrought in Rex by the disappointment of his first love, it was apparently quite secondary to that evidence of more serious ambition which dated from the family misfortune; indeed, Mr. Gascoigne was inclined to regard the little affair which had caused him so much anxiety the year before as an evaporation of superfluous moisture, a kind of finish to the baking process which the human dough demands. Rex had lately come down for a summer visit to the Rectory, bringing Anna home, and while he showed nearly the old liveliness with his brothers and sisters, he continued in his holiday the habits of the eager student, rising early in the morning and shutting himself up early in the evenings to carry on a fixed course of study.

'You don't repent the choice of the law as a profession, Rex?' said his father.

'There is no profession I would choose before it,' said Rex. 'I should like to end my life as a first-rate judge, and help to draw up a code. I reverse the famous dictum – I should say, "Give me something to do with making the laws, and let who will make the songs."'

'You will have to stow in an immense amount of rubbish, I suppose – that's the worst of it,' said the Rector.

'I don't see that law-rubbish is worse than any other sort. It is not so bad as the rubbishy literature that people choke their minds with. It doesn't make one so dull. Our wittiest men have often been lawyers. Any orderly way of looking at things as cases and evidence seems to me better than a perpetual wash of odds and ends bearing on nothing in particular. And then, from a higher point of view, the foundations and the growth of law make the most interesting aspects of philosophy and history. Of course there will be a good deal that is troublesome, drudging, perhaps exasperating. But the great prizes in life can't be won easily – I see that.'

'Well, my boy, the best augury of a man's success in his profession is that he thinks it the finest in the world. But I fancy it is so with most work when a man goes into it with a will. Brewitt, the blacksmith, said to me the other day that his 'prentice had no mind to his trade; "and yet, sir," said Brewitt, "what would a young fellow have if he doesn't like the blacksmithing?"'

The Rector cherished a fatherly delight, which he allowed to escape him only in moderation. Warham, who had gone to India, he had easily borne parting with, but Rex was that romance of later life which a man sometimes finds in a son whom he recognizes as superior to himself,

FRUIT AND SEED

picturing a future eminence for him according to a variety
of famous examples. It was only to his wife that he said
with decision, 'Rex will be a distinguished man, Nancy, I
am sure of it – as sure as Paley's father was about his son.'

'Was Paley an old bachelor?' said Mrs. Gascoigne.

'That is hardly to the point, my dear,' said the Rector,
who did not remember that irrelevant detail. And Mrs.
Gascoigne felt that she had spoken rather weakly.

This quiet trotting of time at the Rectory was shared by
the group who had exchanged the faded dignity of
Offendene for the low white house not a mile off, well
enclosed with evergreens, and known to the villagers as
'Jodson's.' Mrs. Davilow's delicate face showed only a
slight deepening of its mild melancholy, her hair only
a few more silver lines, in consequence of the last year's
trials; the four girls had bloomed out a little from being
less in the shade; and the good Jocosa preserved her
serviceable neutrality towards the pleasure and glories of
the world as things made for those who were not 'in a
situation.'

The low narrow drawing-room, enlarged by two quaint
projecting windows, with lattices wide open on a July
afternoon to the scent of monthly roses, the faint murmurs
of the garden, and the occasional rare sound of hoofs and
wheels seeming to clarify the succeeding silence, made
rather a crowded lively scene, Rex and Anna being added
to the usual group of six. Anna, always a favourite with her
younger cousins, had much to tell of her new experience,
and the acquaintances she had made in London; and when
on her first visit she came alone, many questions were
asked her about Gwendolen's house in Grosvenor
Square, what Gwendolen herself had said, and what any
one else had said about Gwendolen. Had Anna been to see
Gwendolen after she had known about the yacht? No: – an
answer which left speculation free concerning everything
connected with that interesting unknown vessel beyond
the fact that Gwendolen had written just before she set out
to say that Mr. Grandcourt and she were going yachting in

781

the Mediterranean, and again from Marseilles to say that she was sure to like the yachting, the cabins were very elegant, and she would probably not send another letter till she had written quite a long diary filled with *dittos*. Also, this movement of Mr. and Mrs. Grandcourt had been mentioned in 'the newspaper;' so that altogether this new phase of Gwendolen's exalted life made a striking part of the sisters' romance, the book-devouring Isabel throwing in a Corsair or two to make an adventure that might end well.

But when Rex was present, the girls, according to instructions, never started this fascinating topic; and to-day there had only been animated descriptions of the Meyricks and their extraordinary Jewish friends, which caused some astonished questioning from minds to which the idea of live Jews, out of a book, suggested a difference deep enough to be almost zoological, as of a strange race in Pliny's Natural History that might sleep under the shade of its own ears. Bertha could not imagine what Jews believed now; and had a dim idea that they rejected the Old Testament since it proved the New; Miss Merry thought that Mirah and her brother could 'never have been properly argued with,' and the amiable Alice did not mind what the Jews believed, she was sure she 'couldn't bear them.' Mrs. Davilow corrected her by saying that the great Jewish families who were in society were quite what they ought to be both in London and Paris, but admitted that the commoner unconverted Jews were objectionable; and Isabel asked whether Mirah talked just as they did, or whether you might be with her and not find out that she was a Jewess.

Rex, who had no partisanship with the Israelites, having made a troublesome acquaintance with the minutiæ of their ancient history in the form of 'cram,' was amusing himself by playfully exaggerating the notion of each speaker, while Anna begged them all to understand that he was only joking, when the laughter was interrupted by the bringing in of a letter for Mrs. Davilow. A messenger had run with it in great haste from the Rectory. It enclosed a telegram, and as Mrs. Davilow read and re-read it in silence and agitation, all eyes were turned on her with anxiety, but no one dared to speak. Looking up at last and seeing the young faces 'painted with fear,' she remembered that they might be imagining something worse than the truth, something like her own first dread which made her unable to understand what was written, and she said, with a sob which was half relief –

'My dears, Mr. Grandcourt—' She paused an instant, and then began again, 'Mr. Grandcourt is drowned.'

Rex started up as if a missile had been suddenly thrown into the room. He could not help himself, and Anna's first look was at him. But then, gathering some self-command while Mrs. Davilow was reading what the Rector had written on the enclosing paper, he said –

'Can I do anything, aunt? Can I carry any word to my father from you?'

'Yes, dear. Tell him I will be ready – he is very good. He says he will go with me to Genoa – he will be here at half-past six. Jocosa and Alice, help me to get ready. She is safe – Gwendolen is safe – but she must be ill. I am sure she must be very ill. Rex, dear – Rex and Anna – go and tell your father I will be quite ready. I would not for the world lose another night. And bless him for being ready so soon. I can travel night and day till we get there.'

Rex and Anna hurried away through the sunshine which was suddenly solemn to them, without uttering a word to each other; she chiefly possessed by solicitude about any reopening of his wound, he struggling with a tumultuary crowd of thoughts that were an offence against his better will. The oppression being undiminished when they were at the Rectory gate, he said –

'Nannie, I will leave you to say everything to my father. If he wants me immediately, let me know. I shall stay in the shrubbery for ten minutes – only ten minutes.'

Who has been quite free from egoistic escapes of the imagination picturing desirable consequences on his own future in the presence of another's misfortune, sorrow, or death? The expected promotion or legacy is the common type of a temptation which makes speech and even prayer a severe avoidance of the most insistent thoughts, and sometimes raises an inward shame, a self-distaste, that is worse than any other form of unpleasant companionship. In Rex's nature the shame was immediate, and overspread like an ugly light all the hurrying images of what might come, which thrust themselves in with the idea that Gwendolen was again free – overspread them, perhaps, the more persistently because every phantasm of a hope was quickly nullified by a more substantial obstacle. Before the vision of 'Gwendolen free' rose the impassable vision of 'Gwendolen rich, exalted, courted;' and if in the former time, when both their lives were fresh, she had turned from his love with repugnance, what ground was there for supposing that her heart would be more open to him in the future?

These thoughts, which he wanted to master and suspend, were like a tumultuary ringing of opposing chimes that he could not escape from by running. During the last year he had brought himself into a state of calm resolve, and now it seemed that three words had been enough to undo all that difficult work, and cast him back into the wretched fluctuations of a longing which he recognized as simply perturbing and hopeless. And at this moment the activity of such longing had an untimeliness that made it repulsive to his better self. Excuse poor Rex: it was not much more than eighteen months since he had been laid low by an archer who sometimes touches his arrow with a subtle, lingering poison. The disappointment of a youthful passion has effects as incalculable as those of small-pox, which may make one person plain and a genius, another less plain and more foolish, another plain without detriment to his folly, and leave perhaps the majority without obvious change. Everything depends – not on the mere fact of disappointment, but – on the nature affected and the force that stirs it. In Rex's well-endowed nature, brief as the hope had been, the passionate stirring had gone deep, and the effect of disappointment was revolutionary, though fraught with a beneficent new order which retained most of the old virtues: in certain respects he believed that it had finally determined the bias and colour of his life. Now, however, it seemed that his inward peace was hardly more stable than that of republican Florence, and his heart no better than the alarm-bell that made work slack and tumult busy.

Rex's love had been of that sudden, penetrating, cling-ing sort which the ancients knew and sung, and in singing made a fashion of talk for many moderns whose experience has been by no means of a fiery, dæmonic character. To have the consciousness suddenly steeped with another's personality, to have the strongest inclinations possessed by an image which retains its dominance in spite of change and apart from worthiness – nay, to feel a passion which clings the faster for the tragic pangs inflicted by a cruel, recognized unworthiness – is a phase of love which in the feeble and common-minded has a repulsive likeness to a blind animalism insensible to the higher sway of moral affinity or heaven-lit admiration. But when this attaching force is present in a nature not of brutish unmodifiable-ness, but of a human dignity that can risk itself safely, it may even result in a devotedness not unfit to be called divine in a higher sense than the ancient. Phlegmatic rationality stares and shakes its head at these unaccount-able prepossessions, but they exist as undeniably as the winds and waves, determining here a wreck and there a triumphant voyage.

This sort of passion had nested in the sweet-natured, strong Rex, and he had made up his mind to its companion-ship, as if it had been an object supremely dear, stricken dumb and helpless, and turning all the future of tenderness into a shadow of the past. But he had also made up his mind that his life was not to be pauperized because he had had to renounce one sort of joy; rather, he had begun life again with a new counting-up of the treasures that remained to him, and he had even felt a release of power such as may come from ceasing to be afraid of your own neck.

And now, here he was pacing the shrubbery, angry with himself that the sense of irrevocableness in his lot, which ought in reason to have been as strong as ever, had been shaken by a change of circumstances that could make no change in relation to him. He told himself the truth quite roughly:

'She would never love me; and that is not the question – I could never approach her as a lover in her present position. I am exactly of no consequence at all, and am not likely to be of much consequence till my head is turning grey. But what has that to do with it? She would not have me on any terms, and I would not ask her. It is a meanness to be thinking about it now – no better than lurking about the battle-field to strip the dead; but there never was more gratuitous sinning. I have nothing to gain there – absolutely nothing.... Then why can't I face the facts, and behave as they demand, instead of leaving my father to suppose that there are matters he can't speak to me about, though I might be useful in them?'

That last thought made one wave with the impulse that sent Rex walking firmly into the house and through the open door of the study, where he saw his father packing a travelling-desk.

'Can I be of any use, sir?' said Rex, with rallied courage, as his father looked up at him.

'Yes, my boy; when I am gone, just see to my letters, and answer where necessary, and send me word of everything. Dymock will manage the parish very well, and you will stay with your mother, or, at least, go up and down again, till I come back, whenever that may be.'

'You will hardly be very long, sir, I suppose,' said Rex, beginning to strap a railway rug. 'You will perhaps bring my cousin back to England?' He forced himself to speak of Gwendolen for the first time, and the Rector noticed the epoch with satisfaction.

'That depends,' he answered, taking the subject as a matter of course between them. 'Perhaps her mother may stay there with her, and I may come back very soon. This telegram leaves us in an ignorance which is rather anxious. But no doubt the arrangements of the will lately made are satisfactory, and there may possibly be an heir yet to be born. In any case, I feel confident that Gwendolen will be liberally – I should expect, splendidly – provided for.'

'It must have been a great shock for her,' said Rex, getting more resolute after the first twinge had been borne. 'I suppose he was a devoted husband.'

'No doubt of it,' said the Rector, in his most decided manner. 'Few men of his position would have come forward as he did under the circumstances.'

Rex had never seen Grandcourt, had never been spoken to about him by any one of the family, and knew nothing of Gwendolen's flight from her suitor to Leubronn. He only knew that Grandcourt, being very much in love with her, had made her an offer in the first weeks of her sudden poverty, and had behaved very handsomely in providing for her mother and sisters. That was all very natural, and what Rex himself would have liked to do. Grandcourt had been a lucky fellow, and had had some happiness before he got drowned. Yet Rex wondered much whether Gwendolen had been in love with the successful suitor, or had only forborne to tell him that she hated being made love to.

LIX

'I count myself in nothing else so happy
As in a soul remembering my good friends.'
— SHAKESPEARE.

SIR HUGO MALLINGER was not so prompt in starting
for Genoa as Mr. Gascoigne had been, and Deronda on all
accounts would not take his departure till he had seen the
baronet. There was not only Grandcourt's death, but also
the late crisis in his own life to make reasons why his oldest
friend would desire to have the unrestrained communication of speech with him, for in writing he had not felt able
to give any details concerning the mother who had come
and gone like an apparition. It was not till the fifth evening
that Deronda, according to telegram, waited for Sir Hugo
at the station, where he was to arrive between eight and
nine; and while he was looking forward to the sight of the
kind, familiar face, which was part of his earliest memories,
something like a smile, in spite of his late tragic experience, might have been detected in his eyes and the curve
of his lips at the idea of Sir Hugo's pleasure in being now
master of his estates, able to leave them to his daughters, or
at least – according to a view of inheritance which had just
been strongly impressed on Deronda's imagination – to
take make-shift feminine offspring as intermediate to a
satisfactory heir in a grandson. We should be churlish
creatures if we could have no joy in our fellow-mortals'
joy, unless it were in agreement with our theory of righteous distribution and our highest ideal of human good:
what sour corners our mouths would get – our eyes, what
frozen glances! and all the while our own possessions and
desires would not exactly adjust themselves to our ideal.
We must have some comradeship with imperfection; and it
is, happily, possible to feel gratitude even where we discern a mistake that may have been injurious, the vehicle of
the mistake being an affectionate intention prosecuted
through a lifetime of kindly offices. Deronda's feeling

and judgment were strongly against the action of Sir Hugo in making himself the agent of a falsity – yes, a falsity: he could give no milder name to the concealment under which he had been reared. But the baronet had probably had no clear knowledge concerning the mother's breach of trust, and with his light, easy way of taking life, had held it a reasonable preference in her that her son should be made an English gentleman, seeing that she had the eccentricity of not caring to part from her child, and be to him as if she were not. Daniel's affectionate gratitude towards Sir Hugo made him wish to find grounds of excuse rather than blame; for it is as possible to be rigid in principle and tender in blame, as it is to suffer from the sight of things hung awry, and yet to be patient with the hanger who sees amiss. If Sir Hugo in his bachelorhood had been beguiled into regarding children chiefly as a product intended to make life more agreeable to the full-grown, whose conven-ience alone was to be consulted in the disposal of them – why, he had shared an assumption which, if not formally avowed, was massively acted on at that date of the world's history; and Deronda, with all his keen memory of the painful inward struggle he had gone through in his boy-hood, was able also to remember the many signs that his experience had been entirely shut out from Sir Hugo's conception. Ignorant kindness may have the effect of cruelty; but to be angry with it as if it were direct cruelty would be an ignorant *un*kindness, the most remote from Deronda's large imaginative lenience towards others. And perhaps now, after the searching scenes of the last ten days, in which the curtain had been lifted for him from the secrets of lives unlike his own, he was more than ever disposed to check that rashness of indignation or resent-ment which has an unpleasant likeness to the love of punishing. When he saw Sir Hugo's familiar figure des-cending from the railway carriage, the life-long affection, which had been well accustomed to make excuses, flowed in and submerged all newer knowledge that might have seemed fresh ground for blame.

'Well, Dan,' said Sir Hugo, with a serious fervour, grasping Deronda's hand. He uttered no other words of greeting; there was too strong a rush of mutual consciousness. The next thing was to give orders to the courier, and then to propose walking slowly in the mild evening, there being no hurry to get to the hotel.

'I have taken my journey easily, and am in excellent condition,' he said, as he and Deronda came out under the starlight, which was still faint with the lingering sheen of day. 'I didn't hurry in setting off, because I wanted to inquire into things a little, and so I got sight of your letter to Lady Mallinger before I started. But now, how is the widow?'

'Getting calmer,' said Deronda. 'She seems to be escaping the bodily illness that one might have feared for her, after her plunge and terrible excitement. Her uncle and mother came two days ago, and she is being well taken care of.'

'Any prospect of an heir being born?'

'From what Mr. Gascoigne said to me, I conclude not. He spoke as if it were a question whether the widow would have the estates for her life.'

'It will not be much of a wrench to her affections, I fancy, this loss of the husband?' said Sir Hugo, looking round at Deronda.

'The suddenness of the death has been a great blow to her,' said Deronda, quietly evading the question.

'I wonder whether Grandcourt gave her any notion what were the provisions of his will?' said Sir Hugo.

'Do you know what they are, sir?' parried Deronda.

'Yes, I do,' said the baronet, quickly. 'Gad! if there is no prospect of a legitimate heir, he has left everything to a boy he had by a Mrs. Glasher; you know nothing about the affair, I suppose, but she was a sort of wife to him for a good many years, and there are three older children – girls. The boy is to take his father's name; he is Henleigh already, and he is to be Henleigh Mallinger Grandcourt. The Mallinger will be of no use to him, I am happy to say; but the young dog will have more than enough with his fourteen years' minority – no need to have had holes filled up with my fifty thousand for Diplow that he had no right to; and meanwhile my beauty, the young widow, is to put up with a poor two thousand a-year and the house at Gadsmere – a nice kind of banishment for her if she chose to shut herself up there, which I don't think she will. The boy's mother has been living there of late years. I'm perfectly disgusted with Grandcourt. I don't know that I'm obliged to think the better of him because he's drowned, though, so far as my affairs are concerned, nothing in his life became him like the leaving it.'

'In my opinion he did wrong when he married this wife – not in leaving his estates to the son,' said Deronda, rather drily.

'I say nothing against his leaving the land to the lad,' said Sir Hugo; 'but since he had married this girl he ought to have given her a handsome provision, such as she could live on in a style fitted to the rank he had raised her to. She ought to have had four or five thousand a-year and the London house for her life; that's what I should have done for her. I suppose, as she was penniless, her friends couldn't stand out for a settlement, else it's ill trusting to the will a man may make after he's married. Even a wise man generally lets some folly ooze out of him in his will – my father did, I know; and if a fellow has any spite or tyranny in him, he's likely to bottle off a good deal for keeping in that sort of document. It's quite clear Grandcourt meant that his death should put an extinguisher on his wife, if she bore him no heir.'

'And, in the other case, I suppose everything would have been reversed – illegitimacy would have had the extinguisher?' said Deronda, with some scorn.

'Precisely – Gadsmere and the two thousand. It's queer. One nuisance is that Grandcourt has made me an executor; but seeing he was the son of my only brother, I can't refuse to act. And I shall mind it less, if I can be of any use to the widow. Lush thinks she was not in ignorance about the family under the rose, and the purport of the will. He hints that there was no very good understanding between the couple. But I fancy you are the man who knew most about what Mrs. Grandcourt felt or did not feel – eh, Dan?' Sir Hugo did not put this question with his usual jocoseness, but rather with a lowered tone of interested inquiry; and Deronda felt that any evasion would be misinterpreted. He answered gravely –

'She was certainly not happy. They were unsuited to each other. But as to the disposal of the property – from all I have seen of her, I should predict that she will be quite contented with it.'

'Then she is not much like the rest of her sex; that's all I can say,' said Sir Hugo, with a slight shrug. 'However, she ought to be something extraordinary, for there must be an entanglement between your horoscope and hers – eh? When that tremendous telegram came, the first thing Lady Mallinger said was, "How very strange that it should be Daniel who sends it?" But I have had something of the same sort in my own life. I was once at a foreign hotel where a lady had been left by her husband without money. When I heard of it, and came forward to help her, who should she be but an early flame of mine, who had been fool enough to marry an Austrian baron with a long moustache and short affection? But it was an affair of my own that called me there – nothing to do with knight-errantry, any more than your coming to Genoa had to do with the Grandcourts.'

There was silence for a little while. Sir Hugo had begun to talk of the Grandcourts, as the less difficult subject between himself and Deronda; but they were both wishing to overcome a reluctance to perfect frankness on the events which touched their relation to each other. Deronda felt that his letter, after the first interview with his mother, had been rather a thickening than a breaking of the ice, and that he ought to wait for the first opening to come from Sir Hugo. Just when they were about to lose sight of the port, the baronet turned, and pausing as if to get a last view, said in a tone of more serious feeling –

'And about the main business of your coming to Genoa, Dan? You have not been deeply pained by anything you have learned, I hope? There is nothing that you feel need change your position in any way? You know, whatever happens to you must always be of importance to me.'

'I desire to meet your goodness by perfect confidence, sir,' said Deronda. 'But I can't answer those questions truly by a simple yes or no. Much that I have heard about the past has pained me. And it has been a pain to meet and part with my mother, in her suffering state, as I have been compelled to do. But it is no pain – it is rather a clearing up of doubts for which I am thankful, to know my parentage. As to the effect on my position, there will be no change in my gratitude to you, sir, for the fatherly care and affection you have always shown me. But to know that I was born a Jew, may have a momentous influence on my life, which I am hardly able to tell you of at present.'

Deronda spoke the last sentence with a resolve that overcame some diffidence. He felt that the differences between Sir Hugo's nature and his own would have, by-and-by, to disclose themselves more markedly than had ever yet been needful. The baronet gave him a quick glance, and turned to walk on. After a few moments' silence, in which he had reviewed all the material in his memory which would enable him to interpret Deronda's words, he said –

'I have long expected something remarkable from you, Dan; but, for God's sake, don't go into any eccentricities! I can tolerate any man's difference of opinion, but let him tell it me without getting himself up as a lunatic. At this stage of the world, if a man wants to be taken seriously he must keep clear of melodrama. Don't misunderstand me. I am not suspecting you of setting up any lunacy on your own account. I only think you might easily be led arm in arm with a lunatic, especially if he wanted defending. You have a passion for people who are pelted, Dan. I'm sorry for them too; but so far as company goes, it's a bad ground of selection. However, I don't ask you to anticipate your inclination in anything you have to tell me. When you make up your mind to a course that requires money, I have some sixteen thousand pounds that have been accumulating for you over and above what you have been having the interest of as income. And now I am come, I suppose you want to get back to England as soon as you can?'

'I must go first to Mainz to get away a chest of my grandfather's, and perhaps to see a friend of his,' said Deronda. 'Although the chest has been lying there these twenty years, I have an unreasonable sort of nervous eagerness to get it away under my care, as if it were more likely now than before that something might happen to it. And perhaps I am the more uneasy, because I lingered after my mother left, instead of setting out immediately. Yet I can't regret that I was here – else Mrs. Grandcourt would have had none but servants to act for her.'

'Yes, yes,' said Sir Hugo, with a flippancy which was an escape of some vexation hidden under his more serious speech; 'I hope you are not going to set a dead Jew above a living Christian.'

Deronda coloured, and repressed a retort. They were just turning into the *Italia*.

LX

'But I shall say no more of this at this time; for this is to be felt and not to be talked of; and they who never touched it with their fingers may secretly perhaps laugh at it in their hearts and be never the wiser.'

– JEREMY TAYLOR.

The Roman Emperor in the legend put to death ten learned Israelites to avenge the sale of Joseph by his brethren. And there have always been enough of his kidney, whose piety lies in punishing, who can see the justice of grudges but not of gratitude. For you shall never convince the stronger feeling that it hath not the stronger reason, or incline him who hath no love to believe that there is good ground for loving. As we may learn from the order of word-making, wherein *love* precedeth *lovable*.

WHEN Deronda presented his letter at the banking-house in the *Schuster Strasse* at Mainz, and asked for Joseph Kalonymos, he was presently shown into an inner room where, seated at a table arranging open letters, was the white-bearded man whom he had seen the year before in the synagogue at Frankfort. He wore his hat – it seemed to be the same old felt hat as before – and near him was a packed portmanteau with a wrap and overcoat upon it. On seeing Deronda enter he rose, but did not advance or put out his hand. Looking at him with small penetrating eyes which glittered like black gems in the midst of his yellowish face and white hair, he said in German –

'Good! It is now you who seek me, young man.'

'Yes; I seek you with gratitude, as a friend of my grandfather's,' said Deronda, 'and I am under an obligation to you for giving yourself much trouble on my account.' He spoke without difficulty in that liberal language which takes many strange accents to its maternal bosom.

Kalonymos now put out his hand and said cordially, 'So – you are no longer angry at being something more than an Englishman?'

'On the contrary. I thank you heartily for helping to save me from remaining in ignorance of my parentage, and for

795

taking care of the chest that my grandfather left in trust for me.'

'Sit down, sit down,' said Kalonymos, in a quick under-tone, seating himself again, and pointing to a chair near him. Then deliberately laying aside his hat and showing a head thickly covered with white hair, he stroked and clutched his beard while he looked examiningly at the young face before him. The moment wrought strongly on Deronda's imaginative susceptibility: in the presence of one linked still in zealous friendship with the grandfather whose hope had yearned towards him when he was unborn, and who though dead was yet to speak with him in those written memorials which, says Milton, 'contain a potency of life in them to be as active as that soul whose progeny they are,' he seemed to himself to be touching the electric chain of his own ancestry; and he bore the scrutinizing look of Kalonymos with a delighted awe, something like what one feels in the solemn commemoration of acts done long ago but still telling markedly on the life of to-day. Impossible for men of duller fibre – men whose affection is not ready to diffuse itself through the wide travel of imagination, to comprehend, perhaps even to credit this sensibility of Deronda's; but it subsisted, like their own dullness, not-withstanding their lack of belief in it – and it gave his face an expression which seemed very satisfactory to the observer.

He said in Hebrew, quoting from one of the fine hymns in the Hebrew liturgy, 'As thy goodness has been great to the former generations, even so may it be to the latter.' Then after pausing a little he began, 'Young man, I rejoice that I was not yet set off again on my travels, and that you are come in time for me to see the image of my friend as he was in his youth – no longer perverted from the fellowship of your people – no longer shrinking in proud wrath from the touch of him who seemed to be claiming you as a Jew. You come with thankfulness yourself to claim the kindred and heritage that wicked contrivance would have robbed you of. You come with a willing soul to declare, "I am the grandson of Daniel Charisi." Is it not so?'

'Assuredly it is,' said Deronda. 'But let me say that I should at no time have been inclined to treat a Jew with incivility simply because he was a Jew. You can understand that I shrank from saying to a stranger, "I know nothing of my mother."'

'A sin, a sin!' said Kalonymos, putting up his hand and closing his eyes in disgust. 'A robbery of our people – as when our youths and maidens were reared for the Roman Edom. But it is frustrated. I have frustrated it. When Daniel Charisi – may his Rock and his Redeemer guard him! – when Daniel Charisi was a stripling and I was a lad little above his shoulder, we made a solemn vow always to be friends. He said, "Let us bind ourselves with duty, as if we were sons of the same mother." That was his bent from first to last – as he said, to fortify his soul with bonds. It was a saying of his, "Let us bind love with duty; for duty is the love of law; and law is the nature of the Eternal." So we bound ourselves. And though we were much apart in our later life, the bond has never been broken. When he was dead, they sought to rob him; but they could not rob him of me. I rescued that remainder of him which he had prized and preserved for his offspring. And I have restored to him the offspring they had robbed him of. I will bring you the chest forthwith.'

Kalonymos left the room for a few minutes, and returned with a clerk who carried the chest, set it down on the floor, drew off a leather cover, and went out again. It was not very large, but was made heavy by ornamental bracers and handles of gilt iron. The wood was beautifully incised with Arabic lettering.

'So!' said Kalonymos, returning to his seat. 'And here is the curious key,' he added, taking it from a small leathern bag. 'Bestow it carefully. I trust you are methodic and wary.' He gave Deronda the monitory and slightly suspicious look with which age is apt to commit any object to the keeping of youth.

'I shall be more careful of this than of any other property,' said Deronda, smiling and putting the key in his

797

breast-pocket. 'I never before possessed anything that was a sign to me of so much cherished hope and effort. And I shall never forget that the effort was partly yours. Have you time to tell me more of my grandfather? Or shall I be trespassing in staying longer?'

'Stay yet a while. In an hour and eighteen minutes I start for Trieste,' said Kalonymos, looking at his watch, 'and presently my sons will expect my attention. Will you let me make you known to them, so that they may have the pleasure of showing hospitality to my friend's grandson? They dwell here in ease and luxury, though I choose to be a wanderer.'

'I shall be glad if you will commend me to their acquaintance for some future opportunity,' said Deronda. 'There are pressing claims calling me to England – friends who may be much in need of my presence. I have been kept away from them too long by unexpected circumstances. But to know more of you and your family would be motive enough to bring me again to Mainz.'

'Good! Me you will hardly find, for I am beyond my threescore years and ten, and I am a wanderer, carrying my shroud with me. But my sons and their children dwell here in wealth and unity. The days are changed for us in Mainz since our people were slaughtered wholesale if they wouldn't be baptized wholesale: they are changed for us since Karl the Great fetched my ancestors from Italy to bring some tincture of knowledge to our rough German brethren. I and my contemporaries have had to fight for it too. Our youth fell on evil days; but this we have won; we increase our wealth in safety, and the learning of all Germany is fed and fattened by Jewish brains – though they keep not always their Jewish hearts. Have you been left altogether ignorant of your people's life, young man?'

'No,' said Deronda, 'I have lately, before I had any true suspicion of my parentage, been led to study everything belonging to their history with more interest than any other subject. It turns out that I have been making myself ready to understand my grandfather a little.' He was anxious lest the time should be consumed before this circuitous course of talk could lead them back to the topic he most cared about. Age does not easily distinguish between what it needs to express and what youth needs to know – distance seeming to level the objects of memory; and keenly active as Joseph Kalonymos showed himself, an inkstand in the wrong place would have hindered his imagination from getting to Beyrout: he had been used to unite restless travel with punctilious observation. But Deronda's last sentence answered its purpose.

'So – you would perhaps have been such a man as he if your education had not hindered; for you are like him in features: – yet not altogether, young man. He had an iron will in his face: it braced up everybody about him. When he was quite young he had already got one deep upright line in his brow. I see none of that in you. Daniel Charisi used to say, "Better a wrong will than a wavering; better a steadfast enemy than an uncertain friend; better a false belief than no belief at all. What he despised most was indifference. He had longer reasons than I can give you."'

'Yet his knowledge was not narrow?' said Deronda, with a tacit reference to the usual excuse for indecision – that it comes from knowing too much.

'Narrow? no,' said Kalonymos, shaking his head with a compassionate smile. 'From his childhood upward, he drank in learning as easily as the plant sucks up water. But he early took to medicine and theories about life and health. He travelled to many countries, and spent much of his substance in seeing and knowing. What he used to insist on was that the strength and wealth of mankind depended on the balance of separateness and communication, and he was bitterly against our people losing themselves among the Gentiles; "It's no better," said he, "than the many sorts of grain going back from their variety into sameness." He mingled all sorts of learning; and in that he was like our Arabic writers in the golden time. We studied together, but he went beyond me. Though we were bosom friends, and he poured himself out to me, we were as different as the inside and the outside of the bowl. I stood up for no notions of my own: I took Charisi's sayings as I took the shape of the trees: they were there, not to be disputed about. It came to the same thing in both of us: we were both faithful Jews, thankful not to be Gentiles. And since I was a ripe man, I have been what I am now, for all but age – loving to wander, loving transactions, loving to behold all things, and caring nothing about hardship. Charisi thought continually of our people's future: he went with all his soul into that part of our religion: I not. So we have freedom, I am content. Our people wandered before they were driven. Young man, when I am in the East, I lie much on deck and watch the greater stars. The sight of them satisfies me. I know them as they rise, and hunger not to know more. Charisi was satisfied with no sight, but pieced it out with what had been before and what would come after. Yet we loved each other, and as he said, we bound our love with duty; we solemnly pledged ourselves to help and defend each other to the last. I have fulfilled my pledge.' Here Kalonymos rose, and Deronda, rising also, said –

'And in being faithful to him you have caused justice to be done to me. It would have been a robbery of me too that I should never have known of the inheritance he had prepared for me. I thank you with my whole soul.'

'Be worthy of him, young man. What is your vocation?' This question was put with a quick abruptness which embarrassed Deronda, who did not feel it quite honest to allege his law-reading as a vocation. He answered –

'I cannot say that I have any.'

'Get one, get one. The Jew must be diligent. You will call yourself a Jew and profess the faith of your fathers?' said Kalonymos, putting his hand on Deronda's shoulder and looking sharply in his face.

'I shall call myself a Jew,' said Deronda, deliberately, becoming slightly paler under the piercing eyes of his questioner. 'But I will not say that I shall profess to believe exactly as my fathers have believed. Our fathers themselves changed the horizon of their belief and learned of other races. But I think I can maintain my grandfather's notion of separateness with communication. I hold that my first duty is to my own people, and if there is anything to be done towards restoring or perfecting their common life, I shall make that my vocation.'

It happened to Deronda at that moment, as it has often happened to others, that the need for speech made an epoch in resolve. His respect for the questioner would not let him decline to answer, and by the necessity to answer he found out the truth for himself.

'Ah, you argue and you look forward – you are Daniel Charisi's grandson,' said Kalonymos, adding a benediction in Hebrew.

With that they parted; and almost as soon as Deronda was in London, the aged man was again on shipboard, greeting the friendly stars without any eager curiosity.

LXI

'Within the gentle heart Love shelters him,
    As birds within the green shade of the grove,
Before the gentle heart, in Nature's scheme,
    Love was not, nor the gentle heart ere Love.'
    – GUIDO GUINICELLI (*Rossetti's Translation*).

THERE was another house besides the white house at Pennicote, another breast besides Rex Gascoigne's, in which the news of Grandcourt's death caused both strong agitation and the effort to repress it.

It was Hans Meyrick's habit to send or bring in the 'Times' for his mother's reading. She was a great reader of news, from the widest-reaching politics to the list of marriages; the latter, she said, giving her the pleasant sense of finishing the fashionable novels without having read them, and seeing the heroes and heroines happy without knowing what poor creatures they were. On a Wednesday, there were reasons why Hans always chose to bring the paper, and to do so about the time that Mirah had nearly ended giving Mab her weekly lesson, avowing that he came then because he wanted to hear Mirah sing. But on the particular Wednesday now in question, after entering the house as quietly as usual with his latch-key, he appeared in the parlour, shaking the 'Times' aloft with a crackling noise, in remorseless interruption of Mab's attempt to render *Lascia ch'io pianga* with a remote imitation of her teacher. Piano and song ceased immediately: Mirah, who had been playing the accompaniment, involuntarily started up and turned round, the crackling sound, after the occasional trick of sounds, having seemed to her something thunderous; and Mab said –

'O-o-o, Hans! why do you bring a more horrible noise than my singing?'

'What on earth is the wonderful news?' said Mrs. Meyrick, who was the only other person in the room.

'Anything about Italy – anything about the Austrians giving up Venice?'

'Nothing about Italy, but something from Italy,' said Hans, with a peculiarity in his tone and manner which set his mother interpreting. Imagine how some of us feel and behave when an event, not disagreeable, seems to be confirming and carrying out our private constructions. We say, 'What do you think?' in a pregnant tone to some innocent person who has not embarked his wisdom in the same boat with ours, and finds our information flat.

'Nothing bad?' said Mrs. Meyrick, anxiously, thinking immediately of Deronda; and Mirah's heart had been already clutched by the same thought.

'Not bad for anybody we care much about,' said Hans, quickly; 'rather uncommonly lucky, I think. I never knew anybody die conveniently before. Considering what a dear gazelle I am, I am constantly wondering to find myself alive.'

'O me, Hans!' said Mab, impatiently, 'if you must talk of yourself, let it be behind your own back. What *is* it that has happened?'

'Duke Alfonso is drowned, and the Duchess is alive, that's all,' said Hans, putting the paper before Mrs. Meyrick, with his finger against a paragraph. 'But more than all is – Deronda was at Genoa in the same hotel with them, and he saw her brought in by the fishermen, who had got her out of the water time enough to save her from any harm. It seems they saw her jump in after her husband – which was a less judicious action than I should have expected of the Duchess. However, Deronda is a lucky fellow in being there to take care of her.'

Mirah had sunk on the music-stool again, with her eyelids down and her hands tightly clasped; and Mrs. Meyrick, giving up the paper to Mab, said –

'Poor thing! she must have been fond of her husband, to jump in after him.'

'It was an inadvertence – a little absence of mind,' said Hans, creasing his face roguishly, and throwing himself into a chair not far from Mirah. 'Who can be fond of a jealous baritone, with freezing glances, always singing asides? – that was the husband's *rôle*, depend upon it. Nothing can be neater than his getting drowned. The Duchess is at liberty now to marry a man with a fine head of hair, and glances that will melt instead of freezing her. And I shall be invited to the wedding.'

Here Mirah started from her sitting posture, and fixing her eyes on Hans with an angry gleam in them, she said, in the deeply-shaken voice of indignation –

'Mr. Hans, you ought not to speak in that way. Mr. Deronda would not like you to speak so. Why will you say he is lucky – why will you use words of that sort about life and death – when what is life to one is death to another? How do you know it would be lucky if he loved Mrs. Grandcourt? It might be a great evil to him. She would take him away from my brother – I know she would. Mr. Deronda would not call that lucky – to pierce my brother's heart.'

All three were struck with the sudden transformation. Mirah's face, with a look of anger that might have suited Ithuriel, pale even to the lips that were usually so rich of tint, was not far from poor Hans, who sat transfixed, blushing under it as if he had been the girl, while he said nervously –

'I am a fool and a brute, and I withdraw every word. I'll go and hang myself like Judas – if it's allowable to mention him.' Even in Hans's sorrowful moments, his improvised words had inevitably some drollery.

But Mirah's anger was not appeased: how could it be? She had burst into indignant speech as creatures in intense pain bite and make their teeth meet even through their own flesh, by way of making their agony bearable. She said no more, but, seating herself at the piano, pressed the sheet of music before her, as if she thought of beginning to play again.

It was Mab who spoke, while Mrs. Meyrick's face seemed to reflect some of Hans's discomfort.

'Mirah is quite right to scold you, Hans. You are always taking Mr. Deronda's name in vain. And it is horrible, joking in that way about his marrying Mrs. Grandcourt. Men's minds must be very black, I think,' ended Mab, with much scorn.

'Quite true, my dear,' said Hans, in a low tone, rising and turning on his heel to walk towards the back window.

'We had better go on, Mab; you have not given your full time to the lesson,' said Mirah, in a higher tone than usual. 'Will you sing this again, or shall I sing it to you?'

'Oh, please sing it to me,' said Mab, rejoiced that Mirah meant to take no more notice of what had happened.

And Mirah immediately sang *Lascia ch'io pianga*, giving forth its melodious sobs and cries with new fullness and energy. Hans paused in his walk and leaned against the mantelpiece, keeping his eyes carefully away from his mother's. When Mirah had sung her last note and touched the last chord, she rose and said, 'I must go home now. Ezra expects me.'

She gave her hand silently to Mrs. Meyrick and hung back a little, not daring to look at her, instead of kissing her as usual. But the little mother drew Mirah's face down to hers, and said soothingly, 'God bless you, my dear.' Mirah felt that she had committed an offence against Mrs. Meyrick by angrily rebuking Hans, and mixed with the rest of her suffering was the sense that she had shown something like a proud ingratitude, an unbecoming assertion of superiority. And her friend had divined this compunction.

Meanwhile Hans had seized his wide-awake, and was ready to open the door.

'Now Hans,' said Mab, with what was really a sister's tenderness cunningly disguised, 'you are not going to walk home with Mirah. I am sure she would rather not. You are so dreadfully disagreeable to-day.'

'I shall go to take care of her, if she does not forbid me,' said Hans, opening the door.

Mirah said nothing, and when he had opened the outer door for her and closed it behind him, he walked by her side unforbidden. She had not the courage to begin speaking to him again – conscious that she had perhaps been unbecomingly severe in her words to him, yet finding only severer words behind them in her heart. Besides, she was pressed upon by a crowd of thoughts thrusting themselves forward as interpreters of that consciousness which still remained unuttered to herself.

Hans, on his side, had a mind equally busy. Mirah's anger had waked in him a new perception, and with it the unpleasant sense that he was a dolt not to have had it before. Suppose Mirah's heart were entirely preoccupied with Deronda in another character than that of her own and her brother's benefactor: the supposition was attended in Hans's mind with anxieties which, to do him justice, were not altogether selfish. He had a strong persuasion, which only direct evidence to the contrary could have dissipated, that there was a serious attachment between Deronda and Mrs. Grandcourt; he had pieced together many fragments of observation and gradually gathered knowledge, completed by what his sisters had heard from Anna Gascoigne, which convinced him not only that Mrs. Grandcourt had a passion for Deronda, but also, notwithstanding his friend's austere self-repression, that Deronda's susceptibility about her was the sign of concealed love. Some men, having such a conviction, would have avoided allusions that could have roused that susceptibility; but Hans's talk naturally fluttered towards mischief, and he was given to a form of experiment on live animals which consisted in irritating his friends playfully. His experiments had ended in satisfying him that what he thought likely was true.

On the other hand, any susceptibility Deronda had manifested about a lover's attention being shown to Mirah, Hans took to be sufficiently accounted for by the alleged reason, namely, her dependent position; for he credited his friend with all possible unselfish anxiety for those whom he could rescue or protect. And Deronda's insistence that Mirah would never marry one who was not a Jew necessarily seemed to exclude himself, since Hans shared the ordinary opinion, which he knew nothing to disturb, that Deronda was the son of Sir Hugo Mallinger.

Thus he felt himself in clearness about the state of Deronda's affections; but now, the events which really struck him as concurring towards the desirable union with Mrs. Grandcourt, had called forth a flash of revelation from Mirah – a betrayal of her passionate feeling on this subject which made him melancholy on her account as well as his own – yet on the whole less melancholy than if he had imagined Deronda's hopes fixed on her. It is not sublime, but it is common, for a man to see the beloved object unhappy because his rival loves another, with more fortitude and a milder jealousy than if he saw her entirely happy in his rival. At least it was so with the mercurial Hans, who fluctuated between the contradictory states, of feeling wounded because Mirah was wounded, and of being almost obliged to Deronda for loving somebody else. It was impossible for him to give Mirah any direct sign of the way in which he had understood her anger, yet he longed that his speechless companionship should be eloquent in a tender, penitent sympathy which is an admissible form of wooing a bruised heart.

Thus the two went side by side in a companionship that yet seemed an agitated communication, like that of two chords whose quick vibrations lie outside our hearing. But when they reached the door of Mirah's home, and Hans said 'Good-bye,' putting out his hand with an appealing look of penitence, she met the look with melancholy gentleness, and said, 'Will you not come in and see my brother?'

Hans could not but interpret this invitation as a sign of pardon. He had not enough understanding of what Mirah's nature had been wrought into by her early experience, to divine how the very strength of her late excitement had made it pass the more quickly into a resolute acceptance of pain. When he had said, 'If you will let me,' and they went in together, half his grief was gone, and he was spinning a little romance of how his devotion might make him indispensable to Mirah in proportion as Deronda gave his devotion elsewhere. This was quite fair, since his friend was provided for according to his own heart; and on the question of Judaism Hans felt thoroughly fortified: – who ever heard in tale or history that a woman's love went in the track of her race and religion? Moslem and Jewish damsels were always attracted towards Christians, and now if Mirah's heart had gone forth too precipitately towards Deronda, here was another case in point. Hans was wont to make merry with his own arguments, to call himself a Giaour, and antithesis the sole clue to events; but he believed a little in what he laughed at. And thus his bird-like hope, constructed on the lightest principles, soared again in spite of heavy circumstance.

They found Mordecai looking singularly happy, holding a closed letter in his hand, his eyes glowing with a quiet triumph which in his emaciated face gave the idea of a conquest over assailing death. After the greeting between him and Hans, Mirah put her arm round her brother's neck and looked down at the letter in his hand, without the courage to ask about it, though she felt sure that it was the cause of his happiness.

'A letter from Daniel Deronda,' said Mordecai, answering her look. 'Brief – only saying that he hopes soon to return. Unexpected claims have detained him. The promise of seeing him again is like the bow in the cloud to me,' continued Mordecai, looking at Hans; 'and to you also it must be a gladness. For who has two friends like him?'

While Hans was answering Mirah slipped away to her own room; but not to indulge in any outburst of the passion within her. If the angels once supposed to watch the toilet of women had entered the little chamber with her and let her shut the door behind them, they would only have seen her take off her hat, sit down and press her hands against her temples as if she had suddenly reflected that her head ached; then rise to dash cold water on her eyes and brow and hair till her backward curls were full of crystal beads, while she had dried her brow and looked out like a freshly-opened flower from among the dewy tresses of the woodland; then give deep sighs of relief, and putting on her little slippers, sit still after that action for a couple of minutes, which seemed to her so long, so full of things to come, that she rose with an air of recollection, and went down to make tea.

Something of the old life had returned. She had been used to remember that she must learn her part, must go to rehearsal, must act and sing in the evening, must hide her feelings from her father; and the more painful her life grew, the more she had been used to hide. The force of her nature had long found its chief action in resolute endurance, and to-day the violence of feeling which had caused the first jet of anger had quickly transformed itself into a steady facing of trouble, the well-known companion of her young years. But while she moved about and spoke as usual, a close observer might have discerned a difference between this apparent calm, which was the effect of restraining energy, and the sweet genuine calm of the months when she first felt a return of her infantine happiness.

Those who have been indulged by fortune and have always thought of calamity as what happens to others, feel a blind incredulous rage at the reversal of their lot, and half believe that their wild cries will alter the course of the storm. Mirah felt no such surprise when familiar Sorrow came back from brief absence, and sat down with her according to the old use and wont. And this habit of expecting trouble rather than joy, hindered her from having any persistent belief in opposition to the probabilities which were not merely suggested by Hans but were supported by her own private knowledge and long-growing presentiment. An attachment between Deronda and Mrs. Grandcourt, to end in their future marriage, had the aspect of a certainty for her feeling. There had been no fault in him: facts had ordered themselves so that there was a tie between him and this woman who belonged to another world than her own and Ezra's – nay, who seemed another sort of being than Deronda, something foreign that would be a disturbance in his life instead of blending with it. Well, well – but if it could have been deferred so as to make no difference while Ezra was there! She did not know all the momentousness of the relation between Deronda and her brother, but she had seen and instinctively felt enough to forbode its being incongruous with any close tie to Mrs. Grandcourt; at least this was the clothing that Mirah first gave to her mortal repugnance. But in the still, quick action of her consciousness, thoughts went on like changing states of sensation unbroken by her habitual acts; and this inward language soon said distinctly that the mortal repugnance would remain even if Ezra were secured from loss.

'What I have read about and sung about and seen acted, is happening to me – this that I am feeling is the love that makes jealousy:' – so impartially Mirah summed up the charge against herself. But what difference could this pain of hers make to any one else? It must remain as exclusively her own, and hidden, as her early yearning and devotion towards her lost mother. But unlike that devotion, it was something that she felt to be a misfortune of her nature – a discovery that what should have been pure gratitude and reverence had sunk into selfish pain, that the feeling she had hitherto delighted to pour out in words was degraded into something she was ashamed to betray – an absurd longing that she who had received all and given nothing should be of importance where she was of no importance – an angry feeling towards another woman who possessed the good she wanted. But what notion, what vain reliance could it be that had lain darkly within her and was now burning itself into sight as disappointment and jealousy? It was as if her soul had been steeped in poisonous passion by forgotten dreams of deep sleep, and now flamed out in this unaccountable misery. For with her waking reason she had never entertained what seemed the wildly unfitting thought that Deronda could love her. The uneasiness she had felt before had been comparatively vague and easily explained as part of a general regret that he was only a visitant in her and her brother's world, from which the world where his home lay was as different as a portico with lights and lackeys was different from the door of a tent, where the only splendour came from the mysterious inaccessible stars. But her feeling was no longer vague: the cause of her pain – the image of Mrs. Grandcourt by Deronda's side drawing him farther and farther into the distance, was as definite as pincers on her flesh. In the Psyche-mould of Mirah's frame there rested a fervid quality of emotion sometimes rashly supposed to require the bulk of a Cleopatra; her impressions had the thoroughness and tenacity that give to the first selection of passionate feeling the character of a life-long faithfulness. And now a selection had declared itself, which gave love a cruel heart of jealousy: she had been used to a strong repugnance towards certain objects that surrounded her, and to walk inwardly aloof from them while they touched her sense. And now her repugnance concentrated itself on Mrs. Grandcourt, of whom she involuntarily conceived more evil than she knew. 'I could bear everything that used to be – but this is worse – this is worse, – I used not to have horrible feelings!' said the poor child in a loud whisper to her pillow. Strange that she should have to pray against any feeling which concerned Deronda!

But this conclusion had been reached through an evening spent in attending to Mordecai, whose exaltation of spirit in the prospect of seeing his friend again, disposed him to utter many thoughts aloud to Mirah, though such communication was often interrupted by intervals apparently filled with an inward utterance that animated his eyes and gave an occasional silent action to his lips. One thought especially occupied him.

'Seest thou, Mirah,' he said once, after a long silence, 'the *Shemah*, wherein we briefly confess the divine Unity, is the chief devotional exercise of the Hebrew; and this made our religion the fundamental religion for the whole world; for the divine Unity embraced as its consequence the ultimate unity of mankind. See, then – the nation which has been scoffed at for its separateness, has given a binding theory to the human race. Now, in complete unity a part possesses the whole as the whole possesses every part: and in this way human life is tending toward the image of the Supreme Unity: for as our life becomes more spiritual by capacity of thought, and joy therein, possession tends to become more universal, being independent of gross material contact: so that in a brief day the soul of a man may know in fuller volume the good which has been and is, nay, is to come, than all he could possess in a whole life where he had to follow the creeping paths of the senses. In this moment, my sister, I hold the joy of another's future within me: a future which these eyes will not see, and which my spirit may not then recognize as mine. I recognize it now, and love it so, that I can lay down this poor life upon its altar and say: "Burn, burn indiscernibly into that which shall be, which is my love and not me." Dost thou understand, Mirah?'

'A little,' said Mirah, faintly, 'but my mind is too poor to have felt it.'

'And yet,' said Mordecai, rather insistently, 'women are specially framed for the love which feels possession in renouncing, and is thus a fit image of what I mean. Somewhere in the later *Midrash*, I think, is the story of a Jewish maiden who loved a Gentile king so well, that this was what she did: – She entered into prison and changed clothes with the woman who was beloved by the king, that she might deliver that woman from death by dying in her stead, and leave the king to be happy in his love which was not for her. This is the surpassing love, that loses self in the object of love.'

'No, Ezra, no,' said Mirah, with low-toned intensity, 'that was not it. She wanted the king when she was dead to know what she had done, and feel that she was better than the other. It was her strong self, wanting to conquer, that made her die.'

Mordecai was silent a little, and then argued –

'That might be, Mirah. But if she acted so, believing the king would never know?'

'You can make the story so in your mind, Ezra, because you are great, and like to fancy the greatest that could be. But I think it was not really like that. The Jewish girl must have had jealousy in her heart, and she wanted somehow to have the first place in the king's mind. That is what she would die for.'

'My sister, thou hast read too many plays, where the writers delight in showing the human passions as indwelling demons, unmixed with the relenting and devout elements of the soul. Thou judgest by the plays, and not by thy own heart, which is like our mother's.'

Mirah made no answer.

LXII

'Das Glück ist eine leichte Dirne,
Und weilt nicht gern am selben Ort;
Sie streicht das Haar dir von der Stirne
Und küsst dich rasch und flattert fort.

Frau Unglück hat im Gegentheile
Dich liebefest an's Herz gedrückt;
Sie sagt, sie habe keine Eile,
Setzt sich zu dir ans Bett und strickt.'
      – HEINE.

SOMETHING which Mirah had lately been watching for as the fulfilment of a threat, seemed now the continued visit of that familiar sorrow which had lately come back, bringing abundant luggage.

Turning out of Knightsbridge, after singing at a charitable morning concert in a wealthy house, where she had been recommended by Klesmer, and where there had been the usual groups outside to see the departing company, she began to feel herself dogged by footsteps that kept an even pace with her own. Her concert dress being simple black, over which she had thrown a dust-cloak, could not make her an object of unpleasant attention, and render walking an imprudence; but this reflection did not occur to Mirah: another kind of alarm lay uppermost in her mind. She immediately thought of her father, and could no more look round than if she had felt herself tracked by a ghost. To turn and face him would be voluntarily to meet the rush of emotions which beforehand seemed intolerable. If it were her father, he must mean to claim recognition, and he would oblige her to face him. She must wait for that compulsion. She walked on, not quickening her pace – of what use was that? – but picturing what was about to happen as if she had the full certainty that the man behind her was her father; and along with her picturing went a regret that she had given her word to Mrs. Meyrick not to use any concealment about him. The regret at last urged her, at least, to try and hinder any sudden betrayal that

814

would cause her brother an unnecessary shock. Under the pressure of this motive, she resolved to turn before she reached her own door, and firmly will the encounter instead of merely submitting to it. She had already reached the entrance of the small square where her home lay, and had made up her mind to turn, when she felt her embodied presentiment getting closer to her, then slipping to her side, grasping her wrist, and saying, with a persuasive curl of accent, 'Mirah!'

She paused at once without any start; it was the voice she expected, and she was meeting the expected eyes. Her face was as grave as if she had been looking at her executioner, while his was adjusted to the intention of soothing and propitiating her. Once a handsome face, with bright colour, it was now sallow and deep-lined, and had that peculiar impress of impudent suavity which comes from courting favour while accepting disrespect. He was lightly made and active, with something of youth about him which made the signs of age seem a disguise; and in reality he was hardly fifty-seven. His dress was shabby, as when she had seen him before. The presence of this unreverend father now, more than ever, affected Mirah with the mingled anguish of shame and grief, repulsion and pity – more than ever, now that her own world was changed into one where there was no comradeship to fence him from scorn and contempt.

Slowly, with a sad, tremulous voice, she said, 'It is you, father.'

'Why did you run away from me, child?' he began, with rapid speech which was meant to have a tone of tender remonstrance, accompanied with various quick gestures like an abbreviated finger-language. 'What were you afraid of? You knew I never made you do anything against your will. It was for your sake I broke up your engagement in the Vorstadt, because I saw it didn't suit you, and you repaid me by leaving me to the bad times that came in consequence. I had made an easier engagement for you at the Vorstadt Theatre in Dresden: I didn't tell you, because

I wanted to take you by surprise. And you left me planted there – obliged to make myself scarce because I had broken contract. That was hard lines for me, after I had given up everything for the sake of getting you an education which was to be a fortune to you. What father devoted himself to his daughter more than I did to you? You know how I bore that disappointment in your voice, and made the best of it; and when I had nobody besides you, and was getting broken, as a man must who has had to fight his way with his brains – you chose that time to leave me. Who else was it you owed everything to, if not to me? and where was your feeling in return? For what my daughter cared, I might have died in a ditch.'

Lapidoth stopped short here, not from lack of invention, but because he had reached a pathetic climax, and gave a sudden sob, like a woman's, taking out hastily an old yellow silk handkerchief. He really felt that his daughter had treated him ill – a sort of sensibility which is naturally strong in unscrupulous persons, who put down what is owing to them, without any *per contra*. Mirah, in spite of that sob, had energy enough not to let him suppose that he deceived her. She answered more firmly, though it was the first time she had ever used accusing words to him.

'You know why I left you, father; and I had reason to distrust you, because I felt sure that you had deceived my mother. If I could have trusted you, I would have stayed with you and worked for you.'

'I never meant to deceive your mother, Mirah,' said Lapidoth, putting back his handkerchief, but beginning with a voice that seemed to struggle against further sobbing. 'I meant to take you back to her, but chances hindered me just at the time, and then there came information of her death. It was better for you that I should stay where I was, and your brother could take care of himself. Nobody had any claim on me but you. I had word of your mother's death from a particular friend, who had undertaken to manage things for me, and I sent him over money to pay expenses. There's one chance, to be sure' – Lapidoth had

FRUIT AND SEED

quickly conceived that he must guard against something
unlikely, yet possible – 'he may have written me lies for the
sake of getting the money out of me.'

Mirah made no answer; she could not bear to utter the
only true one – 'I don't believe one word of what you say' –
and she simply showed a wish that they should walk on,
feeling that their standing still might draw down unpleasant
notice. Even as they walked along, their companionship
might well have made a passer-by turn back to look at
them. The figure of Mirah, with her beauty set off by the
quiet, careful dress of an English lady, made a strange
pendant to this shabby, foreign-looking, eager, and ges-
ticulating man, who withal had an ineffaceable jauntiness
of air, perhaps due to the bushy curls of his grizzled hair,
the smallness of his hands and feet, and his light walk.

'You seem to have done well for yourself, Mirah? *You* are
in no want, I see,' said the father, looking at her with
emphatic examination.

'Good friends who found me in distress have helped me
to get work,' said Mirah, hardly knowing what she actually
said, from being occupied with what she would presently
have to say. 'I give lessons. I have sung in private houses.
I have just been singing at a private concert.' She paused,
and then added, with significance, 'I have very good
friends, who know all about me.'

'And you would be ashamed they should see your father
in this plight? No wonder. I came to England with no
prospect, but the chance of finding you. It was a mad
quest; but a father's heart is superstitious – feels a loadstone drawing it somewhere or other. I might have done
very well, staying abroad: when I hadn't you to take care of,
I could have rolled or settled as easily as a ball; but it's hard
being lonely in the world, when your spirit's beginning to
break. And I thought my little Mirah would repent leaving
her father, when she came to look back. I've had a sharp
pinch to work my way; I don't know what I shall come
down to next. Talents like mine are no use in this country.
When a man's getting out at elbows nobody will believe in

him. I couldn't get any decent employ with my appearance. I've been obliged to go pretty low for a shilling
already.'

Mirah's anxiety was quick enough to imagine her
father's sinking into a further degradation, which she was
bound to hinder if she could. But before she could answer
his string of inventive sentences, delivered with as much
glibness as if they had been learned by rote, he added
promptly –

'Where do you live, Mirah?'

'Here, in this square. We are not far from the house.'

'In lodgings?'

'Yes.'

'Any one to take care of you?'

'Yes,' said Mirah again, looking full at the keen face
which was turned towards hers – 'my brother.'

The father's eyelids fluttered as if the lightning had
come across them, and there was a slight movement of
the shoulders. But he said, after a just perceptible pause:
'Ezra? How did you know – how did you find him?'

'That would take long to tell. Here we are at the door.
My brother would not wish me to close it on you.'

Mirah was already on the door-step, but had her face
turned towards her father, who stood below her on the
pavement. Her heart had begun to beat faster with the
prospect of what was coming in the presence of Ezra; and
already in this attitude of giving leave to the father whom
she had been used to obey – in this sight of him standing
below her, with a perceptible shrinking from the admission
which he had been indirectly asking for, she had a pang of
the peculiar, sympathetic humiliation and shame – the
stabbed heart of reverence – which belongs to a nature
intensely filial.

'Stay a minute, *Liebchen*,' said Lapidoth, speaking in a
lowered tone; 'what sort of man has Ezra turned out?'

'A good man – a wonderful man,' said Mirah, with slow
emphasis, trying to master the agitation which made her
voice more tremulous as she went on. She felt urged to

prepare her father for the complete penetration of himself which awaited him. 'But he was very poor when my friends found him for me – a poor workman. Once – twelve years ago – he was strong and happy, going to the East, which he loved to think of; and my mother called him back because – because she had lost me. And he went to her, and took care of her through great trouble, and worked for her till she died – died in grief. And Ezra, too, had lost his health and strength. The cold had seized him coming back to my mother, because she was forsaken. For years he has been getting weaker – always poor, always working – but full of knowledge, and great-minded. All who come near him honour him. To stand before him, is like standing before a prophet of God' – Mirah ended with difficulty, her heart throbbing – 'falsehoods are no use.'

She had cast down her eyes that she might not see her father while she spoke the last words – unable to bear the ignoble look of frustration that gathered in his face. But he was none the less quick in invention and decision.

'Mirah, *Liebchen*,' he said, in the old caressing way, 'shouldn't you like me to make myself a little more respectable before my son sees me? If I had a little sum of money, I could fit myself out and come home to you as your father ought, and then I could offer myself for some decent place. With a good shirt and coat on my back, people would be glad enough to have me. I could offer myself for a courier, if I didn't look like a broken-down mountebank. I should like to be with my children, and forget and forgive. But you have never seen your father look like this before. If you had ten pounds at hand – or I could appoint you to bring it me somewhere – I could fit myself out by the day after to-morrow.'

Mirah felt herself under a temptation which she must try to overcome. She answered, obliging herself to look at him again –

'I don't like to deny you what you ask, father; but I have given a promise not to do things for you in secret. It *is* hard to see you looking needy; but we will bear that for a little while; and then you can have new clothes, and we can pay for them.' Her practical sense made her see now what was Mrs. Meyrick's wisdom in exacting a promise from her.

Lapidoth's good-humour gave way a little. He said with a sneer, 'You are a hard and fast young lady – you've been learning useful virtues – keeping promises not to help your father with a pound or two when you are getting money to dress yourself in silk – your father who made an idol of you, and gave up the best part of his life to providing for you.'

'It seems cruel – I know it seems cruel,' said Mirah, feeling this a worse moment than when she meant to drown herself. Her lips were suddenly pale. 'But, father, it is more cruel to break the promises people trust in. That broke my mother's heart – it has broken Ezra's life. You and I must eat now this bitterness from what has been. Bear it. Bear to come in and be cared for as you are.'

'To-morrow, then,' said Lapidoth, almost turning on his heel away from this pale, trembling daughter, who seemed now to have got the inconvenient world to back her; but he quickly turned on it again, with his hands feeling about restlessly in his pockets, and said, with some return to his appealing tone, 'I'm a little cut up with all this, Mirah. I shall get up my spirits by to-morrow. If you've a little money in your pocket, I suppose it isn't against your promise to give me a trifle – to buy a cigar with.'

Mirah could not ask herself another question – could not do anything else than put her cold trembling hands in her pocket for her *portemonnaie* and hold it out. Lapidoth grasped it at once, pressed her fingers the while, said, 'Good-bye, my little girl – to-morrow then!' and left her. He had not taken many steps before he looked carefully into all the folds of the purse, found two half-sovereigns and odd silver, and, pasted against the folding cover, a bit of paper on which Ezra had inscribed, in a beautiful Hebrew character, the name of his mother, the days of her birth, marriage, and death, and the prayer, 'May Mirah be delivered from evil.' It was Mirah's liking to have this little inscription on many articles that she used.

The father read it, and had a quick vision of his marriage-day, and the bright, unblamed young fellow he was in that time; teaching many things, but expecting by-and-by to get money more easily by writing; and very fond of his beautiful bride Sara – crying when she expected him to cry, and reflecting every phase of her feeling with mimetic susceptibility. Lapidoth had travelled a long way from that young self, and thought of all that this inscription signified with an unemotional memory, which was like the ocular perception of a touch to one who has lost the sense of touch, or like morsels on an untasting palate, having shape and grain, but no flavour. Among the things we may gamble away in a lazy selfish life is the capacity for ruth, compunction, or any unselfish regret – which we may come to long for as one in slow death longs to feel laceration, rather than be conscious of a widening margin where consciousness once was. Mirah's purse was a handsome one – a gift to her, which she had been unable to reflect about giving away – and Lapidoth presently found himself outside of his reverie, considering what the purse would fetch in addition to the sum it contained, and what prospect there was of his being able to get more from his daughter without submitting to adopt a penitential form of life under the eyes of that formidable son. On such a subject his susceptibilities were still lively.

Meanwhile Mirah had entered the house with her power of reticence overcome by the cruelty of her pain. She found her brother quietly reading and sifting old manuscripts of his own, which he meant to consign to Deronda. In the reaction from the long effort to master herself, she fell down before him and clasped his knees, sobbing and crying, 'Ezra, Ezra!'

He did not speak. His alarm for her was spending itself on conceiving the cause of her distress, the more striking from the novelty in her of this violent manifestation. But Mirah's own longing was to be able to speak and tell him the cause. Presently she raised her hand, and still sobbing, said brokenly –

DANIEL DERONDA

'Ezra, my father! our father! He followed me. I wanted him to come in. I said you would let him come in. And he said No, he would not – not now, but to-morrow. And he begged for money from me. And I gave him my purse, and he went away.'

Mirah's words seemed to herself to express all the misery she felt in them. Her brother found them less grievous than his preconceptions, and said gently, 'Wait for calm, Mirah, and then tell me all,' – putting off her hat and laying his hands tenderly on her head. She felt the soothing influence, and in a few minutes told him as exactly as she could all that had happened.

'He will not come to-morrow,' said Mordecai. Neither of them said to the other what they both thought, namely, that he might watch for Mirah's outgoings and beg from her again.

'Seest thou,' he presently added, 'our lot is the lot of Israel. The grief and the glory are mingled as the smoke and the flame. It is because we children have inherited the good that we feel the evil. These things are wedded for us, as our father was wedded to our mother.'

The surroundings were of Brompton, but the voice might have come from a Rabbi transmitting the sentences of an elder time to be registered in *Babli* – by which affectionate-sounding diminutive is meant the vast volume of the Babylonian Talmud. 'The Omnipresent,' said a Rabbi, 'is occupied in making marriages.' The levity of the saying lies in the ear of him who hears it; for by marriages the speaker meant all the wondrous combinations of the universe whose issue makes our good and evil.

LXIII

'Moses, trotz seiner Befeindung der Kunst, dennoch selber ein
grosser Künstler war und den wahren Künstlergeist besass. Nur
war dieser Künstlergeist bei ihm, wie bei seinen ägyptischen
Landsleuten, nur auf das Colossale und Unverwüstliche gerich-
tet. Aber nicht wie die Aegypter formirte er seine Kunstwerke
aus Backstein und Granit, sondern er baute Menschen-
pyramiden, er meisselte Menschen Obelisken, er nahm einen
armen Hirtenstamm und Schuf daraus ein Volk, das ebenfalls den
Jahrhunderten trotzen sollte ... er Schuf Israel.'

– HEINE: *Geständnisse*.

IMAGINE the difference in Deronda's state of mind when
he left England and when he returned to it. He had set out
for Genoa in total uncertainty how far the actual bent of his
wishes and affections would be encouraged – how far the
claims revealed to him might draw him into new paths, far
away from the tracks his thoughts had lately been pursuing
with a consent of desire which uncertainty made dangerous. He came back with something like a discovered
charter warranting the inherited right that his ambition
had begun to yearn for: he came back with what was better
than freedom – with a duteous bond which his experience
had been preparing him to accept gladly, even if it had
been attended with no promise of satisfying a secret
passionate longing never yet allowed to grow into a hope.
But now he dared avow to himself the hidden selection of
his love. Since the hour when he left the house at Chelsea
in full-hearted silence under the effect of Mirah's farewell
look and words – their exquisite appealingness stirring in
him that deeply-laid care for womanhood which had begun
when his own lip was like a girl's – her hold on his feeling
had helped him to be blameless in word and deed under
the difficult circumstances we know of. There seemed no
likelihood that he could ever woo this creature who had
become dear to him amidst associations that forbade wooing; yet she had taken her place in his soul as a beloved
type – reducing the power of other fascination and making
a difference in it that became deficiency. The influence

823

had been continually strengthened. It had lain in the course of poor Gwendolen's lot that her dependence on Deronda tended to rouse in him the enthusiasm of self-martyring pity rather than of personal love, and his less constrained tenderness flowed with the fuller stream towards an indwelling image in all things unlike Gwendolen. Still more, his relation to Mordecai had brought with it a new nearness to Mirah which was not the less agitating because there was no apparent change in his position towards her; and she had inevitably been bound up in all the thoughts that made him shrink from an issue disappointing to her brother. This process had not gone on unconsciously in Deronda: he was conscious of it as we are of some covetousness that it would be better to nullify by encouraging other thoughts than to give it the insistency of confession even to ourselves: but the jealous fire had leaped out at Hans's pretensions, and when his mother accused him of being in love with a Jewess, any evasion suddenly seemed an infidelity. His mother had compelled him to a decisive acknowledgement of his love, as Joseph Kalonymos had compelled him to a definite expression of his resolve. This new state of decision wrought on Deronda with a force which surprised even himself. There was a release of all the energy which had long been spent in self-checking and suppression because of doubtful conditions; and he was ready to laugh at his own impetuosity when, as he neared England on his way from Mainz, he felt the remaining distance more and more of an obstruction. It was as if he had found an added soul in finding his ancestry – his judgment no longer wandering in the mazes of impartial sympathy, but choosing, with that noble partiality which is man's best strength, the closer fellowship that makes sympathy practical – exchanging that bird's-eye reasonableness which soars to avoid preference and loses all sense of quality, for the generous reasonableness of drawing shoulder to shoulder with men of like inheritance. He wanted now to be again with Mordecai, to pour forth instead of restraining his feeling, to admit agreement and maintain dissent, and all the while to find Mirah's presence without the embarrassment of obviously seeking it, to see her in the light of a new possibility, to interpret her looks and words from a new starting-point. He was not greatly alarmed about the effect of Hans's attentions, but he had a presentiment that her feeling towards himself had from the first lain in a channel from which it was not likely to be diverted into love. To astonish a woman by turning into her lover when she has been thinking of you merely as a Lord Chancellor is what a man naturally shrinks from: he is anxious to create an easier transition.

What wonder that Deronda saw no other course than to go straight from the London railway station to the lodgings in that small square in Brompton? Every argument was in favour of his losing no time. He had promised to run down the next day to see Lady Mallinger at the Abbey, and it was already sunset. He wished to deposit the precious chest with Mordecai, who would study its contents, both in his absence and in company with him; and that he should pay this visit without pause would gratify Mordecai's heart. Hence, and for other reasons, it gratified Deronda's heart. The strongest tendencies of his nature were rushing in one current – the fervent affectionateness which made him delight in meeting the wish of beings near to him, and the imaginative need of some far-reaching relation to make the horizon of his immediate, daily acts. It has to be admitted that in this classical, romantic, world-historic position of his, bringing as it were from its hiding-place his hereditary armour, he wore – but so, one must suppose, did the most ancient heroes whether Semitic or Japhetic – the summer costume of his contemporaries. He did not reflect that the drab tints were becoming to him, for he rarely went to the expense of such thinking; but his own depth of colouring, which made the becomingness, got an added radiance in the eyes, a fleeting and returning glow in the skin, as he entered the house, wondering what exactly he should find. He made his entrance as noiseless as possible.

It was the evening of that same afternoon on which Mirah had had the interview with her father. Mordecai, penetrated by her grief, and also by the sad memories which the incident had awakened, had not resumed his task of sifting papers: some of them had fallen scattered on the floor in the first moments of anxiety, and neither he nor Mirah had thought of laying them in order again. They had sat perfectly still together, not knowing how long; while the clock ticked on the mantelpiece, and the light was fading. Mirah, unable to think of the food that she ought to have been taking, had not moved since she had thrown off her dust-cloak and sat down beside Mordecai with her hand in his, while he had laid his head backward, with closed eyes and difficult breathing, looking, Mirah thought, as he would look when the soul within him could no longer live in its straitened home. The thought that his death might be near was continually visiting her when she saw his face in this way, without its vivid animation; and now, to the rest of her grief was added the regret that she had been unable to control the violent outburst which had shaken him. She sat watching him – her oval cheeks pallid, her eyes with the sorrowful brilliancy left by young tears, her curls in as much disorder as a just-wakened child's – watching that emaciated face, where it might have been imagined that a veil had been drawn never to be lifted, as if it were her dead joy which had left her strong enough to live on in sorrow. And life at that moment stretched before Mirah with more than a repetition of former sadness. The shadow of the father was there, and more than that, a double bereavement – of one living as well as one dead.

But now the door was opened, and while none entered, a well-known voice said: 'Daniel Deronda – may he come in?'

'Come! come!' said Mordecai, immediately rising with an irradiated face and opened eyes – apparently as little surprised as if he had seen Deronda in the morning, and expected this evening visit; while Mirah started up blushing with confused, half-alarmed expectation.

Yet when Deronda entered, the sight of him was like the clearness after rain: no clouds to come could hinder the cherishing beam of that moment. As he held out his right hand to Mirah, who was close to her brother's left, he laid his other hand on Mordecai's right shoulder, and stood so a moment, holding them both at once, uttering no word, but reading their faces, till he said anxiously to Mirah, 'Has anything happened? – any trouble?'

'Talk not of trouble, now,' said Mordecai, saving her from the need to answer. 'There is joy in your face – let the joy be ours.'

Mirah thought, 'It is for something he cannot tell us.' But they all sat down, Deronda drawing a chair close in front of Mordecai.

'That is true,' he said, emphatically. 'I have a joy which will remain to us even in the worst trouble. I did not tell you the reason of my journey abroad, Mordecai, because – never mind – I went to learn my parentage. And you were right. I am a Jew.'

The two men clasped hands with a movement that seemed part of the flash from Mordecai's eyes, and passed through Mirah like an electric shock. But Deronda went on without pause, speaking from Mordecai's mind as much as from his own –

'We have the same people. Our souls have the same vocation. We shall not be separated by life or by death.'

Mordecai's answer was uttered in Hebrew, and in no more than a loud whisper. It was in the liturgical words which express the religious bond: 'Our God, and the God of our fathers.'

The weight of feeling pressed too strongly on that ready-winged speech which usually moved in quick adaptation to every stirring of his fervour.

Mirah fell on her knees by her brother's side, and looked at his now illuminated face, which had just before been so deathly. The action was an inevitable outlet of the violent reversal from despondency to a gladness which came over her as solemnly as if she had been beholding a religious rite. For the moment she thought of the effect on her own life only through the effect on her brother.

'And it is not only that I am a Jew,' Deronda went on, enjoying one of those rare moments when our yearnings and our acts can be completely one, and the real we behold is our ideal good; 'but I come of a strain that has ardently maintained the fellowship of our race – a line of Spanish Jews that has borne many students and men of practical power. And I possess what will give us a sort of communion with them. My grandfather, Daniel Charisi, preserved manuscripts, family records stretching far back, in the hope that they would pass into the hands of his grandson. And now his hope is fulfilled, in spite of attempts to thwart it by hiding my parentage from me. I possess the chest containing them, with his own papers, and it is down below in this house. I mean to leave it with you, Mordecai, that you may help me to study the manuscripts. Some of them I can read easily enough – those in Spanish and Italian. Others are in Hebrew, and, I think, Arabic; but there seem to be Latin translations. I was only able to look at them cursorily while I stayed at Mainz. We will study them together.'

Deronda ended with that bright smile which, beaming out from the habitual gravity of his face, seemed a revelation (the reverse of the continual smile that discredits all expression). But when this happy glance passed from Mordecai to rest on Mirah, it acted like a little too much sunshine, and made her change her attitude. She had knelt under an impulse with which any personal embarrassment was incongruous, and especially any thoughts about how Mrs. Grandcourt might stand to this new aspect of things – thoughts which made her colour under Deronda's glance, and rise to take her seat again in her usual posture of crossed hands and feet, with the effort to look as quiet as possible. Deronda, equally sensitive, imagined that the feeling of which he was conscious, had entered too much into his eyes, and had been repugnant to her. He was ready enough to believe that any unexpected manifestation might spoil her feeling towards him – and then his precious relation to brother and sister would be marred. If Mirah could have no love for him, any advances of love on his part would make her wretched in that continual contact with him which would remain inevitable.

While such feelings were pulsating quickly in Deronda and Mirah, Mordecai, seeing nothing in his friend's presence and words but a blessed fulfilment, was already speaking with his old sense of enlargement in utterance –

'Daniel, from the first, I have said to you, we know not all the pathways. Has there not been a meeting among them, as of the operations in one soul, where an idea being born and breathing draws the elements towards it, and is fed and grows? For all things are bound together in that Omnipresence which is the place and habitation of the world, and events are as a glass wherethrough our eyes see some of the pathways. And if it seems that the erring and unloving wills of men have helped to prepare you, as Moses was prepared, to serve your people the better, that depends on another order than the law which must guide our footsteps. For the evil will of man makes not a people's good except by stirring the righteous will of man; and beneath all the clouds with which our thought encompasses the Eternal, this is clear – that a people can be blessed only by having counsellors and a multitude whose will moves in obedience to the laws of justice and love. For see, now, it was your loving will that made a chief pathway, and resisted the effect of evil; for, by performing the duties of brotherhood to my sister, and seeking out her brother in the flesh, your soul has been prepared to receive with gladness this message of the Eternal: "Behold the multitude of your brethren."'

'It is quite true that you and Mirah have been my teachers,' said Deronda. 'If this revelation had been made to me before I knew you both, I think my mind would have rebelled against it. Perhaps I should have felt then – "If I could have chosen, I would not have been a Jew." What I feel now is – that my whole being is a consent to the fact. But it has been the gradual accord between your mind and mine which has brought about that full consent.'

At the moment Deronda was speaking, that first evening in the book-shop was vividly in his remembrance, with all the struggling aloofness he had then felt from Mordecai's prophetic confidence. It was his nature to delight in satisfying to the utmost the eagerly-expectant soul, which seemed to be looking out from the face before him, like the long-enduring watcher who at last sees the mounting signal-flame; and he went on with fuller fervour –

'It is through your inspiration that I have discerned what may be my life's task. It is you who have given shape to what, I believe, was an inherited yearning – the effect of brooding, passionate thoughts in many ancestors – thoughts that seem to have been intensely present in my grandfather. Suppose the stolen offspring of some mountain tribe brought up in a city of the plain, or one with an inherited genius for painting, and born blind – the ancestral life would lie within them as a dim longing for unknown objects and sensations, and the spell-bound habit of their inherited frames would be like a cunningly-wrought musical instrument, never played on, but quivering throughout in uneasy mysterious moanings of its intricate structure that, under the right touch, gives music. Something like that, I think, has been my experience. Since I began to read and know, I have always longed for some ideal task, in which I might feel myself the heart and brain of a multitude – some social captainship, which would come to me as a duty, and not be striven for as a personal prize. You have raised the image of such a task for me – to bind our race together in spite of heresy. You have said to me – "Our religion united us before it divided us – it made us a people before it made Rabbanites and Karaites." I mean to try what can be done with that union – I mean to work in your spirit. Failure will not be ignoble, but it would be ignoble for me not to try.'

'Even as my brother that fed at the breasts of my mother,' said Mordecai, falling back in his chair with a look of exultant repose, as after some finished labour.

To estimate the effect of this ardent outpouring from Deronda we must remember his former reserve, his careful avoidance of premature assent or delusive encouragement, which gave to this decided pledge of himself a sacramental solemnity, both for his own mind and Mordecai's. On Mirah the effect was equally strong, though with a difference: she felt a surprise which had no place in her brother's mind, at Deronda's suddenly revealed sense of nearness to them: there seemed to be a breaking of day around her which might show her other facts unlike her forebodings in the darkness. But after a moment's silence Mordecai spoke again:

'It has begun already – the marriage of our souls. It waits but the passing away of this body, and then they who are betrothed shall unite in a stricter bond, and what is mine shall be thine. Call nothing mine that I have written, Daniel; for though our Masters delivered rightly that everything should be quoted in the name of him that said it – and their rule is good – yet it does not exclude the willing marriage which melts soul into soul, and makes thought fuller as the clear waters are made fuller, where the fullness is inseparable and the clearness is inseparable. For I have judged what I have written, and I desire the body that I gave my thought to pass away as this fleshly body will pass; but let the thought be born again from our fuller soul which shall be called yours.'

'You must not ask me to promise that,' said Deronda, smiling. 'I must be convinced first of special reasons for it in the writings themselves. And I am too backward a pupil yet. That blent transmission must go on without any choice of ours; but what we can't hinder must not make our rule for what we ought to choose. I think our duty is faithful tradition where we can attain it. And so you would insist for any one but yourself. Don't ask me to deny my spiritual parentage, when I am finding the clue of my life in the recognition of my natural parentage.'

'I will ask for no promise till you see the reason,' said Mordecai. 'You have said the truth: I would obey the

Masters' rule for another. But for years my hope, nay, my confidence, has been, not that the imperfect image of my thought, which is as the ill-shapen work of the youthful carver who has seen a heavenly pattern, and trembles in imitating the vision – not that this should live, but that my vision and passion should enter into yours – yea, into yours; for he whom I longed for afar, was he not you whom I discerned as mine when you came near? Nevertheless, you shall judge. For my soul is satisfied.' Mordecai paused, and then began in a changed tone, reverting to previous suggestions from Deronda's disclosure: 'What moved your parents—?' but he immediately checked himself, and added, 'Nay, I ask not that you should tell me aught concerning others, unless it is your pleasure.'

'Some time – gradually – you will know all,' said Deronda. 'But now tell me more about yourselves, and how the time has passed since I went away. I am sure there has been some trouble. Mirah has been in distress about something.'

He looked at Mirah, but she immediately turned to her brother, appealing to him to give the difficult answer. She hoped he would not think it necessary to tell Deronda the facts about her father on such an evening as this. Just when Deronda had brought himself so near, and identified himself with her brother, it was cutting to her that he should hear of this disgrace clinging about them, which seemed to have become partly his. To relieve herself she rose to take up her hat and cloak, thinking she would go to her own room: perhaps they would speak more easily when she had left them. But meanwhile Mordecai said –

'To-day there has been a grief. A duty which seemed to have gone far into the distance, has come back and turned its face upon us, and raised no gladness – has raised a dread that we must submit to. But for the moment we are delivered from any visible yoke. Let us defer speaking of it, as if this evening which is deepening about us were the beginning of the festival in which we must offer the first-fruits of our joy, and mingle no mourning with them.'

Deronda divined the hinted grief, and left it in silence, rising as he saw Mirah rise, and saying to her, 'Are you going? I must leave almost immediately – when I and Mrs. Adam have mounted the precious chest, and I have delivered the key to Mordecai – no, Ezra – may I call him Ezra now? I have learned to think of him as Ezra since I have heard you call him so.'

'Please call him Ezra,' said Mirah, faintly, feeling a new timidity under Deronda's glance and near presence. Was there really something different about him, or was the difference only in her feeling? The strangely various emotions of the last few hours had exhausted her; she was faint with fatigue and want of food. Deronda, observing her pallor and tremulousness, longed to show more feeling, but dared not. She put out her hand, with an effort to smile, and then he opened the door for her. That was all.

A man of refined pride shrinks from making a lover's approaches to a woman whose wealth or rank might make them appear presumptuous or low-motived; but Deronda was finding a more delicate difficulty in a position which, superficially taken, was the reverse of that – though to an ardent reverential love, the loved woman has always a kind of wealth and rank which makes a man keenly susceptible about the aspect of his addresses. Deronda's difficulty was what any generous man might have felt in some degree; but it affected him peculiarly through his imaginative sympathy with a mind in which gratitude was strong. Mirah, he knew, felt herself bound to him by deep obligations, which to her sensibilities might give every wish of his the aspect of a claim; and an inability to fulfil it would cause her a pain continually revived by their inevitable communion in care for Ezra. Here were fears not of pride only, but of extreme tenderness. Altogether, to have the character of a benefactor seemed to Deronda's anxiety an insurmountable obstacle to confessing himself a lover, unless in some inconceivable way it could be revealed to him that Mirah's heart had accepted him beforehand. And the agitation on his own account, too, was not small.

Even a man who has practised himself in love-making till his own glibness has rendered him sceptical, may at last be overtaken by the lover's awe – may tremble, stammer, and show other signs of recovered sensibility no more in the range of his acquired talents than pins and needles after numbness: how much more may that energetic timidity possess a man whose inward history has cherished his susceptibilities instead of dulling them, and has kept all the language of passion fresh and rooted as the lovely leafage about the hillside spring!

As for Mirah her dear head lay on its pillow that night with its former suspicions thrown out of shape but still present, like an ugly story which has been discredited but not therefore dissipated. All that she was certain of about Deronda seemed to prove that he had no such fetters upon him as she had been allowing herself to believe in. His whole manner as well as his words implied that there were no hidden bonds remaining to have any effect in determining his future. But notwithstanding this plainly reasonable inference, uneasiness still clung about Mirah's heart. Deronda was not to blame, but he had an importance for Mrs. Grandcourt which must give her some hold on him. And the thought of any close confidence between them stirred the little biting snake that had long lain curled and harmless in Mirah's gentle bosom.

But did she this evening feel as completely as before that her jealousy was no less remote from any possibility for herself personally than if her human soul had been lodged in the body of a fawn that Deronda had saved from the archers? Hardly. Something indefinable had happened and made a difference. The soft warm rain of blossoms which had fallen just where she was – did it really come because she was there? What spirit was there among the boughs?

LXIV

'Questa montagna è tale,
Che sempre al cominciar di sotto è grave,
E quanto uom più va su e men fa male.'
– DANTE: *Il Purgatorio*.

IT was not many days after her mother's arrival that Gwendolen would consent to remain at Genoa. Her desire to get away from that gem of the sea, helped to rally her strength and courage. For what place, though it were the flowery vale of Enna, may not the inward sense turn into a circle of punishment where the flowers are no better than a crop of flame-tongues burning the soles of our feet?

'I shall never like to see the Mediterranean again,' said Gwendolen to her mother, who thought that she quite understood her child's feeling – even in her tacit prohibition of any express reference to her late husband.

Mrs. Davilow, indeed, though compelled formally to regard this time as one of severe calamity, was virtually enjoying her life more than she had ever done since her daughter's marriage. It seemed that her darling was brought back to her not merely with all the old affection, but with a conscious cherishing of her mother's nearness, such as we give to a possession that we have been on the brink of losing.

'Are you there, mamma?' cried Gwendolen in the middle of the night (a bed had been made for her mother in the same room with hers), very much as she would have done in her early girlhood, if she had felt frightened in lying awake.

'Yes, dear; can I do anything for you?'

'No, thank you; only I like so to know you are there. Do you mind my waking you?' (This question would hardly have been Gwendolen's in her early girlhood.)

'I was not asleep, darling.'

'It seemed not real that you were with me. I wanted to make it real. I can bear things if you are with me. But you must not lie awake being anxious about me. You must be happy now. You must let me make you happy now at last – else what shall I do?'

'God bless you, dear; I have the best happiness I can have, when you make much of me.'

But the next night, hearing that she was sighing and restless, Mrs. Davilow said, 'Let me give you your sleeping-draught, Gwendolen.'

'No, mamma, thank you; I don't want to sleep.'

'It would be so good for you to sleep more, my darling.'

'Don't say what would be good for me, mamma,' Gwendolen answered, impetuously. 'You don't know what would be good for me. You and my uncle must not contradict me and tell me anything is good for me when I feel it is not good.'

Mrs. Davilow was silent, not wondering that the poor child was irritable. Presently Gwendolen said –

'I was always naughty to you, mamma.'

'No, dear, no.'

'Yes, I was,' said Gwendolen, insistently. 'It is because I was always wicked that I am miserable now.'

She burst into sobs and cries. The determination to be silent about all the facts of her married life and its close, reacted in these escapes of enigmatic excitement.

But dim lights of interpretation were breaking on the mother's mind through the information that came from Sir Hugo to Mr. Gascoigne, and, with some omissions, from Mr. Gascoigne to herself. The good-natured baronet, while he was attending to all decent measures in relation to his nephew's death, and the possible washing ashore of the body, thought it the kindest thing he could do to use his present friendly intercourse with the Rector as an opportunity for communicating to him, in the mildest way, the purport of Grandcourt's will, so as to save him the additional shock that would be in store for him if he carried his illusions all the way home. Perhaps Sir Hugo would have been communicable enough without that kind motive, but he really felt the motive. He broke the unpleasant news to the Rector by degrees: at first he only implied his fear that the widow was not so splendidly provided for as Mr. Gascoigne, nay, as the baronet himself had expected; and only at last, after some previous vague reference to large claims on Grandcourt, he disclosed the prior relations which, in the unfortunate absence of a legitimate heir, had determined all the splendour in another direction.

The Rector was deeply hurt, and remembered, more vividly than he had ever done before, how offensively proud and repelling the manners of the deceased had been towards him – remembered also that he himself, in that interesting period just before the arrival of the new occupant at Diplow, had received hints of former entangling dissipations, and an undue addiction to pleasure, though he had not foreseen that the pleasure which had probably, so to speak, been swept into private rubbish-heaps, would ever present itself as an array of live caterpillars, disastrous to the green meat of respectable people. But he did not make these retrospective thoughts audible to Sir Hugo, or lower himself by expressing any indignation on merely personal grounds, but behaved like a man of the world who had become a conscientious clergyman. His first remark was –

'When a young man makes his will in health, he usually counts on living a long while. Probably Mr. Grandcourt did not believe that this will would ever have its present effect.' After a moment, he added, 'The effect is painful in more ways than one. Female morality is likely to suffer from this marked advantage and prominence being given to illegitimate offspring.'

'Well, in point of fact,' said Sir Hugo, in his comfortable way, 'since the boy is there, this was really the best alternative for the disposal of the estates. Grandcourt had nobody nearer than his cousin. And it's a chilling thought that you go out of this life only for the benefit of a cousin. A man gets a little pleasure in making his will, if it's for the good of his own curly heads; but it's a nuisance when you're giving and bequeathing to a used-up fellow like yourself, and one you don't care two straws for. It's the next worst thing to having only a life interest in your estates. No; I forgive Grandcourt for that part of his will. But, between ourselves, what I don't forgive him for, is the shabby way he has provided for your niece – *our* niece, I will say – no better a position than if she had been a doctor's widow. Nothing grates on me more than that posthumous grudgingness towards a wife. A man ought to have some pride and fondness for his widow. *I* should, I know. I take it as a test of a man, that he feels the easier about his death when he can think of his wife and daughters being comfortable after it. I like that story of the fellows in the Crimean war, who were ready to go to the bottom of the sea, if their widows were provided for.'

'It has certainly taken me by surprise,' said Mr. Gascoigne, 'all the more because, as the one who stood in the place of father to my niece, I had shown my reliance on Mr. Grandcourt's apparent liberality in money matters by making no claims for her beforehand. That seemed to me due to him under the circumstances. Probably you think me blamable.'

'Not blamable exactly. I respect a man for trusting another. But take my advice. If you marry another niece, though it may be to the Archbishop of Canterbury, bind him down. Your niece can't be married for the first time twice over. And if he's a good fellow, he'll wish to be bound. But as to Mrs. Grandcourt, I can only say that I feel my relation to her all the nearer, because I think that she has not been well treated. And I hope you will urge her to rely on me as a friend.'

Thus spake the chivalrous Sir Hugo, in his disgust at the young and beautiful widow of a Mallinger Grandcourt being left with only two thousand a-year and a house in a coal-mining district. To the Rector that income naturally appeared less shabby and less accompanied with mortifying privations; but in this conversation he had devoured a much keener sense than the baronet's of the humiliation cast over his niece, and also over her nearest friends, by the conspicuous publishing of her husband's relation to Mrs. Glasher. And like all men who are good husbands and fathers, he felt the humiliation through the minds of the women who would be chiefly affected by it; so that the annoyance of first hearing the facts was far slighter than what he felt in communicating them to Mrs. Davilow, and in anticipating Gwendolen's feeling whenever her mother saw fit to tell her of them. For the good Rector had an innocent conviction that his niece was unaware of Mrs. Glasher's existence, arguing with masculine soundness from what maidens and wives were likely to know, do, and suffer, and having had a most imperfect observation of the particular maiden and wife in question. Not so Gwendolen's mother, who now thought that she saw an explanation of much that had been enigmatic in her child's conduct and words before and after her engagement, concluding that in some inconceivable way Gwendolen had been informed of this left-handed marriage and the existence of the children. She trusted to opportunities that would arise in moments of affectionate confidence before and during their journey to England, when she might gradually learn how far the actual state of things was clear to Gwendolen, and prepare her for anything that might be a disappointment. But she was spared from devices on the subject.

'I hope you don't expect that I am going to be rich and grand, mamma,' said Gwendolen, not long after the Rector's communication; 'perhaps I shall have nothing at all.'

She was drest, and had been sitting long in quiet meditation. Mrs. Davilow was startled, but said, after a moment's reflection –

'Oh yes, dear, you will have something. Sir Hugo knows all about the will.'

'That will not decide,' said Gwendolen, abruptly.

'Surely, dear: Sir Hugo says you are to have two thousand a-year and the house at Gadsmere.'

'What I have will depend on what I accept,' said Gwendolen. 'You and my uncle must not attempt to cross me and persuade me about this. I will do everything I can do to make you happy, but in anything about my husband I must not be interfered with. Is eight hundred a-year enough for you, mamma?'

'More than enough, dear. You must not think of giving me so much.' Mrs. Davilow paused a little, and then said, 'Do you know who is to have the estates and the rest of the money?'

'Yes,' said Gwendolen, waving her hand in dismissal of the subject. 'I know everything. It is all perfectly right, and I wish never to have it mentioned.'

The mother was silent, looked away, and rose to fetch a fan-screen, with a slight flush on her delicate cheeks. Wondering, imagining, she did not like to meet her daughter's eyes, and sat down again under a sad constraint. What wretchedness her child had perhaps gone through, which yet must remain as it always had been, locked away from their mutual speech. But Gwendolen was watching her mother with that new divination which experience had given her; and in tender relenting at her own peremptoriness, she said, 'Come and sit nearer to me, mamma, and don't be unhappy.'

Mrs. Davilow did as she was told, but bit her lips in the vain attempt to hinder smarting tears. Gwendolen leaned towards her caressingly and said, 'I mean to be very wise; I do really. And good – oh so good to you, dear, old, sweet mamma, you won't know me. Only you must not cry.'

The resolve that Gwendolen had in her mind was that she would ask Deronda whether she ought to accept any of her husband's money – whether she might accept what would enable her to provide for her mother. The poor thing felt strong enough to do anything that would give her a higher place in Deronda's mind.

An invitation that Sir Hugo pressed on her with kind urgency was that she and Mrs. Davilow should go straight with him to Park Lane, and make his house their abode as long as mourning and other details needed attending to in London. Town, he insisted, was just then the most retired of places; and he proposed to exert himself at once in getting all articles belonging to Gwendolen away from the house in Grosvenor Square. No proposal could have suited her better than this of staying a little while in Park Lane. It would be easy for her there to have an interview with Deronda, if she only knew how to get a letter into his hands, asking him to come to her. During the journey Sir Hugo, having understood that she was acquainted with the purport of her husband's will, ventured to talk before her and to her about her future arrangements, referring here and there to mildly agreeable prospects as matters of course, and otherwise shedding a decorous cheerfulness over her widowed position. It seemed to him really the more graceful course for a widow to recover her spirits on finding that her husband had not dealt as handsomely by her as he might have done; it was the testator's fault if he compromised all her grief at his departure by giving a testamentary reason for it, so that she might be supposed to look sad not because he had left her, but because he had left her poor. The baronet, having his kindliness doubly fanned by the favourable wind on his own fortunes and by compassion for Gwendolen, had become quite fatherly in his behaviour to her, called her 'my dear,' and in mentioning Gadsmere to Mr. Gascoigne with its various advantages and disadvantages, spoke of what 'we' might do to make the best of that property. Gwendolen sat by in pale silence while Sir Hugo, with his face turned towards Mrs. Davilow or Mr. Gascoigne, conjectured that Mrs. Grandcourt might perhaps prefer letting Gadsmere to residing there during any part of the year, in which case he thought that it might be leased on capital terms to one of the fellows engaged with the coal: Sir Hugo had seen enough of the place to know that it was as comfortable and picturesque a box as any man need desire, providing his desires were circumscribed within a coal area.

'*I* shouldn't mind about the soot myself,' said the baronet, with that dispassionateness which belongs to the potential mood. 'Nothing is more healthy. And if one's business lay there, Gadsmere would be a paradise. It makes quite a feature in Scrogg's history of the county, with the little tower and the fine piece of water – the prettiest print in the book.'

'A more important place than Offendene, I suppose?' said Mr. Gascoigne.

'Much,' said the baronet, decisively. 'I was there with my poor brother – it is more than a quarter of a century ago, but I remember it very well. The rooms may not be larger, but the grounds are on a different scale.'

'Our poor dear Offendene is empty after all,' said Mrs. Davilow. 'When it came to the point, Mr. Haynes declared off, and there has been no one to take it since. I might as well have accepted Lord Brackenshaw's kind offer that I should remain in it another year rent-free: for I should have kept the place aired and warmed.'

'I hope you have got something snug instead,' said Sir Hugo.

'A little too snug,' said Mr. Gascoigne, smiling at his sister-in-law. 'You are rather thick upon the ground.'

Gwendolen had turned with a changed glance when her mother spoke of Offendene being empty. This conversation passed during one of the long unaccountable pauses often experienced in foreign trains at some country station. There was a dreamy, sunny stillness over the hedgeless fields stretching to the boundary of poplars; and to Gwendolen the talk within the carriage seemed only to make the dreamland larger with an indistinct region of coal-pits, and a purgatorial Gadsmere which she would never visit; till, at her mother's words, this mingled, dozing view seemed to dissolve and give way to a more wakeful vision of Offendene and Pennicote under their cooler lights. She saw the grey shoulders of the downs, the cattle-specked fields, the shadowy plantations with rutted lanes where the barked timber lay for a wayside seat, the neatly-clipped hedges on the road from the parsonage to Offendene, the avenue where she was gradually discerned from the windows, the hall-door opening, and her mother

or one of the troublesome sisters coming out to meet her.
All that brief experience of a quiet home which had once
seemed a dullness to be fled from, now came back to her as
a restful escape, a station where she found the breath of
morning and the unreproaching voice of birds, after following a lure through a long Satanic masquerade, which she
had entered on with an intoxicated belief in its disguises,
and had seen the end of in shrieking fear lest she herself
had become one of the evil spirits who were dropping their
human mummery and hissing around her with serpent
tongues.

In this way Gwendolen's mind paused over Offendene
and made it the scene of many thoughts; but she gave no
further outward sign of interest in this conversation, any
more than in Sir Hugo's opinion on the telegraphic cable
or her uncle's views of the Church Rate Abolition Bill.
What subjects will not our talk embrace in leisurely day-
journeying from Genoa to London? Even strangers, after
glancing from China to Peru and opening their mental
stores with a liberality threatening a mutual impression of
poverty on any future meeting, are liable to become exces-
sively confidential. But the baronet and the rector were
under a still stronger pressure towards cheerful communication: they were like acquaintances compelled to a long
drive in a mourning-coach, who having first remarked that
the occasion is a melancholy one, naturally proceed to
enliven it by the most miscellaneous discourse. 'I don't
mind telling *you*,' said Sir Hugo to the Rector, in mentioning some private detail; while the Rector, without saying
so, did not mind telling the baronet about his sons, and the
difficulty of placing them in the world. By dint of discuss-
ing all persons and things within driving-reach of Diplow,
Sir Hugo got himself wrought to a pitch of interest in that
former home, and of conviction that it was his pleasant
duty to regain and strengthen his personal influence in the
neighbourhood, that made him declare his intention of
taking his family to the place for a month or two before
the autumn was over; and Mr. Gascoigne cordially rejoiced

in that prospect. Altogether, the journey was continued and ended with mutual liking between the male fellow-travellers.

Meanwhile Gwendolen sat by like one who had visited the spirit-world and was full to the lips of an unutterable experience that threw a strange unreality over all the talk she was hearing of her own and the world's business; and Mrs. Davilow was chiefly occupied in imagining what her daughter was feeling, and in wondering what was signified by her hinted doubt whether she would accept her husband's bequest. Gwendolen in fact had before her the unscaled wall of an immediate purpose shutting off every other resolution. How to scale the wall? She wanted again to see and consult Deronda, that she might secure herself against any act he would disapprove. Would her remorse have maintained its power within her, or would she have felt absolved by secrecy, if it had not been for that outer conscience which was made for her by Deronda? It is hard to say how much we could forgive ourselves if we were secure from judgment by another whose opinion is the breathing-medium of all our joy – who brings to us with close pressure and immediate sequence that judgment of the Invisible and Universal which self-flattery and the world's tolerance would easily melt and disperse. In this way our brother may be in the stead of God to us, and his opinion which has pierced even to the joints and marrow, may be our virtue in the making. That mission of Deronda to Gwendolen had begun with what she had felt to be his judgment of her at the gaming-table. He might easily have spoiled it: – much of our lives is spent in marring our own influence and turning others' belief in us into a widely concluding unbelief which they call knowledge of the world, while it is really disappointment in you or me. Deronda had not spoiled his mission.

But Gwendolen had forgotten to ask him for his address in case she wanted to write, and her only way of reaching him was through Sir Hugo. She was not in the least blind to the construction that all witnesses might put on her giving signs of dependence on Deronda, and her seeking him more than he sought her: Grandcourt's rebukes had sufficiently enlightened her pride. But the force, the tenacity of her nature had thrown itself into that dependence, and she would no more let go her hold on Deronda's help, or deny herself the interview her soul needed, because of witnesses, than if she had been in prison in danger of being condemned to death. When she was in Park Lane and knew that the baronet would be going down to the Abbey immediately (just to see his family for a couple of days and then return to transact needful business for Gwendolen), she said to him without any air of hesitation, while her mother was present –

'Sir Hugo, I wish to see Mr. Deronda again as soon as possible. I don't know his address. Will you tell it me, or let him know that I want to see him?'

A quick thought passed across Sir Hugo's face, but made no difference to the ease with which he said, 'Upon my word, I don't know whether he's at his chambers or the Abbey at this moment. But I'll make sure of him. I'll send a note now to his chambers telling him to come, and if he's at the Abbey I can give him your message and send him up at once. I am sure he will want to obey your wish,' the baronet ended, with grave kindness, as if nothing could seem to him more in the appropriate course of things than that she should send such a message.

But he was convinced that Gwendolen had a passionate attachment to Deronda, the seeds of which had been laid long ago, and his former suspicion now recurred to him with more strength than ever, that her feeling was likely to lead her into imprudences – in which kind-hearted Sir Hugo was determined to screen and defend her as far as lay in his power. To him it was as pretty a story as need be that this fine creature and his favourite Dan should have turned out to be formed for each other, and that the unsuitable husband should have made his exit in such excellent time. Sir Hugo liked that a charming woman should be made as happy as possible. In truth, what most vexed his

mind in this matter at present was a doubt whether the too
lofty and inscrutable Dan had not got some scheme or
other in his head, which would prove to be dearer to him
than the lovely Mrs. Grandcourt, and put that neatly-
prepared marriage with her out of the question. It was
among the usual paradoxes of feeling that Sir Hugo, who
had given his fatherly cautions to Deronda against too
much tenderness in his relations with the bride, should
now feel rather irritated against him by the suspicion that
he had not fallen in love as he ought to have done. Of
course all this thinking on Sir Hugo's part was eminently
premature, only a fortnight or so after Grandcourt's death.
But it is the trick of thinking to be either premature or
behindhand.

However, he sent the note to Deronda's chambers and it
found him there.

LXV

'O, welcome, pure-eyed Faith, white-handed Hope,
Thou hovering angel, girt with golden wings!'
– MILTON.

DERONDA did not obey Gwendolen's new summons without some agitation. Not his vanity, but his keen sympathy made him susceptible to the danger that another's heart might feel larger demands on him than he would be able to fulfil; and it was no longer a matter of argument with him, but of penetrating consciousness, that Gwendolen's soul clung to his with a passionate need. We do not argue the existence of the anger or the scorn that thrills through us in a voice; we simply feel it, and it admits of no disproof. Deronda felt this woman's destiny hanging on his over a precipice of despair. Any one who knows him cannot wonder at his inward confession, that if all this had happened little more than a year ago, he would hardly have asked himself whether he loved her: the impetuous determining impulse which would have moved him would have been to save her from sorrow, to shelter her life for evermore from the dangers of loneliness, and carry out to the last the rescue he had begun in that monitory redemption of the necklace. But now, love and duty had thrown other bonds around him, and that impulse could no longer determine his life; still, it was present in him as a compassionate yearning, a painful quivering at the very imagination of having again and again to meet the appeal of her eyes and words. The very strength of the bond, the certainty of the resolve, that kept him asunder from her, made him gaze at her lot apart with the more aching pity.

He awaited her coming in the back drawing-room – part of that white and crimson space where they had sat together at the musical party, where Gwendolen had said for the first time that her lot depended on his not forsaking her, and her appeal had seemed to melt into the melodic cry – *Per pietà non dirmi addio*. But the melody had come from Mirah's dear voice.

Deronda walked about this room, which he had for years known by heart, with a strange sense of metamorphosis in his own life. The familiar objects around him, from Lady Mallinger's gently smiling portrait to the also human and urbane faces of the lions on the pilasters of the chimney-piece, seemed almost to belong to a previous state of existence which he was revisiting in memory only, not in reality; so deep and transforming had been the impressions he had lately experienced, so new were the conditions under which he found himself in the house he had been accustomed to think of as a home – standing with his hat in his hand awaiting the entrance of a young creature whose life had also been undergoing a transformation – a tragic transformation towards a wavering result, in which he felt with apprehensiveness that his own action was still bound up.

But Gwendolen was come in, looking changed, not only by her mourning dress, but by a more satisfied quietude of expression than he had seen in her face at Genoa. Her satisfaction was that Deronda was there; but there was no smile between them as they met and clasped hands: each was full of remembrances – full of anxious prevision. She said, 'It was good of you to come. Let us sit down,' immediately seating herself in the nearest chair. He placed himself opposite to her.

'I asked you to come because I want you to tell me what I ought to do,' she began, at once. 'Don't be afraid of telling me what you think is right, because it seems hard. I have made up my mind to do it. I was afraid once of being poor; I could not bear to think of being under other people; and that was why I did something – why I married. I have borne worse things now. I think I could bear to be poor, if you think I ought. Do you know about my husband's will?'

'Yes, Sir Hugo told me,' said Deronda, already guessing the question she had to ask.

'Ought I to take anything he has left me? I will tell you what I have been thinking,' said Gwendolen, with a more nervous eagerness. 'Perhaps you may not quite know that

I really did think a good deal about my mother when I married. I *was* selfish, but I did love her, and feel about her poverty; and what comforted me most at first, when I was miserable, was her being better off because I had married. The thing that would be hardest to me now would be to see her in poverty again; and I have been thinking that if I took enough to provide for her, and no more – nothing for myself – it would not be wrong; for I was very precious to my mother – and he took me from her – and he meant – and if she had known—'

Gwendolen broke off. She had been preparing herself for this interview by thinking of hardly anything else than this question of right towards her mother; but the question had carried with it thoughts and reasons which it was impossible for her to utter, and these perilous remembrances swarmed between her words, making her speech more and more agitated and tremulous. She looked down helplessly at her hands, now unladen of all rings except her wedding-ring.

'Do not hurt yourself by speaking of that,' said Deronda, tenderly. 'There is no need; the case is very simple. I think I can hardly judge wrongly about it. You consult me because I am the only person to whom you have confided the most painful part of your experience; and I can understand your scruples.' He did not go on immediately, waiting for her to recover herself. The silence seemed to Gwendolen full of the tenderness that she heard in his voice, and she had courage to lift up her eyes and look at him as he said, 'You are conscious of something which you feel to be a crime towards one who is dead. You think that you have forfeited all claim as a wife. You shrink from taking what was his. You want to keep yourself pure from profiting by his death. Your feeling even urges you to some self-punishment – some scourging of the self that disobeyed your better will – the will that struggled against temptation. I have known something of that myself. Do I understand you?'

'Yes – at least, I want to be good – not like what I have been,' said Gwendolen. 'I will try to bear what you think

I ought to bear. I have tried to tell you the worst about myself. What ought I to do?'

'If no one but yourself were concerned in this question of income,' said Deronda, 'I should hardly dare to urge you against any remorseful prompting; but I take as a guide now your feeling about Mrs. Davilow, which seems to me quite just. I cannot think that your husband's dues even to yourself are nullified by any act you have committed. He voluntarily entered into your life, and affected its course in what is always the most momentous way. But setting that aside, it was due from him in his position that he should provide for your mother, and he of course understood that if this will took effect she would share the provision he had made for you.'

'She has had eight hundred a-year. What I thought of was to take that and leave the rest,' said Gwendolen. She had been so long inwardly arguing for this as a permission, that her mind could not at once take another attitude.

'I think it is not your duty to fix a limit in that way,' said Deronda. 'You would be making a painful enigma for Mrs. Davilow; an income from which you shut yourself out must be embittered to her. And your own course would become too difficult. We agreed at Genoa that the burthen on your conscience is what no one ought to be admitted to the knowledge of. The future beneficence of your life will be best furthered by your saving all others from the pain of that knowledge. In my opinion you ought simply to abide by the provisions of your husband's will, and let your remorse tell only on the use that you will make of your monetary independence.'

In uttering the last sentence Deronda automatically took up his hat, which he had laid on the floor beside him. Gwendolen, sensitive to his slightest movement, felt her heart giving a great leap, as if it too had a con-sciousness of its own, and would hinder him from going: in the same moment she rose from her chair, unable to reflect that the movement was an acceptance of his apparent intention to leave her; and Deronda of course also rose, advancing a little.

'I will do what you tell me,' said Gwendolen, hurriedly; 'but what else shall I do?' No other than these simple words were possible to her; and even these were too much for her in a state of emotion where her proud secrecy was disenthroned: as the childlike sentences fell from her lips they reacted on her like a picture of her own helplessness, and she could not check the sob which sent the large tears to her eyes. Deronda, too, felt a crushing pain; but imminent consequences were visible to him, and urged him to the utmost exertion of conscience. When she had pressed her tears away, he said, in a gently questioning tone –

'You will probably be soon going with Mrs. Davilow into the country?'

'Yes, in a week or ten days.' Gwendolen waited an instant, turning her eyes vaguely towards the window, as if looking at some imagined prospect. 'I want to be kind to them all – they can be happier than I can. Is that the best I can do?'

'I think so. It is a duty that cannot be doubtful,' said Deronda. He paused a little between his sentences, feeling a weight of anxiety on all his words. 'Other duties will spring from it. Looking at your life as a debt may seem the dreariest view of things at a distance; but it cannot really be so. What makes life dreary is the want of motive; but once beginning to act with that penitential, loving purpose you have in your mind, there will be unexpected satisfactions – there will be newly-opening needs – continually coming to carry you on from day to day. You will find your life growing like a plant.'

Gwendolen turned her eyes on him with the look of one athirst towards the sound of unseen waters. Deronda felt the look as if she had been stretching her arms towards him from a forsaken shore. His voice took an affectionate imploringness when he said –

'This sorrow, which has cut down to the root, has come to you while you are so young – try to think of it, not as a spoiling of your life, but as a preparation for it. Let it be a preparation—' Any one overhearing his tones would have thought he was entreating for his own happiness. 'See! you have been saved from the worst evils that might have come from your marriage, which you feel was wrong. You have had a vision of injurious, selfish action – a vision of possible degradation; think that a severe angel, seeing you along the road of error, grasped you by the wrist, and showed you the horror of the life you must avoid. And it has come to you in your spring-time. Think of it as a preparation. You can, you will, be among the best of women, such as make others glad that they were born.'

The words were like the touch of a miraculous hand to Gwendolen. Mingled emotions streamed through her frame with a strength that seemed the beginning of a new existence, having some new powers or other which stirred in her vaguely. So pregnant is the divine hope of moral recovery with the energy that fulfils it. So potent in us is the infused action of another soul, before which we bow in complete love. But the new existence seemed inseparable from Deronda: the hope seemed to make his presence permanent. It was not her thought, that he loved her and would cling to her – a thought would have tottered with improbability: it was her spiritual breath. For the first time since that terrible moment on the sea a flush rose and spread over her cheek, brow, and neck, deepened an instant or two, and then gradually disappeared. She did not speak.

Deronda advanced and put out his hand, saying, 'I must not weary you.'

She was startled by the sense that he was going, and put her hand in his, still without speaking.

'You look ill yet – unlike yourself,' he added, while he held her hand.

'I can't sleep much,' she answered, with some return of her dispirited manner. 'Things repeat themselves in me so. They come back – they will all come back,' she ended, shudderingly, a chill fear threatening her.

'By degrees they will be less insistent,' said Deronda. He could not drop her hand or move away from her abruptly.

'Sir Hugo says he shall come to stay at Diplow,' said Gwendolen, snatching at previously intended words which had slipped away from her. 'You will come too.'

'Probably,' said Deronda, and then feeling that the word was cold, he added, correctively, 'Yes, I shall come,' and then released her hand, with the final friendly pressure of one who has virtually said good-bye.

'And not again here, before I leave town?' said Gwendolen, with timid sadness, looking as pallid as ever.

What could Deronda say? 'If I can be of any use – if you wish me – certainly I will.'

'I must wish it,' said Gwendolen, impetuously; 'you know I must wish it. What strength have I? Who else is there?' Again a sob was rising.

Deronda felt a pang, which showed itself in his face. He looked miserable as he said, 'I will certainly come.'

Gwendolen perceived the change in his face; but the intense relief of expecting him to come again could not give way to any other feeling, and there was a recovery of the inspired hope and courage in her.

'Don't be unhappy about me,' she said, in a tone of affectionate assurance. 'I shall remember your words – every one of them. I shall remember what you believe about me; I shall try.'

She looked at him firmly, and put out her hand again as if she had forgotten what had passed since those words of his which she promised to remember. But there was no approach to a smile on her lips. She had never smiled since her husband's death. When she stood still and in silence, she looked like a melancholy statue of the Gwendolen whose laughter had once been so ready when others were grave.

It is only by remembering the searching anguish which had changed the aspect of the world for her that we can understand her behaviour to Deronda – the unreflecting openness, nay, the importunate pleading, with which she expressed her dependence on him. Considerations such as would have filled the minds of indifferent spectators could not occur to her, any more than if flames had been mounting around her, and she had flung herself into his opened arms and clung about his neck that he might carry her into safety. She identified him with the struggling regenerative process in her which had begun with his action. Is it any wonder that she saw her own necessity reflected in his feeling? She was in that state of unconscious reliance and expectation which is a common experience with us when we are preoccupied with our own trouble or our own purposes. We diffuse our feeling over others, and count on their acting from our motives. Her imagination had not been turned to a future union with Deronda by any other than the spiritual tie which had been continually strengthening; but also it had not been turned towards a future separation from him. Lovemaking and marriage – how could they now be the imagery in which poor Gwendolen's deepest attachment could spontaneously clothe itself? Mighty Love had laid his hand upon her; but what had he demanded of her? Acceptance of rebuke – the hard task of self-change – confession – endurance. If she cried towards him, what then? She cried as the child cries whose little feet have fallen backward – cried to be taken by the hand, lest she should lose herself.

The cry pierced Deronda. What position could have been more difficult for a man full of tenderness, yet with clear foresight? He was the only creature who knew the real nature of Gwendolen's trouble: to withdraw himself from any appeal of hers would be to consign her to a dangerous loneliness. He could not reconcile himself to the cruelty of apparently rejecting her dependence on him; and yet in the nearer or farther distance he saw a coming wrench, which all present strengthening of their bond would make the harder.

He was obliged to risk that. He went once and again to Park Lane before Gwendolen left; but their interviews were in the presence of Mrs. Davilow, and were therefore less agitating. Gwendolen, since she had determined to accept her income, had conceived a project which she liked to speak of: it was, to place her mother and sisters with herself in Offendene again, and, as she said, piece back her life on to that time when they first went there, and when everything was happiness about her, only she did not know it. The idea had been mentioned to Sir Hugo, who was going to exert himself about the letting of Gadsmere for a rent which would more than pay the rent of Offendene. All this was told to Deronda, who willingly dwelt on a subject that seemed to give some soothing occupation to Gwendolen. He said nothing, and she asked nothing, of what chiefly occupied himself. Her mind was fixed on his coming to Diplow before the autumn was over; and she no more thought of the Lapidoths – the little Jewess and her brother – as likely to make a difference in her destiny, than of the fermenting political and social leaven which was making a difference in the history of the world. In fact poor Gwendolen's memory had been stunned, and all outside the lava-lit track of her troubled conscience, and her effort to get deliverance from it, lay for her in dim forgetfulness.

LXVI

'One day still fierce 'mid many a day struck calm.'
– BROWNING: *The Ring and the Book*.

MEANWHILE Ezra and Mirah, whom Gwendolen did not include in her thinking about Deronda, were having their relation to him drawn closer and brought into fuller light.

The father Lapidoth had quitted his daughter at the door-step, ruled by that possibility of staking something in play or betting which presented itself with the handling of any sum beyond the price of staying actual hunger, and left no care for alternative prospects or resolutions. Until he had lost everything he never considered whether he would apply to Mirah again or whether he would brave his son's presence. In the first moment he had shrunk from encountering Ezra as he would have shrunk from any other situation of disagreeable constraint; and the possession of Mirah's purse was enough to banish the thought of future necessities. The gambling appetite is more absolutely dominant than bodily hunger, which can be neutralized by an emotional or intellectual excitation, but the passion for watching chances – the habitual suspensive poise of the mind in actual or imaginary play – nullifies the susceptibility to other excitation. In its final, imperious stage, it seems the unjoyous dissipation of demons, seeking diversion on the burning marl of perdition.

But every form of selfishness, however abstract and unhuman, requires the support of at least one meal a-day; and though Lapidoth's appetite for food and drink was extremely moderate, he had slipped into a shabby, unfriended form of life in which the appetite could not be satisfied without some ready money. When, in a brief visit at a house which announced 'Pyramids' on the window-blind, he had first doubled and trebled and finally lost Mirah's thirty shillings, he went out with her empty purse in his pocket, already balancing in his mind whether he should get another immediate stake by pawning the purse, or whether he should go back to her giving himself a good countenance by restoring the purse, and declaring that he had used the money in paying a score that was standing against him. Besides, among the sensibilities still left strong in Lapidoth was the sensibility to his own claims, and he appeared to himself to have a claim on any property his children might possess, which was stronger than the justice of his son's resentment. After all, to take up his lodging with his children was the best thing he could do; and the more he thought of meeting Ezra the less he winced from it, his imagination being more wrought on by the chances of his getting something into his pocket with safety and without exertion, than by the threat of a private humiliation. Luck had been against him lately; he expected it to turn – and might not the turn begin with some opening of supplies which would present itself through his daughter's affairs and the good friends she had spoken of? Lapidoth counted on the fascination of his cleverness – an old habit of mind which early experience had sanctioned; and it is not only women who are unaware of their diminished charm, or imagine that they can feign not to be worn out.

The result of Lapidoth's rapid balancing was that he went towards the little square in Brompton with the hope that, by walking about and watching, he might catch sight of Mirah going out or returning, in which case his entrance into the house would be made easier. But it was already evening – the evening of the day next to that on which he had first seen her; and after a little waiting, weariness made him reflect that he might ring, and if she were not at home, he might ask the time at which she was expected. But on coming near the house he knew that she was at home: he heard her singing.

Mirah, seated at the piano, was pouring forth '*Herz, mein Herz*,' while Ezra was listening with his eyes shut, when Mrs. Adam opened the door, and said in some embarrassment –

'A gentleman below says he is your father, miss.'

'I will go down to him,' said Mirah, starting up immediately, and looking towards her brother.

'No, Mirah, not so,' said Ezra, with decision. 'Let him come up, Mrs. Adam.'

Mirah stood with her hands pinching each other, and feeling sick with anxiety, while she continued looking at Ezra, who had also risen, and was evidently much shaken. But there was an expression in his face which she had never seen before; his brow was knit, his lips seemed hardened with the same severity that gleamed from his eyes.

When Mrs. Adam opened the door to let in the father, she could not help casting a look at the group, and after glancing from the younger man to the elder, said to herself as she closed the door, 'Father, sure enough.' The likeness was that of outline, which is always most striking at the first moment; the expression had been wrought into the strongest contrast by such hidden or inconspicuous differences as can make the genius of a Cromwell within the outward type of a father who was no more than a respectable parishioner.

Lapidoth had put on a melancholy expression beforehand, but there was some real wincing in his frame as he said –

'Well, Ezra, my boy, you hardly know me after so many years.'

'I know you – too well – father,' said Ezra, with a slow biting solemnity which made the word father a reproach.

'Ah, you are not pleased with me. I don't wonder at it. Appearances have been against me. When a man gets into straits he can't do just as he would by himself or anybody else. I've suffered enough, I know,' said Lapidoth, quickly. In speaking he always recovered some glibness and hardihood; and now turning towards Mirah, he held out her purse, saying, 'Here's your little purse, my dear. I thought you'd be anxious about it because of that bit of writing. I've emptied it, you'll see, for I had a score to pay for food and lodging. I knew you would like me to clear myself, and here I stand – without a single farthing in my pocket – at the mercy of my children. You can turn me out if you like, without getting a policeman. Say the word, Mirah; say, "Father, I've had enough of you; you made a pet of me, and spent your all on me, when I couldn't have done without you; but I can do better without you now," – say that, and I'm gone out like a spark. I shan't spoil your pleasure again.' The tears were in his voice as usual, before he had finished.

'You know I could never say it, father,' answered Mirah, with not the less anguish because she felt the falsity of everything in his speech except the implied wish to remain in the house.

'Mirah, my sister, leave us!' said Ezra, in a tone of authority.

She looked at her brother falteringly, beseechingly – in awe of his decision, yet unable to go without making a plea for this father who was like something that had grown in her flesh with pain, but that she could never have cut away without worse pain. She went close to her brother, and putting her hand in his, said, in a low voice, but not so low as to be unheard by Lapidoth, 'Remember, Ezra – you said my mother would not have shut him out.'

'Trust me, and go,' said Ezra.

She left the room, but after going a few steps up the stairs, sat down with a palpitating heart. If, because of anything her brother said to him, he went away –

Lapidoth had some sense of what was being prepared for him in his son's mind, but he was beginning to adjust himself to the situation and find a point of view that would give him a cool superiority to any attempt at humiliating him. This haggard son, speaking as from a sepulchre, had the incongruity which selfish levity learns to see in suffering and death, until the unrelenting pincers of disease clutch its own flesh. Whatever preaching he might deliver must be taken for a matter of course, as a man finding shelter from hail in an open cathedral might take a little religious howling that happened to be going on there.

Lapidoth was not born with this sort of callousness: he had achieved it.

'This home that we have here,' Ezra began, 'is maintained partly by the generosity of a beloved friend who supports me, and partly by the labours of my sister, who supports herself. While we have a home we will not shut you out from it. We will not cast you out to the mercy of your vices. For you are our father, and though you have broken your bond, we acknowledge ours. But I will never trust you. You absconded with money, leaving your debts unpaid; you forsook my mother; you robbed her of her little child and broke her heart; you have become a gambler, and where shame and conscience were, there sits an insatiable desire; you were ready to sell my sister – you had sold her, but the price was denied you. The man who has done these things must never expect to be trusted any more. We will share our food with you – you shall have a bed, and clothing. We will do this duty to you, because you are our father. But you will never be trusted. You are an evil man: you made the misery of our mother. That such a man is our father is a brand on our flesh which will not cease smarting. But the Eternal has laid it upon us; and though human justice were to flog you for crimes, and your body fell helpless before the public scorn – we would still say, "This is our father; make way, that we may carry him out of your sight."'

Lapidoth, in adjusting himself to what was coming, had not been able to foresee the exact intensity of the lightning or the exact course it would take – that it would not fall outside his frame but through it. He could not foresee what was so new to him as this voice from the soul of his son. It touched that spring of hysterical excitability which Mirah used to witness in him when he sat at home and sobbed. As Ezra ended, Lapidoth threw himself into a chair and cried like a woman, burying his face against the table – and yet, strangely, while this hysterical crying was an inevitable reaction in him under the stress of his son's words, it was also a conscious resource in a difficulty; just as in early life, when he was a bright-faced curly young man, he had been used to avail himself of this subtly-poised physical suscept-ibility to turn the edge of resentment or disapprobation.

Ezra sat down again and said nothing – exhausted by the shock of his own irrepressible utterance, the outburst of feelings which for years he had borne in solitude and silence. His thin hands trembled on the arms of the chair; he would hardly have found voice to answer a question; he felt as if he had taken a step towards beckoning Death. Meanwhile Mirah's quick expectant ear detected a sound which her heart recognized: she could not stay out of the room any longer. But on opening the door, her immediate alarm was for Ezra, and it was to his side that she went, taking his trembling hand in hers, which he pressed and found support in; but he did not speak, or even look at her. The father with his face buried was conscious that Mirah had entered, and presently lifted up his head, pressed his handkerchief against his eyes, put out his hand towards her, and said with plaintive hoarseness, 'Good-bye, Mirah; your father will not trouble you again. He deserves to die like a dog by the roadside, and he will. If your mother had lived, she would have forgiven me – thirty-four years ago I put the ring on her finger under the *Chuppa*, and we were made one. She would have forgiven me, and we should have spent our old age together. But I haven't deserved it. Good-bye.'

He rose from the chair as he said the last 'good-bye.' Mirah had put her hand in his and held him. She was not tearful and grieving, but frightened and awe-struck, as she cried out –

'No, father, no!' Then turning to her brother, 'Ezra, you have not forbidden him? – Stay, father, and leave off wrong things. Ezra, I cannot bear it. How can I say to my father, "Go and die!"'

'I have not said it,' Ezra answered, with great effort. 'I have said, stay and be sheltered.'

'Then you will stay, father – and be taken care of – and come with me,' said Mirah, drawing him towards the door.

This was really what Lapidoth wanted. And for the moment he felt a sort of comfort in recovering his daughter's dutiful tendance, that made a change of habits seem possible to him. She led him down to the parlour below, and said –

'This is my sitting-room when I am not with Ezra, and there is a bedroom behind which shall be yours. You will stay and be good, father. Think that you are come back to my mother, and that she has forgiven you – she speaks to you through me.' Mirah's tones were imploring, but she could not give one of her former caresses.

Lapidoth quickly recovered his composure, began to speak to Mirah of the improvement in her voice, and other easy subjects, and when Mrs. Adam came to lay out his supper, entered into converse with her in order to show her that he was not a common person, though his clothes were just now against him.

But in his usual wakefulness at night, he fell to wondering what money Mirah had by her, and went back over old Continental hours at *Roulette*, reproducing the method of his play, and the chances that had frustrated it. He had had his reasons for coming to England, but for most things it was a cursed country.

These were the stronger visions of the night with Lapidoth, and not the worn frame of his ireful son uttering a terrible judgment. Ezra did pass across the gaming-table, and his words were audible; but he passed like an insubstantial ghost, and his words had the heart eaten out of them by numbers and movements that seemed to make the very tissue of Lapidoth's consciousness.

LXVII

The godhead in us wrings our nobler deeds
From our reluctant selves.

IT was an unpleasant surprise to Deronda when he returned from the Abbey to find the undesirable father installed in the lodgings at Brompton. Mirah had felt it necessary to speak of Deronda to her father, and even to make him as fully aware as she could of the way in which the friendship with Ezra had begun, and of the sympathy which had cemented it. She passed more lightly over what Deronda had done for her, omitting altogether the rescue from drowning, and speaking of the shelter she had found in Mrs. Meyrick's family so as to leave her father to suppose that it was through these friends Deronda had become acquainted with her. She could not persuade herself to more completeness in her narrative: she could not let the breath of her father's soul pass over her relation to Deronda. And Lapidoth, for reasons, was not eager in his questioning about the circumstances of her flight and arrival in England. But he was much interested in the fact of his children having a beneficent friend apparently high in the world.

It was the brother who told Deronda of this new condition added to their life. 'I am become calm in beholding him now,' Ezra ended, 'and I try to think it possible that my sister's tenderness, and the daily tasting a life of peace, may win him to remain aloof from temptation. I have enjoined her, and she has promised, to trust him with no money. I have convinced her that he will buy with it his own destruction.'

Deronda first came on the third day from Lapidoth's arrival. The new clothes for which he had been measured were not yet ready, and wishing to make a favourable impression he did not choose to present himself in the old ones. He watched for Deronda's departure, and getting a view of him from the window was rather surprised at his youthfulness, which Mirah had not mentioned, and which he had somehow thought out of the question in a personage who had taken up a grave friendship and hoary studies with the sepulchral Ezra. Lapidoth began to imagine that Deronda's real or chief motive must be that he was in love with Mirah. And so much the better; for a tie to Mirah had more promise of indulgence for her father than the tie to Ezra; and Lapidoth was not without the hope of recommending himself to Deronda, and of softening any hard prepossessions. He was behaving with much amiability, and trying in all ways at his command to get himself into easy domestication with his children – entering into Mirah's music, showing himself docile about smoking, which Mrs. Adam could not tolerate in her parlour, and walking out in the square with his German pipe and the tobacco with which Mirah supplied him. He was too acute to venture any present remonstrance against the refusal of money, which Mirah told him that she must persist in as a solemn duty promised to her brother. He was comfortable enough to wait.

The next time Deronda came, Lapidoth, equipped in his new clothes and satisfied with his own appearance, was in the room with Ezra, who was teaching himself, as part of his severe duty, to tolerate his father's presence whenever it was imposed. Deronda was cold and distant, the first sight of this man, who had blighted the lives of his wife and children, creating in him a repulsion that was even a physical discomfort. But Lapidoth did not let himself be discouraged, asked leave to stay and hear the reading of papers from the old chest, and actually made himself useful in helping to decipher some difficult German manuscript. This led him to suggest that it might be desirable to make a transcription of the manuscript, and he offered his services for this purpose, and also to make copies of any papers in Roman characters. Though Ezra's young eyes, he observed, were getting weak, his own were still strong. Deronda accepted the offer, thinking that Lapidoth showed a sign of grace in the willingness to be employed usefully; and he saw a gratified expression in Ezra's face, who, however, presently said, 'Let all the writing be done here; for I cannot trust the papers out of my sight, lest there be an accident by burning or otherwise.' Poor Ezra felt very much as if he had a convict on leave under his charge. Unless he saw his father working, it was not possible to believe that he would work in good faith. But by this arrangement he fastened on himself the burthen of his father's presence, which was made painful not only through his deepest, longest associations, but also through Lapidoth's restlessness of temperament, which showed itself the more as he became familiarized with his situation, and lost any awe he had felt of his son. The fact was, he was putting a strong constraint on himself in confining his attention for the sake of winning Deronda's favour; and like a man in an uncomfortable garment he gave himself relief at every opportunity, going out to smoke, or moving about and talking, or throwing himself back in his chair and remaining silent, but incessantly carrying on a dumb language of facial movement or gesticulation; and if Mirah were in the room, he would fall into his old habit of talk with her, gossiping about their former doings and companions, or repeating quirks, and stories, and plots of the plays he used to adapt, in the belief that he could at will command the vivacity of his earlier time. All this was a mortal infliction to Ezra; and when Mirah was at home she tried to relieve him, by getting her father down into the parlour and keeping watch over him there. What duty is made of a single difficult resolve? The difficulty lies in the daily unflinching support of consequences that mar the blessed return of morning with the prospect of irritation to be suppressed or shame to be endured. And such consequences were being borne by these, as by many other, heroic children of an unworthy father – with the prospect, at least to Mirah, of their stretching onward through the solid part of life.

Meanwhile Lapidoth's presence had raised a new impalpable partition between Deronda and Mirah – each of them dreading the soiling inferences of his mind, each of them interpreting mistakenly the increased reserve and diffidence of the other. But it was not very long before some light came to Deronda.

As soon as he could, after returning from his brief visit to the Abbey, he had called at Hans Meyrick's rooms, feeling it, on more grounds than one, a due of friendship that Hans should be at once acquainted with the reasons of his late journey, and the changes of intention it had brought about. Hans was not there; he was said to be in the country for a few days; and Deronda, after leaving a note, waited a week, rather expecting a note in return. But receiving no word, and fearing some freak of feeling in the incalculably susceptible Hans, whose proposed sojourn at the Abbey he knew had been deferred, he at length made a second call, and was admitted into the painting-room, where he found his friend in a light coat, without a waistcoat, his long hair still wet from a bath, but with a face looking worn and wizened – anything but country-like. He had taken up his palette and brushes, and stood before his easel when Deronda entered, but the equipment and attitude seemed to have been got up on short notice.

As they shook hands, Deronda said, 'You don't look much as if you had been in the country, old fellow. Is it Cambridge you have been to?'

'No,' said Hans, curtly, throwing down his palette with the air of one who has begun to feign by mistake; then, pushing forward a chair for Deronda, he threw himself into another, and leaned backward with his hands behind his head, while he went on, 'I've been to I-don't-know-where – No man's land – and a mortally unpleasant country it is.'

'You don't mean to say you have been drinking, Hans,' said Deronda, who had seated himself opposite, in anxious survey.

'Nothing so good. I've been smoking opium. I always meant to do it some time or other, to try how much bliss could be got by it; and having found myself just now rather out of other bliss, I thought it judicious to seize the opportunity. But I pledge you my word I shall never tap a cask of that bliss again. It disagrees with my constitution.'

'What has been the matter? You were in good spirits enough when you wrote to me.'

'Oh, nothing in particular. The world began to look seedy – a sort of cabbage-garden with all the cabbages cut. A malady of genius, you may be sure,' said Hans, creasing his face into a smile; 'and, in fact, I was tired of being virtuous without reward, especially in this hot London weather.'

'Nothing else? No real vexation?' said Deronda.

Hans shook his head.

'I came to tell you of my own affairs, but I can't do it with a good grace if you are to hide yours.'

'Haven't an affair in the world,' said Hans, in a flighty way, 'except a quarrel with a bric-à-brac man. Besides, as it is the first time in our lives that you ever spoke to me about your own affairs, you are only beginning to pay a pretty long debt.'

Deronda felt convinced that Hans was behaving artificially, but he trusted to a return of the old frankness by-and-by if he gave his own confidence.

'You laughed at the mystery of my journey to Italy, Hans,' he began. 'It was for an object that touched my happiness at the very roots. I had never known anything about my parents, and I really went to Genoa to meet my mother. My father has been long dead – died when I was an infant. My mother was the daughter of an eminent Jew; my father was her cousin. Many things had caused me to think of this origin as almost a probability before I set out. I was so far prepared for the result that I was glad of it – glad to find myself a Jew.'

'You must not expect me to look surprised, Deronda,' said Hans, who had changed his attitude, laying one leg across the other and examining the heel of his slipper.

'You knew it?'

'My mother told me. She went to the house the morning after you had been there – brother and sister both told her.

You may imagine we can't rejoice as they do. But whatever you are glad of, I shall come to be glad of in the end – *when* exactly the end may be I can't predict,' said Hans, speaking in a low tone, which was as unusual with him as it was to be out of humour with his lot, and yet bent on making no fuss about it.

'I quite understand that you can't share my feeling,' said Deronda; 'but I could not let silence lie between us on what casts quite a new light over my future. I have taken up some of Mordecai's ideas, and I mean to try and carry them out, so far as one man's efforts can go. I dare say I shall by-and-by travel to the East and be away for some years.'

Hans said nothing, but rose, seized his palette and began to work his brush on it, standing before his picture with his back to Deronda, who also felt himself at a break in his path, embarrassed by Hans's embarrassment.

Presently Hans said, again speaking low, and without turning, 'Excuse the question, but does Mrs. Grandcourt know of all this?'

'No; and I must beg of you, Hans,' said Deronda, rather angrily, 'to cease joking on that subject. Any notions you have are wide of the truth – are the very reverse of the truth.'

'I am no more inclined to joke than I shall be at my own funeral,' said Hans. 'But I am not at all sure that you are aware what are my notions on that subject.'

'Perhaps not,' said Deronda. 'But let me say, once for all, that in relation to Mrs. Grandcourt, I never have had, and never shall have, the position of a lover. If you have ever seriously put that interpretation on anything you have observed, you are supremely mistaken.'

There was silence a little while, and to each the silence was like an irritating air, exaggerating discomfort.

'Perhaps I have been mistaken in another interpretation also,' said Hans, presently.

'What is that?'

'That you had no wish to hold the position of a lover towards another woman, who is neither wife nor widow.'

'I can't pretend not to understand you, Meyrick. It is painful that our wishes should clash. But I hope you will tell me if you have any ground for supposing that you would succeed.'

'That seems rather a superfluous inquiry on your part, Deronda,' said Hans, with some irritation.

'Why superfluous?'

'Because you are perfectly convinced on the subject – and probably you have had the very best evidence to convince you.'

'I will be more frank with you than you are with me,' said Deronda, still heated by Hans's show of temper, and yet sorry for him. 'I have never had the slightest evidence that I should succeed myself. In fact, I have very little hope.'

Hans looked round hastily at his friend, but immediately turned to his picture again.

'And in our present situation,' said Deronda, hurt by the idea that Hans suspected him of insincerity, and giving an offended emphasis to his words, 'I don't see how I can deliberately make known my feeling to her. If she could not return it, I should have embittered her best comfort, for neither she nor I can be parted from her brother, and we should have to meet continually. If I were to cause her that sort of pain by an unwilling betrayal of my feeling, I should be no better than a mischievous animal.'

'I don't know that I have ever betrayed *my* feeling to her,' said Hans, as if he were vindicating himself.

'You mean that we are on a level; then, you have no reason to envy me.'

'Oh, not the slightest,' said Hans, with bitter irony. 'You have measured my conceit and know that it out-tops all your advantages.'

'I am a nuisance to you, Meyrick. I am sorry, but I can't help it,' said Deronda, rising. 'After what passed between us before, I wished to have this explanation; and I don't see that any pretensions of mine have made a real difference to you. They are not likely to make any pleasant difference to myself under present circumstances. Now the father is there – did you know that the father is there?'

'Yes. If he were not a Jew I would permit myself to damn him – with faint praise, I mean,' said Hans, but with no smile.

'She and I meet under greater constraint than ever. Things might go on in this way for two years without my getting any insight into her feeling towards me. That is the whole state of affairs, Hans. Neither you nor I have injured the other, that I can see. We must put up with this sort of rivalry in a hope that is likely enough to come to nothing. Our friendship can bear that strain, surely.'

'No, it can't,' said Hans, impetuously, throwing down his tools, thrusting his hands into his coat-pockets, and turning round to face Deronda, who drew back a little and looked at him with amazement. Hans went on in the same tone –

'Our friendship – my friendship – can't bear the strain of behaving to you like an ungrateful dastard and grudging you your happiness. For you *are* the happiest dog in the world. If Mirah loves anybody better than her brother, *you are the man*.'

Hans turned on his heel and threw himself into his chair, looking up at Deronda with an expression the reverse of tender. Something like a shock passed through Deronda, and, after an instant, he said –

'It is a good-natured fiction of yours, Hans.'

'I am not in a good-natured mood. I assure you I found the fact disagreeable when it was thrust on me – all the more, or perhaps all the less, because I believed then that your heart was pledged to the Duchess. But now, confound you! you turn out to be in love in the right place – a Jew – and everything eligible.'

'Tell me what convinced you – there's a good fellow,' said Deronda, distrusting a delight that he was unused to.

'Don't ask. Little mother was witness. The upshot is, that Mirah is jealous of the Duchess, and the sooner you relieve her mind, the better. There! I've cleared off a score or two, and may be allowed to swear at you for getting what you deserve – which is just the very best luck I know of.'

'God bless you, Hans!' said Deronda, putting out his hand, which the other took and wrung in silence.

LXVIII

'All thoughts, all passions, all delights,
Whatever stirs this mortal frame,
All are but ministers of Love,
And feed his sacred flame.'
— COLERIDGE.

DERONDA'S eagerness to confess his love could hardly have had a stronger stimulus than Hans had given it in his assurance that Mirah needed relief from jealousy. He went on his next visit to Ezra with the determination to be resolute in using – nay, in requesting – an opportunity of private conversation with her. If she accepted his love, he felt courageous about all other consequences, and as her betrothed husband he would gain a protective authority which might be a desirable defence for her in future difficulties with her father. Deronda had not observed any signs of growing restlessness in Lapidoth, or of diminished desire to recommend himself; but he had forebodings of some future struggle, some mortification, or some intolerable increase of domestic disquietude in which he might save Ezra and Mirah from being helpless victims.

His forebodings would have been strengthened if he had known what was going on in the father's mind. That amount of restlessness, that desultoriness of attention, which made a small torture to Ezra, was to Lapidoth an irksome submission to restraint, only made bearable by his thinking of it as a means of by-and-by securing a well-conditioned freedom. He began with the intention of awaiting some really good chance, such as an opening for getting a considerable sum from Deronda; but all the while he was looking about curiously, and trying to discover where Mirah deposited her money and her keys. The imperious gambling desire within him, which carried on its activity through every other occupation, and made a continuous web of imagination that held all else in its meshes, would hardly have been under the control of a protracted purpose, if he had been able to lay his hand on any sum worth capturing. But Mirah, with her practical clear-sightedness, guarded against any frustration of the promise she had given Ezra, by confiding all money, except what she was immediately in want of, to Mrs. Meyrick's care, and Lapidoth felt himself under an irritating completeness of supply in kind as in a lunatic asylum where everything was made safe against him. To have opened a desk or drawer of Mirah's, and pocketed any bank-notes found there, would have been to his mind a sort of domestic appropriation which had no disgrace in it; the degrees of liberty a man allows himself with other people's property being often delicately drawn, even beyond the boundary where the law begins to lay its hold – which is the reason why spoons are a safer investment than mining shares. Lapidoth really felt himself injuriously treated by his daughter, and thought that he ought to have had what he wanted of her other earnings as he had of her apple-tart. But he remained submissive; indeed, the indiscretion that most tempted him was not any insistence with Mirah, but some kind of appeal to Deronda. Clever persons who have nothing else to sell can often put a good price on their absence, and Lapidoth's difficult search for devices forced upon him the idea that his family would find themselves happier without him, and that Deronda would be willing to advance a considerable sum for the sake of getting rid of him. But, in spite of well-practised hardihood, Lapidoth was still in some awe of Ezra's imposing friend, and deferred his purpose indefinitely.

On this day, when Deronda had come full of a gladdened consciousness, which inevitably showed itself in his air and speech, Lapidoth was at a crisis of discontent and longing that made his mind busy with schemes of freedom, and Deronda's new amenity encouraged them. This preoccupation was at last so strong as to interfere with his usual show of interest in what went forward, and his persistence in sitting by even when there was reading which he could not follow. After sitting a little while, he went out to smoke and walk in the square, and the two friends were all the easier. Mirah was not at home, but she was sure to be in again before Deronda left, and his eyes glowed with a secret anticipation: he thought that when he saw her again he should see some sweetness of recognition for himself to which his eyes had been sealed before. There was an additional playful affectionateness in his manner towards Ezra.

'This little room is too close for you, Ezra,' he said, breaking off his reading. 'The week's heat we sometimes get here is worse than the heat in Genoa, where one sits in the shaded coolness of large rooms. You must have a better home now. I shall do as I like with you, being the stronger half.' He smiled toward Ezra, who said –

'I am straitened for nothing except breath. But you, who might be in a spacious palace, with the wide green country around you, find this a narrow prison. Nevertheless, I cannot say, "Go."'

'Oh, the country would be a banishment while you are here,' said Deronda, rising and walking round the double room, which yet offered no long promenade, while he made a great fan of his handkerchief. 'This is the happiest room in the world to me. Besides, I will imagine myself in the East, since I am getting ready to go there some day. Only I will not wear a cravat and a heavy ring there,' he ended emphatically, pausing to take off those superfluities and deposit them on a small table behind Ezra, who had the table in front of him covered with books and papers.

'I have been wearing my memorable ring ever since I came home,' he went on, as he reseated himself. 'But I am such a Sybarite that I constantly put it off as a burthen when I am doing anything. I understand why the Romans had summer rings – *if* they had them. Now then, I shall get on better.'

They were soon absorbed in their work again. Deronda was reading a piece of rabbinical Hebrew under Ezra's correction and comment, and they took little notice when Lapidoth re-entered and seated himself somewhat in the background.

His rambling eyes quickly alighted on the ring that sparkled on the bit of dark mahogany. During his walk, his mind had been occupied with the fiction of an advantageous opening for him abroad, only requiring a sum of ready money, which, on being communicated to Deronda in private, might immediately draw from him a question as to the amount of the required sum; and it was this part of his forecast that Lapidoth found the most debatable, there being a danger in asking too much, and a prospective regret in asking too little. His own desire gave him no limit, and he was quite without guidance as to the limit of Deronda's willingness. But now, in the midst of these airy conditions preparatory to a receipt which remained indefinite, this ring, which on Deronda's finger had become familiar to Lapidoth's envy, suddenly shone detached, and within easy grasp. Its value was certainly below the smallest of the imaginary sums that his purpose fluctuated between; but then it was before him as a solid fact, and his desire at once leaped into the thought (not yet an intention) that if he were quietly to pocket that ring and walk away he would have the means of comfortable escape from present restraint, without trouble, and also without danger; for any property of Deronda's (available without his formal consent) was all one with his children's property, since their father would never be prosecuted for taking it. The details of this thinking followed each other so quickly that they seemed to rise before him as one picture. Lapidoth had never committed larceny; but larceny is a form of appropriation for which people are punished by law; and to take this ring from a virtual relation, who would have been willing to make a much heavier gift, would not come under the head of larceny. Still, the heavier gift was to be preferred, if Lapidoth could only make haste enough in asking for it, and the imaginary action of taking the ring, which kept repeating itself like an inward tune, sank into a rejected idea. He satisfied his urgent longing by resolving to go below and watch for the moment of Deronda's departure, when he would ask leave to join him in his walk, and boldly carry out his meditated plan. He rose and stood looking out of the window, but all the while he saw what lay behind him – the brief passage he would have to make to the door close by the table where the ring was. However, he was resolved to go down; but – by no distinct change of resolution, rather by a dominance of desire, like the thirst of the drunkard – it so happened that in passing the table his fingers fell noiselessly on the ring, and he found himself in the passage with the ring in his hand. It followed that he put on his hat and quitted the house. The possibility of again throwing himself on his children receded into the indefinite distance, and before he was out of the square his sense of haste had concentrated itself on selling the ring and getting on shipboard.

Deronda and Ezra were just aware of his exit; that was all. But, by-and-by, Mirah came in and made a real interruption. She had not taken off her hat; and when Deronda rose and advanced to shake hands with her, she said, in a confusion at once unaccountable and troublesome to herself –

'I only came in to see that Ezra had his new draught. I must go directly to Mrs. Meyrick's to fetch something.'

'Pray allow me to walk with you,' said Deronda, urgently. 'I must not tire Ezra any further; besides, my brains are melting. I want to go to Mrs. Meyrick's: may I go with you?'

'Oh yes,' said Mirah, blushing still more, with the vague sense of something new in Deronda, and turning away to pour out Ezra's draught; Ezra meanwhile throwing back his head with his eyes shut, unable to get his mind away from the ideas that had been filling it while the reading was going on. Deronda for a moment stood thinking of nothing but the walk, till Mirah turned round again and brought the draught, when he suddenly remembered that he had laid aside his cravat, and saying – 'Pray excuse my dishabille – I did not mean you to see it,' he went to the little table, took up his cravat, and exclaimed with a violent impulse of surprise, 'Good heavens! where is my ring gone?' beginning to search about on the floor.

Ezra looked round the corner of his chair. Mirah, quick as thought, went to the spot where Deronda was seeking, and said, 'Did you lay it down?'

'Yes,' said Deronda, still unvisited by any other explanation than that the ring had fallen and was lurking in shadow, indiscernible on the variegated carpet. He was moving the bits of furniture near, and searching in all possible and impossible places with hand and eyes.

But another explanation had visited Mirah and taken the colour from her cheek. She went to Ezra's ear and whispered, 'Was my father here?' He bent his head in reply, meeting her eyes with terrible understanding. She darted back to the spot where Deronda was still casting down his eyes in that hopeless exploration which we are apt to carry on over a space we have examined in vain. 'You have not found it?' she said, hurriedly.

He, meeting her frightened gaze, immediately caught alarm from it and answered, 'I perhaps put it in my pocket,' professing to feel for it there.

She watched him and said, 'It is not there? – you put it on the table,' with a penetrating voice that would not let him feign to have found it in his pocket; and immediately she rushed out of the room. Deronda followed her – she was gone into the sitting-room below to look for her father – she opened the door of the bedroom to see if he were there – she looked where his hat usually hung – she turned with her hands clasped tight and her lips pale, gazing despairingly out of the window. Then she looked up at Deronda who had not dared to speak to her in her white agitation. She looked up at him, unable to utter a word – the look seemed a tacit acceptance of the humiliation she felt in his presence. But he, taking her clasped hands between both his, said, in a tone of reverent adoration –

'Mirah, let me think that he is my father as well as yours – that we can have no sorrow, no disgrace, no joy apart. I will rather take your grief to be mine than I would take the brightest joy of another woman. Say you will not reject me – say you will take me to share all things with you. Say you will promise to be my wife – say it now. I have been in doubt so long – I have had to hide my love so long. Say that now and always I may prove to you that I love you with complete love.'

The change in Mirah had been gradual. She had not passed at once from anguish to the full, blessed consciousness that, in this moment of grief and shame, Deronda was giving her the highest tribute man can give to woman. With the first tones and the first words, she had only a sense of solemn comfort, referring this goodness of Deronda's to his feeling for Ezra. But by degrees the rapturous assurance of unhoped-for good took possession of her frame; her face glowed under Deronda's as he bent over her; yet she looked up still with intense gravity, as when she had first acknowledged with religious gratitude that he had thought her 'worthy of the best;' and when he had finished, she could say nothing – she could only lift up her lips to his and just kiss them, as if that were the simplest 'yes.' They stood then, only looking at each other, he holding her hands between his – too happy to move, meeting so fully in their new consciousness that all signs would have seemed to throw them farther apart, till Mirah said in a whisper: 'Let us go and comfort Ezra.'

LXIX

'The human nature unto which I felt
That I belonged, and reverenced with love,
Was not a punctual presence, but a spirit
Diffused through time and space, with aid derived
Of evidence from monuments, erect,
Prostrate, or leaning towards their common rest
In earth, the widely scattered wreck sublime
Of vanished nations.'
                    – WORDSWORTH: *The Prelude*.

SIR HUGO carried out his plan of spending part of the
autumn at Diplow, and by the beginning of October his
presence was spreading some cheerfulness in the neighbourhood, among all ranks and persons concerned, from
the stately homes of Brackenshaw and Quetcham to the
respectable shop-parlours in Wancester. For Sir Hugo was
a man who liked to show himself and be affable, a Liberal
of good lineage, who confided entirely in Reform as not
likely to make any serious difference in English habits of
feeling, one of which undoubtedly is the liking to behold
society well fenced and adorned with hereditary rank.
Hence he made Diplow a most agreeable house, extending
his invitations to old Wancester solicitors and young village
curates, but also taking some care in the combination of his
guests, and not feeding all the common poultry together,
so that they should think their meal no particular compliment. Easy-going Lord Brackenshaw, for example, would
not mind meeting Robinson the attorney, but Robinson
would have been naturally piqued if he had been asked to
meet a set of people who passed for his equals. On all these
points Sir Hugo was well informed enough at once to gain
popularity for himself and give pleasure to others – two
results which eminently suited his disposition. The Rector
of Pennicote now found a reception at Diplow very different from the haughty tolerance he had undergone during
the reign of Grandcourt. It was not only that the baronet
liked Mr. Gascoigne, it was that he desired to keep up a

marked relation of friendliness with him on account of Mrs. Grandcourt, for whom Sir Hugo's chivalry had become more and more engaged. Why? The chief reason was one that he could not fully communicate, even to Lady Mallinger – for he would not tell what he thought one woman's secret to another even though the other was his wife – which shows that his chivalry included a rare reticence.

Deronda, after he had become engaged to Mirah, felt it right to make a full statement of his position and purposes to Sir Hugo, and he chose to make it by letter. He had more than a presentiment that his fatherly friend would feel some dissatisfaction, if not pain, at this turn of destiny. In reading unwelcome news, instead of hearing it, there is the advantage that one avoids a hasty expression of impatience which may afterwards be repented of. Deronda dreaded that verbal collision which makes otherwise pardonable feeling lastingly offensive.

And Sir Hugo, though not altogether surprised, was thoroughly vexed. His immediate resource was to take the letter to Lady Mallinger, who would be sure to express an astonishment which her husband could argue against as unreasonable, and in this way divide the stress of his discontent. And in fact when she showed herself astonished and distressed that all Daniel's wonderful talents, and the comfort of having him in the house, should have ended in his going mad in this way about the Jews, the baronet could say –

'Oh, nonsense, my dear! depend upon it, Dan will not make a fool of himself. He has large notions about Judaism – political views which you can't understand. No fear but Dan will keep himself head uppermost.'

But with regard to the prospective marriage, she afforded him no counter-irritant. The gentle lady observed, without rancour, that she had little dreamed of what was coming when she had Mirah to sing at her musical party and give lessons to Amabel. After some hesitation, indeed, she confessed it *had* passed through her mind that after a proper time Daniel might marry Mrs. Grandcourt – because it seemed so remarkable that he should be at Genoa just at that time – and although she herself was not fond of widows she could not help thinking that such a marriage would have been better than his going altogether with the Jews. But Sir Hugo was so strongly of the same opinion that he could not correct it as a feminine mistake; and his ill-humour at the disproof of his agreeable conclusions on behalf of Gwendolen was left without vent. He desired Lady Mallinger not to breathe a word about the affair till further notice, saying to himself, 'If it is an unkind cut to the poor thing' (meaning Gwendolen), 'the longer she is without knowing it the better, in her present nervous state. And she will best learn it from Dan himself.' Sir Hugo's conjectures had worked so industriously with his knowledge, that he fancied himself well informed concerning the whole situation.

Meanwhile his residence with his family at Diplow enabled him to continue his fatherly attentions to Gwendolen; and in these Lady Mallinger, notwithstanding her small liking for widows, was quite willing to second him.

The plan of removal to Offendene had been carried out; and Gwendolen, in settling there, maintained a calm beyond her mother's hopes. She was experiencing some of that peaceful melancholy which comes from the renunciation of demands for self, and from taking the ordinary good of existence, and especially kindness, even from a dog, as a gift above expectation. Does one who has been all but lost in a pit of darkness complain of the sweet air and the daylight? There is a way of looking at our life daily as an escape, and taking the quiet return of morn and evening – still more the star-like out-glowing of some pure fellow-feeling, some generous impulse breaking our inward darkness – as a salvation that reconciles us to hardship. Those who have a self-knowledge prompting such self-accusation as Hamlet's, can understand this habitual feeling of rescue. And it was felt by Gwendolen as she lived through and through again the terrible history of her temptations, from their first form of illusory self-pleasing when she struggled away from the hold of conscience, to their latest form of an urgent hatred dragging her towards its satisfaction, while she prayed and cried for the help of that conscience which she had once forsaken. She was now dwelling on every word of Deronda's that pointed to her past deliverance from the worst evil in herself and the worst infliction of it on others, and on every word that carried a force to resist self-despair.

But she was also upborne by the prospect of soon seeing him again: she did not imagine him otherwise than always within her reach, her supreme need of him blinding her to the separateness of his life, the whole scene of which she filled with his relation to her – no unique preoccupation of Gwendolen's, for we are all apt to fall into this passionate egoism of imagination, not only towards our fellow-men, but towards God. And the future which she turned her face to with a willing step was one where she would be continually assimilating herself to some type that he would hold before her. Had he not first risen on her vision as a corrective presence which she had recognized in the beginning with resentment, and at last with entire love and trust? She could not spontaneously think of an end to that reliance, which had become to her imagination like the firmness of the earth, the only condition of her walking.

And Deronda was not long before he came to Diplow, which was at a more convenient distance from town than the Abbey. He had wished to carry out a plan for taking Ezra and Mirah to a mild spot on the coast, while he prepared another home that Mirah might enter as his bride, and where they might unitedly watch over her brother. But Ezra begged not to be removed, unless it were to go with them to the East. All outward solicitations were becoming more and more of a burthen to him; but his mind dwelt on the possibility of this voyage with a visionary joy. Deronda in his preparations for the marriage, which he hoped might not be deferred beyond a couple of months, wished to have fuller consultation as to his resources and affairs generally with Sir Hugo, and here was a reason for not delaying his visit to Diplow. But he thought quite as much of another reason – his promise to Gwendolen. The sense of blessedness in his own lot had yet an aching anxiety at its heart: this may be held para-doxical, for the beloved lover is always called happy, and happiness is considered as a well-fleshed indifference to sorrow outside it. But human experience is usually para-doxical, if that means incongruous with the phrases of current talk or even current philosophy. It was no treason to Mirah, but a part of that full nature which made his love for her the more worthy, that his joy in her could hold by its side the care for another. For what is love itself, for the one we love best? – an enfolding of immeasurable cares which yet are better than any joys outside our love.

Deronda came twice to Diplow, and saw Gwendolen twice – yet he went back to town without having told her anything about the change in his lot and prospects. He blamed himself; but in all momentous communication likely to give pain we feel dependent on some preparatory turn of words or associations, some agreement of the other's mood with the probable effect of what we have to impart. In the first interview Gwendolen was so absorbed in what she had to say to him, so full of questions which he must answer, about the arrangement of her life, what she could do to make herself less ignorant, how she could be kindest to everybody, and make amends for her selfishness and try to be rid of it, that Deronda utterly shrank from waiving her immediate wants in order to speak of himself, nay, from inflicting a wound on her in these moments when she was leaning on him for help in her path. In the second interview, when he went with new resolve to command the conversation into some preparatory track, he found her in a state of deep depression, overmastered by those distaste-ful miserable memories which forced themselves on her as something more real and ample than any new material out

of which she could mould her future. She cried hysterically, and said that he would always despise her. He could
only seek words of soothing and encouragement; and when
she gradually revived under them, with that pathetic look
of renewed childlike interest which we see in eyes where
the lashes are still beaded with tears, it was impossible to
lay another burthen on her.

But time went on, and he felt it a pressing duty to make
the difficult disclosure. Gwendolen, it was true, never
recognized his having any affairs; and it had never even
occurred to her to ask him why he happened to be at
Genoa. But this unconsciousness of hers would make a
sudden revelation of affairs that were determining his
course in life all the heavier blow to her; and if he left the
revelation to be made by indifferent persons, she would
feel that he had treated her with cruel inconsiderateness.
He could not make the communication in writing: his
tenderness could not bear to think of her reading his virtual
farewell in solitude, and perhaps feeling his words full of a
hard gladness for himself and indifference for her. He went
down to Diplow again, feeling that every other peril was to
be incurred rather than that of returning and leaving her
still in ignorance.

On this third visit Deronda found Hans Meyrick
installed with his easel at Diplow, beginning his picture
of the three daughters sitting on a bank 'in the
Gainsborough style,' and varying his work by rambling to
Pennicote to sketch the village children and improve his
acquaintance with the Gascoignes. Hans appeared to have
recovered his vivacity, but Deronda detected some feigning in it, as we detect the artificiality of a lady's bloom from
its being a little too high-toned and steadily persistent (a
'Fluctuating Rouge' not having yet appeared among the
advertisements). Also, with all his grateful friendship and
admiration for Deronda, Hans could not help a certain
irritation against him such as extremely incautious, open
natures are apt to feel when the breaking of a friend's
reserve discloses a state of things not merely unsuspected

but the reverse of what had been hoped and ingeniously conjectured. It is true that poor Hans had always cared chiefly to confide in Deronda, and had been quite incurious as to any confidence that might have been given in return; but what outpourer of his own affairs is not tempted to think any hint of his friend's affairs as an egotistic irrelevance? That was no reason why it was not rather a sore reflection to Hans that while he had been all along naïvely opening his heart about Mirah, Deronda had kept secret a feeling of rivalry which now revealed itself as the important determining fact. Moreover, it is always at their peril that our friends turn out to be something more than we were aware of. Hans must be excused for these promptings of bruised sensibility, since he had not allowed them to govern his substantial conduct: he had the consciousness of having done right by his fortunate friend; or, as he told himself, 'his metal had given a better ring than he would have sworn to beforehand.' For Hans had always said that in point of virtue he was a *dilettante*: which meant that he was very fond of it in other people, but if he meddled with it himself he cut a poor figure. Perhaps in reward of his good behaviour he gave his tongue the more freedom; and he was too fully possessed by the notion of Deronda's happiness to have a conception of what he was feeling about Gwendolen, so that he spoke of her without hesitation.

'When did you come down, Hans?' said Deronda, joining him in the grounds where he was making a study of the requisite bank and trees.

'Oh, ten days ago – before the time Sir Hugo fixed. I ran down with Rex Gascoigne and stayed at the Rectory a day or two. I'm up in all the gossip of these parts – I know the state of the wheelwright's interior, and have assisted at an infant school examination. Sister Anna with the good upper lip escorted me, else I should have been mobbed by three urchins and an idiot, because of my long hair and a general appearance which departs from the Pennicote type of the beautiful. Altogether, the village is idyllic. Its only fault is a dark curate with broad shoulders and broad trousers who ought to have gone into the heavy drapery line. The Gascoignes are perfect – besides being related to the Vandyke duchess. I caught a glimpse of her in her black robes at a distance, though she doesn't show to visitors.'

'She was not staying at the Rectory?' said Deronda.

'No; but I was taken to Offendene to see the old house, and as a consequence I saw the duchess's family. I suppose you have been there and know all about them?'

'Yes, I have been there,' said Deronda, quietly.

'A fine old place. An excellent setting for a widow with romantic fortunes. And she seems to have had several romances. I think I have found out that there was one between her and my friend Rex.'

'Not long before her marriage, then?' said Deronda, really interested; 'for they had only been a year at Offendene. How came you to know anything of it?'

'Oh – not ignorant of what it is to be a miserable devil, I learn to gloat on the signs of misery in others. I found out that Rex never goes to Offendene, and has never seen the duchess since she came back; and Miss Gascoigne let fall something in our talk about charade-acting – for I went through some of my nonsense to please the young ones – something which proved to me that Rex was once hovering about his fair cousin close enough to get singed. I don't know what was her part in the affair. Perhaps the duke came in and carried her off. That is always the way when an exceptionally worthy young man forms an attachment. I understand now why Gascoigne talks of making the law his mistress and remaining a bachelor. But these are green resolves. Since the duke did not get himself drowned for your sake, it may turn out to be for my friend Rex's sake. Who knows?'

'Is it absolutely necessary that Mrs. Grandcourt should marry again?' said Deronda, ready to add that Hans's success in constructing her fortunes hitherto had not been enough to warrant a new attempt.

'You monster!' retorted Hans, 'do you want her to wear weeds for *you* all her life – burn herself in perpetual suttee while you are alive and merry?'

Deronda could say nothing, but he looked so much annoyed that Hans turned the current of his chat, and when he was alone shrugged his shoulders a little over the thought that there really had been some stronger feeling between Deronda and the duchess than Mirah would like to know of. 'Why didn't she fall in love with me?' thought Hans, laughing at himself. 'She would have had no rivals. No woman ever wanted to discuss theology with me.'

No wonder that Deronda winced under that sort of joking with a whip-lash. It touched sensibilities that were already quivering with the anticipation of witnessing some of that pain to which even Hans's light words seemed to give more reality – any sort of recognition by another giving emphasis to the subject of our anxiety. And now he had come down with the firm resolve that he would not again evade the trial. The next day he rode to Offendene. He had sent word that he intended to call and to ask if Gwendolen could receive him; and he found her awaiting him in the old drawing-room where some chief crises of her life had happened. She seemed less sad than he had seen her since her husband's death; there was no smile on her face, but a placid self-possession, in contrast with the mood in which he had last found her. She was all the more alive to the sadness perceptible in Deronda; and they were no sooner seated – he at a little distance opposite to her – than she said:

'You were afraid of coming to see me, because I was so full of grief and despair the last time. But I am not so to-day. I have been sorry ever since. I have been making it a reason why I should keep up my hope and be as cheerful as I can, because I would not give you any pain about me.'

There was an unwonted sweetness in Gwendolen's tone and look as she uttered these words that seemed to Deronda to infuse the utmost cruelty into the task now laid upon him. But he felt obliged to make his answer a beginning of the task.

'I *am* in some trouble to-day,' he said, looking at her rather mournfully; 'but it is because I have things to tell you which you will almost think it a want of confidence on my part not to have spoken of before. They are things affecting my own life – my own future. I shall seem to have made an ill return to you for the trust you have placed in me – never to have given you an idea of events that make great changes for me. But when we have been together we have hardly had time to enter into subjects which at the moment were really less pressing to me than the trials you have been going through.' There was a sort of timid tenderness in Deronda's deep tones, and he paused with a pleading look, as if it had been Gwendolen only who had conferred anything in her scenes of beseeching and confession.

A thrill of surprise was visible in her. Such meaning as she found in his words had shaken her, but without causing fear. Her mind had flown at once to some change in his position with regard to Sir Hugo and Sir Hugo's property. She said, with a sense of comfort from Deronda's way of asking her pardon –

'You never thought of anything but what you could do to help me; and I was so troublesome. How could you tell me things?'

'It will perhaps astonish you,' said Deronda, 'that I have only quite lately known who were my parents.'

Gwendolen was not astonished: she felt the more assured that her expectations of what was coming were right. Deronda went on without check.

'The reason why you found me in Italy was that I had gone there to learn that – in fact, to meet my mother. It was by her wish that I was brought up in ignorance of my parentage. She parted with me after my father's death, when I was a little creature. But she is now very ill, and she felt that the secrecy ought not to be any longer maintained. Her chief reason had been that she did not wish me to know I was a Jew.'

'A *Jew*!' Gwendolen exclaimed, in a low tone of amazement, with an utterly frustrated look, as if some confusing potion were creeping through her system.

Deronda coloured and did not speak, while Gwendolen, with her eyes fixed on the floor, was struggling to find her way in the dark by the aid of various reminiscences. She seemed at last to have arrived at some judgment, for she looked up at Deronda again and said, as if remonstrating against the mother's conduct –

'What difference need that have made?'

'It has made a great difference to me that I have known it,' said Deronda, emphatically; but he could not go on easily – the distance between her ideas and his acted like a difference of native language, making him uncertain what force his words would carry.

Gwendolen meditated again, and then said feelingly, 'I hope there is nothing to make you mind. *You* are just the same as if you were not a Jew.'

She meant to assure him that nothing of that external sort could affect the way in which she regarded him, or the way in which he could influence her. Deronda was a little helped by this misunderstanding.

'The discovery was far from being painful to me,' he said. 'I had been gradually prepared for it, and I was glad of it. I had been prepared for it by becoming intimate with a very remarkable Jew, whose ideas have attracted me so much that I think of devoting the best part of my life to some effort at giving them effect.'

Again Gwendolen seemed shaken – again there was a look of frustration, but this time it was mingled with alarm. She looked at Deronda with lips childishly parted. It was not that she had yet connected his words with Mirah and her brother, but that they had inspired her with a dreadful presentiment of mountainous travel for her mind before it could reach Deronda's. Great ideas in general which she had attributed to him seemed to make no great practical difference, and were not formidable in the same way as these mysteriously-shadowed particular ideas. He could not quite divine what was going on within her; he could only seek the least abrupt path of disclosure.

'That is an object,' he said, after a moment, 'which will by-and-by force me to leave England for some time – for some years. I have purposes which will take me to the East.'

Here was something clearer, but all the more immediately agitating. Gwendolen's lip began to tremble. 'But you will come back?' she said, tasting her own tears as they fell, before she thought of drying them.

Deronda could not sit still. He rose, grasping his coat-collar, and went to prop himself against the corner of the mantelpiece, at a different angle from her face. But when she had pressed her handkerchief against her cheeks, she turned and looked up at him, awaiting an answer.

'If I live,' said Deronda – '*some time.*'

They were both silent. He could not persuade himself to say more unless she led up to it by a question; and she was apparently meditating something that she had to say.

'What are you going to do?' she asked, at last, very timidly. 'Can I understand the ideas, or am I too ignorant?'

'I am going to the East to become better acquainted with the condition of my race in various countries there,' said Deronda, gently – anxious to be as explanatory as he could on what was the impersonal part of their separateness from each other. 'The idea that I am possessed with is that of restoring a political existence to my people, making them a nation again, giving them a national centre, such as the English have, though they too are scattered over the face of the globe. That is a task which presents itself to me as a duty: I am resolved to begin it, however feebly. I am resolved to devote my life to it. At the least, I may awaken a movement in other minds, such as has been awakened in my own.'

There was a long silence between them. The world seemed getting larger round poor Gwendolen, and she more solitary and helpless in the midst. The thought that he might come back after going to the East, sank before the bewildering vision of these wide-stretching purposes in which she felt herself reduced to a mere speck. There comes a terrible moment to many souls when the great movements of the world, the larger destinies of mankind, which have lain aloof in newspapers and other neglected reading, enter like an earthquake into their own lives – when the slow urgency of growing generations turns into the tread of an invading army or the dire clash of civil war, and grey fathers know nothing to seek for but the corpses of their blooming sons, and girls forget all vanity to make lint and bandages which may serve for the shattered limbs of their betrothed husbands. Then it is as if the Invisible Power that has been the object of lip-worship and lip-resignation became visible, according to the imagery of the Hebrew poet, making the flames his chariot and riding on the wings of the wind, till the mountains smoke and the plains shudder under the rolling, fiery visitation. Often the good cause seems to lie prostrate under the thunder of unrelenting force, the martyrs live reviled, they die, and no angel is seen holding forth the crown and the palm branch. Then it is that the submission of the soul to the Highest is tested, and even in the eyes of frivolity life looks out from the scene of human struggle with the awful face of duty, and a religion shows itself which is something else than a private consolation.

That was the sort of crisis which was at this moment beginning in Gwendolen's small life: she was for the first time feeling the pressure of a vast mysterious movement, for the first time being dislodged from her supremacy in her own world, and getting a sense that her horizon was but a dipping onward of an existence with which her own was revolving. All the troubles of her wifehood and widowhood had still left her with the implicit impression which had accompanied her from childhood, that whatever surrounded her was somehow specially for her, and it was because of this that no personal jealousy had been roused in her in relation to Deronda: she could not spontaneously think of him as rightfully belonging to others more than to her. But here had come a shock which went deeper than personal jealousy – something spiritual and vaguely tremendous that thrust her away, and yet quelled all anger into self-humiliation.

There had been a long silence. Deronda had stood still, even thankful for an interval before he needed to say more, and Gwendolen had sat like a statue with her wrists lying over each other and her eyes fixed – the intensity of her mental action arresting all other excitation. At length something occurred to her that made her turn her face to Deronda and say in a trembling voice –

'Is that all you can tell me?'

The question was like a dart to him. 'The Jew whom I mentioned just now,' he answered, not without a certain tremor in his tones too, 'the remarkable man who has greatly influenced my mind, has not perhaps been totally unheard of by you. He is the brother of Miss Lapidoth, whom you have often heard sing.'

A great wave of remembrance passed through Gwendolen, and spread as a deep, painful flush over face and neck. It had come first as the scene of that morning when she had called on Mirah, and heard Deronda's voice reading, and been told, without then heeding it, that he was reading Hebrew with Mirah's brother.

'He is very ill – very near death now,' Deronda went on, nervously, and then stopped short. He felt that he must wait. Would she divine the rest?

'Did she tell you that I went to her?' said Gwendolen, abruptly, looking up at him.

'No,' said Deronda. 'I don't understand you.'

She turned away her eyes again and sat thinking. Slowly the colour died out of face and neck, and she was as pale as before – with that almost withered paleness which is seen after a painful flush. At last she said, without turning towards him – in a low, measured voice, as if she were only thinking aloud in preparation for future speech –

'But *can* you marry?'

'Yes,' said Deronda, also in a low voice. 'I am going to marry.'

At first there was no change in Gwendolen's attitude: she only began to tremble visibly; then she looked before her with dilated eyes, as at something lying in front of her, till she stretched her arms out straight, and cried with a smothered voice –

'I said I should be forsaken. I have been a cruel woman. And I am forsaken.'

Deronda's anguish was intolerable. He could not help himself. He seized her outstretched hands and held them together and kneeled at her feet. She was the victim of his happiness.

'I am cruel too, I am cruel,' he repeated, with a sort of groan, looking up at her imploringly.

His presence and touch seemed to dispel a horrible vision, and she met his upward look of sorrow with something like the return of consciousness after fainting. Then she dwelt on it with that growing pathetic movement of the brow which accompanies the revival of some tender recollection. The look of sorrow brought back what seemed a very far-off moment – the first time she had ever seen it, in the library at the Abbey. Sobs rose, and great tears fell fast. Deronda would not let her hands go – held them still with one of his, and himself pressed her handkerchief against her eyes. She submitted like a half-soothed child, making an effort to speak, which was hindered by struggling sobs. At last she succeeded in saying brokenly –

'I said...I said...it should be better...better with me...for having known you.'

His eyes too were larger with tears. She wrested one of her hands from his, and returned his action, pressing his tears away.

'We shall not be quite parted,' he said. 'I will write to you always, when I can, and you will answer?'

He waited till she said in a whisper, 'I will try.'

'I shall be more with you than I used to be,' Deronda said with gentle urgency, releasing her hands and rising from his kneeling posture. 'If we had been much together before, we should have felt our differences more, and seemed to get farther apart. Now we can perhaps never see each other again. But our minds may get nearer.'

Gwendolen said nothing, but rose too, automatically. Her withered look of grief, such as the sun often shines on when the blinds are drawn up after the burial of life's joy, made him hate his own words: they seemed to have the hardness of easy consolation in them. She felt that he was going, and that nothing could hinder it. The sense of it was like a dreadful whisper in her ear, which dulled all other consciousness; and she had not known that she was rising.

Deronda could not speak again. He thought that they must part in silence, but it was difficult to move towards the parting, till she looked at him with a sort of intention in her eyes, which helped him. He advanced to put out his hand silently, and when she had placed hers within it, she said what her mind had been labouring with –

'You have been very good to me. I have deserved nothing. I will try – try to live. I shall think of you. What good have I been? Only harm. Don't let me be harm to *you*. It shall be the better for me—'

She could not finish. It was not that she was sobbing, but that the intense effort with which she spoke made her too tremulous. The burthen of that difficult rectitude towards him was a weight her frame tottered under.

She bent forward to kiss his cheek, and he kissed hers. Then they looked at each other for an instant with clasped hands, and he turned away.

When he was quite gone, her mother came in and found her sitting motionless.

'Gwendolen, dearest, you look very ill,' she said, bending over her and touching her cold hands.

'Yes, mamma. But don't be afraid. I am going to live,' said Gwendolen, bursting out hysterically.

Her mother persuaded her to go to bed, and watched by her. Through the day and half the night she fell continually into fits of shrieking, but cried in the midst of them to her mother, 'Don't be afraid. I shall live. I mean to live.'

After all, she slept; and when she waked in the morning light, she looked up fixedly at her mother and said tenderly, 'Ah, poor mamma! You have been sitting up with me. Don't be unhappy. I shall live. I shall be better.'

LXX

In the chequered area of human experience the seasons are all
mingled as in the golden age: fruit and blossom hang together; in
the same moment the sickle is reaping and the seed is sprinkled;
one tends the green cluster and another treads the wine-press.
Nay, in each of our lives harvest and spring-time are continually
one, until Death himself gathers us and sows us anew in his
invisible fields.

AMONG the blessings of love there is hardly one
more exquisite than the sense that in uniting the beloved
life to ours we can watch over its happiness, bring comfort
where hardship was, and over memories of privation
and suffering open the sweetest fountains of joy.
Deronda's love for Mirah was strongly imbued with that
blessed protectiveness. Even with infantine feet she had
begun to tread among thorns; and the first time he had
beheld her face it had seemed to him the girlish image of
despair.

But now she was glowing like a dark-tipped yet delicate
ivory-tinted flower in the warm sunlight of content, thinking of any possible grief as part of that life with Deronda
which she could call by no other name than good. And he
watched the sober gladness which gave new beauty to her
movements and her habitual attitudes of repose, with a
delight which made him say to himself that it was enough
of personal joy for him to save her from pain. She knew
nothing of Hans's struggle or of Gwendolen's pang; for
after the assurance that Deronda's hidden love had been
for her, she easily explained Gwendolen's eager solicitude
about him as part of a grateful dependence on his goodness, such as she herself had known. And all Deronda's
words about Mrs. Grandcourt confirmed that view of their
relation, though he never touched on it except in the most
distant manner. Mirah was ready to believe that he had
been a rescuing angel to many besides herself. The only
wonder was, that she among them all was to have the bliss
of being continually by his side.

So, when the bridal veil was around Mirah it hid no doubtful tremors – only a thrill of awe at the acceptance of a great gift which required great uses. And the velvet canopy never covered a more goodly bride and bridegroom, to whom their people might more wisely wish offspring; more truthful lips never touched the sacramental marriage-wine; the marriage-blessing never gathered stronger promise of fulfilment than in the integrity of their mutual pledge. Naturally, they were married according to the Jewish rite. And since no religion seems yet to have demanded that when we make a feast we should invite only the highest rank of our acquaintances, few, it is to be hoped, will be offended to learn that among the guests at Deronda's little wedding-feast was the entire Cohen family, with the one exception of the baby who carried on her teething intelligently at home. How could Mordecai have borne that those friends of his adversity should have been shut out from rejoicing in common with him?

Mrs. Meyrick so fully understood this that she had quite reconciled herself to meeting the Jewish pawnbroker, and was there with her three daughters – all of them enjoying the consciousness that Mirah's marriage to Deronda crowned a romance which would always make a sweet memory to them. For which of them, mother or girls, had not had a generous part in it – giving their best in feeling and in act to her who needed? If Hans could have been there, it would have been better; but Mab had already observed that men must suffer for being so inconvenient: suppose she, Kate, and Amy had all fallen in love with Mr. Deronda? – but being women, they were not so ridiculous.

The Meyricks were rewarded for conquering their prejudices by hearing a speech from Mr. Cohen, which had the rare quality among speeches of not being quite after the usual pattern. Jacob ate beyond his years; and contributed several small whinnying laughs as a free accompaniment of his father's speech, not irreverently, but from a lively sense that his family was distinguishing itself; while Adelaide Rebekah, in a new Sabbath frock, maintained throughout a grave air of responsibility.

Mordecai's brilliant eyes, sunken in their large sockets, dwelt on the scene with the cherishing benignancy of a spirit already lifted into an aloofness which nullified only selfish requirements and left sympathy alive. But continually, after his gaze had been travelling round on the others, it returned to dwell on Deronda, with a fresh gleam of trusting affection.

The wedding-feast was humble, but Mirah was not without splendid wedding-gifts. As soon as the betrothal had been known, there were friends who had entertained graceful devices. Sir Hugo and Lady Mallinger had taken trouble to provide a complete equipment for Eastern travel, as well as a precious locket containing an inscription – '*To the bride of our dear Daniel Deronda all blessings. – H. & L. M.*' The Klesmers sent a perfect watch, also with a pretty inscription.

But something more precious than gold and gems came to Deronda from the neighbourhood of Diplow on the morning of his marriage. It was a letter containing these words:–

Do not think of me sorrowfully on your wedding-day. I have remembered your words – that I may live to be one of the best of women, who make others glad that they were born. I do not yet see how that can be, but you know better than I. If it ever comes true, it will be because you helped me. I only thought of myself, and I made you grieve. It hurts me now to think of your grief. You must not grieve any more for me. It is better – it shall be better with me because I have known you.

GWENDOLEN GRANDCOURT.

The preparations for the departure of all three to the East began at once; for Deronda could not deny Ezra's wish that they should set out on the voyage forthwith, so that he might go with them, instead of detaining them to watch over him. He had no belief that Ezra's life would last through the voyage, for there were symptoms which seemed to show that the last stage of his malady had set in. But Ezra himself had said, 'Never mind where I die, so that I am with you.'

He did not set out with them. One morning early he said to Deronda, 'Do not quit me today. I shall die before it is ended.'

He chose to be dressed and sit up in his easy-chair as usual, Deronda and Mirah on each side of him, and for some hours he was unusually silent, not even making the effort to speak, but looking at them occasionally with eyes full of some restful meaning, as if to assure them that while this remnant of breathing-time was difficult, he felt an ocean of peace beneath him.

It was not till late in the afternoon, when the light was falling, that he took a hand of each in his and said, looking at Deronda, 'Death is coming to me as the divine kiss which is both parting and reunion – which takes me from your bodily eyes and gives me full presence in your soul. Where thou goest, Daniel, I shall go. Is it not begun? Have I not breathed my soul into you? We shall live together.'

He paused, and Deronda waited, thinking that there might be another word for him. But slowly and with effort Ezra, pressing on their hands, raised himself and uttered in Hebrew the confession of the divine Unity, which for long generations has been on the lips of the dying Israelite.

He sank back gently into his chair, and did not speak again. But it was some hours before he had ceased to breathe, with Mirah's and Deronda's arms around him.

> 'Nothing is here for tears, nothing to wail
> Or knock the breast; no weakness, no contempt,
> Dispraise, or blame; nothing but well and fair,
> And what may quiet us in a death so noble.'

This book is set in CASLON, designed and engraved by William
Caslon of WILLIAM CASLON & SON, Letter-Founders in
London, around 1740. In England at the beginning of
the eighteenth century, Dutch type was probably
more widely used than English. The rise
of William Caslon put a stop to the
importation of Dutch types
and so changed the his-
tory of English
typecutting.